Seduced by a ser

DA
DEVASTATING &
DELICIOUS!

Three beloved authors deliver three
glamorous, exhilarating stories

DARK, DEVASTATING & DELICIOUS!

CHRISTINE RIMMER

LEANNE BANKS

DIXIE BROWNING

⦾™ MILLS & BOON®

DARK, DEVASTATING & DELICIOUS! © Harlequin Books S.A. 2009.

First published in Great Britain 2009
Harlequin Mills & Boon Limited,
Eton House, 18-24 Paradise Road, Richmond, Surrey TW9 1SR

The publisher acknowledges the copyright holders of the individual works, which have already been published in the UK, as follows:

The Marriage Medallion © Christine Rimmer 2003
Between Duty and Desire © Leanne Banks 2004
Driven to Distraction © Dixie Browning 2004

ISBN: 978 0 263 87161 6

64-0809

Printed and bound in Spain
by Litografia Rosés S.A., Barcelona

THE MARRIAGE MEDALLION

BY
CHRISTINE RIMMER

Christine Rimmer, before settling down to write about the magic of romance, had been an actress, a salesperson, a caretaker, a model, a phone sales representative, a teacher, a waitress, a playwright and an office manager. Christine is grateful not only for the joy she finds in writing, but for what waits when the day's work is through: a man she loves, who loves her right back, and the privilege of watching their children grow and change day to day. She lives with her family in Oklahoma.

For those who never looked for love,
those who had more important things to do.
I do so hope that love found *you*!

Chapter One

Princess Brit Thorson opened her eyes to find a blurry silver disc hanging directly in front of her face. Beyond the disc she could see the instrument panel of her Cessna Skyhawk.

She blinked. The metal disc still dangled, cold and heavy against the bridge of her nose, blocking the center of her vision. The controls were still there, too. Beyond them, through the windscreen now cross-hatched with cracks, lay rocky ground. Farther away, steep black cliffs jutted downward, softened here and there with stands of evergreens, into a sliver of clear, pale blue Gullandrian sky.

It was cold and it was quiet—too quiet, except for the whispering whoosh of rising wind outside and various odd creaking noises all around her.

Her head hurt—and her arms were dangling over

her head. "Huh?" The world swam and shifted, her addled senses locking at last onto the correct perspective.

She was hanging upside down from the pilot's seat, held crookedly in place by her shoulder harness. The blurry disc? That silver medallion Medwyn Greyfell had given her before she left the palace on her way to the airport. "To keep you safe from all evil," her father's grand counselor had said.

Considering her current situation, the medallion could have done a better job.

Then again, though she hadn't made it to that meadow farther inland where her landing would have been much less eventful, she *was* alive....

Brit groaned and shut her eyes as it all came flooding back: the unremarkable takeoff from Lysgard Airport. The smooth climbout to 6500 feet. Once she'd reached cruising level, she'd banked right, heading northwest, following the curve of the Gullandrian shoreline. At the mouth of Drakveden Fjord, she'd made a right ninety.

And then...

That routine oil-pressure check. The reading: zero.

The awful, hollow feeling of unreality as she went about setting up her best glide speed, running through her emergency checklist, reminding her guide in the rear seat to buckle up, getting on the radio at emergency frequency to broadcast her call of distress.

And all the time, checking below, seeking some viable strip of land where she might bring the Cessna down in one piece. She'd sighted the narrow spit of dry ground at what seemed like the last possible second.

The landing had been rough, but they'd made it down okay. It was during the rollout that she lost it. Some jut of rock must have snagged a wheel. She remembered the sickening lurch, the right wing going up.

About then everything went black…

Brit popped the belt latch and crumpled with a grunt to the deck—scratch that: roof. With some effort, she untangled her arms and legs and got herself into a sitting position. She stared at the dead instrument panel and tried to get her foggy mind to focus.

The Skyhawk was a beautiful, soundly engineered piece of machinery. No way it would completely lose oil pressure out of nowhere—not without help.

Whatever had gone wrong, it wasn't by accident. Someone had tried to kill her. And someone had almost gotten what he—or she—wanted.

Gingerly she poked at the goose egg rising near her hairline. Hurt like hell. But other than that, now the disorientation was fading, she felt all right. Not terrific. Achy and stiff and bruised in places she'd never been bruised before. Also, a little too close to some serious cookie tossing. But passable. Once she and Rutland dragged themselves out of here, she should be able to keep up as the guide led the way to…

The thought trailed off unfinished. *Rutland.* When they boarded for takeoff, Rutland's long, lined face had looked way too pale. "Don't care much for flying, Highness. Think I'll sit in back, if y'don't mind."

After this experience, Rutland would probably never get in a plane again.

Brit shivered. With the heater as dead as the upside-down instrument panel in front of her, the cabin was getting colder by the minute. Outside, the wind kept whining and fading and then rising to whine again.

"Rutland?" Her voice sounded strange—strained and a little shaky—in the unnatural creaking quiet of the cabin, with the eerie wind whistling outside. She wriggled around, getting herself facing aft. "You all ri—" That last word became a tight, anguished cry.

Her guide was rear-end up, knees to the roof along with his head, which was pressed into his shoulders at an impossible angle. He stared at her through sightless eyes.

She'd got it right a moment ago. Rutland Gottshield would never get in a plane again—except maybe to be flown somewhere for burial.

Brit clapped a hand over her mouth. Very carefully, she sucked in a long, shaky breath through her nose. She let the air out. And repeated the process.

She wanted to scream. To throw up. To totally freak. To just give herself over to the sick, swirling combination of pity, panic and guilt that threatened to overwhelm her.

She swore low, and commanded herself through clenched teeth, "No. Don't you dare lose it. You keep it together."

Ignoring as best she could the dead eyes of her guide, Brit took a slow, careful look around. Both left and right hatches were crumpled shut. She moved back and forth, testing the handles. She beat on one and then the other, getting her shoulder into it. Neither gave so much as a fraction.

Okay, so she wasn't getting out through the doors. But she most definitely *was* getting out. And she was taking her pack, her coat and her weapon along with her, all of which waited aft—safe, she hoped—in the baggage net behind the rear seats.

Brit swallowed, sucked in another fortifying breath and wriggled between the front seats. Rutland was squarely in the way. As she tried to squeeze past him, his body crumpled to the side, landing half on top of her with a weird grunting rush of expelled air.

Deadweight, she thought with bleak humor. Never had the meaning of that phrase been so nauseatingly clear.

One deep breath. Another…

And then, with considerable effort, she pushed and prodded the body—still warm, oh, God—until it was rearranged into a marginally more dignified pose, resting against the battered side window, out of her way.

She collapsed the right rear seat back, got the baggage net unhooked and dragged out her stuff. Then, hauling it all along in front of her, she scrambled backward, slithering between the seats until she attained the cockpit area again.

"Weapon," she muttered, breathless, panting. It was wild country out there. Also, she hadn't fallen out of the sky by accident—and she'd do well to remember it.

Yes, she could shoot. Her uncle Cam had taught her, out in the vineyards of his Napa estate, years and years ago. And she kept in practice at a certain San Fernando Valley shooting range. When you lived and worked in one of the rougher areas of L.A., it never hurt to be able to protect yourself—whether at home or on the job. The job being the East Hollywood pizzeria where Brit waited tables to make ends meet.

The painful truth? Though Brit could handle a

weapon and fly a plane, she'd dropped out of UCLA—
and somehow she could never quite manage to live on
the income from her trust fund. There were always too
many things she had to do. Flight lessons. Backpack-
ing trips. Self-defense classes. Shooting range fees.
And then, well, sometimes a friend would need a loan
and she couldn't bring herself to tell them no.

Thus, the Pizza Pitstop had become part of her life.
Paolo, Roberto and the guys always found it so amusing, when she told them to keep hands off or they'd
be looking down the barrel of her trusty SIG 220.
''Macha woman,'' they called her, chuckling with affection.

Not much to chuckle over now. Brit strapped on her
shoulder holster, loaded her weapon and slid it in place
beneath her left arm. Then she pulled on her thick
down jacket. Barely September, and already it was
major nippy in the Vildelund—the Vildelund being the
Gullandrian name for the wild north country of her
father's land.

Weapon loaded and ready, wearing her coat—un-
zipped, so she could reach the gun if she had to—her
pack close at hand, she was ready to go.

Yet she didn't move. Cold as it was in the cabin, it
would be colder still outside. She'd almost rather stay
in here with her dead guide and the increasing chill
and the creepy creaking sounds. At least in here she
knew what she was up against.

She felt in a pocket, sighed in relief when she found
they were still there: a full bag of peanut M&Ms. She
liked to eat them when she was working at her laptop,
writing one of the novels that always started out with

a bang and somehow never got finished, or when she was feeling tense. Or feeling good…

Well, okay. The occasion didn't matter. She liked them, period. Some people smoked. Brit ate peanut M&Ms. She ate them one at a time—very slowly, sucking off the firm shell, getting to the soft chocolate beneath, never biting the peanut until all the coating was gone. She found the process of eating peanut M&Ms so pleasurable. And soothing—and comforting.

She could use a little comfort now. She pulled out the bag, tore off the top, took one out—a yellow one. She liked the yellow ones. Oh, hell, she liked all the colors. Even the greens.

She folded the top of the bag and stuck it back in her pocket and popped the single candy in her mouth. Umm.

Truth to tell, she could almost wish herself back in balmy East Hollywood, safe in her adorably seedy *Day of the Locust*-style courtyard apartment, tying up her duty shoes, ready to head out the door, late as usual for the lunch shift, looking forward to a few harsh words from her boss and an endless stream of—

"No!" Brit sat up straighter, biting the peanut before all of the chocolate was gone. *Don't go there,* she commanded herself silently. *You wanted this. A man has died because you* had *to do this. You don't* even *get to wish it all away.*

And it was time. Time to stop cowering in the crushed cabin of her plane. Time to get a move on, time to be on her way.

Bracing between the upside-down seat and the unbudgeable hatch door, Brit kicked the windscreen's web of ruined Plexiglas out of the frame. That accomplished, she tossed her pack through the hole. And then came the fun part: dragging herself out after it.

As she crawled free of the wreckage, she marveled—better to marvel than to give in to the twin urges to burst into sobbing, desperate tears and start screaming in terror.

She was alive and that was something.

If only Rutland could be crawling out with her....

Shivering, her arms wrapped around herself, she crouched on her haunches on the unwelcoming rocky ground and stared through the ragged hole from which she'd just emerged.

Should she go back, try to drag the guide out, to give him the dignity of a shallow, rocky burial?

She shivered some more, shaking her head. To bury the guide would take time and considerable effort—both of which she needed to conserve at all costs. And Rutland wasn't going to care, either way.

Bracing her hands on her knees, she pushed herself up to a bent-over position. Whoopsy. Her head spun and her stomach rolled. For a few seconds she sucked in cold air and let it out and stared at the ground between her boots, aware of the distant cry of a hawk somewhere far overhead, of the lapping of the fjord waters against the shoreline behind her, the whisper of the wind, cold and misty, smelling of evergreen, the constant creaking of the wreckage that had once been the plane. Somehow, she'd cut the back of her hand. Blood trailed between her fingers. She turned her hand over and studied her palm. Damp, slightly shiny, almost coagulated.

She flexed her hand. *Okay,* she thought. *I'm okay.*

With care, she rose to her height, brushed the dirt and debris off her jacket and jeans.

I can do this, she told herself.

Aside from a few superficial cuts and bruises and a throbbing bump on the side of her head, she was un-injured. Her trusty Timex had a compass feature, and she carried a map scribbled with arrows and instructions on how to get where she was going. The map—and the detailed instructions—had been provided by Medwyn, who'd been born in the Vildelund. She had enough food to last a few days. And she knew how to make a fire. Beneath her jacket was a thick wool sweater and beneath that, good-quality thermal under-wear. Her heavy-duty boots were broken in, and her socks were the best alpaca wool. She had a weapon and she knew how to use it if it came to that.

She may not have finished college, she might have trouble keeping a job, but life and death she could handle.

She *could* do this. She'd backpacked in the Sierras, done both the Appalachian and the Continental Divide trails. She would manage to find her way alone to the Village of the Mystics where Eric Greyfell—Med-wyn's son and hopefully the man to tell her the truth about how her brother Valbrand really died—was pur-ported to be living.

She would find Greyfell and she'd have the up-close and personal little talk she'd been itching to have with him. And when she got back to civilization, she'd find out who messed with the plane—and thus murdered poor Rutland. She'd see that the guilty were punished and that her father's men came for the dead guide, that his remains got the formal burial ceremony he deserved.

Look at it this way, she told herself, as she gauged the rugged upward sweep of craggy land before her. The plane crashing and Rutland dying was about the worst that could have happened. And guess what? It *had* happened.

The worst was over and she was still breathing.

Right then, something whizzed past her ear so close, it stirred her hair.

So much for the worst being over.

Brit went for her .45 as she dropped to one knee. She had the weapon half drawn when she heard a hiss and a *thwack*. Something punched her in the left shoulder.

An arrow! Wide-eyed in sickened disbelief, she stared along the shaft, following it to the head, which was buried in layers of fabric. Blood bloomed high on the front of her jacket. She could feel it spreading, warm and wet, under her sweater.

The good news? She felt no pain. Beyond the shock of impact, the wound itself was numb.

Also on the plus side, she wasn't dead yet.

She scanned the land before her, seeking her attacker—there. Stepping out from behind a big black boulder not fifty feet away. Some guy—way young, seventeen or eighteen, max. Long, tangled gold hair. Rigged out in rawhide leather with a mean-looking crossbow. The crossbow was pointed right at her. But she had her SIG out by then. With some fumbling, as her left hand didn't seem to be working too well, she levered the safety back—at which time, her left hand went limp. Very weird. But she was dealing with it.

Nice thing about the SIG 220. The kick wasn't all that bad. She could shoot it one-handed. She took aim.

It was a Mexican standoff—until everything started spinning.

Now it was her damn *right* hand. Something wrong with it, too. It had gone heavy. She couldn't hold it extended. It fell, nerveless, to her side, the pistol dropping to the rocks.

Well, okay. *Now* she was dead.

But just before the arrow took flight, as her body gave way and she began a strange, slow, nerveless slide to the ground, she heard a gunshot. Her too-young would-be assassin grunted and jerked back. The arrow meant to pierce her heart went wild.

And Brit was flat on the ground—drugged somehow. From the arrow in her shoulder? Must be. She wasn't out yet, not exactly, but hovering in some hazy, halfway place between waking and nothingness.

She lay on the rocks, the wind whistling overhead. She could see that hawk she'd heard before. It soared high up there, in the distant, cold blue yonder, dark wings spread against the sky.

Footsteps came crunching toward her across the rocks. A man was bending over her. An angular, arresting face. Deep-set, hypnotic gray-green eyes. She knew him from the pictures that sweet old Medwyn had made a special point of showing her.

He was Medwyn's only son, Eric Greyfell, the one she'd come to see.

And there. At Greyfell's side. Another. All in black. His face hidden behind a smooth black leather mask.

The things you see when you're probably dying…

And her eyes refused to stay open any longer. They drifted slowly shut.

There was silence.

Peace.

Oblivion.

There was a time of purest silence and velvet darkness.

Then came hot delirium. She burned within, her body ran with sweat.

And there were dreams.

In the dreams, she had visitors. Elli first. Elli was her middle sister. They were three, the sisters, fraternal triplets born within hours of one another: Liv then Elli then Brit.

"Oh, Brit." Elli wore her Viking wedding dress—and her most patient expression. She carried her wedding sword out before her, point down, jeweled hilt gleaming. She floated above the ground, surrounded by light as golden as her hair. "What have you gotten into now?"

"Ell, you look fabulous."

"You don't."

"Well, it's just...I'm so hot. Burning up..."

Elli made a *tsking* sound. "You should have gotten your degree at least, don't you think? Or maybe finished one of those novels you're always starting, before you went off and got yourself killed?"

"Not dead. Uh-uh. Not dead yet..."

"Didn't I warn you?" That was Liv, dressed for success in a cream-colored ensemble and those Mikimoto pearls that Granny Birgit had given her. Liv was bending over Brit, looking down, a scowl on her face, blue eyes narrowed, smooth blond hair falling forward against her cheeks. ''Our dear father, His Majesty the king, has the whole palace bugged. Spies everywhere. How *can* you call him Dad? He as good as abandoned us, the daughters he didn't need…until both his sons were lost.''

''He is what he is….''

''You should have kept your promise to Mom and come home with me in the first place. Then you wouldn't be here. Sweating and delirious. Dying.''

''Hot. So hot…'' Brit shut her eyes.

And when she opened them again, she could see her father. He seemed far away, standing behind his massive desk in his private audience chamber at the royal palace, Isenhalla. But at the same time he was there. With her. Looming over her, looking down at her. Firelight gleamed in his silver-shot dark hair and flashed off the ruby ring of state. Blood-red refractions danced everywhere. ''Brit. Be strong.''

''So hot…''

''Fight. In your veins runs the blood of kings. I have big plans for you. Don't you dare to die and disappoint me.''

''No, Dad. I won't die. I swear I won't….''

But her father only shook his head sadly—and disappeared.

Her mother stood in his place, tall and beautiful and thoroughly exasperated. ''What are you *doing,* Brit? What were you *thinking?*''

''Mom,'' she cried, reaching, crying out again when pain lanced through her shoulder. ''Oh, Mommy, I'm so sorry….'' But like the others, her mother had vanished.

Gentle hands guided her back to lie among the furs. An old woman with kind eyes bent close and whispered coaxingly, "It's all right. Rest. You're safe here."

And there were other voices, soft voices. They whispered of the poison that burned through her body, they murmured that now they could only wait and watch and keep her as comfortable as possible. They spoke to her soothingly. They bathed her sweating face with cool wet cloths.

And then, within the swirling, firelit twilight...

The one whose picture she carried with her, in her pack. The dead brother she'd never know.

Valbrand.

A hot bolt of fiercest joy shot through her. Not lost! Not dead, after all.

Oh, she had known it, though until this moment she hadn't quite dared to admit it even to herself.

Yet it had been there, against all odds, deep in her most secret heart. No one had really believed she would learn anything new when she said she would find the truth about what happened to him—well, okay, her father believed, at least a little. And Medwyn. After all, they had sent her here to find out what she could.

But no one else had any hope. Not her mother. Not her sisters. Not even Jorund Sorenson, the ally she'd cultivated at the National Investigative Bureau.

They all told her the truth was known already: Valbrand had died at sea.

She'd told herself they were probably right, that she only sought Eric Greyfell to understand better *how* her brother had died.

But still, she had *known*.

And she'd been right.

She tried to say his name. But words wouldn't come.

Valbrand. Tall and strong and so very alive. Standing right there, next to where she lay. He was dressed all in black, like the masked figure she'd seen in the heart of the fjord as she stared up, numb and fading, from the cold, rocky ground.

Had that been him, then—the masked one, in the fjord?

Valbrand was looking at Eric Greyfell, who stood beside him.

Eric warned her brother, "She sees you. She *knows* you. You shouldn't be here, not without the mask."

One of the soft-voiced women who tended her whispered, "She knows nothing. She's trapped in her world of fevered dreams...."

Her brother, still looking at Greyfell, smiled. His smile was rueful, sad and teasing all at once. "The littlest of my little sisters..."

Not so little, Brit thought, irritated. Just because she was the youngest by barely two hours didn't give anyone—even her long-lost and recently dead brother—the right to call her "little."

She tried to tell him that, but again the words would not take form. Valbrand was still looking at Eric, still smiling fondly. "Your bride," he said. The two words echoed. They bounced off the rough wooden walls.

Your bride, your bride, your bride, your bride...

Greyfell's expression gave away nothing. "If she lives."

"She'll live," said Valbrand. "Thor and Freyja protect her equally. Hers is the thunder, hers is love.'' He chuckled. ''And war...''

And then he looked directly at her. She saw that something terrible had happened to the left side of his face. It was crisscrossed and puckered with ridges of white scar tissue, the flesh between ruined, ranging from angry red to deep purple. What could do such a thing to a man?

Acid? A blowtorch?

She cried out in pity and despair.

The gentle hands caught her, guiding her down. The soft voices soothed her. ''Rest now, you're safe....''

Chapter Two

Slowly, the burning heat faded. The dreams receded.

Brit woke weak and exhausted. She found herself in a large wooden room, bare rafters overhead. The windows were small and set high up. Thin daylight bled in through them. Very carefully she turned her head.

She saw a big, round-bodied stove in the center of the room, the chimney rising through the rafters above. And a pair of long, plain benches on either side of a plank table made of whitish wood—a deal table, she would have bet. Deal was the pale wood that came from the Norway spruce. There were oil lamps set in sconces on the walls. She lay on a bench-like bed built into one wall. Her blankets? A nest of furs. Someone had dressed her in a soft cotton nightgown.

There was a woman—a slim, straight-backed

woman with white hair. She wore a thick, coarsely woven ankle-length tan dress and good-quality rough-terrain lace-up boots. She sat on a high stool at the far end of the room, her back to Brit. She was working at something that looked as if it might be an old-fashioned loom.

Brit licked her dry, cracked lips. Was this real? Was this actually happening? Or was it just another of her endless, swirling dreams?

She sat up. Her shoulder throbbed, her stomach lurched and her head spun, but she didn't lie back down. "Valbrand?" she managed to croak out through her parched throat. "Eric Greyfell…?"

The woman rose and came to her. "There, there. It's all right. You're safe."

She remembered that kind, wrinkled face, those loving eyes. "I…I know you. You took care of me."

"You've been very ill," the woman said as she guided Brit back down and tucked the furs around her again. "We feared we'd lose you. But you're strong. You will recover."

It came back to her then: the Skyhawk, the forced landing, the death of her guide. "Rutland…my guide?" Maybe that part—the part where she saw the guide dead—was only another of the fever dreams.

The kind-faced old woman shook her head. "What can be done has been done."

"But I…"

The woman had already turned away. She went to the stove, dipped up liquid from an iron pot with a wooden cup. Cup in hand, she returned to Brit's side. "Your guide's body was sent to his family in the valley just south of this one."

So. That part was real. Twin tears dribbled down the sides of her face. "My fault..."

"No. What fate has decreed, no mere mortal can alter."

"It wasn't fate, it was my own arrogance, my own certainty that I could—"

"Here." The woman bent close again, lifted Brit's head and put the cup to her lips. "Drink. This will soothe you."

"But I—"

"Drink."

Brit lacked the energy to argue further. She drank. The warm, sweet liquid felt good sliding down her dry throat.

"There," said the woman. She set the empty cup on the floor. It must have tipped. Brit heard it roll beneath the wooden ledge that served as her bed. The woman ignored it long enough to carefully smooth Brit's furs again. "Rest now." She dropped out of sight as she got down to reach under the bed. In a moment, with a weary little grunt, she was on her feet, cup in hand. She started to turn.

"Wait..." The old woman faced her again, one gray brow arched. "My brother. I want to see him."

The woman shook her head. "Princess, you know that your brothers are gone."

"Kylan, yes." Kylan was the second born. He had died years and years ago, when he was only a child. "But not Valbrand. I saw him. In this room, while I was so sick. His face, the left side, it was...badly scarred."

There was a short silence. The fire crackled in the

stove. Then the woman said, ''A dream, that's all. A dream brought on by your fever.''

''No, he was here. He—''

''Prince Valbrand is dead, Your Highness. Lost to us. Surely you knew. He was taken by the mother sea a year ago this past July.'' The woman spoke so tenderly, with such sincere sympathy.

Brit opened her mouth to argue further, but then the woman leaned close again. A silver medallion dangled from her neck. It must have swung free of her dress when she bent for the cup. Brit couldn't resist reaching out and touching it. It spun a little on its chain, catching the firelight. The sight made Brit smile.

The woman smiled, too, the web of wrinkles in her face etching all the deeper. ''My marriage medallion.''

Marriage? Brit frowned. And then she sighed. ''I have one, too.'' Brit pressed the place where her medallion lay beneath the nightgown, warm against her breast. ''From Medwyn, my father's grand counselor. But mine's only for luck.''

''Ah,'' said the woman, a strange and too-knowing expression on her wise, very lived-in face. ''Sleep now.''

Brit did feel tired. But she had so many questions. ''Where am I?''

''You are where you wished to be, among the ones they call the Mystics.''

''How long have I been...sick?''

''This is the fourth day.''

Her plane had gone down on Monday. ''Thursday? It's Thursday?''

''Yes.''

''How did I—?''

"Eric found you. He brought you to us."

Hope bloomed, a small, bright flame, within her. "Greyfell found me—in Drakveden Fjord?"

"That's right."

"But then, it must be true." The woman frowned down at her, clearly puzzled. "I saw him—Eric Greyfell—in Drakveden Fjord, where I crashed the Skyhawk. Valbrand was with him, I swear he was. Wearing a black mask. And there was this guy with a crossbow…" She laid her hand over the thick bandage on her shoulder. "Someone shot him before he could—"

"Hush." The woman's warm wrinkled hand stroked her brow. "No more questions now. Sleep."

"My father. My mother and my sisters…they'll be so worried…."

"Word has been sent to the king that you are safe with us."

The questions spun in her brain. She needed the answers. But the woman was right. There were too many to ask right now. She could barely keep her eyes open.

"Sleep," the woman whispered. Something about her was so familiar.

"Please…your name?"

"I'm Asta. Medwyn's sister. Eric's aunt."

So, Brit thought. Medwyn's sister. She should have known, of course. Medwyn had told her of Asta, and she could see the resemblance around the eyes and in the shape of the mouth. "Asta." It was pronounced with the *A*s like twin sighs: Ahstah. "It's a pretty name."

"Thank you, Your Highness. Now sleep."

"Yes. All right. I will. Sleep…"

* * *

Brit heard the playful giggle of a child. She opened her eyes in time to watch a mop of shiny blond curls disappear over the side of the sleeping bench.

A few seconds later the curls popped up again, along with a pair of china-blue eyes and a cute little turned-up nose. The eyes widened. "Oops." The small face popped out of sight again. There was more giggling below.

Brit grinned and whispered in a dry croak, "I see you."

More giggles. And then the little head rose into view once more. The rosebud mouth widened in a shy smile. The child raised a thumb and pointed it at her tiny chest. "Mist."

"Hello, Mist. I'm Brit."

"Bwit." The child called Mist beamed with pleasure. "Pwincess Bwit."

"Just Brit will do."

"Just Bwit. Bwit, Bwit, Bwit…"

"Mist," Asta chided from over by the stove where she sat with two younger women, a circle of children playing some sort of game with sticks and a tiny red ball at their feet. "Leave Her Highness to sleep."

"It's all right." Brit winked at the child and pulled herself to a sitting position, wincing at the sharp twinge from the wound in her shoulder. Sunlight slanted in the high slits of the windows. Late morning, Brit thought. Or possibly early afternoon. She let her head fall forward to stretch her stiff neck, and her tangled hair fell over her eyes. She speared her fingers in it to shove it back.

Ugh. A serious shampooing and a little intimate contact with a decent conditioner would do wonders about now. Not to mention a long, hot bath. She heard a growling sound—her stomach. She could eat half a polar bear, or whatever they were serving here in the Vildelund. But first, water. A tall, cool, glorious glass of it.

However, she hesitated to throw back the furs and go looking for a drink in her thin borrowed nightgown with all these strange women and children in the room. "I wonder, could I have some water?"

"Of course." Asta set aside her sewing and went to the big wooden counter against one wall. The sink was there, complete with an ancient-looking pump faucet. Asta pumped clear water into a tall cup and carried it to Brit.

She drank. It was absolute heaven going down.

From her seat on the floor, Mist giggled some more. "Bwit fuhsty." *Fuhsty,* Brit figure out, had to mean thirsty.

Brit swallowed the last of it. "Was I ever. Thanks." She handed Asta back the empty cup. The women by the fire were watching her. She gave them a nod. "I seem to remember you two being here while I was sick…"

"I forget myself," said Asta. "Your Highness, my daughters-in-law, Sif and Sigrid. Mist, whom you've met, is Sif's youngest." She named off the other children. Two were Sigrid's and two, Sif's.

"Great to meet you all." Brit turned to Asta again. "And now…what's for dinner?"

Asta's smile was wide and pleased. "Your health improves."

"It certainly does."

"Bah-wee soup," announced Mist.

"That's barley," Asta explained.

Brit wrinkled her nose. "I was thinking more along the lines of steak and eggs and hash browns."

"Your stomach isn't ready for solid food yet."

Brit sighed. "Barley soup it is." She gave Asta a big smile. "And would you go and tell my brother I'd like to see him now, please?"

It seemed, for a moment, as if the room was too quiet. Then Asta spoke carefully. "We talked of this earlier. Perhaps you've forgotten. Your brother is—"

Brit waved a hand. "Never mind. I remember. So, if my brother's not available, could you track down your nephew, Eric, please? It's imperative that I speak with him."

Sif and Sigrid shared a look. Asta suggested, "Eat first. See how you feel."

Asta dished up a big bowl of broth with barley and cut a thick slice from a loaf of dark bread. She carried it over to Brit on a wooden tray.

By the time she'd eaten half the soup and taken a bite of the bread, Brit was ready to call it quits on the food front. "I guess I sort of miscalculated how much I could eat." Also, she was tired again. This convalescing thing was *so* inconvenient. She handed Asta the bowl. "Thank you."

"You are most welcome, Your High—"

"I wonder, could we dispense with the 'Your Highness' routine?"

Asta looked pleased. "I would be honored."

"It's Brit, then, all right?"

"Yes. Brit. Good enough."

"Now, if you could just get me my clothes and—"

Asta was gently pushing her down. "All that can wait. Rest, now. You're not ready to get out of bed."

Brit found she tended to agree with Asta. So annoying. She felt tired to the bone. She didn't have the energy to get dressed—let alone to deal with Eric Greyfell. She gave Asta a rueful smile. "Sorry, but there's one thing that *can't* wait."

Asta brought her a pair of clogs and wrapped a shawl around her shoulders as the women by the fire continued with their needlework and the group of children played their game and little Mist sat on the floor near Brit's sleeping bench, sucking her thumb and watching wide-eyed.

It was hard work, even leaning on Asta, to get all the way to the door and out into the crisp afternoon beyond. The thin sunlight, after the days inside, seemed blinding. Brit hardly had the energy to glance at the village around her—more long wooden houses, all grouped together along a single dirt street. There were pastures and paddocks behind the houses. Beyond the pastures, a thick forest of spruce flowed up the surrounding hills.

Asta noted her interest in the village houses. "Here we live in the old Norse way. In traditional longhouses—long, one-room dwellings where we eat, sleep, work and gather with our friends and family."

Each house had a small garden to one side of it. The pastureland beyond the gardens was dotted with karavik and sturdy, long-haired white Gullandrian horses. According to the map Medwyn had drawn for her, Drakveden Fjord wasn't far to the north. If she followed the fjord west, she should come to the site where her Skyhawk had gone down.

Not that she had the slightest inclination to go looking for it now. But someday soon. When the annoying weakness left over from her illness had passed.

At the end of the house, they reached a wooden lean-to. It had a sliver of moon carved into the top of the door. Just like in the old days in America, Brit thought. Was the moon on the door the international symbol for outhouse? She grinned to herself.

"Something humorous?" Asta wondered.

"Nothing important. And I don't think I'm going to ask how you handled this while I was so sick."

"We managed," Asta replied with her usual sunny smile. "I'll be right here when you're done."

Brit went in and shut the door. When she came out, Asta was waiting, as promised.

Brit forced a smile. "You are my hero, Asta, I hope you know it."

"I am honored to be of service."

"I have to ask, though I know it's going to make me sound like your classic ugly American—don't you ever think about putting in a bathroom, maybe adding electricity?"

Asta shrugged. "Here we live simply. It's a hard life, yes. But that is our way. We believe the simple life builds strong character and a clear mind—now come. Let's get you back to bed." Asta offered her shoulder. Brit accepted it gratefully. Slowly they shuffled back inside, where Asta helped her to get comfortable and brought her warm water from the stove and a soft cloth to wash her hands and rinse her face.

Brit was already half asleep again when Asta began checking the dressing on her bandage.

"Asta?"

"Hmm?"

"About my brother..."

"Shh. Sleep."

"Sweep, sweep, sweep," chanted Mist, over by the fire now with the other children.

Brit gave in and did as she was told.

The next time she woke, Eric Greyfell was sitting in a chair about two feet from her nest of furs.

She blinked, then muttered, "It's about time you showed up."

He nodded, one regal dip of his head. "My aunt informed me that you wished to speak with me." And then he just sat there, looking at her.

They were alone. The high windows were dark and the lamps were lit. "Where is Asta?"

"My aunt, as you may have deduced, is something of a healer. Her skills are needed elsewhere tonight."

It occurred to Brit that she'd met Asta's daughters-in-law and grandchildren. But she'd never seen a husband. "Your uncle?"

"He died several years ago."

She had assumed as much. "I'm sorry to hear it."

He shrugged. "We live, we die. That is the way of things. For my uncle's death, the time of mourning is long past."

"I see. Well, a good thing, right—I mean, that grief passes?" Sheesh. Talk about inane chatter. She was filling in time as she worked her way around to what was really on her mind: Valbrand.

And the little detail no one seemed to want to talk about—the fact that he wasn't dead, after all.

Greyfell said nothing. The fire crackled in the stove and Brit stared at Medwyn's son, wondering how best to get him to admit that her brother was alive—and to convince him that he should bring Valbrand to her. Now.

As she debated how to begin, he watched her. She found his hooded gaze unnerving. "Why do you look at me like that?"

"Like what, precisely?"

She wished she hadn't asked. "Never mind."

He stood and came closer, until he loomed over her, his deep-set eyes lost in the shadows beneath the shelf of his brow. She stared up at those shadowed eyes and wished he hadn't come so near. She felt like a total wimp, lying there in somebody else's nightgown, weak and shaky and flat on her back.

She sat up—fast enough that her head spun and pain sliced through her shoulder. "Listen."

"Yes?"

His shoulder-length ash-brown hair had a slight curl to it. He wore it loose, though it seemed it had been tied back—in the fjord and that time he stood over her when she was so sick. Now it looked just-combed, smooth and shiny. He smelled of the outdoors, fresh and piney and cool. She didn't want to think about what *she* smelled like. She clutched the furs close to her breast, as if they might protect her from his probing eyes. "Look. I just wanted to talk to you about…well, I mean, my brother…" She waited. Maybe he'd give it up, tell her the truth that everyone kept denying. Maybe he would see in her eyes how badly she needed confirmation that Valbrand lived.

Maybe he would realize that she could be trusted.

But it wasn't happening. He said nothing. She let out a low groan of frustration. "Can we skip the lies and evasions, please? Will you just let me speak with my brother?"

His mouth softened. He lifted his head a fraction, and the lamplight melted the shadows that hid his eyes.

Kind. His eyes were kind. They gleamed with sympathy. She hated that—his sympathy. It made her doubt what she knew in her heart. And it made her soften toward him. She didn't need softening. She was weak enough already.

He spoke so gently, each word uttered with great care. "You must accept that your brother is dead."

"No."

"Yes."

Brit clutched the furs tighter and wished she didn't feel so tired. She wanted to keep after him, to break him down, to get him to admit what they both knew was true. But how?

Her mind felt thick and slow. Weariness dragged at her. All he had to do was stay kind and steady—and keep on with the denials. Eventually she would have to give up and go back to sleep.

She spoke softly, pleadingly, though it galled her to do it. "I saw him. In the fjord, with you, I'm sure of it, though then he was wearing a mask—but here, when I was sick, I saw his face. Please stop lying. Please stop implying that I was too sick and confused to know what I saw. Please admit—"

"I cannot admit what never happened." His deep, rich voice was weighted with just the right measure of regret. He seemed so sincere. She could almost begin to believe he spoke the truth. And to doubt what her eyes had seen…

"He *was* here. I know it."

Gently, so regretfully, he shook his head.

She swallowed. Her mouth was so dry.

And this was a subject better pursued when she was stronger. "I wonder. Would you mind getting me some water?"

"It would be my pleasure."

He went to the sink. While he pumped the water she tried to come up with some new approach, some brilliant line of questioning that would make him open up to her. She drew a complete blank.

And he was back with a full cup. "Do you need help?"

"Thanks. I can manage." She held out her hand, pleased to see that it hardly shook at all. He passed her the cup. She drank long and deep, sighing when she finished.

He was watching, the slightest of smiles tipping the corners of his mouth. "Good?"

"Wonderful."

"More?"

"I would appreciate it." She held out the cup. Their fingers brushed as he took it from her. It seemed, for some reason, a far too intimate contact. He went to the sink again and she watched him go. He wore heavy tan trousers, mountain boots and an oatmeal-colored thermal shirt. He had a great butt. He also carried himself proudly—like the king everyone thought he might someday be now they all believed that Valbrand was gone.

In Gullandria, succession was never assured. All male jarl, or nobles, were princes. Any prince might put himself forward as a candidate for king when the current king could no longer rule and the jarl gathered in the Grand Assembly for the election ceremony known as the kingmaking.

Since childhood, Eric had been groomed, not for the throne, but to one day take his father's place as grand counselor. It had been Valbrand, everyone felt certain, who would win the throne. King Osrik was a respected and effective ruler. The country had prospered during his reign. And the people loved Valbrand. That made him the logical next choice.

But then Valbrand went to sea and didn't come back. And Osrik and Medwyn turned their sights to Eric as the one to claim the crown when the time came. The two had schemed shamelessly. Eric, they decided, should marry one of Osrik's estranged daughters....

The potential king in question had reached the sink. He stood with his back to her, broad-shouldered, narrow-hipped, regal even from the rear, pumping water into her cup.

Brit allowed herself a wide grin.

Her father and Medwyn's schemes kept backfiring. Elli had fallen in love with the man they'd sent to kidnap her. And on Elli's wedding night, Liv had dallied with the notorious Prince Finn Danelaw. She'd become pregnant as a result. And Eric? After months spent in search of the truth about Valbrand's supposed death, Eric had come here, to the Vildelund. He'd resisted his father's repeated requests that he return to the palace and begin preparing for his future as king.

Yes, Brit knew that her father and Medwyn considered her next in line to be Eric's bride. But she'd made it clear to them that romance wasn't on her agenda. She was after the truth about Valbrand. Period.

King Osrik and Medwyn had said they accepted that. And if they didn't, so what? Her father and his grand counselor could plot and plan to their heart's content. She had a goal. Marrying Eric Greyfell wasn't it.

"Brit?"

She blinked. Eric was standing right over her, holding the full cup. "Oh, uh, sorry. Just woolgathering." He wore an expectant look. Maybe he didn't get her meaning. "Woolgathering is an expression. It means—"

"Purposeless thinking." Those deep-set eyes gleamed. "Aimless reverie. The word is derived from the actual process of woolgathering, which entails wandering the countryside, gathering up bits of wool from bushes that karavik—sheep—have brushed up against."

"Very good."

"And where, exactly, did your woolgathering take you?"

She took the cup again and sipped. She was stalling. She really didn't feel up to going into it—especially since it would only lead to the part about how their fathers hoped they'd hook up. "It's not important."

"Somehow I don't believe you."

"Then we're even, aren't we?" She drank the last and handed back the empty cup. "You know what?

I'm really tired. I appreciate your coming and talking to me.'' She stretched out and pulled up the furs. ''You don't have to stay until your aunt gets back. I'll be fine, I promise.'' She snuggled down deeper and shut her eyes. Sleep came almost instantly.

Eric stood over Valbrand's youngest sister and watched her face soften as she drifted into the land of dreams. She had great courage. She'd sought him out in the wild land of his birth, alone but for a single guide to show her the way. She'd lived through the crash that had killed her guide, emerging unaided from the wreckage of her plane, armed and ready to face whatever waited outside. She possessed spirit and stamina—few survived a hit from a renegade's poisoned arrow. And he liked her fine, quick mind.

Her eyes had dark smudges beneath them. A limp coil of lank blond hair lay across her cheek. He dared, very gently, to smooth it back, careful of the still-livid bruise at her temple.

She sighed, a tiny smile curving her cracked, dry lips. He felt the corners of his own mouth lifting in instinctive response.

He supposed he was willing to admit it now. His father had chosen well.

Chapter Three

It was much later when Brit woke again. The lamps were out, though night still ruled beyond the high-set windows. The fire had burned low. It cast a muted glow out the stove door window, spilling soft gold light across the table a few feet away. Where Brit lay, in the far corner, the shadows were thickest.

She sat up. Wow. Her head didn't spin and her shoulder throbbed only dully.

There were three other wide, wall-mounted benches like the one where she slept. One of them—down the wall past another bed, sharp right, then halfway down the next wall—was occupied. And not by the kindly old woman who had brought her back from near death.

Eric lay with his furs to his waist, his eyes shut, face turned toward the center of the room, one arm to his side, the other across his chest.

So had he been sleeping there last night, and the night before? She really hadn't noticed. She'd been far too busy sweating and hallucinating. Strange, to think of him, living here in Asta's longhouse, sleeping in the same room with her and her not even knowing it.

Moonlight from the window across the room slanted down on him, making shadows and silver of the strong planes and angles of his face, defining more sharply the sculpted perfection of his lean, bare chest and hard arms.

The guy really was gorgeous.

And she really, really had to pee.

She figured by now she was strong enough to handle at least that problem on her own. Easing back the furs, she swung her feet over the edge. The clogs were right there, toes peeking out beneath the bench—bless you, Asta.

Brit slid her feet into them. Then, slowly, she stood. Ta-da! Upright and okay about it. So far, so good.

She grabbed one of the furs from her bed and wrapped herself up in it. And then, as quietly as she could, she started for the door.

Ever try to tiptoe in clogs?

She got about four steps when Eric spoke from behind her. ''What are you doing out of bed?''

She sighed. ''Sorry. Didn't mean to wake you. I just have to make a quick trip outside.'' She was pointed toward the door and she stayed that way. She had a feeling he was naked under the furs and she also knew that he was going to insist on getting up and helping her out to the lean-to. If the rest of him looked half as good as what she'd already seen...

Down, girl. Don't go there.

"I'll go with you," he said.

Surprise, surprise. "Make it quick, okay? The situation is getting urgent." She shuffled forward. He must have had his pants nearby, because she only got a few steps before he was taking her elbow. He wore fur-lined moccasin-style slippers over bare feet, the tan trousers he'd worn earlier and no shirt. She cast a meaningful glance at his hard, bare chest. "I'll bet it's nippy out there."

He shrugged, pulled open the door and ushered her out into the starry, cold night. Ten steps and they were at the lean-to.

"Be right out." She hustled in and shut the door.

Boy, was she grateful she wasn't wearing any panties. It was a near thing, but she sat down in time. And after the initial relief, she worried about what women always worry about when they're performing a private function and some guy is standing right outside.

She was sure he could hear everything.

Life in the Mystic village was a little *too* simple for her tastes. Give her insulated walls. And a real toilet that flushed, with a seat that didn't leave slivers in inconvenient places. And a bedroom door to shut when she went to sleep at night, for crying out loud.

When she opened the door again, he was waiting right there, those lean, strong arms crossed over the goose bumps on his beautiful smooth chest. "Ready?" He held out an arm for her.

"I can make it on my own, I think."

He shrugged and fell in behind her.

Inside, she turned for the sink. He followed. Her irritation level rose. Okay, she'd been seriously sick.

But she was well enough now to walk to the sink unattended.

But then he said, "Here," and manned the pump. She rinsed her hands and couldn't resist splashing a little icy water on her face, sipping up a mouthful or two. When she was done, he handed her a towel. She wiped her face. He bent and picked up the fur that had dropped to the rough wooden floor while she reveled in the feel of the water against her cheeks. He gestured toward her sleeping bench. "Back to bed."

It sounded like a great idea. She clomped over, left the heavy clogs where she'd found them and stretched out. He settled the fur over her. "Sleep now."

She couldn't help smiling. "Your aunt's always saying that."

"It's good advice. You've been very ill."

"Is she still at the neighbor's?"

He nodded. "It doesn't look good. A heart attack, we think. The man is young, too. Barely forty."

"Shouldn't he be in a hospital?"

"The man's a true Mystic. No hospitals for him."

"But if he dies—"

His eyes gleamed down at her through the shadows. "It's a choice, to make a life here. With few conveniences. No phones, poor access to emergency care. Most who live here embrace the realities of this place."

They were both whispering. It was nice—companionable. A quiet little chat in the midnight darkness. "Why?"

"They find peace here. And real meaning to their lives."

She smiled, thinking again of what Asta had told

her. A simple life, one that made for strong character and a clear mind. "I was surprised tonight, when I woke up and you were sleeping right over there."

"I live here, in my aunt's house, when I'm staying at the village."

She let a second or two elapse before she asked, "And where does my brother live?"

He didn't answer right away. She had a lovely, rising feeling. He would tell her the truth. And then she would keep after him until he agreed to take her to wherever Valbrand was staying.

But then he said softly, "Your brother lies forever sleeping—at the bottom of the sea."

She bit her lower lip to stop its sudden trembling. "That was cruel."

"The truth is often cruel."

She looked him dead in the eyes. "But it's not the truth. It's a lie. I saw him. You know I did. You were right beside him, standing almost where you're standing now. You said, 'She sees you. She *knows* you.'"

"In your dream."

"It wasn't a dream."

He was already turning away. "Good night, Brit."

Good night, Brit. Damn him, he so easily called her by her first name. Everyone else fell all over themselves Your-Highnessing her to death. But Eric Greyfell had presumed to address her with familiarity from the first.

And come to think of it, why did it bug her so much that he did? As a rule, since she'd come to Gullandria, she was constantly asking people to please just call her Brit.

She heard faint rustlings over by his furs. He would be taking off his trousers, slipping into bed....

"Eric?"

"Yes?" He sounded wary.

And well he should. "You do have some way, don't you, of contacting my father—and yours?"

"There is radio contact, yes. It can be undependable, but eventually we get through."

"Is that how you got hold of my father to tell him what had happened to me?"

"That's right."

"So why didn't he send a helicopter to take me out of here and get me to a hospital?"

He was silent for several seconds. The remains of a log popped in the grate, the sound jarring in the quiet room.

Getting impatient, she prompted, "Eric?"

"Is that what you would have wanted, to be airlifted out of here, had you been able to make the decision for yourself?"

She considered for a moment, then admitted, "No."

"Then it was done as you would have wished."

"But who decided that I would stay here, at your aunt's village, instead of going to a hospital? My brother?"

Did he chuckle then, very low? She thought he might have. "That would have been difficult for him, as he is dead."

She scowled at the ceiling. "This radio—where is it?"

"Here, in the village."

"So. You brought me here, and then you contacted my father..."

"Yes."

"And my father decided that I would stay?"

"Your father. And mine. Your father knows you—better than you might think."

"And *your* father?"

"Some say he has a way of seeing the secrets that lie in the hearts and minds of others. He understood that you were set on a certain course, that if they took you away, you would only return."

"But if I had died…"

"My father also felt certain you were meant to survive. And to grow strong again. There's an old Norse saying…"

As if she hadn't heard it a hundred times already. "'The length of my life and the day of my death were fated long ago.'" He did chuckle then, loud enough that there was no mistaking the sound. She couldn't stop herself from asking, "And you—how did you feel about having to drag an almost-dead woman out of Drakveden Fjord and all the way to your aunt's village?"

"It was a difficult journey over rough country. It took most of a day and into the night. I felt certain, for a time at least, that you wouldn't survive."

"And when my father and your father decided I would stay?"

"I had my doubts it was the right decision—but now, here you are. Alive. Growing stronger. I see that I was wrong to doubt."

"You certainly were. And, Eric?"

"Yes?"

"Your father was right. My course is set. I'm not

going away until I speak with my brother face-to-face.''

There was silence.

Which was okay with Brit. Right then there was nothing more to say.

When Brit woke to daylight, Eric was gone. Asta lay beneath the furs on the bed just down the hall.

Quietly, wanting to let the old woman sleep, Brit got up and tiptoed to the sink. She washed her hands and took a long drink and then went back to bed. She was thinking that maybe she might sleep some more.

Not. Her stomach kept growling. And she wanted a bath. At the same time she didn't really know how to go about getting food or getting clean without Asta's help.

For fifteen minutes or so, Brit lay staring at the rafters, telling herself to ignore her growling stomach and go back to sleep. About then, quietly, the door opened. Eric. He entered on silent feet. His hair was wet, his face freshly shaven. He carried what looked like yesterday's clothing and a small leather case: shaving supplies? He went to his bed and stashed everything beneath it.

She sat up. He glanced her way and she signaled him over. When he reached her and she smelled soap and water on him, she whispered, ''I know you've had a bath. Who do I have to kill to get one myself?''

He crouched to drag her pack out from under her sleeping bench. ''Get what you need,'' he instructed low, pulling her jacket out, too. She saw that the arrow hole had been neatly mended and the blood stain treated. Blood is so stubborn, though. The stain was faint, but still here. "Come," he said. "I'll show you the way."

The village bathhouse—divided in two; one side for the women, the other for the men—was several doors down from Asta's. They had actual indoor plumbing and a huge, propane-burning water heater behind the building, Eric told her. And towels, stacks of them, on shelves along one wall. There were two other women inside, just finishing up. They greeted Brit politely and went on their way.

Brit took off her coat and her nightgown and debated over the large bandage that covered the wound on her shoulder. She decided to leave it, let it get wet, and then figure out what to do about changing it when she got back to the longhouse. She showered, washed her hair and brushed her teeth. Then she put on clean clothes and emerged to find Eric waiting outside for her.

She hadn't expected him to do that. "You didn't have to stay. I can manage the walk back on my own."

"Here," he said, taking her nightgown from over her arm. "That, too." He indicated her vanity pack.

"No, it's all right. Really. I can—"

He waved away her objections, his hand out, waiting for her to give him the pack. With a sigh, she did. He offered her his arm.

Oh, why not? She slipped her hand into the crook of his elbow and they started off.

She clomped along the hard-packed dirt street beside him, shivering a little, eager to get back to the longhouse, to dry her hair by the fire and do something about her uncomfortable soggy bandage—and most important, to find a way to get him to be straight with her.

What, exactly, was he up to here? He refused to stop lying and take her to her brother—a fact that she realized might very well be because Valbrand wanted it that way.

But it wasn't only the big lie he kept telling.

It was also that he was just…such a hottie. And she kept getting the feeling that he was very subtly coming on to her—which was something she *so* didn't need at this point in her life. It would only muck up her focus, add complications she wasn't up to dealing with.

Plus, if he really *was* coming on to her—which, face it, could very well be nothing more than a sort of contrary wishful thinking on her part—why? Because their fathers wanted them to get married and settle down to rule the country? Doubtful. Because she was so incredibly sexy and alluring, with a hole in her shoulder and bruises on her bruises, no makeup and, until about fifteen minutes ago, very dirty hair and serious morning breath? Not.

The deal was, she couldn't figure him out. And until she did, she was going to be wary of him. She didn't trust him. And yet…

It *had* been nice of him to wait. And his arm was warm and strong and steady, his body heat comforting.

They passed a few people as they made their way to Asta's house. A man carrying firewood. A woman with a baby in a papoose-like contraption on her back. Eric nodded, and the villagers nodded back, sparing smiles for Brit, along with murmured Your Highnesses and expressions of pleasure at her improving health.

In the longhouse Asta still slept—a lump beneath the furs, curled up and turned to the wall.

Brit whispered to Eric. "The man she was nursing?"

"It appears he'll survive, after all."

She smiled at the good news as she took off her coat—easing it carefully over her bad shoulder—and hung it on one of the wooden pegs near the door. The clogs made too much noise, so she slipped them off and set them with Asta's pair, beneath the coatrack. In her heavy socks, she padded to her sleeping bench, where she stowed the rest of her things. When she turned back toward the center of the room, Eric was watching her, his gaze tracking to where the water from her soaked bandage was seeping through her shirt. She wondered what else he was looking at. She hadn't taken a bra to the bathhouse. Right now, with her shoulder so stiff, it would have hurt like hell to get into one. And she'd only be taking it off again, anyway. Because as soon as she rebandaged her wound and ate something, her hair should be dry enough that she could climb back into bed.

"Let me change that." His voice was so soft, the verbal equivalent of a caress.

They gazed at each other. It was another of those edgy, what-is-really-happening-here? moments. She blinked and started to tell him no.

But the bandage had to be changed. Asta was asleep. Brit would probably make a mess of it if she tried to do it herself—and, hey, at least her thermal shirt had a zipper front. She should be able to get it out of his way and still keep the crucial parts covered.

"All right, I'd appreciate it—just hold on a minute.'' She turned for her pack beneath her bed. In a side pocket she had three precious bags of peanut M&Ms. She took one out, opened it and got herself a nice, fat blue one. She held out the bag to Eric. Looking puzzled, he shook his head. She put it away.

When she approached the table again, he asked, ''What is that?''

She held up the blue candy. ''M&M. Peanut. I love them.''

For that she got a lifted eyebrow. ''And you must have one...now?''

''I find them soothing—and don't worry. It's not drugs or anything. Just sugar and chocolate and a peanut at the center.'' He still had that I-don't-get-it look. So all right, she was nervous, okay? There was something way too intimate about him tending her wound. ''Could we just...do this?'' She stuck the candy in her mouth.

''As you wish.'' He gestured for her to sit at the table. Then he turned toward the sink area—presumably to get fresh bandages and tape.

Brit seized the moment, perching with her back to him at the end of one of the two long benches, and swiftly unzipping her shirt. She heard the slight creak of the sink pump. He must be washing his hands. She pulled the shirt down her left arm—too roughly, hurt like a mother—and got into trouble trying to reinsert the slide into the stopper thingy.

He was finished at the sink. She heard him approach behind her, moving quietly, halting at her back.

''Just a minute,'' she muttered, already chewing her only half-sucked M&M, hunched over the zipper, feeling exposed and ridiculous and still battling to get the damn thing to hook.

"No hurry."

She felt her face flaming as she continued to struggle, the pain an extra irritant as her injured shoulder complained at the tension. At last she got it in. With a sigh of embarrassed relief, she zipped until she had her breasts covered, the left arm of the shirt hanging beneath her own arm.

She turned to him, certain she would find him smirking or quelling a smarmy chuckle. He wasn't, on either count. He was, however, staring at her chest. He shifted his gaze up to meet her eyes—and she understood.

He'd been looking at her medallion.

She might so easily have lifted it on its chain and mentioned that his father had given it to her. But she didn't. Somehow, the idea of drawing attention to it seemed unwise, even dangerous. "Okay. Do it."

He set his equipment on the table: a roll of gauze, tape, scissors and a tube of ointment. Then he returned to the sink, where he grabbed a cloth from a shelf and filled a wooden bowl halfway with water. At the stove he took the steaming kettle and poured hot water to mix with the cold in the bowl. He returned to her, setting the bowl down, dropping the cloth into it.

He went to work. Once again, with him so near, she became way too aware of the fresh, outdoorsy smell of him. His hands were gentle—quick and skilled. She found herself wondering how many wounds he'd bandaged.

"It's just as well you got it wet," he whispered. "It's not sticking."

She averted her eyes through most of the process, but when he had the soggy bandage off, she looked down at the damage. It wasn't pretty—ragged and red, still draining a little. There was going to be a scar, for sure. "I guess I won't be going strapless to the ball."

He gently cleaned the wound with the warm, damp cloth. "Wear your scars proudly. They speak of what you have faced—and what you have survived."

She looked at him then. Straight on. There were perhaps four inches between his mouth and hers. And his mouth was...so soft looking. Four inches. No distance at all. The slightest forward movement on her part and she would be kissing him.

Oh, now, why did she have to go and think of kisses? She pointedly shifted her gaze to a spot beyond his shoulder.

He went on with his work, finished swabbing the wound with the warm cloth, applied the ointment, which soothed the soreness and gave off a faint scent of cloves.

Finally, he taped on the fresh bandage. "There," he said, stepping back.

Her stomach growled. Loudly.

That mouth she'd almost found herself kissing curved up at the corners. "Oatmeal?"

"Please."

The heavy earthenware bowls waited in plain sight on open shelves. She set the table, doing her best to keep clatter to a minimum as he, equally quietly, fixed the food. They even had milk, which he removed from a small cellar under the floor. There was honey for sweetening. And a lovely tea that tasted of cinnamon—a tea almost good enough to make up for the lack of her usual four cups of morning coffee, strong and black.

She was tired again by the time the meal was over. She helped him clear off, and then he took the single-barreled shotgun from the rack above the door and a pack from under his sleeping bench and left.

Miraculously, Asta hadn't stirred through the changing of the bandage or the meal preparations. Brit plodded to her own furs and stretched out. She was clean and her stomach was full. Life, at the moment, was good.

She was asleep within minutes.

Brit woke again in the afternoon. Asta was up, surrounded by her grandchildren, her daughters-in-law sitting with her near the fire. For a while Brit lay there, feeling cozy and comfortable, listening to the children laugh and whisper to each other—to the women talk. Sigrid was the quiet one, very controlled, it seemed to Brit. Sif, on the other hand, chuckled and chattered and spoke of the neighbors, of what she had heard about this one or that one. Sif was the one who saw that Brit was awake. She looked over and smiled.

Brit smiled back. Then she rose, put on her boots, got a bra from her pack beneath the sleeping bench and excused herself to visit the lean-to. When she returned she washed her hands at the sink, enjoyed a big drink of water and turned to gesture at the two forlorn-looking piles of feathers lying on the table. "What have we here?"

"Eric brought them," said Asta, confirming what Brit had already guessed. "A pair of fine partridges. Aren't they beautiful?"

"They certainly are." She couldn't keep herself from asking, "He's been back again since morning, then? Eric, I mean."

Sif and Sigrid shared what could only have been called a sly, knowing look. Asta nodded. "He'll return for the evening meal."

Brit set her cup on the counter—firmly. Enough about Eric. "So how 'bout I make myself useful and pluck those birds for you?"

Asta tried to talk her out of it. It wasn't necessary, she said. She'd do it herself in a little while.

But Brit insisted. In the end, when she had sworn she could handle it, she was allowed to do the plucking. Eric had already gutted them in the field, which, her uncle Cam always said, was the best time to do it. The birds cooled faster that way; less chance the meat would sour.

"I'm guessing you have some sort of game shed," Brit said when the task was done.

Asta, still near the stove with her daughters-in-law, sent her an approving look. "We do. Out in the back."

Brit took them out and hung them in the wire cage behind the longhouse, where they'd be safe from scavengers until the meat had aged properly. When she returned, Sif was preparing to take Asta's laundry to the community washhouse.

Brit added her borrowed nightgown and a few other items to the big net bag. "I wonder—could I tag along?"

Sif, who had skin like fresh cream and wore her long red hair in two fat braids wrapped around her head, looked doubtful. "Are you certain you feel well enough?"

"Positive."

"She's a determined one," Asta remarked, never dropping a stitch. "Take her with you. Fresh air will bring the color back to her cheeks."

"I go, too," announced little Mist, rising from her seat on the floor and tucking her rag doll beneath her arm.

"All right," said her mother fondly. "You may come along."

"Don't overextend yourself," Asta told Brit. "If you tire, return immediately."

"You bet." Brit grabbed her coat from the peg and followed Sif and Mist out the door.

The washhouse was just beyond the bathhouse. Inside, there was running hot water and six deep concrete sinks, set up in pairs, one for washing, one for rinsing. Hooked between each pair of sinks were old-fashioned, hand-cranked clothes wringers. A washboard waited in each washing sink. Clotheslines ran everywhere, crisscrossing back and forth, about half of them hung with drying garments. One wall had a long table tucked against it—for folding the dry clothes, no doubt. And there were metal racks where sweaters, blocked back into shape, were drying.

Sif explained that each family had washhouse hours. They hung their clothes on the lines and came back for them after they'd had time to dry.

Brit wasn't much use at the wringer or the washboard. Her shoulder was still way too tender for that. But she helped feed the clothes into the roller while Sif cranked the handle. And then later, she shook out the wet things and handed them to Sif for hanging on the line.

And of course, while they worked, the two women talked. The usual getting-to-know-you chatter. Brit insisted she preferred to dispense with the Your Highnesses and asked how long Sif had been married and if she was born in the village.

"Gunnolf and I have been married eight years—and no, I come from a village to the east, near Solgang Fjord." Asta's wasn't the only village where the people known as Mystics made their home. There were several in the Vildelund.

Brit spoke of her sisters and their new husbands. And then she asked quietly, "Why is it neither Asta nor Eric will talk to me about my brother?"

Did the other woman's eyes shift away—just a fraction? After a moment Sif said carefully, "I think it's more that you were so insistent you'd seen him. They didn't know what to say about it, except to tell you that you couldn't have seen him, as he is dead."

He wasn't, of course. He lived. She knew it. She *had* seen him. But constantly insisting that she knew he was alive didn't seem to be getting her anywhere. A new approach was called for. "Did you ever meet my brother?" She shook out a wet shirt—from the size and cut, probably Eric's—and handed it to Sif.

Sif took so long to answer Brit began to think she wouldn't. But then she said, "For our wedding trip, Eric took Gunnolf and me over the Black Mountains to the south, to see Lysgard. We stayed for seven nights at Isenhalla. Gunnolf already knew your brother, since His Highness had visited this village often as a boy. But I had never had the honor." Sif hung the shirt on the line. Brit shook out a gray gathered skirt and glanced up to find Sif staring off toward the sinks, a musing smile on her full mouth. "It was a wondrous time for us. Newly wed. So happy. Looking forward to our life together here, in the village of Gunnolf's people. And being honored to tour our country's capital city as guests of the royal family."

Brit handed her the wet skirt. "You met Valbrand during that trip?"

"Yes. He was…so very handsome. And kind. Thoughtful for one so young—he was barely twenty at the time, I believe. On more than one occasion he paused to speak with Gunnolf and me. He would ask how we were enjoying our stay at Isenhalla. He even advised us on things to be sure to see in Lysgard." The blue eyes were misty. "Yes. I can tell you that." As opposed, Brit thought with some irony, to what you *can't* tell me? Sif sighed. "Prince Valbrand was a good man. What a king he would have made."

"Dawk Waiduh," said Mist. The child sat in a chair a few feet away, near the long table. She held her doll in her lap and she smiled proudly at Brit. "Pwince Vawbwand. Dawk Waiduh."

Sif gave a nervous laugh. "Children. The things they say…"

"What is a Dawk Waiduh?"

"Dawk Waiduh!" Mist insisted, as if Brit wasn't getting it right.

"She means Dark Raider, I think," Sif said, too casually, giving the gray skirt an extra shake, then turning to hang it on the line.

"Yes!" Mist was beaming again. "Dawk Waiduh."

Brit vaguely remembered hearing stories of the Dark Raider—way back when, at her mother's knee. Ingrid had made it a point that her California-raised daughters should know the myths, the basic history and at least some of the customs of the land where they were born. "A legend, right? A masked hero, all in black on a rare black Gullandrian horse."

"That's right," said Sif. "A legend. It is said that the Dark Raider is reborn to the people in troubled times to save them from corrupt men and tyrants without honor."

Dressed all in black, Brit was thinking. Both times Brit had seen her brother—those times that everyone kept insisting never happened—he'd been dressed in black. And that first time, well, hey, guess what? He'd been wearing a mask. She said lightly, "And the correlation between my brother and this legendary figure?"

Sif laughed again. "None that I know of—except in the mind of my two-year-old daughter."

Brit laughed, too. Then she looked at Sif sideways. "So tell me—seen the Dark Raider around the village lately?"

Sif blinked. Trapped, Brit thought. Hah!

And then, a gossip's gleam in her eye, Sif admitted, "I must confess, there have been…stories."

Brit leaned a little closer to Asta's daughter-in-law. "Tell me."

Sif waved a hand. "Oh, just rumors. Tall tales. An old man from three valleys over, attacked in the forest by thieves. He claimed the Dark Raider rescued him. And then there have been reports of a number of incidents involving renegades—you know about the renegades?" She must have seen by Brit's expression that she didn't. "You've been told that, in Gullandria, troubled youths are sent north, to our Mystic communities?''

"Yes." Just a month ago Brit's sister Liv had arranged to have a certain seventeen-year-old boy sent to the Mystics in hopes they might be able to help him change his ways.

"Sometimes," said Sif, "those difficult boys run away from us. They live wild, causing trouble whenever they come upon other people. We call them renegades."

Brit brought her hand to her injured shoulder, remembering the boy with the crossbow in Drakveden Fjord.

Sif was nodding. "Yes. The boy who shot you was a renegade." Brit had a few questions concerning that boy, but she didn't want Sif straying too far from the subject of the Dark Raider. Sif went on, "There have been stories of renegades stealing from local villagers, or groups of them coming in from the wild to wreak havoc on good folk. In a valley to the east of here, one renegade group is said to have staged a small reign of terror, threatening innocent people, killing livestock, breaking into longhouses when the owners were gone."

"And the Dark Raider stopped them?"

"Yes. The story goes that he caught them, one by one, that he took them where they could cause no more harm."

"And that would be where?"

"The Mystic village northernmost in all the Vildelund. We send the most incorrigible young ones there, to be shown—more forcefully—a better way."

"The boy who shot me—did Eric have him taken there?"

"I believe so. Yes."

"And the Dark Raider himself…if it's true he's returned, where would he be living now?"

Something happened in Sif's pretty face—a mental turning away. A retreat. Brit knew she was thinking she had said too much. "Eric would be the one to speak to of this." Asta's daughter-in-law bent to the pile of clothes, took out a nightgown, shook it and turned to hang it. "We must finish the laundry now."

Brit didn't press her further. She figured she'd gotten about as much as she was going to get from Sif, for the time being, anyway. And yes, it was all vague stuff. But it was vague stuff that matched up with what her own eyes had seen: a masked man in the fjord with Eric; her brother, in the longhouse, the same height and build as the man in the fjord, wearing the same black clothing.

And Eric warning him, "She sees you. She knows you. You shouldn't be here. Not without the mask…."

Now Sif spoke of an old legend come recently to life.

Was it totally crazy to imagine that her brother might have taken on the guise of the mythical Dark Raider? Not the way Brit saw it.

What better way to keep the fact that he still lived a secret from his enemies than to wear a mask?

Chapter Four

Another day passed. And another after that.

Brit's impatience was growing. She had come to the village for a reason. And since that one conversation with Sif Saturday afternoon in the washhouse, she hadn't moved a fraction of an inch toward her goal.

No one would talk to her. Not about Valbrand, anyway. The mention of his name brought long silences and significant looks. And then whoever she'd asked would answer that she already knew everything *they* knew on the subject.

She'd even gone so far as trying to get some small shred of information out of the children—and okay, that was kind of pitiful. But she was getting desperate.

They told her they'd seen Valbrand. That he came sometimes to visit—and that at night he turned into the Dark Raider. She almost got her hopes up, almost dared to imagine she might be getting somewhere.

But then the little darlings proceeded to tell her they'd also seen Thor in the sky, throwing his hammer, and Freyja riding through the clouds in her cat-drawn chariot.

So much for asking the kids.

Finally, on Tuesday, a week and a day after her plane went down, as she was sitting at the breakfast table with Asta and Eric, she decided she'd had about enough of getting nowhere. She looked across the table at the man who had carried her out of Drakveden Fjord.

Those haunting eyes were waiting, as usual. Over the past few days, she was constantly glancing up to find him looking at her, his gaze both measuring and intent.

Now he wore the strangest expression. Expectant and yet wary. As if he already knew what she would say.

"I would like to speak with you alone please—after breakfast if that's all right."

He nodded in that regal way of his. "As you wish."

And Asta beamed, as if the thought of the two of them speaking alone after breakfast just tickled her pink. "Well," the old woman said. "At last."

Now, what was for Asta to be so thrilled about? She had to know that they'd be talking about Valbrand.

Whatever was up with her, Asta couldn't get out and leave them alone fast enough. She had the table cleared and their breakfast bowls draining in the wooden rack on the counter in record time. "I'll be at Sigrid's," she announced breathlessly as she grabbed her heavy shawl from the row of pegs by the door.

Brit gave her a puzzled look and a wave as she went out.

The door clicked shut, and it was just Brit and Eric, facing each other across the plain wooden table.

"Well then." Those green-gray eyes looked at her probingly. "You have something to say to me?"

Something to say? Oh, you'd better believe it. She had a hundred questions, at least. Was it possible he was finally ready to fork over a few answers?

Jorund, the agent from the Gullandrian National Investigative Bureau she'd befriended, had warned her about this. "He's a Mystic through and through," the NIB special agent had cautioned. "Plays it close and tight. You'll have trouble getting anything out of him." But, hey. What did Jorund know? Hadn't he told her any number of times that she was chasing shadows, that her brother had met his end out there in the ocean, off the coast of Iceland somewhere? He'd been wrong on that count. Brit would prove him wrong about Eric, too.

She hoped.

Brit folded her hands on the table and leaned toward the silent man across from her. "You—and everyone else around here, as a matter of fact—keep claiming that my brother is dead, that I never saw him. Not here. Not in the fjord…" She let her voice trail off. Hey, who could say? Maybe he'd actually volunteer something. He didn't. "Well, okay, just for the sake of moving on, let's say that you're telling me the truth."

He nodded again. It wasn't an answer—but she hadn't really asked any questions. Yet.

"Okay, then, Eric. So let's go back aways."

"Back aways." He looked amused.

She quelled the urge to raise her voice in frustration and explained evenly, "That's right. If you won't admit my brother's alive, then will you tell me what you do know? Tell me what you found out, after he went missing. Tell me what you learned when you went searching for answers to what had happened to him."

"I learned nothing. Except that he is truly dead."

"Got that. But *how* did he die?"

"I'm sure your father must have told you."

"He did. But I want *you* to tell me. Please?"

He studied her for a long moment, then shifted on his bench and rested his forearms on the table. "The truth about Valbrand is exactly what His Majesty, your father, has told you. Valbrand went a-Viking—in the modern-day sense of the word, anyway. Every prince who plans to put himself forward as a candidate for the crown in the next kingmaking must accomplish such a journey. It is tradition. A holdover from the old days when kings themselves went a-Viking, when, as the old saying goes, 'Kings were made for honor, and not for long life.'

"Thus, Valbrand set out with a trusted crew in an authentic reconstruction of a Viking longship, from Lysgard harbor to the Shetland Islands, and on to the Faeroes. From there, he made for Iceland. Somewhere in the North Atlantic, he encountered a bad storm. During that storm, your brother was washed overboard, never to be seen again."

"And you know this for certain because?"

"I tracked down the survivors of the storm and spoke with them, in person. They told me what everyone already knows. I heard their stories and each one corroborated the one before. It all fit together and it all made sense. As I have told you time after time after time, I now have no doubt at all that Valbrand's death happened in a storm at sea.'' He leaned closer across the table. ''There. Are you satisfied?''

''Never.''

He made a low sound in his throat. ''Freyja's eyes. When will you abandon this witless hope that you'll somehow find a dead man alive?''

Witless, huh? She was leaning forward, too. She leaned farther. They were nose to nose. The air between them seemed to crackle and snap. ''I'll have you know that your own father—and mine—sent me here to try to find out what really happened to my brother.''

''Is that what they told you?''

She scowled at him. ''What do you mean, is that what they told me? Why else would I be here?'' He was looking at her strangely again, frowning, his head slightly to the side. She reminded him, ''And just in case you've somehow forgotten, my plane was *sabotaged*. And then there was that juvenile delinquent with the wicked-looking crossbow. Sif called him a renegade. Are you sure about that? Are you sure he wasn't someone sent by whoever messed with my plane, to finish me off in the event I managed to crawl out alive?''

Now he wore a patient look. ''The boy was a renegade. One of a small number of ill-behaved young ruffians who roam the Vildelund committing murder and stirring up mayhem whenever they get the chance.''

''So you're saying it was just the Gullandrian version of a random drive-by shooting? Oh, puh-lease. If you think I buy that, I've got a statue in New York harbor I can sell you.''

He seemed very sure. ''The boy is a renegade. I spoke with him myself, before I sent him to the northernmost village where he'll receive the discipline and teaching he so obviously needs.''

''How did you manage that?''

''Manage what?''

''Well, you had me to drag out of there—and a wounded renegade to *send* to the north. I'm just trying to figure out how one man accomplished all that.''

''I was not alone. There were other men with me, men from the village. They took him north.''

''I didn't see any other men—well, except for my brother, all in black, wearing a mask.''

''Your brother is dead. He wasn't there.''

''He was. You and him and no one else.''

He shrugged. ''The men were there, whether you saw them or not. And it's unfortunate that your plane crashed. But it doesn't mean the plane was sabotaged.''

''It was a fine plane in perfect working order. No way it would have gone to zero oil pressure out of nowhere like that.''

''Perhaps there was something wrong with your oil gauge—and as for why my father sent you here, we both know the reason. You have only to look as far as the medallion you wear around your neck to know the intentions of my father *and* yours.''

Brit stiffened. She felt for the chain at her neck and dragged the medallion out into the light. Her fingers closed around the warm, comforting shape of it.

"What are you talking about? Your father gave me this for luck, to keep me safe from all evil, he said."

Eric was wearing that odd expression again—that sort of bemused half frown, his head tipped to the side. "You really don't know, do you?"

"What?" she demanded. He went on looking at her. She said it again, louder, *"What?"*

And then, at last, he told her. "That medallion is mine. My father gave it to you so I might know you as my chosen bride."

Chapter Five

Should she have known? Probably.

"I see you have been…misled," he said softly. Brit only clutched the medallion and stared. Very patiently he went on, "We Mystics cling more closely to the old ways than do the people of the south. For us marriage is, first and foremost, an alliance between families. In the past millennium or so, it's been the custom for the father of the groom to present the future bride of his son with a special pendant—a marriage medallion that was wrought of silver in the first months after the son's birth. Each medallion is different, because each was made specifically for one treasured infant son."

He paused for a moment, his gaze holding hers. Then, as if he could see it, though she still had her hand wrapped around it and he continued looking right in her eyes, he said, "A circle in quadrants, a ribbon-like creature, twisting and twining over the whole—the world serpent, perhaps, that coils at the roots of the guardian tree, holding together all the nine worlds. Four animal heads—snakes, dragons, rams? Perhaps. Or perhaps these are creatures of fancy, of myth. And at the center, the symbol for Saint John's arms—like a cross, with four equal sides, each coiling and turning into the next. St. John is said to keep its bearer safe from all evil, did you know?"

She had, of course. Medwyn had told her—that much. But no more.

Eric said, "The medallion you wear used to hang on the wall above my blankets when I was an infant. As a child, I wore it against my flesh. When I turned eighteen, I gave it to my father—to be returned to me only around the neck of the woman I would wed. You."

It came to Brit, suddenly, why she hadn't figured it out before: she hadn't wanted to know. She'd been so proud and sure that her father and his grand counselor believed her—believed *in* her. That they'd seen her purpose and her determination to find her brother, or at the very least, to learn the truth of his death. She'd allowed herself to believe that they respected her quest—and yes, damn it, it *was* a quest.

But apparently, only to her. To them—to her father the king and Medwyn and this too-attractive man sitting opposite her, she was *only* a woman. And to them, as to far too many men, Gullandrian or otherwise, a woman was to be taken seriously in only one context.

In relationship to a man.

"Let me get this straight." She kept her voice low.

Moderate. Controlled. "Medwyn and my dad sent me here to *marry* you? I was almost killed in a plane crash, my guide *died,* I was just about finished off in a…a *hike-by* shooting, and you're trying to tell me it's all for the sake of *wedding bells?*"

"It is of great importance, whom you marry. The fate of our country may hang upon that choice."

"I'm not here to find a husband."

"Yet a husband is what you shall have."

"You can't force me to marry you."

"I will not have to force you."

She shoved back from the table, knocking the bench over behind her. The sound of it crashing to the floor was satisfying in the extreme. "Get this. I'll say it slowly. It's. Not. Going. To. Happen."

He frowned, just the slightest downward curl at each side of his fine mouth. "You are angry."

Major understatement. "You are right."

"You will come, over time, to accept—"

She raised a hand, palm out. "Uh-uh. Don't you even try to tell me what I'll accept."

He hadn't moved. He remained in his seat across the table, looking up, his expression patient enough to set her teeth on edge. "Perhaps now you wish to rest."

Rest after *this* conversation? "As if."

Shaking his head, he rose and carefully stepped free of the bench on his side of the table. "I fear there will be yelling and recriminations, if I stay."

"No kidding—and don't you dare leave yet."

He was already striding for the door.

She flew at him. "You are not walking out of here. Not now. Not until I say what I have to say." She grabbed his arm.

Big mistake. He stopped and looked right at her.

And there it was, that…energy. That…connection. Hot. And dangerously delicious.

Forget that, she told herself. She gave his arm a good yank and got her face right up to his, so she could stare squarely into those mesmerizing eyes. "He's alive, my brother. I know he is. I saw him. He was here, in this very room. He stood over my bed and he called me your *bride*. Now, how could I dream that, when I didn't know a thing about it until right now?"

Eric did not so much as blink. "Some things are known by the heart before they are known by the mind."

"Oh, don't give me that Mystic baloney. Valbrand's alive. Admit it."

"You delude yourself."

"The left side of his face is scarred. Terribly. What did that to him?"

"Turn your mind to what matters here."

"My brother. *He* is what matters. And I'm here to find him."

"Your brother is dead. Accept it. You are here because you are mine, as I am yours. The fates have decreed it."

"*Yours?* I don't even *know* you."

"You will. Over time."

"No."

He went on, not even pausing. "You are brave and strong. Of obvious intelligence, though sometimes too quick to act, when to watch and wait would be wiser. I have seen you with the children. You like them, you have a kind heart. To look at you pleases me. You are of a good age for breeding, though a bit younger might have been better.''

"Breeding? I'm a good age for *breeding?*''

"Overall, I am more than content with my father's choice—and I see in your eyes, in the quickening of your breath when you are near me, that I am not totally repellent to you.''

"This is insane.''

"No. This is as it was meant to be. It is our mutual fate that we be bound, each to the other, as man and wife.''

She let go of his arm and stepped back, mindful not to trip on the bench she'd overturned. "Listen, it's not my fate to be *bound* to anyone. I need serious breathing room. For me, settling down goes under *later.* When I'm older. And slower. But by then, I won't be such a good *breeder,* will I? So from your point of view, what good would I be?''

He smiled at that, straight teeth flashing white. "Your point is well taken. I have been too blunt. Months in the wilds will do that to a man. And it's always possible no children will come of our union. Yet there will be a union—in time. That much I know.'' His smile vanished. "And it seems I have said too much too soon. You are not ready to hear the truth.''

She dragged in a long, dramatic breath and let it out slowly. "Hear *that?* That's a deep sigh. It means, as I keep trying to tell you, that as far as this you-and-me thing goes—it's not. And it's never going to be.''

"It is.''

"It's not.''

He closed the distance she'd opened between them.

He did it slowly enough that he didn't spook her. Too bad. If he'd moved a little faster, she might have backed up. But she held her ground. And then he was right there, in front of her. His strong hand closed over hers.

Slowly he raised her hand to his lips.

She shocked herself. She let him do it. And when she felt his mouth against her skin, a hot and hungry shiver went shimmering through her.

"No!" She jerked away and cradled her hand as if he'd injured it. "Uh-uh. Not. No way…"

Eric made no effort to recapture her hand.

No progress was being made here.

Her fine eyes were wild, her wide mouth set in a scowl. He would very much have enjoyed kissing that mouth. But he'd had several days—to watch, to assess and to learn to admire; to accept the fact that this woman was meant for him. She had only just been informed of her fate, and that made her far from ready for kissing. For now he'd said what needed saying— and more. It was enough. He went to the door and put on his shearling coat, then took down the rifle racked beneath his shotgun.

She spoke then. "Wait."

He turned back to her slowly that time, holding the rifle with care, barrel to the floor.

She was guiding the silver chain over her head. "I'm not going to marry you, Eric." She held out the gleaming disk, the heavy chain trickling over her hand, the links falling through her fingers. "I want you to take this. Give it to the right woman when she comes along."

He felt again the urge to smile. This time he quelled it. "The right woman already has it."

Her face was flushed, blue eyes flashing. "Eric—" There was nothing to be gained by staying to hear more. He pulled open the door and went out.

Brit was left standing in the longhouse alone, the marriage medallion shining in her outstretched hand.

No problem, she thought, her fist closing tight over the silver disk. He won't take it. Doesn't matter. He's getting it back, anyway.

She marched over to his bed and dropped the medallion onto his furs, turning quickly away from it— from her own ridiculous reluctance to part with it. She righted the bench she'd kicked over and sat on it to put on her boots. Then she grabbed her jacket from its peg. She needed a long walk. A head-clearing dose of cold, fresh Vildelund air.

With her hand on the latch, she hesitated. No way strolling up and down the single village street, trying not to scowl at every friendly villager she happened to pass, was going to do the trick. She needed space and a total absence of other people. And if she was going to wander a little farther afield than the cluster of buildings that made up the tiny town, she'd be wise to do it armed. Renegades, apparently, *were* a problem around here. And from what she'd been told, there were bears. And wolves. And the legendary white Gullandrian mountain cats—and who knew what else?

Better armed than dead. She got her weapon from her pack, loaded it, put on her shoulder rig and holstered the SIG. Only then did she put on her coat and head for the door again.

Outside, it was in the high thirties. She felt in a

pocket and came up with that bag of peanut M&M candies that she'd opened before she climbed from her wrecked plane. She took one out—a red one—and put it in her mouth to savor. Delicious. She might want more. Maybe she'd eat them all on her walk, indulge in an orgy of chocolate and peanuts to soothe her frayed nerves, ease her troubled mind. She emptied them into the pocket and then wadded the bag and stuck it in the front pocket of her jeans to throw in the fire later.

Another pocket of her jacket yielded a wool beanie. A third, a pair of red wool gloves. She was pulling them on as she turned away from the street toward the back of the house, the M&M sweet in her mouth, her spirits already lifting.

At the rear of the house, about ten yards beyond the game cage, she reached a small barn. To either side of it rough plank fencing bordered a narrow paddock where a few horses grazed. One—a gelding with a dove-gray blaze between his big dark eyes—turned to watch as she climbed the fence and dropped to her feet inside. Then, with a snort that showed as mist on the icy air and a toss of his snow-white mane, he went back to cropping the short grass. None of the other horses seemed the least interested in her.

It was good, she decided, to be outside again, on her own, with the sun a rim of gold just making its climb over the crests of the hills to her right, the brown grass crackling with frost beneath her boots, the cold air sharp and bracing in her lungs and the inviting shelter of tall evergreens ahead.

She reached the back fence and hoisted herself over it with minimal awkwardness, though her left shoulder was still tender and any pressure on the muscles near the wound caused a definite twinge. When she dropped to the grass on the other side, she was perhaps thirty feet from the thick, close-growing forest of spruce that surrounded the village on all sides and grew up the flanks of the hills.

She stopped to press the compass button on her watch. The trees ahead were due north, Asta's house to the south. She should be safe to walk in the forest a little, as long as she was careful to keep her bearings and to watch out for predators—human or otherwise. She walked on into the shadows of the tall, proud trees, the thick blanket of short brown needles crunching underfoot.

The drop in temperature was immediate. Her breath came out as thick mist. She hunched down into the warmth of her jacket and picked up the pace a little—more exertion, more body heat.

A squirrel scolded her from a branch up ahead, tail twitching. She smiled as it jumped to the next tree, scampered inward to the rough red bark of the trunk and shot upward, vanishing from sight.

She felt better already. It was good, to be alone for a while, outside in the clean air, with only the sentinel trees and the chattering squirrels for company.

Her M&M was down to the peanut. Brit bit it good and hard and chewed it to a pulp. She swallowed. The situation stunk. There was Eric, who was too sexy and too tempting—and had some crazy idea that the two of them were meant for each other. And there were Asta and her daughters-in-law, sending Brit hopeful, dreamy-eyed looks every time Eric's name was mentioned. Worst of all, there was her father, who had

tricked her into thinking he believed in her quest—
well, no. Worst of all was the quest itself, her search
for her lost brother, which was going nowhere fast.

"Take 'em off, sweetling."

Brit froze on the shadowed path. The voice, from
up ahead, was male, unfamiliar—and full of youth and
meanness.

"I am not your sweetling, lout." A woman's voice.
Angry. Proud.

Someone laughed, low and harsh. And then came
another voice, male and young, like the first, but more
nasal. "We have you. Surrender."

"Never."

A silence. And then the unpleasant sound of a fist
hitting flesh. A grunt. Scuffling.

"Hold her, Trigg…"

"Loki mock her, she's slippery as an angry ot-
ter…"

The blows and grunts continued. Brit didn't like to
shoot with gloves on, but there was no time to remove
them. She drew her SIG, levered back the safety. Carefully, gun at the ready, she crept forward toward the
sound. At the next curve in the path, she came upon
them. Two boys—renegades, no doubt.

And one young woman, dressed much like them, in
rawhide leather, high lace-up moccasin-like boots on
her feet. The woman struggled against the grip of the
larger boy as the other tore at her clothes.

Rape in progress? Apparently.

Her pulse pounding in her throat, Brit acted. What
else was there to do? She stepped out into the open,
gun straight out, aiming steady with both hands.
"Stop. Now."

The boys froze and turned. "Balls of Balder, who are *you*?" demanded the one with the nasal voice.

Brit gestured, a twitch of the gun barrel. "Hands up. Now."

The boys, looking sullen and snarly, did as instructed.

"On the ground," Brit said. "Facedown." The boys dropped to a sprawl. "Spread your arms wider. And your legs." They complied.

The woman, whose blond hair had come loose from a thick braid, and half-covered her face, spared not more than a glance at Brit. She seemed totally unmoved by what had almost happened to her. "I'll bind them."

Brit didn't argue. "Great idea."

The woman, who was about Brit's size, was already striding to a leather pack that waited on the ground a few feet away. She dropped to her haunches and took out several lengths of leather twine. Brit held her gun on the pair as the woman swiftly and expertly tied their hands and ankles.

When she finished, she stood tall and spat on the ground between the two would-be rapists. "There. That'll hold 'em." She raked her wild hair off her face and looked directly at Brit for the first time.

Brit gasped. "My God."

The woman had an ugly cut on her full lower lip, a deep scratch on her cheek and an angry bruise rising at her jawline. But it wasn't her injuries that had Brit staring, openmouthed. It was the woman herself.

Injuries aside, she was the image of Brit's mother. She was Ingrid Freyasdahl Thorson, just as she looked in the old pictures in the family albums at home. Brit's mother. Twenty-plus years ago.

How could that be?

''Princess Brit?'' The woman smiled. It was Brit's mother smiling, Brit's mother in her midtwenties, with a cut lip and a naughty gleam in her sea-blue eyes. ''Don't answer,'' she said. ''There's no need. I know you by the look of you. And isn't this a story to be told around the tent fire on a cold winter's night? The gods must be pleased with us. They have sent you out to meet us.''

Us?

Right then, from directly behind Brit, another woman said, ''Drop your weapon, Your Highness. Or I'll be forced to send my arrow flying straight to your heart.''

Chapter Six

One hand in the air, Brit knelt and carefully set the SIG on the ground. Still grinning, the woman who looked like her mother darted forward and snatched it up.

She pointed it at Brit. "Got her, Grid."

The other woman—Grid?—came around in front of her, an arrow in her bow, but pointed at the ground. She was much older than the first woman, with graying brown hair, broad shoulders and thick legs. "By the wolves of Odin, Rinda," she said. "I dare not leave you on your own for the span of a minute."

Rinda shrugged. "No real harm done. And look who has come to my aid."

"Of that," said Grid, "I cannot complain."

Brit cleared her throat. "Look. I'm on *your* side. There's no need for you to take my—"

"Silence," barked Grid.

"But I only—"

Three words. That was as far as she got. By then Grid had drawn her free hand across her barrel chest. *Smack.* The back of Grid's hand caught Brit hard on her right cheek. Brit went spinning. She landed on her face in the dirt.

"Get up," growled Grid. "And don't speak again unless you are first spoken to."

The whole right side of Brit's face felt numb. Lovely. Brit brought her hands up to push herself to her knees. Her right hand brushed against a few hard little balls—M&Ms, fallen from her pocket as she dropped. She managed to drag them along with the back of her glove and to grab them in her fist before she scrambled upright. Neither of the women seemed to notice. Good. She really needed them. Nothing like a peanut M&M when a girl was under stress....

Eric checked his traps in the woods east of the village, finding one angry white fox. He released it, chiding himself for a too-soft heart.

Then, hoping the rage of his reluctant bride would have cooled somewhat by then, he returned to his aunt's longhouse. The women were there, clustered near the fire, busy with their sewing, the children playing quietly around them. There was one woman missing.

The most important one.

The others looked up from their stitching and saw him. A small silence followed, one brimming with expectation.

Asta broke the silence. "Why, where's Brit?"

"Bwit," said little Mist, who was sitting on the floor near Eric's sleeping bench. "Gone, gone, gone."

Eric frowned. "She was here when I left."

The women shared quick glances. Sif said, "And we assumed she was with you."

He looked at the pegs by the door. Her big blue jacket wasn't there. Her boots should have been waiting on the floor beneath the missing jacket. They weren't there, either.

The women were shaking their heads.

Mist had gotten to her plump little feet beside his sleeping bench. She reached for something among the furs and then held up a silver chain. His marriage medallion turned at the end of it. "Ohh, pwetty, pwetty."

Eric approached the child and knelt before her. "Mist. That is mine."

Mist frowned, but then, with a long sigh, she offered the chain. "Ewic take."

He plucked the dangling medallion from the air, winking at the winsome child as he rose. He slipped the chain over his neck and tucked the silver disk beneath his leather shirt. When Brit wanted it back, it would be waiting, warm from his body, charged with all the energy his strong heart could give it.

Right now, though, he had to find where the irksome woman had gotten herself off to.

Asta and his cousins' wives were watching him.

"Asta," he said. "Stay with the children. Sif. Sigrid. Come and help me find my runaway bride."

Eric and his cousins' wives searched the village, knocking on every door, looking through the bathhouse and the washhouse, the various small barns and other outbuildings. When they'd checked everywhere to no avail, he and the women returned to his aunt's house, where they found the older children playing outside near the front step.

Asta signaled him inside—alone. "Word has come."

Mist was sitting under the long deal table, cradling her yarn-haired doll. "Dawk Waiduh," she said, with a happy little laugh.

Asta said, "In the woods just north of the back pasture you'll find a pair of renegades. They are bound hand and foot—and they have quite a tale to tell."

The two women had horses. They rode bareback. Brit, her hands tied before her, rode double with the one named Rinda. Grid took the lead.

There had been little explanation. They were taking her to their camp, they said. The news of Brit's arrival over a week ago had spread through the Vildelund. The two women had been sent to the village in search of her.

It didn't take a Mensa candidate to figure out what they were. Anyone who knew anything of Gullandria had heard the tales of the *kvina soldars*—the nomadic warrior women who lived in the Vildelund, who fought with great skill and lived free, never binding their lives to any man. As a child at her mother's knee, Brit had loved to hear the tales of the *kvina soldars*. In her soft bed in her mother's house in Sacramento, she used to dream of someday coming to her father's land, of traveling to the wild north country, of meeting a *kvina soldar* face-to-face.

Well. Be careful what you dream of, as they say.

Brit had the front position on the sturdy mare, her "cousin's" slim body pressed close at her back. They'd been on the trail, moving mostly northeast and climbing, for over an hour.

Brit was following Grid's orders and staying quiet. She concentrated on the easy rhythm of the horse beneath her. Riding came natural as breathing to her, always had. Her legs did the work, so even with her hands tied, she had little trouble keeping her seat. For balance, she wrapped her fingers in the mare's braided mane. She listened to the sound of the wind in the tall trees, felt the warmth of the woman who might be a lost cousin at her back—and she tried not to worry.

Strangely, it wasn't so hard not to worry about herself. She'd looked into the eyes of both Rinda and Grid and seen no cruelty there. They were tough women, women who lived by their wits, their strength and their fighting skills. Her instinctive assessment of their basic decency had been bolstered by the way they ended up dealing with the two renegade boys.

To the *kvina soldars,* from what Brit had learned as she sought to understand the different peoples of her father's land, rape was a crime punishable by death. And not only that. After killing a rapist, the warrior women frequently mutilated the man's body, cutting off both his head and his offending male parts.

By their lights, Grid and Rinda had every right to kill the renegade pair. But they hadn't. They'd decided to leave them to the mercy of chance. Whoever—or whatever—found them, would get to deal with them. To Brit this seemed more than reasonable, given the circumstances.

It was less reasonable of the women to carry Brit

off. After all, she'd done nothing but come to the aid of one of them. They might have been a little grateful and let her head back to Asta's place in peace.

But no. Their "leader" wished to speak with her. And their job was to make that happen. What Brit wanted counted for nothing with them.

From overhead came the cry of a hunting bird. Brit glanced up to see a hawk soaring in the clear blue, and she thought of that other hawk in Drakveden Fjord the day this big adventure had begun.

She thought of Eric's face that first time she'd seen him in person, of the worry in his eyes as he'd looked down at her—injured, fading fast, on the rocky, cold ground. Now she was the one worrying. For him. Because Eric was going to blame himself when he found out she was missing.

Their disagreement back at the longhouse seemed of no importance now. So what if he thought they were getting married? It didn't matter, let him think it. What mattered was that Eric Greyfell was the kind of man who took his responsibilities seriously. He would consider it his duty to keep her safe and he would torture himself for failing in his duty.

He was an exasperating man. But still, she didn't want him torturing himself.

He would come after her, of course—at least, he would if he could figure out where to look. She was doing what she could to help him with that, though she doubted her little attempt to lead him along would work. But it seemed only right to at least give it a try.

She was thinking of it as the "Hansel and Gretel" technique. Instead of a trail of bread crumbs or pebbles to show the way, she was dropping peanut M&Ms. So far she'd dropped three. One in the clearing just as they were leaving. One about twenty minutes later. And one several minutes after that.

Okay, it was kind of pitiful if she gave it too much thought. What were three little M&Ms in an hour's worth of traveling? Not a lot. But hey, she was doing the best she could with what she had.

And as of now, her hands were empty.

For the first time since Grid backhanded her for talking, she dared to speak. "Ahem. Sorry, but I really have to have a moment in the bushes."

Neither Grid nor Rinda responded. The horses labored upward on the trail. Perhaps five minutes passed. Brit was debating how soon she dared to ask again, when Grid pulled to a stop. "Right there." Grid pointed at a clump of bushes beside the trail. "Relieve yourself. Make no sudden movements. We will be watching."

Terrific. Should she ask to have her hands untied? Uh-uh. If they did free her hands for the moment, they would only tie them again before she got back on the horse. And then they would be too likely to spot her trick.

Brit went into the bushes. It was quite the fun adventure, getting her pants down with her hands tied and the wool gloves making her fingers all fat and awkward. Lots of wiggling and squirming involved.

Which actually worked out fine. All the jerking around provided cover for that split second after she had her pants back up and zipped, when she shoved both hands in her jacket pocket and got what she needed.

Two minutes later she was back on the horse. She

waited several minutes more before she let the next M&M roll from her fisted hand.

Twenty minutes after her break in the bushes, they reached the crest of the hill they'd been climbing. Below them the land fell away sharply into a deep tree-shrouded ravine. They started down, moving west, then switching back, going east, following the zigs and zags of the trail as it took them to the bottom.

At the bottom, they crossed a swift-running stream and started climbing again. At the top of that hill, they went down in a series of switchbacks, the same as before.

And so on, for hours.

Finally, in late afternoon, they descended another hill and began moving east along the narrow strip of relatively flat land at the bottom. They were deep in the trees. Brit hunched into her jacket and shivered and let go of another M&M. After that she had only one left.

It was perhaps ten minutes later—by then she was tired enough she hardly glanced at her watch anymore—that another woman, dressed much like Rinda and Grid but with skin the color of richest mahogany, materialized from the bushes at the side of the trail. The woman stood, hands on hips, dark eyes flashing, squarely in their path.

"Greetings, sisters."

Grid reined in and saluted, the tips of her fingers to the center of her forehead. "Freyja guide your sword arm, Fulla guard your hearth."

"You have her," said the woman on the trail.

"We do."

''Come, then. Ragnild awaits.''

The warrior on the trail turned and vanished into the trees. Grid—and Rinda and Brit—followed. Brit let go of the final piece of candy, right there, a few yards after they turned into the trees.

They all three had to duck low to the horses to keep from being unseated by the thick, low-hanging branches. They rode for five minutes or so, Grid and Brit with cheeks to the necks of their mounts, Rinda with her head pressed against Brit's side.

At last, the trees opened up into a clearing: the camp of the *kvina soldars.*

Brit saw teepee-style tents arranged in a circle, smoke spiraling up through the tops of them. In addition to whatever fires burned within, there were open fires, rimmed by rocks, before the tents. Beyond the tent circle, hobbled horses nibbled the short grass. Warrior women of various ages moved in and out of the tents. Some of the women were black, some were of Asian descent, some Middle Eastern. There were dogs. And there were children, two of whom—at first glance, anyway—appeared to be little boys. In the center of the circle, someone had pounded in a tree trunk about a foot in diameter and around seven feet tall.

Grid dismounted.

''Get down,'' said Rinda from behind her.

Stiffly—after all that time riding bareback with bound hands—Brit slid to the ground. Rinda dismounted last. The dark-skinned woman who had found them on the trail led the horses off.

''This way,'' said Grid.

Brit fell in step behind her. Rinda took up the rear. Grid led them across the central area between the tents, to one slightly larger tent on the eastern side of the circle. As they passed, the children stopped their play to stare. The other women either ignored the newcomers or paused to salute, fingers to forehead, as Grid had done on the trail.

At the tent, they ducked inside.

A woman waited beyond the central fire, on the far side of the tent. She wore a white leather robe over her clothing. The robe was decorated with red runic-looking symbols. She sat cross-legged on a pallet of furs. Her hair was auburn, loose and full around her handsome face. Brit would have guessed her to be about forty.

"Unbind her," the woman in the robe commanded.

Grid turned to Brit, a knife in her hand. One clean swipe and the leather thongs fell away. Brit slid off her gloves, stuck them in a pocket and rubbed her tender, leather-abraded wrists.

The woman in the robe saluted Grid and Rinda. "Thank you. You may leave her here with me."

"But—" Rinda began.

The woman on the pallet cut her off with a slow shake of her head. "Discipline, my daughter. The first cornerstone of a life of power."

Rinda said nothing more. She followed Grid out.

"Do you thirst?" asked the auburn-haired woman. "Do you have need to relieve yourself?"

Brit was not at her best by then. Her thighs ached and her shoulder throbbed and she hadn't a clue where she was or what was going to happen next. Also, if she'd thought the Mystic villagers lived primitively, well, hel-lo. The *kvina soldars* had them beat by a mile. "Do I get to talk now?"

The handsome woman frowned. ''You are angry?''

''Uh, yeah. You could say that. There I was, walking in the woods, minding my own business. And I come upon what is about to be a rape. I step in, stop the rape—and get kidnapped for my trouble.'' She touched her cheek. ''Plus, Grid backhanded me for asking questions about what, exactly, was happening. And no, I don't have to relieve myself and we stopped to drink at a spring not far back down the trail.''

The woman gestured at her pallet, which was big enough for more than one. ''Please. Will you sit? I apologize for the...zealousness of my women. I requested that they bring you to me. They only did what I asked of them.''

''So you're saying you're the one to blame?''

The woman smiled, the fine lines around her eyes etching deeper. ''Yes. I am Ragnild, leader of this camp. And I am to blame for everything. Now. Will you sit?''

Brit blew out a breath. ''I suppose.'' She circled the low fire and dropped to the furs with a tiny groan. She really wasn't used to riding without a saddle. Everything was going to be way sore by tomorrow. But back to business. ''Okay, Ragnild. What is going on?''

The woman put up a hand. ''Please. Be still now. Look me squarely in the eye.''

Brit stifled a second groan—one that had nothing to do with her physical discomfort. She wanted answers, damn it. And she deserved them.

But something in the leader calmed her. Made her willing to just sit there—for a moment, anyway—and stare straight into Ragnild's hazel eyes.

"Yes," said Ragnild, after a long, strangely peaceful span of time. "It is as my dreams have foretold. You will be a great queen, the first in our nation's history to rule *with* her king."

Chapter Seven

Brit opened her mouth to argue—but decided against it. What Ragnild predicted would happen or it wouldn't. And the future wasn't the issue right now.

Now she had questions. Lots of them. "Rinda called me her cousin…"

"Because you are. As I am her mother."

"But how are we related?"

"Your mother had a brother named Brian. Have you been told of him?"

Brit made a face. "More than I wanted to know, to be honest." Her mother had finally told Liv, only weeks ago, why she had left their father, why she had split their family in two—baby triplet daughters to Ingrid, sons to Osrik. Brian Freyasdahl, a real piece of work, as it turned out, had been at the center of the problem. She frowned. "You're saying that my rotten uncle Brian was Rinda's father?"

Ragnild sighed.

Brit understood. "You're the one, aren't you? The one who killed him, the one who cut off his head and his—"

Ragnild waved a hand. "It was long ago."

"But then…he must have raped you, right?"

"He did. And for that I did what any *kvina soldar* will do to a man who dares to take what it is a woman's sacred choice to give. A few months later I realized that I would have his child."

She thought of Rinda, with her bold attitude and her naughty smile. "That makes your daughter illegitimate."

Ragnild nodded. *"Fitz,"* she said softly, with distaste. In Gullandria, a bastard child was called a *fitz* and was considered the lowest of the low. "Among us, among the warrior women, there is no judgment on the child for being born outside of a marriage. No *kvina soldar* can marry and remain with us, anyway. Sometimes, for whatever reason—the dishonor of rape, the lusts of the flesh, the true call of love—we find ourselves with child. When that happens, should we choose to have the child, we love that child and bring her or him up strong and capable and proud, as much as we can." She smoothed the soft white leather of her robe. "With girl children, it usually works well, since they most often choose to stay with us. The life of the boys is more difficult. They are sent away at the age of eight and they suffer at the cruelty of the outside world."

Brit was thinking of her brother-in-law, the king's warrior, Hauk Wyborn. Her father had recently legitimized Hauk, but before that Hauk's last name had been *Fitz*Wyborn. "My brother-in-law's mother was a *kvina soldar*."

Ragnild smiled softly. "Valda Booth. I knew her. She was a great warrior."

And really, there were more important things to be talking about than the plight of the *fitz* in Gullandrian society and what a dirty rat her creepy long-dead uncle had been. "What do you know of my brother, Valbrand?"

If the abrupt change of subject bothered Ragnild, she didn't show it. "They say he died at sea."

"Do you believe that?"

"Shouldn't I believe it?"

"I don't. I think someone tried to kill him. And I know in my heart that that someone failed."

"The heart is often wiser than the mind."

"So you're saying you think I'm right?"

"I am saying that you must do…what you must do."

"You know, you're like a lot of people in Gullandria. Big dreams of what the future will be, not very helpful in the here and now."

Ragnild chuckled. "I fear you speak the truth."

Brit sent her cousin's mother a sideways look. "What about the Dark Raider? Heard any stories about him showing up in the Vildelund lately?"

Ragnild nodded. "Rumor has it he rides among us again—that he rescued an old man from thieves, that he dealt with a group of renegades who were terrorizing one of the nearby Mystic communities."

Okay, great. Ragnild had heard the same stories as Sif. A confirmation. But nothing new. "Another question."

"Ask."

"When am I allowed to go back to the village where I came from?"

"Will tomorrow be acceptable? You'll stay with us tonight, share a meal, get to know your cousin a little. Rinda and Grid will take you back in the morning."

"So…this is it, then? You had me abducted so you could look in my eyes and reassure yourself that your dreams will come true?"

Ragnild laughed full out. It was a strong, rich sound. "I fear you have it exactly right—to look in the eyes of our future queen, to forge, you might say, the beginnings of a bond between us, for the sake of the future of my women. And to meet my daughter's blood cousin. I find I am well satisfied, on all counts."

Brit grumbled, "Rinda took my SIG 220, you know. I'm really fond of that gun."

"I'll have it returned to you immediately."

"Good. But getting my pistol back isn't the only problem. There are people who have to be seriously freaked by now, worrying about me."

"You'll return to them tomorrow, none the worse for wear."

Brit got a tour of the village and a lesson in the practice of the dragon dials.

The dragon dials was an exercise system developed in the seventeenth century by the *kvina soldars*. It was a specific sequence of slow, controlled movements that the warrior women believed promoted strength, calmness, discipline and mental clarity.

After the exercise session, Brit shared a meal in Ragnild's tent with the camp leader, Rinda, Grid and several other women. They had reindeer stew. Brit found it tasty, if a little tough. After the meal, Rinda invited Brit to the hot springs not far from camp.

Brit went gratefully, looking forward to soothing the aches and pains from a long day on the trail. Rinda brought a fresh dressing along for Brit's shoulder wound and changed it for her once they'd had a long soak.

Really, Brit was feeling pretty good about everything as she and Rinda strolled back to camp. Tomorrow she'd return to Asta's place.

And the day after tomorrow, she was heading out again. For Drakveden Fjord. It was time to have a look at what was left of the Skyhawk, to see if she could find a clue as to who had sabotaged her plane.

They heard the commotion as they came out of the trees and into the clearing where the circle of tents stood. Something was going on in the center of the circle.

Rinda grinned. "Looks to me like they've caught a man."

Brit walked faster—and stopped dead when she saw.

They certainly had caught a man. And that man was Eric. He was tied to the big stake in the center of the circle. The children of the camp darted around him, taunting him, and now and then striking him with stones and sticks.

Brit took off at a run. "Hey, stop that!" She hit the center of the circle yelling, making shooing motions with her hands. "Cut that out, you little brats. Go on, go on. Get away from him!"

The children backed off, though a couple made grotesque faces and stuck out their tongues.

Brit turned to Eric. "Are you all right?"

"Most assuredly," he replied. His expression was subdued. She couldn't read his eyes. "Especially now that my champion is here."

She grunted. "Oh, yeah, right."

About then, Ragnild emerged from her tent. "There you are. We've been awaiting you. This man has said your name in hopes that you might claim him."

"This man is…my friend. He's only here to rescue me. Untie him. Now."

Ragnild was shaking her head. "I regret that I can't do that—at least, not yet."

"Why the hell not?"

"This man strode boldly into the center of our camp. No man is allowed such a liberty. And he can't even plead ignorance. I know him. He is the son of the grand counselor, born of Mystic stock. He knows our ways."

Brit turned to Eric. A trickle of blood slid down his neck where some cruel child had struck him. "What is she talking about?"

Instead of an answer, she got one lifted sable eyebrow.

Argh. What was up with him? He could help her out a little here. She faced her aunt again. "I'm afraid I'm confused. *Why* is he tied up? What did he do?"

Ragnild was frowning. "I have explained that. He belongs to no woman here, yet he dared to walk boldly among us. Such behavior cannot be allowed."

Rinda stepped forward. She was grinning that naughty grin of hers. "You have to claim him." She tipped her head to the side and looked Eric up and down. ''Hmm.'' She licked her split lip. ''Perhaps I shall claim him—that is, cousin, should you reject him first.''

''What is this? *Claim* him? How do I do that?''

''You say, 'I will claim this man.'''

''Okay. And then?''

''Then we untie him. You take him to your tent— Grid and I shall be pleased to have you borrow ours.''

''Okay. I take him to my tent…''

''And then—'' Rinda's grin widened ''—you have your way with him.''

''My *way?*''

Rinda laughed. ''You do take my meaning. I see it in your eyes.''

Brit sighed. ''And after I have my way with him?''

''Then you may keep him for as many as seven nights, though I suppose, in your case, it would only be the one night, as tomorrow you are leaving us. If you are pleased with his performance, it is the custom that you let him go.'' Rinda's grin got wider. ''If he doesn't please you, you can offer him to another of us. Or simply kill him for being useless as a lover.''

Bizarre. ''And what if I *don't* claim him?''

''Well then, if no one else wants him, we'll kill him right now.''

''You're not serious.''

No one said anything. Ragnild looked determined. Rinda continued to look way too amused. The blood-thirsty children watched with wide, eager eyes. And Eric simply waited, his angular face a patient mask. As if it made no difference to him whether she took him or the warrior women stabbed him in the heart.

Finally Ragnild asked somberly, "Cousin to my only daughter, will you claim this man?"

The choices were severely limited. "Okay, all right. I claim this man."

Chapter Eight

"What are you, nuts?" Brit demanded. "I really think they might have killed you." They were alone in the tent Grid and Rinda had given them for their supposed night of sexual delights.

Eric stood over the low central fire, warming his hands. Firelight glinted off his clubbed-back hair, bringing out bronze gleams in the ash-brown strands. "No harm is done, for you have saved me."

Was he *smiling?* Brit swore, a very bad swear word. "You have blood on your neck."

"And you have a new bruise on your cheek."

Lightly she touched the swollen spot where Grid's knuckles had struck. "I spoke when not spoken to."

"A good thing you don't receive a blow every time you do that."

"Chuckle, chuckle."

He took a handkerchief from the pocket of his shearling coat and wiped until only a faint smear remained. "Better?" He stuck the cloth back in his pocket.

"Not particularly. How can you stand there and grin? That was stupid, what you did. Those women out there take their beliefs seriously."

"I had complete faith in you."

"What if I wasn't here, what if I hadn't come back to the camp, for some reason? What if I had refused to claim you?"

"But you *were* here. You *did* come back...and you *have* claimed me." That haunting deep-set gaze was on her.

She felt her skin grow warmer, felt the hungry shiver sliding through her. "Stop that."

"Stop what?"

"You know what. That...look. You give me that look and I get all..." She let the sentence die unfinished, since she was getting herself deeper in trouble with every word.

He showed no mercy. "You get 'all' what?"

"Just...don't, okay?"

"Don't...?"

She flung out both hands. "Don't give me the bedroom eyes. Don't get...ideas."

"Bedroom eyes? You Americans. Such amusing figures of speech." He took something from another pocket, then shrugged out of the coat and tossed it on the pallet that lay against the side of the tent, to his left. His leather shirt was the same one he'd been wearing that morning. It had lacings at the neck. She could see a slice of firm, smooth chest.

And a few links of silver chain, shining. "I see you found your medallion."

"Would you like it back now?"

"Uh. No, I would not."

He circled the fire and came toward her. She debated: shrink back or stand proud?

As usual, before she made a choice, there he was. Right in front of her, mesmerizing eyes and broad shoulders filling the world. "Give me your hand."

"I said I don't want the medallion."

"I have something else of yours."

She should probably take issue with the word *else*. Then again, better not to belabor a point made far too many times already. She settled for a sneering curl to her lip and a surly, "What?"

He simply waited.

"Oh, all right." Grudgingly she held out her hand.

He cradled her palm, his hand warm and firm around the back of hers.

The problem was, she did like it. When he touched her. She gloried in the shivery feelings he aroused, though she kept trying to tell herself she shouldn't, that her obvious response to him only egged him on when it was absolutely paramount that she keep him at a distance.

Carefully, so as not to spill them, he laid a pile of peanut M&Ms in her cupped hand.

She looked down at them and back up at him. He was smiling again. And so was she—now. It was just too rich. "Pretty good, huh?"

"You are a woman of greatest resourcefulness."

"That I am."

"Not that I wouldn't have found you without the

bright-colored trail you left for me. I would find you anywhere.''

"Oh, I'll bet.''

The fire behind him crackled cheerily. Thin gray curls of smoke drifted up through the tent hole above. Outside, faintly, she could hear the sounds of the women of the camp as they prepared to settle in for the night. A woman called for a child and a thin voice answered, "Coming, Mama!" Brit stared at Eric and he stared back at her and they smiled at each other like a couple of fools.

"I was curious," he said. "I ate one.''

"Did you like it?''

"It was excellent. That smooth outer shell, the silky, melting ball of chocolate, the crunch of the nut within…''

He had it exactly. She confessed, though it was the last thing she ought to be telling him, "I like to suck them. Slowly.''

He whispered, his voice rubbing, velvet soft, along her every nerve, "Show me.''

She made herself frown. "Oh, puh-lease. They've been on the ground.''

"So fastidious…''

"That's me.'' She was thinking of that big plate of night crawlers in blood balls she'd lapped up that time on *Fear Factor*. Fastidious. Oh, yeah. Fershure. At least when she could afford to be.

She noticed that he was bending his head.

And yes, it was true. She was lifting hers.

Their lips met.

Well, what do you know?

She was doing it. Kissing Eric, though she knew she shouldn't.

Okay, all right. It was a problem she had. Just ask her mother. There was always what she *should* be doing: college, finishing one of her novels, stuff like that. And the various dangerous activities that tempted her: to learn to fly, to earn a black belt, to explore what was left of the world's wildernesses, the kinds of places where if you didn't know what you were doing, you could end up dead.

Oscar Wilde had said it best: "I can resist everything except temptation…"

You go, Oscar!

His mouth to hers…so lightly. Just brushing. And what a mouth it was. Exactly as she'd imagined it, velvety soft as his voice could be.

He spoke between those brushing kisses. "My dreams. At last. Coming true."

She pulled back. "Don't get your hopes up. It was only a—"

He silenced her by taking her mouth again. She let him do it.

Only a kiss, she promised herself. It's only a bone-melting, sweet, tender kiss….

Oh, and it was…all that.

Really, she had to be honest—at least, with herself. *He* was…all that.

His lips settled in, covering the whole of her mouth. She heard an eager, needful sound—a sound that came from her own throat. And her mouth was opening—just a little, she promised herself. Only enough to let in the wonderful moist heat of his breath.

But then, what do you know? His tongue came in, too. And she didn't close her lips against it.

In fact, she slid her own tongue beneath his.

Oh, my, yes.

Their tongues sparred and slid, up and over each other. His retreated.

Hers followed. Into the wet cave beyond those beautiful, tempting, velvet-soft lips.

Chaka-boom, she was going.

Going, going…

Gone.

With a hungry cry, she grabbed for him, wincing a little as her hurt shoulder complained. She slid her eager hands up over his hard chest, his strong shoulders, until she had him around the neck, until her body was pressed to his, her breasts to his chest, her hips just below his. Against her belly she could feel his desire. Heaven, that hard ridge. At the center of herself, she was warming, softening, hollowing out. Melting like the chocolate beneath the outer shell of an M&M, the sweetness spreading…

She opened her hand. The candies rolled down his back and hit the dirt floor with soft plopping sounds.

He chuckled at that.

She pulled back enough to grant him a mock scowl. "You know we shouldn't be doing this."

He laid a finger against her mouth. "No. You have it wrong. We *must* do this. I must please you. Or you'll have to kill me."

She stuck out her tongue and licked that finger of his—it tasted salty and a little bit dusty. Altogether lovely.

Fastidious? Brit Thorson? Not right this minute…

She felt his low groan as it rose from his chest. Delicious. Perfect.

No, she would not marry him, no matter what the fates predicted. But this…

How could she turn away from this?

He brought up his other hand and cradled her face in his warm, cherishing palms. His eyes looked into hers. She was falling. Down and down…

"You have claimed me. You shall have me."

Oh, well. All right.

But then again…

"I have an idea." Her voice came out husky, hungry, low.

"Share it."

"How 'bout we don't? And just say we did."

He only shook his head at that, his eyes so deep, his mouth swollen with kissing.

Crazy, she told herself. Way, way insane.

A leather strip held back his hair—another temptation, more of the only thing she couldn't resist. She took that strip and pulled. It slid away. His hair fell loose around his shoulders. She let the bit of leather drop, down there to the dirt, with the scattered M&Ms. She combed her fingers through the strands—so silky, alive with the warmth of him.

"You don't need this coat," he said.

She didn't argue. She let him push it from her shoulders and toss it to the pallet where his own coat lay.

He gathered her close again, enfolding her in those lean, strong arms. And he kissed her, his tongue pushing in, finding hers waiting. To welcome him.

To play…

He had her sweater by the sides. He raised it, fingers

trailing over the bumpy fabric of her thermal shirt, thrilling her with the simple pressure of his touch. The kiss was interrupted as he pulled the sweater over her head. She lifted her arms straight up too fast.

A small cry of pain got away from her.

He tossed the sweater away, his brows drawing together. "Your wound…?"

"No. Nothing. It's…"

But he was bending close again, pressing his lips to her shirt, right over the bandage that covered the place where the arrow had struck. He blew out a breath. She felt it through the layers of cloth and the bandage. It was lovely. Warm and moist. So tender. So soothing. So right…

She cradled his head against her shoulder and stroked his hair. "Oh, Eric…"

He pulled back and took her by the arms. And he looked into her eyes, deeply. For an endless span of time.

She shook herself. Really, she had to clarify things a little. "This doesn't mean—"

"Shh." His finger sealed her lips again. "Explanations are for strangers. We are not strangers. We never were that." She put her hands flat against his chest. She had a thousand things to say. But they all kept flying away. His eyes were so deep. They went down and down forever. "I assume nothing. You needn't fear."

He *did* assume. She could see it there. Shining in his spruce-green eyes.

But—right then, did she care?

Uh-uh.

He was holding her. He wanted her, and, oh, she

did want him, want his hard body against hers, his strong arms around her. For this night, in her cousin's tent, in the camp of the *kvina soldars.*

It was not such an easy thing, this quest of hers. Mostly it seemed she was getting nowhere—except in trouble. And in one sense, he *was* her adversary, keeping from her what she needed to know.

But in another, deeper way she truly did feel bound to him. Beyond being adversaries, they were also comrades. He would fight at her side if it came to that. He would willingly lay down his life for hers.

And as she looked up at him, she knew she would do the same for him.

It *was* a bond between them. A powerful one. Wherever this all might lead in the end, it would be an honest thing, to be with him tonight.

She felt the smile of acceptance curve her lips.

In response he whispered her name. "Brit…"

She took the sides of his shirt and gathered the soft leather, sliding it upward, fingers skimming the firm, hot flesh along his ribs, pulling the shirt over his head and tossing it in the corner with the rest of their things.

His smooth bare chest gleamed in the darkness. And there was the medallion….

The sight of it—of the twining serpent, the four mystic animal faces, the cloverleaf cross at the center—took the shivery, sexual moment and twisted it. Ruined it.

She turned her head away.

He caught her chin, guided her back. "Look. Know. It is there for you when you want it. And only then."

She pushed at his chest—regretfully. But firmly.

He dropped his hands to his sides.

They stared at each other, inches—and now suddenly, miles—apart. They were both breathing heavily.

"I can't do it," she said at last. "It just wouldn't be right."

He cocked an eyebrow at her. "And so, when the warrior women learn I have failed to please you, I die."

Like she could let him get away with that one. "Oh, please. You know that is *so* not going to happen."

"But I must—"

"Please me? That's right. And you have. Thoroughly. End of problem."

"I'd like to do more." He looked so sincere. And so devastatingly sexy. Damn him.

She shrugged, the gesture cool—everything she wasn't inside. "Get over it."

"So much bravado. Strange how it suits you."

"Bravado? This is not bravado. This is me. Trying, against all odds, to get through to *you*."

"And I have heard you. No more pleasuring. Not tonight."

"Not tonight, not *ever*."

"Ah," he said, as if he understood. But he didn't. He was absolutely certain tonight had been only the beginning of the *pleasuring* they'd share. He didn't believe for a moment that she meant what she said.

And how could she expect him to? She didn't believe it herself.

She pointed at the pallet where their things were piled. "You can sleep there. I'll take the other one."

"I am yours to command."

Oh, yeah, right. "Go to bed then."

"As you wish, so shall it ever be."

* * *

The hawk dropped from the sky. Its eyes were dragon eyes, burning red. Flames shot from its beak, searing all in its path. She put up her arms to shield her face and a single cry escaped her.

Brit woke sitting up, arms across her eyes. Slowly she lowered them.

The fire was down to a low glow of coals. Her pallet was a mess, the furs and blankets wrinkled and lumped up beneath her.

And Eric was awake, lying on his side, his head propped on a hand…watching her. The medallion hung to the side. His gorgeous chest gleamed at her. His blankets were down to his waist. She'd made a concentrated effort *not* to look as he got ready for bed. And now, she couldn't help but wonder…

If those blankets slipped a little lower, would she get a view of what she'd felt against her belly earlier?

She jerked her gaze—and her thoughts—away from where they had no business going.

His eyes were waiting, way too alert, unsettlingly aware. "Bad dream?"

She grunted. It was answer enough. And then she concentrated on straightening her bedding. At first, she tried to do it without getting up. She only made things worse.

"Allow me to help you with that."

"No, thanks." At least she'd had the sense—unlike *some* people—to keep everything but her boots on when she crawled beneath the blankets. She was showing him nothing as she stumbled to her feet and tugged on the heavy pallet until it was reasonably smooth again.

She was just about to slide back in, where it was warm, when he said with infuriating good humor, "Always such an angry sleeper."

She shot him a look. *Always,* he'd said. That meant he must have watched her sleep, at Asta's house....

"Not angry. Restless." She lifted the covers, got under them and settled them over herself. "Good night." She shut her eyes.

"Brit?"

Outside somewhere an owl asked "Who, who, who," as she considered not responding. But in the end, she gave in and muttered, "What?"

"The blond warrior woman, the one called Rinda..."

"What about her?"

"She called you 'cousin.'"

"Because I am."

He was quiet for a moment. Finally he said, "She looks like you."

Brit stared through the smoke hole above. The night sky was cloudy, a deep grayness, hiding the stars. "She's the image of my mother at twenty-five or so."

Eric made a low noise in his throat. "I have it. Brian the Blackhearted..."

Brit felt a funny little sadness, a heaviness near her heart. "They called my uncle that?"

"They did. And he was."

"Blackhearted..."

"Yes. And was he Rinda's father?"

She could see no reason—beyond a petty desire to goad him—to keep what she knew to herself. "Yes. He raped Ragnild."

"Ah," he said, as if that explained everything. And really, it probably did. "So Ragnild wished to meet you."

"That's right." *She believes that I'll someday be queen,* she thought. But she didn't say it. Many, after all, believed that Eric would one day be king. If Brit were to be queen, then that would mean...

No. Better not even go there. And besides. Since Valbrand lived, *he* would most likely be the next king, once all this confusion got straightened out. No way Valbrand would be marrying his little sister. Even in Gullandria, they weren't into stuff like that.

So much for Ragnild's dreams.

And what, Brit wondered, was Valbrand doing right now?

Really, there was so much she wanted—*needed*—to know. "Eric?"

He made a noise that told her he was listening.

"How old were you when you first met my brother?"

He didn't answer for a moment. But the silence was a musing one. Then he said, "So young, I don't even remember a time when I didn't know him. I was two when he was born. And it seems, in my memory, that he is always there. We played together, from the time he was old enough to crawl. And then, for a while, it was the three of us."

"Kylan, too?"

"Yes. And then Kylan was gone. It was only us two again, your brother and me. From wooden swords to swords of steel. We shared the same teachers, in the classroom, in the training yard. We were bloodbound when I was twelve and he was ten—do you know what it means, to be bloodbound?''

She repeated what she'd read in one of the books she'd found in the palace library about life in Gullandria. ''To be bloodbound is to share with another a blood oath of loyalty and commitment. It's an oath that binds equals, makes them brothers in the truest sense—as opposed to bloodsworn, which binds one of lesser rank to a ruler or a leader.''

''You have it right.''

''I wonder…''

''Ask.''

''Well, did Valbrand ever speak of us—of his sisters and his mother, in America?''

There was complete silence, suddenly, as if the night itself held its breath.

''Eric?'' she prompted at last, when she was sure he would never answer.

He said, ''It was bad for Valbrand, when your mother left—you three princesses were only babies. He didn't know you. So your loss he could bear. But the loss of a mother… It leaves a ragged hole of longing, a scar that never completely heals. And then, so shortly after that, for him to lose your brother, Kylan, as well…'' Eric's voice trailed off, as if no words could express how terrible that had been. ''I was fourteen when my mother died. Valbrand got me through it. Because he *knew*. He understood…'' Eric made a low sound. ''And I haven't answered your question, have I?''

Her question seemed unimportant by then. She was thinking how bad it must have been for Valbrand. And for Eric, too. Brit and her mother had issues—but the thought of Ingrid not *being* there. That would be way hard to get through. "It's okay. I can understand why he wasn't thinking much about his baby sisters."

"The truth is, he did think of you. And he spoke of you. More and more often as we came into manhood. He spoke of the time he knew would come someday, when you and your sisters would venture across the sea to visit the land of your birth. He spoke now and then of going to visit you in America. But he never quite got around to it. I think, perhaps, there were traces of bitterness, still, within him—bitterness at your mother, for leaving him, for never coming back."

"Bitterness…" Such a sad word. A word full of *might have been,* of *if I had only,* a word heavy with hurt and regret.

"Only traces." Eric's voice was warm with reassurance. "Nothing that couldn't be healed, given time and tenderness. He wasn't a man to hold grudges, not a man to let bitterness own him. He was bigger… better than that."

Was.

How easily he spoke of her brother in the past tense. Was it shrewdness on his part, to maintain consistency with the original lie?

Or merely the sad truth?

No.

She'd never believe that. She'd *seen* her brother. Valbrand still lived. All Eric Greyfell's clever lies wouldn't steal the truth she knew in her heart.

She rolled to her right side, facing the dying fire— she would have rather faced the shadows, but her sore shoulder wouldn't let her. She stared at the glowing embers until sleep closed her eyes and carried her off into dreams again.

The next morning the clouds had cleared away. The sky was the startling blue of a newborn baby's eyes. They went to Ragnild's tent for an early breakfast of porridge and jerky.

Eric was ordered to wait outside while Ragnild questioned Brit concerning his performance the night before.

"How well did he pleasure you?" Ragnild demanded.

Brit had her answer ready. "He is a lover without peer. I am well satisfied."

Yeah, okay. The well-satisfied part was an outright lie. But from the kisses they'd shared, she felt justified in making the leap to calling him a good lover.

As for the bit about him being without peer? Well, hey. That was one of the great things about Gullandria. You could call a man "without peer" and nobody would think you were being pretentious.

Satisfied with Brit's answer, the camp leader allowed Eric to join them in the tent. Ragnild even granted him permission to sit with the rest of them and share the meal, as though he was more than a mere man, fit only to provide sexual pleasure and children.

After the meal Ragnild had a fine mare—white, the cutest gray boots on her front hooves—brought from the camp's remuda.

"For you, my daughter's cousin," said the leader proudly, stroking the mare's silky forehead. "May she carry you without stumbling, onward to meet your destiny.''

A horse was a very big gift—one that Brit accepted gratefully. A good horse would come in handy during her stay in the Vildelund. Also, having her own horse meant she wouldn't have to share a ride with Eric to get back to the village. They'd travel faster if they each had their own mount—not to mention that she could skip the forced intimacy of having his body pressed against her back for the next six or seven hours, providing a constant reminder of what she'd promised herself she was not going to do with him.

''Thank you, Ragnild. Does this fine horse have a name?''

''Svald.''

''And that means?''

''Why, whatever you would have it mean.''

Brit took the reins.

Rinda handed her three small, hard apples. ''Here, cousin. A few apples always smooth the way between a horse and her new owner.''

Brit offered the apples to Svald. The mare lipped them up and chomped them, then nuzzled for more. Brit stroked her fine, sleek neck and blew in her nostrils.

Eric said he'd help her to mount.

''No, thanks. I can manage.'' She grabbed a handful of braided mane and hoisted herself to the horse's strong back. The muscles of her legs and buttocks complained. But the long soak in the hot spring the night before had helped a lot. The stiffness wasn't as bad as it might have been.

Brit promised to visit again, and she and Eric set out through the trees.

At the top of the first rise, they paused to survey the rugged, tree-covered land before them. Eric said, "You will have trouble finding those women again."

"I know the way."

He smiled. That smile warmed her—intentions to the contrary. "They will move camp now. They're probably packing things up as we speak."

"But why?"

"They live free. They can't allow outsiders to know where to find them."

"They can trust us. We'd never betray them."

"*We?* High praise." He was grinning.

"I never mistrusted you. I know you're an honest man—well, except for that big lie you keep telling me about Valbrand." She put up a hand. "Don't say it. I don't need to hear it—and are you telling me I've found Ragnild and my cousin only to lose them again?"

"You *will* see them, in the future. On that I would wager my best hunting rifle."

"But you just said—"

"That you would have trouble finding them again. I didn't say anything about *them* finding *you*. I'm certain they will, when next they feel a need to seek you out."

They reached the village at a little past three that afternoon. Asta came running out, followed by her daughters-in-law and a chattering knot of children. There were glad cries of greeting and warm hugs all around.

Mist grabbed Brit around the knees and squeezed. "Bwit, I miss you. Miss you, miss you, vewwy much…"

Brit scooped her up and held her close. "Give me a big squeeze. See? I'm right here—and you are so strong!"

The little one was already squirming to get down. Brit let her go with some reluctance, glancing up to see that Eric was watching, looking way too smug.

Oh, right. Back to what a wonderful wife she was going to make. Because she loved kids and would no doubt be yearning to *breed* a passel of them. Yeah, sure. As in, don't hold your breath.

Asta took her arm. "Eric, see to the horses. Brit, come inside immediately. I must check your bandage, and then you are to eat a hearty meal. After the meal no doubt you'll enjoy a trip to the bathhouse. And after that you'll have a long, healing night's rest."

"Sounds terrific," said Brit. "Good food, a bath and some rest." She might as well drop the bombshell now. "I'll need all that to be fresh for the big day tomorrow."

Asta's eyes narrowed. Eric looked bleak.

"Oh," Brit said, with an offhand wave. "Sorry. I've been meaning to tell you. Tomorrow I'm heading for Drakveden Fjord. I want to have a look at what's left of my plane."

Chapter Nine

Asta let out a small cry of outrage. Then she started objecting. "Brit, you'll do no such thing. It isn't safe for you to be wandering all over the Vildelund."

"My safety isn't the issue here. I'm going."

"Of course your safety is the issue. You are the daughter of our king, and your life is precious above all else."

"Asta. There's no sense in arguing about this. I'm heading out tomorrow at first light."

"Eric." Asta was actually wringing her hands. "Talk to her."

Eric looked as if he wouldn't mind strangling someone—and Brit had a good idea who that someone might be. "Take her inside," he commanded. "Feed her. I'll see to the horses. Then she and I will share an evening stroll."

* * *

The "evening stroll" happened an hour later, in waning daylight. And as it turned out, there was no strolling involved. Eric must have decided he didn't want to argue with her on the village street, where anyone might hear them going at each other. So he shooed the others out. They faced off as they had the morning before, alone in Asta's longhouse, on either side of the deal table.

"What is the point of this?" Eric demanded. "You put yourself in harm's way for the mere thrill of it."

"No, I do not. And there *is* a point, since you asked. I want to have a look at that plane."

"To what purpose?"

"I want to see what was done to it, to make it lose oil pressure out of nowhere like that."

"Ah," he sneered. "Not only a licensed pilot, but an airplane mechanic, as well."

"I just want to have a look, okay? I just want to see if I can—"

"No." His voice was carefully controlled—but his expression was thunderous. "It is not, in any way, *okay.*"

"Well, fine. It's not okay. But I'm going, so get used to the idea."

"You will learn nothing. And you might very well get yourself killed."

"So be it. A little danger I can handle. It's way preferable to hanging around here, twiddling my thumbs, getting the brush-off every time I dare to ask a question about my brother." She was leaning toward him, knuckles braced on the table. "Unless…"

He looked bleak. "Tell me."

"Well, I might be willing to change my mind, if you were to decide you're finally ready to trust me. If you'd agree to take me to my brother…"

"How can I do that? Your brother is dead."

"You keep saying that. Why don't I believe it?"

"You don't *want* to believe it."

"That's right. I don't. Because it's not true."

They enjoyed a short, angry stare down.

Brit was the one who looked away. She pushed herself back from the table and stood fully upright, wrapping her arms around herself, turning from him, toward the stove. "I'm sick of it." She tossed the words over her shoulder. "I'm *through* with it. I'm not going to learn anything more staying here."

"Your injury—"

She whirled on him. "Is better. Better every day. Yes, it's still tender. But it's not going to stop me from doing what I need to do. I prevented a rape yesterday. I was slapped to the ground by a big, bossy *kvina soldar*. I rode bareback for hours—yesterday *and* today. My shoulder is no worse for all the activity. Don't you even try to use it as an excuse to keep me here. There is nothing more for me to do here. I've asked all my questions and I've gotten too few answers. I've got to look elsewhere. Otherwise, what's left for me but to return to my father's palace with nothing to show for all I've been through but an ugly burden of guilt over my dead guide and a gross-looking scar from a renegade's poisoned arrow?"

The look of fury had left his face. Now he regarded her with dangerous tenderness. "There could be more than that. There could be—"

"I know where you're going." She was shaking her

head. "Don't." Just because she couldn't stop imagining what it might be like to roll around on the bed furs with him didn't mean she was ready to wear his medallion and bear his children.

When she bound her life to a man, that man was going to respect her as a full equal. And he was *always* going to be able to trust her with the truth.

He was coming around the table toward her. He stopped about three inches away.

She groaned. "Why am I always standing here waiting when you get to me?"

He lifted a hand.

She should have backed away. But as usual, she didn't.

His finger brushed the line of her jaw, leaving delicious little tingles of longing in its wake. "Perhaps you like it, when I'm near you."

She lifted her chin and looked at him dead-on. "Maybe I do. Maybe I wish…" Oh, what was she saying?

"Don't stop now." His voice had gone velvety, lovely, warm.

She pushed his tender hand away and stepped back as she should have a moment before. "Forget all that. What you need to accept right now is that tomorrow I *am* going to have a look at my plane. Short of locking me up and throwing the key away, you're not going to stop me."

He was looking bleak again. "It's more than thirty kilometers from here, over rough, steep terrain. The hazards are endless. You won't only have to worry about the occasional renegade and other fierce bands of *kvina soldars*. There are also large meat-eating animals with sharp claws and long teeth.''

''In case you haven't figured it out by now, I've spent my life going to places where the terrain is rugged, the animals predatory and the locals restless. And yet, here I am. In one piece. And ready to go.''

He was the one who stepped back then. ''There is no stopping you, is there?''

''Finally. You're getting it.''

He gave her one of those long, unwavering looks—to let her know he was about to make a point that would not be negotiable. ''If you're going, I am going with you.''

She smiled then.

He grunted. ''So. That was your plan all along.''

''Well…''

''What?''

''I have to admit, the idea makes me a little edgy. You know how it is with us….'' She let him finish that thought for himself. ''I don't need the distraction. However, you know the way and I don't. I can use a good guide, not to mention…''

''What?'' he prompted, when she didn't finish.

She shrugged. ''You're quick and strong. I have no doubt you know how to handle a weapon. You're a good man to have on my side if I have to fight my way out of a sticky situation.''

He didn't look happy, exactly. But he definitely looked a little less fed up. ''Let us hope for good weather, for an absence of 'sticky situations.'''

''Hope for the best, be ready for the worst. It's the only way to go, if you ask me.''

* * *

They set out at six the next morning, before the sun crested the hills to the east. Asta had loaned Brit a saddle. She stood outside to tell them goodbye.

"Bad weather coming," she warned, as they mounted the horses. "If you must go, then leave on the morrow."

"Oh, Asta." Brit stroked the side of Svald's sleek neck. "Come on. There's not a cloud in the sky."

Eric, on a muscular gelding, gestured at the barometer beside the front door. "Falling fast." Brit only looked at him. He turned to his aunt. "It appears the coming storm will not stop us. We are going today."

Asta's frown deepened, but she said no more. She stood out in the street and waved as they rode away. Pure foolishness, she'd called the venture the night before, when she returned to her house to learn that Eric had failed to talk Brit out of going. An idiot's quest.

To a certain degree, Brit had to agree with her. But she wasn't going to learn a damn thing sitting around the Mystic village, being coddled by Asta and the other women, getting no answers to her questions, daydreaming too much about Eric while she plucked the occasional game bird and helped Sif with the wash.

And wait another day in case the weather turned bad? No, thanks. A little rain wasn't going to slow her down. And, anyway, it was warmer than it had been. Felt like in the low forties already. A much more pleasant temperature for traveling than yesterday or the day before.

She felt eager. Ready. Felt…a sort of happy shiver running beneath her skin to think that they were on the way.

She glanced at the man on the gelding beside her. Taking her daydreams right along with her. Oh, yes, she was. Hey. Couldn't be helped. A girl's gotta do what a girl's gotta do. She needed a guide, and he knew his way around the Vildelund.

They rode with the rising sun at their backs until they reached the forest that rimmed the village and its fields. About a mile into the deep, cold shadows of the tall trees, the trail came to a three-way fork. Eric laid his reins to the gelding's neck and the horse, bridle wise, took the right fork, to the north. Brit followed his lead.

At first the horses jogged easily on level ground, the trail wide enough that they could ride side by side. But soon enough they began climbing. The trail narrowed and Brit fell in at the rear. Above, through the lacy branches of the trees, clouds gathered. The wind was rising.

For a couple of hours it was much the same kind of travel as the day before and the day before that— up and down the sides of steep hills, on trails that led them in zigzagging switchbacks—much the same, only darker and windier.

They had just reached the base of a hill when Eric reined in and put up a hand. Quietly he slid to the ground. Brit followed his lead. He indicated a clump of black boulders faintly visible through the trees, perhaps fifteen feet from the trail. He took his horse by the bridle. Brit did the same.

They moved cautiously into the trees. When they reached the black rocks, Eric signaled her in close. They held the muzzles of the horses and were silent. Waiting.

Eric tipped his head, gesturing at a gap in the high, sloping rocks. Two quiet steps to the side and she could peer through.

She saw four men—young, on foot, three armed with crossbows, dagger hilts visible in sheaths tied at the thigh. The third had a rifle. Two carried a rough pole between them; a slain doe, gutted, was tied to it, dangling.

"Renegades?" She mouthed the word, careful to make no sound.

"Perhaps," he mouthed in answer.

She understood. No percentage in finding out. Better to just keep their heads down and their mounts quiet until the potential threat could pass on by.

The wind rushed down the canyon, keening. Svald shifted, nervous, ready to dance. Brit laid her face to the silky muzzle and whispered very low. "Shh. Easy, my darling, easy my sweet girl." The mare quieted.

They waited some more, as the wind whipped around them, singing eerily through the trees. Lightning flashed and booming thunder followed. The first drops of rain began to fall. Finally, after the four men were long gone, Eric led her around the stand of boulders and onto the trail where the men had passed.

"How did you know they were there?" she asked before they mounted up again.

He shook his head as lightning blazed in the sky above. Thunder boomed and rolled away. "Later. Now we must move on." They mounted and went in the opposite direction from the four men.

They covered what was left of the ravine floor quickly and within minutes they were climbing again. The wind tore at them, lightning speared the sky, angry thunder booming in its wake. The sky opened up and the rain poured down—fat drops, coming harder and faster.

They fought their way upward as the downpour intensified. In no time the trail was awash in mud. The mud turned to rivulets, then to small, rushing streams.

"We must leave the trail. It will soon be a river," Eric called over his shoulder, shouting against the wind.

Brit followed him into the trees, her head low against the mare's neck, smelling rain and wet horse, her beanie and the hair beneath it plastered to her skull.

Eric led her on, through the close-growing evergreens. More than once she got whacked by low-hanging branches. And even there, in the thickness of the trees, the rain got through, whipping at their faces, driven by the relentless wind. Svald, bless her sweet heart, was a surefooted animal. They picked their way along the steep slope of the hill, moving east now, climbing as they went.

They were practically upon the mouth of the cave before she saw it: two shelves of rock surrounded by trees, a tall, dark hole between. Eric dismounted and climbed the rest of the way on foot, leading the gelding, slipping a little on the soggy ground, but jumping at last to the lower shelf at the cave's entrance and urging the gelding up after him. There was space on the ledge for him, his horse, Brit and Svald, with room to spare.

He waved her on. She slid from the saddle and followed, leading her horse, landing on her feet at the cave's entrance, Svald scrambling a little, but ending up at her side.

"Stay here." Eric handed her the gelding's reins and vanished into the darkness. Brit surprised herself by letting him go without a word of protest. Truth to tell, she thought as she stood there in the mouth of the cave, dripping wet and shivering with cold, she was feeling more than a little discouraged with herself. Concerning the weather, Asta had been all too right. Maybe she should have listened.

But she'd always been that way. When she was ready to go, there was just no stopping her. A character flaw? Well, yeah. In some circumstances.

Like, for instance, this one.

The horses shook the heavy, soaked braids of their manes, flinging icy water everywhere, including on her. Beyond the ledge, the rain was turning slushy— a snow and rain mix.

Terrific. Perfect. Wonderful. Would they end up snowed in here, thanks to her pigheadedness?

Now, wouldn't that be lovely? Way to go, Brit.

"This way," Eric said from behind her. He stood about fifteen feet into the cave. He was carrying...a flaming torch?

"Where did you get that?"

"It's always wise to keep safe places, stocked and ready, for times like this one. We're fortunate. No scavengers have found this cave since last I was here." Really, the guy never ceased to amaze her. "Come," he said.

She went, leading the horses into the darkness, toward the tall, proud man with the blazing light.

Chapter Ten

The cave was a tunnel for about a hundred feet. Then it opened to a wide, shadowy chamber. Eric went directly to the circle of stones at the center. Within the circle a fire was laid and waiting to be lit.

He lowered the torch to the kindling and the fire caught. The smoke spiraled up and disappeared into the shadows above. Apparently, there were gaps in the rocks up there, a natural flue that let the smoke escape.

Brit swiped off her wet beanie, dropped it to a nearby rock and raked her fingers back through her hair. Ugh. Dripping and tangled. She really should have taken a moment, back there when it started raining, to unzip her collar and make use of the waterproof hood built into her jacket.

Eric stuck the torch into the dirt. He turned it until the flame went out, then dropped the heavy stick beside the ring of stones. He glanced up to find her staring at him and returned the favor with a dead-on kind of look.

Well, okay, she thought, shrugging and raising her hands, palms out. All my fault we're here. Message received. My bad.

He didn't seem particularly mollified by her show of meekness.

So fine, she thought. Be that way.

She shifted her glance to the licking, rising flames of the fire and her low spirits lifted a fraction—at the brightness and warmth and the cheery crackling sounds it made. She took a look around. Gleaming in the far shadows, near another tunnel opposite the one they had come through, she could see a small pool.

"A spring?" she asked, and then wished she hadn't. He probably wouldn't even bother to answer.

But he did. "The water is clear, very cold—and safe to drink." He took the reins of his horse from her. "We must see to our mounts." There were supplies stacked on a ledge of rock near the cave wall: a pile of blankets, a bag of oats, a bucket....

From his saddlebag Eric produced a brush and a curry comb. "Put your pistol aside."

She did as he instructed, removing her coat so she could take off her shoulder holster, setting the gun and the holster on a flat-topped rock a few feet from the fire. She was shivering, so she put her coat back on.

They unsaddled, wiped down and brushed the long-haired horses, unbraiding and combing out their manes so they would dry. It took a while. They had to share the comb and brush. Midway through, no longer cold, she took off her coat and set it on a rock, the outside spread toward the fire to dry.

They were silent as they worked. Eric wore a grim look the whole time. Did she blame him?

Not really.

"I'll feed the horses," he said when the job of getting the animals dry and groomed was done. "Take off your wet clothes. Lay them out to dry." He tossed her a blanket to wrap herself in.

Her socks were dry, thanks to her heavy boots. But upward from there to her waist she was wet to the skin.

On top, the news was better. Her water-repellent jacket, though damp on the outside, had protected her underneath. Water had gotten in around her neck, but not a lot. It would dry quickly if she stood near the fire.

Her bandage was fine. Hooray for small favors.

She retreated to a corner of the cave, where she took off her boots and then hopped around in her socks, getting off the clammy jeans and thermal pants. Eric never glanced her way—or if he did, she didn't catch him at it.

Yeah, okay. It was kind of childish, to keep darting suspicious looks his way to make sure he wasn't peeking. As if it mattered if he watched her hopping around without her jeans on. He wouldn't have seen much, anyway—just her looking seriously awkward, with bare legs. And given his current mood, why would he bother?

She wrapped her lower body in the blanket, put her boots back on and hobbled to the fire carrying her two sets of soggy pants. Once she'd spread the clothes on the rocks several feet from the flames, where they could soak up the heat without getting singed, she got her comb from her saddlebag and perched on a rock to work the tangles from her hair.

About then Eric finished with the horses and withdrew to a corner of his own to hop around getting out of his wet things—not that she watched him. Of course she didn't. She just knew what the procedure entailed, having done it herself a few minutes ago.

Soon enough, a blanket tied at his waist, he joined her at the fire. He was bare-chested. His thick shearling jacket didn't have a zipper. Water must have gotten through…

She realized she was staring at him again—and no, not at the medallion, though it gleamed against his skin. She was looking at his beautiful, muscular, smooth chest.

She blinked, jerked her glance downward and regarded her boots as she yanked at the tangles in her hair.

He chuckled.

She looked up, glaring, sharp words rising to her lips.

"You have something to say?" His eyes were gleaming.

She cleared her throat. "Uh, no. Not a thing."

Really, why rag on him? She was *grateful* to him, she truly was. If she'd been on her own, she'd have ridden right up on those four mean-looking characters with that poor dead doe. And even if she'd somehow gotten past them, she'd be out in the rain right now, soaked to the skin, wondering what to do next—instead of safe in a warm, dry place, reasonably comfortable while she waited out the storm.

"Well," she said cautiously, daring to hope they might manage to be on good terms while they were stuck here. "I guess you're not *that* mad at me."

He was laying his clothes on the rocks, the lean, strong muscles of his arms and shoulders bunching and releasing as he worked. He sent her a glance.

She realized she was doing it again—staring at his body. She jerked her gaze downward.

"A fine pair of boots you have there."

She couldn't help smiling. "I like 'em." She lifted her head. His eyes were waiting. "So. We're okay then—I mean, you and me? You're not totally furious with me for getting us into this jam?"

He seemed to consider, then replied. "I confess, I was angry. But while you were looking at your boots, it occurred to me that I might as well blame the rain for falling as be angry at you for going where you think you have to go." He half sat on a steeply sloping rock.

She worked a final stubborn knot from a damp lock of hair. "I don't just *think* I have to go there." He only looked at her. She read his expression and couldn't help grinning. "Determined to avoid an argument, are we?"

"I am trying with all my might."

The knot came free. "I can see that. And I've got to say you're doing an excellent job."

They had jerky in their saddlebags and dried apples and grain bars—pressed oats and nuts, sweetened with honey. They spread blankets on the floor and sat down for lunch, using their saddles for backrests.

Brit had two sticks of jerky, several dried apple slices, a grain bar and a precious bag of M&Ms laid out on a handkerchief at her side. She took one of the jerky sticks. "So now can you tell me how you knew those men were on the trail?"

He was chewing on a bite of grain bar. He swallowed. "The truth is, I don't *know* how I knew. They might have made a noise that I heard somewhere below the threshold of my conscious mind. Or maybe it was the quality of the silence."

Silence? The wind had been blowing, making the tree branches sway and sigh. And what about the jingle of their bridles, the soft clop-clop of the horses' hooves?

He must have seen by her expression that she didn't understand. "It's…an instinct, I suppose. An instinct one develops, over time. When we pass through the forest, the smaller creatures—all but the foolish squirrels and some of the cheekier birds—go quiet, wary of us as potential predators. Though there is the noise of our passing, there is also a circle of silence around us as we move. When those men got too close, they brought their own circle with them. I sensed it."

She gestured with her piece of jerky. "Ah. Well. Now, that explains it."

"You still do not follow?"

She stared into his eyes for a moment. "Yes. I follow, at least to a degree…"

He tore off a bite of jerky and so did she. They both chewed. Great thing about dried meat—really kept the old jaw muscles in top form.

She swallowed. "So you've spent a lot of time here, in the Vildelund, over the years?"

"I have."

"Your father brought you?"

He shook his head. "My father had his work at the king's side in the south, demanding work that left few opportunities for family trips. But my mother loved the Mystic life. She would come often to the Vildelund for lengthy visits. Much of the time I would come with her."

She thought of her brother and wondered. Sif had said he used to come here. "And Valbrand? Did he come, too?" He sent her a look. She bristled. "What? Now I can't even ask you about him? We talked about him the other night."

He considered for a moment, then granted, "That we did."

She set down her half-eaten grain bar. "I just want to…know about him. Please. It means a lot—to hear how he felt about things, about how he was." She used the past tense without the slightest hesitation, though she didn't for a minute believe her brother was really dead. It only seemed to her the best way to show Eric that, right now at least, she wasn't leading him anywhere, wasn't trying to trip him up. She was only a sister longing to learn about the brother she had never had the opportunity to know. She asked again, "Did Valbrand used to come to the Vildelund with you?"

And he answered. "Yes. Many times."

"Did he like it here?"

"He did."

"Why?"

"He liked the wildness of the land, I think, the peace that can be found in living simply."

"The same things you like."

"Yes."

"He didn't think much of the life at court, then?"

A ghost of a smile haunted Eric's fine mouth. "Ah, but he did. He loved the life at court."

She made a small sound in her throat. "Well. Easy to please, wasn't he?"

"You could say that, I suppose. Valbrand had a talent for living within each moment. Wherever he was, he never wished himself elsewhere. He always seemed to enjoy himself at functions of state. No matter how long or tedious the event, he would be alert and smiling, thoroughly engrossed." Eric stared into the fire as though looking into a kinder past. "That was your brother. Always interested. And seeing the good first, in every man."

Though it was off the all-important subject of her brother, she couldn't stop herself from asking, "And what about you? Do you enjoy the life at Isenhalla?"

"Not as much as Valbrand did." They shared a glance. He added, "But I do find it stimulating. After all, His Majesty and my father are responsible, to some extent, for the well-being of every Gullandrian. It's important work that they do. I grew to manhood knowing that the time would come when I would step forward to assume the sacred duty of helping my king— your brother—to rule this land. I was content in that knowledge. I was committed to preparing myself fully for the future I knew awaited me."

"And now?"

His mouth had a rueful curl to it. "Now I would

say that I no longer see my future as a clear, straight road before me. There are twists and turns, corners I cannot see around.''

''You mean, since my brother was lost at sea?''

He studied her face for a moment, his eyes narrowed. And then he stuck out his right arm, wrist up. She saw the white ridge of scar tissue. He said, ''Valbrand had a scar to match this one.''

''From when you were bloodbound to each other?''

He nodded. ''In the bloodbinding ceremony, each of us was bled—a copious bleeding, believe me—into the same deep bowl. Then, our wounds still open, we took turns, the blood running free down our arms, passing the bowl back and forth, drinking our mingled blood until every drop was gone.'' He let his arm fall to his side. ''So I have drunk your brother's blood— as he drank mine. When he was lost, I lost not only my dearest friend and bloodbound brother, but also my future partner in the work of ruling this land. It was a terrible blow, a cleaving at the center of who I am. As if half of my true self was slashed away.''

She didn't know what to say, so she said nothing, only reached out and brushed her fingers down the side of his arm in a wordless acknowledgment of his loss. Though she remained certain Valbrand had returned, she had no doubt Eric had once believed him dead—and that that belief had changed him in a deep, irrevocable way.

Eric caught her hand, clasped it briefly, then let it go.

She felt a warmth all through her. A closeness to him that had nothing to do with desire. This was something else. It was what she'd sensed between them two nights ago, in Rinda's tent in the camp of the *kvina soldars*.

The closeness of comrades…

There was wood—maybe half a cord—stacked near the supplies against the cave wall. And a much smaller pile of logs nearer the fire. He rose with surprising grace, given the way the blanket was wrapped so close around his legs, and got a fresh log from the smaller pile. He crouched to add it to the flames.

She let herself admire the fine, strong shape of his back, the play of light and shadow on the bumps of his spine, the healthy bloom on his smooth skin as he positioned the log in the fire. A few winking sparks shot up, weaving toward the darkness above for a brave, soaring moment, then surrendering to gravity and gently showering back down.

He returned to the blanket and got comfortable against his saddle. "And what of you, oh fearless one? To whom are you bound?"

She rolled her eyes. "Fearless. Right." She met his eyes. "No, really. I'm far from fearless."

"Yet you never let your fear rule you."

"That's right. Hey. Talk to my mother. She claims I actually seek out the things that scare me."

"And you would do this because…?"

"Well, my mother would say, for the dangerous thrill of confronting my own fear."

"And does your mother have it right?"

She sighed. "Maybe. Sometimes. I've always felt…out of place, I guess. As if I'm looking for something and it's never there." She swallowed, though her mouth was empty.

He asked, his voice gentle, "What things truly frighten you?"

She thought for a moment. "Oh, dying. Original, huh? I guess I'm like most people—not up for that yet."

"Yet you could face it. You *have* faced it. Recently."

Her hand went automatically to her shoulder. He nodded and she found herself nodding in response.

He said, "You will face death again, there is no escaping that."

"Yeah. But I'd seriously prefer if I didn't have to do it anytime soon."

"Your mother might say otherwise."

"She would *definitely* say otherwise."

"Mothers can be so irritating—they are too often right."

She made a humphing sound. "Unfortunately."

He shrugged. "The time will come, for all of us, when death will win the day. Our forefathers understood this. They asked only for the chance to die fighting."

Our forefathers. If she closed her eyes, she could almost see them. The bold Norsemen of old in their serpent-thin ships, brutal men bound only by their warrior code, eyes on the far horizon, rowing hard and steady toward the next settled, prosperous, ripe-for-the-picking coastal town.

Eric said, "Death is the one constant, the thing to which we all ultimately surrender, even as we spend our lives denying that death will have us in the end."

What was there to say to that? Nothing—which was exactly what she said.

He asked, "And my original question—to whom are you bound?"

That was a fairly easy one. "My family. My mother, my sisters. My father. Strange. I never knew him for all those years. But the moment I met him, I felt that I'd known him all of my life." She glanced away. She was thinking that she felt the same way about the man who sat beside her. But she didn't want to say it. It would be way unwise, given the circumstances—the two of them, alone by the fire until the storm passed, wearing blankets instead of their clothes.

"Who else?" he prompted.

She did look at him then, chin high, defiant. "My brother." It came out sounding like a taunt.

He didn't rise to the bait. "And...?"

One more person came to mind. "A friend. She lives in Los Angeles. Her name is Dulcie Samples. I met her at a writers' workshop. She has red hair and honest hazel eyes and the biggest heart in California."

"A friend and a true one."

"You got it."

"A friend found at...a writers' workshop?"

"That's right."

"You are an author?"

"Wannabe."

"Wanna—"

"Want to be," she clarified. "I've started ten novels. Haven't finished a one."

"You say that with such bravado. Why?"

"I didn't finish college, either. Some have remarked that there seems to be a pattern here."

If there was a pattern, Eric didn't seem particularly

concerned about it. He asked, "And your friend, Dulcie?"

"She's written three, I think—all the way through to the end. Hasn't sold one yet, but I really believe, for her, that day will come."

"For her—yet not for you?"

She waved a hand. "I gotta be honest. All that sitting, I just can't stick with it."

"A woman of action."

"Well, yeah. I guess so." A few feet away, Svald shook her head and snorted. "See? I get no respect. Not even from my horse."

"I respect you." He was looking at her teasingly, but it didn't matter. She knew he meant what he said. His expression changed, turned more serious. "And what about men? Other than your father...and your brother. Is there a man to whom you feel bound?"

"Not...at the moment." Was that a lie? Maybe. Maybe she did feel bound. Just a little bit—to Eric.

Did he sense she felt that way? If he did, he let it pass. "But there have been men you have...cared for?"

Was this somewhere they ought to be going? Probably not. Still, she heard herself answering, "A few. Somehow, it just never seemed to work out."

"Good," he said.

She couldn't resist. "Fair's fair. What about you?"

"A dalliance or two. Foolish. Long over. For the past seven years, I've been waiting for you."

Oops. No doubt about it now. Time to change the subject.

But she didn't. "Eric. Come on..."

His grin was slow and lazy. "Lead the way."

''Oh, puh-lease. Seven years is pretty close to a decade—and you're how old?''

''I am thirty.''

''That's...wild.''

''No. It is simply the truth.''

''I gotta ask, when you say you were waiting for *me,* you don't really mean me, specifically?''

''That is exactly what I meant. You. Specifically.''

''Get outta town.''

''Since we are not *in* town, I will assume that is simply one of your American expressions.''

''Good thinking. But seriously, at the age of twenty-three, you suddenly decided, 'Hey, enough of this dallying. I'm waiting for Brit.' Is that what you're telling me?''

''Ah. I understand your question now. The truth is that I was waiting for you, specifically. But I didn't know who you would be until you came here, to the Vildelund, in search of me. Until I saw that you wore my medallion.''

She found she was staring at his chest again. Staring at the medallion, she told herself.

Yeah, right.

Their saddles almost touched. It was way too easy for him to slide over next to her. He cupped the back of her neck, his warm fingers gliding up into her almost-dry hair.

She gulped. ''Get back to your own saddle.''

He whispered, ''You say that with no conviction.''

Well, and how was she supposed to say *anything* with conviction? When his warm, strong body was brushing against hers, when the scent of him was all around her, when she gloried in the feel of his fingers in her hair. "This is *so* not fair…"

"Ah, but it *is* fair. It is fair and right. And exactly as it was meant to be."

"Can we just stay away from the meant-to-bes?"

One sable eyebrow lifted. "If you insist. For now." His fingers stroked down through her hair.

She whispered, suddenly breathless, "When you get so close like this…"

"Yes?"

"I can't…"

"What?"

"Damn you, you'd better just go ahead and kiss me."

"As you wish, so shall it be." He said that—and then that tempting mouth of his stayed right where it was. The medallion was touching her, the weight of it pressing through her sweater and her shirt, to a spot right above her breast.

The other night, in Rinda's tent, the sight of that medallion had been enough to make her put a stop to the magic between them.

Not tonight, though.

Tonight she felt the warm weight of it and it was good. Right.

The only problem? His mouth was three whole inches away.

She slid her hand around his neck. It took just one small tug and—at last—his lips met hers.

Chapter Eleven

A kiss.

His kiss.

How did he do it? He kissed her as if he would never kiss another. As if this kiss was the only kiss that had ever been.

Or would ever be.

The thing was, when he kissed her, she could almost believe that ''meant to be'' was exactly right. Exactly what they were, the two of them.

Meant to be. And together at last. After all the long, lonely years spent waiting. For this moment.

For all their moments to come....

When he kissed her, she could almost forget her quest to bring her brother home, almost accept his lie that Valbrand was no more. When he kissed her she heard violins, saw sparks leaping, showering down.

When he kissed her, she was certain that this man and this kiss would last forevermore…

He lifted his head, just a little, enough that he could look down at her.

Oh, his eyes…

Nobody had eyes like that. Eyes the color of spruce. Or maybe jade. Eyes that looked into hers so deeply.

Way, way deep. Deeper than anyone had dared—or even cared—to look before.

"Come back here, please," she whispered. "Kiss me some more…."

He answered by again lowering his mouth to hers.

She held his mouth with hers and she slipped a hand up, her fingers brushing the medallion.

Oh, the wonderful smooth, hard skin of his chest, so marvelous to touch. The *heat* of him. She laid her palm flat against his left breast—there. She felt it. The strong, steady beat of his heart.

It was glorious. Impossible. Right.

She could feel how he wanted her—in the way his tender hands stroked her nape and caressed her shoulders, in the needful rhythm of his heartbeat, in the hardness that was pressed against her thigh.

He pulled back again.

She frowned at him. "Don't do that."

"What?"

"Don't pull back."

He bent close again—but only for a fleeting moment, only long enough to quickly brush his lips across hers. Then again he pulled away. He shook his head. Slowly. "I regret that now is not the time."

She felt a stab of irritation. "Night before last you

didn't say that. Night before last you thought it was very much *the time*.''

He retreated to his own saddle.

She sat up. ''Okay, what's going on? What did I *do*?''

''Nothing. I could kiss you forever....''

She wrinkled her nose at him. ''Well, hey. That clarifies it for me.''

He found a twig on the blanket, tossed it into the fire. They watched the flames lick around it, claim it, consume it.

Finally he said, ''The other night, I knew you wouldn't have me. I knew you weren't ready. But you would give me kisses. A few sweet embraces. So I took them. I understood that in the end you would push me away. Tonight...I don't want you to do what you might later regret.''

She really wanted to argue. But that was only pure pettiness talking. What he said was the truth. She wasn't ready to get naked with him.

And she might never be. Certainly she wouldn't be until he told her the truth that mattered most—the truth that, for whatever reason, he kept choosing to deny her.

She settled back against her saddle with a sigh. ''So, how long do you figure we're going to be stuck here?''

''Until the storm plays out. Tomorrow, at the earliest. That would be my guess.''

She looked at her watch. Barely noon. Whoopee. ''Got a deck of cards with you?''

''I regret to say I don't.''

''So, then. What shall we talk about now?''

''Is it necessary that we talk?''

"Not in the least." However, at that moment silence seemed a bad choice. She slanted him a look. "Read any good books lately?"

He played along. "A few. I recently finished Hawking's *A Brief History of Time.*"

"No kidding. I didn't know anyone had actually read that one."

"Black holes. Fascinating."

"Oh, yeah, I'd imagine. What about music?"

He put up a hand. "Your turn."

"Okay. Eminem."

"Isn't that a candy?"

"No. I mean the rapper." She fully expected him to think she'd said *wrapper.*

But he surprised her. "Ah, rap—talking in rhythm to music. So distinctly American. And I remember. This rapper you mention spells Eminem phonetically. But it means 'M and M,' for his full name, which is Marshall Mathers."

"Hey. Right on the money."

Eric was frowning. "This Eminem is controversial. I have heard his songs are disrespectful to women— and yet he's a favorite of yours?"

She shrugged. "He's got a bad attitude and problems with his mother. Let's just say I can relate." She picked up the bag of candy beside her, tore off the top and held it his way. "M&M?"

"I believe I will, thank you."

"Go ahead, take five or six."

"I see you are feeling generous."

"Yes, I am."

He looked right at her. "I'd rather have them one

at a time.'' He grinned at her nod of approval and popped the candy into his mouth.

She took one for herself. They sat back on their saddles and stared into the fire. Sucking. Slowly.

The sound was very faint. It came from the far tunnel, beyond the gleaming underground pool. A sound like a pebble tossed against a rock. Eric recognized it for the signal it was.

Careful to be absolutely silent, he pushed back the blanket beneath which, but for his boots, he was fully dressed. Their clothes had dried by midafternoon. They'd wasted no time in putting them on. For both of them, too much bare skin presented way too much temptation.

His boots waited where he'd left them, near his bedding. He reached for them, pulled them on and tied up the laces.

The fire had burned low. Quietly he rose, got more wood and set the heavy logs gently on the glowing coals. There was rustling behind him, followed by a long, soft sigh. And then a groan. He turned from the fire to look at his woman.

She lay on her back, both arms flung out on the blanket beneath her spread bedroll. Her tangled pale hair fell across the down coat she had used for a pillow. She was scowling. ''Ugh,'' she grumbled. And then she smiled.

He felt his own smile taking form from hers. She slept as she did everything else. Restlessly. With enthusiasm.

Her foot in its heavy wool sock appeared from beneath the covers. She grumbled some more, gave a kick—and her slim denim-clad leg was exposed all the way to the thigh. He resisted the urge to go to her and straighten her blankets, to cover her again. The logs behind him were already catching. If she was chilly now, the freshly stoked fire would warm her soon enough.

He waited, watching to see if she might wake. Though she constantly mumbled and sighed and tossed and turned, after a time he became certain she was deeply asleep.

Only then did he dare to snatch his coat from the rock where he'd left it and move stealthily past her, donning the coat as he went. He crossed the dirt floor of the cavern, went past the small pool formed from an underground spring and on into the pitch black of the far tunnel.

He didn't need light. He knew the way. The tunnel first took him deeper into the hillside. But then, about twenty meters along, it turned sharply to the right.

Within minutes of leaving Brit by the fire, he emerged from the tunnel onto a ledge quite similar to the one through which they'd first entered the cave.

The storm was over, the still night air bracing. His breath came out as mist. The rain had become snow at some point. But it must have stayed a slushy mix almost through to the end; the ground was white, but not to any depth. It wouldn't last. Tomorrow, if the sun came out, the thin layer of snow would melt away to nothing by noon.

In the hush, the trees made faint crackling noises. He waited, every sense attuned.

There he heard it: the slightest movement on the hillside, above him to the left, the sound so small it might have been only the scrabbling of some foolish night-foraging squirrel.

But the sound, Eric knew, was intentional. And not made by a squirrel.

It was made by something much larger, something that walked on two legs, a creature feared throughout the Vildelund by youthful renegades—by all men of flawed character and evil intent.

Eric turned. Saw.

Deep in shadow, beneath the thick branches of a spruce tree, invisible to anyone who didn't know what to look for: black boots.

The boots were attached to a pair of black-clad legs. At about hip height, the rest of the dark figure melted into the tree.

Eric cupped his hands around his mouth and blew. The sound was part whistle, part an echo of wind in the trees. It was their signal from when they were boys.

It meant all clear—no need to hide.

At the signal, Valbrand ducked free of the sheltering tree branches. Sure-footed as a mountain cat, he descended, moving sideways for easy balance, jumping at last to Eric's side at the mouth of the cave.

Chapter Twelve

The black leather mask had been stitched by Asta's talented hands. The seams were almost invisible. It fit the ravaged face beneath like a second skin, the holes at the eyes carefully crafted to a catlike slant.

At the mouth there was little more than a slit. Valbrand's voice came out low, slightly muffled, on a thin cloud of mist. "You are certain she won't wake?"

Eric almost smiled. "As certain as one can be about anything that concerns your contrary youngest sister."

Dark eyes gleamed behind the mask. "I think you are positive now of one thing—that she is yours."

Eric lost the urge to smile. "She knows the truth. Though I tell your lie for you at every turn, she remains certain that she saw you—at the crash site, and in my aunt's longhouse. Nothing will shake her belief."

Valbrand backed away a step. "Must you look at me like that? Yes, I should have heeded your warning and worn the mask when she was so ill. But I was confident that she wouldn't recall what she'd seen."

Eric couldn't let that pass. "Why take such a chance? Unless, in some part of your heart, you *wanted* her to see you—to know that you still live."

The dark gaze shifted away. "The answer is no."

Eric cast his own glance upward toward the star-scattered sky. Somewhere out there in the limitless night, black holes waited to suck down unknowing universes into swirling oblivion. Sometimes he felt it was the same here on earth.

He wondered at his own choices. He had been born to follow the man who stood beside him, conditioned all the years of his life to forge onward at all cost toward a shared central goal: Valbrand would be king, Eric his grand counselor. One to lead and one to provide balance and the objective view, as it was with their fathers before them.

Could the goal ever be realized now? More and more, Eric doubted.

He looked at the dark figure beside him. "Did I ask?"

"You were coming to it."

Denials would be useless. They knew each other too well. "Yes. I grow impatient. Can you blame me?"

"Blame *you*?" Valbrand's voice was gentle, heavy with regret. "Never."

"Then when will you show yourself to her?"

"I cannot say."

The same answer. Always. For too long now, Eric

had dared to hope that his friend would eventually recover from the damage inflicted on him.

But like sand in an hourglass, hope was running out.

It was six months since he had at last found Valbrand, a haunted shell of the man he had been, living in a cave on a tiny island off the coast of Iceland, whispered about by the local fisherman—rough and independent men who knew the old Norse ways.

At first Valbrand would not even emerge from the shadows of the cave to speak with him. Slowly, over long weeks, as one might build trust in an injured wild animal, with gifts of food and blankets to lure the wild man ever nearer, Eric had broken through enough that Valbrand allowed him close.

Weeks more were spent in rebuilding the old trust, in convincing Valbrand to come home. The price? Eric's vow to stay near him and keep the secret that he lived. Until Valbrand declared himself ready, only a chosen few—Mystics all—would know that he survived.

Eric had made the trip south to Isenhalla after leaving his friend—only briefly, Valbrand made him swear—safe with Asta. There, at the silver slate palace of Gullandrian kings, Eric had lied—to his father and to his king. He said his time of seeking was over; he'd at last come to accept the fact that Valbrand was no more. The lie had chafed him from the first, but never so much as now when that lie stood, unbreachable as a mile-high fortress wall, between him and the woman destined to be his.

Valbrand spoke then. "I have been again to the crash site." They had agreed the night before that Valbrand would go.

"And?"

"Men still guard it—six of them, NIB." During Brit's illness, they had returned to the crash site together. They'd spotted the guards, who had come through the fjord by boat. "The boat remains moored three kilometers west of the site. While I watched, they had two with the boat and four on the site. Then the two on the boat went out to relieve two of the men near the plane."

"You're certain now—that they're NIB?"

Valbrand nodded. "I slipped aboard the boat during the brief time it waited empty and stole a quick look around."

"The king's men, then?"

"At least in appearance."

"You don't trust them."

"I trust no one but you. You know that. And I wonder. Surely my father must have sent a mechanic to examine the wreckage. That would be routine procedure. What did that mechanic report?"

The question was purely rhetorical. They could not know what the king might have learned without asking him. And Eric couldn't ask His Majesty such a question, as King Osrik would only become suspicious of his claim that he was certain the crash had been an accident.

Any suspicions on King Osrik's part were dangerous until Valbrand declared himself ready to set aside the mask.

Valbrand said, "What of your plans for the morrow?"

"We go on, to the plane."

The eyes behind the mask narrowed. "Are you mad? She can't be allowed there."

"Your sister cares not what she is allowed. She won't be stopped."

"I thought your plan was to—"

"She has a compass and knows how to use it. She has an accurate map drawn by my father. If I lead her on a fool's chase, she'll only find the way herself in the end."

"Then you must make her understand that the danger is too great. She must go back."

With considerable effort, Eric schooled his voice to a patient tone. "You are the one who refuses to understand. Her way is set. She won't return to the safety of the village until she's examined for herself the wreckage of her plane."

Valbrand shook his head. "There's nothing to be gained by that. Even if the men who guard it turn out to be friendly and go so far as to allow her access, she will find nothing of use."

"Why are we discussing this?" Eric found it ever more challenging to keep the irritation from his voice. "You seek to convince me of what I already know. Perhaps *you* would like to try persuading her?"

A low sound came from behind the mask. "Sarcasm, my friend?"

"Born of frustration. She must be told that you live. Our fathers must know, as well. We tread water while all our hopes drown."

Valbrand chopped the air with a black-gloved hand. "I cannot. Not yet."

"You can. You *choose* not to." Eric leaned closer to the man beside him and spoke lower, with greater intensity. "Don't imagine I think it will be an easy thing. I know that for you to stand bare-faced before your father the king and the eyes of the court will be, in its way, a greater feat than surviving the horror that has already been done to you. I *have* been patient. I have waited on your readiness, by your side as I promised. But there is so much to do. Traitors to expose. Wrongs to make right. None of that will be accomplished while you hide behind a mask."

Valbrand's gaze had shifted away again. "This mask has served me—and our people—well. I have saved lives wearing it."

There was truth in those words. At first, when Valbrand had laid claim to Starkavin, the rare black horse he'd taken from renegades, when he'd asked that Asta create for him a black leather mask and clothing to match it, Eric had been heartened. It had seemed a first step: Valbrand, incensed by raiding renegades and ready for action at last. In the guise of a legendary hero, he would ambush the troublemakers and protect the innocent from harm. Surely, in time he'd be ready to put the mask aside, to reunite with his father, to find and vanquish his enemies—and to claim his rightful place as the most likely successor to the Gullandrian throne.

But the sand trickled downward in the hourglass of time. And Valbrand showed no inclination to give up the mask and emerge from the wilderness. Eric said, "I have kept my vow to you, to remain at your side. I have lied for you. But I refuse to help you tell lies to yourself. The greatest evil awaits you in the south. You must root it out and face it without the Dark Raider's mask."

"When I am ready." Valbrand's tone brooked no further argument.

Eric felt a weariness, a heavy dragging on his soul. "Then I fear that right now there is nothing more to say." He turned for the tunnel.

Valbrand spoke to his back. "I'll stay close tomorrow, in the event of trouble."

"I know it." Eric paused, but he didn't turn.

"You may yet convince her to give up this foolishness."

"It won't happen."

Surely Valbrand had to realize that *he* was the only one who could make Brit go back—by revealing himself to her.

In his mind's eye, Eric saw her—tall, strong, proud...and so very determined.

Then again perhaps it was too late to stop her. Even should Valbrand put aside the mask and show himself to her, she'd still have to try to discover who had sabotaged her plane.

And he'd left her alone for too long. She could wake. If she did, who could say what kind of mischief she'd get up to?

Eric moved into the shadows, never once turning to glance back at his friend. He'd said more than perhaps he should have.

And he knew that Valbrand was already gone.

In her dream Brit rode a fleet black horse. She urged the horse onward, cold wind on her face, her blood pumping in time to the hollow beat of hooves drumming the frozen ground. She saw the sheer cliff before them, the limitless sky beyond. She didn't even try to draw a halt, only urged her dark mount onward, faster and faster toward the yawning chasm ahead.

The horse leaped, hooves churning empty air.

She woke as they fell, twisting, into nothingness.

She lay, covers a tangled mess as usual, on her back. For a dazed moment or two she stared blankly at the cave ceiling above her—arching, uneven, lit by the fickle light of dancing flame shadows.

She turned her head, first to the fire, then to where Eric should have been sleeping.

He wasn't there.

She shot to a sitting position—and saw movement—someone emerging through the tunnel by the underground pool. She was reaching for her pistol when she realized it was only Eric.

She left the pistol on the rock and demanded, "Okay, what's up?"

"Nature calls. I but answer."

She stifled a groan. Leave it to Eric to make a poem of letting her know he'd just stepped out to take a whiz. He approached. She watched him coming, feeling a little curl of warmth down inside. He moved with such sure, easy grace. Dropping his jacket on a rock, he crouched beside her, the action boneless. Fluid.

Her silly heart beat faster. "Looks dark back there. You should have taken a light."

"I know these hills blindfolded—and the tunnels within them."

"How convenient."

"You've made chaos of your bedroll."

"As usual—I was having this incredible dream. I rode a black horse. Over the side of a cliff."

"Were you frightened?"

"Only at the very end. As I fell."

"There are those who believe lessons seek us out in dreams."

"Maybe so. But what a way to go."

"You amaze me."

"Hmm. Amazement. That's good. Right?"

He lifted his hand. It didn't even occur to her to flinch away. The back of his finger traced the line of her jaw, making her flesh warm and tingly, causing those delightful little flares of sensation that faded slowly after his finger had moved on.

She stared into his eyes as his hand moved higher— a light caress against her cheek and then he was smoothing her tangled hair out of her eyes. It took conscious effort not to catch that hand and press her lips to it.

"So brave," he whispered. "And so foolish."

She did flinch away at that. He dropped his hand to his side.

"I gotta wonder," she muttered. "Why is it when a man does what he has to do, that's okay? But when a woman does the same, she's a fool?"

"I didn't call you a fool."

"Close enough."

He frowned. "Is this an argument beginning?"

She lifted her good shoulder in a half-shrug. "Could be."

"Must we continue?"

A moment before, she'd felt all quivery and tender. Now she only felt tired. "You're right. Let's get some sleep."

He rose, went to his own bedroll, dropped down and untied the lace of his left boot. He slanted her a glance as he pulled the boot off. "Will you sit there glaring at me all night, then?"

"Sorry," she mumbled. She pushed the tangle of blankets away from her legs, got up on her knees and set to work straightening out her bed.

They rose before dawn, stoked the fire, fed the horses and ate a cold breakfast of oatcakes, jerky and icy spring water. Together, by the light of the fire, they restacked the blankets and supplies and laid the makings of a fire within a fresh circle of stones. Once they'd prepared the cave for the next time it was needed, they braided the long manes of their horses and tacked up. Through all of it, Eric hardly said a word.

They were ready to head out when, out of nowhere, he announced, "I must speak with you."

Oh, goody. "I was starting to think you never would."

He dropped his horse's reins and sat on a rock near the fire. She holstered her pistol, pulled on her jacket and took a rock next to him.

"Okay," she said. "Spill it."

He stared into the licking flames—clearly in preference to looking at her. "I had hopes you might be convinced to go back before we reached the site where your plane crashed."

"Message received. Loud and clear. You've been telling me I have to go back practically the whole way."

"I wasn't counting on my words alone to make you change your mind. There was also the sight of those men on the trail, the difficult terrain, the storm."

She sighed. "So much for your hopes."

He lifted his head and looked at her then. "I confess, I even had plans to lead you on something of a wild-goose chase."

She gave him a look. "I do have a general idea of where we're supposed to be headed, you know. If you led me off in some totally wrong direction—"

He put up a hand, palm out. "I know. I have finally come to accept that you won't be frightened, overwhelmed or argued from your goal." *About time,* she thought. He said, "So I have reevaluated."

"Which means?"

"There are things you must know."

"Such as?"

"I believe as you do. I think your plane was sabotaged."

She gaped at him for about two seconds. What he'd just admitted was a vindication, of sorts. "Send up the bottle rockets. We're on the same page at last." She started to stand. "Can we go check it out now?"

"No."

She sank back to the hard rock. "Because…?"

"There are guards on it. It isn't safe."

She asked the pertinent question. "Guards sent by…?"

He answered grudgingly. "Your father."

"And that's a *problem?*"

"They're NIB," he said—presumably by way of explanation.

This wasn't adding up. "NIB? But…then they're on *our* side."

He looked at her coolly. "As a whole, the Bureau *is* on 'our side', as you put it."

"But there are traitors inside it? Is that what you're saying?"

"I don't know that, not beyond a doubt."

"Well, that's reassuring."

"Think. What better way to work against the throne than to infiltrate a governmental organization? All that secret information, right there, at the traitor's fingertips. It's too perfect. We have to assume it has happened."

She looked at him sideways. "This 'we' you mention…it includes my brother, doesn't it?"

For the first time he didn't give her an outright denial. "I am not speaking, at the moment, of your brother."

"No. But I am." She gave it up when he scowled at her. "All right. For now, let's leave my brother out of it." She leaned toward him. "Listen. Really, what's so suspicious here? The guards are NIB, sent at my father's command. They're looking for just what we're looking for—clues as to what made the plane go down."

"They could be doing exactly that."

She waited. He didn't explain himself. She gave up and prodded impatiently, "So? What's your point?"

"The problem is that those men could be working under orders His Majesty never gave them. They could be counteragents—men who have infiltrated the NIB, men who work for your father on one level but on a deeper level are not on his side at all."

She threw up both hands. "How do you know all this?"

"I don't know it, not for certain. But all indications point in that direction."

"What *indications?*"

He only looked at her—an If-I-told-you-that-I'd-have-to-kill-you kind of look.

"That does it." She jumped to her feet. "Let's go. I want to see these guys for myself."

Eric glared up at her. "You are surely the most contrary woman in all this land. Why do you always have to see things for yourself?"

"Indulge me, please. And don't look at me like that." Her request had zero effect. He told her nothing and he went on glaring. She gave up and dropped to the rock again. "I have to say, at this point I just don't know what to believe. For days you've been telling me you're certain my plane going down was an accident. Now you say you think maybe it wasn't—and that there are men guarding it—NIB, but also traitors. You won't tell me how you know this, you just lay it out and expect me to buy it. Why should I? The NIB has been a lot more helpful to me in finding out what I need to know than you've ever been."

His eyes narrowed. "How?"

"Excuse me?"

"How has the NIB been helpful to you?"

"What? That's so surprising? That someone would actually try to *help* me to find out where my brother is?"

"This someone…who is it?"

Brit had had about enough. "You know what? I'm totally, utterly one-hundred percent not getting this."

"I want you to tell me—"

"Uh-uh. Wrong. Not." Now she was the one glaring. She glared and she waited. When he let several seconds elapse without giving any orders, she asked, too sweetly, "Are you listening?"

He nodded.

"Good. Because I have a few points to make and I'd like your undivided attention while make them."

"You have it."

She cleared her throat. "Last night you said I was amazing. Let me return the favor. *You're* amazing. And not in a good way. This is insane. For a while there I thought you and my brother and my father and *your* father were up to something together. Now I don't. Now my take is, you're out of the loop and my father hasn't got a clue. My father and Medwyn indulged what they consider my pointless quest to find my dead brother because it meant I would come here—and hook up with you, thus resulting in wedding bells and the uniting of our families.

"And you and my brother? Well, for some reason that's completely beyond me, you two are just... hanging out up here in the hills. My brother is letting everybody think he's dead while he rides around masked on a black horse playing superhero to the Mystics. I have to say, hel-lo. I don't get it. It makes zero sense to me. If somebody tried to kill me—and I'm guessing they tried to kill Valbrand, too—then there's lots more that's rotten in Denmark than a few renegades. We ought to be working together to deal with the main problem, don't you think? My father and your father should know—not only that my brother's alive, but that there have been nearly successful assassination attempts on his life and on mine."

She paused for a breath—and okay, maybe also because she was hoping he'd speak up and tell her something she didn't already know.

But he kept that fine mouth firmly shut. She looked in his watchful eyes and knew he wasn't going to tell her squat. And for the first time since she woke from her illness and Asta confirmed that her guide had died, she felt hot tears pushing behind her eyes.

Damned if she'd let them fall. "Oh, Eric. When are you going to get honest with me? When are you going to trust me? When will you tell me what you know so we can finally start working together on this?"

Chapter Thirteen

Eric longed for nothing so much as to open his mouth
and tell her that she had it exactly right. What he
couldn't say left a bitter taste on his tongue—a bitter
taste he would simply have to bear, for he was bound
by his vow of silence.

And not only his vow. There was also the hope that
had not yet completely run out: that in time Valbrand
would come back fully to his true self and willingly
reveal himself to the family—and the nation—that
thought him dead.

If Eric admitted to Brit now that her brother did live,
what would that be but a betrayal of a lifelong friend
to whom he'd sworn undying loyalty? And not only
that; not just a sacred vow broken; not just the possibility that Valbrand might never forgive him. Were
it that alone, at this point, he might have told her
anyway.

No. It was what his broken vow might do to Valbrand's fragile equilibrium. He had seen Valbrand living like a creature only half-human. Eric, alone, had lured him from his cave, had coaxed and cajoled until the creature stood upright again and behaved as a man. Eric's vow of silence had been the linchpin that had brought Valbrand home to Gullandria. Eric simply wasn't ready to take the chance of pulling that pin.

Brit was up from her rock again, pacing back and forth before the still-bright fire. She stopped and whirled on him. "Okay, so much for a little give and take. Let me tell you what I intend to do. I'm going— today—to have a look at my plane. And then, once that's done, I'm going back to Isenhalla. I figure I've learned all I can around here."

He knew once she made up her mind to a thing, there was no stopping her. What could he say? *Please don't tell our fathers what you think you know?* Hardly. "You will do what you must."

"You got that much right. Let's go."

"Not yet. Not until you tell me who has *helped* you at the NIB."

She pushed back the sides of her thick jacket and braced her slim hands on her hips, revealing the butt of the weapon she never let get too far from her reach. "Let me get this straight. I get to wander around in the dark—but I'm supposed to tell *you* everything I know."

Eric didn't answer; no words would serve him as well as silence right then. There was no pettiness in her. Given a little time to think it over, she would see that, even in the face of all he hadn't said, it gained her nothing to keep this information from him.

She made a small, grumbling sound. "I keep asking myself, why do I trust you? You won't answer my questions, you won't stop lying to me about my brother...."

"My actions have been trustworthy. Actions should always carry more weight than words."

She plopped to the rock again. "Right. Of course. Thank you for explaining it to me."

"Concerning this person at the NIB..."

"You are relentless."

"The same could, most assuredly, be said of you."

Brit stared into the fire. She *was* going to tell him and she knew it. Putting it off only postponed their getting out of here. "Okay..." She glanced over to meet those waiting eyes. "I have a...what? An ally at the NIB, I guess you could say. Someone I've even started thinking of as a friend."

By then, he was scowling. "This 'ally.' A man?"

"I said a *friend*. It's not a man-woman kind of thing—not that you'd have any business getting heated up about it, if it was."

He didn't argue. But she saw in his eyes that he thought he had every right to object if it turned out there was some other guy on the scene—and, okay, maybe she could understand why he felt that way. Maybe she kind of felt that way herself. He said, "Tell me about this *friend*."

"His name is Jorund Sorenson—Special Agent Jorund Sorenson. I met him about two weeks after I first came here to Gullandria, in July."

"How did this meeting come about?"

"Jorund didn't instigate it, if that's what you're getting at."

"Just tell me how it happened."

"I was nosing around a little, asking questions about Valbrand. And, well, you know how my father is. He got nervous I was going to get myself into some kind of trouble."

"Now, where would His Majesty get an idea like that?"

"Ha-ha. Shall I continue?"

"Please do."

"So...first my dad gets Hauk—my brother-in-law?"

"I know Hauk."

"Well, my dad gets Hauk to put some of his people on me." Hauk Wyborn was the king's warrior. In Gullandria, the king's warrior was the head of an elite fighting squad—a sort of Gullandrian Secret Service, referred to by many as King Osrik's Berserkers—who took their orders directly from the king. "Hauk's men can fight with the best of them. They can also be very discreet. Still, I recognized one of them and had a little talk with my father. Dad promised there'd be no more bodyguards on me. Right. So next, he calls in the NIB—figuring, I suppose, that I wouldn't recognize any of those guys. I didn't. But after four or five days I couldn't help but notice the goons in bad suits tailing me everywhere, looking away whenever I tried to catch their eyes. I got tired of it, so I waylaid one of them. Ducked into a hallway at the National Museum of Norse History and when he came by, looking worried, trying to figure out where I'd gone, I jumped out and shouted, 'Boo!'"

"Charming."

"Believe it or not, I did surprise him. While he was

still sputtering and backing up, I demanded to know who his superior was. He blurted out Jorund's name. I tracked Jorund down at the Bureau offices. At first, you can imagine, he was reluctant to…work with me. But I had a little talk with my father and soon enough I had Special Agent Sorenson checking my rooms at the palace for bugs—even though the bugs were put there at my father's orders. Jorund told me what he knew about Valbrand's disappearance.''

Eric sat up straighter. ''What did he know?''

''Not a lot, really. Only what you said the other morning. That Valbrand went a-Viking and was killed in a storm at sea. Nothing I hadn't already learned. But Jorund would…talk with me about it. You know, we'd take the facts we had and brainstorm with them.''

''Brainstorm…''

''That's when you—''

''Never mind. I'm aware of what the word means. I'm just trying to understand why an NIB special agent would decide to be your 'ally.'''

''You know what? So am I—now. Though you've really told me nothing that proves there are traitors within the NIB.'' Still, Eric had planted the seeds of doubt. It wasn't a good feeling, to find herself wondering at the true loyalties of a man she'd come to trust.

''What else did you learn from this *friend* of yours?''

''We talked about you. Jorund said I'd have trouble getting anything out of you.'' She licked her finger and drew a mark in the air, putting her tongue to the roof of her mouth to make a sizzling sound. "Point for Jorund on that score."

Eric was looking excessively patient. "Did he offer to accompany you here?"

"We talked about it. And we agreed that my showing up with an NIB agent in tow would only make it harder for me to get you to tell me anything."

"Whose reasoning was that?"

"You know, I don't remember."

"Is it possible he simply didn't want to be on that plane with you—or anywhere nearby when you met your tragic end?"

Defensiveness curled through her, tightening her stomach, making her edgy and fed up with talking. "Anything's possible—can we go now?"

Those watchful eyes were on her. She thought for sure he would have more to say. But in the end, he only stood. "As you wish. Let me douse the fire."

They emerged from the cave to find the dawn coming, the sun not yet risen, a soft glow on the far horizon. The thin layer of snow from yesterday's storm crunched beneath the horses' hooves as they picked their way upward to the crest of the hill and then down the other side.

The new day was starting out warmer even than the day before. As the sun rose, the snow melted. Within a few brief hours it lay in shrinking patches here and there on the trail. They reached the rim of Drakveden Fjord at a little past ten and paused, still mounted, to admire the view. It was a sheer drop-off, walls of rough black rock going down and down through layers of mist. Far below, faintly, Brit could see a thick ribbon of water, gleaming. Across the yawning misty space, a waterfall tumbled from the facing cliffs, white and foaming, roaring as it fell.

Brit checked her compass. They'd been traveling parallel with the fjord for several miles, but this was the first time the trail had met up with it. She spoke to Eric, raising her voice to compete with the roar of the falls. "Where do we go down?"

"We follow the rim for another two kilometers. Then the trail begins a slow descent."

"We're close."

He nodded, turning his horse to the trail once more.

Soon they reached the place where the trail began going down. They followed the twists and turns, ducking hanging tree branches, until they reached a spot about midway along. For another hour they moved due west, climbing awhile, then moving down, then up again, most of the time with the waters of the fjord in sight below them.

Finally, when they'd been climbing for some time, Eric turned his horse from the trail, away from the water. They wove their way through the trees for several yards and came to a small clearing.

He dismounted, taking his rifle from the saddle holster and binoculars from his saddlebag. "Hobble your horse. We go down now, to the crash site. The trail is narrow from here on, little more than a rocky ledge. It's safer—and quieter—to go on foot."

She thought of the roving bands of renegades, of the bears and Gullandrian mountain cats that she knew roamed the hills. "You think it's safe to leave the horses here alone?"

"Safer than to try to ride them any closer to the

crash site. We'll be quieter on foot." He must have read her look. "Yes, they could be gone—stolen, or attacked by predators—when we return, if that's what you're wondering."

She swallowed. "Yeah, that was what I was wondering."

"We have to take that chance—unless, that is, you'd prefer to turn around?"

"Nice try." She dismounted. "Let's go."

They went back the way they'd come, rejoining the trail at about the same spot they'd left it and forging on to the west. In half a mile or so, they came out onto a point with a clear view of the gorge floor and the fjord below.

"Stay low." Eric dropped to a crouch and signaled her to follow. They crept to the edge, where two waist-high boulders blocked the view as they ducked behind them.

"What now?"

"First, look between the space in the rocks. Down there. Do you see?"

She saw the narrow spit of land where she'd brought down the Skyhawk, saw the crumpled fuselage not far from the trees at the end of the rocky ground. "My plane," she said, "or what's left of it." A moment of silence elapsed and then she asked, "What else?"

"We wait," he said.

"For...?"

He set his rifle carefully aside and indicated the binoculars he'd taken from his saddlebag. Then he pointed to a wide gray-bellied white cloud drifting near the sun. "That cloud will soon cover the sun and minimize the chance that sunlight will reflect off the lenses and give our position away to anyone below.''

''Waiting. Great. Not my favorite activity.''

He grunted. ''I have noticed.''

Time crawled by. About five endless minutes later, the sun slipped behind the outer edge of the cloud. Eric brought up the binoculars and peered with them through a gap in the rocks. He scanned the terrain below. ''There,'' he whispered, more to himself than to her. ''And there…'' He gave her the binoculars. ''Look for yourself. There are three of them visible from this vantage point.'' He guided the binoculars to her face. ''First look straight across, to the opposite slope, then down a little…''

She picked out an armed man, in the trees on the hillside opposite, but below the point where they crouched. ''I see him.''

''Lower now. Track west—to your left.''

She found him. ''Okay. That's two.''

And the third…he's difficult to make out, near the base of this trail, after it flattens out, still in the trees, a short distance before they give way to bare ground.'' He took hold of the binoculars again, just enough to lower them to the right place. ''There? You see him?''

She focused. Found the man. He was dressed like the others, in camo fatigues, dark boots and a plain black watch cap, a rifle in his hands. His broad back was to her—at first. But then, for a moment, he turned his head. She got a look at his face, a three-quarter view. It was a fleshy, roundish face, with a blunt jaw, a small mouth and close-set eyes…

She lowered the binoculars. ''I know him. I mean, I've seen him before.''

"Where?"

"That first day I went to the Bureau offices. He was coming out of Jorund's office as I was going in."

"So...a subordinate of your supposed friend?"

"It's as good a guess as any—and I don't like the way you say *supposed*."

"But you are willing now to admit those men are NIB?"

"Since I know one of them and I saw him at the Bureau offices—sure. It's not a big leap. But you know what? It's pure paranoia to think that means they're automatically traitors."

"They've been guarding this area for days now. And there is a fourth man, somewhere nearby, probably on the hillside below us, not visible from here. And not only those four—there are two more, at the boat they used to get here. They rotate in guarding the plane. We can't be certain when they'll change shifts—or if, right now, there are five of them nearby, or even all six."

"How do you know all this?"

His response to that was another of those oh-so-patient looks. He said, "The plane is unsalvageable. Your father believes you had an accident, that's all. Word has been sent that you survived the crash and a renegade's attack and are safe at my family's village. Those men have had plenty of time to look things over and remove any equipment His Majesty might have wanted saved. They should have been gone days ago. Yet they remain. Why else would they stay except in hopes that you might return—as you are doing—and give them another chance to finish what they started?"

"Eric, you don't know what my father thinks. You

have minimal communication with him. You send him radio messages, right, telling him your version of what's up? And he replies in kind.''

"That is correct."

"Maybe he suspects what you and I suspect. That somebody helped my plane to go down. Maybe he has those men guarding it so that, if any of the real assassins show up to look over their handiwork, those men can deal with them.''

"Your reasoning is faulty."

"Gee, thanks. Why?"

"You know His Majesty. If he believed you'd survived an assassination attempt, he'd have ordered you back to Isenhalla. He'd want you near him, where he could make certain you were safe. And he'd want to interview you in depth to learn everything you know in order to find and punish the ones who dared to do such a thing.''

His argument made sense. Too much sense. "I'm still not going to just *assume* that those men are traitors. I'm not going to—''

Eric cut her off by muttering grimly, "Enough. You've seen them. We can't risk hailing them and we can't be sure how many more of them are out there than the three we can find. We will return now to my aunt's village."

"The hell we will."

He was glaring again. "What more can we do?"

"We've got to find out if they're really my father's men—or not."

"There is no way to find out for certain without the chance of—''

She cut *him* off that time. "I have a plan."

His lip curled in distaste. "I don't like it."

"You haven't even heard it yet."

"I know by the look in your eye that I'm not going to like it."

"Just listen. Just let me explain."

"Do I have a choice?"

"Not about this. Oh, Eric. We have all these suspicions—suspicions that mean nothing without some kind of proof."

"I see it in your eyes. To get your proof could mean your death."

"Not if we're careful—and we might just find out those guys down there are on our side, after all."

"No. It's too dangerous." He dropped the binoculars and took her by the arms. "Listen. Let me take you back. I'll gather some men. We'll return here. We'll capture the agents below and question them. We'll discover—"

"Zilch." She pulled free. "They'll just tell you that they're NIB sent to guard the plane."

His square jaw was set. "If they're traitors, we'll find out."

"By torture? No, thanks. My way's a lot more direct and my way no one has to get hurt."

"I don't like it," he said for the third time.

"You haven't even heard me out yet. Please. Just listen for a minute." He looked at her as if he wanted to strangle her—but he kept his mouth shut. It was her chance. She took it. "We'll go down there now—carefully, making sure the guys on the opposite slope don't spot us, watching for any others as we go. We'll circle the one I recognize—yes, we'll have to be careful, not give him any chance to signal the others. You go behind him, get up close. I'll step out and say hello.''

He blinked. ''Hello. You'll say…hello.''

''That's right. If he was sent here to kill me, he'll probably try it. Then we'll both get a chance to stop him.'' She said the rest, though she hated to have to say it. ''And we'll know if my friend at the NIB wasn't really any kind of friend at all.''

He stared at her as if she'd suddenly sprouted horns and a tail. ''This is madness.''

''Not madness. Dangerous, possibly. But we're going to make it work. And no one is going to get hurt.''

He made a growling sound. ''You delude yourself. You could be killed. If the three Norns of destiny smile on us, you might survive. But in any case, if that fellow down there points his rifle at you, he will die. I will see to it.''

''No. Now, that isn't the plan.''

''He will die.''

''Eric. You're not listening.''

''Because you are talking dangerous nonsense.''

She decided to let that insulting remark pass and stick to the point. ''I don't want anyone to get hurt. I mean it. There's been enough bloodshed around here lately, thank you very much. If he points his gun at me, you can jump him. We'll shoot to wound if we have to—but the idea is to get through this without a shot being fired. Shots will only bring the others down on us.''

''It's madness.''

''You keep saying that.''

''I won't be a part of it.''

''Oh, no? Then what.''

"I am going back to the village. Now. You are coming with me."

"No. I'm not. Go back by yourself if you think you have to, but—"

He put up a hand. There was silence. Somewhere in the trees behind them, a bird warbled out a brief, bright song. At last he spoke. "What, by all the frozen towers of Hel, is a man to do with you?"

"Eric."

He didn't really answer, just made a low, furious sound and muttered what must have been a truly bad Gullandrian oath, though he spoke too low for her to make out the words.

"It's the only way," she said.

"It's not—and I have it. You'll stay here. I'll go down and—"

"No. It has to be me he sees. He might or might not attack you for any number of reasons. But if he tries to shoot me, well, the only reason he'd do that is because he—and most likely Jorund Sorenson—is part of the plot to get rid of me."

Something happened in his eyes.

"Don't," she said.

He was utterly still.

"I mean it, Eric. If you try to…stop me now, if you do something to physically restrain me from going down there, you will only be putting off the inevitable. I'm going to go. And if you mess with me now, I'll just end up doing it alone as soon as I can escape you."

The look on his face at that moment was frightening. And then, in a movement so tiny she barely saw it even though she was looking straight at him, he shook his head. Or maybe not shook it, exactly. Just gave it a sharp, minute jerk to the left. It might have been a twitch—except that Eric Greyfell was not a man prone to twitching.

She didn't dare turn from him, didn't trust him not to try to knock her out, or jump her for her own good. But she was absolutely certain that there was someone behind her, and that Eric had just signaled that someone—in the negative.

Like a bright light exploding on in darkness, she got it. "Valbrand?" she asked Eric quietly. He only went on looking at her, barely controlled fury in his eyes. So she spoke, still not turning, to the presence behind her. "Valbrand. It's you, isn't it?"

Chapter Fourteen

No one answered—until Eric said, "You're mistaken. There's no one there."

It was true, of course. There was no longer anyone behind her. She had a clear sense that whoever it was had melted back into the trees. She turned and saw exactly what she expected to see: nothing but bare ground and, a little farther on, tall, thick evergreens. She turned to Eric again. "So then," she said cheerfully, "we do have backup—the, uh, Dark Raider would be my guess."

"I said there is no one." He was really, really mad.

She strove to keep it light. "Well, yes. You did. But just because you said it doesn't make it true."

He hooked the binoculars to his belt beneath his jacket and reached for his rifle. "If you're determined to do this, let's go." He remained utterly furious. It occurred to her that she'd never seen him so enraged. And all at once, she had the hollow, awful feeling that he would never forgive her for forcing him to do this.

Heartsickness, all the more powerful for being totally unanticipated, washed over her in a heavy, dragging wave. Without thinking, she grabbed his arm. "Do you have to be so angry?"

He froze. His hand was on the rifle. She clutched his coat and the hard forearm beneath it. He looked down at her grasping fingers as if they repulsed him. Then he said, very quietly, "As much as I crave your touch, now is not the time."

She knew he was right. She shouldn't have touched him. She let go. He looked in her face then, his eyes green ice. She stared into those eyes and discovered something about herself she would have preferred not to know.

She wanted—*yearned*—to give in to him. To let him lead her away from the precipice, back to the safety of his aunt's friendly village. To say what women have said since the beginning of time: *Yes, all right. You're bigger and stronger and you want to take care of me. We'll do it your way....*

She yearned to.

But she couldn't. It wasn't in her to follow—not when she was certain that she was in the right. Yes, it was dangerous. But not to take the chance would leave them with their suspicions and their theories and not much else. This way, they might inch a fraction closer to discovering who their real enemies were.

"Can't you see, Eric? We have to do this."

He gave her no answer. His face remained closed against her. He would only say, again, "Let's go."

* * *

Eric on point, Brit right behind him, they made their way down slowly, watching where they put their feet, catching branches before they ran into them, pushing them aside, releasing them gently, exercising constant vigilance to make as little sound as possible. Careless footfalls could dislodge rocks and pebbles that would tumble to the gorge below, gathering momentum, collecting other bits of debris as they went and signaling their presence to the men with the guns.

The trail was narrow—hardly more than a sliver of ledge in places—cut raggedly into the rocky side of the hill. Luckily for them, rather than the bare black rock that rimmed so much of the fjord, here, the trees grew close all around, providing cover from seeking eyes.

The farther they got without incident, the more certain Brit became that something very bad was going to happen any second now. Her whole body felt prickly, the skin tight and twitchy at the back of her neck. She was wet beneath the arms—and it wasn't all that warm out. No, this was the sweat of pure animal fear. She knew it was coming—from behind or above: someone would jump on her or shoot her or throw a knife, *thwack,* right between her shoulderblades.

Still they kept moving. Nobody attacked them.

She tried not to obsess on that other guy, the fourth guard they'd never spotted, the one Eric had said had to be around there somewhere. Really, where else would be as logical as lurking close to the trail?

But the miracle happened: nothing. They kept moving downward. They were almost to the bottom, perhaps fifty yards from where the ground flattened out. Very soon now they'd be closing in on that cohort of Jorund's—that is, if he was anywhere near where he'd been when they pinpointed his location from above.

She heard rustling—ten or twelve yards up and behind her. She stopped, stood absolutely still. So did Eric. They waited—straining to see. But the trees were too thick.

And then—in a few seconds that only seemed like a lifetime—the rustling stopped.

They waited some more. Brit wondered if the Dark Raider had just taken on that mysterious fourth guard—or if it was only some unwary creature, scrabbling along the hillside.

They went on, stopping dead again when Brit stepped on a rock wrong and it went sliding off down the hill. But fortune smiled on them. The rock caught in an exposed tree root before it really got rolling.

Silence. They went on.

At last they reached the floor of the gorge. There were maybe twenty yards of forest ahead of them. And then the open rocky ground, her plane and, farther on, the jewel-blue fjord waters.

Now, to find Jorund's associate before the associate found them. Eric gestured for her to follow. They left the trail and moved into the trees, creeping along, every slight crunch at each footfall sounding loud as cannon fire.

Eric stopped, ducked, signaled her down. She crouched beside him. He pointed.

She picked out the combat boots and the fatigues tucked into them—maybe twenty feet from them, facing away. Way close. Way scary. Her heart pounded in her ears. The boots began to move, turning with agonizing slowness, as if the man who wore them had heard something and was cautiously seeking the source of the sound.

Brit held her breath—realized she was doing it—let it out with slow care. The boots had stopped, blunt toes facing their direction, as if the agent knew they were lurking there.

Thank God for Eric ordering her down—crouched as they were, the man must be looking right over their heads. The boots began to move again. In a few seconds she and Eric stared once more at the heels.

Eric touched her, the slightest brush of his hand against her good shoulder, to get her attention. She looked at him and he gestured, a circular movement, tracing in the air the path he would take through the trees to get around to the other side of the owner of the heavy boots.

It seemed such a long, long way to go soundlessly. The crack of a broken branch or a foot placed wrong, and the man who wore the boots might spot him, open fire....

Eric could die doing this.

The simple sentence ricocheted its way around her brain.

She had known it before, of course she had. As she had known that she herself might die.

But right now, it was...too real, too imminent. It was the sweat beneath her arms, the shiver down her back, the too-loud, too-fast, hurtful beating of her heart....

Eric could die.

And how would she bear it?

He looked at her. And she looked back at him.

She knew that he knew how close she was…to shaking her head. To mouthing, *No. Let's not do this, after all. Let's just go back.*

But somehow she didn't shake her head. She didn't mouth anything. She only looked into his eyes until the moment passed.

And then, very deliberately, she nodded.

He began to creep away from her. It was incredible, how quietly he could move. He wove his way through the trees, his steps without sound. She alternately watched him…and the boots. The boots did move, this way and that. The movements of a man on guard with no perceived danger nearby.

Too soon, she couldn't see Eric anymore.

She crouched there, watching the boots, her pulse a tattoo in her ears, reminding herself now and then to breathe, slowly realizing she had no clue when she ought to make her move.

Was Eric in position yet—was there even a position for him to *get* into? A tree big enough to hide behind, a crouch low enough that the man in the heavy boots wouldn't look down and see him?

Silently she railed at herself. It was a bad plan. An exceedingly stupid plan. It was so bad and so stupid it was no plan at all. Eric would die and she would either die right after him—or wish she had.

Oh, why hadn't she listened to him? Why had she insisted her way was the only way?

She swallowed. And then, carefully, silently, she reached under her jacket and wrapped her fingers around the grip of her SIG.

No. She let it go, smoothed her jacket down to cover

it. Its weight might feel reassuring in her hand, but she couldn't be carrying it in plain sight when she hailed the agent. He mustn't feel threatened. And if he saw the gun, how else would he feel? He might shoot her just because he thought she was planning to shoot him.

And then what would they learn from executing this bad, stupid plan of hers?

She strained all her senses, listening.

Nothing but a slight wind whispering in the trees, a bird calling far off. The boots faced the other way— not moving.

Were those boots…too still?

She thought, *He's seen something, in the trees. Let it not be Eric.*

And surely Eric must be in position—whatever that meant—by now.

And the boots…the boots were starting to move, cautiously, away.

It was the moment to act. She knew it. She didn't know exactly *how* she knew. But this was no time to question her instincts.

Right now her instincts were just about all she had.

As quietly as she could, she crept forward, bent at the waist, but up on her feet. Each step took an eternity, yet somehow, between one breath and the next, she was there. Close enough that three more steps would bring her to where she could reach out and touch the man with the rifle, in the combat boots and the camo fatigues. He had his back to her, his rifle ready in his hands. He had heard something. He peered into the trees.

Time to do it.

She stood to her height and boldly stepped forward. "Ahem."

The agent went still—and then he turned. He saw her, standing no more than six feet from him. The close-set eyes widened. The small mouth formed an O. Under less scary circumstances, his expression might have brought a chuckle.

Now, though, she didn't feel like laughing at all. She had to force a wide grin. "Hey. Am I ever glad to see you."

The agent blinked. "Your Highness?"

"You bet."

The agent raised his rifle.

So much for my *ally* at the NIB, she thought. And then everything happened at once, in that strangely slow way that things tend to happen when you have to act and act fast—or die.

She ducked—well, that was the bad, stupid plan, wasn't it? And Eric rose soundlessly from behind the agent, seeming to materialize out of thin air with the butt of his rifle held high in both strong hands. He slammed the rifle butt into the back of the agent's head before the agent could readjust his aim and fire down at her.

There was the awful thick sound of the something hard connecting with the agent's skull. And the man dropped like a safe, without managing to get off a shot. His rifle fell with him, unfired, to the forest floor.

Slowly she straightened and stared down at the slack face below her. There—his chest moved. Yes! Still alive. Her bad, stupid plan had worked perfectly. They knew what they needed to know and everyone was still breathing.

She didn't get all that much time to pat herself on the back, though. It appeared that things weren't so perfect, after all. Eric had dropped to a crouch, set his rifle aside and whipped something thin and black from his boot. *Snick.* A gleaming blade shot from the black handle.

Sheesh. Hauk had a knife like that. She hadn't had a clue that Eric had one, too.

Brit stared down, not quite believing what she was seeing as Eric hooked the unconscious man beneath the chin, yanking his head farther back, knocking his watch cap off in the process—and exposing a too-vulnerable expanse of bare neck.

"No!" Brit whispered the word with such force it echoed in her ears like a shout. She went to her haunches and grabbed Eric's knife arm before he could slit the unconscious agent's throat. "Nobody dies."

Eric's eyes glittered with a feral light. "That's the second time you've grabbed me when you had no business doing it."

She didn't let go this time. She couldn't. "Eric. I beg you. Don't kill him."

His lip curled, wolflike. "*He* would have killed *you.*"

"But he didn't. Eric. *Please.*"

For a terrible moment she was certain there was no way she could stop him. He would shake her off and slit the unconscious man's throat.

But then, with a low grunt of pure disgust, he flicked the blade back into the knife handle and let go of the man's chin. There was blood, on his pants, at the knee, where the agent's head had pressed against him. She wondered if the fellow would survive in any case.

The knife disappeared in Eric's boot. He grabbed his waiting rifle, then took the agent's pistol from its shoulder holster, dropped out the clip and threw it into the trees. He tossed the pistol in the opposite direction. Then he picked up the man's rifle and shoved it at Brit. She took it.

"We dare not linger," he muttered. His fury was palpable, like the beating of hot wings on the chill air. "The others will be on us." He turned without another word and headed for the trail.

She put the safety on the rifle and followed.

The unconscious man groaned. He was waking at last from his abrupt, unwelcome sleep.

Valbrand, safe behind the mask, crouched a few feet from the man's boots. He had two lengths of cord and a gag at his side and the traitor's own pistol, loaded again and pointed at the traitor's heart, in his hand. It had been approximately fifteen minutes since his bold and cheeky little sister and his angry bloodbound friend had strode off toward the trail. By now they should be almost at their waiting horses. And safe.

Yes, there was another agent, up higher on the trail. But he would present no challenge to them. Valbrand had considered killing him, but in the end had left him alive, unarmed, gagged and tied to a tree, for his colleagues to find—if something with sharp teeth and claws didn't get to him first. If he lived, that traitor would have an interesting story to tell.

Behind the mask Valbrand smiled. He knew his smile, once thought the most charming in all of the land, was hideous now. He could feel the ugliness of it, ruined flesh pulling in the most bizarre ways. That was the wonder of the mask. The ugliness hidden behind smooth black leather.

Would the bound agent on the hillside dare to tell his comrades that the Dark Raider had attacked him? Would they think he'd gone mad if he did?

Valbrand had an intimate knowledge of madness. For a long while, until Eric had found him and begun the endless, unhappy process of luring him back to the bleak world of sanity, he'd found a certain wild comfort in madness.

But then, being mad was not the same as merely having others believe you to be. More frustrating, most likely. Less…consuming.

And, since Valbrand had decided to let the man before him live as well, this one and the agent on the hill could corroborate each other's stories. That made them at least a fraction more likely to be believed. Less likely to be thought out of their mutual minds.

And that was good.

Let them all believe and let them fear and wonder….

Let whoever lurked—a puppet master pulling lethal strings—behind these recent deadly games, beware.

The time *was* coming. Valbrand knew it and hated that he knew it. And yes, Eric had it right: Valbrand dreaded facing his father and his people. It *would* be a thousand times more difficult than the bleak horror of what had gone before.

But he would do it. Somehow. When the time was right.

For now, though, there was the consoling feel of the

mask against his ruined face. And this traitor, groaning at his feet.

The traitor opened his eyes. They widened. Good.

Valbrand rose to his height, pistol trained on the stunned face below him. "Your name, traitor."

The man groaned.

Valbrand cocked the pistol. It wasn't necessary to cock it, not with a gun like this one. But cocking it did make such a satisfying sound. "Your name."

The man lifted his head. "Agent…Hans Borger."

"And whom do you serve, Hans Borger?"

Borger groaned again and let his head drop. "My king."

"You lie. I should kill you now." Valbrand gestured with the gun. "Over. To your belly, dog, where you belong."

With another groan, the agent started to roll, sliding one hand down as he did it. Valbrand chuckled and held up the contact device in his left hand. "Looking for this?" The dog's eyes widened—then narrowed in defeat. Valbrand dropped the device to the ground and crushed it under his boot. "Now roll."

Hans Borger obeyed. Swiftly, aware of the danger of temporarily setting the weapon aside, Valbrand took the waiting lengths of cord and bound the agent hand and foot. He tied the gag last, tightly.

Then he picked up the gun and rose again to his feet. "When they find you, tell them that Princess Brit and Prince Eric Greyfell disarmed you with ease. They spared your worthless life, as do I, the Dark Raider. This game that you and your cohorts may have thought almost over has only now begun. It will end in shameful defeat and slow, painful death for all who dared to dream they could bring down the House of Thor.''

The dog on the ground grunted behind his gag and struggled fitfully against the cords that bound him. There was blood matting his close-cut pale hair.

Valbrand holstered his weapon. ''Would that I had more time. We could speak…in depth. I would show you the many ways I know to make a sharp knife sing. But I fear the dogs you run with will come looking for you soon. So I shall leave you now, to the mercy of the traitors who own you. May they punish you cruelly for your failure, after they laugh in your face when you tell them that the princess you were sent to kill outsmarted you and that you let Eric Greyfell come up behind you without your knowing, armed only with the wrong end of a rifle.'' He paused, considered, then advised, ''Perhaps you shouldn't even mention your conversation with me. So many believe I am only a myth, a story told to children, by firelight, on long winter nights. So if you were to tell them that you spoke with me…hmm. Were I your superior, I might begin to think you mad.''

Agent Borger had little constructive to contribute in reply. A gag will do that. He grunted and struggled, a pitiful sight.

Valbrand had said all that needed saying. Grinning behind the mask, he turned and vanished into the trees.

Chapter Fifteen

Eric, grim-faced and speaking to Brit only when absolutely necessary, kept them on the move for the remainder of the day. They crossed paths with no dangerous animals—on two legs or four. And they made good time.

Still, the long fingers of twilight had slipped down the slopes of the hills when they rode their tired horses out of the trees and onto the hard-packed dirt street of Asta's village. Light glowed, warm and welcoming, from the high-set narrow windows of the longhouses, and Sigrid's oldest boy, Brokk, named after his father, came running out to meet them.

"Grandmother Asta asked me to wait for you." The redheaded, freckle-faced boy, all of eleven, smiled in pride at being granted such a great responsibility. The boy said Asta was tending one of the village women.

"She makes a new baby tonight." The boy beamed. "I've left the fire well tended. And I'm good with the horses. Will you allow me to see to your mounts?"

For the first time since their argument at the lookout point above the wreckage of the plane, Eric smiled. "We would be pleased and grateful to leave our horses in your capable hands."

They dismounted and the boy took both sets of reins.

Eric turned to her, his smile a memory. He spoke curtly. "Take the traitor's rifle and whatever you need from the saddlebags."

She did as he told her, feeling exhausted and heartsick—and aching for the sight of Asta's kind, wrinkled face. It looked like a long, grim night ahead, with Asta gone to another longhouse and Brit alone with Mr. Cheerful.

Brokk said, "There's shepherd's pie waiting in the warming oven. I will see to the horses, then tell Grandmother that you've returned safely. She'll be glad of the news." The boy headed for the horse barn behind Asta's longhouse, leaving the two of them standing in the street.

After a moment, not even sparing her a glance, Eric turned for the house. Reluctantly Brit trailed after, feeling like a very bad child and resenting it—a lot.

Inside, Brit went straight to her sleeping bench and dropped her things on her bed furs. She still had the rifle.

"Give it here," Eric grumbled.

She handed it over, and he put it, along with his own rifle and the shotgun, in the rack above the door.

She took off her coat, hung it on a peg and then went to put her things away.

They shared a truly toxic silence as they washed their hands and faces and got out the pie, set a simple table and sat down to eat. She stolidly chewed and swallowed and avoided Eric's eyes—which wasn't difficult. He didn't show any eagerness to look at her, either.

It was really bad. She wished she could do something, say something, to try to get him to...

What?

Forgive her for being right about her admittedly wild plan that had given them the first piece of solid information as to who might be behind the plot to kill her?

And maybe, while he was forgiving her, he could stop being mad at her because she stepped in before he could slit a man's throat?

The problem was, the longer he scowled and growled, the more she started thinking that she was getting pretty mad herself. Okay, she was an action junkie. She didn't like to sit around, considering all the angles, when something could be *done*.

Her plan had been far from well thought out. But damn it, it had worked, hadn't it?

She sent him an angry glance. He glared back at her.

They ate the rest of the food, cleared off and washed the heavy plates. By then she was certain that if she stayed cooped up with him much longer, there would be yelling and throwing of plates.

''I'm going over to bathhouse,'' she announced into

the awful, furious silence. "I'll be back in an hour or so."

"I'll go with you."

"No. I'll go alone. I don't need you to—"

"I'd like a bath myself." He said it flatly. The look in his eyes said he'd also like to grab her and shake her till she pleaded for mercy and never again dared to have a plan of her own.

"Fine. Whatever. It's a free country—more or less."

They gathered what they needed and went out into the night.

In the bathhouse, Brit took off her clothes and her bandage and indulged in a shamefully long, hot shower. Her wound was healed enough by then that she could handle bandaging it herself. And she did, with gauze and tape, before she put on clean clothes, her lightest long underwear first. The underwear was made of silk, but it was still your basic long johns design, a long-sleeved T-shirt and super-lightweight knit bottoms. Over the long johns, she pulled on a sweater and jeans. Bedtime was coming, so she dispensed with a bra.

She emerged into the night again, hoping she had taken long enough that Eric would have already gone back. The short walk to the longhouse would have been much more pleasant without him scowling at her side.

But no. There he was, waiting, his face a bleak mask. He saw her and he turned without a word and headed up the street.

Oh, boy, wasn't this fun? She hung back, walking

slowly, hoping he would charge on ahead and leave her, for a few precious moments anyway, alone.

He didn't. When he realized she wasn't hustling to catch up with him, he stopped and glared back at her. ''Are you coming?'' In spite of the question mark at the end, it was an impatient command.

She pressed her lips together—hard—to keep something loud and shrill from getting out. And then she picked up her pace.

Back in the longhouse, it was more of the same. Silence and total avoidance of anything resembling eye contact.

The night might be young, but it showed no likelihood of turning the least bit enjoyable. And the day had been long. And tomorrow, she was going to have to figure out how she'd get out of the Vildelund and back to Isenhalla. Maybe Eric would contact her father and have him send some small aircraft to pick her up.

Or maybe she'd have to head for the Black Mountains. The high, snow-capped range about twenty miles due south of the village stood between the Vildelund and the more civilized world on the other side.

Whatever. One way or another, she was out of here tomorrow. Jorund had to be dealt with. And she wanted to have a long heart-to-heart with her father. It was about time somebody told the king what the hell was going on.

She brushed her teeth and went to her sleeping bench, took off the top layer of clothes and climbed beneath the furs wearing her socks and her long johns. With so much hostility thickening the air, it took a while to get to sleep.

But she was tired. Her bed might be hard, but she'd grown used to it by then. And the furs felt so soft and comforting around her....

Eric waited until he was certain she slept. Then he pulled on his coat and grabbed his boots and slipped out the door, pausing at the stoop to put the boots on.

In the trees behind the horse paddock, Valbrand waited, a darker shadow among shadows. His rare black Gullandrian gelding was hobbled a few feet away, nosing and nibbling the cold ground.

"The traitor?" Eric asked.

"He lives. I left him bound and gagged and awaiting the tender mercies of the others."

"The one higher on the hillside?"

"I did the same for him."

"Did you get anything from either of them?"

"There was no opportunity to ask questions of the one up on the hill. I took his rifle and his pistol."

"And the other?"

"His name. Agent Hans Borger. I regret there was no time to learn more."

"At least we know now that our suspicions concerning the infiltration of the NIB have merit."

"Thanks to the clever actions of my irrepressible little sister."

Eric heard the rare smile in Valbrand's voice and didn't like it—not now, not on this subject. "Can't you see that the woman rushes headlong toward her own death at every opportunity? She is suicidal in her heedlessness."

"She looked quite healthy to me when you led her away."

"Yes, she came away unharmed. This time." Eric

stuck his fists in the pockets of his coat. "She leaves tomorrow for the south."

"Your choice—or hers?"

"She has said she will go. It is probably, at this point, the only issue on which we agree."

"What of your marriage?"

"What of it? She refuses me at every turn."

"Perhaps you give her reason to refuse you?"

An angry rejoinder rose in his throat. He swallowed it. "I only want to keep her safe."

"Even I can see she's not a woman who seeks safety. Perhaps if you wish finally to claim her, you will have to take her as she is."

Eric glared straight-on into the dark eyes behind the mask. "Do you lecture me now, my friend?"

"I but offer…an objective view."

An objective view. Now, there was an irony. Valbrand was supposed to be the leader. Providing an objective view had always been Eric's responsibility. He grumbled, "I am in no mood to take what you offer with any grace."

"As you wish." The black horse tossed his fine head and snorted. Valbrand spoke to the animal softly, "Easy, Starkavin. All is well." Then he turned to Eric again. "By what route will she return to the palace?"

"We've yet to speak of that."

"Whichever way she goes, there will be danger."

"Must you remind me?"

"When danger is inevitable—why not make use of it?"

An owl hooted, somewhere in the dark. Overhead, beyond the trees, the quarter moon dangled from a star. The night was cloudless and very still.

Eric asked, "What are you getting at?"

Valbrand moved closer and pitched his voice to a whisper. "Why not guide our enemies to waylay us on our terms?"

Brit was sitting at the table in her long johns and heavy socks, one of Asta's knitted shawls thrown across her shoulders, when Eric came sneaking through the door, his boots in his hands.

She had a pretty good idea where he'd been: out to meet Valbrand. But she wasn't going to challenge him about it. She was a little sick of challenges at the moment, thank you.

He said, "What are doing out of bed?" The question was pure challenge. Of course.

What business is it of yours? she thought. She stared at the lamp she'd lighted. It sat on the table before her, giving off a warm golden glow that didn't comfort her in the least. "I woke up. I was alone. For the first time since late this morning, there was no one here to glare or bark at me." She looked at Eric. "I found it kind of…pleasant. I decided to get up and enjoy the peace and quiet." Sadly, she hadn't enjoyed the absence of hostility as much as she'd hoped to. She'd started thinking about Jorund and what a complete idiot she'd been on that score. Yeah—duh. Sure, an NIB special agent had just been longing to be her *friend*….

Eric shrugged. He turned to hang his jacket on a peg and set his boots beside the door. When he faced her again, it was only to say, "I bid you good-night, then."

It came to her on a wave of frustrated misery that this was impossible. It really had to stop. "Eric…"

He paused a few feet from her—on his way to his sleeping bench. "What is it now?"

Her irritation spiked again. Oh, why even bother to try to get through to him?

Because I care for him—a whole lot—and I can't stand to leave it like this.

She gathered the warm shawl a little closer around her, seeking a comfort she didn't find. "Look. Can we just get past this? I'm leaving tomorrow. We've been…friends, haven't we? Friends shouldn't part in anger."

His gray-green gaze swept over her, burning where it touched. "We are much more than friends. And you know it. Why will you constantly insist on belittling the bond between us?"

She wanted to shout at him—and she held it back; to reach out to him—but he wouldn't like it.

Stifled at every turn, she couldn't sit still. She stood from the end of the bench. He backed up a step, as if he thought she might dare to put her hands on him.

And really, the voice of fairness whispered in her ear, why wouldn't he think it? She'd grabbed him twice today, both times when the last thing he wanted was her touching him.

She bit her lip and went to the stove. Behind the window in the stove door, she could see the red flames licking. She stared into them, gathering calm about her like the shawl around her shoulders, thinking that this was for sure a first: Brit Thorson, striving for calm and reason.

Wouldn't Liv and Elli have a great big fat laugh? And her mother? Ingrid would never believe it.

She turned to him again and spoke slowly, choosing

each word with care. "I don't belittle what's between us. I swear I don't. I do think of you as a friend and I think it's important—to be friends with a man who…I care for so much."

His face remained set against her, but his gaze ran over her, furious—and hungry. She knew he wanted to shout rude things at her. And that he also wanted to do things—sexual things—the kind of things a man like Eric would never do to someone who was only a *friend*.

And she? All right, yes. She wanted him to do those things. With all of her yearning body.

And every beat of her aching heart.

But first there was what had to be said. She pleaded, "Look. Just say it, will you? Whatever you want to say to me, just do it, just get it out."

"You are serious?"

"As a bullet through the heart."

"You won't like it."

"I don't expect to like it. I just think it's what you have to say…and what I've got to stand here and take."

It must have made sense to him. He laid it on her, his voice low and deep, his tone as intense as the hunger in his eyes. "I fear for you—fear you see this trouble before us as some kind of tempting, risky game. I begin to think that there is but one thing that you do with slow care, and that is eat those bright candies you love. I close my eyes—and I see you dead, your pretty neck slit for some chance you just had to take. You are…never cautious. You fling yourself, all unwary, at the next test, the next confrontation with deadly forces. I cannot be forever looking out for you—and yet I'm terrified to leave you alone. By Thor's mighty hammer, who can say what trouble you'll get into next? I find I don't want to know, don't want to be there when the price of your heedlessness is finally your life.''

He fell silent. The room seemed to echo with his words. *Calm,* she reminded herself. *Calm and reason. And honesty.*

''Eric. I'm so sorry I scared you. At this moment I can almost regret that I am who I am, that the time will come when I'll scare you again. But, Eric, what I did today that you hated so much—it worked. And it needed to be done. And I'd do it again, in the same circumstances.''

With a low oath, he turned from her. She thought for a minute he would keep going, that he'd grab his boots and his coat and stalk back out the door.

But he didn't. He stopped in midstride—and whirled on her again. ''You don't realize, you refuse to understand the magnitude of what lies before us. The danger has only begun. That traitor you forced me to spare today could be the one who kills you in the end.''

''Yes,'' she said softly, ''he could.''

''Then why in Odin's name didn't you let me cut his throat?''

''Because we didn't *have* to. Because he was already out cold.'' She ached to touch him. But she wasn't going to make that particular mistake again— not until he *wanted* her touch. She fisted her hands at her sides. ''Eric, you just can't do it—can't protect me from every threat. And it's not what I want from you. It's not...what I need. If we're ever going to really be together, you and me, you're going to have to learn to take me as I am.''

He stared at her, his gaze green fire, hotter, somehow, than the red flames in the stove beside her. And then he blinked.

''What?'' she demanded. ''Say it.''

He waved a hand. ''It's nothing.''

''Don't lie to me, please. Not now. Now I really need you to help me to understand.''

He glanced away.

''Look at me. Please…''

He dragged in a breath. ''It's only… Someone else said something similar to me recently—that you were not a woman who sought safety, that I would have to learn to accept you as you are.''

''Someone else?''

But he only looked at her.

It must have been Valbrand who said it, she thought. The idea pleased her, that while her brother hardly knew her, he understood her so well.

And if Valbrand had been the one, Eric wasn't going to tell her so. She let it go and moved on. ''*You've* taken chances—chances that anyone might call insane. Remember, in the camp of the *kvina soldars?* If what you did—walking right into that camp when you knew they might kill you for it—if that wasn't reckless, I don't know what is.''

''That risk was well calculated. I knew you were there, knew you would claim me and knew the warrior women to be honorable.''

''The risk we took today was calculated, too. And you can't deny that it worked. It gave us information we badly needed. I would do it again in a heartbeat—

and I think you have to get used to the fact that I'm going to keep on doing what I have to do.''

"No," he said, closing the distance between them in two long strides and grabbing her hard by the shoulders.

His fingers dug into her healing wound. She cried out at the sharp stab of pain.

He let go—but only to grab her again, by the arms. The shawl slid to the floor. "I will never get used to it, not if the price could be your life. You almost died today." He spoke low and furiously, his twisted face inches from hers. "That NIB bastard son of a fitz could have killed you." She saw the murder in those burning green eyes.

And the blazing desire.

"Oh, Eric," she whispered. "When will you see? The rules have to be the same for both of us. Or it's no good."

He released her and stepped back. She watched the bright fury drain from his eyes, leaving them suddenly lightless. Dull. "There is no point in this talk. It goes in circles, leading us nowhere. And you leave tomorrow."

"Come with me." The words were out almost before she knew she would say them.

His answer was just what she expected. "It's not possible."

"Why not?"

"You know why not."

She stared at him. It was the closest he'd ever come to admitting that Valbrand lived. "Because of my brother, right? Because he—''

"I cannot speak of it." He put up a hand. "Please. Let it go."

Let it go?

She made a scoffing sound. He should know by now that letting it go was just not her style.

He had to get it through his thick head. Time was running out. They couldn't afford to hang around in the wilds anymore. There were traitors to deal with, a kingdom to save. They needed to go, the three of them, united, to the south. Every day they put off facing their enemies only made their enemies stronger.

It was all there, on the tip of her tongue, what he needed to hear, what she *had* to say.

And then, in a flash of blinding insight, she saw all her righteous arguments for what they really were: cruel taunts, and no more.

Why torment him when she could see the anguish in his now-lightless eyes? Why goad him when at last she understood that she wouldn't be saying anything he didn't already know?

"All right." She spoke softly. "I'll let it go." She crouched to snare the fallen shawl and then stood to her height again, the shawl trailing from her fingers. "I'll just…" She met his eyes again and forgot what she'd been meaning to say.

She was…captured.

By the sight of him, so tall and proud, his ash-brown hair shining in the lamplight, his mouth a bleak line, his jade eyes shadowed and infinitely sad.

She whispered the truth that lay waiting in her heart. "I…oh, God. I will miss you."

A ridiculous flush crept up her cheeks—she could feel it, burning red. Oh, now why had she said that?

Now he would get macho on her again. He'd bark out some surly command: *Then stay* or *Don't go.*

But he only whispered, "As I will miss you."

His stark and gentle words blasted through all her defenses. She heard herself say way too dreamily, "I wish—"

He shook his head before she could get out the rest, the sweetest, most tender of smiles curving the bleak mouth to softness. "Remember, I am but a man. If you tell me your wishes, I will only strive to make them come true."

Astonishing. All their battles, his constant refusal to accept her as she was, and yet at that moment he knew her better than she knew herself. He understood before she did that her wishes and their fulfillment had to be up to her. Well, mostly...

All at once she felt absurdly shy, couldn't even make herself look at him. She stared down at the red knit toes of her socks and didn't know if she dared to raise her eyes again to his. Finally she managed it, though in a shamelessly girly way, glancing up at him from under her lashes. "There is one wish that you could, uh, help me with."

He knew that, too. He understood. She heard it in the quick, indrawn rush of his breath, saw it in the sudden hot light that shone from his eyes. "You're certain?"

She swallowed, nodded. "Even if I can't...be what you want me to be, I've got to have your arms around me. I can't just go away from you tomorrow without..." She let out a small moan. Where were the right words when she really needed them? She dragged the shawl upward, clutched it to her breasts. "Oh, please, Eric. At least for tonight?"

He looked so gorgeously, infinitely regretful. "I am Gullandrian."

No kidding. She gulped. "And that means…?"

"No child of mine will be born a fitz. And I have nothing to protect you from pregnancy. Are you saying that you do?"

Well, as a matter of fact she didn't. She'd come to the Vildelund prepared for action—just not this kind. "Sorry," she muttered, feeling silly and sheepish, "but I don't."

"Then I would want your vow first. Should there be a child from this, you will become my wife."

Her first response was suspicion. Was this a setup? She got pregnant and they got married, as he'd been insisting they were going to do for days now?

No. It didn't add up. If he'd wanted to pull something like that, he would have let nature take its course in Rinda's tent—not to mention in the cave last night, while they waited out the storm. She'd hardly been a shy, blushing flower either time.

Uh-uh. This was no trick. It was only Eric being Eric. Honorable and straightforward…well, at least, about the two of them.

He was offering her the clear chance to back out. If she had any sense at all, she'd take it.

And tomorrow would come and she would go back to the palace. With traitors lurking everywhere, anything could happen. The possibility was achingly real that they would never see each other again—at least, not alive.

Sometimes you just had to go for the old *carpe*

diem—or maybe, in this case, it was the *night* getting seized.

She clutched the shawl all the tighter, a regular Linus response. Next, she'd be sucking her thumb. "Ahem, well. It just occurred to me..." He waited. He wasn't going to help her out at all with this. He was letting it be completely her choice. Big of him. "I mean, well, I guess I have to admit it. Who else would I marry—if I ever do get married—but you?"

He didn't look particularly impressed with her stammered, astonishingly wimpy admission. "No buts," he said. "No ifs. I want your word that, should you become pregnant, you will be my wife."

She had to hand it to him. The guy had no trouble making his position crystal clear.

The least she could do was stand up tall and tell him straight out what she was willing to do. She pulled back her shoulders and dropped her arms to her sides, letting the shawl trail again to the floor. "All right. We're agreed. If I become pregnant, we'll get married."

"You will contact me immediately. We'll be married as soon as I can arrange to come to you."

"Okay. All right. If I get pregnant, we'll get married right away." She still held the shawl by a corner. She let it drop. "So...what do you say?"

He answered without uttering a word, by the simple action of holding out his hand.

Chapter Sixteen

Eric led her to his furs.

They undressed quickly, not quite daring to look at each other, tearing off their clothes and tossing them aside, as if they both feared any hesitation might mean the other would think twice about the wisdom of their actions.

But somehow they made it out of their clothes and, in a scurrying flash of bare flesh and goose bumps, beneath the soft furs.

The bed was narrow, only a smidgen wider than a single. Brit, on the inside, scooted over as close as she could to the rough-hewn wall. She stared at the whirling patterns in the wood and shivered, wondering—though she'd all but begged for this—if it was, after all, a bad idea.

Things weren't really right between them.

And Asta could walk in on them at any time....

Then Eric whispered, so tenderly, "Your sweet body speaks of second thoughts."

She gulped. "Well, yeah." She realized she'd just said that to the wall. She turned her head and there he was—just inches away, smelling of soap and manliness. Looking good enough to eat. She cleared her throat and hated the sound. She'd been doing it so much lately. "Uh, well, we were fighting each other, all day. And we don't know what will happen tomorrow. And now we're here and I..." She didn't know how to finish.

He didn't seem to mind, didn't seem to need her to finish. He canted up on an elbow and gazed down at her, the furs falling away a little. The silver chain slipped to the side, and the medallion dangled along the flexed muscle of his bracing arm, catching somehow a random ray of light and gleaming.

Medwyn had promised the medallion would keep her safe. She sent up a silent prayer that the wise old man had told her the truth when he said that. If the one who wore it was protected, then it would keep Eric safe.

Oh, please, God. Whatever happens, won't you keep this man safe?

Eric touched her forehead—so warm, so right, whenever he touched her—and traced the line of her hair as it fell along her temple and back against the furs. His eyes crinkled at the corners. "Shall I put out the light?"

"No." She forced a smile for him. "It's not the light."

"Then...?"

"Eric…?"

"Yes?"

"Whatever happens…"

He bent close, brushed a kiss at her temple, at the spot where the faintest bruise still remained—where she'd hit her head and been knocked out cold the day her plane went down.

He kissed the tip of her nose, brushed his mouth, too briefly, across her waiting lips.

And she gave him the impossible truth, the one she hadn't known fully until just that moment. "Eric. I love you. I will love you, always. No matter what."

He lifted away—a fraction. And he whispered, "As I love you."

Equal parts joy and sadness swirled through her. She would do what she had to do. But this moment, right now, beneath his furs, naked beside him, their bodies not quite touching, yet still sharing warmth… Her words of love—and his given back to her—no one and nothing could take this away.

He pushed the furs away a fraction. She felt his gaze on her, moving, hungry and tender, along her neck and lower. He bent his head to her left shoulder and pressed a kiss, gentle, lingering, on the white bandage, right over the wound.

With the touch of his lips there, at the warmth of his breath through the white gauze, her sadness vanished.

There was only joy.

She freed her arm from the prison of fur and laid her hand on the warm, hard curve of his shoulder, pulling him closer, moaning a little as his body touched hers, all the way down, in one branding caress.

He had that leather strip tying back his hair. She took it and slipped it off and the silken strands trailed to her shoulder, brushed at her breasts. She let go of the leather strip, had not a care where it fell. He kissed his way along the curve of her collarbone, licked a trail up her throat, over her chin to her waiting mouth.

His tongue dipped in. She drew on it as the medallion pressed itself, warm and heavy, against her upper chest.

He touched her as he kissed her, his hand moving along her eager flesh, leaving waves of longing and delight in its wake. He stroked her arm, learned the shape of each rib, the inward curve of her waist, the swell of her hip...

And lower...

He brushed the side of her thigh.

And then he wrapped his arm around her and rolled until she was on top and he lay beneath her, still kissing her, his lean body a cradle for hers.

She felt him, the hardness of him, pressed at the cove where her thighs joined. It was the most natural thing, to spread her legs and brace her knees to the furs on either side of him.

He groaned into her mouth. And they both went still. She lifted her mouth from his and looked down at him, at his flushed, yearning face, at his eyes, gray-green now as a stormy sea.

She whispered his name. He took her hips and levered her upward, seeking her breast.

He captured it in that tender mouth and drew on the nipple. She felt the wonderful, shimmering shock of connection, as if a thread of sensation pulsed between her breast and her womb. She moaned as his fingers slid over her belly and combed through the curls between her spread thighs.

He found her, long fingers sliding along the wet folds and then entering her. She gasped and then she shuddered. His fingers stroked, so slowly, in and out. The fleshy pad at the base of his palm rubbed knowingly at the center of her pleasure.

She was so wet and so eager. She moaned and moved in a liquid slide against his rubbing hand, at first holding her breast to his mouth and then, unable to go another second without kissing him, bending her legs a little more, taking her breast from him so she could have his mouth pressed to hers.

Another kiss. Endless. Wet. Seeking…

His hand went on stroking, sending waves of pleasure shivering through her.

Until she could bear it no longer.

She reached down and found him and guided him home.

There was a low, guttural moan. His? Hers? Who could tell? The rough, hungry sound echoed in her head. His tongue stroked the wet surfaces beyond her lips.

She lowered herself onto him, inch by slow, delicious inch.

When at last she had him fully, she stilled, her legs folded beneath her, her body holding him, hard and deep. She pushed at his shoulders.

He held her tightly, at first. And th n, with clear reluctance, he surrendered. Let her go.

She threw back the sheltering furs and rose above him. He opened his eyes and looked up at her.

''Fearless one,'' he whispered, the sound ragged and needful and a little bit angry.

She put her fingers against his mouth—to silence him? Maybe.

Or maybe just to feel the hot scrape of his tongue against her fingerpads. She moaned. He sucked her fingers into his mouth, his hips pressing up, as if he couldn't get far enough, deep enough, inside her.

Oh, she could not bear it. She had to move....

She pulled her fingers, dragging, wet, from his mouth, and braced her hands on his shoulders. The medallion had fallen to the side of his neck. It lay, facedown, gleaming, on the furs.

She shut her eyes against it and she began to rock her hips.

They both moaned then. There were hard sighs and soft cries. His strong arms came up and closed around her.

She gave in to him, let him guide her to the side— somehow, he managed it so they remained joined. They faced each other, her outer leg draped over him. He pushed in hard.

She threw back her head and groaned.

He chuckled then—a hot, knowing sound that slid along her nerve endings, striking sparks as it went. She dragged her head back so she could glare at him.

And then she was smiling, too.

And then she *couldn't* smile. She couldn't glare. Her eyes drooped shut and her lips went slack. She could only moan and sigh.

He took her by the nape and pulled her mouth to

his and rolled her the rest of the way until she was under him and he was rocking into her and she didn't care…who was up, who was down.

It was all one, a river of joy and sensation, flowing from him into her and pulsing back again.

She cried out at the finish and he called her name.

There was a silence like snow drifting softly down, a luxurious feeling of floating on air. She was, for that moment, exactly where she wanted to be.

He cradled her close and she snuggled against him.

They were one, as it ought to be.

As it might never be again.

At the hour when the night is darkest, not long before dawn, Asta at last returned to her longhouse. She had her heaviest shawl wrapped tightly around her, yet still she shivered with the cold. Her breath came out as a cloud.

Her steps were heavy with weariness—but her heart was light. A new baby—a girl—was born and cradled in the loving arms of her exhausted mother.

And Brokk—a good boy, that one—had brought the news that Eric and Brit had returned safe and sound.

Asta saw the light gleaming through the narrow slits of the high windows as she trudged up to the door. Were the young people still awake, then? She frowned.

Perhaps having some kind of argument?

They were at odds far too often, in Asta's opinion. Life was so much shorter than the young could ever realize. Young people grabbed every day—and sometimes each other—by the throat.

Of course, it was clear as fresh springwater that Eric

loved Brit and the king's willful daughter loved him back. Still, they had to fight about it, worry their love between them like two greedy dogs with a single bone.

Yes, there were real impediments to their happiness. Brit knew the false story of Valbrand's death for the lie it was. And Eric—like Asta herself—was sworn to vouch for the lie at every turn. It didn't make for trust or easy communication.

That Valbrand. Asta clucked her tongue at the night. Damaged so deeply. And not only his ravaged face. He ought to at least be staying in her longhouse, enjoying the civilized comfort of a sleeping bench and thick furs, eating at her table, where she'd soon put some healthy fat on that too-lean frame.

Instead, almost from the day Eric had brought him to stay in the village five months ago, he'd taken off to live wild, in the woods and in hillside caves, his only constant companion that black horse, Starkavin.

Asta paused at the stoop, reluctant to enter on some moment of discord, straining her ears for the sound of harsh words.

She heard only silence within.

With a small sigh of relief she pushed open the door to the warmth of the fire and the light of the lamp, which waited on the table, burning low.

And what was that? A lump of wool on the floor…

She recognized her old gray shawl. But where were the young people?

Ah.

With great care, so as not to disturb them, Asta shut the door. Her weariness had vanished, her body was no longer cold. Wearing a look much too soft and full of dreams for a woman who'd raised her sons and set her husband's funeral boat afire, she started back up the street.

There was always a sleeping bench for her at Sif's. Or at Sigrid's, for that matter....

Chapter Seventeen

Brit woke to daylight. She turned her head to see Eric, already up and dressed, spooning bowls of steaming oatmeal from a cast-iron pot.

He glanced her way and smiled. All of last night was there, in that smile. In those deep, knowing eyes.

God, she hoped she wasn't blushing. Her cheeks felt way too warm. She sat, raking her hair back from her forehead and pulling the furs with her to cover her bare breasts—which was kind of silly, if she thought about it. It wasn't as if he hadn't already gotten an up-close-and-personal look at them.

At all of her, for that matter.

"Come," he said. "Eat."

"Ahem." Oh, great. Throat clearing again. She had to stop doing that. "Where's Asta?"

"At Sif's." How did he know that? Did it matter?

Probably not. He set the pot on the stove and went to the counter by the deep, old-fashioned sink.

As soon as his back was turned, she leaned over and snatched up her long johns from where she'd dropped them the night before. Under cover of the furs, she wiggled into them.

When Eric turned around again, she was perched on the edge of the bench, pulling on her socks.

"Gotta make a quick trip outside."

He nodded, poured himself a cup of tea and sat down to eat. Brit slid on the clogs Asta had loaned her, grabbed the gray shawl from the peg where somebody had hung it and went out into the brisk, bright morning.

She was back in no time. She went to her own sleeping bench and got a bra from the pack beneath it. Turning to the wall, she pulled her arms out of her shirt and put the thing on. She added her jeans and sweater over the long johns and then ran a brush through her hair.

Well, hey, wow. Ready to face the day.

More or less.

She washed her hands and joined Eric at the table. They ate. They cleared off and washed their bowls and cups and spoons. She was setting the second bowl in its place on the shelf when he touched her—a breath of a touch, the back of his finger to the side of her throat and gone.

"At night, a temptress. In the morning, a little anxious—and trying to pretend that she's not."

She felt a smile quiver across her mouth. "Oh, Eric…" She set the towel on the counter and turned to him.

He gathered her into his arms.

It felt really good to be there. She nuzzled his warm neck and breathed in the scent of his skin and tucked her head against his strong shoulder. "What are we going to do about us?"

He held her away a little so he could look down at her. "Do you really want me to answer?" She didn't, and they both knew it. He took her hand and pressed it to his chest. She could feel the round shape of the medallion beneath his heavy wool shirt. He gave her his answer, whether she wanted it or not. It was only one word. "Stay."

The crazy, insane truth was, she wanted to do exactly that. She could admit that now, for all the good it did. But...

"You can't," he said, finishing a sentence only begun in her mind. "You have set yourself a task and you will see it through, no matter how bitter the end."

She looked deep into his eyes. "And you should be with me. You know that you should..." He started to speak. She put her fingers to his lips. "Never mind. Believe it or not, I kind of understand. My brother needs you near him. And you won't desert him."

He caught her hand again and kissed the pads of her fingers, one by one. "I never said that."

"It's all right. I forgive you."

He was frowning—but playfully. "Did I ask for your forgiveness?"

"It doesn't matter. You have it, anyway." She pulled her hand free of his gently. "I hope it keeps you warm at night when I'm not here."

He smiled at the taunt. "Your mouth is forever uttering barbed words. I like it better when you use it for kissing.'' He tipped his head down.

She tipped hers up.

And there. Her mouth was doing what he liked—kissing him. Actually, she liked it, too.

A lot.

With a long sigh, she slid her arms up his broad chest and wrapped them around his neck so she could stroke his nape and toy with the idea of pulling the leather cord from his silky hair.

She never got a chance to decide if she would do it. He lifted his head too soon. "I've contacted your father with our plans.''

She pushed at his chest and his arms dropped away. "You contacted him by shortwave?''

"Yes.''

"I am a little curious about this shortwave setup I've never seen that you're always sending my father messages on.''

"Gunnolf has a work shed behind his and Sif's longhouse. We have it rigged with a generator. The radio is there. I suppose you'd like to see it?''

"Not really. I just wondered where it was.'' She stepped back. "And what, exactly, are these plans of ours?''

"We'll leave as soon as you're ready, you and I, on horseback. We'll go through the Black Mountains, by way of the Helmouth Pass.''

The Helmouth Pass. Such a charming name.

She knew where the pass was. At least, she'd seen it on the map. It twisted through the mountains, beginning about twenty miles south and slightly east of the village.

Eric went on, "The mountains are still passable. The snows have yet to close them off. We'll stay about midway through the pass, high in the mountains, in a traveler's hut I know of, for tonight. By tomorrow, at late morning, we'll be on the other side. Your father is sending Hauk Wyborn to meet you and accompany you the rest of the way to Isenhalla."

"I gotta ask, whatever happened to the option of a nice, efficient helicopter? Seems like a helicopter could easily land in one of the pastures out back—and I could just climb on and be at the palace in no time."

He looked very serious. "You'd prefer that, then?"

"I'm just saying, it seems a lot simpler."

"Good enough." Did he sound...too casual? "Would you care to come with me while I send a second message?"

She studied his face. Yeah. Way too guileless. "What's going on?"

"I thought you would perhaps want to take your horse with you. But if you prefer the helicopter, I promise you that Svald will be well cared for here."

Her horse. Right. "Eric, is there some valid reason you can't tell me what you're up to here?"

Now he was the one studying her. And frowning. Finally he admitted, "I suppose not...beyond the usual unswerving desire to protect you—thoroughly misguided, at least in this case. My apologies." He was so handsome when contrite. "We very well could get through the mountains without incident. Still, you should understand the danger."

"The bears and the mountain cats, right? And let's not forget all the fine young renegades and—I think

I've got it. The biggest threat of all. That would be the bad guys with the guns who call themselves NIB.''

He shrugged. ''And there you have it.''

''Traveling overland, we get to be bait.''

He nodded. ''So you see? Here I am, suggesting that you put your life in danger. After this you must never again accuse me of trying to keep you safe.'' He spoke teasingly. He was making a truly valiant effort to keep things light.

But she saw in his eyes what he didn't say. Should they meet up with Jorund's men, there was a very good chance she'd never again be accusing him of anything.

It's hard to do much accusing when you're dead.

Chapter Eighteen

Asta and her family—Sif and Gunnolf, and Sigrid and her husband Brokk the elder, and all the little Borghilds—came out to say goodbye. There were hugs all around.

Little Mist instructed, "Bwit. You come back soon."

"I will," she promised, feeling only the slightest twinge of guilt that it was a promise she had no idea if she'd be able to keep. She looked up from the child into Asta's worried eyes.

"I don't like this," the old woman said. "The pass through the mountains is dangerous. And why must you leave us so soon?" Brit had no answer for her. She held out her arms. With a grunt of disapproval, Asta allowed a second goodbye hug.

"Thank you," Brit whispered against the old woman's thick white hair. "For everything…"

"Humph," said Asta. When Brit let her go, she fumbled in the pocket of her skirt and came out with a kerchief. "Oh, now—" she dabbed her eyes and blew her nose "—you keep safe. You hear me?"

"Absolutely, Asta. I will."

She caught Eric's reproachful look as she mounted her horse. Well, and what was she supposed to say? He swung up into the saddle as Asta chided him, "Take care. Keep well...."

They started off along the dirt lane in the opposite direction from the way they'd gone two days before. Brit turned to glance back more than once. Each time she looked, the Borghilds remained in the middle of the dirt street, waving goodbye. Gunnolf had lifted Mist to his shoulder, and the child's small frame rose above the rest. She had her plump arm held up, her tiny hand swaying back and forth.

Too soon they reached the trees. The Mystic settlement—and the small knot of well-wishers—was lost to view.

They reached the next village to the south two hours later. It looked much like Asta's village: a single dirt street lined with matching rows of longhouses, pastures and barns and livestock pens spreading out behind the houses to the edge of the trees.

Brit remembered what Asta had told her that first time she woke from her fever—that her guide's body had been sent to his family in a village to the south. "Is this the village where Rutland Gottshield's family lives?"

Eric gave her a bleak look. "We haven't time to linger here."

"Only for a moment. I'd just like the chance to pay my respects."

"Be quick."

He led her to the second house on the left side of the street. A woman, her long red hair streaked with gray, came out to meet them. Brit introduced herself and explained that she'd only come to offer condolences, that they couldn't stay, had no time even to come inside. The woman, Rutland's widow, who said her name was Trine, saluted, fist to chest, in the Gullandrian way and spoke of how honored she was that Her Highness had stopped. Trine said the king had seen to her well-being and the future of the four sons—working in the pastures now, and out hunting—who had lost their father. She murmured shyly that she would forever mourn her husband, but knew great pride that he had died bravely in the service of his king.

In her mind's eye, Brit saw Rutland's pale face and shaking hands when they had boarded the Skyhawk. "Yes," she told the widow. "Your husband died a hero's death." Her next words came to her, stolen from the stories she'd heard at her mother's knee. "May he feast and fight forever in Odin's great hall."

The widow stood in the street, waving, when they rode away. Brit glanced back once and thought of the Borghilds, waving, as they'd left Asta's village. She had a strange, sinking feeling. As if she and the man beside her rode toward something huge and horrible, as if they were leaving all kindness and goodwill behind.

The way was much easier than the trip into Drakveden Fjord—at least at first. The hills sloped gently, with small valleys between. The road, well traveled, lay before them wide enough to ride abreast.

No bands of renegades attacked them. Mountain cats and bears kept to the shelter of the trees off the trail. If traitors lurked nearby, it must have been only to watch and wait for some later opportunity.

They stopped briefly for a quick meal of jerky and trail mix at noon. About an hour later they reached the base of the jutting, jagged mountains crested at the highest points with white, and began climbing. Soon the trail narrowed. The steep black cliffs soared up and up on either side, the sky a slice of blue between them. Eric took the lead.

They rode mostly in shadow. The sunlight couldn't reach them between the high rock walls. The wind kicked up, whistling down on them. And clouds began to gather.

So inconvenient. Brit could almost start to feel that Mother Nature didn't like her much. Every time she had someplace important to go lately, the weather had to up the stakes. She pulled her beanie down more securely over her ears and hunched into her jacket— which, as usual, she didn't dare zip up all the way as she'd have poor access to her weapon.

Most of the time they were traveling south, protected somewhat by the rock walls around them. But when the trail jogged north, they headed into the wind. The cliff faces on either side made a tunnel through which the icy air rushed at them hard and fast as a runaway train. Brit's lips went numb, and her chin ached with cold. She worried that her eyeballs would freeze in their sockets. She marveled at her own idiocy; she could have brought a damn ski mask, for goodness' sake.

And then—but of course—the snow started to fall, stinging flakes that beat against her cheeks and gathered on her eyebrows. She got the hood free of her collar and pulled it up, tightening the strings and tying them beneath her chin with gloved hands that felt like slabs of ice. It didn't help a whole heck of a lot. But it did keep the snow from slipping in around her neck.

The snow came down thicker—well, maybe *down* wasn't the word for it; it swirled around them on the angry wind. Brit gave up on the weapon-ready angle and zipped her coat to the neck. Her fingers were so cold and stiff she doubted she could deal with her gun right then, anyway.

They went on forever, into the cold, blustery white, sometimes moving down into a steep canyon or a rocky gorge, but mostly, it seemed to Brit, moving ever upward toward the stormy sky and the high cliffs that rose tauntingly above them.

Okay, all right. She wasn't as tough as she liked to think she was. She'd have ordered Eric to stop a hundred times by then, if there'd only been anywhere *to* stop. But the snow was piling up on the trail and there was zero shelter that she could see. If they stopped, they'd probably end up freezing to death.

They went on.

For hours. Sometimes the snow abated and there was only the freezing wind. But it always started up again.

The snow was blowing at her again, thick and white and blinding, when she pulled back her sleeve and checked her watch. Nearly seven. It must be getting dark. But who could tell? The clouds above were so thick and black, the cliff walls so steep around them, it had seemed like the middle of the night since about three in the afternoon.

And then, out of the stinging white and the howling wind—shelter. Around a sharp turn, in a little cove of flat land to the side of the snow-white trail, an old wood shack materialized, silvered with weathering, out of the storm.

Brit had never in her life been so thrilled to see four walls and a roof. And was it possible? Could that be a stone chimney she saw on top of that beautiful roof? A chimney would mean a fireplace, and a fireplace just might mean...

Oh, be still, my beating heart.

Eric led her around to the most protected side, facing the cliff. A crude porchlike structure consisting of a roof and side walls, about ten feet deep and covering the entire cliff-facing wall, led into yet deeper shadow.

They slid from their horses to the snow-covered ground and went beneath the shelter of the roof.

Eric handed her his reins. "Watch the horses. I'll only be long enough to get the fire started."

The fire...

Then that *had* been a chimney. And if there was going to be a fire, she would literally melt with gratitude. He opened the door on the wall of the shack, stepped in and shut the door.

The horses snorted and shook their snow-thick manes. More good news: the snow slid right off and left them hardly wet at all. Less work for her and Eric. Oh, yay, hooray! Plus, it wasn't nearly as bad standing here as out there in the storm. Pretty darn cold, yes.

But bearable. The horses would be fine out here. And there were railings suitable for hitching to either side of the door.

And speaking of the door—it wasn't set in the frame all that straight. Golden light glowed around the edges of it. Oh, yes, yes, yes!

The door opened. Eric stood there, holding a lighted kerosene lamp. Behind him, on the side wall, the fire in the fireplace was already crackling away.

They unsaddled the horses, brushed them down quickly and fed them the oats Eric had brought outside. Then they lugged their gear inside, where the cheery fire was blazing, and Brit dared to hope she might actually get warm again sometime very soon.

The one-room shack had two doors: one led to the shelter where they'd left the horses. The other, on the wall opposite, faced the trail—two doors, no windows. Like the cave the other night, the shack had been stocked with the bare necessities. The furniture wasn't much: a small table and a couple of roughly made ladder-back chairs.

Eric took one of the chairs and braced it under the knob of the door that faced the trail. "It won't stop anyone," he said, "but it will give us a little warning." The door they'd come in through opened out. Bracing a chair against it would accomplish nothing. Eric must have caught the direction of her gaze. "It's doubtful they'll use that door, anyway, too much chance they'd spook the horses and give us warning."

"If things get crazy, they'll probably be coming at us from both sides."

He didn't argue. "We'll put the table against that one, then."

He put out the lamp and set it in the corner with the blankets and the bucket, the can of lamp oil and the bag of feed. They positioned the table, legs out into the room, against the lean-to door. It wasn't big enough to reach the top of the door frame—but, hey, they had to make do with what was available. Once the table was in place, they spread their bedrolls before the fire. They sat, backs against their saddles, to eat their dried meat and oatcakes.

"Shh," Eric said a while later. "Listen."

Had he heard boots in the snow? Brit felt a shiver, like ice water trickling down her spine. She whispered, "I don't hear anything."

He saw her wide eyes and smiled. "Easy. I only meant the wind has died. The storm is passing. We'll have a clear day tomorrow, I'd lay odds on it, and no more than six inches of snow on the ground. It should be passable."

She let herself slump against her saddle. "And not a peep from Jorund and crew."

"The night is young."

She stared into the dancing flames of the fire. "I suppose, if they're out there, the smoke from our chimney will lead them right to us."

He gave her a wry look. "That *is* the idea...."

"So we...keep our weapons close and our eyes open?"

"Well said." He had his rifle beside him. "They'll fall on us—or they won't. We'll live. Or we'll die."

A licking warmth tingled through her—and not from the fire. At last he was accepting her as an equal, someone he trusted to be ready, willing and able to fight at his side. She could almost get starry-eyed.

"Be ready," he said softly.

She sent him her best come-and-get-me smile. "I will."

He reached across the distance between them, wrapped his warm hand around the back of her neck and pulled her toward him. Their lips met in a hard, hungry kiss. He whispered against her mouth, "I would like nothing better than to drive you wild with pleasure tonight—and increase the odds you might be forced by your own vow to marry me."

"Hmm. We're back to the breeding issue again, are we?"

He let out a long, aggressively rueful sigh. "But, alas, one should never get undressed when under the threat of being set upon by traitors."

"Oh, I don't know. It sounds kind of…exciting."

"Too exciting. And distracting. Plus, it's discouraging to be attacked while naked."

"Happened to you before, has it?"

He chuckled. "Not recently, no."

"I have to admit I'd rather die with my boots on."

"Then keep them on. And get back into your jacket."

"I suppose next you'll say I have to keep my shoulder rig on, too."

He nodded. "You want to be ready to defend yourself—and ready to run, too. And that means you'll need—"

"Outerwear. All of it."

"That's right."

Another thought occurred to her—a not-very-pleasant one: *the Freyasdahl signs.*

Ho-boy, now there was an issue she really should have considered last night.

The Freyasdahl signs had been named by her father, when her mother, who had been a Freyasdahl, experienced them, though the signs came down through the women in her family...

Which got way confusing and wasn't the point. The point was, when a woman in her family got pregnant, she also got the signs within twenty-four hours. First, she threw up, and then she fainted and then a bright red rash would appear across her chest. Brit had been there when it happened to her oldest sister, Liv.

But really, the chance that might be happening to her in the next few hours had to be minimal, didn't it?

Yeah, right. Ask Liv about that. She'd gotten pregnant after one wild night with Finn Danelaw....

Eric was watching her. He read her too well. He knew something was wrong.

Why, oh, why hadn't she thought of this last night?

Well, hey, last night she hadn't realized that tonight she'd be holed up in the Helmouth Pass waiting for a gang of traitors to bust in the door.

She didn't want to tell him. It was one more thing to worry about, and there were far too many of those already.

But if the signs did put in an appearance, they could be grossly inconvenient. He needed to know there was a remote possibility that she'd be throwing up and fainting in the middle of the part where they were fighting for their lives.

"Ahem," she said.

He regarded her for a moment. "I fear that doesn't sound encouraging."

"Well, it's like this…" She told him, in as few words as possible. When she was done, she added sheepishly, "I just…thought of it and realized you should know."

He took her hand and kissed the knuckles. He did have the softest lips in the world. "Put it from your mind."

Hah. "Sure."

"It's only one dire possibility among so many."

He had it right there. "Eric?"

"Yes, my only love?"

"How many would you guess there are going to be?"

"It depends on how good they think they are. There could be only one or two—trained and experienced assassins—to slip in on us and cut our throats. Or perhaps the six, from the crash site…"

"And what about my *friend,* Agent Sorenson?"

"Ah yes, possibly Agent Sorenson as well. They'll have horses, perhaps leave one to tend them. And they could leave another one or two outside, to stand guard."

"So what you're really saying is, you haven't a clue how many there'll be."

"Yes. That's what I'm really saying."

"Are we crazy to be doing this?"

"Oh, yes. Beyond the darkest shadow of a doubt."

At a little after midnight Eric told her to try to get a little sleep.

Great idea. Get some sleep. Be fresh when the assassins arrive. "What about you?"

"Later. I'll wake you and you can have your turn on guard."

"Goody."

"Sleep."

"I can't bear not to ask…we do have backup, don't we?"

He answered with a wide smile. "We do."

"I guess I don't get to ask who?"

He only looked at her and softly repeated, "Sleep."

To be a good sport about it, she settled against her saddle and shut her eyes.

Unbelievable. She must have actually dropped off.

Because the next thing she knew, Eric's hand was on her shoulder. "They come…"

There was a clattering noise—the chair at the door.

Brit sat bolt upright, going for the SIG.

Eric had already turned and shouldered his rifle. His first shot exploded, deafening in the small space, as the chair gave way and the door flew inward.

A man, his features covered by a ski mask, fell half into the room. Another came after him. Eric fired and he fell back, out of sight, into the darkness beyond the doorway.

There was silence—one awful, endless second of it.

And then a voice from the back door said, "Drop your weapons or die."

Chapter Nineteen

There were two men at the back door, one with a rifle and one with a combat pistol. They'd used the confusion of the frontal attack to open the door and get themselves in place. The table, smaller than it should have been and still right where she and Eric had put it, covered them both to chest height. Like the others—the man who lay, too still, in the doorway and the one who had fallen back—they wore ski masks over their faces.

"Set your weapons on the floor. Do it now."

Eric sent her a glance, an almost-imperceptible nod. Together they crouched and set their guns down.

"Now stand up. Hands high."

They obeyed. Brit's heart pounded as if it had plans to escape from her chest. She hadn't gotten off a single shot. And why the hell hadn't she had sense enough to cover the other door? Things had happened too damn fast. Next time—if there was one—she'd know better.

And hey, wow. At least she wasn't throwing up and fainting. She did kind of have that whoopsy feeling in her stomach. But the Freyasdahl signs had nothing to do with it.

That was pure terror talking.

It was her first gun battle. Her performance? Far from impressive. But at least she and Eric were still breathing—for the moment, anyway. She glanced at the fallen man in the front doorway and knew a twinge of regret—mostly that she couldn't help being glad he was probably dead.

"Safe to enter, sir," said the man with the rifle trained on them. About then the man in the front doorway pushed himself up, groaning. Not dead, after all, though he didn't look too healthy. His face had a bluish cast and things looked real bad at about belt level. Gut shot. She'd seen a lot of action movies. Gut shot was not a fun way to go.

He fell backward, groaning, into the night behind him.

Another man—about five-seven and powerfully built—appeared from the darkness and came through the wide-open front door. He stood opposite Eric and aimed his pistol right at him. Yet another, taller and leaner, followed after him, crossing behind him to take a position opposite Brit. Both, like the two in the back doorway, were armed.

Four men, in combat boots and camo, ski masks covering each face. Four guns, all trained on Brit and

Eric. Brit's pulse showed no signs of slowing down soon.

The short, beefy one—whom Brit had already recognized by his height and build and the confident way he carried himself—reached up and yanked off his mask to reveal his shaved head.

A bullet of a man, she'd thought the first time she saw him. Compact and deadly—but with such a winning smile. Weeks ago, which seemed like centuries now, she'd sat across from him at Loki's Laughter, the homey neighborhood pub near the Bureau offices that the agents liked to frequent. With a tall glass of sweet Gullandrian ale on the scarred oak table in front of her, she'd told him her theories about what might have happened to her brother, tickled pink with herself to have been so clever as to cultivate a connection with him.

"Hello, Jorund."

Special Agent Sorenson grinned, showing straight white teeth and a lot of friendly laugh lines. "Your Highness. So good to see you again—though I'm certain you're *not* pleased to see me. But then, it's your own fault. You should have killed Hans here when you had the chance." The man beside him took his left hand from his rifle just long enough to drag off his mask and let it drop to the floor. Good old Hans Borger.

Hans wasn't smiling. He had her in his sights again, just waiting for the order to blow her head off—the order that, she had a sinking feeling, would be coming very soon.

Jorund had more to say. "Fortunately for me, Princess, you are too softhearted. You let Hans live. And, once he was through babbling nonsense about a legend come to life, he remembered that you had seen him that first day you visited my office and thus would be…oh, how to put it? 'On to me,' now. And with you 'on to me,' well, I knew that it wouldn't be long before the king's soldiers came knocking at my door. I found it expedient to come looking for you before you had a chance to speak with your father.'' Jorund indulged in a little cheerful chuckling. He appeared to be having a very good time. 'A legend come alive?' He must mean the Dark Raider. Valbrand must have paid Hans a visit after she and Eric left him yesterday.

Jorund turned his ice-blue eyes to Eric and clucked his tongue. "Radio messages…so easy to intercept." He gestured at the two still-masked agents waiting at the back door. "We'll take over here. Stand guard." They lowered their weapons, backed into the shadows and were gone.

Brit really hoped that the backup Eric had mentioned would be showing up shortly. In the meantime, well, nothing ventured… "Who do you work for, Jorund?"

Jorund found her so amusing. He chuckled some more. "Questions, questions. Your Highness has always asked far too many questions. And what good will the answers do you now—on the night of your death?"

"Hey, you know, just wondering…."

Jorund tipped his head to the side, considering. "Well, and then again, why not? A tidbit or two— before Hans dispatches both you and Prince Greyfell. This is really too, too good. To be rid of you both in one night. Together, you know, you represent a very large threat to the plans of certain important people. Should you be allowed to live and perhaps to marry, and thus unite your two houses…'' He shook his head. ''Disaster. Prince Greyfell, here, would in that case most assuredly be named our next king.''

Brit shrugged. She was proud of that shrug. It was cool and offhand and spoke nothing of the way her stomach twisted and her pulse raced. All she had to do was *not* look at Eric, not let herself even think that in a few minutes he could be dead. If she didn't look at Eric, she could do this. ''But then again, if we're dead, we can't get married.''

Jorund indulged in another jovial chortle. ''Your Highness, you astound me with the brilliance and clarity of your powers of deduction. You've cut right to the heart of the matter.''

''These important people you just spoke of—they want the throne?''

Jorund was clucking his tongue again. ''Well, now, *someone* has to claim the throne when the next king-making occurs. Sadly, both Thorson princes are dead. After tonight, there'll be no Greyfell to step forward. *Someone* must take over. And the kingmaking could come at any time—some would say, sooner than you'd think….''

Brit used her brilliant powers of deduction. ''You're planning to assassinate my father.''

''Not to worry. That won't happen for a while yet. He'll have time to suffer and mourn some more first— over another child gone forever. How very, very sad.''

''Valbrand? You're responsible for that, too?''

Jorund heaved a big, fake sigh. ''So unfortunate. Lost at sea. Just as you and Prince Greyfell here will be lost, vanished forever in the Helmouth Pass.'' He gestured at Hans, who had his rifle pointed at Brit's heart. "Ready?"

"Yes, sir." Hans spoke flatly, still sighting, finger ready on the trigger. This close, Brit was going to have a very big hole in her chest. The irony was perfect. It was just as Eric had predicted.

She'd spared the agent's life—so he could be the one to kill her.

"And now, Princess, I'm afraid it's time to bid you fare—"

Something thudded against the north wall of the shack. Both Jorund and Hans glanced back toward the sound.

It was all the opening they needed. Eric dived for Jorund. Brit went for Hans.

Weapons fired and shots went wild—ricocheting off the stone fireplace. Brit managed to knock the rifle out of Hans's grip as it fired. He let it go—and dealt with her.

It was a fight she knew she couldn't win. Sure, she'd had a few self-defense lessons. But Hans was bigger and stronger and combat trained. Hand-to-hand, he would take her. She tried to kick him where it mattered, but he was ready. He jerked his hips away and then threw a leg over her, trapping her beneath him. In a split second he was looming above her. His fist connected—hard—with her jaw.

Spots spun and danced before her eyes. He hit her again. Her head bounced against the floor.

She saw double—Hans shifting and fading in and out of himself, two right fists coming at her at once. She knew she was done for.

And then a sound like the world coming apart—
a shot.

Hans had a red hole in the center of his face. Blood
was spraying everywhere. He collapsed on top of her,
his ruined face smacking the floor above her bad
shoulder a few inches from her head, sending more
blood spattering. Dazed, bloodied, her suddenly limp
would-be murderer pinning her to the floor, she saw
Eric standing a few feet away, her own trusty SIG in
his hand.

She blinked, because everything still kept going
double, and behind Eric…

Valbrand—minus the Dark Raider's mask, his poor
face as she remembered it, a horror on one side—in
the doorway. Valbrand had a gun, too. He had Jorund
in a neck lock, the gun pointed at his head. Valbrand
was backing out, dragging Jorund with him.

"Brit." Eric filled the world as he crouched beside
her. He pushed the limp man off her. She looked up
into his face, her head spinning, her heart aching—but
aching in a *good* way, really. Because he was alive
and she was alive, at least so far. Because she'd just
seen her brother, alive, too, and not hiding behind a
mask.

She blinked as she heard a sudden soft roar. She
lifted her head, blinked again.

What was this?

The fire had…escaped. It was a bright ribbon, eating up the floor, sizzling out from the fireplace.

How could that be?

"Come. Now." Eric held out his hand. She put hers
in it. He pulled her up.

She swayed on her feet. The room went round and round and the flames...

They were licking at the old, dry boards of the floor, creeping ever closer. Smoke curled up, billowing. She coughed as Eric wrapped a strong arm around her and half dragged her to the open door.

They stumbled over the sill. She fell—but he caught her and dragged her up again, up and away from the flames, out to the snow-thick trail.

At last. Safe. She sucked in a great breath of the cold, fresh night air. Eric's strong arm was tight around her, holding her up. She clung to him, so tight. They watched the shack burn.

Her dizziness slowly faded. She looked at Eric. His eyes blazed, reflecting the flames. "The fire...how?"

"The lamp oil. I kicked it over when I grappled with Sorenson. The lid must have come off."

"Hans..."

He gave her a dark scowl. "Dead. You saw his face. His blood is all over you. Don't you dare ask me to go in there and pull his body out."

"I'm not. I promise." She huddled against his warmth and shook her head, trying to clear it, to understand it all. Then she turned enough to gape at the empty doorway beyond which the bright flames danced. "The two men you shot...when they first burst through the door?"

A voice from behind her said. "Wounded but alive. One might even survive. The other, shot in the belly, most likely not."

Eric released her. She swayed a moment, then steadied. She turned, slowly, her heart kicking hard against her ribs, knowing that voice though she'd heard it only once, when she was so ill. "Valbrand."

Her brother nodded.

With a glad cry she took one step and then another. At the last minute, her brother held out his arms.

Chapter Twenty

As the shack burned, the flames licking high toward the last of the night, Valbrand led them around to the back, near the face of the cliff, where Gunnolf and Brokk the elder and two other strong men from Asta's village were waiting with the horses. At their feet a row of traitors, Jorund among them, lay bound in the snow.

"It is important work we've done tonight," Gunnolf announced with pride. Svald, as if in thorough agreement, tossed her braided mane and let out a joyful whinny.

Brit turned to the brother she'd found at last. "And now what?"

He smiled. It was a hideous smile—and the second most beautiful she'd ever seen. "We go, with the daylight, all of us together, to the south. There are traitors to bring to justice. And our country to save."

It was exactly what she'd hoped, schemed—and nearly died—to hear. For tonight there was only one more thing that needed settling.

She turned to the man at her other side. "I wonder, could we have a moment...just the two of us, alone?"

Brit and Eric left the others and went back, hand in hand, around the front of the blazing shack.

They stopped, of one accord, at the place they'd stood before, on the trail, opposite the glowing rectangle of the open front door. They watched the consuming flames, the sparks shooting high into the darkness, bright spots drifting down, winking out into ash.

Eric wrapped an arm around her and pulled her close to his side. "The night seems black as ink now." He breathed the words against her blood-matted hair. "Yet dawn will be on us in the wink of Odin's good eye."

Keeping tight in the circle of his strong arm, she turned until she was facing him, sliding her arms around his waist to link at the small of his back. With a long sigh, she leaned fully against him—the best place in the whole world to be—her head on his shoulder, her heart so close to his.

She breathed in the scent of him: smoke and sweat, the blood of their vanquished enemy. "Oh, Eric. All I wanted was to find my brother. And I did—and so much more...."

He caught her chin, tipped it up. She winced—her jaw was way tender, from Hans's deadly attentions. "You've blood in your brows, on your cheeks, in your lashes. And you'll be black-and-blue from ear to ear.

And yet, as always, you are so very beautiful.'' Behind her, the fire roared. The flames danced in his eyes.

''My dad will freak when he sees me.''

''The blood will wash off. And the bruises will heal.''

''They'd better. I want to be lookin' good when I hand you my wedding sword.''

His brows drew together—though he was smiling. ''Could this mean…?''

''Oh, yes. It most definitely could.''

''And since you have neither been sick, nor fainted—''

''Well, I came pretty close to both, when I was sure we were done for—and then when Hans started punching me. But that was stark terror and a couple of mean right hooks.''

''So. You don't carry my child.''

''Not if I'm like the rest of the women in my family—and anyway, it doesn't matter. I don't want to marry you because I'm pregnant. I don't want to marry you because it's supposed to be fated. Or because it could strike a telling blow against the enemies we haven't even routed out yet. Oh, no. I want to marry you because—'' She sighed, swallowed. Now, where had the words gone?

He waited, knowing she would find them.

And she did. ''Because I love you. Because you're the guy I've been waiting for when I didn't even know that I *was* waiting.''

''As I have waited, only for you.''

He bent his head. She lifted hers. The kiss was long and so very sweet. It pushed back the night and warmed the snowy mountaintops.

When they moved apart, it was only so he could take the medallion from around his neck and settle it over her head.

"Forever," he said.

"And always," she whispered.

He smoothed the silver chain, pressed the medallion in the place it was meant to be, near her heart. Then he took her hand again and twined his fingers with hers.

They turned to the fire as the shack gave way, collapsing inward with a heated rush. Sparks shot skyward, a million tiny points of hot light that, winking, fell. Hungry red flames licked higher, a moment of false triumph—then faded downward to the rubble with a sound like a surrendering sigh.

And in the east, the sliver of paleness along the rim of the mountains signaled the coming day.

* * * * *

BETWEEN DUTY AND DESIRE

BY
LEANNE BANKS

Leanne Banks, a *USA TODAY* bestselling author of romance and 2002 winner of the prestigious Booksellers' Best Award, lives in her native Virginia with her husband, son and daughter. Recognised for both her sensual and humorous writing with two Career Achievement Awards from *Romantic Times*, Leanne likes creating a story with a few grins, a generous kick of sensuality and characters that hang around after the book is finished. Leanne believes romance readers are the best readers in the world because they understand that love is the greatest miracle of all. Contact Leanne online at leannebbb@aol.com or write to her at PO Box 1442, Midlothian, VA 23113, USA. An SAE with return postage for a reply would be greatly appreciated.

This book is dedicated to all of those who have
served in the United States Marine Corps.
I'm humbled by your discipline and dedication.

Prologue

"In war, you win or lose, live or die—and the difference is an eyelash."
—General Douglas MacArthur

The moon shone over the desert, reflecting on the land. As usual, Staff Sergeant Rob Newton was talking about his wife, Callie. Captain Brock Armstrong smiled inwardly at the story Rob told while the two of them conducted their routine patrol. Rob was clearly crazy about his wife. Brock's gaze shifted constantly around them and scanned the distance. He might be amused, but that didn't mean he wouldn't be careful.

Rob was laughing. An explosion split the air. Pain tore through Brock at the same time he heard Rob's scream. "Callie! Callie!"

His flesh burned and ached so much he couldn't

speak. Time crawled by in a haze of pain. Images blurred. He couldn't see out of his right eye. He tried to move, felt himself lifted, and heard the whir of a helicopter propeller. Help was on the way.

"Callie," he heard Rob mutter and managed to turn his head.

"Rob, you okay?"

"Don't let her crawl back in her hole and hide," he said desperately. "Don't let her be a hermit. Don't let her—"

"You need to calm down," another voice said. A medic? Brock wondered, feeling his sense of reality slip and slide. "You need to conserve your energy."

Everything went black.

Brock awakened, drenched in sweat. He opened his eyes, but the darkness closed around his throat like a vise. He reached for his bedside lamp and turned it on, then sat up in bed, breathing like he was running a marathon. Even though the wound was long healed, he instinctively rubbed his right eye. He hadn't been able to see out of the eye that night because blood from his head wound had pulled a curtain over his vision.

After months of physical therapy, he still limped. He might always limp. It didn't stop him from running. It wouldn't stop him from much, except being a Marine. He'd always known he wouldn't stay in the Corps forever, but he hadn't expected to receive a discharge with honors quite this soon.

He raked his hand through his hair. It was long and

needed a cut. Or not, he reminded himself. He wasn't required to keep it regulation length anymore.

He glanced around his room in the rehabilitation center and felt an edgy restlessness. He'd been here long enough. He was ready to move on, to leave this sense of shock and weakness behind. His body was growing stronger and his will was catching up.

He was sick of focusing on himself, sick of talking about himself during his sessions with the head-doctor.

Sighing, he slid to the edge of the bed and limped to the small window. He looked out into the night and remembered the last night he'd seen Rob Newton alive. The land mine had taken Rob and left Brock. Brock still didn't understand why, though he asked himself the question approximately every five minutes.

The staff shrink had told him he was suffering from survivor's guilt and it would take time.

Brock swallowed over a knot in his throat. "Thanks for nothing," he muttered.

Rob's cries for his wife echoed inside his brain. He closed his eyes against the clawing sensation inside him. Maybe he was never going to get over this. Maybe he was never going to feel at peace again. Sitting here in the rehab center wasn't going to solve anything. He could finish the rest of his therapy on his own.

He had to find a way to live with himself, a way to assuage his guilt. He snorted. *Mission Impossible*. What could he do for a dead man?

He thought again of Rob's widow. Maybe, just maybe, he could live with himself a little more easily if he honored Rob's last request.

One

Marine Lingo Translation
Alpha Unit: Marine's spouse.

He knew her favorite color was blue.

He knew she was allergic to strawberries, but sometimes ate them anyway.

He knew her hazel eyes changed colors depending on her mood.

He knew she had a scar at the top of her thigh from a bike wreck she'd had when she was a child.

Brock knew Callie Newton intimately, even though he'd never met her. That would change in approximately ninety seconds, he thought, as he lifted his hand to knock on the weathered wooden door to her South Carolina beach cottage. The salty scent of the ocean was a nice change from the antiseptic smell of the rehab center.

His leg aching from being wedged into the small seat in the commercial jet that had brought him here, he leaned against the outside wall of the house for a moment. When there was no answer, he shifted and knocked again, this time more loudly.

He heard the sound of scrambling feet and a muffled shriek, then more scrambling and the door finally flew open. A woman with mussed shoulder-length strawberry-blond hair shielded her eyes with her hands as if she were seeing the sun for the first time today. Dressed in a wrinkled oversize white T-shirt and faded denim shorts that emphasized long lithe pale legs, Callie Newton squinted her eyes at him. "Who are—"

"Brock Armstrong," he said, wondering if she had any idea that the white T-shirt she wore revealed her nipples. He lifted his gaze from her chest. "I knew—"

"Rob," she finished for him, her voice softening. Her eyes darkened with sadness. "He talked about you in the e-mails and letters he sent me. The Dark Angel."

Brock felt an odd twist at hearing his nickname again. His buddies had given it to him because his hair and eyes were dark, along with his mood. Hell, before the accident, he'd been angry for as long as he could remember. He had been locked in combat with his stepfather since puberty. The "angel" part of the name was given because he'd pulled several guys out of tough spots.

Not Rob, though, he thought, feeling another hard

tug in his gut. He hadn't been able to pull Rob out of his tough spot.

Callie chewed the inside of her bottom lip and waved her hand toward the house. "Come in."

Brock followed her into the dark interior of the cottage. He heard her whack her leg against an end table and she made a quick hissing sound of pain.

"You want me to turn on a light or open one of the blinds?" he asked.

"No. I'll do it," she muttered, moving toward a large window and adjusting the blinds so that the sun illuminated the room. The couch was covered with a dark throw, the walls were bare of pictures and the hardwood floor was rugless. "I worked late last night—well, really into the morning," she added. "I guess I overslept." She whipped around to face him, stumbling again.

Brock instinctively grabbed her arms to keep her upright. With one red-gold strand over one eye, she looked at him and he was close enough to count her eyelashes and freckles. He'd heard stories about the placement of some of those freckles.

"What time is it anyway?" she asked in a sleep-husky voice that reminded him of sex.

Hell, everything reminded him of sex. It had been too damn long since he'd gotten any. "Fourteen hun—" He stopped, remembering he didn't need to speak in military time. "Two o'clock in the afternoon."

She winced. "I didn't realize it was so late." A cat prowled into the room and wrapped around her ankles. "Bet you're hungry, Oscar," she said to the feline then glanced at him. "I'll start some coffee."

She took a step, nearly tripped over the cat, righted herself then left the room.

A little klutzy in the morning, he recalled Rob telling him and felt a twitch of humor. Only this wasn't morning, at least not for most people.

Brock glanced around the spare, bare room. It didn't feel right. Rob had described Callie as if she never took a break from creating and decorating. Every room had a theme. She didn't know the meaning of the word bland. He frowned. This room was definitely bland.

He wandered down the hallway where he heard water running from a faucet. The kitchen was small, but sunny with a clean sink and clean counters. There was no kitchen table. Instead a chair stood at the end of the counter where he spotted a sketch pad, a box of Frosted Lucky Charms and Little Debbie Swiss Cake Rolls.

Uh-oh. Swiss Cake Rolls were PMS and deadline food. Brock approached her warily. "Are you on deadline?"

She nodded. "I got behind when Rob—" She broke off and sighed. "I couldn't draw for a while. I can now, but I'm not sure any of it is right. I'm still not reaching for happy, light colors and I'm supposed to be illustrating happy, light books. Three of them. I've done all the rainy, sad, gray scenes," she said, staring expectantly at the coffee aker. "Four times."

A suspicion was forming in his gut. "Looks like

a nice little island," he ventured. "Do you like your neighbors?"

She ran her hand through her hair. "I haven't had time to meet them. I don't get out much."

His suspicion intensified. "I'm staying here for a while. Can you recommend a couple of restaurants?"

She bit her lip. "Y'know, I haven't had a lot of time. I've done most of my grocery shopping at the quick-mart."

He nodded, rubbing his chin. So Rob's concern for Callie had been justified—she'd turned into a hermit.

The coffee flowed into the carafe and she pulled two mugs out of the cabinet. Pouring the coffee, she looked up. "I don't have cream. Would you like sugar?"

He shook his head and accepted the mug she offered. "Black is fine."

She cradled her mug in both hands and took a quick sip then glanced up at him. "Rob really admired you."

"It was mutual. Rob was well-liked and respected. He was a mechanical whiz and he talked about you all the time."

She rolled her eyes. "He must have bored you guys to death."

He shook his head. "He gave us a nice break from the tension." He paused. "I'm sorry I couldn't make it to his funeral. The doctor wouldn't let me out of the hospital."

"Understandable," she said, lowering her gaze to

her cup so that her eyelashes shielded her expression from him. "You were hurt when the mine…" She shrugged as if she didn't want to finish. "I didn't want Rob to join the Marines. It was one of the few things we argued about."

"Why? Too dangerous?"

"At the time he joined, I don't think I realized how dangerous it could be. I just didn't want to move and move and move. I wanted us to make a home, a haven, and stay there forever."

"But you moved here after he died," Brock pointed out.

She shook her head. "Too many memories. I felt like I was bumping into him, into our dreams, every three minutes." She met his gaze. "So why are you here?"

Not ready to reveal Rob's last request, he glanced down at his leg. "I'm almost finished with my rehabilitation and I couldn't stand being tied to the center one more minute. I decided a few weeks at the beach before I take my job sounded good."

"Why this beach?" she asked, her eyes skeptical. She was waking up and she wasn't stupid.

"It's quiet, not too commercial." He cracked a grin. "If I fall on my face when I take my morning run, no one will see me and laugh."

Her gaze shifted. She was still skeptical, but more amused. "Something tells me you don't have much experience falling on your face."

"Not until this year."

Her half smile faded. "I'm sorry."

"I'm sorry about Rob."

"Thanks. Me, too," she said and gave him a con-sidering glance. "If this was a duty call, consider it done."

He nodded, but inside he was shaking his head. The woman lived at the beach, but her skin was as white as the sand and the circles under her eyes were vio-let. She looked too thin and as though she were stuck in neutral. He needed to at least get her into first gear.

Brock settled into his condo which was about a quarter-mile north of Callie's. Sitting on the balcony, he watched the waves rhythmically rolling in and felt a measure of peace wash through him. The ocean wasn't about war. It changed every second, but in many ways remained constant. Watching the tide provided the best therapy he'd been given in months, and Lord knew the military had made damn sure he'd received a truckload of therapy.

As he climbed into bed and fell asleep, an image of Callie Newton drifted through his mind. He won-dered what she was doing right this minute. Was she staring at a blank canvas? Was she drawing yet an-other dark picture? Or was she falling asleep just like he was? He remembered being fascinated by the photograph of her that Rob had proudly displayed. She'd been laughing with abandon. She'd looked like the female equivalent of sunshine. She and Rob could have posed for matching bookends of the all-

American boy and girl. Rob had miraculously managed to get through boot camp without having his upbeat attitude beat out of him. Rob had been a nice uncynical guy, not like Brock. Brock had enough cynicism for a dozen men. Maybe that was why he'd been drawn to Rob and his stories about his wife. They'd seemed fresh and innocent. Brock couldn't remember feeling fresh and innocent, not since his father died when he was seven years old.

His mind drifted back to Callie. Even though the sadness in her eyes twisted his gut, something about being in her presence made him breathe a little easier. He sensed she might demand perfection of herself and in her work, but she didn't demand it of others. He frowned, wondering why she seemed sexy to him.

Her hair was a seductive red-gold curtain and her white skin emphasized her femininity. Her lips reminded him of a juicy plum and that damn T-shirt had made him want to play hide-and-seek with her curves.

He felt himself grow hard and swore under his breath. His attraction to Callie wasn't personal. He was frustrated—sexually, personally, mentally. Tossing off the covers, he walked naked to the shower. *Forget the cold water.* He turned on the warm spray and stepped inside where he could take care of at least part of his frustration with any woman he chose to picture in his mind.

* * *

The following morning, he rose at six o'clock. The Marine Corps had conditioned him to rise early. He didn't know if he'd ever be able to sleep in again. He fixed a breakfast of scrambled eggs, toast and coffee and read the newspaper, showered and dressed in running shorts and a tank, then walked down the beach to Callie's cottage at ten o'clock.

The first step to feeling normal was sleeping at night and working during the day. Callie was like a baby who had her nights and days mixed up. She needed a little help to deconfuse them. He rapped on the front door to the darkened, quiet house and waited. And waited. He rubbed the toe of his running shoe on a rough place in the concrete on her porch then knocked again.

He heard a loud bang and "Ouch!" and shook his head. The door jerked open and she squinted up at him. "Why do I feel like I've done this before?"

"Sorry. I thought you'd be awake by now," he fudged. "I remember hearing that you liked to run, so I wondered if you would like to join me this morning for a slow jog. My leg's not a hundred percent, so I have to move a little more slowly than I'd like."

"Run?" she echoed and looked outside. "Now? What time is it?"

"Ten o'clock," he said.

"Oh," she murmured, pushing her hair from her face. "I had a late night last night working on a drawing," she said. "That I probably won't use," she added in a dark, disgusted tone, and sighed.

"If you're not up to it…" he ventured, checking to see if she had enough fire in her to rise to the challenge.

She frowned. "I'm up to it," she retorted waspishly. "I may be a little rusty because it's been a while, but I'm up to it."

He nodded, approving the hint of a kick in her response. That was a good sign. "You want me to wait out here while you change?"

She glanced down at her nightshirt as if she'd just realized she still had it on. Her cheeks colored. "Yeah, I should have— I was—" She shrugged and waved him inside. "You can come in. It won't take me long."

"Thanks," he murmured and followed her in the door, catching a draft of her sweet, sleepy scent. It was a fresh, sexy smell that made him want to bury his face in her hair. The thought took him by surprise and he shook his head.

She hurried down the hallway and the cat greeted him with a sniff then dismissed him. He'd never understood the appeal of cats. Felines didn't come when they were called. They expected to be fed and sheltered, yet pretty much disdained their owners. Now, dogs were a different story.

Callie returned with her hair pulled back in a ponytail. She wore a tight sporty tank top and a little pair of shorts that rode below her belly button. A few of the nurses at the rehab center had come on to him, but none of them had been dressed like this.

Damn, he'd been locked up entirely too long. He was beginning to feel like a raging bundle of hormones. Before the accident, he'd had his share of women. He'd never had any problem finding a willing woman. Rob had said he went through women with the same ease a lot of men went through a six-pack of beer. It wasn't far from the truth. He'd always made it clear he wasn't making any promises—he didn't want to put in the time a *relationship* required.

Ungluing his gaze from Callie's bare belly, he raked his hand through his hair. "You ready?"

She moved her head in an indecisive circle. "Let's go."

They hit the beach and twenty-three minutes later Brock was afraid she was going to keel over before she'd tell him she'd had enough. "There's a coffee shop. You want to stop?"

She came to an abrupt stop and met his gaze with a mixture of wariness and relief. "Do you?"

She was clearly prickly, so he took a light approach. "If you get heat exhaustion, it would be a real hassle to have to haul you back to your cottage with my bum leg."

She frowned. "Are you denigrating my level of physical fitness?"

"Not at all. You look physically *fine* to me. You just might be a little out of practice."

She opened her mouth as if to protest then seemed to think better of it.

"Let me buy you breakfast," he said, moving toward the coffee shop.

She groaned. "I'm so overheated I'll never be able to eat," she muttered.

"We'll see," he said.

Twenty-five minutes later—after Callie had downed three glasses of ice water, a glass of orange juice and a cup of coffee—she was tearing into her hotcakes, eggs and bacon as if she hadn't eaten in days.

"More syrup?" he asked, lifting the small pitcher.

She shook her head. "Thanks, no."

"More pancakes?" he asked, unable to keep his humor from his voice.

She glanced up at him with her mouth full of pancake and searched his gaze. She chewed and swallowed. "Go ahead and say it," she said, taking a sip of coffee.

"Say what?"

"That you told me I'd want breakfast. How did you know, anyway?"

"If what I saw on your kitchen counter was any indication of what was inside the cabinets then you must be craving some substance. Cereal can't satisfy forever. How long has it been since you've had some protein?"

"Not that long," she said with a trace of defensiveness in her voice.

He nodded. "Good. What'd you have?"

Chewing another bite of pancake, she blinked then looked away. "Last week I had some cheese…"

Her words had faded and turned unintelligible. "Excuse me? You had some cheese what?"

She frowned at him and played with the strawberry garnish on her plate. "I had some cheese crackers last week."

"Oh," he said, swallowing a grin. "Good to know you're sticking with the pyramid diet plan."

She picked up the strawberry then set it down. "I don't put a high priority on eating when I'm on deadline."

"Hey, I'm with you. When I've been in a crunch, I've eaten peanut M&M's and coffee."

"Well it's good to know you bow to your baser urges every now and then. I suspect it doesn't happen very often."

Not as often as he'd like to give in to his baser urges, he thought as he watched her lift the strawberry to her lips.

"Are you sure you want to itch all day?"

Her eyes widened and she set the strawberry down. "How did you know I was allergic to them?"

"Rob told me."

She rolled her eyes in disgust. "What a big mouth. What else did he tell you?"

"Just your complete family, health, educational, professional and romantic history."

"Well that stinks," she said. "You know everything about me and I don't know diddly about you except how smart he said you were and what a good leader he said you were and how fast he said you could run."

Brock felt an itchy discomfort at the thought of Rob's praise. "Can't run all that fast anymore."

"You can outrun me."

"Yeah, but you're totally out of sh—" He broke off as her eyes widened.

"I didn't have any Marine training to get your buff body," she said, lifting her chin. "Look at those muscles," she said, pointing to his arms. "You're just a show-off."

Brock chuckled at the same time he felt a strange rush of pleasure at her backhanded compliment. He gave her feminine curves a once-over then a twice-over for good measure. "Trust me. Your body is no hardship on the eyes."

She met his gaze and something snapped and flickered between them.

She cleared her throat and took a sip of ice water. "You're too kind," she murmured. "Thanks for breakfast. I think I can walk back to my cottage now." She smiled. "See, now I have the excuse that I shouldn't exercise after I've just eaten."

"True," he said, tossing a few bucks on the table to cover the tip. "Must have felt great, though, your blood pumping through your veins, the ocean breeze on your face, the sun shining down," he teased.

"The onset of heatstroke," she added, deadpan. "Are you sure the Marines don't train you to have a sadistic streak a mile wide?" she asked over her shoulder as they left the coffee shop.

"Nah," he said, his gaze latching onto her curvy backside. *You can look, but you can't touch.* "Masochists. We're all masochists."

Two

Marine Lingo Translation
Semper Gumby: Unofficial motto—
Always Flexible.

The next morning when Brock knocked on Callie's door, she was still in her nightshirt, but she was awake. *Progress,* he thought as she opened the door. "I'm running a little late. I got on a roll and didn't go to bed until the middle of the night," she said. "Although I'd planned to go to bed early so I wouldn't embarrass myself during our run this morning. Looks hot out there."

"Eighty-two and the humidity is—"

"Three hundred percent," she said with a wry grin. "One of the charms of living at the shore. It won't take me but a minute to change. Are you sure you don't want to go by yourself? I'll just hold you back."

No, she wouldn't. He'd already gone for a run

once this morning. "Not a chance. Hey, when are you going to show me your etchings?"

"I don't know," she said warily. "I haven't been feeling all that confident about my work lately. I think I'd rather show my scars than my art."

"Is that your appendectomy scar or your bicycle accident scar?" he asked.

Her eyes widened like saucers. "There you go again. Geez, was there anything he did *not* tell you?"

"I'll tell you when I notice something."

She gave a grumble of disgust. "Well, this has got to change. It's not fair. You're going to have to cough up some information about yourself."

He shrugged. "No problem. There's not much to tell though. I'm not nearly as fascinating as you are."

She rolled her eyes. "Yeah, right." She wagged her finger at him. "Give me a minute and be prepared to answer some questions while we're running."

A few minutes later, they hit the beach and she immediately started shooting questions at him. "Favorite color?"

"Same as yours, blue," he said.

She smiled and shook her head. "Birthplace?"

"Columbus, Ohio. You were born in Pine Creek, North Carolina."

"What will you do now that you're out of the Marines?"

"Architecture. I majored in architecture in college and specialized in structural analysis. I'll be working for a major firm in Atlanta."

She wrinkled her nose. "I don't like big cities."

"Yeah, I know. Rob mentioned that. Atlanta's got a lot going on. That was my best job offer and it seemed like a good place to start over."

She slowed. "Do you mind when people mention your military career?"

"No," he said, shaking his head. "I just don't want to talk about it a lot. As you know, it didn't end the way I thought it would."

Her gaze softened with sadness and sympathy. "You've had a rough recovery, haven't you?"

He wanted to say that it could have been worse, but he didn't want to make her feel bad. "My drill instructor from boot camp visited me when I'd been in the hospital just a couple of weeks and told me if I started feeling sorry for myself, he was going to round up his men and hold a Victoria's Secret panty party for me."

"How charming. Was that supposed to be motivation?"

He chuckled. "In a way. Sergeant Roscoe is an expert at motivation. He called us all kinds of flattering, uplifting names in boot camp. Ladies, knuckleheads, maggots— I probably shouldn't repeat any more."

"What a jerk. Every time Rob told me about boot camp, it made me nuts. It's so barbaric, so disrespectful."

"The point was to learn respect and loyalty in a short amount of time."

"Well, I don't see why they had to be so rude about it."

"It offends your artistic sensibilities," he said, unable to keep a grin from his face.

"It offends my every sensibility," she huffed, shaking her head. "Okay, another question. Your favorite food? Let me guess, steak and potato."

He couldn't resist teasing her. "I was going to say quiche or those little cucumber sandwiches they serve at tea."

She did a double take. "Oh, you're pulling my leg."

"You have two very nice legs. Why can't I pull one?"

Her lips lifted in a smile and she chuckled. "You're funnier than I would have predicted," she said.

He looked at her eyes. Still not sparkling the way they had in that photograph he'd looked at so many times when he'd been in the desert. *You're sadder than I expected,* he thought, but didn't say it aloud. He wanted to change it. It was strange as hell, but he wanted to see her laughing with abandon again. He wondered what it would take.

"You're trying to distract me into slowing down, so you don't get a good run," he said, picking up the pace just a little.

She made a face. "Haven't we already had a *good* run?"

Brock just gave an evil chuckle.

By the time they returned to her cottage, she had extracted from him bits of his family history and even some of his romantic history. His leg was starting to ache.

She must have noticed his limp. "Come in and have something to drink before you leave."

"Do you have anything?" he teased, reminding her of her bare cupboards.

She gave a moue of reproach. "Of course I do. I have water and coffee. I may even have a flat soda."

"How can I resist? Throw in a tour of your studio and it's a deal."

She wrinkled her nose as she pulled open her screen door. "Do I have to?"

"You could always show me your scars," he suggested.

Her gaze met his and he felt the crackling sensation zip between them again. "Okay, I'll show you my studio, but make it snappy."

Curious, he accepted a glass of water and followed her into a back room with only bedsheets for window coverings. It was filled with drawings, and the floor was carpeted with discarded, balled-up sheets of paper. A large table sat before the window.

He drew closer to a casually arranged collection of drawings of a little girl with wide eyes and blond hair that stuck out. In one, the clouds hovering over her had wispy faces that looked like monsters. In another, the wind whipped her against a tree. In another, rain drenched her even though she carried a red umbrella.

"She doesn't look like she has a lot of luck with weather," he said.

"Those are the dark pictures I told you about. Now I need to do the bright, happy, sunny pictures. I'm not sure how."

"You could fake it," he suggested.

"Fake it?" she echoed in disapproval.

"You could pretend to be in a bright, happy, sunny mood for a few hours and see what happens. We had to pretend to like a lot of things we really didn't like when I was on active duty."

She looked skeptical. "I don't know. Art is about being authentic."

He nodded and shrugged. "Just a suggestion." He glanced around the room and his gaze fell on a picture of the ocean on a cloudy day. The way she'd mingled blue, gray and white drew him. A discarded red life preserver drifted aimlessly.

"What do you think of it?" she asked.

"Do you want me to be honest?"

"Yeah, I can take it," she said with a smile in her voice.

"There's something moody and sexy about it. The red of the life preserver reminds me of red lipstick. This isn't going in your kid book, is it?"

"No." She laughed. "I guess you could say this is one of my few grown-up pictures."

"Ever thought about having a show?" he asked.

"Not unless I'm forced."

"Why not?"

She shrugged. "I don't know. I think it might be easier to walk naked down Main Street. I put so much of myself in my paintings."

"Hmm," he said, looking again at her grown-up picture.

"What does 'hmm' mean?" she asked, looking at him curiously.

"I just had a philosophical thought," he said and grinned. "Don't worry. It'll pass."

"What?" she asked. "What's your philosophical thought?"

"What do you see as the purpose of your art?" he asked, thinking back to the art appreciation course he'd taken in college.

She paused thoughtfully. "I think my art may be multipurpose. There's self-expression, of course, and with Phoebe over there, there's sympathy and emotion. Identification. Haven't we all had a bad day when the weather was horrible?"

"So your pictures make people feel less alone," he said.

She paused again then slowly smiled. "I guess so."

"And a show might give some different people the opportunity to enjoy your drawings and feel less alone," he said.

"I hadn't thought of it that way. I just break out in a cold sweat thinking about exposing myself." She wrapped her arms around herself. "Rob always wanted me to do a show." She closed her eyes. "But Rob also wanted me to skydive, ride a bicycle with no hands and go skinny-dipping in high school."

"Extreme boyfriend," he said with a chuckle.

She smiled and met his gaze. "That would be

right. He was always dragging me off on one adventure or another."

"Did you like it?"

"Sometimes. Sometimes I just wanted to be my little boring self drawing on a pad of paper while I sat under the kitchen table."

"Now, see, I would think it could get a little cramped under the kitchen table."

"Think of it as a pup tent. It felt safe."

She was so freakin' cute he had the overwhelming urge to take her in his arms and make her feel safe. Which wasn't like Brock at all. Maybe that concussion had left permanent damage? "How'd the skinny-dip turn out?"

She tossed him a sideways glance. "We got caught. Well, I guess I should say I got caught. When we heard someone drive up, Rob pulled on his shorts, but my clothes had disappeared. I stayed in that creek so long my entire body turned blue."

Brock swallowed a chuckle. "That's a new one. I never heard that story."

"Probably because I told Rob I wouldn't speak to him again if he told anyone."

Brock saw her expression change from amused frustration to wistfulness and felt his gut twist. He shifted his stance and the papers rustled beneath his feet, distracting her.

"Look at this mess," she said. "I need to pick these up and toss them."

He bent down to help her. "I noticed there was more on the floor than on the walls or easels."

She laughed. "A lot more. One of the secrets of

getting past a block is not being afraid to waste some paint by drawing something that really stinks."

He started to uncurl one of the balled-up pieces of discarded paper and she immediately caught his hand.

"Oh, no. Absolutely not. I let you look at my studio, but I draw the line at allowing you to look at my stinkers."

"How do you know they're really stinkers? I might think they're good."

"It doesn't matter what you think. It matters what I think."

He glanced down at her slim, artistic fingers over his larger hand and felt an odd stirring inside him. He looked up into her resolute don't-mess-with-me gaze. "Are you sure you've never been a drill instructor? You sure can be bossy for a little thing."

"I may not be able to control what goes on outside this room, and I'm not always happy with what I create inside this room, but I make the rules for this room."

"The goddess of your little corner of the universe," he said, understanding her need for control.

"I wouldn't use the term 'goddess,'" she said dryly.

"You're not looking at you," he said and surrendered the ball of discarded paper even though he was curious as hell.

She stared at him and he felt the electrical zap between them again. She must have felt it, too, because he saw her catch her breath. She quickly pulled her hand from his.

"He told me you were good with the ladies," she said. "Flattering a woman must be second nature to you."

He shrugged, but didn't say anything. He knew a no-win conversation with a woman when he saw it coming.

"What? No answer? What are you thinking?"

"You don't really want to know."

"Yes, I do."

He shook his head and scooped up another piece of paper. "Nah."

He felt her hand on his arm. "I want to know. Fair is fair. You know all about me."

Uncomfortable, he sighed. "Okay, you're gonna think this is cocky as hell, but I don't have to flatter women. I haven't had to work that hard to get a woman's attention."

She opened her mouth then shut it. "That's pretty cocky."

"I told you."

"Right," she said. "Rob told me you didn't keep any of them around too long, either."

He shouldn't care what she might think of his lack of commitment, but he did. "I never made promises I couldn't keep. Everything always felt temporary—in college, in the Corps."

She nodded, but he could tell she didn't understand and it bothered him. "I don't know why I always had it easy with females."

"Oh, I know," she said. "They want to tame you. You have this dark, restless look about you that makes women want to domesticate you."

"You said women," he told her in a low voice. "Does that include you?"

"N-no, no no no," she said, taking a step back. "I may illustrate children's books, but I don't live in never-never land. I've never gone for the dark, brooding type. They always seemed like too much work and angst."

Glimpsing a reluctant fascination in her gaze that belied her words, he casually took a step toward her. "You think I'm dark and brooding?"

"Well, you're not exactly a laugh a minute," she said, biting her lip.

"Do I make you nervous, Callie?"

Her eyes said *yes,* but she shook her head. "Not really."

He shook his head and narrowed his eyes. "Why do I make you nervous?"

She crossed her arms over her chest. "I just said that you don't."

"I'm not convinced."

She looked away from him and sighed. "You're just different than what I'm used to."

"You're used to the boy-next-door dragging you off on little adventures."

"Yeah." She pushed a strand of hair behind her ear, and the expression in her eyes held warring glints of grief and a forbidden curiosity that was all too easy for him to understand, because he felt the same burning curiosity about Callie.

Three

Marine Lingo Translation
Commando: Not wearing underwear.

Brock didn't see Callie for more than ten minutes during the next three days. Shin splints prevented her from running on Tuesday and it rained nearly non-stop on Wednesday and Thursday as tropical depression Bettina revved up to tropical storm Bettina.

Brock ran despite the rain. He struggled with what he needed to do next to get through to Callie. He also struggled with how much he thought about her when she wasn't around. He put it down to unfinished business. As soon as he could help Callie out of the hole she was hiding in, she wouldn't occupy so much of his mind and he would be able to move on.

When the lights started flickering in the afternoon, he thought about her bare cupboard and nearly bare refrigerator and made a quick trip to the grocery store before everything shut down. By the time he knocked on her front door, he and the bags he carried were drenched.

Callie opened the door and stared at him. "What are you doing—" She broke off and tried to take one of the bags from his arms, but he held tight.

Her eyebrows puckering in a frown, she tugged on his arm. "Come in, you nutcase. Don't you know there's a hurricane coming?"

"That's why I brought you some food," he said, allowing her to guide him to the kitchen where he set the bags on the counter. "I figured by the time you realized you didn't have anything to eat the convenience store would be closed and you would be hungry and SOL."

"SOL?" she repeated with a confused expression on her face. "Oh, *surely out of luck,*" she translated.

"That's the Disney version," he muttered.

She shook her head. "I could get offended by your lack of confidence in my ability to take care of myself," she fumed as she began to unload the bags.

"I got bread, milk, eggs, cheese, pancake mix, a couple of steaks, a few frozen and canned staples and chocolate-covered peanuts."

Her eyes rounded and she dug through the second bag and pulled out the box. "Double dipper chocolate-covered peanuts! Oh, you have no idea how much I love—" She broke off and tossed him a sideways glance then rolled her eyes. "Oh, yes you do. Rob must have told you."

Brock nodded.

"Okay, in exchange for your gift of double dippers I can forgive your lack of faith in me."

His lips twitched at her cockeyed point of view. "That's mighty generous of you," he said, feeling a strange warmth from seeing her again even though she'd scolded him.

Her gaze fell over him and she gasped. She touched his damp cheek with her soft hand. "You're drenched and I've been standing here fussing at you. Do you want to shower? No, don't answer. You should shower before the electricity goes completely out—and it will," she said knowingly. "If you hurry, I can put your clothes in the dryer. So hurry," she said, shooing him into the hall. She grabbed a couple of towels from the closet and pushed them into his hands.

"Just toss your clothes out the door as soon as you get undressed."

"I can handle being wet. It's not a big deal," he said.

"It is when you don't have any dry clothes to change into."

"I've got plenty back at my cottage."

She blinked. "Oh, I thought you were going to join me for dinner."

Her husky invitation did something weird to his gut. "I guess I could."

Her lips curved in a slow smile. "Then if we want to eat, we'd better hurry before the electricity goes out."

His stomach growling at the thought of steak, he stepped into the bathroom, shucked his clothes and tossed them in the hall as she'd suggested. He turned her shower on hot, quickly lathered his body and rinsed. He had to concede Callie had been right. The shower felt great. It reminded him of how good a shower had felt coming in from the field. A shower followed by a couple of cold beers, a hot meal and a hotter woman provided a little respite from the uncertainty.

He rubbed himself dry with one towel and ran his fingers through his hair. Glancing around her bathroom, he saw her silk bathrobe hanging on the back of the door and gave in to the urge to touch it. He suspected her skin was just as soft, only warmer. He thought of her rosebud mouth and licked his own lips. Where were these thoughts coming from? Shaking his head to clear it, he wrapped the second towel around his waist and ventured into the hallway. He heard the rattle of pots and pans in the kitchen and turned in that direction.

"Need some help?" he asked as he rounded the corner.

Callie looked up from the bag of frozen mixed vegetables she was pouring into a pot and stared openmouthed at him. He could feel her hazel gaze track every inch of his bare skin from his throat and shoulders to his chest down to his abdomen over the towel that covered him to just above his knees.

Her hand shifted and the vegetables began to spill onto the stove top.

"Whoa," he said, stepping forward to reposition her hand.

Her hand trembled beneath his.

"Sorry, I didn't mean to startle you."

She jerked her hand away from his as if he'd scorched her. She shook her head and backed away, her gaze drifting to his chest repeatedly. "No, I just—uh—" She swallowed and met his gaze.

Brock glanced down at his bare torso and saw the tracks of his wounds from the explosion. He'd grown accustomed to the scars, but Callie hadn't ever seen them. His gut twisted. Maybe his scars made Callie think of Rob. "Is it the scars?"

She blinked and shook her head. "Uh, no," she said sounding surprised. "No, it's—"

"It's what?"

Embarrassment crossed her face and she looked away. "It's the muscles."

It took him a moment to comprehend what she'd said and when he did, he felt a roar of pleasure he couldn't recall feeling in a long time. So, her emotions weren't totally dead after all. That was good. It was part of the plan. Her attraction to him, however, wasn't part of the plan, but he wasn't inclined to discourage it at the moment.

"Thanks for the compliment," he said quietly, feeling a grin play around his lips.

She risked a glance at him. "I'm sure tons of women have complimented your body."

"Not lately," he said.

"Whose choice is that?"

He shrugged. "It hasn't been a priority." His body would disagree.

"Do you think you're not as attractive because of your scars?"

"I haven't really cared," he said, and it was true. "I feel different now. It's more than the limp and the scars. I haven't figured it all out yet."

"Inside," she said thoughtfully.

"Yeah." He inhaled and caught a whiff of beef broiling. "The steaks aren't burning, are they?"

"Oh no!" Her eyes widened and she jerked open the oven door. A sizzling sound immediately filled the air and she pulled the steaks from the oven. "They don't look too bad, but you're out of luck if you wanted yours rare."

"If it's not as tough as shoe leather, I'll consider it perfect," he said and glanced at the toaster oven. "You think the bread—"

"Yes, I do," she said, pulling out the biscuits. "Oh, look, the veggies are boiling. They won't take any time. I think you got some margarine," she said, pulling a stick from the refrigerator. "We're almost set."

Brock grabbed plates and cups from the cupboard, Callie collected the flatware and, within moments, they took their plates into the den to eat.

"Sorry I don't have a kitchen table," she said as she sat on the floor across from him. "That's on my to-do list."

The lights flickered and he could almost feel her hold her breath. They came back on and she sighed.

"I know they'll probably go out for hours, but I want it put off as long as possible."

"Are you afraid of the dark?" he asked, then took a bite of steak that was slightly overcooked, but still tasty.

"No," she said, taking a sip of water. "And yes.

"I'm not really afraid of the dark. I just don't like not being able to have light when I want it."

He nodded, amused. "So it's more of a convenience issue."

"For the most part," she said. "There's also the side effect of how other senses are sharpened to compensate for the one you can't use."

"Things that go bump in the night."

"Yeah, aliens under the bed, in the closet." She took a bite of steak and swallowed.

"But you're not really afraid."

"Right," she said, as she opened a biscuit and poured honey on it. "If I keep telling myself that, it will come true, right?"

Brock chuckled. "Yeah, right."

"Are you afraid of anything? Oh, wait, you're a Marine, so you're not allowed to be afraid."

"Everybody's afraid of something, Callie."

She met his gaze, and understanding and something more flickered between them.

"I just try not to let my fears get in my way, and when they do, I do something about them." He took another bite of steak and thought about why he was here with Callie right now. It was because he was afraid he would never be able to sleep at night and face his image in the mirror each morning if he didn't at least try to help Rob's widow. He knew he couldn't bring back Rob, but he could at least make sure the woman his buddy left behind wasn't hiding from humanity for the rest of her life.

The lights flickered again and again, and the house turned dark. "Looks like you got the food ready just in time. Where do you keep your candles and flashlights?"

"In the kitchen," she muttered and he heard her stand.

"I can help."

"No, that's okay. Just guard my plate so the cat doesn't get my food."

He chuckled. "I can do that."

He heard her stumble around in the kitchen, bumping into things, opening and closing drawers. After a couple of minutes, he couldn't stand it anymore and he picked up both plates and carefully walked into the kitchen.

"I'm right behind you," he murmured, not wanting her to back into him and upset the plates.

She gave a squeak of surprise and he successfully avoided her then set the plates on the counter.

"Matches," she said. "I can't find the matches. They should be in this drawer."

"Let me try," he said, finding her arm with his hand and following it to the drawer. Some part of him was reluctant to trade the smooth sensation of her skin for the articles in the drawer, but he did. His hand brushed hers in the search for the matches and he felt an odd sensual thrill. He heard her catch her breath and wondered if she felt it, too. His fingers closed around a small rectangular cardboard object. "Got it. Where are your flashlights anyway?"

"Bedroom," she said.

"Ah, to ward off the aliens under the bed."

"Right. I've got the candle right here."

Brock struck the match, lighting it on the first try, and quickly lit the candle. He looked at the soft light illuminating Callie's features and felt a warmth grow in his belly. "You look like an angel." The words spilled out impulsively and he immediately felt self-conscious.

"It's the candlelight. Everyone looks angelic."

"Not me," he said dryly.

She smiled. "Maybe a dark angel."

"That's a stretch."

She laughed. "Here," she said, putting the wick of another candle against the lit one. It hit him that this was what some people did during wedding ceremonies. Alarm rushed through him. Now that was just too weird.

"I'll go get the flashlights now."

She returned with the flashlights and a battery-operated radio. "Good girl," he said.

"I may seem like an unprepared flake, but I'm not. We'd better finish eating before the food gets cold."

Finishing before she did, he messed with the radio and found an AM station where the deejay reported massive blackouts. The electric company warned that power might not return until morning.

"Oh, goody," she muttered. "I guess I won't be working tonight."

"Do you have any cards?"

"Somewhere. I haven't played in a while."

"I thought you might like to try to beat me at James Bond Junior."

She gave a double take. "I always beat Rob at James Bond Junior."

"But can you beat me?"

She lifted an eyebrow. "We'll have to see."

He won the first two games and she was not at all happy. The way she fumed reminded him of a buzzing honey bee.

"I demand a rematch. Those first two games were flukes."

"Flukes?" he echoed, enjoying taunting her just a little. "You're just peeved because I'm beating the pants off of you."

"My pants are staying exactly where they are," she retorted. "You're the one who's still not dressed. That's your secret weapon."

"What *are* you talking about?"

"Your chest. It's distracting. That's why you're winning. You play dirty."

He brushed her backhanded compliment aside, although he felt flattered as hell. "I wouldn't call it dirty," he said. "I just always play to win. You want to go again?"

She met his gaze and he saw her bite her lip as she glanced at his chest then back to his face. Her expression was shockingly hungry and sexual. He immediately turned hard. He wanted to bring her small artist's hand to his chest and feel her touch. He wanted to take that plump lip she was biting with his mouth and tongue. He wanted to slide his hands over the wonderland of her body and feel every inch of her skin against every inch of his. Then he wanted to sink himself so deep inside her—

"Go again," she said in a husky voice. "I'll win this time."

The game began and he heard her breath and inhaled her scent. With every flip of the cards, he felt himself grow hotter. The image of her hair hanging around his face like a curtain, skimming over his bare skin, down his belly. He told himself to stop, but his body spurred his mind on. He wanted her small breasts in his mouth. He wanted to be inside her where it was warm and good.

"James Bond Junior," she said triumphantly. "I told you I would win."

"So you did," he said.

"What do you want to do now?"

"Nothing, I ought to—" he muttered under his breath.

"Pardon? I didn't hear you."

"Nothing," he said, moving his tight shoulders. It felt like his entire body was stretched tight. He suddenly felt her hand over his and his heart stopped.

"Brock?"

"Yeah?"

"If I ask you a question, would you answer it with the truth?"

His heart started beating again, way too fast. Her hand felt like a branding iron and he grit his teeth to keep from turning his palm over and pulling her to him. "What is this? Truth or dare now?"

"Just truth. Why did you come to see me?"

He sighed, conflicted. "Why do you ask?"

"Because I want to know."

"He was afraid you would turn into a hermit if something happened to him."

She made a sound of disgust and jerked her hand away. "I haven't become a hermit. I've been independent. I even moved to the beach. I always told him I'd wanted to live at the beach."

He raked his hand through his hair. If they were going down this road, then he was going to make her face the truth. "How many people have you met since you moved here?"

"My landlord and a boy who was looking for his dog," she said defensively.

"Callie, you haven't even spent more than thirty minutes in a grocery store. You're white as a ghost because you sleep all day and work at night."

"Maybe I'm part vampire," she joked.

She was sucking the restraint out of him. "You've done what Rob was afraid you would do. You've become a hermit. You haven't made any friends. You haven't gotten involved with anything or anyone. You've cut yourself off from the rest of the world."

"I have not. It's just taking me a while to find my—" She broke off as if she couldn't find the word.

"What? Your mojo?"

She snorted. "I never had a mojo."

"That's a matter of opinion."

She stared at him. "What do you mean?"

"You've obviously got some kind of mojo going with your art," he said with a shrug. "And I'm sure there are plenty of men, given the opportunity," he added meaningfully, "who would like to help you explore your mojo."

"I don't want anyone but Rob," she whispered, and the pain in her eyes chipped at his heart.

"I know, but he wants you to go on. He wouldn't want you to live this way."

She closed her eyes. "I can't love anyone."

Unable to keep himself from touching her, he took her hand in his. "If ever someone was made to love, it was you, Callie. I could have told you that just by looking at the photo Rob kept of you."

"But how do you love when you don't feel like living?" she asked him, opening her eyes to search his.

"You wake up every morning and you put one foot in front of the other. You go through the motions until you start to feel again, and you will."

She took a careful breath. "So your coming here was a pity call, after all."

He shook his head. "You've got your pain. I've got

my demons. I can't help thinking I should have been the one to die."

She turned her head away from him and he had the odd sensation of the sun turning its back on him. He couldn't blame her if she thought he should have been the one to die instead of Rob.

She turned back to him, lifting her chin. "Rob wouldn't want you to be thinking that way, would he?"

He let out a breath he hadn't known he'd been holding. "No, Rob was a great guy," he said. *And I want his wife so bad I can taste it.*

Four

Marine Lingo Translation
RON: Remain Overnight

"I'm an introvert. I was born an introvert. What if I don't want to be friendly and meet new people?" Callie argued as they took a fast walk on the beach the next morning.

After her electricity finally came on near midnight, Brock returned to his cottage, downed a beer, willed his brain not to think and fell asleep. His Marine conditioning was unforgiving, however, and he'd awakened early. After a run on the beach, he read the newspaper and visited Callie to coax her out for a walk.

The sun shone like diamonds on the water while the tide washed over the beat-up beach. "You have to make yourself. You need to meet new people whether you want to or not."

Her jaw tightened and she frowned. "I shouldn't have to if I don't want to."

"That's a selfish attitude," Brock said bluntly.

Her eyes rounded and she stopped dead in her tracks. "I'm not selfish. I'm just not outgoing. I'm more comfortable by myself."

He stopped, squaring off with her. She was probably going to think he was a nut, but he could speak from experience. He didn't totally understand it, but looking at her photograph when he'd been overseas had given him a little lift even though he'd never really met her. "Did you ever think that there are some people who could benefit from knowing you? Did it ever occur to you that there could be people on this planet who need you in some way? People you haven't ever met?"

She blinked and stared at him for a long moment. "No. Why would anyone need me?"

Brock swallowed an oath. He could give her a thousand reasons. "For starters, there's your art. Those pictures you draw impact a lot of kids and parents. Those people are counting on you."

She squinted her eyes against the sun. "I guess I can see that. But I still don't see why I have to go out and meet people. I can just stay in my cottage and draw."

"Yeah, that's worked out real well the last several months, hasn't it?"

She shot him a dirty look and began to walk again. "That wasn't nice."

He shrugged. "May not be nice, but it's true. You've said you're not happy with what you've created."

"I'm recovering from my husband's death," she said, nearly spitting the words at him.

"You could spend your whole life recovering."

"I may just do that," she retorted.

He caught her by the arm. "You can't cut yourself off like this. Rob didn't want it."

"Well, Rob didn't get what he wanted and I didn't get what I wanted, either." She closed her eyes. "I don't want to feel anymore. I don't want to feel sad. I don't deserve to feel hap—" She broke off and opened her eyes.

Brock's heart clenched in his chest at the lost expression in her eyes. "You have to," he said. "You're gonna laugh. You're gonna cry. You're still alive, Callie. You may even love again."

She shook her head vigorously. "Even if I found someone, I wouldn't want to. It just hurts too much to lose."

He nodded. "Well, you're one up on me there. I haven't lost anyone except my father. I never had anything special with a woman."

"Was that because of you or the women?"

"I don't know," he said with a shrug. "Maybe I scare all the good girls with hearts and attract the bad girls like mosquitoes."

A chuckle bubbled from her throat. A reluctant

one, he thought, looking into her eyes. "Mosqui-toes?" she echoed. "Bloodsuckers. Not the most flat-tering description of your past girlfriends."

"Girlfriend may be elevating the position." He nodded and snagged her wrist. "C'mon, let's keep walking."

"I'm starting to get the impression that I'm a how-to project for you."

"That's not all bad," he said lightly. "I've been commended for developing strategies that achieve goals."

"But what if your goal and mine are different?"

"Then we'll negotiate," he lied.

She looked at him skeptically. "You don't strike me as a particularly flexible kind of guy."

"Maybe I'll surprise you," he said, determined to keep the exchange light. If she knew what he really had planned, his life just might be in danger.

"You already have surprised me," she said darkly.

An impulse he couldn't ignore bit at him and he whisked her up into his arms.

She gasped, squirming in his arms. Her body felt soft and warm. "What are you doing?"

He carried her swiftly to the ocean as she started to kick and scream so loudly the seagulls squawked and flew away. Despite her struggle, he couldn't re-member holding a woman who felt so sweet.

"What are you doing?" she demanded.

He kept walking and lowered both of them up to their shoulders into the cool water. She shrieked again and shook her head at him. With all her huffing and puffing, her breath played over him like a little breeze. "Why did you do that? The water's cold from the storm. I'm all wet."

"I am, too."

"So?" she said frowning.

"Think of it as a demonstration," he told her. "If my strategy gets you wet, I'll get wet, too."

She opened her mouth and her jaw worked, but no sound came out. Her eyebrows knit together. "I think you may be insane," she said.

He *knew* he was insane. He wanted to run his hands over all her curves and secret places. He was burning with need. Just having her in his arms was incredible temptation. Yep, he was definitely insane.

"I have no idea what your point is."

Sighing, he stood up and carried her from the ocean. "You'll understand soon enough," he said as he reluctantly set her down on the sand. He didn't want her to know he was hard. She would think he was a pervert.

Her teeth chattered and her nipples puckered against her tank top. "I don't like being told what's best for me."

It took all the self-discipline Brock possessed to lift his gaze from her small breasts. "As soon as you realize what's best for you, then nobody will need to tell you."

She scowled and turned away from him. "I'm a grown woman. I don't need you telling me what to do."

"Start acting like it then," he dared her.

She did a double take. "What do you mean?"

"I mean start acting like a grown woman."

She crossed her arms over her chest and gave him a long, considering glance. "I don't agree with your methods, but you may be kinda right."

"Kinda?" he asked.

"Okay, mostly. I probably should start acting like a grown woman, a live grown woman."

He nodded. "Yep."

She took a deep breath and nodded. "Yep. Even if it kills me."

Or kills me, he thought, as he watched her turn and treat him to the inviting sight of her backside encased in nearly transparent white shorts. Her underwear looked like it was a light lilac color. Brock felt himself harden again and groaned. If this was supposed to be the cure for his ravaged conscience, he wondered if boiling himself in water would be easier.

"I think you should start by going to a bar," Brock said that evening. He'd always been told the best way to get over a woman was to go to a bar, drink too many beers and meet a new woman. He figured the reverse would be true for Callie.

Looking at him as if he'd lost his mind, she shook her head. "No. That's like stealing home before you go to first, second or third base. I thought a nice quiet trip to the library—"

He shook his head. "Nope. Too solitary. The objective is to get you back and involved with *humans,* not books."

She made a face and sighed. "I agree that I need to get out more, to try to have more of a life, if for no other reason than my art. You're right. I've isolated myself. But I want to take it slowly at first. There's this cute little restaurant that serves all these different kinds of teas—"

Brock rolled his eyes. For Pete's sake, punitive night drills during boot camp had been easier than this. They negotiated for another five minutes and finally decided on a trip to the grocery store.

"Pitiful," he muttered under his breath as she pushed the cart through the produce section. "Pitiful."

"Hey, don't knock it. This is the first time I've been to a real grocery store in ages. You have to crawl before you can walk. Oh, look. Fresh peaches. I love fresh peaches."

"I know," Brock said and chuckled when she stuck out her tongue at him.

"Okay, smarty-pants, what's your favorite fruit?"

"Cherries," he said.

"No surprise there," she said dryly. "Given your way with the ladies."

He dropped his jaw in mock surprise. "I'm shocked that your mind would sink so low. My mother baked a great cherry pie. I usually had cherry pie for my birthday instead of cake. And my grandmother had a cherry tree in her backyard."

"Oops. Sorry. It was a natural connection to

make—cherries, ladies." Her cheeks bloomed. "Or not. Tell me about this pie your mother used to make. Did she make the crust from scratch? I never could figure out how to make a good crust."

He nodded, swallowing his humor over her chatty effort to cover her gaffe. "She made the whole thing from scratch. I have the recipe and I can make it."

Her eyes widened in disbelief. "You're kidding. You can bake a cherry pie from scratch?"

"Yeah. What's so unbelievable about that?"

She shrugged her shoulders. "You just don't seem the domestic type."

"I'm not, but I don't like to starve. And I don't get home much anymore, so if I want hot cherry pie, I make it myself."

She studied him. "You really don't get along with your stepfather, do you?"

"Tough relationship. I've accepted it."

"I bet your mom misses you, though."

He nodded, thinking how frequently she'd written him when he'd been in the hospital.

"Maybe you should go see her," she said.

He wasn't accustomed to women giving him advice about his mother. "Maybe I will after I get settled in Atlanta."

They turned the cart onto the dairy aisle and she picked up a couple of cartons of yogurt and a small jug of milk. "I could never live in Atlanta. Too busy. Too crowded. Too much traffic."

"Depends on your point of view. There's a lot of stimulation in Atlanta, lots of things to do."

"As an artist, I prefer the quiet of a smaller town."

"One of the things I learned as a Marine was to create the quiet inside me. That way, I take it with me wherever I go. I'm not dependent on my environment."

She looked at him thoughtfully. "I never thought of it that way."

They continued through the store and completed her shopping. One more aisle to go and it was the cookie aisle. "Are you going to be a good girl and avoid the sweets?"

"Absolutely not," she said, grabbing a box of cookies. He grinned. "For such a little thing, you sure like your sweets."

"High metabolism," she said and grabbed one more box. "That's all," she said, but stopped suddenly near the end of the aisle.

"What is it?" he asked, seeing her features tighten with pain.

She held her breath. "It's silly, really silly. But he loved animal crackers. Even when he grew up, Rob loved animal crackers. I sent them to him when he was overseas."

Brock felt a sharp twist in his chest at the lost expression on Callie's face. She and Rob had known each other for so long that there would be many memories that would ambush her at odd times. It occurred to him that she might feel barraged with those memories when she ventured outside her cottage.

"Breathe," he said. "It's worse when you freeze up."

She glanced at him in surprise and took a shallow breath.

"Take another one, deeper," he coached, and watched her make the effort. He reached across her and took the small box of animal crackers from the shelf.

"Why did you—"

"We're going to eat these in Rob's memory," he said.

He drove her back to the cottage and they unloaded her groceries. She pulled out the box of animal crackers, opened it and solemnly ate a lion. She offered Brock a giraffe. She munched on a monkey then swallowed.

"This is probably very disrespectful to mention at this particular moment, but—" She lowered her voice to a whisper. "I don't like animal crackers."

Brock chuckled. "Neither do I. They taste like cardboard."

She smiled. "Rob must've liked them because his mother got them for him."

"That's possible. You know me and cherry pie."

Her eyes sparkled. "Yeah. For me, it's chocolate chip cookies. Great big, fat, hot cookies loaded—and I mean loaded—with chocolate chips."

Her voice was husky with a sexy indulgence that made his blood race to his crotch. He bit back an oath. Just hearing her talk about a cookie made him hard.

Callie closed the box and put it in the cabinet. "I'll save these for someone else."

"Just make sure you don't leave them in there until they're museum quality."

She laughed. "Duly noted. I think I'd like to play some music. Do you mind? It's a nice evening. Would you like some lemonade to wash down the cardboard?"

"Sure," he said, accepting the glass she offered and wandering out onto the patio. The sensual sound of a song by the artist Seal eased through the speakers of her stereo. In another situation, he would be drinking a beer or a glass of wine and getting his date ready for some time between the sheets. Instead he'd eaten animal crackers, was drinking lemonade, and was probably going to be taking a cold shower when he returned to his cottage tonight. The irony was sweet, he thought, shaking his head.

He heard Callie step onto the patio behind him. She sighed. "I need to thank you," she said in a low voice.

"Why?" he asked, turning to look at her. Her hair was pale in the moonlight, her eyes glowed with mystery. Looking at her made something inside him twist and something else inside him ease all at the same time.

"It's embarrassing to admit, but I realized it at the grocery store. It's like I've been totally locked up. Can't breathe, can't eat," she said with a lopsided smile. "Well, can't eat much anyway. Can't sleep. Can't do much of anything." She took a deep breath. "Breathing is a good place to start."

She was so charming with her vulnerability. He

wanted to pull her in his arms and tell her she would be okay, but he knew he shouldn't. He crammed his fists into his pockets.

"Thanks."

"No problem," he said and downed the rest of his lemonade. "Well, I should probably head back to my cottage."

"Do you have to?"

His heart stuttered at the expression in her eyes. "Why?"

She shrugged. "Sounds wussy, but I don't want to be alone yet tonight."

"Okay," he said, mentally girding himself for more sexual temptation—and deprivation. "What do you want to do?"

"Cards, Scrabble, Monopoly."

"Monopoly," he said decisively. If he couldn't have sex, he would dominate the real estate world.

An hour and a half later, she shook her head at him. "Whew! You're ruthless and you own everything," she complained. "I can't land on anything where I don't have to pay you rent. And I'm nearly broke. How'd you get to be so good?"

"This was how I got kisses when I was thirteen," he said, rolling the dice. "I played with a couple of neighbor girls. They always ended up owing me and I allowed them to pay some of their rent in trade."

"You dirty dog," she said. "You started young. Well, I'm not trading my kisses to pay your obscene rent."

"I hadn't asked," he said lightly, even though he felt himself go tight inside.

"That's right. You haven't," she said, meeting his gaze with a hint of curiosity in her eyes. That curiosity did dangerous things to his gut. She bit her lip. "I'm not at all your type."

He nodded and glanced away, focusing on moving his token. "Yep."

"You prefer uncommitted, undemanding, sexually experienced women with healthy appetites," she continued.

"You hit the nail on the head," he said, telling himself it was the truth. *Why did it feel like a lie?*

"Do you dance?"

He blinked and looked at her. "What?"

Her smile was a little self-conscious. "Do you dance?"

He nodded. "Yeah. Why?"

"Rob didn't."

"Really? I didn't know that, but then I never asked him to dance."

She laughed and then the silence stretched between them. His heart picked up the pace. He tried to ignore it, tried to ignore the expectant tension between them, tried not to think about holding her in his arms for a few moments. No kissing, no making love, just a dance. She hadn't gotten that from Rob. Maybe he wouldn't mind. The words were out before he could stop them.

"Wanna dance?"

Five

Marine Lingo Translation
Cinderella Liberty: An authorized absence that
expires at midnight.

He took her small hand in his and pulled her into
his arms. She slid her other hand over his shoulder then behind his back as he drew her closer. She
fit against him as if she were made for his body.
Made for his soul, something inside him whispered. Brock stopped himself. *What crazy
thoughts.* He inhaled and caught a draft of the
sweet, citrus scent of her hair. He felt the silky
strands brush his chin.

Her breasts glanced his rib cage and his abdomen
tightened. Her thighs slid against his and his heart
pounded.

He tried to swallow the knot of need forming in

his throat. The song playing on the radio would have provided a perfect accompaniment to a long French kiss or an afternoon spent in bed. It was slow and sexy, not the kind of music for twirling.

He cleared his throat, needing to break the tension, the magic. "Who is this artist? I don't think I've heard him before."

"I can tell you've been out of the country," she said with soft amusement in her voice. "John Mayer. He's very popular."

"Do you like him?"

He felt her nod. "Yes. His voice is expressive, so are his lyrics."

It would be so easy to rub his lips over her forehead, Brock thought. So easy. She might not even notice. He gave in to the temptation and a surge of illicit pleasure raced through him. He swallowed an oath at the strength of it. If kissing her forehead did this to him, then what would kissing her other places do to him?

Brock closed his eyes and tried to close his mind to all the possibilities. She just probably needed a little human contact. A brotherly hug. He shouldn't think about nudging her chin upward and tasting her mouth, or sliding his hand down to her bottom to draw her against the part of him that grew harder with each breath she took.

He heard her murmur something and opened his eyes. "What'd you say?"

Feeling her pull her head back slightly, he looked

down at her. A strand of her hair clung to his chin.
Pulling it free, she smiled and lifted her fingers to his
chin. "Five o'clock shadow. Rob must have been
jealous of you. I think he had about ten whiskers on
his face and three hairs on his chest."

Fighting a twinge of self-consciousness, Brock
rubbed his jaw. "I've always had to shave often or—"

"Or you get scrubby."

"Yeah," he said and noticed that her gaze fell to
his chest. It was a little thing, but it grabbed at his gut.
She was aware of him as a man, perhaps just because
of his beard, but the awareness was there. He could
see it and feel it. All of his instincts pushed him to
take this further, to lower his mouth to hers and rub
his hands over every inch of her body.

His conscience jabbed at him. He would be taking unfair advantage. Unfair advantage of Rob's
wife. Of Rob.

Clenching his jaw, he pulled back. "Song's over,"
he muttered.

This would have been so much easier if Callie was
a guy. He could pat her on the back, watch some
baseball games on television with her, go to a bar,
help her pick up somebody so she could get laid.
After that, if she were a guy, she'd be as good as new.

Guys were simpler than women. Sports, beer and
a good lay could solve a lot of problems. Women,
however, were much more complicated. And Callie
was no exception. During his training, he'd been

taught that in order to defeat the enemy, he needed to understand the way the enemy thought. Callie wasn't the enemy, but he sure as hell didn't think the same way she did. He racked his brain for a way to pull her out of her slump and even resorted to something he'd never done before—he called the one woman he could trust for advice.

"Hey, Mom, how's everything?"

"Brock! I wondered where you'd gone. I called the rehab center and no one knew. I was worried sick—"

Brock winced. He'd been in such a rush to leave he'd forgotten to tell her. "Sorry, Mom. I'd had enough. I had to get out of there. I decided I needed a change of environment before I moved to Atlanta."

"So where are you?"

"Down in South Carolina. It's a little place on the beach."

"Oh, the ocean," his mother said longingly. "That sounds nice."

"Yeah, you should get Sam to take you sometime. Listen, I was thinking about you the other day."

"That's sweet of you to say, dear. You know I think of you all the time. Sam and I miss you terribly. We were hoping you would come see us when you left the rehab center."

Brock felt a pinch of discomfort. "I was thinking about trying to get up to see you after I get settled in Atlanta. I'll have a lot to do. But I was thinking about when Dad died. I was wondering how you kept it all together. I remember catching you crying a few times, but you didn't ever fall apart."

Silence followed. "Well, that was because of you, Brock. If it had been left up to me, I would have curled into a ball and never left the house. I was lost without your father. But I still had my precious son and I needed to be strong for you."

Brock's heart tightened at the memory. He remembered that period of time just after his father's death. He'd been confused and lost, but his mother had seemed so strong. He was surprised to learn how hard it had been for her. "You did a good job, Mom. I didn't know."

She sighed. "Everyone needs a reason to get up in the morning. You were mine," she said, and he heard the smile in her voice. "When someone close to you dies, it's a struggle to go on, but you just have to. You have to get up, get dressed and go out in the world. Sometimes it's little things that help. Smelling flowers, holding a baby, striking up a conversation with someone you don't know. And for women, shopping can be a panacea, even if we don't buy anything. I remember going shopping twice a week after your father died. I didn't usually buy anything, but it got me out among people. And then I joined a garden club and got a job. And when I met Sam, I thought he could be a good father for you."

She didn't sound too sure with that last reference to his stepfather. "He was in a tough position," Brock conceded.

"And you're both bullheaded," his mother said.

"True. Maybe that's why you love us both so much," he said.

She laughed with pleasure and the sound pleased him. "You've always been a rascal. Are you taking care of yourself? Eating good food? Taking your vitamins and getting your rest?"

"Yes, Mom," he said, stifling a groan.

"Don't you *yes, Mom* me," she fussed. "We nearly lost you, so I'm allowed to worry."

"You didn't lose me. I'm still ornery as ever."

"So when will you come to see me?"

"Soon. Two or three months."

"Promise?"

"Promise. Thanks, Mom."

"Anytime, dear. Take care of yourself."

"You, too," he said and hung up the phone.

He thought back to the conversation and made a mental list of what his mother had said. *Smelling flowers, joining clubs, getting a job, shopping.* He wrinkled his nose in distaste at the last activity, and Callie already had a job. He would try the others first.

Brock didn't know much about flowers, so he got two of each, along with a couple of big pots, some bags of dirt and gardening tools. After he hauled everything onto Callie's front porch, he rang the doorbell.

She answered more quickly than ever, and she actually looked as if she'd been awake for a while. His heart lifted at the sight of her. Her hair was pulled back in some kind of messy bun. He wished she would wear it down. Her legs looked lean and shapely despite her loose shorts.

Glancing at the flowers for a long moment, she finally met his gaze. "Just a guess, but I'm thinking Rob didn't tell you that I have a black thumb."

"He told me you don't have a black thumb. You just get distracted and forget to water plants."

She crossed her arms over her chest. "Well, they're not like pets. They don't remind you to give them water—until it's too late."

"I have a solution for that," he said.

"What?" she asked skeptically.

"I'll tell you after we plant the flowers."

She gave a put-upon sigh, but joined him on the porch. "Is this part of my recovery?"

"Yes." He gave her a trowel and opened one of the bags of dirt.

"Where'd you get this idea?"

"My mother." He dumped some dirt into each of the large pots.

She looked at him with her eyebrows raised. "Your mother? I didn't know you ever talked with your mother."

Brock resisted the urge to growl. "What is it with women? All or nothing. I call my mother every now and then. I even wrote her when I was overseas and when I was in the physical rehabilitation center. I called her last night and—"

"Bet she was surprised," Callie interjected.

Brock shot her a quelling glance that didn't appear to dent her challenging, impish expression.

"Betcha she was surprised," she said, shaking her trowel at him. "Betcha she didn't even know where you were calling her from."

"And your point is?"

She wiggled the trowel in a circle as if she were trying to come up with something, but couldn't. "Nothing really, except you don't call her as often as she'd like. Did you talk about me?"

"No. I just asked her what she did to keep going when my dad died."

The silence that stretched between them had a sweet quality to it. He glanced up and saw sympathy in her gaze. He usually hated the very idea of someone feeling sympathy for him, especially after all his time in the hospital, but it felt different coming from Callie. He would have to figure that out later.

"That must've been a rough time for both of you," she said.

He nodded. "It was. I don't think I realized how tough it was for her until lately."

"So how did she get through? Gardening?" Callie asked with a smile on her face. She shifted one of the flowers into the larger pot.

"That and some other things," he said.

"Do I have these other things to look forward to?" she asked warily.

"Some. Not all," he said, thinking that the way she looked at him with her hair partly covering one eye was sexy as all get-out.

"What won't I be doing?"

He felt a ripple of discomfort. "Well, you don't have a kid, so…"

She met his gaze again, realization glinting through her eyes. "Yeah, I can see that. I bet you were her biggest motivation for getting up in the morning."

"I guess that's what mothers are supposed to say."

She smiled. "I never have understood why guys hate having their moms fuss over them a little."

"Because it's never a little. It starts out small and innocent with her fixing my favorite pie, then it progresses to grilling me about my health, fussing over me eating vegetables, then before you know it, she's trying to pick out a wife for me and begging for grandchildren."

"And by then, you're choking on your cherry pie," she said, chuckling. "How are we going to arrange these flowers?"

He shrugged. "You're the artist."

"With a black thumb," she added.

"Okay, these are annuals," he said, pointing to the flowers next to him. "The ones next to you are perennials. So some of them will come back again next year and some of them won't."

"Kinda like you," she murmured.

He could have let it pass, but he was curious. He set down his trowel. "How are they like me?"

"The annuals are pretty for a season, but they won't be back next year."

"Are you saying I'm pretty?" he teased.

"I'm saying you're temporary," she emphasized, and he couldn't tell if she was saying it more for him or for herself. "Then again," she said, instantly lightening the mood with a rueful smile. "They may *all* be temporary due to my black thumb."

He shook his head. "This time is gonna be different. The annuals will last all season and the perennials will be back next year."

If he couldn't be here with her next spring, then at least the damn flowers would, he thought. *Now that was insane. Purely insane. Why did he give a rip if these flowers bloomed next year?* And he sure didn't want to be here next year wanting another man's woman and not having her.

Insisting she wasn't a joiner, Callie didn't bite at the club suggestion, even after he read a list compiled by the local newspaper. He subscribed to the local paper for her, figuring it would be worth the cost if she read the comics and just one of them made her smile.

When he knocked on her door one afternoon, she answered with a pink nose, pink cheeks and tearful eyes. His gut clenched. "What's wrong?"

"This isn't a good day," she said in a wobbly voice. "I don't think I'm going to be very good company. You'd probably better go back to your place."

"I'm not going back to my place. What is it?"

She bit her lip. "It's his birthday," she whispered. "It's Rob's birthday. I've spent nearly every birthday with him since he was ten."

His chest tightened at the pain he saw in her eyes. She looked like a lost child. Unable to stop himself, he pulled her into his arms and she sobbed against him. She sniffled and snorted and wept. "I'm sorry. I'm really sorry. I told you that you should go back—"

"Hush," he said, holding her tighter. "This is why I'm here."

She inhaled deeply and let it out in a jagged, uneven breath.

He stroked her hair the same way he would comfort a child, all the while aware—terribly aware—that she was a woman. "Does this mean we have to eat the animal crackers in his honor?"

She gave a weak chuckle and looked up at him. "No. He didn't usually have animal crackers on his birthday. Just the regular birthday cake, yellow cake, white frosting, candles." She rubbed the tears from her cheeks. "Sorry."

"It's okay. What do you want to do this evening?"

"I don't know. Maybe look at some photographs. I'd toast him, but I don't think I have any alcohol."

"I can take care of that," he offered.

She took a step back and shook her head. "Oh, no. You can't stay. This is really going to be maudlin and I'll just keep this to myself."

He immediately felt the gap where she'd been. "Are you saying I'm not invited?"

She opened her mouth and worked it, but nothing came out. "Well, it's not going to be a fun time."

"I miss him, too," he confessed.

She looked at him for a long moment. "Okay. You can come to my pity party if you really want to."

"Let me go pick up something for toasting first," he said, pointing at her. "I'll be back in a flash. Don't start without me."

She shrugged. "Whatever you say."

Twenty-two minutes later, he returned with tequila, salt, lime, a birthday cake and two shot glasses.

She raised her eyebrows at his purchase. "That looks like an interesting taste combination."

"After you drink a couple shots, your taste buds will be numb and it won't matter."

She gave a weak laugh. "That's good to know."

Brock washed out the glasses and sliced the lime while she cut a couple pieces of cake. "Where's the party?"

"The den," she said, licking the frosting from one of her fingers.

"I'm ready when you are," he said and followed her out of the kitchen.

Crossing her legs over each other, she set the pieces of cake aside and picked up a large photo album. "Let's start with the first birthday. He was cute even when he was a baby."

"He was," Brock agreed, seeing the same sparkle in the baby's eyes that he'd seen in Rob's eyes.

"He walked early and loved anything on wheels," she continued.

"Yep, he got a kick out of the vehicles the Marines used."

"He drove a motorcycle before he was old enough to get his driver's license, but he didn't get caught." She shook her head. "He never got caught."

Except when he stepped on that mine. He got caught then. Brock's chest contracted so sharply he couldn't breathe. He shook some salt on his hand, licked it, poured a shot of tequila, downed it and sucked on a lime.

He felt Callie's gaze on him. "That always looked like it required a lot of coordination to me."

"You've never had tequila?"

"That would require me going to a bar, and the only times I went to bars I was with Rob. He always got me one of those drinks with the little umbrellas."

"You want to try a shot?" he asked.

"Okay, but you'll have to coach me," she said.

Brock talked her through the salt and the shot and watched her face after she tossed back the tequila. "Ewww. That's gross!" She coughed.

"Suck the lime," he told her, lifting her hand.

She obeyed and her lips puckered and eyes watered. She coughed again. He gently thumped her on her back.

"That's disgusting. Why would anyone drink more than one of those?" she asked in a hoarse voice.

After viewing several more pages of photographs of Rob, however, she took another shot when Brock did. She shared memory after memory with Brock. Some were funny, some were bittersweet, but they all made him ache because she obviously missed him so much. It hit him again that Callie hadn't just lost a lover or husband—she'd lost her life partner. And nothing, and no one, would ever be able to totally replace everything Rob had been to her.

The knowledge tore at him and he felt his own eyes burn when she turned the page to show Rob in his uniform, fresh out of boot camp.

Callie scrubbed at her eyes with the backs of her hands and took another shot. "I think I'm starting to feel the effect of the tequila now. I should probably eat something," she said. "Cake. I'll eat the cake."

"I'm not sure that's really gonna help," he said, amused, despite the fact that she'd been weeping like a child just moments before.

"Better than nothing," she said and took a couple of bites.

He watched her and got distracted by the little bit of frosting on her cheek. He rubbed it off with his finger then licked it.

Her gaze locked with his in fascination. "After this cake, I bet that tequila will taste more bitter than ever."

"You bet right," he said with a grin.

She sighed and took another bite of cake. "Well, I can say that I did something adventurous on Rob's birthday by trying tequila."

"Hear, hear," he said, pouring himself another shot. "And you can feel good that you didn't do anything too bad, like body slammers."

She swallowed over her bite of cake. "What's a body slammer?"

"Nothing you want to do," he told her. A dozen forbidden images flew through his mind of places on her body he would like to taste.

She leaned toward him with her hand on his thigh. She probably didn't even realize she was touching him, he thought. "Tell me what a body slammer is," she demanded.

Her eyes were sexy, smoky and her voice had a husky tinge that rattled his nerve endings. "It's when you put salt on another person's body, lick it off, drink the shot of tequila and follow it up with the lime." His brain ran down the road to temptation again.

She blinked. "Now let me get this straight. You pour salt on someone else's body and lick it off. Doesn't it just fall off?"

"You have to do it fast."

She was quiet for a long moment. "I can honestly say I've never had a body slammer."

Brock felt a punch of arousal along with an uh-oh sensation. She had that same look on her face she'd worn when he'd danced with her. That one little dance had nearly killed him. He would swallow his tongue before he offered her a body slammer.

She bit her lip and eyed the tequila then her gaze slid over him again. She'd had enough alcohol to lower her inhibitions, which could be a damn dangerous state for him. Her expectancy was so palpable, it twisted between them like a coiled wire. "I really don't know when I'm going to have this opportunity again," she said and licked her lips. "And I can trust you. If I don't choose anything obscene, would you let me body slam you?"

Six

Marine Lingo Translation
Devil Dog: a name for Marines that signifies
the dogged determination of Marines.

*And I can trust you...would you let me body slam
you?*

Brock swallowed every swear word he'd ever
heard along with a few he made up. *She could trust
him? She damn well shouldn't trust him.* He felt like
the biggest, baddest wolf on the planet and he wanted
this Little Red Riding Hood for breakfast, lunch and
dinner.

Squeezing in a breath, he willed his lips to form
the word *no,* all the while looking into her sexy eyes.
He glanced at her mouth and felt his libido roar like
an overbuilt engine.

"Go ahead," he said, his voice sounding rough to his own ears. "Body slam me."

Her face lit up and she smiled. "Okay, I'll try it on your hand." She poured her shot then grabbed the salt shaker and sprinkled some on the back of his hand. Leaning forward, she lowered her mouth and stuck out her tongue. She started to laugh and backed away. "Sorry," she said. "This is just one of the most bizarre things I've done in a long time."

Her laughter was as seductive as everything else about her. Brock was amused and aroused. Unbearably so.

She pressed two fingers over her mouth as if to force herself to stop giggling. "I can do this. I want to be able to say I've body slammed."

Lowering her head again, she leaned forward and slid her tongue over his skin. The sight and sensation of her pink tongue on his flesh tightened every cell inside him. She rubbed her tongue from side to side and he felt his temperature rise with every stroke. *Damn, she was just licking his hand. What if she'd been licking his…*

She pulled back and a groan escaped his throat. She tossed back the tequila with a grimace and quickly followed by sucking on another slice of lime. "Well, that was interesting," she said with a smile.

"I think you've had enough," he said, tossing back one more shot himself.

"Maybe," she said. "How many have I—"

"One clue that you've had enough is when you can't remember how many you drank."

She moved her head in a circle. "Are you gonna body slam me?"

She had no idea how much he wanted to body slam her—and his idea of body slamming had nothing to do with tequila.

"Fair's fair," she said, lifting her hand.

Unable to resist, he poured another shot and got his lime ready then sprinkled salt on her and lowered his head.

She started to giggle and the salt fell off. "It tickled."

Caught somewhere between agonizing arousal and amusement, he laughed. "Give me your hand," he said and turned her wrist over. Holding it steady, he sprinkled salt on the inside of her wrist and lowered his mouth to her skin.

Her soft intake of breath was like an intimate touch. He slid his tongue over the inside of her wrist, savoring the flavor and texture of her skin mixed with the salt. He licked the tiny blue vein beneath her fair skin.

"Oh, my," she whispered.

Reluctantly pulling back, he tossed back the shot and sucked the lime. She looked at him with a mixture of curiosity and sensual wariness, as if he were some wild animal she should avoid but found fascinating, all the same.

"That's some drink. A body slammer. I think I better get a drink of water." She stood and lifted her hand to her head. "Whew! I feel wobbly."

Brock caught her hand and tugged her back onto the couch. "Stay here. I'll get it."

"You had more tequila than I did. How come you aren't woozy like me?"

He stood. "Men metabolize alcohol faster than women do."

"But you didn't even eat any cake," she protested.

He went into the kitchen and filled two glasses with ice water, then returned. Still standing, he drank his water, hoping it would bring him a little sanity. He was tempted to pour the stuff over his head to cool himself down.

He felt Callie's gaze on him as she sipped her water. She patted the cushion beside her. "Would you stay a little longer? I don't want to be alone yet."

He sank down onto the sofa and felt the silence between them.

"Could I ask a favor of you?"

"Sure," he said, knowing there wasn't much she could ask that he wouldn't do.

"Would you hold me for a little while?"

His heart turned over at the vulnerability in her sweet features. "Sure," he said and pulled her into his arms. Her body was soft and pliable. She relaxed against him as if she had no idea how much he wanted to undress her and make love to her. She stuck her face against his throat and inhaled deeply then lifted her hands to his shoulders. Her hair felt like silk beneath his chin. His heart hammered in his chest while her breaths evened out and she drifted off to sleep.

Hours later, the low sound of a motor awakened him. Brock opened his eyes, immediately aware that Callie was spread over him like a blanket. Something gray moved beside him and he turned his head to see the cat. The cat, whose whiskers were covered in white frosting, stared at him unblinkingly and purred.

Brock shifted slightly, but Callie continued to sleep. He shifted again and, when she didn't move, he thought about putting a mirror under her nose to make sure she was breathing. The tequila must have delivered a knockout punch.

His body groaned in protest at the crumpled position he'd been in for the last several hours. He had an ugly suspicion his body was going to exact a heavy punishment. Grimacing, he carefully slid Callie off of him and onto another cushion on the couch. She stirred, but continued to sleep.

Rising from the couch, he stretched and felt pain shoot through his back and leg. His head throbbed. Yep, he probably shouldn't have downed that last shot of tequila. He took the remainder of the cake sitting on the table and tossed it in the trash in the kitchen. Returning to the den, he looked at Callie and felt his chest tighten. Her hair spilled over the dark upholstery, looking like wildfire. Her rosebud lips were slightly parted.

Lord, how he wanted her.

But he couldn't have her.

Heaving a sigh, he went to the sofa and carefully picked her up and carried her toward the back of the house, where he suspected her bedroom was.

"What are you doing?" she asked as he stepped through the doorway.

"Putting you to bed."

"What time is it?"

"Very late or very early, depending on your perspective," he said.

"My head feels like the hunchback of Notre Dame is ringing cathedral bells inside it."

"Yeah, I feel like crap, too."

"I feel dizzy when I open my eyes."

"Then keep them closed," he told her, and lowered her onto her bed. "I'm going to bring a glass of water and some aspirin and put it on your bedside table."

"Why?"

"If I don't, you may kill me in the morning," he muttered, and collected the items. He returned to the bedroom to find her under the sheet and tossing articles of her clothing on the floor. Her shirt flew through the air, followed by her bra and shorts.

His temperature climbed several degrees as his mind stripped down the covers to her bed and he found her naked, warm and waiting. Inviting.

"You can sleep on the sofa if you think you shouldn't be driving," she said.

Not exactly the invitation his libido had been wishing for. "That's okay. I'm gonna walk home."

Her eyes still closed, she frowned. "It's too late for that."

"Nah, the fresh air will do me good." Hopefully it would get his brain out of his shorts.

She sighed.

"Sit up just a little," he coaxed.

"I don't want to take anything. I'm too sleepy."

"You don't even have to open your eyes," he told her and she lifted her head slightly.

He touched her bottom lip and when she opened her mouth, he placed the aspirin on her tongue. He held the glass of water to her lips and she swallowed. After repeating the process, he lowered her head to the pillow. "Thanks, Brock. Did you know you taste a lot better than tequila?" she asked, tossing her panties over the edge of the bed and rolling onto her side.

Brock rubbed his hand over his face in frustration. *…you taste a lot better than tequila.* In any other situation, he would be in that bed and on her in three seconds flat. But not in this situation, he told himself. Not with this woman.

"I'm never drinking tequila again," Callie said as she opened her door to him the next morning. With her hair sticking out in no less than ten directions, she put her hands on either side of her face and shook her head. She wore a little robe and Brock suspected she was naked beneath it. The knowledge cranked up his body temperature.

"You didn't warn me that I would feel like my body had been slammed the next morning."

"I encouraged you to stop, but you wanted to continue," he pointed out, following her inside. "Are you ready for your run?"

She looked at him in disbelief. "What are you? The Terminator or something? Are you sure you aren't hiding steel underneath that skin?" Callie asked, poking at one of Brock's biceps.

He caught her finger and shook his head. "No steel. Just the regular combination of blood and guts."

"No way," she said. "You're not regular anything."

Her compliment felt like a soft stroke on his skin. He cracked a smile. "It's my Marine training. C'mon. Let's go. The fresh air will make you feel better."

Callie made a face. "A twelve-hour nap would make me feel better."

"Go get dressed," he told her.

"We're not really going to run, are we?"

"We'll take it easy," he promised.

She made another face. "Your version of easy and my version of easy are very, very different," she grumbled, but headed toward her bedroom. "Did you know Oscar got into the cake last night?" she yelled from the bedroom.

"Yeah, his purring was what woke me up."

"Who would have thought a cat would like birthday cake?"

He heard her walk from her bedroom to the bathroom, followed by the sounds of water and a little shriek. "Oh, my hair! I look like something out of a horror movie."

Chuckling at her dismay, he strolled closer to the hallway. "It wasn't that bad. You just looked like a wannabe rock star."

"Cute, very cute," she retorted and opened the door, her hair pulled back in a high ponytail and a scowl on her face. "This is really all your fault. Tequila."

He lifted his hands. "I encouraged you to stop."

"Hmmph. Okay, Dr. Torture, let's go."

They took a short jog on the beach and slowed to a walk after a short time. Callie wandered closer to the edge of the tide and looked out on the ocean. "I'll say one thing for how I feel today. I feel so cruddy physically that I can't focus on whining about Rob."

"You don't whine," Brock said as he joined her. "At least, not about Rob."

Her lips twitched. "You're so kind."

He shrugged. "Your grief is valid."

"Yeah, but I've made a full-time job of it. He wouldn't want it that way. Plus, it's exhausting and unproductive."

"So what are you going to do?"

She met his gaze. "I'm already *doing*. I've allowed myself to get suckered into the Brock Armstrong recovery program, haven't I?"

"Kicking and screaming every inch of the way."

She studied him. "I just wish you didn't feel like you had a penance to pay for surviving when Rob didn't."

Her words hit too close and he looked away. "It's more complicated than that."

"Okay. Whatever it is, thanks."

"It works both ways. Helping you helps me."

"Penance," she said.

He shook his head. "I told you it's more than that. You've probably forgotten this, but being with you can be nice."

"Oh, yeah, a laugh a minute."

An urge to touch her rippled through him like the ocean breeze. He wanted to pull her against him. The strength of the instinct irritated him. He shoved his hands into the pockets of his shorts.

She touched him lightly on his arm. "It means a lot that I can trust you."

Don't trust me too much, he thought, craving her. His pulse raced at her nearness and he was careful not to move a millimeter. He didn't want her to pull away. "It works both ways, Callie," he said in a low voice.

"You're so strong that I sometimes forget that you're recovering, too." She searched his face then put her arms around him.

He sucked in her closeness like a man who'd been stuck in the desert for days and she was his first drink of water. Her embrace knocked him sideways. She was sober and not crying. This was the first time she'd flat-out hugged him, and his heart and body were overwhelmed. He pulled his hands out of his pockets to put them around her, then thought better of it and returned them. He shouldn't encourage her.

On the other hand, he knew a human touch was part of healing.

Holding his breath, he slowly eased his hands out of his pockets and slid his arms around her.

She made a little sound of satisfaction and squeezed him. "This is embarrassing to admit, but I think I must be starved for hugs."

"I'm sure you can find lots of volunteers to give you hugs," he said dryly.

"Yeah, but they're not—" She broke off and pulled back slightly, looking into his eyes.

"They're not what?"

She moved her shoulders and confusion shimmered in her eyes. "I guess I don't want hugs from just anyone."

"Picky," he said, trying to lighten the conversation, even though his chest felt strange as the dickens.

She gave a lopsided smile. "Choosy. I've always thought it was a good thing to be choosy."

"Choosy's just a nice word for picky," he told her, thinking that if she decided he was going to be her hug supplier, he was in for pure torture. Heaven help him.

She began to spontaneously hug him and touch him. Every once in a while he could see it coming and brace himself for his response to her, but she often ambushed him. She clearly had no idea of her effect on him.

Brock was starting to think that the cure to his survivor guilt just might put him over the edge. She was so soft and feminine in his arms. He inhaled her scent as if it were a drug. After feeling dead for so long, she made his every cell feel alive. He spent an inordinate amount of energy trying to ignore just how alive she made him feel. He had a mission. There were steps to take, goals to be accomplished.

"You need to make some friends," he said, as they went for their run on the beach one cloudy morning.

"I probably should, but I'm not sure how. It's not really one of those things you can do through a classified ad."

"You could volunteer or join a club," he suggested.

Callie made a face and slowed to a walk. "I already told you I'm not much of a joiner."

He struggled with a ripple of frustration. "You may need to change that."

"I don't know. I don't fit in with groups real well. I didn't fit in with the military wives. They thought I was weird." She shrugged and looked at him. "And I guess I am a little weird, but isn't everyone?"

"Some are more weird than others," he said dryly.

"Oh, thanks!" She swatted him playfully. "Just the encouragement I needed to go out among the rest of humanity."

Brock laughed at her indignation then felt a few drops of rain on his shoulders. He looked up at the sky. "Oops. I think we're gonna get caught."

"And I'm not running the rest of the way back to my cottage," she said.

Glancing around, he spotted a stand of trees. "C'mon, that looks like it will be better than nothing."

The rain suddenly burst through the clouds and he

tugged her toward the trees. Water dampened her hair and face. She pulled at her T-shirt as it clung to her, then glanced at him. "This is your fault. If you hadn't dragged me out here—"

"You'd be inside moping," he finished for her.

She opened her mouth then closed it. "Maybe not. Maybe I would be working. I've been productive lately."

"Good for you."

"Probably thanks to you," she said reluctantly.

"You're welcome," he said with mock sweetness.

She stuck out her tongue at him.

Pleased to see some fire in her exchanges with him, he shook his finger at her playfully. "Don't stick out your tongue unless you plan to use it."

"How should I use it?" she asked, with a sensual curiosity in her eyes that made him regret teasing her.

"That's for you to figure out," he muttered, irritated at how quickly she made his temperature rise.

He barely saw her coming when she lifted her mouth to his mouth and kissed him quickly. She drew back, looking as surprised at her action as he was.

He stared at her in disbelief. "Why'd you do that?"

"Because you dared me to do it," she said defensively.

"I did not."

"Yes, you did," she argued, her cheeks heating. "You dared me to kiss you when you said something about using my tongue. If you didn't like it, you'll just have to get over it because you asked for it."

The combination of her indignation, embarrassment and impulsive kiss set off a chain reaction inside him of gut-clenching want. The sensations inside him were a mixture of arousal and excruciating tenderness.

Instinctively reaching for her, he pulled her against him. "I didn't ask for that kind of kiss, Callie," he told her in a voice that sounded rough to his own ears.

"What kind of kiss did you ask for?"

He lowered his mouth and showed her. He rubbed his lips over hers, relishing the shape and texture of her mouth. Gently squeezing the nape of her neck, he coaxed her lips to a more accessible position.

He had the sensation of danger as he took her mouth. It should have made him more careful, but there was too much that had been pent up inside him for too long. He slid his tongue over her lips, then inside her mouth to taste her. Surprising the hell out of him, she pressed the front of her body flush against him as if she couldn't get close enough. With each stroke of his tongue, he felt as if he were standing at the edge of a volcano ready to erupt.

She made a sound of need that affected him like an intimate touch, and went wild in his arms. Matching him caress for caress, she drew his tongue deep into her mouth the same way she would draw his hardness into her body. The knowledge made him sweat.

She squeezed his forearms with a sexy kind of desperation, then slipped her hands up under his tank top to touch his chest.

Brock felt his heart hammer in his chest. Swollen with need, he slid one of his hands down to her bottom, guiding her pelvis against the place where he ached. Feeling the tight tips of her breasts against his chest, he was filled with the need to touch her all over at once. He skimmed his hand over the edge of her breast and she turned toward him, clearly begging for more.

On fire, he wanted nothing more than to strip off her clothes and plunge inside her.

After one kiss.

She pulled away to gasp for air. "Oh, wow," she whispered.

Oh, wow was an understatement. A minuscule amount of oxygen seeped into his brain. He saw the dark arousal in her eyes, her lips were already swollen from their kiss. *He could take her now if he wanted,* the devil inside him said. *He could have Rob's woman.*

Seven

Marine Lingo Translation
Soup Sandwich: A mess. Not squared away.

He needed a beer. He needed to watch a ball game on a giant screen. He needed to get laid. Two out of three wasn't bad, he thought, as he chugged his second cold one and sat on a stool at Smiley's Bar. His Braves were having a tough time.

Hearing a chorus of feminine laughter, he glanced over his shoulder and saw the cute brunette giving him the eye again. He glanced away, thinking he could probably get something going with her if he was so inclined. He'd been walking around with a hard-on for the last two weeks. He should be inclined but, for some reason, he didn't have the stomach for anonymous sex anymore. Brock wondered if his change in attitude was due to the explosion. More than his body had been affected by it.

Sighing, he took another swig and focused on the game.

"The Braves aren't doing very well tonight, are they?" a feminine voice beside him said.

He glanced up to see the brunette who had been watching him all evening. "Yep. They can't seem to pull it together tonight. Happens to most everyone once in a while."

"I'm Candace McDonald," she said, and extended her hand. "You looked lonely over here, so I thought I would come say hello."

"Hi. I'm Brock," he said, and glanced at the screen again.

"Are you new here?" she asked, sitting next to him.

"Kinda. I'm just here for a few weeks. What about you?"

She smiled. "Darn, I should have known. All the good ones are temporary. I live here full-time and trust me, there's not much going on in the winter."

He nodded. "I can see how that would happen. It gets cold and all the visitors go away."

"And there's my job. I teach kindergarten and most of my colleagues are female. Makes it tough for a girl to meet a guy."

He looked at her again, this time from a different perspective. Maybe she could become a friend of Callie's. "You haven't been here long?"

"This is my first job out of college. I'm working this summer with an enrichment program."

"Enrichment?" he echoed.

"We do art projects and introduction to foreign languages, elementary science experiments. That sort of thing."

"Art," he said, thinking of that old saying, *if the mountain won't come to Mohammed, then Mohammed must go to the mountain.* "I know a woman, a local woman who draws art for children's books."

Her eyes widened with interest. "Really? I bet my kids would love for her to visit. You think she would be interested?"

"I think you should ask her," he said. "She's a little shy, but I bet she would say yes." He thought for a moment. "You know, you might even invite her out to lunch sometime. Here's her name and phone number," he said, and wrote down Callie's information on a paper napkin.

The young woman took the napkin and gave him a considering glance. "I wouldn't mind having lunch with you, but I get the impression you're otherwise engaged, or at least otherwise distracted." She tapped her fingernail against the napkin and lifted her eyebrow in a questioning way.

He almost denied it. He definitely wasn't engaged, however he couldn't honestly say he wasn't distracted by Callie. "Give her a call. You'll be glad you did."

"Okay," she said, taking another napkin and writing her name and phone number on it. "You give me a call if you change your mind."

"Okay," he said, accepting the napkin. But he knew he wouldn't call her.

Brock came to the conclusion that the only way he was going to be able to keep his hands off of Callie was by helping her get a life and by helping her get a man. Although part of him vehemently rebelled at the notion of Callie being with another man, he knew that was what she needed. Sure, no man would ever be able to replace Rob, but another man could hold her, kiss her and cherish her. Another man could make love to her. The very thought of it made his blood pressure spike, but he believed it was necessary for her reentry into the land of the living.

Callie was an affectionate woman and she needed someone, besides a cat, on whom to pour all her affection.

After getting a look at her wardrobe of T-shirts, jeans and sweats, he faced another hard truth—Callie needed to go shopping for clothes, and he was going to have to accompany her.

Arming himself with the *Atlanta Constitution,* he picked her up on Wednesday afternoon and drove to a shopping mall about thirty miles away. He had told her he was taking her for a drive, not out to get a new wardrobe.

When he pulled into a parking space, she looked at him in confusion. "Why are we stopping?"

"We're going shopping."

"What do you need?"

His lips twitched. "I don't need anything. You need some new clothes."

"No, I don't."

"Yes, you do. You're going to start participating in more activities than walking on the beach, feeding the cat and painting. You need a couple of dresses and some shirts that fit you instead of hanging off you."

She frowned at him. "Are you criticizing my style?"

"Yes," he said flatly, and opened the car door and got out.

"I didn't bring any money," she protested.

"That's okay. You can use my credit card. If you dent it too much, then you can pay me back." He opened her car door. "Your adventure awaits."

With narrowed eyes, she glanced at the newspaper he'd tucked under his arm. "You think you're just going to cruise through this with a newspaper while I do all the work?"

"They'll be your clothes. You should do the work," he told her.

She stood up and got in his face. "Uh-uh. You, Mr. Smarty-Pants, are going to have to shop, too. Yes, that four-letter word that men hate so much. You're going to have to make suggestions and offer opinions. If I have to suffer through this, then you do, too."

Brock quickly realized he'd unleashed a shopping she-devil. She dragged him with her to every women's clothing store. Not content to let him find a seat in the food court so he could read the sports section, she consulted him on colors and styles, hem length, pants versus dresses.

"You're an artist. You know a lot more about color and stuff like that than I do."

"Well, you must have an opinion," the shopping she-devil said. "Since you're convinced I need a new wardrobe. Lingerie is next," she said with an evil smile.

He groaned as he followed her into a shop filled with satin, silk and lace.

"What do you think of this?" she asked him, pointing to a black bra. "It's supposed to do miraculous things for your breasts without surgery. I'm so small," she complained.

"Small isn't all bad," he murmured, running his fingers over the satin cup, imagining taking the bra off of her and teasing her nipples into tight buds, wrapping his tongue around them and... His internal body temperature shot up several degrees.

"Which color do you like best?" she asked, holding up a black thong in one hand and a red thong in the other.

His throat tightened up when his mind easily produced the image of her tight little bottom in either of those scraps of satin. "Either," he said hoarsely. "Both."

"Okay. I'll go try some of these on. You're in luck," she said, scooping up another couple of bras.

"How?" he asked, unable to see any vestige of good luck for him in this situation.

"You can read your newspaper now. I'm way too shy to model this stuff for you."

He watched her leave and tried to decide if that meant he was lucky or not. He went outside the store and found a bench. Sitting down, he took out his paper and turned to the sports section. Was he really lucky because he wasn't actually seeing her in the satin bras and thongs? His mind conjured an image of Callie wearing the black thong and black satin bra, her fiery hair in disarray and her lips painted red, but smudged from his kisses.

He could feel the silk of her skin beneath his fingertips, the taste of her tongue as he took her mouth again. He loved the way her hands felt on his bare skin, the feminine wanting she expressed with every little movement she made. The way she drew his tongue into her mouth made him think about how she would draw him deep into her body.

He wanted more. He wanted to caress her nipples. He wanted to taste them until she was wet and swollen with wanting between her thighs. He wanted to touch her in her secret places and make her bloom with so much need she trembled from it.

In some corner of his perception, Brock noticed the newspaper twitching. He glanced down at his hands clenched around the edges of the paper, crumpling it. He was hard. He was sweating. Swearing under his breath, he shook his head to clear it. He hadn't even seen her try on that lingerie, but he knew he would be tormented with his own images for a long, long time.

Two days later, he knew he was going to have to be firm with her. He decided to try yet another strategy to get past his strange feelings toward Callie. He'd decided to pretend she was his sister. "It's Friday night," Brock told her, expecting protests, excuses and reasons to procrastinate. "We're going to a bar."

She wrinkled her nose. "I don't really feel like going out tonight. Besides, I'm going to have to be social in another way. I got a call from some teacher at a local elementary school today and she asked me to come and help with a special program for her kindergarten class. I can't figure out how she got my name."

Good, he thought. The woman he'd met the other night had followed up.

"We started talking and she asked me to meet her for a drink sometime. So, see, it's not necessary for me to go to a bar tonight."

"You need practice," he said. "You need practice interacting with adults."

She shot him a look of disapproval. "That's not very nice. My social skills are fine."

"I wasn't talking about your social skills. I'm talking about social experience. You need practice. Can you tell me that isn't true?"

"Well, maybe, but—"

"Face it, Callie. Most of your social experience is with Rob. You need to start getting some of your own experience."

She sighed. "I was hoping you wouldn't push for this so soon, but I had a very bad feeling about that shopping spree. Like payback was going to be hell."

"Fair is fair," he said, remembering how she had relished putting him through his paces during the shopping trip, too.

"I don't know where any bars are," she protested. "And I really need to spend some more time in the studio tonight and—"

"Excuses," he said, shaking his head. "Procrastination. Get your butt into one of those new dresses, brush your hair and put on some of that war paint I bought for you and we'll head out."

Fifteen minutes later, Callie tottered into the room on a pair of stiletto heels and wearing a blue dress that faithfully followed her every curve. She bit her lush painted lips and Brock thought of a thousand reasons *not* to take her to a bar tonight. His goal was to get Callie out among adults and find a guy or two she could spend some time with. He was trying to help her find a man to dance with, maybe kiss, maybe more…

Regret burned in his gut. He didn't want some other man pawing her. Clenching his jaw and sucking in a mind-clearing breath, he reminded himself that this wasn't about what he wanted. It was about what Callie needed.

"Good job," he said, forcing himself to use the same tone he would use when a PFC performed well.

"I shouldn't have gotten these shoes. I'm going to break my neck," she said.

"You'll be fine. I imagine there will be at least a half-dozen guys willing to catch you if you fall."

"And if there aren't?"

"Then I will," he promised, but part of him wondered who was really doing the falling.

He escorted her out the door, to his car and toward a dance bar down the beach. Glancing at her, he noticed she was clasping her hands together so tightly he wondered if she would draw blood.

"Nobody's going to bite you—unless you want them to," he told her.

She shot him a hostile look. "Thanks for the reassurance. I feel so much better."

He shrugged and turned on the radio to help calm her nerves. "Approach it from a military point of view. What's the worst case scenario?"

"Just one worst case scenario?" she asked. "I thought there were at least a dozen. I could trip over these heels and fall down in front of everyone."

"We covered that one. Several someones will help you up."

"It would still be embarrassing."

"But you would live. If it bothered you that much,

you could go to a different bar where no one had seen you fall."

"What if someone makes a move on me?" she asked in a tense voice.

"Before I answer that question, I need to know if you would want them to make a move or not."

She glared at him. "Not, of course."

"No of course about it, Callie. You're single now."

"I don't feel single."

"That's because you haven't gotten out enough."

She sighed. "You still haven't answered my question."

"If some guy makes a move on you, you can turn him down, or I can help," he said.

"Then there's the opposite end of the spectrum. What if nobody talks to me and I sit there all alone feeling like a dud?"

"Is it better to sit alone feeling like a dud at home?"

She gave an exaggerated nod. "It's much better to feel like a dud in the privacy of my home. That way, I'm just lonely, not lonely and humiliated."

Brock pulled into the gravel parking lot of the bar and rubbed his hand over his face. This could be more challenging than he'd predicted. "Tell you what, I'll buy you a drink and talk to you for a half hour, then give the other guys some room."

She frowned, but nodded. "Okay."

"Okay, scoot."

She wrinkled her brow in confusion. "What do you mean, scoot?"

"I mean go make your entrance."

"By myself?"

"Of course. If you walk in with me, everyone will assume we're together and that will defeat the purpose of this exercise."

"And just so I'm clear on this, what is the purpose of this exercise?"

"The purpose is for you to engage in conversation with adult males and females, dance if you're so inclined, and possibly make arrangements for future dates or—"

She held up her hand. "Let's just work on the conversation part first. I'm not interested in dating. I'm not sure I ever will be," she said firmly.

Brock didn't bother to correct her. No use arguing over home plate when he had to get her to first base. He cocked his head toward the bar. "Stalling time is over."

She made a face. "You, you, you better come in after me, just in case…" Her mouth hung open as if she were searching for the right words.

"Just in case you get stampeded by every male in the place," he offered for her.

She snorted in disbelief and shoved open her car door. "Yeah, right. Like that's ever going to happen to me."

Brock watched her get out of the car and walk toward the entrance to the bar, her hips swinging from side to side as she planted one high heel in front of the other. Second—and third—thoughts chugged through his mind. Maybe this hadn't been a good idea after all. Maybe she wasn't ready.

Maybe *he* wasn't ready.

Eight

Marine Lingo Translation
Crumbcatcher: Mouth.

Brock gave Callie three minutes before he strolled into the bar. Spotting her from the doorway, he was surprised to see her already chatting animatedly with a man. He sidled over to an empty table that gave him a good view but wasn't too close to the bar, and watched the two of them talk.

After a few minutes, it became clear that they were talking about a couple of paintings hanging from the walls. The man carried her drink and his beer and guided her to one of the pictures. They appeared to discuss the painting for several minutes then returned to the bar. Callie wrote something down on a napkin and handed it to the man.

Brock raised his eyebrows and took a swig of his Corona. If she'd given him her phone number, the guy must have been smooth. He studied the man carefully. He looked midthirties, a little on the short side, dressed more appropriately for the city than this beach bar where drinks were served in plastic cups, and he'd slicked back his hair with gel.

The man kept moving way too close to Callie for Brock's taste, but she didn't seem to mind. She smiled and laughed.

Brock frowned. A restless sensation skittered through him. It was all well and good to get Callie out and dating again, but she needed to develop some self-protective skills toward men. He didn't want anyone taking advantage of her.

Acting in her best interest—at least that was what he told himself—he ambled to Callie's side. She smiled at him. "Brock, I've met another artist. He did those paintings on the far wall. Aren't they fantastic?"

Brock nodded in a noncommittal way. "Yeah. Are you from around here?"

The man shook his head and extended his hand. "No. Just passing through. I have a gallery in Atlanta. I'm Rick Lowry."

"Brock Armstrong," he said.

"Brock is moving to Atlanta soon. He's an architect."

"It's a great city. I prefer Boston or New York, but I have other reasons for staying." He glanced toward the other side of the bar and his face lit up. "There's

George waving me over." He turned back to Brock and pulled a card out of his pocket. "Listen, if you need anything when you get to Atlanta, give me a call. I know the best bars." He smiled at Callie. "Keep in touch. Let me know when you want to do a show. Bye now."

Brock took a deep gulp of his beer as he felt Callie looking at him.

"I think George is his partner," Callie said.

Brock nodded. "I got that impression. I imagine he won't be asking you to dance."

"No, but he might ask you," she said and chuckled.

Brock shot her a sideways glance. "Aren't you the funny one? I send you in here to hook up with a guy and you immediately find the one who doesn't like women."

Her lips twitched. "I wouldn't say he doesn't like women at all. He just may not like them—" she waved her hand "—romantically."

At that moment, the band on the patio geared up, filling the area with loud music.

"That's not a…"

Brock leaned closer, straining to hear her. "What did you say?"

"I said that's not all bad since this is my first time out and I told you I'm not interested in—"

"Excuse me," a male voice interjected.

Callie and Brock looked up in surprise.

The man cocked his head toward the dance floor. "Wanna dance?"

Brock watched the man's gaze slide over Callie's body like a laser-guided missile, not missing a curve. He fought a sudden strange urge to cover her with something—a blanket, on oversize beach towel, his body. Taking a deep breath, he dismissed the instinct and told himself this was what he'd wanted for her. He glanced at Callie and saw her jaw hanging slightly open in surprise.

She started to shake her head and Brock intervened. "Sure she will. Callie loves to dance."

Callie blinked then glared at him. "I, uh—"

"She's just a little shy," Brock said.

"I can help with that," the guy said in a seductive voice that made Brock grind his teeth. The man extended his hand and Callie hesitantly accepted.

No big deal, he told himself. This was what he'd wanted for Callie. Besides, the band wasn't playing a slow song, so the guy wouldn't be putting his hands all over her.

Sighing, Brock ordered another beer and watched Callie. Twenty minutes later, he glanced at his watch. The guy must have been persuasive if he'd hung on to her this long. Brock heard the music slow and watched the man pull her into his arms.

His gut clenched and he held his breath. Swearing at himself, he deliberately took a breath. Why was he overreacting like this? It was just a dance. It was what he'd wanted for her.

Glued to the sight of her, he felt her gaze connect with his when the man's back was facing Brock.

Even from this distance in the darkened bar, he saw emotions churning in her eyes. He glimpsed a combination of discomfort warring with need. She bit her lip and pulled away. He could practically hear the apology. He saw it written on her face as she left the dance floor.

She sat next to him and took a sip of her now-melted margarita. "Are you happy now?"

Not exactly, he thought. "It's a step," he said. "The first one is the hardest."

"I guess," she murmured. "Can we walk out on the beach for a couple of minutes? I need some air."

"Sure," he said. "Do you want your drink?"

She shrugged, but shook her head. "No."

They walked past the band and dance floor to the back door. Callie slipped off her shoes and carried them in one hand as she stepped onto the sand. "Oh, barefoot on the sand feels so much better than these heels."

Glad he'd skipped socks, Brock ditched his loafers and joined her. They walked closer to the shore and he watched her inhale the ocean breeze. She seemed restless and edgy.

"Was it that bad? I thought you told me that you like to dance," he said.

"I do like to dance, but I didn't feel comfortable with that man."

"Probably because you didn't know him. You might have grown more comfortable."

She shrugged. "I felt a lot more comfortable with you," she said and met his gaze.

He saw flickers of hunger in her eyes that matched what he was feeling for her. His gut tightened. "Maybe you shouldn't feel quite so comfortable with me."

"Why?" she asked, cocking her head to one side.

Brock looked away and stifled a groan. How did he explain that he wanted her so much, he went to bed every night burning with it? How did he confess his carnal need for her and still have her trust him?

She put her hand on his arm and he instinctively tightened his bicep. He'd spent so much time denying himself, he hadn't realized how much her touch could effect him.

"Why?" she repeated, her gaze imploring.

Brock sighed. "Because I may be doing my damndest to look after you, but I'm still a man. It's been a long time since I've been with a woman and being around you—" He broke off. "Being with you reminds me of what I'm missing."

Her eyes widened in disbelief. "You want me?"

He felt a scratchy irritation skitter down his neck. "What's so surprising about that? You're warm and sexy. You're beautiful."

She lifted her hand to his forehead. "Are you sure you're not ill? Delusional? I'm not beautiful. And I couldn't be sexy if I tried."

"You don't have to try. You haven't been looking at yourself like I have," he muttered, covering her hand with his and lowering it to his mouth. He rubbed his mouth over her palm, then darted his tongue over the inside of her wrist. He did the seductive move as a warning. *Know the limits, he was trying to tell her. Don't push the boundaries or you might get something you don't want.*

Expecting her to gasp and jerk her hand away, he was surprised when she stared at him in fascination and allowed him to continue to hold her hand in his.

Moving closer, she licked her lips and the sight of her pink tongue made him hard. "I want you, too," she whispered. "I feel guilty about it. Like I shouldn't," she continued in a rush.

Her confession made his heart jump. "You shouldn't want me," he told her. "I'm not the right kind of guy for you."

"The right kind of guy died," she said, her voice turning bitter. "I may fight it, but I'm still breathing, still living, still hurting and now wanting. I'm tired of feeling guilty for living when Rob died."

"You shouldn't feel guilty for living, Callie," he said, cradling her jaw, fighting the urge to draw her to him.

She closed her eyes. "Sometimes I think I must have turned into the worst woman on the planet. I want you. I don't love you, but I want you. I want to kiss you and touch you. I want you to touch me and get rid of this frustration and dissatisfaction that never goes away. I want to be one of those women you've had where they know the game and don't care."

Brock's temperature climbed several degrees. It would be so easy to take advantage of her now. So easy. He could pull her against him and touch her. He could kiss away the guilt and any vestiges of resistance. "You're not that kind of woman," he told her.

"Maybe I am," she said, opening her eyes, and he could feel the heat of her arousal between them. It thrummed with a dark and desperate need that matched his. "Maybe I've changed. Maybe I'm terrible and wicked because I want you, but I'd just be using you." She inhaled audibly and pulled her hand from his. "Oh, I can't believe I'm telling you this. It's crazy. I've gone crazy," she said and turned away.

She was his for the taking. The knowledge was unbearably tempting. She could ease the burning inside him. But how could he justify taking Rob's woman?

Rob was dead, a voice inside him ruthlessly reminded him. Rob couldn't take care of Callie's needs anymore. Brock couldn't take care of her the way she needed to be cared for, but he was confident he could take care of her in bed. He could let her use him.

What a joke, he thought. As if he would be doing her a favor. He was dying to get close to her, inside her.

Swearing under his breath, he scraped his hand through his hair. Maybe he was making this too complicated. Maybe this was part of the healing process for Callie. Maybe she needed to have sex with him so she could be ready for the guy she would really fall for. The thought pinched, but he brushed the sensation aside. Maybe he was looking for a justification where there was none.

Maybe it was time to stop thinking so damn much.

His heart pounding in his chest, he moved closer

to her, right behind her so he could smell a hint of her soft, sweet fragrance. "Are you sure about this?" he asked in a low voice against her ear.

"Yes," she said. "How horrible am I?"

Feeling like Satan himself, he lifted her hair from the side of her neck and lowered his mouth to brush his lips over her skin, while he slid his other hand around to her belly. "Maybe we should skip the recriminations and just agree to be horrible together."

He felt her shudder in his arms, then she turned around to face him and lifted her hands to cradle his head. "I've never been with a man like you."

"So we're even. I've never been with a woman like you," he said, seeing the lack of confidence in her eyes. "Maybe you can teach me something."

She gave a short, catchy laugh of disbelief. "Fat chance."

"You can try," he said, moving his hands around to the back of her waist and pulling her against him. "C'mon, Callie," he taunted. "Give it a try." Lowering his head, he pressed his mouth against hers and rubbed from side to side, absorbing the taste and texture of her lips. The kiss was a tease to himself, to her, and as she slid her fingers through his hair and gave a soft moan, he wanted more.

Opening his mouth, he drew her lips into his, tasting her, wanting to inhale her sweetness. She responded by sliding her tongue against his in a shy, but sensual shimmy that did crazy things to his nerve endings. Another moan escaped her lips and he felt the fire in his belly burn higher.

He opened his mouth and consumed her lips and tongue with his. As if there was a raging inferno pushing him onward, he rocked against the cradle of her femininity. The friction made him even harder. She ground against him in response, sucking his tongue deep into her sweet recesses.

She was so warm, so sexy, so ready. He felt the fringe of her desperation ripple through him. She caught him off guard when she tugged his shirt free from his jeans. Her hands on his belly were a welcome surprise.

He slid his hands lower to cup her sweet bottom as they moved against each other. He grew harder with each movement, each stolen breath she took. Unable to resist the temptation of her bare skin, he slipped one of his hands up under the hem of her dress, higher, finding her naked derriere. She was wearing the damn thong.

He broke into a sweat. The image of her naked bottom jerked him into third gear. He slid his fingers over the silky rounded contours. She undulated against him, as hot and bothered as he was. He could ditch this little scrap of silk and slide inside her right now. She wasn't at all cognizant of their proximity to the public bar, and he barely was.

He should stop, show some sanity, but oh—she felt so good, and she was wiggling against him like she couldn't get close enough. He wanted just a little more. *Just a little more,* he thought, as he slid his fingers between her legs and found her warm and wet.

"Oh, you feel so good," he muttered.

She moaned into his mouth and he stroked her, finding her bead of femininity swollen. He rubbed her with his thumb and plunged his finger inside her. The pitch of her voice changed, higher, more desperate. More than anything, he wanted to take care of the need he felt and heard coming from inside her.

He French-kissed her as he stroked her sweet spot and she opened her mouth gasping. He felt her contract intimately in his hand. "I—I—ohhhhhh." He covered her mouth with his to conceal the volume, drinking in her cry of pleasure.

"Oh my G—" She broke off and gasped for air, clinging to him. She ducked her head in his shoulder. "I don't know whether to die from embarrassment or just thank you," she finally managed in a husky breath.

"Why embarrassment?" he asked, trying unsuccessfully to nudge her head upward. "Embarrassment," he muttered, still hard as a brick. "Do you have any idea how sexy you were?"

"Yeah, right," she said in disbelief. "Sexy like a cat in heat. Screaming and mewing. Did I leave claw marks?"

"No," he said and chuckled. "But the evening's young."

She slowly lifted her head, her eyes full of pleasure and shimmering with the beginning of desire.

"I've never done that—" she cleared her throat self-consciously "—on the—"

"Beach. There's a drink called Sex on the Beach. I take it you've never had it."

She shook her head. "I never had body slammers, either."

"Looks like I'm leading you down the road to perdition. Are you sure you wanna go?"

Her eyes darkened. "Race ya," she said. "Can we go to your place?"

Nine

Marine Lingo Translation
Mattress pressing: Sleeping.

Brock drove them to his condo. Callie didn't say a word, but he could practically hear her emotions rattling inside her with the force of a hurricane.

He was still aroused, raring to go, ready in every way. He took a deep breath and worked at putting out the fire, or at least bringing it under control.

She'd lost her nerve. He felt a sinking disappointment, and something deeper, and shook it off. Maybe it was for the best.

He pulled into a spot in front of his condo and shifted into a Park. Sighing, he turned to her. "Hey, I can take you home. It's no problem."

"Why?" she asked.

Confused by the note of surprise in her voice, he looked at her. "You haven't said anything. You're having second thoughts. I understand."

"I'm not having second thoughts," she said.

Growing impatient, he rolled his eyes. "Callie, you've been completely silent."

"Well, excuse me, but maybe I'm a little nervous. It's been a while for me. And you're, well, you're different," she said in a huffy voice. "What if you end up thinking I'm a dud in bed and—"

He couldn't hold back a chuckle.

"And now you're laughing at me. Maybe I *am* having second thoughts," she said, crossing her arms over her chest.

Laughing again in some crazy combination of relief and frustration, he pulled her against him. "Don't worry about being a dud."

"Easy for you to say, Mr. Romeo."

He pressed his forehead against hers. "I told you I'm no Romeo. I didn't have to work that hard. Romeo had to try harder."

"That's right. The women fall into your hands like water from the faucet. I'm just like the rest of them, Brock."

"No you're not," he said. "No—"

She lifted her finger to his lips to stop his words. "I'm just like the rest of them. I need to be just like the rest of them."

She wasn't, but he wasn't going to argue with her about it. Not right now, anyway. This was one freakin' weird situation, but Brock had the odd feeling that he needed to let Callie see what a woman she was—in every sense of the word.

He kissed her and her response was warm and inviting. His banked arousal flared again. "Let's go inside," he murmured.

He led her inside and into the den. "Can I get you something to drink?"

"That would be nice," she said.

He pulled out a bottle of white wine he'd bought a week ago and poured two glasses. The wine wasn't going to do a damn thing to dampen his libido. He figured he would need to be run over by a truck in order to lose this edgy gotta-have-her feeling. Maybe not even then.

He found her on his balcony, enjoying the ocean breeze, and offered her a glass of wine.

"You have a great view," she said, accepting the glass and taking a long sip.

"I do," he said, looking at her.

She caught his gaze and smiled, shaking her head. "I meant the ocean."

"It's okay. I like what I'm looking at better."

"You're a flatterer," she chided, taking another sip.

"Not me. Just call 'em like I see 'em." He stepped closer to her, inhaling her scent as he slid his arm around the front of her and drew her against him.

"Hmm. You're warm," she murmured.

"You cold?"

"Not really. But your warmth feels good."

He planned to make her feel a helluva lot more than *good*.

"Have you ever made love on a balcony?" she asked.

Surprised by her question, he grinned in the darkness. "No. Why?"

"Just curious. I imagine you've had sex in more interesting places than I have."

Setting down his glass of wine, he turned her to face him. "Do you wanna make love on the balcony?"

"Maybe," she said a little defensively. "What if I do?"

He felt his grin grow. "Then we'll make love on the balcony."

She bit her lip. "Or maybe I'd like to sometime."

Bold, then timid. She was going to kill him. *Ah, but what a way to go.* Backing against the wall, he pulled her with him. "I'll make a note to check the security of the railing," he said, lowering his mouth and French-kissing her. She tasted of wine and sweetness.

He pulled the wineglass from her hand and put it on the small wrought-iron table beside them. Her lips and tongue chased his, and with every little stroke of her tongue, he grew hotter and harder.

He ran his hands down her back to her bottom. "You feel so good," he muttered.

"You do, too," she said, her body flush with his.

He continued to dally with her lips, driving himself a little more crazy. He could feel her warming up, growing hotter and more restless. Her fingers squeezed his biceps then slid up to his shoulders. She rubbed against him and he could feel the hard tips of her breasts even through her clothing. He wanted to rip off those clothes and plunge inside her.

Slow, he coached himself. It's been a while for her. It'll be better if it's slow.

She made a sound of frustration and tugged at the buttons of his shirt. He heard the sound of one clicking on the concrete floor as it fell.

"Sorry," she murmured.

"No problem," he managed in a voice that sounded hoarse to his own ears.

"I like your chest," she whispered, her hands floating over his bare skin like a breeze. She buried her face in his chest then slid her tongue over his throat. "I like the way you taste."

Brock swallowed an oath at the surge of arousal that pumped through him. He was supposed to be the experienced one, the one in control.

She tugged her straps down and pressed her small, bare breasts against his chest and sighed as if in relief. "Sorry, I just needed to feel you."

"No apologies necessary," he said, thinking she was hotter than a firecracker and he wanted all her heat and fire. He lifted his hands and slid his fingers between them to touch the hard tips of her breasts.

She moaned against his throat. *Sensitive,* he thought, a rush of delight running through him. He played with her nipples and kissed her until her gasps made him sweat. Blindly, he groped for a chair and sank down onto it, pulling her onto his lap.

He sucked her hard nipple into his mouth and she made a sexy, keening sound of pleasure. She pressed her breast against him and he gently nipped the tip and laved it with his tongue.

Each sound she made was like another intimate stroke. He slid one of his hands between her legs and found her wet and warm. "I want to be inside you, Callie. As deep as I can get."

Shuddering, she gave him an openmouthed kiss that made him feel as if he were going to explode. Pushed to the edge of his restraint, he stood and carried her to his bedroom. He put her down on his bed and shucked his jeans, then reached to his bedside table for the condoms he'd bought last week. He tore one open and put it on, then followed her down onto the bed.

He wanted to plunge inside her this second, but he wanted to make sure she was ready for him. He found her swollen nubbin of femininity and rubbed it with his thumb. She arched against him.

"Brock."

She said his name in a hot, restless, needy whisper that felt like a drug flowing through his veins. He wanted to consume every inch of her. He stripped off her thong and buried his face between her legs, kissing her intimately, licking and sucking her hot spot.

He felt her come apart, and her climax was the biggest turn-on he'd ever experienced. Rising, he spread her legs farther apart and plunged inside her.

He distantly heard her barely audible sound of relief mingle with his. She paused a moment, her eyes widening as if his size was more than she'd expected.

Then she undulated beneath him.

Brock swore at the tight sensation. Her hair scattered over his bedspread like wild red-gold ribbons, her mouth swollen from his kisses, her eyes dark with arousal, her small breasts and tight nipples all a picture of the darkest, most forbidden fantasy he'd conjured.

She moved again in invitation.

"Take me," she said.

And he did, plunging into a rhythm that stretched and caressed. When she wrapped her legs around his waist, he felt something inside him tear at the sexy display of trust, and his orgasm ripped through him like buckshot.

Several moments passed before he could breathe or think. His heart still pounding as if he'd run a race, he rolled onto his back beside Callie. He swore.

"Is that bad or good?" she asked.

He took her hand and laced his fingers through hers. "Great. Amazing."

"Do you think it was so intense because it's been so long for both of us?"

"It could have been part of it," he said, but he knew that wasn't all. The dark, driving need he felt for her wasn't just because he'd been abstinent for a long while. He turned onto his side and looked at her. "There's one way to find out."

She looked up at him and smiled. "Really? You could do it again tonight?"

Her question made him wonder what her love life with Rob had been like, but he didn't want to go near the subject—not with his mind, certainly not with their conversation.

"Yeah, we can go again. If you want…" He lifted her hand to his mouth and kissed it.

She slid her hand over his jaw and the combination of how sexy she looked and how sweetly she touched him undid something inside him. "I think I want," she said and urged his mouth down to hers.

Hours later, after they'd made love more times than he'd thought possible, he looked up to find her sitting at the bottom of his bed with her arms holding her knees close to her chest. He suddenly felt a distance between them and a painful sensation tightened his gut. Regret. She regretted being with him. He could practically taste it.

"I think I should go home now."

He wanted to ask why, but he wasn't sure he wanted the answer, so he didn't. "Okay. Let me pull on my clothes."

He got dressed and she did the same, her eyes never meeting his as she stepped into her thong and zipped her dress. She ran her fingers through her tangled hair and winced.

"You want a brush?"

"No, I'll just wait until I get home."

They'd been as close as a man and woman could get, yet she wouldn't look at him. He felt oddly snubbed, irritated.

They walked to his car and he noticed how careful she was not to brush up against him. That irritated him more. He started the engine and drove the short distance to her cottage. He cut the engine and they sat in silence for a full moment.

"Thank you for bringing me home," she said in a small, stilted voice.

Brock clenched his jaw. An hour ago, she'd been crying out his name, begging him to come inside her. "No problem. I'm at your service."

She must have heard the slight edge to his voice. She looked at him. "I've never had an affair. I'm not exactly sure how to do this. What do I do now?"

He relaxed a millimeter. "What do you want to do?"

"I don't know. I feel weird."

He nodded, thinking in all the times he'd been intimate with a woman, the evening had never ended like this. But then, he'd never been with Callie before.

He leaned closer to her and lowered his head, brushing a kiss to her forehead. "Don't try to figure it all out tonight."

"It would give me a headache."

He chuckled. "I'm flattered."

She looked at him blankly then her eyes widened. "Oh, I'm probably supposed to tell you that you were great in bed, aren't I?"

He lifted his hand. "No, not necessary at all. It's

just if you're gonna get the headache complaints, they're usually before."

"Well you were very good." She looked away then back at him as if something was troubling her. "Maybe too good. Thank you for the evening. G'night," she said and slipped out of the car.

As he watched her walk into her house, he wanted to go after her and ask her what she'd meant by *too good. How could a man be too good in bed?* She hadn't said it in a complimentary way.

Brock frowned and started the car, jerking it into gear. By the time he arrived back at his condo, every other word flying through his mind was an oath. What a kooky, weird woman. *Too good, my ass,* he thought. She hadn't been exactly shabby herself.

Stomping into his house, he headed for the refrigerator and poured himself a glass of wine. He swore again. After the amount of sex he'd had tonight, he should be dead on his feet, ready for a coma. Instead, he was irritated, wondering what her problem was. He knew she'd wanted him, she'd matched his eagerness. He hadn't misread her.

Scowling, he paced the den. He collected their abandoned glasses from the balcony and tried not to focus on how she had felt in his arms, how she had tasted. Pulling the patio door shut, he turned on the television to a late-night infomercial. He needed to fill up his brain with something besides Callie.

Taking a gulp of his wine, he paced from one end of the den to the other. He paced to the bedroom and came to a stop. The bed mocked him. He smelled her scent and she was there—her hair splayed out on his bedcover, her legs tangled with his, her voice urging him on.

Damn her. He stripped the bed and put on fresh sheets, but before he tossed the sheets into the washer, he couldn't resist inhaling another draft of her. She had told him she wanted to be just like all the other women he had known. He'd never had any problem putting a woman behind him.

He'd better not start now with her.

The next morning, after another restless night, he grimly refocused and reminded himself that he was trying to help Callie recover from her grief. It was her prerogative to act strangely. He needed, however, to keep her on track. Last night had been about healing and want.

It sure as hell hadn't been pity sex, his brain screamed at him with the same lack of pity he would expect from a drill instructor. He had relished every minute of it and would have gone back for more if...

He swore. He needed to stop thinking about it. After taking an early morning run, he waited awhile and decided to get Callie moving. One of the keys to getting her out of a rut was keeping her moving, even if that meant a run on the beach.

He pounded on the door and waited. Several moments later, she appeared at the door in a robe, her hand shielding her eyes from the sun.

"Why are you here now?"

"Time for your run." He pointed at his watch. "I gave you an extra hour."

She groaned, covering her face. "I don't feel like running today." She held the door open for a half-second then turned back into the house.

Brock caught the screen door just before it slammed shut and followed her inside. "You'll feel better once you get moving."

"No, I won't. I drank some of that nasty tequila you left here."

He lifted his eyebrows in surprise. "Why?"

"So I wouldn't think and so I would sleep. My head feels like someone is slamming it with a hammer."

"How much did you drink?"

"Just two shots, but I think it combined with the margarita and the glass of wine and—" she glanced at him then looked away "—and the activity to be too much."

"I'll get you some aspirin," he said, heading for her medicine cabinet. In some sick way, it comforted him that she'd had problems sleeping, too. After he collected the medicine, he stopped by the kitchen to fill a glass with water and grab a few crackers.

"Crackers first," he said as he stood in front of her.

She sighed. "Do you have to be so nice when I'm feeling so cranky?"

His lips twitched. She reminded him of a child that had been woken too early from her nap. "You can walk a little when the meds kick in."

She shook her head. "No, I can't."

"Why not?"

"Because my head isn't the only thing that's hurting," she said bluntly.

It took a moment for her meaning to sink in. "Oh, muscles or—"

"Try everything. Everything that hasn't been exercised that way in a long time, or maybe everything that's never been exercised that way. And I know they're necessary, but I think the condoms made it worse."

He gaped at her.

"So when we do this again, I prefer it barefoot."

He blinked, his stomach taking an odd dip. "From the way you acted last night, I didn't get the impression you wanted to do it again."

She sipped her water and pushed her hair from her face. Slowly, she met his gaze and he saw the stark emotion stamped across her fine features.

Guilt. She felt guilty as hell.

He felt it like a kick in the gut. "You really don't have—"

She shook her head and bit her lip. "I don't have it all figured out, but the thing that bothered me most was that I liked it better with you than I remember liking it with Rob."

Ten

Marine Lingo Translation
Cool beans: Everything is fine.

She could have knocked him over with her pinkie finger. Brock stared at her. No, make that her pinkie fingernail.

Her eyebrows furrowed. "I don't really want to talk about it. It feels disrespectful or dishonorable or scuzzy."

"Okay," he said, not eager to hear the intimate details of Callie's sexual experiences with Rob.

"But it just always seemed to go too fast and just when I started to get into it," she said with a shrug, "it would be over."

Speechless, Brock nodded. "I understand if you don't want to talk about it."

"I really appreciate it, but it's a sensitive subject. It always was. Rob never really wanted to talk about it and I just figured something might be wrong with me."

"Trust me, Callie, there's nothing wrong with you. Nothing at all," he said, remembering how hot she'd been in his arms last night.

"Are you sure?" she whispered.

Her uncertainty ripped at something inside him. The fragility of the moment required a careful response. He sank onto the sofa beside her. "I'm pretty sure," he said, "but there's only one real way to be sure. We'd have to do it again."

She punched his arm and laughed. "Not today. I'm too sore."

The telephone rang and she glanced toward the kitchen. "I wonder who that is," she said, rising. "Back in a minute."

He heard her pick up the phone. "Oh, Mama Newton, how are you?"

His ears perked up at the mention of Rob's last name.

"They've built a memorial in front of the library in honor of Rob?" Callie said, her voice tightening. "That's wonderful."

"You want me to come to the dedication ceremony?" he heard her ask, her voice tightening even more. Funny how his gut tightened each time he heard the tension rise in her voice.

"Of course I'll come," she said and paused. "Mama Newton, you're sweet to offer, but we've been through this before. I can't come live with you. My messy art would drive you crazy."

The conversation continued for several more minutes with a few muted responses from Callie. He heard her hang up the phone. A long moment passed before she returned to the den with her face and spirit matching the muted tone of her voice.

"Your mother-in-law?" he prompted.

She nodded, looking as tense as an overdrawn bow with her arms crossed over her chest. "Problem?"

"No," she said in a clipped, small voice. "She's a lovely person and she's always been very kind and generous to me."

"I hear a but," he said, standing, concerned at the shift in her mood.

"No buts," she insisted.

"Callie," he said, putting his hand on her shoulder. "You're acting like an overwound jack-in-the-box."

She sighed. "It's hard to hear her pain. She still can't believe he's gone and I think one of the ways she tries to keep him alive is by talking with me about him." She pushed her hair behind her ear. "I don't want to be unkind, but I always feel so sad after I talk with her." Her voice broke and she audibly swallowed. "Sometimes I think she wants me to live the rest of my life in Rob's memory. Live with her, stop drawing, stop laughing, stop—"

"Breathing," he finished for her.

She met his gaze with desperation in her eyes. "I feel bad talking about her this way."

"You wouldn't go live with her, would you?" he asked, his instincts telling him that would be one of the worst things Callie could do.

She shook her head. "I thought about it, but I took the coward's way out," she said with a short laugh. "I ran away and moved to the beach instead."

"Good choice," he said.

She shrugged her shoulders and gave him a lop-sided smile that had the ability to move past skin, bone and muscle to his heart. "We'll see. I've been drawing more lately. This kind of thing usually slows me down, though."

"Okay. What club do you want to join so you don't slow down?" he asked.

Callie wrinkled her nose. "I think I'm going to go to a meeting of the sand castle builders' club. Wanna come?"

He nodded, unable to swallow his grin. "Yeah, just remember I'm an architect, so I'm opinionated about construction."

They spent the next three hours constructing an elaborate castle made of sand. Brock had argued for something more modern, but Callie insisted on turrets and moats. Soon enough, a group of children asked if they could help and the castle became a community project.

Brock enjoyed watching Callie's interaction with the children and he became more determined than ever to nudge her to get regularly involved. She exclaimed over their diligence and creativity.

"Photographs," she said. "I've got to have photographs. Wait here while I get my cameras," she said, and ran to the cottage.

She returned with two cameras. "Okay, crowd around the back of the castle. You, too, Brock!"

He shook his head. "No. You should be in this."

She shook her head. "No, you designed it so—"

"Your nose is burned," he said, lightly touching her pink nose. "I told you that you should have put on more sunscreen."

"I'll take it," a woman said, stepping forward. "That way, both you and your husband can be in the picture."

Out of the corner of his eye, Brock saw Callie open her mouth at the same time he opened his. "Thanks," he said, beating her to the punch and tugging Callie toward the castle. "We'd appreciate that."

"You shouldn't have let her think we were—"

"The ocean would have washed away the castle by the time we explained our relationship to her," he muttered. "Just let the woman take the picture."

The passerby took several photos with each camera.

"That one's digital," Callie said. "For immediate gratification."

"Is that what you want?" Brock asked in a low voice. "Immediate gratification."

She gave a cheesy smile for the camera then turned to him with fire in her eyes. "You have a wicked mind."

"You didn't answer my question," he said.

"I like it slow."

Brock made a note of it.

* * *

Brock still wasn't happy with Callie's lack of involvement and in the back of his mind, the clock was ticking. He would be leaving for his job in Atlanta in a couple of weeks. Although it wasn't his first choice, he took Callie to visit a senior citizens' center.

"I don't like public speaking," she told him as he escorted her inside the small brick building.

"Just talk a few minutes," he told her. "The director told me the main thing these people will enjoy will be some personal interaction with you."

Sighing, she shook her head. "Do you ever think you're taking this grief treatment service to the extreme? Shopping, sex, trips to the senior citizens' center."

His mind tripped on the middle item on her list. "We only had sex one time."

"It was one night," she corrected. "But it was definitely more than one time. That's why we haven't had it again."

He'd wondered. He'd told himself she was teasing him about having sex again with him, but he spent a lot of time looking for any sign of invitation from her. None so far.

The director met them and led them to a sunny room. She introduced Callie to the surprisingly large group of people. Callie spoke for a few minutes and showed the group examples of her work. Afterward, she invited the group to experiment with the easels and pads of paper available throughout the room.

Brock watched her talk with nearly every person in the room. Her patience and the way she focused her attention on each individual impressed him. He tried to think of one woman he'd dated who would have spent more than five minutes at a senior citizens' center. None came to mind.

The men flirted with her. The women mothered her. Two hours later, he finally drove out of the parking lot.

Callie leaned her head against the headrest and sighed. "That was more fun than I expected."

"You were great," he told her.

She glanced at him. "I didn't really do much. They mostly wanted to talk."

"You paid attention. You laughed at corny jokes and acted like you were interested when you were looking at photographs of grandchildren and great-grandchildren."

"I wasn't acting. It's fun to hear people talk about things or people they're enthusiastic about."

"So maybe you're not the superintrovert you profess to be," he said.

"Do you have to rub this in?"

"I'm not gonna be here forever and I don't want you crawling back into your cave when I leave."

She turned quiet. "I keep forgetting you're going to be leaving soon."

"Are you afraid you're going to miss me?"

He felt her glance at him thoughtfully. "Well, I

think you're one of those people you get used to having around."

The note of tenderness in her voice made a knot form in his chest. He didn't know if it was longing or something else.

"Sort of like a pet allergy."

He tossed her a sideways glance.

"Or a reaction to poison ivy," she said cheerfully.

"You little witch."

"Well, if you're going to get all sloppy and sentimental about me missing you."

"I didn't get sloppy and sentimental."

"Brock, you're moving just over the state line. I can hunt you down if I want."

She wouldn't want to hunt him down, though, he knew. "You don't like Atlanta."

"That's right. So you're probably safe."

"Unless you quit being such a chicken and show some of your work besides your illustrations for the children's books."

"You're starting to remind me of a pet allergy again."

He gave a dry grin. "It's my mission in life. How am I doing?"

"Great. I'm starved."

"Would you like to go to dinner?"

"That would be nice."

"To a real restaurant in public. Two public outings in one day. Are you sure you're up to it?"

She shot him a level gaze. "I've turned a corner."

"But you're not all the way onto the new road."

"Nag, nag, nag," she said.

"Is this okay?" he asked, pointing to a seafood restaurant.

She nodded. "Looks good to me."

She ordered a Hurricane. He ordered a beer. While they waited, she doodled on a napkin. He wanted to know what she was drawing, but she snatched it away before he could see. They split an appetizer of coconut shrimp. She ordered a second Hurricane and he raised his eyebrows. "You going for another headache?"

"No," she said, and muttered something under her breath. When the waitress returned with her drink, Callie pulled the cherry from her glass and offered it to him. "You told me you liked cherries?"

He choked on the beer he'd just swallowed. He couldn't read her expression, but the way she dangled the cherry from the stem made him think about forbidden fruit. Hers in particular. He grew warmer. "Yeah," he said and popped the plump cherry into his mouth.

"Just curious," she said, stirring her drink with the straw. "When was the last time you were tested for sexually transmitted diseases?"

He dipped his head in disbelief. "Excuse me?"

"When was the last time you were—"

His heart stuttered in his chest. He waved his hand for her to stop. "They tested me for everything when I was in the hospital. Why do you ask?"

She paused for a long moment, still stirring her

drink, then met his gaze. "Because I'm not sore anymore."

Brock felt his libido jump the equivalent from one to two-hundred-and-fifty miles per hour. "Is that why you've been drinking Hurricanes?"

"It would be more gallant of you not to point that out," she said, taking a sip.

He grabbed her hand and held it in his. "You want me to be gallant?"

She bit her lip. "Not really."

He leaned toward her. "Callie, it's okay to ask for what you want."

"I guess I'm not used to feeling free to ask."

"What would you like?"

Taking a little breath as if she were shoring up her nerve, she smiled. "I would like you to please take care of the check while I go to the powder room, and then I would like to go back to your place, if that's okay with you."

Her combination of shyness and boldness did dangerous things to his heart. "Okay," he said, and signaled for the waitress while Callie left the table.

When they arrived at his condo, the sun was just beginning to set and they sat in the car to watch it. "Look how pretty the sky is," she said. "Hot pink, coral and gray-blue."

"Ever get the itch to do landscapes and watercolors?"

"Every once in a while. I often joked with Rob that I needed to go to the Caribbean so I could be inspired by the sunset, but we never went." She cleared her throat and shrugged. "It didn't really matter. My strength is drawing people. I like showing emotion in facial expressions, posture, even what they wear. And with kids, I don't have to be too subtle. It's fun." She looked at him. "What about you? Did you ever want to do a different kind of architecture?"

He nodded. "Skyscrapers, like everyone else."

"Do you ever sneak and draw a building on a napkin when you're supposed to be doing something else?" she asked.

"I used to," he said, her question reminding him of times in his life that hadn't been so driven, so serious. "I haven't had a chance in a while."

"Did you when you were in the hospital?"

"A few times," he admitted and narrowed his eyes at her. "How did you know?" he teased. "Were you watching me?"

"Well, architecture is a kind of art, so I figured you had to be a doodler at some time in your life." She met his gaze, and her eyes held a combination of fragility and resolve. "I've started doodling again," she told him.

"In the restaurant," he said with a nod. "What were you drawing?"

She hesitated. "Come on," he coaxed.

"I did it quickly, so don't expect too much." She fished the napkin out of her purse and showed it to him.

Brock stared at the portrait she'd drawn of him. It had a slight cartoon quality. His chin and cheekbones were exaggerated, but she had softened his scowl with a glint in his eye. His shoulders were overly broad and she'd emphasized his pecs. "You made me look like a superhero."

"How?" she asked, frowning as she turned the napkin around to study it.

"My shoulders aren't that broad," he said.

"Yes, they are."

"You exaggerated my pecs," he said.

"Did not," she protested. "You've got a killer body and you know it."

He knew he was in shape, but it was damn nice hearing her compliment because he knew it wasn't idle flattery. After all, this same woman had compared him to the itch associated with poison ivy. "Are you trying to seduce me?"

"With this drawing?" she asked in disbelief, then chortled with glee. "Are you that easy?"

"Depends on the woman," he said, meeting her gaze and holding it. The temperature in the car went up several degrees. He saw the wanting in her eyes. "Ask for what you want," he told her.

"Kiss me," she told him, lifting her lips to his.

He took her mouth and kissed her, searching for answers to the questions she aroused in him. How did she manage to make him feel lighter just by smiling? How did she know just what to ask him that reminded him of a more carefree time in his life? How did she make him crave being with her? Even when she was sad. She was so real. Sometimes he felt as if he'd never held a real woman until her. He flicked his tongue over hers and she responded immediately, tasting him, licking his lips as if she craved him the same way he craved her.

It wasn't possible, he told himself, but it sure felt good.

"I've never done it in a car," she murmured against his lips.

"Are you saying you want to?" he asked, pulling back slightly.

Her cheeks lit with color. "Maybe sometime."

"Not tonight?" he clarified.

"Not tonight. Can we go up to your condo now?"

"Oh, yeah," he said, his body temperature climbing at the expression in her eyes.

She slid her hand into his and walked with him up the steps. He liked the way her small hand felt in his. He liked the way she felt beside him. He felt the hum of anticipation between them.

Brock was getting the impression that Callie hadn't been encouraged to be adventurous in bed, but she was eager to experiment.

He might go to hell for it, but she could experiment on him all she wanted.

Eleven

Marine Lingo Translation
Pucker Factor: The degree of stress in a given
situation.

As soon as Brock got Callie inside his condo door,
he pushed her against the wall and French-kissed her
until they could barely breathe.

Her lids heavy with arousal, she sighed. "Oh, wow.
I'm starting to understand why you don't have trouble
getting women to do what you want," she murmured.

Her comment flattered him at the same time it
bothered him. He pushed the bothered part aside and
sank his hands into her hair and kissed her again. It
was easy to forget everything when he kissed Callie.
Her taste, her scent, her response, filled him up. He
slid his knee between her legs and she wriggled
against him.

She made him want everything at once. He wanted to kiss her everywhere, take her every way, all at once. Frustration and desire he'd never before experienced rolled through him.

"Oh." She moaned against his throat, and he felt her tempting little cat tongue slide over his skin.

"What do you want, baby?" he asked, wanting to give her everything.

"I can barely think straight. How can I tell—" She broke off when he ground her against his swollen hardness.

"I want you to tell me what you want."

"You're doing pretty good without me telling you what to do."

He took a mind-clearing breath. "I mean it. I want you to tell me what you want. I have this feeling you haven't always gotten what you wanted or needed, and I'm going to make sure that changes. Especially tonight."

She looked up at him uncertainly. "Anything? I can ask for anything?"

"Anything," he said, but he was determined she would want him inside her before the night was over.

"Okay." She licked her lips then closed her eyes. "Looking at you is distracting. I want music. I want one glass of wine for us to share. I want the lights down low."

"Have a seat while I get the wine," he said, and handed her the remote control to the stereo system.

He heard her flick through several radio stations until she landed on jazz.

Brock's fingers fumbled as he opened the bottle of white wine he'd bought after he and Callie had made love the first time. He had thought it might happen again and he'd been in a state of anticipatory lust.

He wanted this to be so right for her. His gut tied in knots, he shook his head at himself. He couldn't remember the last time he'd been nervous with a woman. He'd always taken his signals from the woman and acted on instinct, but for some reason, with Callie, it was different. He wanted to be everything she wanted and needed.

He swore under his breath as he spilled some of the wine. He was thinking way too deeply about this. Returning the wine bottle to the fridge, he walked into the den where the lights were low and found Callie in a large overstuffed chair.

"Here it is," he said, extending the wineglass to her.

"Thanks," she said and scooted over. "Join me."

"Sure." It took some rearranging, but soon she was sitting on his lap and they were taking turns sipping the wine.

He teased her with slow, mind-drugging kisses that left him hard and her limp. She accidentally spilled some wine on his shirt.

"Oh, I'm sorry. I didn't mean to—"

"No problem," he said, pulling off his shirt and tossing it aside.

Shaking her head, she skimmed one of her hands over his chest, sending a shiver down his spine. "You are incredibly built."

"A lot of scars," he muttered. He generally ignored them, but sometimes when he stepped out of the shower, the marks on his body still caught him off guard.

"They don't bother me," she whispered, and darted her pink tongue over a jagged scar on his chest.

Every muscle inside him tightened at the soft, sensual stroke.

She paused, glancing up at him. "Hurt?"

He shook his head. "Not at all."

Her lips curved in a slow, sexy smile and she lowered her mouth to his chest again. She dropped openmouthed kisses over his chest and torso. With each millimeter lower that she traveled, he felt himself grow harder. When she dipped her mouth just above his navel, all he could think about was her wrapping her busy tongue around him, and exploding.

That would last a whopping three seconds and she wouldn't get a thing from it. Sighing, he drew her back up to his mouth.

"You didn't like the direction I was going?"

"Too much," he said, and slid his hands under her blouse while he kissed her. He found her nipples, tight little buds already, and fondled them until she was squirming in his lap.

As if she couldn't stand the teasing sensation, she pulled off her shirt and bra and tossed them aside.

She immediately pressed her breasts against him and sighed in pleasure.

Determined to make the rest of their clothes evaporate, Brock unfastened her jeans. Following his lead, he felt her tug at the button and zipper for his jeans, too. Her fumbling only made him harder.

With a growl of frustration, she pulled away from him and ditched her own jeans then tugged at his. That primitive growl sent thunder through his pulse, and after he got rid of his jeans, he pulled her back onto his lap and drew one of her breasts into his mouth.

"Oh, wow." She moaned. "They're so small, but you make them feel so good."

"They're not too small. Just right," he said, nibbling gently on her nipple.

She moaned again and squirmed. He could feel her moistness brush against him. It would be so easy to pull her over him and slide inside. The very thought of it made him feel like he would explode.

Pushing away from him, she stood naked in front of him, tugging at his hand to join her.

"What?" he asked, fascinated by the sight of her, bare and pale with her fiery red-gold hair mussed and hanging down to her shoulders.

"Dance with me," she coaxed. "Dance naked with me."

The invitation was so sexy it almost hurt to accept. As soon as he took her hand in his, she pressed herself flush against him and urged his mouth to hers.

Brock couldn't think of anything more erotic than having Callie kiss him while her silky legs slid against his and her bare belly brushed him intimately. She stretched on tiptoe, inviting him to slide against her where she was wet and swollen.

Brock accepted the invitation. She felt like warm honey on him. He wanted so badly to plunge inside… He swore.

"I need to get a condom," he muttered, loath to move away from her.

"No, you don't," she said, brushing her lips over his in a teasing caress.

"What do you mean?"

"I mean I got something from the doctor so we don't have to use anything else."

"The pill?"

She shook her head and made a little sound of frustration. "No. I took care of it. No worries. No babies."

For an instant, the image of Callie, big and pregnant with his baby, flashed through his mind. His heart squeezed tight in a strange way. Alarm shot through him. *Where the hell had that thought come—*

She brushed against him again, distracting him.

She was a delectable, wiggling, irresistible combination and she was so hot he could barely stand it. He could feel her heat, her want, and it drove his excitement level straight through the roof.

"Oh, babe, you're making it hard for me to take my time," he said, both tortured and stimulated as she rocked against him. "What do you want, Callie?"

Her shiver of anticipation sent his libido up another notch. "I like it all," she murmured, rubbing her mouth over his chest. "I like the way you touch me, the way you kiss me. I like it all."

The dark sensual expression in her eyes tore his already shredded restraint. He pushed her back against the chair they'd shared and kissed his way down her silky, smooth skin. Her flat belly rippled as he tasted her belly button and when he went lower, she gasped. He tasted her intimately, rubbing his tongue over her swollen bead.

She arched against his mouth and her breath came in sexy little gasps that made him crazy with need. She said his name over and over again as he felt her climax against him.

"Brock, pleeeeeeease."

"Please what?" he asked, his body bucking with the need to be inside her.

She slid her hands over his hips and pulled him between her legs. "I want you so bad."

"How, Callie?" he asked at the edge of his control. He felt his muscles bunch and coil with the effort to restrain himself.

"In me," she said, arching her hips upward in a glorious feminine invitation that he would have to be dead not to accept.

Unable to hold back any longer, he plunged inside her. He heard her moan mingle with his at the delicious sensation. She was wet, tight and irresistible. He pumped inside her, groaning at the way she tightened around him intimately, as if she couldn't get enough of him, as if she were stroking and holding him in the most sensual, intimate way possible.

The combination of her rocking movements and her little, breathless gasps undid him. He felt the force of his peak vibrate from head to toe. Feeling aftershocks rocking through both him and Callie, he rolled to his side and held her tightly against him.

Her breath tickled his throat and he felt an odd warmth unfurl from inside him. He couldn't remember feeling so satisfied, so complete.

Callie wiggled slightly and slid her arms underneath his. "I know guys like you probably hate this, but could you hold me a little longer?"

Brock frowned. "What do you mean *guys like me?*"

"Well, I mean experienced guys, love-'em-and-leave-'em types. You probably would prefer me to jump up, give you a quick kiss good-night then leave you in peace, but—"

Brock swore and shook his head. "You must have one helluva low opinion of me."

Callie looked up at him. "Not at all. I just understand that you don't want a cling-wrap kind of lover."

Brock felt the stab of truth in her words. She wasn't that far off. With just about any other woman, right now he'd be thinking about how to get her out the door. But not with Callie. He liked the way she felt wrapped around him like cling wrap. He liked feeling every inch of her and he wasn't inclined to move one millimeter away.

"There's no rush," he said, and liked the way her eyes softened.

"Are you sure?" she asked in a husky voice that felt warm and fuzzy inside him.

"Yeah," he said and pulled her against him. She gave a soft sigh of contentment that seeped through him like brandy. He wanted another shot.

They made love frequently over the next few days. Callie seemed determined to make love with Brock in every way she'd been denied in the past, and Brock was perfectly willing to indulge her every request. For a woman who claimed limited experience and previous sexual shyness, she sure was knocking his socks off on a regular basis.

It would have been one hundred percent pleasurable if he hadn't detected an undertone of desperation. He wanted to ask her about it, but some form of self-preservation told him not to go there.

One night after she'd burned up his bed, she sat up and wrapped her arms around her legs. "I have to go to my mother-in-law's house tomorrow morning."

Her announcement felt as if she'd thrown a bucket of ice water on him. He sat up slowly. "Why is that?"

"The memorial for Rob is this weekend. I promised I would come."

He nodded, feeling a tightness form in his chest. He'd spent a lot of time running from thoughts of Rob and how he would feel about Brock making love to his wife. If he spent more than ten seconds thinking about it, Brock felt like the very devil himself. "Do you want me to go with you?"

"No," she said immediately, and he felt the cut as if she'd sliced him with a switchblade. "I think it would be hard for his mother to see you. She's still so hurt. She doesn't understand why—"

"Why I lived and he didn't," he finished for her, bitterness backing up in his throat.

She swallowed audibly, clearly dealing with her own emotions. "I was going to say that she doesn't understand why he had to die. I know that his death and your life aren't really related, but she might react to you out of her pain. Nobody needs that to happen."

"If I had never met Rob, would you want me to go with you?"

She bit her lip and shook her head.

Something inside him cracked and it hurt like hell.

"I have a role to play for my mother-in-law and for the community."

"Grieving widow."

"Right," she said. She reached out and took his hand. "I'm not exactly the grieving widow when I'm with you."

"You have been," he said, soothed just a little by her stroking fingers.

"Not lately."

"You sound like you feel guilty."

"I do, some. If I think about it, but I try not to."

She took a deep breath and exhaled. "I feel very alive with you."

"That's not all bad, Callie," he said, leaning toward her and nuzzling her head.

"I guess," she said, and was quiet for a long moment. "When do you start your job in Atlanta?"

"Nine days."

She gave a forced laugh and pulled away. "Well, at least you won't have to put up with my craziness anymore."

He hated her withdrawal. He wanted her back, close to him, depending on him. "You haven't heard me complaining, have you?"

"No."

"It doesn't have to end when I move to Atlanta," he ventured, tugging at her hand.

"Yes, it does," she said firmly. "You and I have given ourselves permission to be lovers for a limited time. You need to start your life and I need to get on with mine. We both knew this was going to be tempor—"

He covered her mouth with his, cutting off her words with a kiss. His heart pounded in rebellion at the thought of being temporary to her. For the first time in his life, Brock didn't want to be temporary and he didn't know what to do about it.

The following morning, despite Callie's protests, Brock checked the oil and fluids in her little Nissan. He filled up the gas tank and added some air to one of the tires. "Take care of yourself," he said, and watched her drive away. She was going to North Carolina. He would drive to Atlanta in preparation for another change. It was almost time to move on. His job with Callie was nearly done.

Twelve

Marine Lingo Translation
Crucible: A grueling 54-hour training exercise
for recruits during boot camp characterized by
lack of sleep, little food, forced exercise and
teamwork.

Within twelve hours, Brock drove to Atlanta, turned
in his rental car, bought an SUV and signed a three-
month lease for a furnished executive condo. He
wanted to live somewhere temporary and convenient,
so he could take his time figuring out where he eventually wanted to settle. Everything he did, everything
decision he made, he wondered what Callie would
choose.

She would probably turn her nose up at the SUV,
preferring something smaller and more fuel efficient,
but she might approve of the executive condo. She

would change the furnishings, but she would like the skylights and generous expanse of windows.

She would, however, hate the traffic and the busy pace. She would miss the ocean.

He would miss it, too, he thought, as he returned to South Carolina. But he would miss Callie a whole lot more.

As he returned to the small coastal town, Brock gave himself a harsh lecture, reminding himself of the mission he'd intended to complete with Callie. He had accomplished his goal of prying her out of her hermitlike existence. She was able to work now. When he left, she would go out with people. She'd already met the kindergarten teacher for lunch once. He was confident she wouldn't hide away in her little cottage like she had before. He wondered when she would start dating again, and the prospect bothered him so much he turned the radio on full blast to drown out his thoughts.

Instinctively drawn to her place instead of his, Brock pulled into her driveway and noticed that her car wasn't there. She hadn't returned. He wondered how the weekend had gone for her. It was silly as hell, but he wished she had let him join her. More than that, it had stung when she'd told him not to come.

Noticing he was tapping his foot against the floor and drumming his thumb on the steering wheel, he shook his head at his restlessness and got out of the car. He walked toward the beach. It was dark outside, but the smell of salt filled his nostrils and the breeze moved over him with a cleansing rush.

The wind, however, couldn't wash thoughts of Callie from his mind. He hadn't realized how deeply she'd burrowed her way under his skin. Before he'd met her face-to-face, he'd been drawn to her. He'd envied Rob, then when Rob had died, he'd been tormented by visions of her. When he'd become her lover, he'd thought she would quickly lose appeal. He kept waiting, but it wasn't happening.

His gut tightened at the realization. The reflection of a headlight flashed to his left and he turned, spotting a car pulling into her driveway. His heart picked up. She was back.

Brock walked to the house just as she got out of her car and stretched. "Long drive?"

She stopped midstretch and looked at him. "Oh, I thought it might be you. New wheels?" she asked, tilting her head in the direction of his SUV.

He nodded as he moved toward her. "Yeah. I decided it was time to ditch the rental and make a commitment."

"Definitely a guy car," she said.

He'd predicted this. His lips twitched. "You don't like it. Too big, and bad gas mileage."

"Exactly," she said. "And I would have preferred you choose a different color than black."

"Why? Not artsy enough?" he asked, inhaling her scent and wanting to get closer so he could smell her more.

She shook her head. "Safety reasons, knuckle-head," she said, gently stabbing her finger against his chest. "Black is one of the least visible colors for cars. There's a time for stealth and a time to be seen."

His heart twisting, he grabbed her hand and held it against his chest. "Aw, Callie, I didn't know you cared," he said, making sure he used a playful tone.

She rolled her eyes. "Don't get excited. I care for my cat, too."

"Thanks," he said dryly. "I'll remember that."

He looked at her for a long moment that stretched into two and told his stomach to unknot itself. "You okay?" he asked in a low voice.

She sighed and her eyelids fluttered down, shielding her gaze from his. "Yeah." She swallowed. "It hurt, but I didn't feel so lost." She shrugged and looked up at him. "It's hard to explain."

"You don't have to if you don't want," he said, lifting his hand to touch her hair.

"Let's go inside. I've been sitting in that car a long time and I need to tinkle."

Brock chuckled. "You go on in and I'll unload your car."

"Don't forget the wine. I picked up some on my way into town," she said as she dashed for the front door.

"You did?" he muttered in surprise, not sure what to make of that. Not sure he should make anything of it. Maybe she'd planned to drink a glass of wine in solitude after her long drive. Maybe the wine purchase had nothing to do with him.

Brock swore under his breath. He was overthinking stuff way too much. Grabbing her overnight bag, a backpack and the small grocery bag, he took them into her cottage. He set her overnight bag and backpack in her bedroom then took the grocery bag into the kitchen. He stuck the wine in the freezer, setting his mental timer for twenty minutes. He was about to throw away the grocery bag when he spotted four chocolate chip cookies from the deli.

"I had a burger on the way home, but I thought cookies and wine sounded good," she said from the doorway. "Two for you and two for me."

He chuckled. So she had thought of him after all. "You could save the other two for tomorrow night."

"I can share," she said, almost flirting with him. "Tell me about your trip."

He shrugged. "Not much to tell. I bought the SUV and rented a furnished condo."

"Furnished," she echoed, wrinkling her nose in disapproval.

"It's temporary," he said. "It's pretty nice. Got skylights and a Jacuzzi."

"Ooh, I could be a little jealous of the Jacuzzi, but I'll console myself with my ocean and lack of traffic."

"Your ocean," he returned, laughing. "When did it become yours?"

"Okay, my access to the ocean." She crossed her arms over her chest. "I know I've been a pain in the butt fix-it project for you, but you'll miss me more than you plan on."

He sure as hell hoped not, Brock thought. He'd missed her so much this past weekend it had taken his breath away a few times. "Sure I'll miss you. Like a toothache," he teased her as he pulled her against him. He was tired of waiting to hold her.

She thumped his chest with her fist. "It's gonna be weird not having you around."

"I'm only a phone call away. Just a four-hour drive."

She bit her lip and shook her head. "I'm not going to bug you when you're starting your new adventure."

"What if I don't think of it as bugging me?"

She shook her head again. "That's just your over-developed sense of responsibility talking."

He wanted to argue, but shelved it for another time. Now, at least, she was in his arms. "I'm not feeling responsible right now," he said and lowered his head.

"Oh, really? Wha—"

He took her mouth with his, stopping her words. She immediately lifted her hands to the back of his neck and his heart turned over. He took his time with her mouth, kissing her so long he had to pull back for air.

"You feel so good," she whispered. "The whole drive home, I thought about how good you feel."

The sensual need in her voice pulled every chain inside him. "I thought about you a lot, too," he muttered.

"You don't sound happy about it," she murmured, running her lips over his throat.

Brock wasn't happy about it. He felt his body temperature rise another degree. Impatient with her clothes, with his clothes, with anything between them, he slid his fingers over her nipples and approved the ripple that raced through her.

He felt her tug his shirt loose and slip her hands underneath. He felt so hot he wondered if his skin sizzled at her touch. A groan escaped his throat when she pulled at the buttons on his shirt.

"I was planning on wine, cookies then you, but…" Her voice trailed off as she pressed her open mouth on his chest.

Brock groaned again. "We can have the wine. It just needs to chill a little longer."

"That'll take too long," she protested, lowering her mouth to his belly.

Brock swore. "No, it won't. I put it in the freezer."

She glanced up at him. "How long?"

"Fifteen or twenty minutes," he said, his heart pounding at the dark, wanting expression in her eyes.

She bit her lip and lowered her palm to the front of his pants. "I think you're ready now."

Unbearably aroused by her boldness, he held his breath. "Seems like I'm always ready around you."

She closed her eyes and pressed her mouth against his chest. "But I'm ready, too. I've been ready for you for hours."

Brock started to sweat. "You're making it impossible for me to go slow with you."

"I don't want slow tonight," she said, pulling her shirt over her head and tossing her bra aside. "I just want you."

Something inside him snapped. He felt hard and

urgent, almost desperate. No almost about it. He felt lust and something more. He wanted to give and take, to possess. He couldn't rebel against the primitive need. He wanted Callie to be his and no one else's. He wanted to mark her as his. Feeling his muscles twitch from the strain of restraint, he argued with himself. Until she took his mouth. And then he was lost to everything but her.

Sliding his hands under her bottom, he picked her up and strode to her bedroom. It was dark except for the light streaming in from the hallway. He tumbled her onto the bed and immediately followed her down. His mouth seeking hers, he helped rid her of her clothes and his. Her skin felt like the softest satin beneath him—hot satin. He touched her between her thighs and found her damp and ready.

"Do I need a con—"

She shook her head. "I took care of—"

Unable to wait one more second, he thrust inside her. Her sigh mingled with his.

"Take me," she pleaded. "Let me take you."

She already had taken him, he thought, as he began to move inside her in a rhythm guaranteed to send him over the edge in no time. He held her as she urged him on and from the corner of his eye, he saw her bedside table with Rob's photo, his medals and his cover... Even as Brock tumbled over the edge, something inside him whispered *you'll never really have her.*

That didn't keep him from trying. Remembering

the bottle of wine in the freezer, he collected it along with some glasses and toasted every inch of her starting with her hair. He toasted her eyes and nose, which made her giggle. He toasted her lips several times, then her chin. He spilled a little wine on her and kissed it away. She returned the favor, and pretty soon he ditched the wine. She tasted better anyway.

He made love to her again and again throughout the night, trying to get enough of her, trying to fill himself up enough that maybe he wouldn't want her so much.

When dawn slipped through her bedroom window he was sexually satisfied, sated. Sighing, he looked at her, but she was turned away from him. He felt an odd gnawing sensation in his gut. He wanted to see her face. Her hair spilled over the pillow behind her and she was very still. Sleeping, he thought, until he saw her chest rise in a jerky movement and heard a tight choking sound.

Alarmed, Brock sat up. "Callie?" He glanced in the same direction she was looking and his heart sank. She was looking at Rob's medals and his cover, his photo. He heard her sniff and his stomach twisted. "Callie," he said, reaching for her.

She flinched away from his touch.

That slight movement sliced him.

Pulling the sheet with her, she sat up, swiping at her cheeks. "I'm sorry. It just hit me all of a sudden." Her voice was strained and tight. "I kept it together all weekend. I got a little sad at the memorial when

I thought about Rob and me and some of the things we did when we were kids, but—" She broke off and closed her eyes, taking a steadying breath. She opened her eyes and met his gaze. "I'm really starting to lose him," she whispered, desperation oozing from her. "I don't think about him every other minute anymore."

He took her hand in his even though it hurt not to pull her into his arms. "You're not losing him, Callie. You're just starting to live again. He'll always be a part of you, your art, the way you look at people. He'll always be with you even when you're not thinking about him."

There was so much more he wanted to say, more he wanted to be to her. Rob may have been Callie's history, but Brock wanted to be her future. The desire was starting to consume him. He was beginning to think that going through the grueling Crucible training in boot camp had been nothing compared to what he'd gotten himself into with Callie.

He met her for a midmorning walk. It was a windy, sunny day and she chattered excitedly about how much progress she was making with her art. Her voice sounded like music to him. One more thing he would miss like hell. He hated the way his gut felt, like it was being twisted and torn out of him.

She reached for his hand and pulled him to a stop, laughing. "You haven't said a word and you're walking like you're headed for Egypt. What's up?"

He paused, memorizing how her hand felt on his—soft and small, yet firm. "Not Egypt," he said, meeting her gaze. "Just Atlanta."

Her smile fell and she brushed her hair out of her face. "How soon?"

"Today."

Her eyes widened and she looked away. "Wow."

"Callie," he began, wanting to reassure her.

She lifted her hand and shook her head. "No, no, no. You don't have to baby me. I knew this was coming. I'll be okay. I *am* okay," she corrected, lifting her lips in a forced, but determined smile. "You don't have to worry. I won't weep and wail. I won't act like Velcro. I won't be plastic cling wrap around you."

What if that was what he wanted? "You know you can call me for anything," he said. "I can be here in no time if you need me."

"But I won't," she insisted, lifting her chin. "I appreciate everything you've done. You pulled me out of my hole and—" She broke off and shook her head smiling. "God rest Rob's soul, but you gave me the best sex I've ever had."

"Same," he said.

Her eyes widened in surprise. "I find that difficult to believe."

"Believe it," he said.

She met his gaze and the electricity between them hummed as if a power line ran straight through them. Her face turned pink and she lifted her hand self-consciously to her throat. "Watch out," she warned. "It'll go to my head."

"That's fair. You've gone to my head." That was as close as he would get to telling her how he really felt about her. He wouldn't make promises she wouldn't want him to keep. He wouldn't make a profession that would make her faint in disbelief.

She rolled her eyes and snagged his arm. "Come on. I don't want you worrying about me while you go off on your new adventure," she said as she urged him toward her cottage. "I'm going to be fine. I have another luncheon date and I've somehow gotten myself committed to working with kindergartners once a week."

"I guess that means you'll at least start your car once a week."

She tossed him a dirty look then continued with a driven air. "Don't pull that innocent routine with me. I know you're behind it. I'm also going back to the retirement center. But I have something I want you to take with you. There were actually two things I wanted to give you, but I didn't know you were leaving so soon."

Brock shook his head as they entered the back door of the cottage. "I don't want anything, don't need anything. Really. It's not—"

"This isn't anything that big, just a reminder," she said, guiding him to the kitchen. "I'm glad I went ahead and got them developed." She grabbed a packet of photographs from the counter and flipped through them. "Where is it…here it is!" she said, pulling out one and thrusting it at him.

"What was I saying?" she murmured, lifting her hand to her head. "Oh, it's a reminder. Not of me," she said firmly, "but of you."

Distracted by the unusual frantic pace of her conversation, Brock looked down at the photograph and wrinkled his brow in confusion. It was the photo of him and Callie and all those kids who had worked on the sand castle. His gaze automatically returned to Callie, with her sunburned nose, windblown hair and laughing smile.

"Are you looking at yourself?"

He nodded, lying, his gaze still fastened on her.

"See how relaxed you look, how happy," she said, pointing at him.

Brock glanced at himself in the photo. She was right. He looked happy. "Yeah," he muttered.

"Don't forget the sand castles," she said.

He looked at her. "What do you mean?"

"I mean you are one of the most driven men I've ever met. You're intense, sometimes too serious, and almost always too hard on yourself. Don't forget what your dreams were when you were a kid." She took a quick breath then lifted her lips to his in a kiss that didn't last nearly long enough. "Draw some high-rise sand castles during some of those endless meetings."

A terrible knot formed in his throat, but he smiled over it. "I'll do that," he said, and lifted his hand to touch her cheek, memorizing her features one more time. "Call me for any reason."

She shook her head. "This is your new adventure. I refuse to butt in." She bit her lip. "Thank you for everything. Good—"

Unable to bear hearing those words from her, he covered her mouth. "Don't say it."

"What do you want me to say?" she asked, her voice reflecting a hint of the desperation he felt.

"See you soon," he said.

"What if that's not true?"

"Say it anyway."

"See you soon," she said, and he pulled her into his arms and held her in silence for two and a half minutes. It took him that long to get himself squared away enough to walk away.

Thirteen

Marine Lingo Translation
Semper Fi: Marine Corps motto—
Always Faithful.

The late November rain pounded against the window of Brock's corner office. His leg always ached when there was a cold rain and today was no different. Reports waited for his review, but he picked up the photograph of Callie and him with the super sand castle instead. He'd touched it so often, the edges had started to show some wear, so he'd put it in a Plexiglas frame. If he closed his eyes, he could smell the ocean and hear her laughter.

"Brock?" a male voice called from the doorway, interrupting Brock's trip to the South Carolina shore.

Sighing, he turned toward the door. He knew the

voice belonged to the managing partner's intern. "What do you need, Eugene?"

"Mr. Robertson just wants your opinion on this as soon as you can take a look at it," Eugene said, setting down a thick file and glancing over Brock's shoulder. "Pretty lady," he said. "I didn't know you were married."

Brock set the picture down. "I'm not."

"Significant other? Fiancée?" Eugene paused. "Sister? She doesn't really look—"

"No, she's not my sister," he said, feeling irritated. "She's just a woman I know."

"An acquaintance," Eugene clarified, nodding his head.

"Yes," Brock said, knowing the description wasn't right. "And—"

"More," Eugene said, waving his hand. "A friend."

"Why are we playing charades?" Brock asked.

Eugene shrugged. "I've never noticed that photograph before."

That was because Brock had kept it in his drawer until he'd put it in a frame. "You can tell Mr. Robertson I'll get this done by tomorrow."

Eugene scratched the back of his neck. "If you're not romantically involved, I know a woman who would like to meet you for a drink."

Brock immediately rejected the idea. He wasn't interested. He wasn't sure when he would be interested again. He was starting to wonder if he might as well become a monk. "I've got a lot of work—"

"Before you say no," Eugene said, "remember, it's just a drink. I'll pay."

Brock frowned in confusion. "Why?"

Eugene sighed and looked over his shoulder as if to make sure no one was listening. "Because I want Linda in Accounting to go out with me. She said she would meet me for drinks if I could get you to come along for Beth. We could all go together."

Brock couldn't remember meeting Beth personally, but she looked exactly like the kind of woman who would have attracted him before Callie. Killer body, clearly experienced, hot. Not feeling a lick of interest, Brock shook his head. "Sorry, Eugene, you're gonna have to—"

"Oh, come on. It's no skin off your nose. One drink." Eugene pointed to the pile of papers on Brock's desk. "It's not like you'll be doing anything better. It looks like all you do is work."

In other circumstances, Brock would be tempted to deliver a kiwi-injection—otherwise known as a swift kick in the rear—to Eugene, but he couldn't ignore the pinch of truth in the graduate student's words. Was he becoming a hermit, buried in his work? Disliking the thought, he frowned. "Okay, tomorrow after work. One drink."

Eugene immediately brightened, swinging his fist through the air. "Great. You won't regret it." He lowered his voice in a confidential tone. "I hear Beth is downright easy for the right guy. You could get lucky."

Quit while you're ahead, Brock thought, but stifled the words. "One drink tomorrow after work," he repeated. "If you don't mind, close the door on your way out," Brock said, scowling as the young man left.

Scrubbing his hand through his hair, he picked up the photo again and drank in the sight of Callie. His gut twisted with longing. What he wouldn't give just to see her again, but she'd made it clear he was temporary. She didn't want anything permanent with him.

He missed her.

Yes, he could function without her. Yes, he was able to feed himself, get his work done and even watch a ballgame. But nothing was half as much fun.

Heaven help him, he was one sorry sonofabitch. He shoved the photo into a drawer so he wouldn't see it. Maybe he needed to forget her. Maybe he needed to go out with Beth and have a few too many and then maybe have Beth, too.

The following afternoon it rained again. His leg was killing him as he held an umbrella and escorted Beth Pritchard to a trendy bar two blocks away from the office. He and Beth followed Eugene and Linda. She had great legs, a killer body and a voice that made him want to chew glass. He'd only noticed her across the room before, so he hadn't known she possessed such a nasal, grating tone.

She chatted about her family and college background and attempted to engage Brock in conversation. By the time the foursome arrived at the bar, Brock was ready for a double of anything hard to drink.

"Eugene tells me you were a Marine," Beth said, scooting her bar stool close to his. "Did you see any action?"

Brock nodded. "What do you want to drink?"

"A sour apple martini," she said.

"Whiskey," he said to the bartender. "Double."

"Tell me what it was like being a Marine," she said. "I have a thing about men in uniform."

"I don't wear it anymore," he said.

She slid her hand onto his thigh. "That's okay. It's what's underneath that really matters."

Caught off guard at her brazenness, he swiveled toward the bar, away from her touch. "The drinks are here."

"Do you like to dance?"

I did with Callie, he thought, remembering dancing with her and how she had felt like magic in his arms. "I haven't done much dancing since I left the Corps. One of my legs was injured and—"

"Oh, that's too bad," she said. "I bet you could slow dance, though."

With the right woman, he thought. *Aw, hell, this wasn't going well at all.* He downed his whiskey in two gulps. "Listen, I don't really feel like being here tonight, so—"

She leaned closer and slid her hand onto his thigh again. "We can go to my house."

He sighed. "Beth, I'm—"

"Excuse me," a familiar female voice said from a few feet away. "Pardon me. Is Brock Armstrong here?"

Unable to believe his ears, he swiveled around to find Callie standing in front of the bar looking like a drowned rat as she gripped a drooping bouquet of roses in one hand and the heel of her shoe in the other.

"Callie?" was all he could say.

Her gaze swiveled away from the bartender to his and his heart tripped over itself.

"Surprise," she said with an unsteady smile. "It's me. I got a makeover at one of the salons this morning, but the rain washed it away. I broke the heel of my shoe on a manhole." She glanced at Beth. "Am I interrupting?"

"Not at all," he said.

Beth frowned. "I'm Beth Pritchard. Brock and I work together."

Callie nodded. "How nice for you. I'm Callie Newton. Brock and I got to know each other this summer." He saw the moment she noticed Beth's hand on his thigh. She bit her lip, looking suddenly uncertain. "You know, maybe this is a bad time. Maybe this was a bad idea."

Feeling a slice of desperation cut through him, he stood and reached for her arm. "No, it was a great idea. I've picked up the phone to call you too many times to count."

She glanced at Beth again. "Uh-huh," she said,

clearly unconvinced. She squeezed her forehead. "I think I've been way too impulsive and—"

"Callie," he interrupted, putting his hands on both her shoulders and gently shaking. "Why are you here?"

She met his gaze and opened her mouth, then closed it. Her gaze slid to Beth and back to Brock. "Are you and her—" She broke off and shook her head. "Oh, I shouldn't ask. I have no right to ask. It's none of my business and—"

"We're not," Brock said. "We're not anything. This is the first time I've been out since I moved to Atlanta. Eugene twisted my arm because he wanted to get with Linda. This was part of the trade-off."

Brock held his breath while Callie paused and studied him. "So you're not involved," she said.

"Not at all," he said. "Why are you here, Callie?" he asked, unable to take his gaze off of her.

She took a careful breath and lifted her chin as if she were fortifying herself. "I want to ask you a favor," she said.

"A favor?" he echoed, confused as hell.

"Well I wasn't going to say favor," she amended and swore under her breath. "I had this all planned out and practiced it on the drive down and I can't remember a freakin' word of it now. Here," she said, thrusting the roses into his arms. "These are for you."

Touched and surprised, he gaped at her. "For me?"

"Yes, and this, too," she said, pulling a CD from the purse hanging on her shoulder.

"Whoa. What's—" He glanced at the CD. "Jimmy Buffet?"

"I'm here to kidnap you. I'm going to the Caribbean and I would like to take someone very special with me." She bit her lip. "That someone very special would be you."

Too shocked for words, all he could do was stare at her, his heart pounding so hard he could hear it throb in his brain.

She pulled back slightly, color rising to her cheeks. "See? I told you it was impulsive, insane, crazy. I shouldn't have—"

"When does the plane leave?" he asked, finally finding his voice.

She blinked. "Tomorrow."

"You want to go back to my place and help me pack?"

Her turn to be speechless. She opened her mouth and her jaw worked, but no sound came out. "Are you sure?"

He lifted his hand to cup her jaw. Her skin was so soft, her heart so sweet and his chest squeezed so tight it hurt. This was his chance with her and he was going to take it. He hoped Rob wouldn't mind. "I'm sure," he said.

Twenty-four hours later, they were sharing a chaise lounge watching the sun set. He was drinking a beer. She was drinking a Hurricane.

Sitting between his legs with her hair against his chest, she gave a long sigh. "I'm glad I did this."

"Me, too," he said, burying his face in her hair and inhaling her scent. They'd made love three times, but hadn't talked about anything important.

"I was scared you would say no."

"What gave you the *cojones* to do it then?"

She turned slightly and looked at him. "Well, you did tell me to call you for any reason."

"Yeah," he said with a nod, wanting more from her, but not wanting to ask.

"Regrets?" she asked, searching his face.

"I regret that we've been apart for the last three months," he said quietly, finding it more and more difficult to cover how deep his feelings were for her.

Setting her drink down on the balcony floor beside her, she turned the rest of the way around onto his lap so that she was facing him. "I do and I don't," she said.

He frowned in confusion.

She lifted her hands to his shoulders and traced them with her fingertips. "I know it sounds strange, but I was such a mess when I first met you. You helped pull me out of my black hole and I think I needed to be by myself for a little bit."

His gut tightened. "And now?"

"I want to be strong enough for you," she said, meeting his gaze.

"What?"

"I don't want to always be leaning on you. I don't want you to always lead with me always following." She bit her lip. "I've done that before."

Her eyes were dark with an emotion he sensed was almost as deep as his, but he was almost afraid to hope. "So what do you want, Callie?"

"I want to take turns." She searched for his hand and laced her fingers through his. "What do you want?"

"I don't want to be temporary," he said, hearing the huskiness in his voice, but unable to do a damn thing about it.

"Oh."

Brock put it all on the line. "I'm in love with you," he said. "I want to marry you."

Her eyes widened. "Are you sure?"

"Yeah, I am. But I'm not sure how you feel about me, how you feel about Rob."

She took a deep breath. "I'll always love Rob and he'll always be a part of me. I didn't think I could love again, but I was wrong. This may sound strange to you, but I kinda feel like Rob gave me you."

Something eased inside Brock. Maybe Rob wouldn't hate him for loving Callie.

He lifted her hand to his lips. "When you're near me, it's like the sun is shining even if it's pouring down rain."

"Really?" she asked, her smile lighting her face.

"Yeah, really."

She threw her arms around his shoulders and hugged him. "You're so strong. I had to make sure I was strong enough for you."

"There's brute strength and there's magic. You're the magic."

* * *

Twelve months later, Brock kidnapped his wife and took her on a trip to the Caribbean. She was sipping lemonade and he was drinking a beer. It was afternoon, and she lay between his legs on a chaise lounge with her gorgeous seven-months-pregnant belly exposed to the waning afternoon sun.

She touched her belly and gave a breathless chuckle. Brock had watched her often enough to know what that meant—the baby had moved.

He slid his hand over her stomach and felt a kick. He smiled and stroked her hair with his other hand. "How does cupcake like the Caribbean?" he asked. *Cupcake* was Callie's name for the baby.

She turned slightly and looked up at him with loving eyes that still made his heart turn over. "Cupcake loves the Caribbean. Cupcake is going to be a weekend beach baby."

"Just like Momma," he said. "Have you hated the city as much as you thought you would?" He'd worried about that. She'd been so emphatic about detesting the traffic and noise.

She shook her head. "How could I hate it when I'm with you? Besides, you lured me with such a nice house in a nice woodsy neighborhood and tucked me into a cul de sac. You come home every day and love me every night, and sometimes you even cook dinner. You made peace with my cat and let him move in with us, too."

He lowered his head to taste her lips. Heaven help him, he still couldn't get enough of her.

She sighed in pleasure against his mouth. "Plus you let me kidnap you to the beach almost every weekend." She paused a half beat. "My only complaint is that you won't let me include my drawings of you in my show next month."

Brock chuckled. He knew she was teasing. "I thought your nude drawings of me were supposed to be just for us."

"The artist in me wants to share them. After all, they took so long for me to complete because you kept interrupting me while I was drawing."

He skimmed his hand down her throat to her now-blooming cleavage. "I don't recall you complaining too much at the time."

"Well, you didn't—"

He slid his finger underneath her halter top to touch her nipple. Her breasts had become delightfully sensitive to his touch due to her advancing pregnancy.

She closed her eyes and made a soft breathy sound.

He toyed with both stiff peaks, enjoying her sensual movements.

She opened her eyes. "You're distracting me again."

"It's one of my favorite things to do."

Sighing, she shifted slightly and lifted her lips to kiss him. "I am totally crazy for you, Brock Armstrong."

His heart melted in his chest the same way it did every time she assured him how much she loved him. Sometimes he still couldn't believe she was his.

"I love how you encourage me with my art. I love

how you take care of me and let me take care of you. I love how you helped me make the memory box for Rob and hung it on the wall in the den."

"He's a part of you. I'll always be grateful to him, Callie. I'm sorry we lost him, but he gave me something more precious than I could have dreamed."

Her eyes filled with tears. "I can't believe how lucky I am to have you."

"Same for me, sunshine. I guess we'll just have to keep showing each other." He dropped a kiss on her soft, sweet mouth. Showing her how much he loved her would be his favorite mission for the rest of his life.

* * * * *

DRIVEN TO DISTRACTION

BY
DIXIE BROWNING

Dixie Browning is an award-winning painter and writer, mother and grandmother who has written nearly eighty contemporary romances. Dixie and her sister, Mary Williams, also write historical romances as Bronwyn Williams. Contact Dixie at www.dixiebrowning.com, or at PO Box 1389, Buxton, NC 27920, USA.

To all the wonderful printmakers whose works I've collected over the years. (And the artists whose reproductions I own because I can't afford the originals.)

One

Maggie Riley was nobody's victim. She knew all about situation awareness, having once interviewed a police officer for her column. For the past half hour or so the same dark green pickup truck had been behind her. Traffic had been unusually light all the way from Winston-Salem, but when she'd turned off the interstate onto the state road and the green truck had turned, too—and then it had followed her onto a glorified cowpath that led to her destination—well, she'd started to wonder. Maybe the driver just wanted to tell her that her license plate had fallen off or that a tire was going flat.

On the other hand, he might see her as a potential mugging victim, a woman driving alone. Of course there was always the possibility that he was headed for the same place she was. Peddler's Knob, in the foothills of the Blue Ridge Mountains, site of the Perry Silver Watercolor Workshop. So far as she knew there was no law against artists driving big 4x4 muscle trucks with muddy license plates.

"So enough with the paranoia," she muttered, watching as the dark truck pulled into the small parking lot.

She set the emergency brake and turned her attention to the three-story Victorian house where she would be living and studying for the next six days. A wedding cake of a house, it was riddled with turrets and cupolas, gingerbread and stained glass windows, not to mention a dozen fancy lightning rods.

"Beam me up, Scotty," she murmured.

Two weeks ago when she'd mailed in the application, it had seemed like the perfect solution, even though Maggie knew as much about art as she did nuclear physics. Workshops were for learning, right? So maybe she would actually learn how to paint—not that it was a priority.

Now that it was too late—several hundred dollars too late—second thoughts were swarming thicker than fruitflies at a watermelon bust.

"On your mark, get set—go," she said softly, eyeing the steep, badly graveled path that led to the house where she was scheduled to spend the next six days as an embedded journalist.

She did like the term embedded. It might be stretching it a bit, although she really was here on a covert mission. Never in a million years would she have thought of enrolling in a watercolor workshop if some smooth-talking jerk hadn't targeted her best friend, who was not only gullible, but rich as chocolate mocha pie.

Leaning over, Maggie tied on her sandals. She knew better than to try to drive in three-inch platforms after getting one of them stuck between the brake pedal and the accelerator the first day she'd worn them.

With one last glance at the dark green truck again, she told herself that if the driver had been planning to do her bodily harm, he would hardly have waited until there were witnesses. All the same, she waited to see if he would approach her or drive off in a spray of gravel, or...

"Holy mackerel, would you look at that," she murmured admiringly. Maggie had enjoyed thinking of herself as an embedded journalist, out to save her best friend from being left high and dry with a broken heart and an empty bank account.

The term embedded took on a whole new concept as she watched the long, lean figure wearing faded jeans, western boots and a shirt that barely stretched across his shoulders as he leaned back inside the cab. She had yet to see his face but from the waist down, he looked scrumptious. If this was an example of a male artist, no wonder Mary Rose had flipped out. And if this guy turned out to be Perry Silver, she was licked before she even got started.

Being an advice columnist, Maggie had heard tales that would curl the hair on a billiard ball. She'd tried to reason with her friend, to no avail. On the other hand, if this was the scoundrel in question, she could almost understand.

Thank goodness she was both experienced and

tough as old boots, because it looked as if she had
her work cut out for her. Determination reconfirmed,
she got out, stretched and began unloading her luggage, watching from the corner of her eye for the man
to turn around so she could see his face. With any
luck he'd be ugly as homemade sin.

The picture on the front of the Perry Silver Watercolor Workshop brochure had been of a tall, nice-
looking fellow with a toothy smile and a French beret.
According to Mary Rose, who had met him at an art
exhibit her father had sponsored—the Dilyses were
big on corporate sponsorships—he was every
woman's dream come true. "Oh, Maggie, he took my
hand and held it the longest time, while he stared right
into my eyes without saying a word. I felt like the
most beautiful woman in the world. Did I tell you his
eyes are this brilliant shade of turquoise?" Mary Rose
had said when she'd called that evening.

Sure they were. With a little help from Lens-
Crafters.

"Oh, I wish you'd been there." Maggie had declined the invitation using the excuse of having a column to write. "We talked and talked, and then when
I had to leave to drive Daddy home, Perry took my
hand and said I was the reason he'd been drawn to
Winston-Salem, because his soul knew there was a
kindred spirit waiting for him here."

Maggie had snorted, but covered it with a cough.

"It was like—oh, how can I say it without you
thinking I'm crazy? It was like we were lovers in
another life and recognized each other instantly.
That's the only way I can describe it."

At that point Maggie's gag reflex had threatened.

Using all the tact at her command, she had tried to talk her friend down from cloud nine, but tact had failed and reasoning hadn't made a dent. She'd been about to leave when Mary Rose mentioned endowing a Perry Silver art scholarship at her alma mater. That was when Maggie had realized that quick action was called for.

Oh-oh, tall, dark and dangerous was finally looking her way. Maggie pretended not to be staring as she dragged her big suitcase from the trunk of her dusty hatchback. This job wasn't going to be quite the cinch she'd expected. The man was flat-out gorgeous.

"And you're flat-out dumb as dirt," she muttered as she reached back inside for her art supplies.

Three cars over, the unknown hottie lifted out a small canvas bag and a large plastic shopping bag. Turning her way, he set them on the ground. Maggie caught her breath. Holy mackerel, if this *did* turn out to be Perry Silver it was no wonder Mary Rose had flipped out. He was *better* than handsome—although if her life depended on it, Maggie couldn't have explained what that meant—and words were her business.

"Need another hand?" he called across two sedans and a hardtop convertible. His voice matched his looks. Slow, sweet and gravelly.

"No, thanks," she said airily.

She needed six hands, not three. As usual, she'd packed far too much, but she wasn't about to accept a favor from a stranger, not until she'd had a better chance to size him up. When it came to people, Maggie trusted her instincts, which was why she was here in the first place.

While she was still trying to prioritize the load, he strolled over to join her. "I think you do."

She looked him square in the face, and was sorry she did. The guy flat-out took the breath right out of her lungs, he was that striking. A full head shorter than he was, Maggie managed to look down her nose at him. "I beg your pardon?" Haughty was hard to achieve when you were barely five foot four and a hundred and two pounds only after a big meal. "You're not…"

She started to ask if he were Perry Silver. She knew for a fact that publicity shots were usually heavily retouched, but this man's eyes were the color of clear amber—which also could be due to contact lenses. He was bareheaded, and according to Mary Rose, Perry Silver always wore a beret.

"He wears this beret, and honestly, Mag, he's the most romantic man I've ever seen outside of the movies. Think of a young Gregory Peck. He told me if Raphael had met me first, my portrait would be hanging in the Louvre today. Don't you think that's the sweetest thing you ever heard?"

"Miss?"

"What?" she snapped, jerking her thoughts back in line. He was leaning against her car, staring down into her open trunk, which was half-full of newspapers she kept forgetting to take to the recyclers and other junk she always carried in case of a road emergency. A short length of rope, a flashlight—she reminded herself to check the batteries—and a pair of the world's ugliest shoes.

"Like I said, if you need a hand, I happen to have a free one."

"Then thank you, if you can carry that—" she pointed at her small, tapestry toilet case— "I can handle the rest."

Ignoring her suggestion, he reached for her big suitcase, her computer case and the bundle of art supplies she'd bought at Wal-Mart, leaving her to bring her shoulder bag and her toilet case. She followed him up the hill, studying his lean backside in those jeans that were strategically worn in all the right places.

If he *did* turn out to be Perry Silver, then she might as well give up now and go home. No way could she change any woman's mind about this man, even if she caught him, figuratively speaking, with his hand in the cookie jar.

"Watch the gravel," he warned.

"I'm watching." She tore her gaze from his trim behind and scowled at the rocky, uneven path.

Maggie's idol was Farrah Fawcett, one of the original *Charlie's Angels*. Farrah had never once tripped during the entire series. Maggie knew, as she'd practically memorized the reruns.

Maggie Riley, advice columnist for the *Suburban Record* and investigative journalist-in-training, had tripped a few times. Actually, more than a few times, usually because her attention was elsewhere.

As it was now.

Aside from getting the goods on Perry Silver, she intended to take advantage of the opportunity to learn something about art. The *Suburban Record* didn't have an art critic, but that was not to say they couldn't use one.

Only in her most painfully honest moments did Maggie admit that her "Ask Miss Maggie" column, like the *Record's* few others regular features, served mainly as fillers between ads, school news, meeting announcements and cents-off coupons.

On the other hand, even Woodward and Bernstein had had to start somewhere.

M. Riley, art critic.

Critic of art?

Too self-conscious. She'd settle for art critic.

"This place needs stair steps." He had a dark molasses drawl. Southern, but not Carolina.

"Or an escalator," Maggie said. His legs were roughly a mile longer than hers, even without those slant-heeled cowboy boots. He stopped to wait for her to catch up. "I guess you're here to learn how to paint, too," she ventured. By now she was all but certain he wasn't Perry Silver. Mary Rose would have mentioned more than just his hands and his eyes.

All the same, she introduced herself. "I'm Maggie Riley. I guess we'll be…studying together for the next week."

Several steps ahead of her, he glanced over his shoulder, throwing into relief a profile fit for a Roman coin. "Pleased to meet you, ma'am."

Ma'am? "I didn't catch your name?"

"Ben Hunter. You ready to tackle the last stretch?"

Maggie looked at the last stretch of badly graveled path. "I guess." She was readier for that than she was for her first art lesson. The brochure had described the scenic splendor, which they'd probably be asked to paint. She glanced suspiciously at the misty mountains, the dense forest and the blooming rhododendron. No big deal, she told herself with faux bravado. Splash of blue, splash of green, maybe a streak of pink, and she'd call whatever she created abstract. Who could argue with that? Art was in the eye of the beholder, hadn't somebody famous said that?

Looking ahead, she sized up the group on the porch as she panted up the last few yards. She wasn't particularly surprised to see mostly women. The trouble was, most of them appeared to be middle–aged or older. The only one who looked anywhere near Maggie's age was the blonde in the bandanna bra, but she'd be perfect as bait if Maggie could convince her to cooperate.

It would all work out somehow, she assured herself. She would *make* it work. Mary Rose might be as gullible as a newborn calf, but Maggie wasn't about to be taken in by any smooth-talking leech with turquoise eyes, sensitive hands and a line that would gag an alligator.

Or by a cowboy with whiskey-colored eyes, come to that.

"You okay?" the whiskey-eyed cowboy asked. He paused to wait for her near the rusty wrought iron gate that was half-buried under a jungle of trumpet vine and honeysuckle.

To avoid looking directly at him, Maggie stared up at the house, which appeared to be somewhat shabby up close. "I'm fine," she assured him just as her foot slipped on the gravel.

She staggered, flailed her arms, dropped her toilet kit and managed to regain her balance before tall, dark and devastating could lay a hand on her. When it came to recoveries, she'd had plenty of practice. Graceful, she wasn't.

"It's this darned gravel," she complained. Hopping on her right foot, she ran a finger between her left shoe and her bare foot to dislodge whatever had stuck there.

"Here, let me help," Ben Hunter said, and before she could stop him, he took her foot in his hand and eased a finger between her sole and the platform. "Got it," he said, brushing out a bit of pea gravel.

Clinging to the vine-covered gate for balance, Maggie thought, talk about getting off on the wrong foot!

Before she could catch her breath to thank him, he picked up her bags and set out again, leaving her to follow...or not. She watched as he climbed the steps, strode across to the front door and disappeared inside the house with her luggage.

"Who put a burr under your saddle?" she muttered. He'd been the one to offer his help, she hadn't asked him to grab her ankle and run his hands all over her bare foot.

Nice going, Maggie. You really made a terrific first impression.

Scowling, Ben dumped the bags just inside the door, hooked his thumbs in his hip pockets and waited for his eyes to adjust to the dim interior light. Where the devil had he parked his brain? Now he had to make another trip down the hill to retrieve the gear he'd left on the ground beside his truck.

Silly woman. High heels were one thing—Ben appreciated a sexy shoe and a well-turned ankle as much as the next guy—but a woman who had no better sense than to wear something like that on her feet, well, you had to wonder about her, that's all.

He looked around for whoever was in charge of this tea party. Maybe this hadn't been such a great idea after all. He'd done his share of undercover work—been damned good at it, too. That is, he had until he'd stumbled across evidence that not only were more than half the cops on the force crooked as a corkscrew, the rot went all the way up to the mayor's office—possibly even as far up as Austin. Sick at heart, but not particularly eager to be a dead hero, he'd reported his findings along with documentation to the proper authorities and turned in his badge.

That was when things had started falling apart, including his relationship with the woman he'd been seeing for nearly a year. Not that it had been serious on either side, but they'd been well matched in bed, and Leah hadn't seemed to mind his being a cop.

Then, as if all that weren't enough, he'd had a call from his grandmother, back east. He hadn't seen her in years, but he tried to call a couple of times a month and always wired flowers for her birthday and holidays.

"Benny, I think I might have made a mistake," she'd confided. That's when he'd learned that she'd been bilked out of her savings by some eel posing as an artist who had talked her into "investing" in a bunch of overpriced prints, swearing that within five years they would easily triple in value.

At least, that was Ben's interpretation of what Miss Emma had told him. Personally, he didn't know bad art from good art, but he knew what he liked. What he *didn't* like was any creep who preyed on retirees, especially women. And from what he'd been able to find out, this guy Silver had all the earmarks. In his thirteen-year career as a lawman Ben Hunter had nailed any number of scam artists. He figured that even though he no longer wore a badge, he might as well make it one more for good measure.

He had yet to meet this Silver guy, but he'd studied the picture on the brochure. Big, toothy smile, French headgear, probably to cover a bad comb-over—and a "Trust me" expression.

Oh, yeah, Ben trusted him, all right. About the length of his own shadow, no farther.

There was a string of awards listed on the inside of the three-fold brochure, but who was to say the guy hadn't made them up? The Better Business Bureau didn't have time to check up on every hit-and-run operator.

Standing there in the front hall getting his bearings, his thoughts wandered back to the blonde—not the one with the dark roots and the skimpy red top he'd seen out on the porch, but the other one. Miss Independent in the dumb shoes. Shaggy, dark blond hair, thick, pale lashes and a pair of hazel eyes that kept zapping out messages he interpreted as, "Back off, buddy."

If he was smart, that was a message he'd do well to heed.

Two

If Ben Hunter was an artist, then she had chosen the wrong career, Maggie thought as she signed the roster in the front hall, chose which blanks to fill in and which to leave blank. She picked up her luggage where he'd left it and followed the blonde she had noticed earlier to the room they had both been assigned.

"Oh, my, is this it?"

"Cozy might be an understatement." Suzy James indicated one of three cots in the cramped room off the kitchen. "This one's mine. You might as well take your pick. Whoever we're supposed to share with hasn't shown up yet."

Maggie stacked her luggage beside the cot nearest the small window. Dismayed, she looked around.

"Real bedrooms and bath are on the second floor,

but those rooms are all taken. I must've been one of the last to sign up.''

''Me, too,'' Maggie admitted, wondering if even the best of intentions was worth a week in this claustrophobic environment. *Mary Rose, you owe me, big time.*

While Suzy James perched on the end of her cot and watched, making occasional comments, Maggie unlatched her suitcase and looked for a place to hang the dresses she'd brought.

''Is this your first workshop?''

Warily, Maggie laid aside the flowered sun hat she'd just taken out of her suitcase. The crown had been filled with her underwear. ''Um…is that a problem? I'm probably not what you'd call experienced.''

''Hey, we're here to learn, right?'' Suzy stretched her arms over her head. She had the kind of figure Maggie had given up on achieving when she'd reached her twentieth birthday still wearing a size thirty-two A cup bra—that is, when she wore one at all.

Maggie got out a few packages of the snack food she'd brought along for emergencies and stacked them at one end of the shelf that served as a dressing table. ''Help yourself,'' she offered. ''I wasn't sure what to expect, mealwise.''

''Sure, thanks. Um…who's your cowboy?''

''My cowboy?''

''Long drink of water with the shoulders and those bedroom eyes. Did y'all come together? I noticed he toted your stuff up the hill.''

''We just happened to pull into the parking lot at the same time.'' Maggie could feel her cheeks growing warm. Her cowboy, indeed. *Don't I wish!* "All I know is he said his name was Ben Hunter."

At least that was all she knew other than the fact that he had a way of moving that could melt the tires on a tractor-trailer. More than once, following him up the path to the house, she had nearly tripped because instead of watching where she was going, she'd been watching the way he moved.

She happened to know he had the kind of voice that resonated in places that sound was not supposed to affect. She also knew she'd do well to keep her mind on her mission and not allow herself to be distracted.

"Have you met Perry Silver yet?" she asked. Seeing no sign of a closet, she folded the dress she'd been holding back into her suitcase. Considering what this week was costing her, was it too much to expect a few coat hangers and maybe a nail or two on the wall?

"Not yet. They say he usually comes in late so he can make this grand entrance."

"Then I guess we'll know when he gets here." Maggie had taken to thinking of him as Perry the Paragon after hearing Mary Rose carry on about everything from the length of his eyelashes to the shape of his fingernails.

Stepping into the adjoining half bath, she set out her toilet articles and then washed her hands. "What now?" she asked, drying off on the towel she'd brought from home.

"We go back out and mingle, I guess. Dibs on the cowboy if you don't want him."

"Help yourself." Maggie had an idea the cowboy

would have something to say about that. Besides, she would much rather Suzy James drew a bead on Perry Silver.

That might have to wait, though. First she needed to explain about Mary Rose and how she was hoping to catch Silver making a play for some other woman, using the same tired old line, so that her friend might wake up before it was too late. Maggie wasn't a meddler, but it was hardly meddling, she rationalized, to expose the truth to spare a friend from future heartbreak.

A dozen or so people had gathered on the deep porch that surrounded three sides of the house. Maggie had intended to join them, but Suzy nodded to the roster where everyone was supposed to sign in and list a few vital statistics. Maggie had put down Clemmons as her hometown and journalist as her occupation. Suzy had listed East Bend and student. Most of the others had put down Retired under occupation.

Ben Hunter had evidently signed in while she'd been unpacking. He'd given Texas as his home address and security as his occupation. "Not real free with details, is he?" Maggie murmured.

"Security," Suzy said thoughtfully. "Wonder what kind of security. Maybe border patrol. He doesn't say where in Texas, but it could be near the border."

"Probably a security guard at a shopping mall," Maggie retorted. She didn't think so, though. He hadn't developed that sexy, loose-limbed walk pounding the terrazzo in some fancy-schmancy shopper's heaven. If she didn't watch out, he was going to prove a major distraction.

"Are you really a journalist?" Suzy indicated Maggie's entry on the roster.

"Well...sort of. That is, I write a weekly column."

"Oh, wow, that must be exciting. Which paper, the *Journal Sentinel*?"

Maggie hated to name the small weekly rag she actually worked for, but she was nothing if not honest. "Just the *Suburban Record* so far. I write the 'Ask Miss Maggie' column." She waited to see if Suzy had ever heard of it. "You wouldn't believe some of the letters I get."

"No kidding? So tell me..." Her voice trailed off as she looked over Maggie's shoulder.

Maggie turned to find herself ensnared by a pair of honey-brown eyes. Ben Hunter said, "I see you're still wearing those shoes."

"I see you're still wearing those cowboy boots. They must have rubber soles, the way you sneak up on people." She closed her eyes and muttered, "Sorry. That was rude."

"It's kind of noisy in here." Evidently he hadn't taken offense. "You might want to wear something a little more sensible when you go outside. Not much level ground around here, and what there is is rocky."

Maggie's eyes flashed a warning. She had heard similar warnings all her life. *Don't climb up on that table, Margaret Lee. Don't run up the stairs! Watch your step, sugar—oops!*

Her entire life had been filled with "oopses," but that didn't mean she was going to change the way she dressed just because some whiskey-eyed cowboy didn't like her style.

Suzy looked from one to the other like a spectator

at a tennis match. "Hey, I'm wearing flip-flops," she said brightly.

Both Ben and Maggie ignored her. Maggie tried to come up with a smart comeback, but before she could think of anything really clever, Ben turned away to join a group of senior citizens.

One of whom, Maggie noticed with interest, wore her pink hair in a single braid along with gold ear hoops, black tights, a peasant blouse and cross-trainers. "Now there," she said softly to Suzy, "is my idea of what an artist should look like."

So saying, she turned, tripped over a pair of big feet and flung out her arms. The elderly gentleman whose feet had been in her way said, "Steady there, little lady."

Smiling weakly, Maggie didn't bother to tell him she was a congenital tripper. Everything from pot-holes to campaign posters. If she'd heard the words, "Look where you're going" once, she'd heard them a million times. Once she'd even skidded on grains of rice while she was backing up to take a picture and landed on her keester in front of an entire wedding party. Graceful, she wasn't, but after twenty-seven years she had learned to live with her shortcomings.

What was it with women and their crazy shoes? Ben wondered as he edged through the crowd, sizing up the likely candidates for Silver's pitch. He'd seen women dance all night on ice-pick heels and then limp for days. Somebody should've warned her that on anything rougher than a dance floor, stability was more important than style.

On impulse, he worked his way past a gaggle of

gray-heads until he was standing behind her again. Leaning over, he said softly, "You ready to rumble?"

Startled, Maggie Riley spun around. He grinned. "Ready to commit art, that is."

"That's what I came here for," she said defensively.

"Right. Me, too."

The way she looked him over, from the toe of his good-luck boots to the scar on his chin, compliments of a dirtbag armed with a beer bottle, Ben got the idea she was somewhat skeptical about his artistic abilities.

Smart lady. Granted, he was working at a slight disadvantage here, but having once gone undercover with a ring of transvestites who were drugging and robbing businessmen at a restaurateur's convention, he'd considered playing the role of an art student a cinch.

Besides, under the mattress of the room he was sharing with a retired biology teacher was a newly purchased book entitled Watercolor Painting in Ten Easy Lessons. He intended to have at least one of those lessons under his belt by the time the first class was called to order.

"I heard somebody say the maestro's supposed to be here for supper," Suzy James whispered as they found a small table with their names on it a few hours later. "Oh, hell, they've put us right next to the kitchen again. Who do they think I am, Cinderella?"

"At least the food should be hotter." Maggie glanced around the dining room. She made a point of not looking at Ben Hunter, but evidently she wasn't fooling anyone.

Suzy said soulfully, "Is that prime stuff, or what?"

Maggie shrugged. "Good-looking men are always so vain." As if she had firsthand experience. On a scale of one to ten, she was about a four. The best she could hope for was another four—at most, a five.

"So he likes mirrors. I can live with that. I'm not into kinky, understand, but a few mirrors are okay, right?"

Just then there was a stir out in the hall. Both women glanced up expectantly. Suzy whispered, "They say Perry always makes this grand entrance, like, 'Tah-dah, here I am, folks, in all my glory!'"

"You don't sound too impressed. Why'd you sign up for his workshop?"

"Because it was either that or spend another summer working for Daddy in his lumberyard. He's been trying for years to get me interested in taking over the office, but I ask you—a lumberyard?"

"I know what you mean. My father sells insurance and I'm his only offspring. I'm not about to follow in his footsteps, though." Not that he'd ever asked her to.

"I guess not, when you're already a journalist."

"A columnist," Maggie said modestly. Her gaze strayed again to the other side of the dining room, where tall, dark and delicious was frowning. And wouldn't you know it? The man even had a gorgeous frown. Move over, Hugh Jackman. Not for the first time, Maggie told herself that Ben Hunter could easily become a major distraction if she allowed herself to be distracted.

Service was slow. Maggie said, "After seeing the rest of the accommodations I'm surprised we weren't asked to serve ourselves."

"That starts tomorrow. First night's supposed to be special because not everyone gets here in time to pitch in. Didn't you read the fine print in the brochure?"

Maggie had a tendency to skim over fine print. Besides, she'd been too busy studying the picture of Perry the Silver-plated Paragon. "Only enough to know that one week cost an arm and a leg, and you have to bring your own art supplies and linens."

A grim-faced woman slapped two cups of coffee onto the table. Maggie had wanted iced tea, but she wasn't about to make waves, not on the first night.

Suzy murmured, "Judging from the stir out in the hall, I think you-know-who's about to make his entrance. If you've never seen him before, don't be taken in by his looks."

"You've met him?"

"He came to our house once last spring trying to get my father to donate a prize."

"A prize for what?"

"You know—different businesses donate prize money for the advertising. The more prizes, the more entries—the more entries, the more entry fees are collected and the more our guy Perry takes home after expenses. He's a genius when it comes to boosting sponsors."

Which was precisely how he had come to meet Mary Rose, Maggie reminded herself. "Sounds like you're not exactly his biggest fan. You sure you wouldn't rather work for your father?"

"No way. I give him two weeks every summer while his secretary goes to Myrtle Beach, but that's it. You don't meet guys like Texas in a lumberyard office." She nodded toward the table where Ben Hunter was seated and smacked her lips. "I wonder what he's doing here."

"Same thing we are. Trying to learn how to paint."

"Uh-uh. I bet he's ATF. I've heard there's still some white liquor being produced around here."

"Alcohol, tobacco and firearms? How is studying art supposed to help him locate a hidden still?" Maggie sipped her coffee. It was cold and weak.

"Who knows? Maybe he just needed an excuse to hang around in the area. There's nothing much around these parts but this place, and you know what? I wouldn't be surprised if whoever built the place back in the twenties made his fortune in moonshine whiskey." Elbows on the table, Suzy was getting into the conspiracy thing.

"Maybe, but who makes the stuff anymore when you can buy whiskey in any ABC store?"

"White lightning, my de-ah, is an acquired taste. Once you've acquired it, Jack Daniel's pales by comparison."

Maggie hooted with laughter. From the corner of her eye she saw Ben Hunter turn and look her way. Feeling her cheeks burn, she studiously applied herself to the stewed chicken and overcooked vegetables.

"Don't look now, but here comes the maestro now," Suzy whispered a few minutes later. "I've heard he makes the rounds introducing himself, so smile and be sweet. You might even get a passing grade."

Maggie looked up into a pair of turquoise eyes that had to be—simply had to be—contacts. God didn't make eyes like that.

"Ah, we meet again, Miss James." Perry Silver smiled at Suzy, then turned to Maggie. "Let me guess. This would be Miss Riley, right? Margaret L. Riley, the journalist? I'm honored, my dear. May I join you for a few minutes?"

From the far side of the dining room, Ben frowned as he watched Silver make his way across the room to the table by the kitchen door. The slick jackass was hanging all over the Riley woman, ignoring the bleached blonde.

Conversation continued around him. One of the women said, "I remember thinking at the time that ten thousand was a fortune. Nowadays it wouldn't even last six months, not at today's prices."

"What? Oh, right," someone else said. "GI Insurance."

Ben had been gently sounding out his dinner partners, trying to squeeze in a subtle hint about a few of the scams that targeted senior citizens. New ones cropped up every day, and for any seniors who went online, the dangers tripled. On his left sat Janie Burger, whose husband, a World War II veteran, had died a couple of years ago, leaving her with an eighty-six Plymouth van, a house in need of rerooting and a ten-thousand dollar GI life insurance policy. Her daughter had treated her to Silver's workshop in order to—as Janie put it—haul her up from the slough of despond, which Ben interpreted as depression. Although the lady didn't strike him as depressed. Far from it.

"I'll certainly never get rich as an artist," she said with a self-deprecating chuckle, "but at least I won't have to worry about buying Christmas gifts this year. They'll all get bad watercolors and won't have the nerve to tell me what they think of my talent. Works every time."

Pulling his attention away from the table by the kitchen door, Ben made an ambiguous, hopefully appropriate comment. He admired the lady's spunk, as well as her unlikely pink hair.

"We're supposed to be intermediates, aren't we? Didn't it say so on the brochure?" That from Charlie Spainhour. The two men had been assigned a room together. "I took a few courses some years back, but haven't done any painting since my late wife decided the bathroom needed a pink ceiling."

Ben glanced again at the table by the kitchen door, where little Ms. Riley was smirking up at Silver, batting her eyelashes like she'd caught a cinder and was trying to dislodge it. If she wanted to play teacher's pet, it was no skin off his nose. Hell, she wasn't even all that pretty.

The conversation eddied around him while he watched the Riley woman's reaction to whatever Silver was saying. Lapping it up with a spoon. He shook his head and forced his attention back to his own dinner companions.

Charlie said, "I don't know if it'll come back to me or not. Like I said, it's been a while."

"Don't worry, if he's as good a teacher as I've heard he is, he'll fill in the gaps," said the white-haired woman at the end of the table—Georgia something or other. "By the end of the week we'll all be intermediates—some of us already are. I guess you can fake it that long.''

Evidently, Ben was the only one present who had never tried his hand at painting before. He was beginning to feel more than ever like a fish out of water.

Janie, Ben's favorite so far, removed her red-framed bifocals and cleaned them with a napkin as her eyes crinkled in another smile. ''Frankly, my dear, I don't give a darn. I painted my first bad watercolor before that boy was even out of diapers. Been painting them ever since.''

It garnered a few chuckles, including Ben's. Not that it was all that funny, but who knew better than an undercover specialist how to fit in? So far it looked like a pretty decent group, ready to lighten up for a week instead of sitting home watching their IRAs bottom out while they waited for the monthly social security stipend. Maybe he should have brought Miss Emma along. So far as he knew, the only thing she'd ever painted was her kitchen chairs, but who was to say she wouldn't discover a latent talent?

The desultory conversation continued with only an occasional comment from Ben. It turned out that Georgia and Janie were friends; both widows, both retired teachers. Janie and Charlie had met before, evidently having taught at the same school.

Placing his silverware on his plate, Ben angled his chair slightly for a better view of the other diners. He was beginning to see a pattern in the enrollment. Retirees took precedence, with just enough variety, such as himself and the pair across the room, to throw off suspicion.

On the get-acquainted roster on the hall table, more

than half the enrollees had listed Retired under occupation. Ben had put down Security, which wasn't actually a lie. Not that he couldn't lie with the best of them when the occasion demanded, but he preferred not to. Less to trip over.

He glanced over at the Riley woman again. She had dressed for the occasion in a long button-front dress with a matching scarf. He couldn't see her feet, but no doubt she was still wearing those same dumb platforms with the loop around her big toe, in spite of his good advice.

At the moment, she was fussing about something. Now why did that not surprise him? He didn't know much about her disposition, but it hadn't taken him long to learn that she bristled with attitude. In a guy, he'd heard it referred to as a Napoleon complex—not necessarily a bad thing, depending on how it was used. It could turn a guy into an overachiever or make him a real pain.

Where Riley was concerned, he had a feeling it might be the latter.

With one last long look at her profile—short, straight nose, well-defined jaw, a tempting speck of a mole and full lips that at the moment were clamped tighter than a—

Yeah, well…he was going to have to watch his similes, too. This place was filled with respectable grannies. His own had peeled the bark off him when he'd forgotten and let slip a few choice words the other day when a damn-fool driver nearly shaved the paint off his front fender by cutting in front of him on the way to the grocery store.

He might not be able to recover Miss Emma's

losses, but he could make damn sure the same thing didn't happen to anyone else's granny. Not on his watch.

"Our resident genius seems mighty interested in that table over by the kitchen," Charlie, high school biology teacher, murmured. He nodded toward where Silver was still hanging over the two younger women. The platinum blonde with the dark roots had tossed on a white shirt over the red bra, but hadn't bothered to button it up.

It was the other one that held Ben's attention. Maggie Riley. According to the roster, she was from Clemmons which, if memory served, was less than a half hour's drive from where his grandmother lived in Mocksville. Under occupation, she'd written journalist. Interesting, he mused.

None of your business, he reminded himself firmly. She could be a nuclear scientist and it still wouldn't matter. It was the blue-haired ladies, including Janie, whose shoulder-length hair just happened to be pink, who were his real targets. Those were the ones Silver would go for if Ben's predictions proved accurate. If he could wise them up in time, they could go forth and spread the word any way they chose to. Senior citizens' groups, newsletters—whatever. This was at best a borderline case of fraud, but for individuals on fixed incomes, it could be devastating.

"What? Oh, yeah—I'll take natural hair over nylon any day," he said as if he knew what the devil they were talking about. He figured at least half the women here weren't wearing the hair color they were born with. Wigs or not, Georgia, with her white brush cut, and Riley with the attitude and the shaggy, straw-colored hair were probably among the very few who were wearing their natural color.

"Some like a flat, but me, I prefer round."

It took him a moment, but he got it. They were talking about brushes, not wigs. He had one. Didn't remember if it was flat or round, as it came with the set of paints he'd bought. He figured as long as you wet it, rubbed it on the paint and wiped it across the paper, one shape was as good as another.

Although rice pudding was about six yards down on his list of favorites, he lingered over dessert while the others went out to watch the sunset. Technically, the sun had set about half an hour ago, but according to Janie, there was something special about the last rays of color that shot up from behind the mountains.

When he saw the two at the back table rake back their chairs, he collected his dishes, stacked them with the others on the table, and headed toward the kitchen. The lady in the kitchen looked as if she could use a hand, and his were available. And if it happened to take him within a couple of feet of Ms. Riley and her haystack hair, so be it.

She glanced up when he passed by with his hands full of dishes. "Oh, are we supposed to do that?" Rising, she started gathering up the dishes on her table.

Suzy looked from Ben to Maggie and lifted a brow. "See you later, okay?" she said with what could only be called a smirk.

Riley followed him out to the kitchen, where the cook was elbow deep in suds. Evidently, the place didn't run to a dishwasher, mechanical or otherwise.

"Here's these," he said.

Without glancing around, the woman said, "Scrape 'em in the can, leave 'em on the counter."

Ben looked at Maggie. Maggie looked at Ben. That's when he noticed that her eyes had almost as many different shades as her hair. By tomorrow, he might even be able to name a few, but for now he'd have to settle for brown, yellow and blue-green. The eyes, not the hair.

"What, do I have dirt on my face?" The multi-colored eyes flashed a warning.

He forced himself to look away. "Sorry—just thinking about tomorrow."

"Oh. Well, sure. Me, too. That is, I'm really looking forward to, uh—wetting some paper."

"Gimme them cups," the woman at the sink said, and they both reached for the thick white cups they'd just placed on the counter. Ben's arm struck Maggie's hand, which struck the stack of cups. They watched them bounce on the sagging linoleum floor. Fortunately, only one broke. They were the thick, white institutional kind.

"Sorry," he said. Quickly, he rounded up the un-broken cups while Maggie ripped off a handful of paper towels and moped up a splash of coffee. They ended up kneeling head to head, and he caught a faint whiff of apples and something else—maybe coco-nut—that hadn't been on the menu tonight.

And neither is she, he reminded himself.

Fleeing before they could do any more damage, neither of them waited for the thanks that probably wouldn't be forthcoming anyway, judging from the way the woman was scowling. Maggie said, "Oops."

Ben said, "Yeah," and grinned.

The others were beginning to straggle inside after watching the sunset. Janie with the pink hair was guffawing. She had a great laugh, apparently oblivious to the fact that her face crinkled up like used wrapping tissue. She probably had better sense than to invest in any of Silver's junk anyway, but Ben would watch over her, just in case. He liked her.

Her friend Georgia, too. Ben sized her up as a likely candidate. White hair, flowered dress, embroidered button-front sweater, support hose and cross trainers. Not to mention a rock the size of a golf ball on her third finger, left hand. With her swollen knuckles, she probably couldn't get it off, poor woman. He'd keep a special eye out for her. First time he caught Silver spending an unusual amount of time with her, he'd follow up with a word of caution.

Okay, Janie and Georgia and who else? There were at least a dozen candidates, not counting the two blondes and the two guys, including Charlie and himself.

Maybe he should hold an impromptu seminar on how not to be drawn into a sucker's trap. He had yet to work out a plan for getting the goods on Silver, but he was used to going in without an ironclad plan. A good cop left plenty of maneuvering room; he'd learned that his first year on the job when he'd walked in on a convenience store robbery and got a face full of Reddi-wip. Since then he'd at least had sense enough to work the perp around to the bagged goods before trying to cuff him. A face full of corn chips couldn't do a whole lot of damage.

"Wanna join the others out on the porch?" he asked.

Riley looked at him a full thirty seconds before shaking her head. "No thanks," she said, and walked off.

Nice going, Hunter. From now on, keep your mind on the job you're supposed to be doing.

Three

It was a good hour earlier than her usual bedtime when Maggie headed for her assigned quarters. Beginning tomorrow the students would be responsible for meals. They were to work out a plan among themselves. Suzy, seated in the middle of her cot, was painting her toenails. She suggested that some of the older women would naturally want to take charge.

"Why?"

"Well…because, I mean, most of them have been married, so they're used to cooking."

So was Maggie, not that she intended to advertise it. Her mother had left home when Maggie was eleven, after announcing that life was a fleeting thing. Several weeks later she'd written from a commune out in Idaho, something about being free to become herself. She still came home occasionally, never staying more than a few days. Actually, she hadn't been home in several years, but at least she still wrote when she remembered to. Handmade postcards for the most part, filled with colored drawings of moons and stars and rainbows and elves.

So maybe, Maggie mused, she had inherited some artistic talent after all.

She considered unpacking her laptop to record a few first impressions to work into a special column once the week was over. With any luck, her editor might accept it—might even spring for a small bonus. If she earned enough to pay income taxes she could write off this whole horribly expensive week as research—but first she would have to write about it.

She found a place to set up her laptop by shifting Suzy's array of cosmetics, then looked around for an outlet within reach. Her batteries were probably dead. Since she rarely used them, she rarely remembered to check them. Why didn't someone invent a computer that plugged into a cell phone? Or maybe they already had. Technology wasn't her thing, but that would bear checking out.

She might even get a column about that, too. Technology for the technophobe. Not that she was really phobic, she was simply too busy to keep up with the stuff.

"I still don't think he's an artist," Suzy announced out of the blue.

"Who?" As if she didn't know. "All the famous artists have been men." Maggie continued checking the pockets of her computer case to see if she'd brought along any batteries. If so, they were too old to have any juice left in them.

"They say that about chefs, too, but what about Julia Child?"

"What about that Western artist, whatsisname?"

"You're asking me?" Suzy was using Crayolas to hold her toes apart to keep the polish from smearing.

"You know who I mean—he's named something to do with guns. Colt? Browning? Oh, yeah—Remington."

"He probably carries one. A gun, I mean. He said he was in security." Carefully, Suzy began pulling out the Crayolas. "Man, I wouldn't mind a taste of that kind of security."

"Maybe he's a model," Maggie suggested.

"In that case, I'm devoting the rest of my life to art."

Maggie said, "How did we get off on this subject, anyway?" As if she didn't know. "I need to take some notes in case I want to write about it."

"Okay, first note—your heroine's name is Suzy and your hero's name is Ben. Is that a virile name, or what?"

Maggie threw a small instruction leaflet, which she'd never bothered to read, across the room. It landed among the shoes near the bed. Four pairs of Suzy's, one pair of hers.

"I'm going to grab a shower while everybody's still out on the porch." Collecting soap, shampoo and a loose cotton shift that doubled as a robe, Maggie headed upstairs where one of the larger rooms had been turned into a communal bathroom. There was a single claw-foot tub, three lavatories, three commodes and three shower stalls. The men evidently had a tiny

bathroom down the hall, which was a rough indication of the usual ratio between men and women.

Lathering her hair, she wondered if Silver culled
through the applicants, deliberately choosing the ones
he wanted to include. Using what criterion, she wondered. She hadn't been particularly surprised to see
so few men. The surprising thing had been that so
many of the women were over fifty. It only solidified
her suspicion that he was far more interested in
money than in sex or romance.

On the other hand, he'd been hanging all over Suzy
at supper tonight. At this point Suzy was more interested in Ben Hunter, but maybe that didn't mean she
wouldn't cooperate for the good of the mission. Lumber money was as good as pickle money, especially
when the only heir just happened to be an attractive
daughter of marriageable age.

It never occurred to Maggie to consider herself a
candidate. Her father sold insurance. He didn't own
the company—didn't even manage the three-man
agency, which was one of the reasons Maggie had
attended a community college instead of university;
why she'd gone to work for a pittance at the *Suburban
Record* until she could get a real job at the *Twin-City
Journal.* Even in-state tuition cost a fortune, and besides, her father needed her at home. Left to himself
he'd have ended up eating bacon and eggs and real
butter and drinking four-percent milk in spite of
knowing better.

Before her mother had left they'd dined more often
than not on things like tofu, tahini and soybeans in
one form or another. Maggie had joined her father in
pigging out on junk food between meals, but now that

she was older she had settled on a more moderate path. Whole-grain, low-fat, with lots of fresh fruit and vegetables. If she occasionally backslid when she was away from home, that was nobody's business but her own. As long as she had only one functional parent, she fully intended to keep him that way. Let her mother go on drifting from one mushroom field to another, playing her zither, smoking pot and remembering every six months or so that she still had a family back east. Fortunately, Maggie had inherited a broad streak of practicality from her father, enough to take care of him and anyone else who needed it.

"Any hot water left?" Suzy was in the room when Maggie got back from her shower.

"Gobs. Look, I need you to do me a favor." And so she explained about Mary Rose and why she was really here.

"Geez, I don't know, Riley." Leaning back on her elbows, Suzy admired her colorful toenails. "I sort of had my eye on the cowboy. Besides, Perry spent most of his time with that lady with the buzz cut and the three-carat diamond."

"Georgia, I think her name is." Maggie sat on the room's only chair, which lacked a back and could more properly be termed a stool. She toweled her hair. "The cowboy will wait. All I need is one good example of Perry reeling out the same old line he used on Mary Rose, and I'll have him dead to rights."

"Would she believe you?"

"If I could get it on tape, it would be even better." Maggie waited hopefully for Suzy to offer her body to be wired. When no such offer was forthcoming,

she shrugged and said, "She knows I never lie...
unless it's absolutely necessary."

"If I get the goods on Silver, do I get dibs on the
cowboy?"

"Unless he's married or otherwise out of the running, he's all yours," Maggie said magnanimously,
as if it were up to her. If she had anything to say
about it, she might not be so generous.

"He's not wearing a ring." Suzy went through a
few lethargic yoga movements. "There's my day's
exercise. I'm a firm believer in moderation in all
things."

Maggie continued to towel her hair, her mind on
the man who kept popping into her thoughts like a
sexy poltergeist. "He's probably not going to model,
since he signed the register like all the rest of us."

"Besides, if he were a model, he'd be busy trying
on jockstraps."

"Perish the thought," Maggie said, grinning.

"I don't want to perish the thought, it's too tempting."

"About tomorrow—" Maggie was determined not
to lose sight of her mission. "We're all going to have
to paint something. How good are you?"

Suzy shrugged. "It's been a while."

"I've never even tried to draw anything since I
used to do stuff in school, mostly stick figures standing under a rainbow."

"What do you bet we're not the only amateurs
here?"

"Um-hmm..." Maggie was having trouble picturing Ben Hunter as an artist, although she couldn't
have said quite why. Maybe because of his boots. Or

maybe those powerful arms. She'd be willing to bet those strong hands and muscular forearms had done more than wield a paintbrush.

"But then, hey—if it weren't for us amateurs, Perry would be out of a job, right?" Suzy said brightly.

After that, they talked about clothes—whether or not they'd brought the right kind—and boyfriends. Suzy was currently juggling three; Maggie didn't have time for even one, although she had her eye on a young high school coach.

By the time the new roommate, Ann Ehringhaus, showed up, Maggie was already yawning. After introductions all around, Suzy pointed out the amenities, such as they were. When Ann sneezed for the third time, Maggie murmured something about allergies. While the other two women talked softly, Maggie fell asleep and dreamed of a Ben Hunter who segued into one of those famous male statues wearing a fig leaf and a strategically draped shawl, with a quiver full of watercolor brushes on his back. He was leering at her.

Mercy! No wonder she woke up even before the alarm went off with the mother of all headaches.

Leaving the other two women still sleeping, Maggie dressed quietly and tiptoed into the kitchen, following the beguiling aroma of freshly brewed coffee. When a shaft of sunlight slanting through the window struck her, she winced and shut her eyes.

"Not a morning person, hmm?"

Her stomach did a funny little lurch and she blinked at the figure silhouetted against the open back door. Wouldn't you know the first person she'd see before she could even wash down a handful of pills would be Apollo in person. If he'd been wearing a fig leaf and shawl, she'd have run screaming off down the hill.

Instead he was wearing the same faded jeans he'd worn yesterday, which were as good as a roadmap pointing out strategic points of interest. Her good-morning sounded more like the snarl of a pit bull.

"It's probably the altitude," he told her solicitously.

She shot him a suspicious look, and he said, "Headache, right? Flying does it to me, even in a pressurized cabin. We're not all that high here, but—"

"Thanks, I don't need a diagnosis," she growled. "Lack of sleep always gives me a headache." With any luck, it would be gone before the first class started—and so would he.

"Me, I slept like a log."

She shot him a saccharine smile. "Goody for you."

"We're on our own from now on." Reaching inside a cabinet, he took out a box of sweetened cereal and frowned at the picture of tiny, pastel-colored shapes.

Maggie had brought her own cereal. It was whole grain and probably not as tasty as the one he was holding. His arms and his hands were tanned. There was no lighter circle on his third finger, left hand, to indicate he had recently worn a ring.

He said, "I checked the refrigerator. The kitchen's stocked with basics, but they're pretty, ah—basic. Eggs, bacon. Bunch of green stuff."

"Do you have to talk so much?" She winced as she crossed through the patch of sunlight again.

"Reckon not. Reckon we could just dance."

She goggled at him. No other word to describe it. She did her best to blot out the memory of the impressive creature with his undraped loins and his quiver of brushes, that had haunted her early morning dreams. The image was already losing the sharp edges, but she could still see those muscular calves and the flat, ridged abdomen where the shawl draped low on one hip before swinging up to his shoulder.

"If you don't mind," she said haughtily, "I'd rather not talk before I've had my morning pint."

"Yes, ma'am. Better warn you, though—it's pretty strong. You might want to water it down some. Be somebody along pretty soon to start the bacon and eggs."

She mimicked talking with her fingers. He looked suitably chastened and covered his mouth with his hand. And darn it, he really did have gorgeous hands. Maggie wasn't entirely certain what an artistic hand was supposed to look like, but artistic or not, his long, square-tipped fingers were perfectly proportioned for the square palm.

And if she'd ever even considered a man's hands in that respect, she had to be plum out of her mind. What the devil was happening to her normally sharp-as-a-tack brain? She was here on a mission. She didn't have time for this kind of distraction.

She poured herself a mug of coffee and by the time she turned around, Ben had placed a jug of whole milk and a can of evaporated on the table, along with a sugar bowl, a jar of honey and a stack of pink packets of sweetener. He grinned as if he'd offered her the crown jewels.

"Thank you," she croaked. Croaked because her voice was always rusty first thing in the morning. She was used to seeing her father off to work in silence and taking her pint of coffee into the ex-utility room she laughingly called her office, where she worked on her column until noon. If any calls came in, she let the machine take them.

"Really," she said when he continued to look at her as if she were something he'd found under a microscope. Or under a rock.

"Look, you're a nice man and I'm a grungy curmudgeon. I'm sorry, but that's just the way it is, okay?"

Bemused was the only word she could think of to describe the way he looked at her. As if whatever it was he'd discovered under the microscope—or the rock—had suddenly launched into a full orchestra rendition of the "Star Spangled Banner." She sometimes had that effect on men. They didn't know what to make of her, and so mostly, they made nothing. Which suited her just fine, it really did. It always had.

Until just recently...

Without a word, Ben Hunter eased up from the spoke-backed kitchen chair, tipped her a nod and let himself out onto the side porch. A few moments later she could hear the creak of the swing.

Darn it, why did she do that? She knew all about women who were their own worst enemy. So certain men wouldn't like them that they went out of their way to prove they didn't care. She'd written about that kind of behavior. The thing was, she'd never before realized she followed the pattern.

As the first class began to take shape, each of the several long tables filled, some with three students, a few with four. Maggie, Suzy and the latecomer, Ann Ehringhaus, chose a smaller table near the back of the studio. Without intending to, Maggie looked around for Ben and found him setting up several tables away with two women and a guy who looked like G. Gordon Liddy—same bald head, same beetle brows, but a smaller mustache.

There were no easels. There were also no chairs. Suzy muttered something about a half-ass operation. Ann sneezed. Maggie shifted restlessly and considered giving up on this whole crazy idea. What had started as a simple rescue mission and expanded to a story op—M. L. Riley, embedded somewhere in the foothills of the Blue Ridge Mountains—was looking more like an expensive mistake.

Hardly her first. She simply hadn't thought things through, and now she was about to be exposed as the fraud she really was. She could no more paint a picture than she could hop on a broomstick and fly. What on earth had made her believe she could pull it off?

From somewhere off-stage, music started up, screeched to a halt and then started again. To the strains of something vaguely Celtic, vaguely New Age, Perry made his grand entrance, scattering smiles all around. He was wearing his trademark beret, even though the temperature was already in the mid-seventies and the old house evidently didn't run to air conditioning. He took his place at a table in front that had been set up with a child's plastic beach pail filled with water, a big, smeary palate, an enormous sheet of paper on a drawing board and an alabaster vase filled with at least a dozen brushes of all sizes and shapes.

"So that's what all the plastic pails are for," Maggie murmured indicating the yellow one beside her stack of stuff.

"You'll have to fill and empty your own. Perry's the only one who gets serviced," Ann whispered.

"Now," the tall, willowy artist said, his mellifluous voice blending with the music, "I'll start off with a demonstration and then you'll all have half an hour to do your version of what I've painted. We want quick and sloppy today. This is just a loosening-up exercise. By the way, how many of you can still touch your toes?"

Maggie looked at Suzy, who shrugged. For the first time since she'd arrived the night before, Ann smiled. "Wait, you'll see," she whispered.

Across the room, Ben wondered what the hell the guy meant by that question. And what was with all the flutes and harps? To cover up the groans from people who hadn't touched their toes in decades? Hell yes, he could touch his toes. He might be on the shady side of thirty, but he could still take down a cream puff like Silver with one hand tied behind him.

Only this time he was going to do it nice and legal. Scare the hell out of him so that nobody's gullible granny would get taken for a ride on Hi-Ho Silver.

Bracing his feet apart, Ben crossed his arms over his chest and waited for the show to begin. Beside him, Janie Burger planted her hands on her hips and did the same. Georgia said something about not enough liniment in the world to make her try it, and Charlie chuckled.

Meanwhile, in the front of the room, Perry Silver had already started on the morning's masterpiece, working flat on the table. From time to time he pursed his lips, stepped back, tilted his head and muttered an unintelligible incantation, after which, while his audience tried vainly to see what he was doing, he would lunge forward to add another touch. Gradually a streak of muddy color appeared on the floor where he repeatedly slung wet paint from his brush.

"No wonder the floors in here look like sh—like sugar," Ben muttered. "Why the devil doesn't he hold the thing up so we can see what the—so we can see what he's doing?" Out of respect for his associates, he was trying to cull the profanity from his vocabulary, but it wasn't easy.

"With watercolor, mostly you do it flat so you can tilt it whatever way you want the paint to flow," Janie whispered.

"Oh. Right." Going undercover as an artist might not be the swiftest idea he'd ever had.

Georgia nudged him and whispered, "Did the brochure say anything about having to pass a physical first?"

With a slow smile, Ben shook his head. The lady with the white buzz cut smelled like his granny. Combination of almond-scented hand lotion and arthritis-strength liniment. It reminded him of why he was here.

Silver glanced up with a boyish grin and said, "I know, I know, it seems like forever, but this little bit over here just simply isn't working. Give me another minute, dears, all right?''

Dears?

There was a general shuffling of tired feet. Someone sneezed—the latecomer with the allergies, probably.

Someone snickered. Had to be Maggie. He glanced around, and sure enough, her hand was covering her mouth and her eyes were alight with mischief. Today she was wearing a sleeveless blue chambray thing with what looked like a man's undershirt underneath. On her, it looked just fine.

Ben winked at her. Last time he remembered winking at a woman he'd been about fifteen, all beered up and looking for action.

Found it, too, if memory served.

God, he'd had some narrow escapes. This just might turn out to be one more in a long list, unless he could keep his mind on his mission.

''You're at the wrong table, hon,'' Janie whispered. Her pastel-colored hair was held back this morning with a twisted scarf. She was wearing black tights again along with a baggy pink sweatshirt sporting a risqué slogan. It occurred to him that maybe no one had told her she was pushing seventy.

You go, lady, he encouraged silently.

''Did you say something, Miss...Riley, isn't it?'' The maestro looked up, light from the north-facing windows emphasizing the bags under his eyes. Ben figured the picture on the cover of the brochure had been either heavily retouched or taken quite a few years earlier.

"Sorry. I was just—just eager to see what you've done."

Bless her heart, she was lying through her pearly whites. Ben winked again. It had to be a twitch. Maybe an ingrown eyelash.

Then Silver whipped out a hair dryer, switched it on and waved it over whatever he'd just done. Probably another "investment" like those Miss Emma had paid a whole slew of social security money for. If there was any way he could squeeze a refund out of this cheesy bastard he intended to do it.

"Oh, my, he's done it again," murmured Georgia as Perry propped his drawing board up on the easel so that it faced the class. She applauded. A few others picked it up, but Silver waved his hand and the applause quickly faded.

"Now, using my feeble attempt as an example, let's all see what we can come up with. Quickly, quickly—let the medium know who's boss."

Let the medium know who was boss? What the hell was *that* supposed to mean? Ben glanced over his shoulder and happened to catch Maggie's eye. She shrugged. He shook his head. At least this time they were in agreement. A regular meeting of the minds. He could think of several other areas where he wouldn't mind meeting her.

"You have thirty minutes," Silver said. "Impressions only, we'll get to details later in the week."

Charlie, on the far end of Ben's table, asked if there were any chairs. Perry lifted his eyebrows, but Charlie, a high school biology teacher a year away from retirement, was not intimidated. "In my classroom I stand," he stated. "On vacation, I sit unless I've got a golf club in my hand."

Ben wondered what the hell the older man was doing here when he could be outside in the fresh air beating the stuffing out of a little white ball?

"Is anyone else unable to stand for more than fifteen minutes? If so, you might want to consider dropping out now." Adjusting his beret, the instructor surveyed the room as if daring anyone to take the challenge.

"Do I get a refund if I drop out?" Charlie asked.

"I believe the terms were clearly stated in your application."

"I guess that means no."

Sounds of disapproval moved through the room on the pollen-laden breeze, drawing a variety of responses. Janie uncovered what she called a watercolor block—a stack of rough pages glued together on the edges. She leaned past Ben to smile at Charlie.

Ignoring a few murmurs of discontent, Silver pointed out first one area and then another in his landscape, over which he had quickly taped a white mat, as if to lend it legitimacy. "Note the contrasts," he instructed. "Dark against light, light against dark."

Hard to get one without the other, Ben thought, but then he wasn't feeling particularly charitable.

"Gradation, there's your sense of depth. Note the sharpest areas—in other words, the greatest contrast—falls near the center of interest, while everything else seems to soften. Blended washes. Do we see this?"

"With or without my trifocals?" someone asked, to the accompaniment of a few snickers.

And then, Lord bless her, Maggie spoke up. "Which part wasn't working…sir? If you don't mind my asking."

Janie bit her lip. Charlie said something about his feet not working, plus a few other parts he could mention, but wouldn't. Georgia dipped a brush that could easily be used for window trim into her plastic pail and dragged it over a pan of colors that looked as if it had been caught in the middle of a paint war.

By the time they broke for a glass of sweetened iced tea, everyone had committed their thirty minutes' worth of art. Ben had done his share of cursing, but fell silent after the first remonstrative look from Georgia. "Sorry," he said. "I'm trying to break the habit, but the damn paper—darned paper keeps puckering."

Charlie offered a few euphemisms, several of which were biological terms which, translated to street parlance, wouldn't pass muster. Janie called him a dirty old man, but grinned when she said it. She handed Ben a couple of clothespins and showed him how to use them to control the swelling of wet paper. All three of his tablemates commented freely, the comments for the most part flying over Ben's head.

Washes, bleeds, drybrush? Hell, he couldn't even manage the lingo. How the devil was he supposed to learn how to paint a picture?

Answer? He wasn't. No point in getting too caught up in the action. That wasn't why he was here.

He added a long squiggle of red across his mountain just because he'd always liked the color. It turned brown. "Well, shi—ucks," he grumbled. "I know damned well I dipped my brush in red."

Janie laughed and pointed out that mixed together, the colors he'd used make mud.

And then Maggie was there, peering over his shoulder to see how badly he'd embarrassed himself. He felt like covering it up, but he had too damn much pride.

"Oh, wow," she breathed reverently. "You're almost as good as I am. Does either of us really need to be here?"

"I'm seriously startin' to wonder," Ben growled.

Maggie felt like patting him on the head—or maybe somewhere more accessible. It made her feel better about her own charade to know that she and Suzy weren't the only two in the room without a clue. Mr. Spainhour wasn't bad, and the two ladies were actually pretty good, not that she was any real judge.

But Ben Hunter was awful. Purely awful! For some reason, that delighted her.

"I understand we're going to have a student exhibit at the end of the week," she said softly, leaning closer to Ben so that Perry the Paragon wouldn't overhear. He was wandering from table to table, scattering his pearls of wisdom. "Word of advice," she murmured. "If you enter this morning's effort in any exhibit, sign somebody else's name to it. That way nobody can hold you responsible."

He glowered at her, but midglower, his eyes warmed into a smile. "Yeah, it's pretty ugly, isn't it?"

"I wouldn't say it's exactly ugly…but then, I was taught that if you couldn't say something nice, it's better not to say anything at all."

He turned to reexamine his morning's work

while Maggie stepped back to study the man himself. If ever a man looked out of his element it was Ben Hunter with his bristly jaw, his honey-colored eyes and a pair of shoulders that threatened to burst the seams of his shirt. Not that artists couldn't be manly, but if Hunter had the slightest bit of artistic talent he was working hard not to let it show.

He raked his fingers through his hair, causing it to flop back on his brow. "Warm up exercise," he said gruffly. "I haven't painted in a while, so if you don't mind, I'll take a few days to get back in practice."

Yeah, sure you will. She thought it, but knew better than to say it out loud. No point in issuing a direct challenge. For all she knew, he might be really good, only not in any style she recognized. It looked like someone had dumped a bowl of scrambled green eggs on his paper and then tromped through it with muddy boots.

But then, her effort didn't look much better.

One of the women said something about the music, which was pretty cloying. "A little Vince Gill would suit me better," Maggie said.

"That reminds me, I understand there's dancing after dinner," said the woman with the pink hair. "There's a stack of old records, some of them 78s. Does anyone else remember those?"

Dancing, with a dozen women and three men to go around? That ought to be interesting, Maggie mused. They talked about music for a few minutes, and then a thoughtful Maggie wandered back to her own table. Not for the first time, it occurred to her that something about Ben Hunter didn't quite ring true. An artist, he wasn't. So why was he here?

The man would bear watching, she thought, and for some idiotic reason, found herself smiling.

Four

By mutual consent everyone migrated to the side porch, where a tray of glasses and another pitcher of tea was waiting, compliments of Ann, who seemed to spend more time in peripheral duties than she did in class. Could there be another nonartist who, for reasons of her own, had enrolled in Silver's circus? No wonder Silver spent so much of his time with the older members of his class. Apparently those were the only ones who were serious about learning.

Maggie felt Ben's presence even before he reached past her to scoop two glasses into the ice bucket. He filled them with the sweetened tea and handed her one, saying, ''Here you go.''

''Thank you,'' she said stiffly. Then, with false conviction, ''This is really nice, isn't it?''

His eyes sparkled with hidden laughter. The jour-

nalist in her—not to mention the woman—wanted to
ask him why he was pretending to be an artist when
obviously he was no better at it than she was, and
evidently no more interested in learning.

But then, he might ask a few questions she'd just
as soon not answer.

He leaned against the porch rail, his gaze moving
over the clusters of chattering women. She wanted to
shout, *"I'm right here—look at me!"*

Instead, she backed away to perch on the arm of
an Adirondack chair. The chair tipped, tea splashed
over her lap, ice cubes skittered across the porch floor
and Maggie swore silently. If there happened to be a
spill, a splash or a drip anywhere in the vicinity, her
body would attract it like a magnet.

When Ben leaned forward and began mopping at
the icy liquid with a handkerchief, she shoved his
hand away. "Don't bother. It's only tea, it won't kill
me." Judging from what she'd seen of the facilities,
any laundry equipment would probably consist of a
washtub and a clothesline.

The older woman with the pretty pink hair strolled
over. "Hi, you're Maggie and I'm Janie—I think we
met yesterday. Are you having as much fun this
morning as I am?" She held up her glass. "I don't
think it'll stain. It's mostly sugar syrup." She kicked
a few ice cubes under the railing without making a
big production of it.

When Perry Silver joined them, the temperature
seemed to drop several degrees. It had nothing to do
with a few ice cubes melting in the shrubbery, or even
the clammy mess plastered to her thighs. As uncomfortable as she was, Maggie sensed Ben's hostility.

Which was odd, as she'd never before been particularly sensitive to the feelings of others.

Well, except for Mary Rose. And her father. And the elderly widow she visited two or three times a week with library books and treats from the bakery. And maybe a few others.

"Are you enjoying yourself, Hunter?" Perry asked with a smile that easily qualified as a smirk.

"I was," Ben said. He hadn't moved a muscle. Maggie was reminded of a sleeping lion she'd seen at the Asheboro Zoo.

"Good, good." Turning to Janie, the artist said, "And you, little lady? This morning's effort showed definite promise. We'll have you painting like a pro by week's end, I guarantee."

Janie waited until he moved on to another group before murmuring a reply. "Sonny boy, if you're an example of a pro, I'll pass." With a shrug, she added, "He really is a good teacher, though."

"That's what everybody keeps saying," Maggie said. "Sure can't prove it by me."

When Janie wandered off to join Charlie and Georgia, Maggie turned to Ben, wishing she had half the poise of the older woman. Poise was tough enough when she was all dressed up in her Sunday best. Wet from the waist down, it was impossible. "Well…I guess I'll see you around."

Ben stood. He'd stood when Janie joined them until the older woman had pressed him back down again. Someone, Maggie thought—his mother, probably— had taught him good manners.

"Maggie," Ben said just as she was about to disappear inside. She glanced over her shoulder, and he grinned at her. "You're not all that bad. Honest."

"As if you'd know."

But she was smiling when she hurried to her room to wash off the stickiness and change clothes. Lord, the man was something. Trouble on the hoof. How was she supposed to concentrate on getting the goods on Perry Silver when all she had to do was catch sight of Ben Hunter for her knees to go weak and her brain to turn to gravy?

"Answer me that, Wonder Woman," she muttered.

Suzy was just coming from the room they shared, having shed the shirt she wore over her halter top as the day warmed up. Today's top was blue, and even skimpier than yesterday's. "What'd you say?"

"Nothing," Maggie snapped.

"I saw you drooling over our cowboy. Hey, there's going to be dancing tonight. Wanna draw straws for him?"

"This isn't drool, I spilled my tea."

"Whatever," the younger woman said with a knowing grin.

"Yeah, whatever," Maggie muttered as she hurried past to clean off the sticky mess. She'd do well to keep her mind on her mission.

A critique was no worse than the average root canal, Maggie told herself some forty-five minutes later, coolly admiring her own objectivity. Silver found something kind to say about almost every single work until he got to the last three examples, namely, hers, Suzy's and Ben Hunter's. After a lot of hemming and hawing, he called Ben's effort problematic, and to be fair, even Maggie could see that Ben's was easily the worst of the lot.

Silver would set up each student's work on his easel in turn. Then, using a brush handle as a pointer, he would indicate the parts that "worked" and those that didn't, and explain why. While Suzy's sky was nicely done and Maggie's colors weren't *too* muddy, evidently nothing in Ben's painting worked. Not a single thing.

Maggie put it down to jealousy. Both men were attractive, but there was really no comparison. Without lifting a finger, Ben attracted women of all ages. Maybe he was the son or grandson the older ones wished they'd been lucky enough to have, but there was nothing even faintly maternal in Maggie's feelings. Never having experienced it before, at least not to this degree, she recognized it as sheer, unadulterated lust.

"I don't know about you, but I kinda like my picture." Ben murmured in her ear, his warm breath sending tendrils of hair tickling her cheek—not to mention certain other ticklish parts of her body. "Reckon my granny would like to have it?"

"As a Halloween decoration, you mean? Tell me something—what is that wiggly streak across the front of the page? A rusty train track?"

"Now you're deliberately trying to hurt my feelings. It's a—"

Maggie never did find out what the jagged streak was supposed to be, as Ben glanced up just then and saw Silver in a huddle with the two women he had seemingly adopted. "'Scuse me," he said, and sauntered off.

Sauntered was a word Maggie rarely had an opportunity to use in her general advice column, but it came closest to describing that easy, loose-limbed way Ben Hunter had of moving, as if he were so comfortable in his skin he might actually fall asleep in transit.

Watching him make his way through the crowd, she could think of several methods she might employ in an effort to keep him awake.

Suzy sidled up beside her. "You think he's got a mother fixation, or whatever they call that thingee? Some kind of a complex?"

In Maggie's estimation, Suzy's four years at Chapel Hill had left her largely untouched, education-wise. But then, sometimes a college education took a while to filter through. As with whiskey, maturity often made a difference. She'd used that little gem of wisdom in one of her columns just last month.

"You mean Janie and Georgia? They're nice, aren't they?" *Be generous, Maggie—he could be going after Suzy or Ann.* "I wouldn't mind having either one of them for a mother."

When Suzy lifted one penciled eyebrow, Maggie shrugged. "My mother was never your standard cookie-baking, PTA-meeting, do-your-homework type of mother, if you know what I mean."

Suzy nodded, indicating she understood, then said, "Not exactly."

"Never mind. Look, how about doing me a favor? Remember what I told you about my friend, Mary Rose Dilys."

It was hardly a promising beginning, Maggie thought a few hours later as she dressed for supper—

starting with having to expose her total lack of talent, followed by a lapful of cold, sticky iced tea. After that came the afternoon session, which only confirmed what the morning class had hinted at. She'd bought the wrong kind of paint, the wrong kind of paper and her one and only brush was about as useful as a secondhand Q-Tip. Add to that the fact that of the only two men enrolled, the only attractive one—devastating, really—attractive didn't begin to describe him—preferred older women. As in about forty years older.

Catching sight of Ben and Janie wandering around outside while she tried to tame her hair, she thought, maybe if I were to use a rinse...

Her brush-hand fell still as she stared out the tiny window at the pair highlighted by the setting sun. Ben was definitely a saunterer, but Janie's walk defied description. Viewed from the back, with her pink, shoulder-length hair—which was really more of a peach-color—she didn't look a day over twenty-five. Maybe thirty. Even with those ugly cross-trainers. Heads together, the two of them were as chummy as a pack of Nibs.

Oh, well, Maggie rationalized, she hadn't come here looking for romance. From now on she'd pay strict attention to her mission, she vowed as she fished through her suitcase for something suitable for supper and dancing. Dancing was one of the few sports in which she excelled.

Lifting out her stiletto heels, she remembered the last time she'd worn them. She'd got one heel jammed between the boards in the deck of a nice couple who'd invited her to supper to meet their nephew.

No point in courting disaster. She'd be just as tall in her everyday platforms.

Suzy breezed into the room, still wearing her high-cut skintight shorts and the skimpy low-cut halter. "Hi, you getting ready for tonight?"

"For supper. I thought maybe—"

"Right. You thought maybe you'd get dressed up for the big diesel."

"The big—" Maggie felt her face grow warm.

Suzy said dryly, "You need to keep your eyeballs on a shorter leash. I mean, the man's a serious stud muffin, but he has this hang-up about older women. You said so yourself."

Maggie dropped back onto the cot. It threatened to tip and she grabbed the wooden sides. This was not her lucky day. "Are you going to do it?" she asked, referring to their earlier conversation.

"What, troll my bait in front of Silver?"

"Well, yeah...sort of. Nothing outrageous, but just let him know you might be interested. See how he reacts. In a house full of people you'll be safe enough, and I'll be standing by to rescue you if it comes to that."

"Now if we were talking about the mighty Hunter, I'd be way out ahead of you." She rolled her eyes. "Okay, okay. If things get too tense I can always take a cue from Ann and sneeze real loud." Their room-mate had serious allergies.

Maggie sighed heavily. "It seemed like such a per-fect plan when I started out. Now I've blown all this money—my dad's home alone eating junk food and

smoking too much, and I'm not sure that even if I get
proof that Perry's a—a philanderer, it will make a
speck of difference.''

''A philanderer?''

''Skunk. The two words are interchangeable. My
dad says I'm a meddler, but honestly, I'm not. It's
just that I get these brilliant ideas that occasionally
don't work out quite the way I'd planned.''

''Okay, I'll try my hand at being skunk bait. Beats
working in an unair-conditioned office that smells like
turpentine. I keep telling my dad that a window unit
wouldn't exactly bankrupt James and James Lumber
Company.''

''Who's the other James?''

Suzy grimaced. ''Moi. He hopes. You wearing
that?'' She indicated Maggie's ankle-length, button-
front, straight-line shirtwaist. ''Hate to tell you, but if
you're looking for any action tonight, that dress has
to go. Sexy, it's not, and besides, the skirt's too tight
for line dancing. If those boots are anything to go by,
that's probably all our cowboy knows how to do.''

Maggie tossed a Perry Silver Watercolor Workshop
brochure at her. It sailed under the cot.

Seating arrangements had been slightly modified
for the second night. Seated at the head table, Perry
Silver had the only chair with arms, thus denoting his
rank. Janie was on his right with Ben beside her,
Georgia to his left, with Charlie beside her, with a
retired public health nurse at the far end.

''How come all the men have to be at one table?''
Suzy asked as they made their way to the small table

by the kitchen door. "Why can't we share the good-ies?"

"Ask whoever arranged the seating." Maggie wondered, too, but she wasn't about to make an issue of it. Charlie, she wouldn't have minded—at least he had a sense of humor, but either of the other two would have made her too nervous to eat, for entirely different reasons.

"I wonder how I'd look with pink hair," Suzy mused as she dug into the entrée, which tonight was pork chops and sweet potatoes with bagged coleslaw and biscuits from a tube, compliments of the two librarians and a retired accountant.

"If you mean like Janie's, it's more peach than pink."

"Whatever. Our cowboy sure seems to like it." She shot Maggie a sly look.

Our cowboy?

"So?" If she sounded preoccupied, it was because she was. Preoccupied with trying to keep her mind focused on the reason she was here.

Ann slid into the empty chair beside Maggie, her allergies apparently subdued. "I signed the three of us up for tomorrow, is that okay?"

Maggie said, "I thought when I signed up that meals were included."

Ann shook her head. "Read the fine print. Meals are provided, some assembly required. Words to that effect."

"If worse comes to worst I guess I could micro-wave," Suzy admitted.

Maggie sighed. "I can cook. Plain country, nothing

fancy. I've been doing it for years, else my Dad would have cholesterol up the wazoo.''

Without cracking a smile, Ann said, ''I didn't know there's where cholesterol settled. Live and learn.''

''You probably didn't know Maggie was jumping off tall buildings to save the weak and helpless by the time she cut her permanent teeth, either,'' Suzy said dryly.

''Then I vote we elect her chief cook, you can do the serving and I'll do the bottle washing,'' Ann said. ''Maggie? Okay with you?''

Maggie shot her a telling look. The fewer people who knew about her covert mission, the better.

They talked about men and about food and about the best shops in Hanes Mall. And about men again. ''You know what?'' Maggie said quietly. ''I don't think he's all that great.''

''Who, Ben Hunter? Trust me, he's great.'' The observation, not surprisingly, came from Suzy.

''I was talking about our leader,'' Maggie said. ''Do you like his work?''

''Actually, he's considered quite good if you like realism—and lots of people do,'' said Ann, who seemed surprisingly knowledgeable considering she'd skipped most of the day's classes.

Maggie was about to mention a certain calendar in her father's office that reminded her of Perry's work when Suzy held up a hand. ''Save it, we've got incoming.''

He came up behind Maggie's chair. She didn't have to look around. Couldn't if she'd wanted to, not without brushing against him. Seated, her head was at belt level—or slightly lower.

"Hi," drawled Suzy. "You know everybody here, don't you, Ben? Ann, this is Ben—Ben, Ann. She came in late yesterday."

"We've met, thanks." Ben touched Maggie on the shoulder and she stopped breathing. "Got a minute? Something I'd like to talk over with you, if you'll excuse us."

Ann said, "Sure."

Suzy smirked.

Maggie was having trouble regulating her air intake, but she raked back her chair and followed him out onto the porch.

Fool, fool, fool!

Five

There was still enough of an afterglow from the spectacular sunset to cast shadows. "This really is a beautiful place," Maggie said brightly. She was nervous. Maggie was *never* nervous.

"Yeah, it's kind of pretty. Green, at least. Big change from where I came from." Ben sounded oddly distracted. He wasn't looking at the scenery, he was looking at Maggie.

"Which is?"

"Hmm? Oh—West Texas. Little town nobody ever heard of. It's pretty much flat if you don't count the anthills."

If anything could make her clumsier than she already was, it was feeling self-conscious, and the intent way he was staring at her made her wonder if the label at the back of her neck was sticking out. "I'm sure it's lovely," she murmured.

What she was sure of was that Ben hadn't brought her out here to talk about geography, his or hers. Why *had* he brought her outside? What could he possibly have to say to her that couldn't be said in front of the others?

"Maggie?" Was it her imagination, or did he sound as if he had a sore throat? He lifted his hands and dropped them.

She stopped breathing.

He lifted them again, and this time they made it all the way up to her face. Clasping her cheeks, he tilted her face up and lowered his own. Her eyes remained open until he went out of focus, and then all she was conscious of was the incredibly soft feel of his lips on hers.

Soft, warm, moist, they moved over her mouth, back and forth—undemanding. He didn't try to taste her, to involve her in anything more than a simple kiss.

Never—*ever*—had anything so simple been so complex.

He lifted his head and she wanted to pull him back, to lick his lips and then go from there—to follow this crazy thing that had blossomed inside her to wherever it might lead.

He cleared his throat. His hands rested loosely on her shoulders and his eyes, those warm whiskey-brown eyes, looked dark as night under his half-lowered lids. She couldn't have spoken if her life depended on it.

"How about you and me teaming up?" he rasped.

She blinked in confusion. It was the last thing she expected to hear. "You mean—cooking?"

He laughed, and it was as if someone had trailed a feather duster from the sole of her foot to the tip of her ear. "No, not cooking, although if you insist, we might give that a shot, too."

Omigod, he really was hitting on her. Teaming up. Was he talking switching roommates or...or something more permanent? "I'm not sure what kind of team you're talking about," she said cautiously, her head already reeling with possibilities. Would she or wouldn't she?

Well, of course she wouldn't. Where could they go for privacy? Besides, even without Mary Rose's example she knew better than to "team up" with a man she'd known for less than two days.

She stepped away, hoping she could think more clearly if he wasn't touching her. It helped...but not very much. Her lips still tingled and she wanted to feel it again—that incredibly soft pressure. She'd been kissed before, plenty of times—well, enough times so that she knew most kisses were pretty much alike. Open mouth, probing tongue, thrusting pelvis— the whole works.

Ben's kiss was totally different. The wild optimist hiding deep inside her pragmatic exterior wanted to believe he was reaching out to the woman she really was instead of simply reacting to a marginally attractive, marginally available member of the opposite sex.

He was no longer gazing into her eyes. Using the toe of his boot to dislodge a small rock from the red clay matrix, he said, "You might have noticed, I'm sort of out of my league here."

With his looks, he could hold his own in any league. He couldn't possibly be talking about...

"Oh...you mean art-wise?"

"Art dumb would be more like it." When he smiled, he had a crease in one cheek that almost qualified as a dimple. "You might even say I'm here under false pretenses."

The lawn immediately surrounding the house was unkempt—a little chickweed, a little grass and a lot of exposed rock. They reached the edge of the cleared area and Maggie waited for him to continue. Okay, this wasn't about sex. That kiss had been merely a— a bonding gesture. Like a handshake, only more personal.

It occurred to her belatedly that she might not be the only one here with an agenda that didn't include qualifying for membership in the Watercolor Society. Something was going on—something that probably didn't involve diving into the nearest bed.

Well...shoot!

She let him talk, trying not to notice the way he stood, with his feet braced apart in those well-worn boots and thumbs hooked into his hip pockets. Sort of an 'I-shall-not-be-moved' stance, with overtones of 'But-I-can-be-tempted'.

Yeah, right. Obviously she didn't have what it took to tempt him.

"See, I have this grandmother," he said.

Her jaw fell, and she snapped it shut. How did he get from a kiss that was like nothing she had ever experienced before to telling her about his relatives? Was he inviting her home to meet his family?

"Miss Emma—she likes for me to call her that— she's in her late seventies and lives alone. Not that she needs a caretaker or anything like that. I mean, she still does all her own housework, gardening—you name it. Gets involved in local politics, goes to these arts and crafts affairs. She just finished taking a computer class with some friends.''

Back to earth with a dull thud. ''So that's why you're here, right? You're checking this workshop out for your grandmother? Aren't there any workshops in Texas?''

''She lives in North Carolina.''

''Oh. Well, that's stretching family obligations, isn't it? Bringing a grandson all the way from Texas just to be sure a course is suitable? What was she afraid of, nude male models?''

He looked away, and she was tempted to grab that rock-bound jaw of his and force him to look at her. *I'm here—your granny isn't! Look at me, darn you!*

''See, she's taken all these classes in fancy sewing, lace-making, stuff like that. She goes to a lot of exhibits, too. Something to do with her time, I guess.'' He raked his fingers through his hair, dislodging a lock that fell across his brow. Maggie had already noticed that he did that when he was shaping his next statement. ''Anyway she told me about this guy she met at an art show last fall and how she came to buy a bunch of his pictures.''

''Paintings,'' Maggie corrected absently. ''When they're painted by hand they're called paintings.''

''Well, sure, I knew that.'' Ben rocked on his heels like a kid with a guilty conscience. Maggie thought it was endearing in a big, tough-looking guy from West Texas…or wherever.

''Thing is, these weren't real paintings, they were some kind of prints, I guess, but he wrote his name on them and sold a bunch of 'em. Miss Emma shot her wad buying one of everything. Things weren't even framed, just matted and sealed in plastic. Most of 'em looked pretty much like that thing Silver did this morning. Not much color, mostly browns and grays. Dead trees, log cabins, cornfields and patches of snow, maybe a mountain or two in the background."

Now that she'd finally got her feet planted firmly on earth again, Maggie wondered where he was going with this. She didn't find Perry's work particularly exciting, either the one he'd done as a demonstration or those she'd seen hanging on the downstairs walls. But then, she was no art critic. Not yet, at any rate.

And neither, if his own effort was any example, was Ben Hunter.

"So you see where I'm going with this," he said.

"Uh...not really."

Just then something small and dark swooped silently out of nowhere. Maggie flinched and hid her face. Ben grabbed her arm. "Steady there," he cautioned. "Some of those rocks are slippery—easy to lose your footing."

Breathless, she said, "It's not my feet I'm worried about. Was that a—a bat?"

"Not a bloodsucker, just the ordinary bug-eating kind. You didn't twist your ankle, did you?"

She was shaking her foot. "I'm fine, stop fussing." She staggered slightly. She was wearing her clogs again. She'd packed only two pairs of shoes, not counting the old pair she kept in the trunk of her car for emergencies that were practical, but ugly as sin.

"I've got a pebble in my shoe," she admitted when the thing refused to fall out.

Ben squatted and took her foot in his hand. She grabbed his shoulder for support while he ran his finger between the platform and the sole of her foot.

"That's got it. I'm fine now, honestly," she said breathlessly. She'd be fine if he would remove his hands from her ankle and stop tickling her foot. On the other hand, if he wanted to kiss it and make it all better, she wouldn't complain.

When another bat swept past, she hardly even noticed.

Ben said, "You're sure?" He levered himself up, all six-feet whatever of lean, clean-smelling male. He really wasn't the handsomest man she'd ever seen, but there was something about him...

Maggie decided on the spot that starting tomorrow she would dig around in her car under the accumulation of junk and retrieve the hideous shoes with the thick soles, the padded tongues and the stripes on the sides. She'd tossed them in along with her space blanket, a flashlight and a first aid kit in case she ever got stranded on the road and had to walk. With her skinny legs, they made her look like Minnie Mouse, but then, even Minnie would have better sense than to go all mooney-eyed over a long-legged Texan.

"Could we get on with whatever it was you brought me out here to discuss? Something about teaming up?"

"Right," he said slowly, as if he were mentally skimming down a long page, trying to find his place. He was probably as rattled by that bat as she'd been, only being a man, he'd never admit it.

"You were telling me about your grandmother and her taste in art," she prompted when he stood there staring down at her as if he'd forgotten who she was, much less what he'd been about to tell her.

"Oh yeah. Well, like I said, Miss Emma's big on independence and all that. Once she retired, she bought herself an annuity and a bunch of CDs—not the music kind, the ones you get from a bank."

Maggie only nodded. There was probably a point here somewhere. Being a slow-talking, slow-walking Texan, it took him a while to get to it.

"Right. But then along comes this slick hustler, tells her one-percent interest or whatever she was getting, was peanuts. What she needed to invest in was art. In other words, his stuff. So bless her sweet, gullible heart, she cashes in a few CDs, throws in a couple of Social Security checks and buys herself a bunch of bad wallpaper, thinking she can resell it in a year or so at a huge profit."

"Why am I not surprised?" Maggie murmured. Any man who would sweet-talk a woman he'd just met with one eye on her trust fund would definitely do something like that. The old-fashioned term "gold digger" was usually applied to women, but it was definitely an equal opportunity appellation. Given enough material, she could write an exposé that might earn her a place on a real newspaper instead of a few double-column inches between Belk's white sale and the weekly specials at Mount Tabor Food Market. "How much did your grandmother, uh—invest?"

Why don't we try that kiss again? As long as I'm going to be remembering it for the next hundred years, I want to be sure I've got it right. Oh, and this

*time, put your arms around me. As long as I'm re-
membering, I might as well get the sizzle in all the
right places.*

"Get taken for, you mean? Not a fortune, but per-
centage-wise it was still way too much. Things cost
a couple of hundred bucks apiece, depending on the
numbers scribbled in pencil on the lower left-hand
margin. His autograph—"

"Signature," Maggie supplied. "You mean he actually puts the price right on the painting, or whatever?" She was finding it hard to concentrate on art,
much less on her personal mission—much less on *his*
personal mission—when he was standing there, looking so sexy and appealing. She didn't need the distraction, she really, really didn't.

"It's not exactly a price, but the numbers in the
left-hand corner have something to do with how valuable the thing is. Lower the numbers, the higher the
price, according to my source."

His *source?* This was sounding more and more serious.

"The one she paid the most for was marked eleven-
slash-one-twenty. Means there were only a hundred
and twenty of the things printed, issued, whatever you
call it—and hers was number eleven. Don't ask me
why it matters."

He took her arm and steered her toward an old-
fashioned wooden swing under a vine-covered arbor.
The fragrance of blooming wisteria was almost too
sweet. Maggie started to sit, thought about bees, and
stepped back, bumping into Ben. Excusing herself,
she sighed. "Look, could we just go inside where

there aren't any rocks, bees or vampire bats? I really can't concentrate when my life's in danger.''

When it came to distraction, bats, bees and pebbles couldn't hold a candle to the man who towered over her. It wasn't enough that he was a supermagnet for any woman with a viable hormone in her body and that he could kiss like an angel—he had a granny he cared enough for to go the extra mile. That was like triple chocolate mousse—with nuts and brandy-flavored whipped cream.

''Sure, if you'd rather. I just didn't want to take a chance on being overheard.''

''This is beginning to feel like a spy thriller,'' she said as she matched her short stride to his longer one. If he could ignore that kiss, than she could ignore it, too. It never happened. ''You're not undercover for James Bond, are you?''

At the sound of his deep, rusty chuckle, she sighed. Okay, so it had happened. The guy was worse than an epidemic of Spanish flu. She was definitely going to need a booster shot, and the sooner, the better.

''Art police, you might say. Matter of fact, until about six weeks ago I was wearing a badge.''

That stopped her cold. By then they'd reached the porch steps, with Maggie leading the way as if she could outrun temptation. Mounting to the top step, she turned. Ben was two full steps behind her, which meant for once she could look him square in the mouth—that is, in the eyes. And from the light shining out the window, his eyes were…

Oh, hell, Maggie, eyes aren't magnificent! Bodies, maybe—even faces, but eyes were just…

He was probably nearsighted. Or farsighted. Whatever, no man was all that perfect. She said, "So you're a cop." It sounded more like an accusation.

"Was. I resigned."

"You're too young to retire."

He looked away then, saving her from making a fool of herself—again. "Let's just say it was time to move on."

Well, that certainly rang false, but she knew better than to try to pin him down, figuratively *or* literally. Her hands might itch to touch that crease on his cheek—or even the small scar on his jaw—but it was an itch she wasn't about to scratch. "You know what? Usually when someone begins a sentence with 'Let's just say,' it means they're not telling the truth—at least not all of it."

He turned to look at her again. "You know what? Whenever someone starts a sentence with 'you know what,' I figure they're getting ready to dodge the issue."

He moved up another step, which made her feel for the step behind her. *Uh-uh. No way. You're not going to draw me in with another kiss.*

Turning, she headed toward the far end of the wraparound porch, where another wisteria-draped trellis enclosed an old-fashioned wooden swing. The place was booby-trapped!

Warily, she said, "You might as well tell me the rest of it."

"Why I resigned?"

"That, too, if you want to, but I mean about teaming up. And your grandmother, and her being taken in by…whatever."

"Bottom line—Silver might be a good painter, but

his real art is flimflam. I had a feeling something like that might be going on, but now that I've seen the way the enrollment shapes up, I'm dead certain. Didn't you notice anything unusual about it?''

''It's my first workshop, so I don't have anything to compare it to. If you're talking about the fact that six days of cooking your own meals and sleeping on a torture device costs almost as much as an ocean cruise, then yeah, I definitely noticed that.''

''Torture device, hmm?'' There was a long pause, during which her mind took off on a wild tangent. Then he said, ''What I'm talking about—Silver's culled the applicants so he has just the right mix. Mostly women, mostly retirees.''

She waited for the punch line.

''What's the most vulnerable portion of society these days?''

''Babies? Kids who do dumb stuff and think it's smart?'' Women who get themselves kissed and are ready to send for the preacher? ''I give up, who?''

''Senior citizens, that's who. Like my grandmother and all those other grandmothers he cons into signing up for his so-called art lessons. A captive audience, that's who. Give him a week to soften them up and he'll have at least two-thirds of them lining up to buy his pictures.'' He shook his head. ''And yeah, I know—if they're done by hand they're paintings, but the ones he sold my grandmother weren't. The only thing done by hand was his signature in pencil, so if it's his autograph he's selling, why not just say so?''

''Because he's not famous enough, so nobody would want it?''

''Bingo. Trust me, I know what I'm talking about

here. I didn't just walk into this thing cold, I checked it out with a reputable source.''

She nodded knowingly. ''Reporters have sources, too. I could do some more checking if it would help.'' Not even to herself would she admit to being disappointed. He'd led her out into the moonlight to talk to her about teaming up. Could she help it if her imagination had slipped its leash for a moment? ''All right, so exactly what is you want me to do?''

''Just keep your ears open, that's all for now, and if Silver comes on to you, give him the brush-off. I want him to go after the older women, they're his real target. Before any damage gets done, I'll have him cold.''

Avoiding the shadowy swing, Maggie sank down into one of the cane rockers. It was already damp with dew. ''That's it? You can actually arrest him for trying to talk people into buying his art?'' She shook her head slowly. ''I don't know, Ben...''

Ben didn't know either. It wasn't like him to jump on his horse and ride wildly off in all directions without so much as a roadmap. It's just that when he'd realized that his own grandmother had been taken in by a scam artist, he'd seen red. Not until he'd signed up for this wingding and written a hefty check did it dawn on him that he couldn't just haul the guy in for making a sales pitch, even if he caught him in a flat-out lie. Fraud could be tricky as hell to prove. Not only was he out of his element with this art business, he was out of his territory.

Didn't even have a territory, for that matter.

''It's a work in progress, okay?'' he said. ''I'll think of something.'' He blew out a frustrated sigh, then inhaled deeply, aware of the heavy scent of the purple blossoms and the lighter fragrance of the woman beside him. "So, will you help me out here?"

He couldn't have felt more helpless if he'd been fifty miles out in the flats with a lame horse and no cell phone. Not that he hadn't worked with a partner before—he had. But this time his so-called partner wasn't a cop, and he didn't actually need her help. What he'd wanted to do when he'd led her out in the moonlight was kiss the living daylights out of her and go from there. Fortunately, after one brief sample, he'd had sense enough to back off. There was something about Maggie Riley that didn't add up. Whatever it was, it shorted out his brain and sparked a major reaction below the belt at a time when he needed all his powers of concentration.

Whatever else she was, Riley was a major distraction.

Touching his toe to the porch rail, he set the rocker in motion. A month ago he'd been holed up in an unused lineshack on a friend's ranch, firing off letters to the Attorney General's office, half expecting a sawed-off shotgun to poke through the door at any moment. Shoot, shovel and shut-up. It wouldn't be the first time a lawman had disappeared when he'd stumbled into something he wasn't supposed to see.

Maggie's voice came out of the shadows, yanking him back to the present. "The thing is," she said, "I sort of have my own mission."

"You're covering it for your paper? You said you were a journalist, right?" He was sitting far enough away so that there was no danger of touching her. It didn't help a whole lot.

"Well, that, too. I mean, I'd planned to write about it, but that's not why I'm here."

"If you're wanting to learn how to paint, Janie says Silver's a better teacher than he is a painter. She says he's even a pretty good painter if you happen to like his style. From what I've seen, he paints the same scene, just rearranging the parts and changing the sky a little."

"She's your special friend, right?"

Was that a wishful question? Ben stopped rocking, wondering how he could find out. They'd only just met. With some women, all you had to do was buy 'em a beer and it was off to bed, but Maggie was different. In spite of that impulsive kiss he'd stolen, she really wasn't his type. He usually went for long legs, big boobs and lots of bleached hair. Dolly Parton on stilts. Women who were good for a few laughs, a few rolls in the hay, but nothing more serious, because he was nowhere near ready to settle down.

Trouble with Maggie, the more he got to know her, the more he wanted to know. Whatever the attraction, it sure as hell wasn't her legs or her boobs. Although her hair was nice, even if it wasn't piled up like a bleached blond helmet. He had a sneaking suspicion she had brains and heart and all those other organs he tried so hard to steer clear of in his relationships with women.

"Yoo-hoo, y'all want some dessert?"

Saved by the bell, Ben thought. Good thing, too, because he didn't particularly like the way his thoughts were wandering all over the road. He was definitely losing his edge.

He said, "Sure, Janie, what're you offering?"

Six

Dessert was store-bought cake that was too dry and too sweet. Maggie ate it anyway, because it was something to do and she was feeling edgy. Ben poured himself a glass of cold coffee, iced it, and stayed with her while the other stragglers left the kitchen and wandered into the large front room where someone was playing records. Not CDs, or even audiotapes, but vinyl.

Tapping rhythm on his glass with the blade of a table knife, Ben hummed along while Maggie finished her cake. He had a deep, gravelly voice—nice, actually, and only a few notes off-key.

"Care to join 'em?" he asked.

"Might as well," she allowed, feeling a shimmer of tension at the thought of dancing in Ben's arms. Slow dancing, not line dancing. Then maybe they would wander out onto the porch and he would kiss her again.

Several of the women were dancing together while Charlie looked over a selection of records, including some old 33 1/3s and even a few 78 rpms. Janie was dancing alone, clicking her fingers and swaying to the tune of something Maggie remembered her mother singing a long time ago.

Perry was nowhere in sight, nor was Ann.

Suzy came up behind them and said, "You wouldn't believe this record collection. If they weren't all scratched up, they'd probably be worth a bunch." She touched Ben on the arm and said, "Dance with me, cowboy. You don't mind, do you, Maggie?"

Maggie minded more than she cared to admit, but she smiled, nodded and knelt beside Charlie, who said, "Look at this, will you? I haven't heard this one since I was in grad school."

Maggie must have said something appropriate, but disappointment ate at her. Ed Ames tried to remember and the Mamas and the Papas went through their repertoire while Ben danced with Janie, with Georgia and with half the other women in the room, apparently having a wonderful time. She refused to look over her shoulder, but she could hear their laughter over the sound of the scratchy old records.

Someone called out, "Play 'Moon River' again, will you? It was my husband's favorite."

All dressed up and nowhere to go, Maggie thought, dismally amused. The dress she'd worn tonight was one of her favorites, bought on sale last fall. She hadn't been sure it would still be in style this year, but it was.

For all the good it did her.

Janie hadn't even changed for supper, much less for dancing. She was still wearing tights and a sweatshirt, but she'd slipped off her shoes. She had bunions, Maggie noticed, and then felt horribly guilty for being jealous of a woman who was more than twice her age.

Charlie was still making discoveries in the stack of old vinyl when someone tapped her on the shoulder. "My turn," Ben said. "Charlie, stop hogging my woman."

Which was so totally absurd Maggie felt like taking a poke at him. Instead, she melted into his arms and they circled the small area that had been cleared for dancing. She couldn't think of a thing to say—nothing that made any sense, at least. She wasn't about to ask why he had danced with practically every woman there—with Suzy twice—before he'd remembered to ask her.

He was a surprisingly smooth dancer. Nothing fancy, just holding, swaying and shuffling, mostly, but she still liked the way he moved. The disparity in their heights should have made it awkward. Instead, she was in a perfect position to rest her cheek on his chest and hear his heartbeat.

Pa-bum. Pa-bum. Pa-bum, pa-bum, bum, bum, bum!

Evidently exercise got him all…exercised, she thought, savoring the thought that holding her in his arms might have something to do with his accelerated heartbeat.

His warm breath stirred her hair and when her left arm got tired of reaching up to his shoulder, she looped it around his waist. The record—one of those old LPs that had half a dozen different songs on each side—shifted into something with a jazzy beat, but Ben's rhythm never changed. Slow and slower, feet barely moving at all, they swayed in place.

Maggie was aware of little outside the feel of his lean, hard body, the scent of one of those fresh-smelling soaps, and the thump of his heart under her cheek. She was pretty sure the shape of his hand would be branded on her back for weeks. She could have drifted this way forever, not thinking beyond the moment.

Ben started to hum again. The sound—more a vibration, really—triggered a response in parts of her body that had no business responding to sound. Under her dress she wore only a pair of briefs and a silk camisole. Her breasts, as small as they were, seemed to swell as if begging for attention. Her nipples actually throbbed.

When the record finally came to an end, Ben led her toward the French doors that opened out onto the porch. His breathing was audible, even over the murmur of conversation coming from three of the women in the corner who had set up a table under a yellow bug-light and were playing gin rummy.

Suzy had evidently given up and gone to bed. Maggie wondered if she should feel guilty for hogging the most attractive man on the premises for so long.

No way. Regardless of what happened next, the last hour was going to be tucked away in her memory box for a long, long time. Her life wasn't exactly a hotbed of romantic moments.

By silent mutual consent they headed for the swing this time. Ben's arm was still around her as if he'd forgotten where he'd left it. She hadn't forgotten, not when every cell in her body was dancing the cha-cha-cha. Nearby, a whippoorwill tuned up. Through some trick of acoustics, she could hear the sound of sporadic traffic out on highway 52, several miles away as the crow flew.

Pausing in the shelter of the wisteria vines, Ben turned her in his arms. "Maggie, there's something you need to know."

I already know everything I need to know, she thought. I know I'm in serious trouble if you're not feeling the same way I am. I know I've never been so attracted to any man before, not this soon. I know I've got no call to accuse Mary Rose of—

"Hey, do you two *mind?*"

The sound of Charlie's voice was like a dash of ice water. Ben tensed, but didn't release her. Maggie, her face burning, tipped her head forward to rest on his chest.

Ben said, "Sorry, man. I didn't know the swing was taken."

Maggie said, "It's late anyway." She pulled away, fighting disappointment. "I'd better—that is…"

At first she thought he wasn't going to release her, but in the end he let her go with a quick kiss on the top of her head. "Tomorrow," he promised. Actually, he only said it, but she wanted desperately to believe it was a promise.

She didn't slam the door. She didn't even stomp as

she made her way though the house to the glorified pantry where she was billeted. She had long since outgrown childish tantrums, but that didn't mean she'd outgrown being disappointed, much less being sexually frustrated. She *wanted* the man. She hadn't actually wanted a man since...

Since never.

Suzy was adding another coat of polish to her toenails. Glancing up, she raked back her short hair and grinned. "I thought by now you two would be getting down to some serious kanoodling."

Maggie slipped off her sandals and reached for the shirt she wore to sleep in. "Try finding any privacy in a house with fifteen people."

"There's always the basement or the attic."

"Forget it, I didn't come here to waste time kanoodling."

So much for all her splendid plans to spare Mary Rose from heartbreak and poverty.

"Wanna talk about it?"

Maggie hung up her dress, and without turning around, said, "I don't even want to think about it."

She slept like a log and woke hearing the sounds of laughter coming from the kitchen. Evidently, Suzy and Ann were already up, dressed and ready to start cooking breakfast for anyone who wanted something more than dry cereal. Feeling guilty, Maggie dashed upstairs, waited for a shower to be free, and then hurriedly dressed, this time in her oldest jeans and a yellow camp shirt that was wrinkled from being crammed in her suitcase under a box of graham crackers. She tucked her damp hair behind her ears and put on a tinted lip balm. If anyone thought she was going to take any special pains with her looks on account of last night, they were sadly mistaken. Anyone being Ben Hunter.

As early as it was, several people had gathered in the front hall to watch a uniformed man laboring up the front path carrying a large carton. Charlie said, "If that thing's as heavy as it looks, we're going to have a seriously herniated brownie here."

Ann had already brewed the coffee and Suzy was staring at the big iron skillet as if she'd never seen one before.

"Hey, can somebody take this thing and sign for it?" the deliveryman called through the front screen door.

Ben came in from the side porch and said, "Sure thing. Let me help you set it down." If he noticed Maggie's presence, he ignored it.

She shrugged off a stab of disappointment, although she didn't know what else she could have expected. Nothing had really happened between them last night. Occasionally she got swept away by her own creative imagination.

As Silver had yet to put in an appearance, Ben signed for the delivery and tipped the deliverer, which Maggie considered generous of him. Charlie said, "Don't try to pick it up. Those guys know how to carry stuff like that. You can throw your back out without half trying."

"What is it?" Janie murmured from halfway down the stairs. She looked fabulous. Maggie made up her mind on the spot that if she had to grow old, she was going to use Janie Burger as a pattern.

Charlie obviously liked her style, too, she thought, remembering the two of them swinging away on what she'd come to think of as her and Ben's private place.

Janie leaned over and studied the label on the carton. "Hong Kong? Jeepers, who does he know in Hong Kong?"

But by then the first batch of bacon was starting to burn. Suzy yelled for help and Maggie hurried back to rescue it and to start whipping up eggs. The delivery was forgotten as talk turned to today's assignment and other esoteric topics, such as whether or not Ginko biloba improved the memory, and the lack of anything but white bread.

Perry arrived late. He seemed distinctly put out on finding the front door partially blocked by the delivery. "Leave it," he snapped when Ben offered to set it out of the way. "Where's Ann?"

"She made the coffee, but she was sniffing and sneezing. She's probably gone back to the room," said Suzy. "Have you had breakfast yet?"

Instead of replying, he stalked off in the direction of the room the three youngest class members shared. Maggie nearly scorched the eggs, wondering what was going on. It wasn't the first time she'd noticed the interaction between Ann and the instructor. She'd even asked about it, but Ann had brushed off the question and asked, instead, what being a reporter was like. Not that she'd seemed particularly interested in the reply, but then, when Maggie got onto a topic that interested her, she tended to lapse into essay mode.

Janie and Georgia offered to help clear up after breakfast so that they could all get started on today's assignment, which was painting on location. "I'm sorry, dears, but they're predicting rain starting late tonight, so I've decided to push things along a bit,'' Perry had said by way of explanation.

"I could've told him it was going to rain. My bones gave me fits last night, I couldn't sleep a wink,'' remarked one of the retired teachers.

Maggie had had trouble sleeping, too, but more on account of painful thoughts about Ben than painful joints.

Painting on location turned out to involve dragging all their gear from the studio outside. A few students produced clever contraptions that appeared to be a combination stool and easel, but most, including Maggie, were assigned card tables which were neither large enough nor steady enough to be practical. The second time her water pail sloshed over, Ben suggested she either dig holes for two of the legs or prop up the other pair.

"Smart, aren't you?'' She flashed him a nasty look that had him grinning. "I already thought of that.''

It would probably have occurred to her sooner or later, but she enjoyed sparring with him. At least it helped dispel the awkwardness after last night.

Ben helped Georgia find a place that was more or less level, helped her set up her equipment, and then helped Charlie wrestle a heavier picnic table into the shade for the two librarians. For all he looked like the hero of one of those action movies—rough, ready and more than slightly dangerous—Ben Hunter was a genuinely kindhearted man. He would make some woman a wonderful—

Don't even go there.

"Ann's going to work inside today,'' Suzy said

when Maggie asked about their roommate. "Pollen count's too high."

One of the blue-haired ladies mentioned that the coming rain would probably help reduce the pollen count, never mind how it affected various joints and sinuses. Soon they were all busy rendering the mountain scenery in a medium that had Ben cursing and Maggie muttering about paint with a mind of its own.

"Look at that!" she snarled after some twenty minutes had passed. "The blasted paint refuses to stay where I put it! The sky keeps washing away my mountain and when I try to push it back up where it belongs, the darned stuff fights back!"

"Here comes Perry, he'll tell you what you're doing wrong." That from Georgia, whose sky was behaving the way a sky should instead of trickling down the mountain where there wasn't even a valley, much less a blasted waterfall.

"This is for the birds," Ben growled. He stepped back, hands on his hips, and glared at the buckling sheet of thin watercolor paper.

"That reminds me, we'd better watch out for dive bombers." Charlie nodded toward a flock of grackles squabbling over a stand of pokeberry bushes.

"Purple, right? Couldn't hurt. Might even help." Ben happened to catch Maggie's eye. He winked and gave her a thumbs-up, his thumb stained with what she now recognized as alizarin crimson.

Where the dickens did he see anything red out there? Was he color blind?

Wearing a crisply ironed smock and his usual beret, Silver meandered among his students offering a word of advice here, a compliment there. He went lighter than usual on criticism, which in Maggie's estimation was a good thing. It wouldn't take much for her to throw everything into her hatchback and head home, mission or no mission. Suzy had reluctantly agreed to cooperate, but so far Silver had shown surprisingly little interest. Today he ignored her completely, probably figuring that like Maggie and Ben, she was beyond help.

Instead, he spared most of the time and attention for his older students. Not Charlie—not Janie or Georgia, either, but as they were all adequate painters, they didn't really need him. Janie, in particular, had a style Maggie liked. She called it her "who gives a hoot, I'm having fun!" style.

Silver spent most of his time with a small group of students who lapped up his every word as if it were nectar. Ben caught her eye and nodded at the cluster of appreciative women. At least his mission appeared to be on track.

A few minutes later Silver moved to the edge of the rough lawn, stepped up on a low granite outcropping and clapped his hands for attention. "All right, children, lunchtime is critique time. When you're finished here, make sure your work's dry and take it in to the studio." He glanced at the sky. "Leave everything else outside, we'll try to squeeze in another hour after lunch before the rain starts."

There were a few groans, but the overall response was muted excitement. Evidently artists were masochists, willing to endure everything from gnats to glaring sunshine to swollen ankles and aching feet for their art.

Ben tucked something in his shirt pocket, rolled up

his morning's work, dry or not, and joined Maggie, who was scowling at the mess she'd made on a perfectly good piece of white paper.

She said, "Is there some secret to keeping your skies from wandering downhill and messing up your mountains?"

"What you have to do, see, is learn to go with the flow." He draped a companionable arm across her shoulder. The magic was still there, but today there was an added quality. A sort of best-buddies warmth that was almost—not quite—as potent.

"I read that on a T-shirt somewhere." It had been her mother's T-shirt, worn with a long, flowered skirt. Come to think of it, long flowered skirts were back in style again. Going with the flow never would be, not as far as Maggie was concerned. She had too much ambition. Too many people depending on her. If she went with the flow the way her mother had done, her dad would end up living on junk food and clogging his arteries and Mary Rose would probably end up broke and brokenhearted.

"What's that in your pocket?" she asked, watching the rocky terrain carefully so as not to trip. She didn't have a whole lot of dignity left; she'd just as soon hang onto whatever she could salvage.

"Show you later," he promised, which only perked up her curiosity.

Seven

It was devastating. Maggie laughed aloud at the caricature of a willowy man in a beret and a flowing smock. His long, thin nose was exaggerated, his eyes baggier and too close together, but the resemblance was striking. "I thought you said you didn't have any artistic talent."

"I don't. A friend of mine is a police artist and she taught me a few things. Mostly she used composites in her work, but she had a great eye when it came to summing up a particular set of features."

Maggie tried to see Ben through the eyes of a caricaturist—or a police artist. The way his thick, dark hair grew, with that bit he was always shoving back off his forehead. The winged curve of his eyebrows, the angular cheekbones, a nose that was not too big, but not too small, either—and the shape of his mouth.

Oh my, yes, the shape of his mouth…

She wanted to ask what else the woman had taught him—if he'd had a special relationship with her and if so, what had happened to it.

None of your business.

She had her own past, such as it was; he had his. If there was one thing she'd learned over the years since she'd first noticed that boys were a different and rather interesting species, it was that the really good-looking ones were usually vain and immature. Not that many of the really good-looking had given her a second glance, much less asked her out on a date.

Suzy was setting out sandwich components when they reached the kitchen, "Where's Ann?" Maggie asked. She got out a pitcher of iced tea and opened the freezer compartment. "She said she'd help."

"Dunno. Her coffee mug's missing, so maybe she's back in the room."

After filling a bucket with ice, Maggie slipped away to check on the missing member of the team, trying to remember anything she'd read about allergies that might be helpful. Ann wasn't in the room they shared, nor was she in the studio. Maggie dashed upstairs to check the bathroom, called a few times in both directions, then hurried back down to do whatever else was needed. Lunch was usually a do-it-yourself meal, but the team-of-the-day was supposed to make the process easier.

"Maybe she drove into town for a prescription or something." Suzy was layering cheese, onions and peanut butter on a poppyseed roll.

Maggie stared at it and shuddered. "If she's smart she'll have lunch while she's out. Who did the grocery shopping for this place? Why isn't there any low-fat mayo?''

"How about rye bread? Next time anybody goes to town, how about picking up a loaf?" Charlie asked.

Bumping elbows, begging pardons and discussing everything from arch supports to the best source of ready-cut mats, everyone pitched in before wandering away, sandwiches and drinks of choice in hand.

Suzy and Maggie remained in the kitchen, finishing off leftover slices of cheese and a box of stale vanilla wafers.

"I might as well clean out this peanut butter jar. We can open a fresh one tomorrow," Suzy said.

Maggie picked up wafer crumbs with her thumb. "Wonder what Perry meant when he asked if we could touch our toes. Was he trying to be cruel? I mean, just look at this class—most of the women probably wear support hose, and the men aren't much better."

"Charlie might wear support hose, but I betcha Ben doesn't." Suzy grinned, leaned back in her chair and stretched her arms. "Be glad to check it out for you, though. Wasn't that what you were wanting me to do? Check out the guys?"

"One guy only," Maggie reminded her.

"Oh, yeah, I keep forgetting."

"Surrre you do," Maggie teased.

Once the kitchen was put in order, the two women joined the others in the studio where the morning's efforts had been laid out on the tables, ready for a critique. Maggie pointedly didn't look at Ben, but her peripheral vision was excellent. He stood, feet braced apart, hands on his narrow hips, silently challenging Perry to do his worst.

Perry was just hitting his stride when someone near the window noticed that it had started to sprinkle outside. In the rush to rescue whatever had been left behind after the morning's session, Maggie heard Ben tell the two women at his table to stay put, that he'd collect their things.

And that was another thing—he was so darned decent!

She beat him to the front door by half a step and was headed down the wet steps when he caught her by the waist and swung her to the ground. Over her protests he said calmly, "Crazy shoes, slick steps, sure recipe for disaster." He set her down on the broken concrete walk, then jogged off to gather up anything the rain might damage. Staring after him, Maggie had a sinking feeling that the kind of trouble she was in had nothing to do with slick steps and three-inch platforms.

"What about your boots?" she called after him.

Without turning around, he waved a dismissing hand and began gathering up painting equipment. Maggie glowered. "Talk about vanity, there's not a horse within fifty miles of this place."

Suzy dashed past her, both arms full, a knowing grin on her piquant face. "Oh, shut up," Maggie grumbled. Grabbing the supplies she'd left on her rickety card table, she glanced around to see if anyone needed help. The rain was falling harder now, plastering her hair to her head, her shirt to her back. Dodging others on the same mission, she collected whatever she saw that looked in need of rescuing and hurried back inside.

Charlie helped her unload and distribute materials, then Ben came up behind her, laid a big, warm hand on her shoulder and said, "You get everything in? Need me to go back out and bring in the rest?"

"Thanks, I'm fine," she said, sounding breathless and hoping he put it down to exertion. "I guess we don't need to worry about the tables."

Charlie grumbled, "Maybe I should've left my morning's work out in the rain. Couldn't hurt—might even help. Did I tell you about the time I was painting on a dock down in Southport and a gull flew over and made a deposit on the seascape I was working on? Actually, it didn't look too bad. I had to wash off some of the texture, but the gray cloud worked out pretty well."

Ben chuckled and placed his hand on Maggie's back, ushering her into the front hall where the others were examining their belongings for rain damage. A rash of goose bumps shivered down her spine, radiating outward from his hand. She ducked away and was considering dashing back to her room for a dry shirt when a loud thump sounded from overhead. Several people looked up. One woman fingered her hearing aid.

Someone said, "Thunder?"

Charlie said, "Perry dropped his attitude?"

"Sounded more like he dropped a load of bricks," offered a woman whose work Maggie had admired in yesterday's critique.

Before anyone could go investigate, Perry appeared

at the head of the stairs, attitude intact. "No problem, dears, just some paper I had delivered."

So that was what was in that carton. Maggie had heard all about the advantages of three-hundred-pound watercolor paper over the cheap pad she'd bought at the discount store. She hadn't thought it meant the stuff literally weighed three hundred pounds.

Rubbing his hands together, Silver beamed down at them. "Everyone finished with lunch? Good, good—shall we get on with the afternoon session then?"

"Do we have any choice?" Ben muttered softly.

"Amen," Maggie echoed. Considering how much it was costing her, she really should try to get something out of it. So far, she hadn't collected a speck of evidence that would convince Mary Rose that this skunk was risky marriage material. All she'd learned was that she had the wrong kind of paints, the wrong kind of brush and the paper she'd paid nearly ten bucks a tablet for was barely a step up from newsprint. Evidently imported was the only way to go.

Add to that the fact that she was highly susceptible to slow-talking, slow-walking Texans who were also totally out of their element, and she was in so far over her head she needed a snorkel just to breathe.

Ann slid into place almost an hour into the afternoon lesson. Maggie didn't hear her approach, as the rain that had started shortly after noon drummed steadily on the roof so that it was hard to hear anything at all.

"Hi. We missed you this morning," she murmured, noting that the young brunette looked even more tired than usual. "I set up your stuff there on the end of the table. We've been working on graded washes. You've studied with Perry before, haven't you?"

Without answering, Ann said, "I think I'll pass. My hands are—that is, my head's really stopped up."

At the other end of the eight-foot table, Suzy swiped a wet brush across the streak of burnt sienna and tipped her paper up the way Charlie had shown her. After his opening demonstration, Perry had spent most of his time with a retired dental technician and the two librarians.

"Hey, you know what?" Suzy whispered. "I figured it up last night. Not counting room and board, each one of these so-called classes is costing us eighteen dollars an hour. Multiply that by fifteen. What I want to know is, how much is overhead and how much is pure profit?"

"Are you sure you don't want to manage your father's office?" Maggie teased. "I can probably name one of the operational expenses—liability insurance. My dad does that sort of thing."

"How's your wash coming along?" Ben joined them after glancing over at the instructor, who was still holding his elderly students in thrall. "Hi, Ann, you feeling better?"

Ann's gaze slid away. She mumbled an excuse and left the room. Ben shrugged and looked after her. "Was it something I said? Suzy-Q, this little place right here's not working." He waved a big, square-palmed hand over what was supposed to be a graded wash, but looked more like a fallow field after a deluge.

Suzy struck a pose, batted her lashes and thrust out one shapely hip. ''Do me a favor, Texas—stuff it in your saddlebags.''

Ben grinned, flashing that not-quite-a-dimple again. ''Yes, ma'am.''

Something that felt uncomfortably like jealousy churned in Maggie's stomach. But then, with Suzy's figure, she could have read the label on a can of motor oil and made it sound like the *Kama Sutra*.

Maggie didn't have a figure. She'd reached the pinnacle of figurehood at the age of thirteen and been stranded there ever since. With enough makeup she could improve on her face, but she drew the line at enhancing her bustline, surgically or otherwise. Occasionally she used a temporary rinse, but it was hardly worth the effort as the result was simply ordinary Maggie with different colored hair. Unadorned, at least she blended into the scenery, which was a definite advantage for an investigative reporter. Beauty faded. Brains only grew sharper. She'd been telling herself that for years.

Janie wandered over and tucked her arm through Ben's. She'd ponytailed her hair, making her look like a teenager whose face had inadvertently been left too long in the water, causing it to pucker.

''I'm thinking of adopting him, ladies. What do you think? I can't talk him into eloping with me, but I'm not about to give him up.''

Ben kissed her on the cheek and winked at Maggie. ''I'll have to introduce her to Miss Emma. Might make for a pretty interesting relationship, right?''

He was a magnet, no two ways about it. Suzy latched on to his other arm while Ben, the big jerk,

ust stood there soaking up adoration like Roy Rogers
after he'd saved Dale Evans from a fate worse than
death.

If he said, "Aw, shucks, ma'am," Maggie vowed
silently, she might do him serious bodily harm.

"Children, children, time's wasting. Now, let's see
how we're doing with our graded washes, shall we?
Suzy, doll, I'm afraid you weren't listening. You
must—now listen, class, this is crucial—you simply
must learn how to master your medium, otherwise it
will get the best of you every time. Watercolor's not
like oil or acrylic—it won't just sit there meekly and
let you push it around. You must be *trick-y, trick-y,
trick-y* if you want to master watercolor!" Perry was
fond of speaking in triplicates.

Trick-y, trick-y, trick-y, Maggie mimicked silently,
feeling distinctly uncharitable at the moment. Let's
just see how masterful he was when Mary Rose and
her humongous trust fund slipped through his fingers.

While Maggie, Suzy and Ann, who showed up
again after class, began putting together the evening
meal, Ben sat at the kitchen table and entertained
them by drawing quick caricatures. Janie was easy—
Charlie, too, as he was the only other man in the class
besides Perry. The rest weren't quite as easy to identify, but everyone got a laugh as they picked out the
one they thought represented them.

Maggie looked at the figure that was supposed to
represent her. Was he trying to be kind? Afraid of
hurting her feelings? She was the original stick-figure,
but instead of drawing her that way, he had given her
a sexy shape and a headful of wavy hair.

She didn't have waves, she had a shaggy cut and dozens of cowlicks. And surely her eyes weren't *that* large.

When she glanced up, all ready to ridicule his efforts, he was tipped back in his chair, hands laced across his flat belly, staring at her. From any other man, toward any other woman, she might even call the look smoldering. A practiced pragmatist, Maggie put it down to either distraction or a possible astigmatism.

Charlie spoke up admiringly. "Hey, man, you're good."

"Who's good?" Perry joined them without his usual Perry-like entrance. Quickly searching the room, he pointed toward Maggie, Suzy and Ben. "You, Maggie—and you, darling—you, too, Hunter. A few of you still haven't caught on. Tonight after supper, we'll talk about some of the physics involved."

The *physics?*

Maggie glanced at Ben, this time for reassurance and not whatever it was that set her hormones to sizzling whenever he was around.

Ben shrugged and mimed, "Beats me."

Then Perry leaned over and murmured something quietly to Ann, who slipped away, leaving the salad for Suzy to finish.

Knife in hand, Suzy turned to Ben. "Help out here cowboy. Grab me an onion from that sack." She did a perfect Mae West, complete with a modified bump and grind, the only difference being a few years, a few pounds and the paring knife in her hand.

Maggie managed to produce a passable vegetarian

chili, one she'd often served her father. Dessert was canned peaches, and as no one complained—at least not in her hearing—she felt free to relax. Ann never reappeared, not for the meal itself or for the clean-up after. Maggie was seriously starting to worry. If her allergies were that bad, she didn't need to be here.

Between finishing the dishes and assembling for the evening session, Maggie settled into the porch swing and gave it a gentle shove with her toe. The rain had stopped, leaving behind a layered fog that reminded her of the cover of a Gothic romance. All it lacked was a veil-clad heroine fleeing some unspecified evil.

Stealing a moment to brace herself before facing Perry's criticism, she shoved off with one foot. She wasn't really surprised when Ben appeared, caught the chain and held it still long enough to settle in beside her.

"You think Ann might be allergic to this house?" she asked.

"Could be. It's old, probably full of all kinds of mold spores. Now she's complaining about her hands, too."

"Pretty young to be a hypochondriac."

Maggie set the swing in motion again, needing an outlet for the restless energy that always seemed to assail her whenever he was near. All along the shadowy porch others were settling in the rockers and Adirondacks. One or two perched on the railing.

Ben inhaled deeply. "Something smells good."

She opened her mouth to tell him it was the wisteria, but she heard herself saying, "Insect repellent."

Anything to break the spell that was stealing away
her objectivity. "Where's Suzy?" she asked brightly.

"Haven't seen her in the past few minutes."

Feeling his gaze on her, she tried to act like the
adult she was instead of the adolescent she had never
quite left behind. "Maybe she's with Perry. I guess
it's time to go back in."

"Jealous?"

She planted both feet on the floor, causing the
swing to jerk on its chains. "Of what?"

"Hey, just because the guy's a crook, that doesn't
mean women don't like him. Part of the problem is
that they like him too much."

"Yes, well this woman thinks he's a creep." And
then, because she felt guilty for not leveling with him
after he'd told her about his grandmother, she blurted,
"If you must know, my best friend thinks he's in love
with her."

Long pause. "And?"

"Well...I don't think he is, that's all."

"Because...?"

How could she explain tactfully? "For one thing
she only met him once for a few hours, and I'm pretty
sure she hasn't seen him since then."

"You don't believe in love at first sight?"

Maggie set the swing in motion again. As Ben
wasn't ready, the movement was jerky. Well, shoot.
With a moon creeping over the mountain, layering the
valley with silver veils of fog, any woman with half
a brain would know how to take advantage of the
moment.

Not Maggie. Oh, no, not Maggie the klutz, Maggie
the skinny kid whose hottest date in her senior year

had been with a certified nerd who'd taken her to a science fair.

"Look, my friend just happens to be rich, all right? I mean her father's this big pickle magnate and she's as sweet as she can be, and I don't want to hear any jokes about sweet pickles. With the name Dilys, she's heard every pickle joke in the book. The thing is, she doesn't know a lot about men."

Some of her belligerence faded when Ben's fingers closed gently on the back of her neck, pressing ever so slightly. It hurt, but in a delicious way. He said, "And you know all there is to know about men, mmm?" Finger-walking along her tense muscles, he said, "Don't you ever relax?"

For a few heavenly moments she let him work at untying the knots at the base of her skull because it felt so good, and because his voice was murmuring abstract words that didn't seem to relate to anything. Before she could melt into a disgusting puddle of liquid desire, she cleared her throat and said, "Uh— where was I? Oh yes, Mary Rose. Well as I was saying, her father's so overprotective he still vets all her dates. She's twenty-five, for goodness sake! You'd think we were back in the Dark Ages." Closing her eyes, she let her head roll forward as Ben worked his magic. "Ah, right there…"

Against the creak of the swing and the murmur of voices farther along the porch, a whippoorwill tuned up for his evening serenade. Maggie shifted slightly so that Ben's hand left her neck, his arm resting along the back of the swing.

"I'm probably overreacting, but you see, she's always let her folks run her life. I keep telling her, you don't learn anything that way.''

"Who runs your life, hmm?"

She had to smile. ''Me. At least since I graduated from kindergarten. Okay, maybe from the sixth grade.'' His fingers brushed her hair again. She would have moved away, but moving required too much energy. To cover what could only be called a stealth attack of lust, she said, ''Mary Rose graduated from college with honors. Besides that, everybody always says she has the prettiest face, and she does.'' If she sounded slightly belligerent it was only because she was trying to stay focused in spite of a major distraction.

''So where's the problem?'' His fingers brushed her nape, then moved through her hair. Did hair have nerve endings?

Hers obviously did. That's what came from having the dead ends whacked off every six weeks. ''The problem is—'' she said, ignoring the urge to curl up in his arms and let nature take its course ''—the problem is that I think Perry's only after her money. Maybe I'm doing him an injustice, but if she marries him and finds out he's not what she thought, it's going to break her heart.'' As an advice columnist, she had heard the same sad tale too many times. About the way men changed after marriage. All the promises they made before and how quickly they were forgotten once the honeymoon ended. Broken promises that led to broken marriages and broken hearts, never mind the poor children left broken and bewildered in the wreckage.

Think about all that, Maggie Riley, and stop think-

ing about jumping into bed with a man you've known for all of two days!

"Let me see if I've got this straight," Ben murmured, his fingers slowly massaging the back of her head. "You're going to rescue this woman whether or not she wants to be rescued, right?"

Instinctively, Maggie pressed her head against his touch. "Isn't that what you're doing for your grandmother?"

"Nowhere close. I was too late to keep Miss Emma from getting snookered. Best I can do is spare other grannies from the same fate by reminding this jerk that there's a thin line between hyping a product and fraud, and he might have stepped over it when he started touting his pictures as investments."

"Fine. You do your thing, I'll do mine. And I'm really sorry about your grandmother, but that's already done. If I can keep Mary Rose from being married for her money—and don't tell me he's truly in love, because from what I've seen, Perry Silver wouldn't know love if it jumped up and bit him on the keester."

Ben's hand fell away as he started to laugh. Maggie could have sunk through the floor. Here she was sharing a swing with the handsomest man east of the Mississippi, with a big moon coming up over the mountain and wisteria blossoms perfuming the air, and what did she do?

She blew it, that's what. No wonder she'd never had a serious relationship in her entire life, if you didn't count the one that had ended in the back seat of Larry Beecham's Pontiac when she was seventeen.

Go with the flow, her mother used to say, especially after she'd enjoyed one of her hand-rolled cigarettes.

Maggie had never learned to go with the flow. She'd been too busy fighting the waves. Hiding from her parents' noisy arguments. Keeping her father's spirits up after his wife left him—reading all those articles about depression and leaving them where he would be sure to see them. Studying hard so that in case she could scrape together enough money to go to college she'd be eligible. Taking courses in the local community college and working for a miserable little freebie paper for a pittance while she waited for a chance to get on with a real newspaper.

"Maggie?" Ben's raspy drawl crawled down her spine sending shock waves to the most vulnerable parts of her body.

"What!" she snapped. And then, letting her head fall back again, she closed her eyes. "I think I'm having a premature midlife crisis."

"You'd be surprised what we could do if we teamed up." The words were whispered. Just as the meaning sunk in, his face went out of focus, and then he was kissing her again. And not just any old kiss, but one of those magical Ben-kisses—incredibly soft, warm and moist—pressing, lifting, moving so that she wanted to climb onto his lap and have her way with him.

And he wanted the same thing, she could tell by the way his heart was thundering. Or was it hers?

She was in way over her head, drowning in a sea of desire. Without lifting his face from hers, he drew her onto his lap. She tugged at his shirttail, hungry to touch his body—to slide her hands over that broad, warm chest. To press herself against him, to follow wherever he led—

To lead the way…

From inside came the sound of music from the old wind-up Victrola as someone opened a door. Maggie opened her eyes wide. Breaking away, she gasped, "'Scuse me," and reluctantly pulled free.

He didn't try to hold her. She thought she heard him utter a swearword, but he might have been laughing, instead. She had no intention of hanging around long enough to find out. She wasn't rated for this much temptation.

In fact, she'd do better to head for the studio so that Silver could tell her what a miserable failure she was as an artist. At least her ego wouldn't suffer, because it wasn't involved.

He chuckled, which was just as bad. The mere sound of his voice saying anything at all punched all her buttons, including a few she didn't even know she had. "Like I said before, why don't we team up?"

She turned to confront him and discovered that he was closer than he'd been only moments before. "How? You want to catch him selling a bill of goods to Janie and Georgia and the others. I want to catch him trying to seduce Suzy and get it on tape."

"Which is illegal," he reminded her gently.

"Whatever. I just don't see how we can do both, do you?"

Eight

Half an hour later, Ben glanced into the living room where Charlie was entertaining the ladies by playing disc jockey. Maggie wasn't there. Probably just as well. He had some thinking to do, and clear thinking wasn't an option as long as Maggie was anywhere around.

What the devil was it about the woman, anyway? Technically speaking, she wasn't particularly pretty. Over the years he'd arrived at certain standards, and Maggie Riley didn't meet a single one. So why was it that he could look at her from across the room and be so turned on he had to pull his shirttail out and hope it covered the evidence.

Not only that, but he liked hearing her laugh. Liked hearing her talk—got a kick out of her irreverent comments about Silver and his pretentions.

Hell, he just liked being around her. Trouble was, just being around her wasn't enough, and that was a distraction he didn't need.

The sound of laughter came from the large room they used as a studio. From somewhere else in the house he heard the strains of something jazzy and pictured Maggie kicking off her shoes, snapping her fingers and moving to the music.

Why not join her? Maybe do a little moving himself?

No way. Given a choice of hearing Silver blow him off as a no-talent jerk or making even more of a fool of himself with a woman he barely knew, he opted to use the rare privacy to sift through what little evidence he'd collected. So far, most of it was circumstantial, including the discreet sign announcing that signed and numbered prints would be available for sale at the end-of-the-workshop exhibit. Not signed and numbered copies, which might have given him something to go on.

Okay, so maybe he was crazy. Maybe he was totally off-base. But when Miss Emma had told him how much she'd spent, and he'd checked around and found out that her chances of ever recovering her investment were about as good as his chance of being elected president, he'd had to do something.

It boiled down to shades of gray. The ones here were paler than the ones he'd uncovered in Dry Creek, but people were still getting hurt. People like Miss Emma who had done nothing to deserve it.

Both in his law career and on the streets before Mercy had hauled his butt out of the fire, Ben had seen about every shade of gray there was. He didn't

like any of them, but only a fool believed the world
was all black and white. That didn't mean he could
quit fighting gray where he found it.

And then there was Maggie, whose face kept getting in the way of his deliberations. With Maggie Riley, what you saw was what you got, which might
even be a part of the attraction. Because what he saw
was a small, gutsy woman with an understated brand
of beauty all her own. Whatever it was, it could sneak
up on a man and zap him with a sucker punch before
he knew what hit him.

Ben had a long-standing policy, based on the experience of his friends, of keeping his personal life
impersonal. What he hadn't counted on was a small
distraction by the name of Maggie Riley.

Lying there half-asleep, he pictured her as a skinny
kid in wrinkled tights, a mask and a homemade cape,
determined to save the world. She must have been a
real handful growing up. Still was, come to that. Super Woman minus the tights and cape, determined to
save a friend from being hoodwinked by a smooth-
talking flimflam artist. Oddly enough that was also
his goal. Trouble was, they might need to take different routes to get there.

Charlie came in while he was still picturing Maggie
in different costumes, mostly filmy, lacy stuff that en-
hanced rather than concealed.

"Hi, sport, d'you get your message? You left your
cell phone on the dresser. It was ringing when I came
in before supper."

Ben sat up and raked his hair back. "You're looking bright-eyed and bushy-tailed."

The older man grinned. "Here's hopin'," he said

cheerfully as he changed into a clean shirt, splashed on a palmful of Old Spice and checked his billfold. "You seen that moon yet? It's a doozy."

A doozy? Right.

Ben levered himself out of bed and retrieved his cell phone. He'd quit wearing the thing since he'd come east. Didn't know of anyone who might try to reach him unless it was Miss Emma, calling to remind him to eat a good breakfast, wear a raincoat if it clouded over and put on a sweater if it turned cool.

While he was checking to see if he recognized the number, Charlie said something about not waiting up. Ben nodded absently. He recognized the area code. And then he recognized the number.

Charlie said, "Wish me luck, sport. It's been a while."

"Yeah, sure," Ben muttered. Now why in hell would Internal Affairs be calling him? He'd turned over everything he had, knowing it probably wasn't going any farther up the ladder. He might as well have buried it in a time capsule.

With one last glance in the mirror, Charlie said, "Nothing serious, I hope. I tried to find you, but you weren't in the house."

Ben glanced at his watch. Even with the time difference it was too late to call back. He'd like to think it was only a glitch in the paperwork. He'd misspelled a name or failed to cross all his *t*'s. He glanced up and said, "Yeah, sure—thanks, Charlie. Uh—you going out somewhere?"

The older man sighed and shook his head. "Ben, Ben, Ben—wake up and smell the flowers, boy. Life don't last forever." He closed the door quietly behind him, leaving Ben in a cloud of aftershave to ponder a few more imponderables. Like why I.A. would suddenly want to contact him. They'd grilled him thoroughly, going over and over every speck of evidence before he'd been allowed to leave Dry Creek. By that time, sick at heart and mad as hell, he'd felt like a traitor for turning in fellow cops he knew and liked and had once respected. He'd grilled steaks with several of the guys, even attended the christening of their kids.

But that was before he'd happened to see a couple of the older ones deliberately turn away at a critical moment so as not to witness a crime going down. Wondering what the hell had happened, he'd started to tackle them on it, but something had stopped him. That crazy sixth sense that warned an experienced cop when something was out of alignment.

Over the next few months he had quietly observed certain transactions taking place in dark alleys, in empty buildings—even on the damn country club golf course. That's when he'd realized just how high up the ladder the rot went. Feeling like a traitor but knowing he had no choice, he'd gone first to I.A., then to the chief himself. He owed him that much and more.

"Figgered you had us made, boy. Always was a smart one, that's why I hauled you out of that gang before you got in too deep."

At fifteen, Ben had been running with a gang of jackers, doing body work—mostly disassembling and filing off VIN numbers. Another few months and he would have been in too deep. Alvin Mercer, called

Mercy by those on the right side of the law, had taken his age into consideration and gone to bat for him.

What made it worse when Ben had confronted his mentor with indisputable evidence was that the chief hadn't even tried to deny it. If anything, he'd seemed almost relieved. "Times a man goes along to get along, son, but it don't pay. Nosiree, in the long run, it's more trouble than it's worth."

So now here he was, an unemployed ex-cop, more than a thousand miles from home, taking a damned art workshop in an effort to catch some creep who was ripping off senior citizens by mislabeling a product.

Old habits died hard. Some never died at all. One of the last assignments he'd worked before pulling the roof down on his own head was the classic borrowed-bank-account scam. Working with a veteran officer—one who'd been clean, incidentally—they had set up the scene. Three days later the mark had taken the bait. This good-looking kid had approached Abbie, who was dressed in civvies and sitting in her car in the bank parking lot pretending to be adding up a deposit before going inside.

The perp had walked up and introduced himself and asked if she could help him out, explaining that he was new in town and his mama had just sent him a check to live on while he interviewed for jobs. Trouble was, he didn't yet have an account and the bank wouldn't cash his check.

Eight out of ten times the women fell for it. The perp would hand over the check, the woman would deposit it in her own account, withdraw the amount—usually a few thousand—and hand it over. A day or so later she'd hear from the bank that the check she'd deposited was no good. Not only was the account phony, the bank it was written on didn't exist.

Ben had warned his grandmother against the borrowed-bank-account scam, but he'd been too late to warn her against investing her life's savings in a bunch of pictures that were supposedly guaranteed to triple in value in a year's time.

He'd smelled a rat as soon as she'd told him what she'd done. Just to be sure—hell, he knew as much about art as he did about toe dancing—he'd gone online and checked out a few things. Then he'd placed a call to an art teacher he'd met when her fifteen-year-old kid got in trouble for shoplifting.

Mona Hammond had summed it up for him. There were legitimate prints, several different types whose names he couldn't recall—some of them extremely valuable, depending on the artist and the rarity. But if an artist painted a picture and then had copies made, then the copies were just that. Copies. Names and numbers scribbled on the margin didn't change the fact that they were no more valuable than the knockoff Rolexes peddled on street corners.

"That's not to say that some of them aren't lovely," Mona had told him. "But even when they're printed on all rag paper using the finest quality inks, they're still technically reproductions, copies of the original painting."

"What about as an investment?" he'd asked, and she'd just laughed.

"No way, hon. I might buy one if I liked it and wanted to live with it, but then, that's the best rationale for buying any art. I wouldn't recommend buying one as an investment, though. So, when are you coming back home? We miss you here. Mike was asking about you just the other day.''

He'd told her his plans were still on hold and hung up, wondering just when his life had taken a turn for the bizarre.

Unlike Maggie, Ben hadn't grown up with a save-the-world complex. Instead, he'd grown up on the streets of a small town that had started out as a farm community more than a hundred years ago and grown when a big manufacturer had moved in. He barely remembered his father, although he clearly remembered driving all the way to North Carolina with him in a pickup truck with a busted muffler to meet Miss Emma. Just him and his old man. He must have been about eight or nine.

It had been like dropping in on another world. They'd stayed about a week before heading west again. His father had been a long-haul truck driver, gone more than he was at home. One day he was gone for good. Just forgot to come home.

Ben's mother hadn't been much on discipline, either her own or her son's. When she'd been arrested on a drug charge a year or so later, a social worker had called Miss Emma, who had paid his fare east. He'd stayed with her until his mother was released. A few years later when she'd skipped town with one of her boyfriends, Ben had stayed on in their trailer until it had been repossessed, then moved into an empty warehouse, which was how he came to get mixed up with the jackers.

If he hadn't been bailed out by Alvin Mercer, a heavyset, soft-voiced cop who went on to become chief of police, he might have ended up doing hard time—or worse. Instead, he'd ended up going back to school and eventually wearing a badge.

Years later he'd been compelled to rat out his mentor and most of his friends on the force. God, he'd hated that! He happened to know Mercy had been trying to hang on until retirement, fighting prostate problems and a few other symptoms that had him pushing more pills than a backstreet dealer. Ben would like to think he'd done the chief a favor, but some days he still felt lower than pond scum.

He wondered what Maggie would say if she knew about him. About where he'd come from and what he'd done back in Dry Creek. He wondered if she'd consider him a traitor or just a guy trying to do the right thing in a situation that was neither all black nor all white, but too many shades of gray.

He finally drifted off, half-thinking, half-dreaming of a crime-fighting duo wearing midnight blue capes, uncovering scams and writing them up in comic book format.

Sometime in the night he roused enough to roll over, aware of the faint sweet, spicy scent and the sound of someone humming softly. At that point his dreams took a decidedly different track. Just after daybreak he woke drenched in sweat, his pulse pounding like a jackhammer. Charlie was snoring in the bed across the room. Without arousing him, Ben collected a handful of clean clothes and tiptoed down the hall to shower and shave before going in search of caffeine.

The first class wasn't scheduled until nine, but the new cooking team was already in the kitchen when he followed the tantalizing aroma of dark-roasted coffee. The pot was institutional size. A few hardened addicts would be drinking the stuff all day, but after the third reheating, Ben couldn't handle it.

"Yes, ma'am, three strips if you don't mind, and however you're cooking the eggs this morning, that'll be fine, too."

The cook-of-the-day patted him on the shoulder. "Sit down, honey, I'll have it for you in a minute."

Breakfast and lunch were served in the kitchen; dinner in the dining room that also served as a gallery for Silver's art and a few select pieces of student work. Ben was still musing on what it would have been like to grow up in a home with a mother who cooked breakfast and called him "honey" when Maggie wandered in, looking as if she hadn't slept any better than he had.

Considering the part she'd played in his early morning dreams, Ben thought it was no wonder she was looking kind of used up. Wearing her clunky toe-ring sandals with a shapeless blue dress that covered her down to the ankles, she still managed to look sexy as hell. Wet hair had left damp patches on the shoulders, as she hadn't bothered to dry it, much less use those fat rollers and sticky sprays his last lady friend had used. Maggie's hair, roughly the color of desert camouflage, usually looked like she'd stepped outside in the wind and forgotten to brush it when she came back inside.

On Maggie, it looked good. Everything about her looked good.

In his usual place at the end of one of the long kitchen tables, Ben remembered his manners and lurched to his feet. There was room to spare, but she bumped against his shoulder on the way past. "You're blocking traffic," she muttered, her voice gruff with sleep. "Where's my mug?"

"Morning to you, too, sweetheart." He sat down again, wondering what she'd do if he hauled her down onto his lap and stroked her until she purred. He might be tempted to try it if it weren't for a room full of chaperones.

"Has Ann been in yet?" Maggie asked the woman who was lifting bacon from a fourteen-inch iron skillet.

"Lord, yes, she was in here when I came down to start the coffee. She'd already made herself some instant—I think she might've taken it upstairs."

Aware of him with every cell in her body, Maggie ignored Ben as she poured herself a mug of coffee, diluted it with milk and added two spoonfuls of sugar. One mystery was solved, anyway. Last night when she'd gone to the room they shared, Ann had been nowhere in evidence. According to Suzy, she was up on the third floor doing office work for Perry to pay for the workshop. "Ask me, she's not getting much for her efforts. I doubt if she's spent more than five hours in class since we started." Suzy had gone on patting moisturizer on her throat.

"I don't know…that thing she painted yesterday looked pretty good to me. Better than Perry's, anyway."

Shrugging, Suzy had said, "So maybe we should change teachers. By the way, when are you going to stop hogging our cowboy? Perry won't give me the time of day, so I might as well have some fun while I'm here if you're not interested.''

Oh, Maggie was interested, all right. Which was not to say she intended to do anything about it.

That had been last night. Now, sipping her coffee, she tried to remember whether or not she'd answered. At the time she'd still been under the spell of that romantic, wisteria-scented fog, wondering what would have happened if the two of them had been alone instead of surrounded by fully half the class.

Disgusted, she dumped in another spoonful of sugar and reminded herself that, while imagination was a great advantage for a novelist, too much of the stuff could pose a danger for an objective journalist.

She stole a glance at Ben, caught him looking at her and lowered her flushed face.

Cool, Maggie—really cool.

Just then Perry made his entrance, pausing in the doorway to beam at his audience. ''Morning, morning, morning! Remember the first day when I asked how many of you could touch your toes?'' Without even looking around, he accepted the steaming pottery mug of coffee someone handed him.

General groans were heard. Several more people had wandered in during the past few minutes. ''What is this, the inquisition?'' asked a woman in a flowered muumuu.

''Methods, methods, methods,'' Perry sang. ''Loose, loose, loose!''

''Trick-y, trick-y, trick-y,'' Suzy said, snickering just loud enough so that several people turned to look at her as she reached for a cup. She'd applied lipstick and eye shadow, but hadn't bothered to brush her hair. On some women, Maggie thought rancorously, bed-head looked good.

Pointing at the far end of the long table, the instructor indicated a group of four women, all well past middle age, none with any noticeable degree of talent. "Remember yesterday when I told you that the object of art is not to copy nature, but to comment on it? To interpret what you see? A few of you seem to be having problems with the concept."

"Does he mean we're supposed to color outside the lines?" Maggie whispered.

"Maybe he should practice what he preaches," Suzy replied. "You see the way he interpreted that old barn hanging in the front hall? He even painted the splinters in the wood and the shadows under the rusty nails. Might as well use a camera with a close-up lens if that's the kind of interpretation he wants. Be a lot faster, that's for sure."

One of the cooking team set a plate on the table before him and Perry took his seat and applied himself to breakfast. "Thirty minutes," he warned, fork poised over the mound of scrambled eggs. "Everybody be ready to make great strides today."

Yesterday's efforts were still spread out on the tables when the class straggled into the studio. Rather than face a critical review, Maggie tucked her drab, colorless blobscape under her tablet. As an artist, she was hopeless. Even Suzy was better. The only one worse was Ben Hunter, who didn't give a hoot. Maggie probably shouldn't, either, but then she'd always hated to fail at anything.

"It's the quality of your paints, Maggie," Janie

said softly. "Too much filler. Let me give you a few tubes of artists grade paint, it'll make all the difference in the world."

"Thanks, but it won't, not really. I shouldn't even be here."

"I was wondering about that," the older woman said with a lift of one carefully penciled eyebrow. "There are some excellent beginner's classes available in Winston. Had you thought about signing up for one at the Sawtooth Center?"

Before she could come up with a reply that wasn't an outright lie, Perry waltzed into the studio brandishing his brush as if it were a baton. "All right, ladies...and gentlemen," he added as an afterthought. "Now, here's what we're going to do today, even those of you who don't need loosening up. It won't hurt and it just might help give you a different perspective."

"The hell it won't hurt if it's that toe-touching crap." Charlie's grumbling voice could be heard all the way across the room.

Perry glared at him. Then, lifting his drawing board from the table at the front of the room, the instructor dropped it onto the floor, a fresh sheet of three-hundred-pound d'Arches already taped in place. Beside it he set his water pail and his big messy palette. "Now, bending from the waist—" He swayed from the hip several times in case anyone was in doubt of the location of the waist. "I want you to swe-e-eep in the sky, using plenty of color in a big, juicy wash!"

He demonstrated with a few broad strokes, clearly visible to those at the front tables. Those in the back of the studio hadn't a clue.

"You, Mr. Hunter—are you amused at something I said?"

"Who, me? Amused? I was just wondering why anyone who wants to can't sit on a chair and straight-arm down to the floor. Get pretty much the same result, wouldn't we?"

"*Must* I explain all over again? We need *free*-dom of movement. That simply can't be had sitting down."

But when three women left the room and returned with kitchen chairs, he only shrugged and went on with his demonstration.

Some forty minutes later as the class broke, some moving to the front of the studio to view the morning's masterpiece, others heading for the doors, Ben came up beside Maggie and slipped an arm around her shoulders. "You gotta admit, what he did this morning looks a hell of a lot better than these things he's got hanging on the wall. If that's an example of loose, I like it a whole lot better than tight."

Maggie felt as if someone had touched her with a live wire. Somehow she was going to have to drum up some resistance before she did something foolish. "I wouldn't know, since I couldn't see past all his admirers," she said, trying for blasé and missing it by a mile. And then, "Ben..." She looked up and found herself captured by his warm brown eyes. "Um—Charlie looks like he's coming down with something. You think he might be catching whatever Ann has?" She hated it when her voice sounded as if she'd just run a three-minute mile, but that was the way Ben affected her. Maybe she was the one with the allergies.

"He was out late last night. Probably just needs more sleep. C'mon, I want to show you something."

"Out where? What about the next assignment?"

Ben just shrugged. "It'll wait."

"Where are we going?" Not that she cared as she hurried after him. Obviously, mountain air had a deleterious affect on the immune system.

He led her out the back door, away from the house, to the vine-covered arbor. "If you're talking about the view," she said breathlessly. "I saw it the other night, remember?"

What if he tried to kiss her again?

What if he *didn't?*

So much for her powers of resistance.

"You put fifteen people—sixteen counting Silver—in one house, and it's damned near impossible to find any privacy."

Her breath snagged in her lungs. He *was* going to kiss her again! Her lips softened in expectation.

And then he reached into his pocket and pulled out a sheet of paper that looked as if it had been crumpled, smoothed out and then folded. Without another word, he handed it to her.

Puzzled, Maggie stared at the scribbled words, all in pencil, all similar, but with slight variations. "What am I supposed to see?"

"What does it look like?"

Trying to hide her disappointment, she looked again, frowning. "Somebody practicing cursive writing?"

"Try again."

"A...signature?"

"Bingo," he said softly. "And who needs to practice a signature?"

"Physicians?" she said half-joking, still puzzled.
She looked up to see him smiling down at the top of
her head. The smile faded from his mouth, then from
his eyes last of all, leaving in its place something
edgier.

"How about forgers?" he said softly.

Nine

"You're kidding, right?" Still holding the scrap of paper, Maggie searched his face. "You're not kidding," she said softly. Thunder echoed in the distance. Neither of them noticed.

"On a scale of one to ten, this probably rates about a two. This art scam, I mean." A slight breeze ruffled his hair, tempting her to smooth it back from his brow.

"If it is a scam." Regardless of what he'd said, Maggie, as an objective journalist, tried to keep an open mind. Marrying a wealthy, inexperienced woman for her money was one thing, but art forgery? She didn't have a clue. "How can it be forgery? Those prints hanging on the walls are obviously Perry's work. We've both seem him painting pictures that look almost identical. They've all got his signature. In fact, come to think of it, on the prints—reproductions, whatever—he's written his name twice, once on the picture itself and once in the margin. So what's the problem?"

"I'm not quite sure, but I intend to find out," he said grimly. His face softened and he continued to look at her.

Her breath quickening, Maggie waved away a bee that seemed more interested in her hair than in the nearby blossoms. Another rumble of thunder rolled across the valley. Forcing herself not to stare at his mouth, Maggie said, "So what do you think? He's practicing bending over from the waist to sign his name?"

"Hold still," Ben murmured.

She froze, her eyes darting to the nearby arbor, half expecting an armed forger to be lurking in the shadows.

Armed with—what, a loaded fountain pen? All this talk of forgers and scams was distracting her from her primary mission.

Slowly, Ben lifted his hand to her head. He said, "Shoo." And then he growled, "Scat, dammit."

A bee lifted off and droned away, moving heavily, as if it had pigged out on nectar. Ben went on staring at her hair. He said, "Raw sienna."

She blinked. "Raw what?"

"Your hair. I've identified three of the colors, but this one right here...I'm not quite sure." He fingered the tendril of hair she had tucked behind her ear as it dried. "There you've got your burnt sienna, your burnt umber and your yellow okra—it's this one right here I can't quite identify."

"Ochre," she corrected absently. The class had not entirely been wasted on her. "It's called yellow ochre."

"Yeah, that's what I said. I figure you've got all the colors they used in the desert cammy uniforms."

"Am I supposed to thank you for the compliment, or whack you and march off in high whatchamacallit?"

"High gear?"

"High dudgeon. It's what ladies and English butlers are known for in regency romances." And then, before he could come back at her, she closed her eyes. "Forget I said that, will you?"

He laughed, and just like that, all thoughts of forgers, gold diggers and desert camouflage evaporated.

But not romance, regency or otherwise. For one tingling moment Maggie's world narrowed to include only the man who was standing so close she could see the shards of gold in his whiskey-brown eyes, the iridescent gleam in his crow-black hair and the crease in his left cheek that was almost, but not quite, a dimple.

Without thinking, she reached up and touched it. He caught her hand and held it against his face. Heat sizzled between her skin and his. Just before he lowered his lips to hers, she heard him whisper, "This is crazy…"

This time there was nothing tentative about the kiss. It was carnal right from the start. And it felt so good, so right in the cool, fragrant morning air. She only wished she were taller so that everything would fit better. It occurred to her that if they were lying down, everything would fit perfectly.

But misaligned height had nothing to do with taste, and he tasted like coffee and mint and something wildly intoxicating. When his hand moved up and down her back, cupping her hips, she wanted to rip off her clothes to allow him better access. Her meager breasts swelled eagerly as his hands moved over her body.

And then he discovered that she wasn't wearing a bra and the exploration expanded. His thumbs feathered across her hardened nipples, zinging messages to the place between her thighs, preparing her for what was about to happen…

Only it wasn't. It couldn't. Not in broad daylight, in plain view of anyone who happened to glance out the window. Maggie could have wept with frustration. Never had she been kissed so thoroughly, so deliciously. Never before had she realized what a potent instrument a tongue could be.

Slowly, Ben lifted his face to stare down at her, his breath as ragged as her own. "Come on," he whispered roughly, and before she could protest—not that she would have—he led her through the patch of mountain laurel down a narrow path.

"Where?" she panted, barely able to keep up.

"Waterfall," he said. He stopped, turned, and drew her into his arms again. This time when the kiss ended there wasn't the slightest question of where they were headed.

Someplace private. Someplace *very* private.

Someplace where they wouldn't shock anyone who stumbled across their naked bodies. Because sure as the sky was blue—well, gray at the moment, and getting grayer—they were going to be naked and all over each other the minute they found a patch of level ground.

It was level only by comparison. Covered with dark green moss, surrounded by rocks worn smooth by time, it was barely wider than her cot. Ben lowered her and followed her down. Somewhere nearby, Maggie could hear the sound of moving water, but she had eyes only for the man kneeling beside her. With a soft oath, he ripped his shirt off over his head. Cloud-filtered sunlight splintered off his powerful shoulders.

He said, "Maggie...?"

"Yes." Just that one whispered word. It was all he needed; all either of them needed.

Buttons and zippers were dealt with, and Maggie waited impatiently while Ben tugged off his boots in order to pull off his jeans. Wearing only a scrap of yellow lace—lingerie was her one secret indulgence—she lay back on the velvety moss and watched as he finished undressing.

His hands were shaking. For some odd reason, which she didn't even bother to explore, that made her feel empowered. Mighty Maggie strikes again. Weak men fall to their knees; brave men quail in terror.

There was nothing faintly weak about Ben Hunter. Even in areas where the sun couldn't reach, his skin was the color of a rich latte. Flat black curls T-ed across his chest and arrowed down toward his groin, where...

"Oh, my," she whispered as he tossed his jeans aside and came down over her.

"Don't talk—don't think." His voice sounded like torn canvas. "Just let me…"

She couldn't have spoken then if her life depended on it. So she let him…and he let her. Coals that had smoldered since the first time she'd noticed him when he'd been leaning into the cab of his truck quickly burst into flames. In a single moment, Maggie went from being a mature, sensible woman to being a wild, irresponsible creature, heedless of all but her own burgeoning needs. Oblivious to the warm breeze that played over her naked body—to the cool moss beneath her, she was conscious only of Ben's arms, his hands—his fiercely aroused body moving over hers.

Her hands fluttered over his back, urging him on. *Now, now—please!*

He took his time. His mouth drove her wild with a series of soft, maddeningly gentle kisses before tracing a path of wildfire down her heated body.

"Please?" she managed to squeak when his lips moved over an exquisitely sensitive place.

"I—wait a minute," he said gruffly, and pulled away.

Frantic with need, she clutched at him as he reached over to drag his jeans closer. "Don't you dare leave me now," she cried softly.

"I used to carry—not sure it's still there, but—"

And then he was back, and she closed her eyes.

Ben suited up swiftly, his hands unsteady, his heart thundering visibly. He knew something about explosives, but never had he experienced anything as incendiary as the touch of this one small woman. If they'd both been dressed in asbestos it wouldn't have mattered. One kiss—one touch, and he would have gone up in flames.

He moved over her again, parting her thighs to kneel between them. "Beautiful," he whispered raggedly. "So beautiful."

He kissed her eyes and her throat, inhaling the intoxicating scent of soap, shampoo and aroused woman. He kissed her breasts, paying homage to the small pink nipples that rose hungrily to meet his lips. He placed kisses in the hollow beside each hipbone and one on her soft belly before moving on. By the time he lifted himself over her again, her heels were softly pounding the earth. She was whimpering with need.

And he was trembling with it. "I want it to be good for you, sweetheart," he said huskily.

"Yes!" she exploded, pulling him down to her with small, but surprisingly strong hands. Those were the last words either of them uttered until the wildfire died away.

As soon as either of them was able to move, Ben rolled onto his back, taking her with him. She lay draped over him like a damp blanket. If she was anywhere near as replete as he was, neither of them would be moving for the next few days.

Thunder rumbled across the mountains. A cool draft stirred the treetops around them. Once his breathing returned to normal, Ben whispered, "Maggie...I think it's about to rain on us."

"Mmm."

"You want to head back?"

She shook her head—managed to do that much, at least. "Uh-uh."

Eyes closed, he grinned. "Me, either."

She felt a drop of rain on her bottom. Just one, though. And she felt him stir to life beneath her. This time, since she was already on top, she took the line of least resistance.

Neither of them spoke on the uphill trek to the house. Maggie probably because she was too winded, Ben because he knew better. Anything a man said at a time like this was apt to land him in trouble.

He thought it, though. *What the devil have you done to me, woman?*

If she had any idea he was thinking things no cop, ex- or otherwise, should be thinking about, she'd high-tail it down the mountain. The odds were lousy. Four of the seven men he'd worked with over the past ten years had at least one busted marriage behind them. A couple more were in counseling. Hell, even in a small town like Dry Creek, where most of the problems were either drug-related or domestic, the stats were lousy.

And he was due back there on Monday. Barely time enough to throw a wrench in Silver's smooth little operation and say goodbye to Miss Emma. No time at all to figure out what was going on with Maggie, much less to try and explain why it would never work.

Who was it who'd said something about east being east and west being west, and the trains never running? One more pothole in his formal education.

Maggie marched past him without a word. Probably had a head full of second thoughts herself. Pure devilment made him call after her. "Hey! See you in class this afternoon, right?"

No reaction.

Just as well.

Charlie was in the men's john trying to wash a spot of something off one of his shirts. "You missed lunch," he said. "I don't know who made the last supply run, but we're already running short of a few things. I put down rye bread. You showering now? Didn't you shower this morning?"

"Poison ivy."

"Bad stuff. They got a washing machine in the basement if you want to use it. Be sure you use hot water, though, else it just spreads the oils."

Ben stepped in the shower stall and turned on the water to keep from having to lie any more, either by omission or commission. He had a feeling that if he were to look the older man in the eye, Charlie would be able to see right through him.

Maggie had never been so confused in her life.

Actually, she had, only not about sex. She was hardly promiscuous, but neither was she wildly experienced. Of all the men she had ever slept with— all three of them—no one had ever made her feel the way Ben had. Just thinking about him made her feel warm and gushy all over.

Class was already in session by the time she showered and changed into her last clean outfit. She should have packed more clothes and fewer snacks, but then, live and learn.

She slipped into the studio just as Silver was winding up a demonstration. Suzy made room for her and whispered, ''Where've you been? Do you know where Ben is? Janie was asking.''

Maggie's gaze flew to the left side table near the front of the room. One peach-colored head, one white one and one bald one. She'd heard Charlie laughing last night telling someone that that circle of skin on top wasn't a bald spot, it was a solar panel for a raging love machine.

No Ben. Speaking of raging love machines. Maybe he'd tossed his things into his pickup and fled, leaving Janie and all the other grandmothers to fend for themselves. A clear case of committal-phobia. She tried to think of all the advice she'd ladled out for her readers about men who were afraid to commit, but failed to come up with a single piece of wisdom other than that some men—maybe even most men—were.

Opening her watercolor pad, she stared at the blank page and tried to remember if she'd said anything that would lead him to believe she expected anything of him. She didn't, not really. Not to say she wouldn't have considered some sort of a relationship, but not every relationship had to end in marriage. That was foolish idealism, and while she had her ideals, she was nobody's fool.

Somehow she managed to get through the class without attracting any further attention. Suzy was doodling on the back of a horrible watercolor. Janie waved at her, but didn't come over. Charlie looked at her, smiled, turned away and then turned back to look some more.

Merciful Heaven, did it show? Men talked...

Of course women talked, too, but Maggie would curl up and die if she thought anyone knew where she'd been for the past hour, much less what she'd been doing. For two cents she'd throw everything in the car and go home, mission unaccomplished.

When the session ended she headed for the shelter of the side porch. And wouldn't you just know it? Ben had beat her there. He was staring out at the distinctive profile of Pilot Knob, barely visible in the distance. Before she could sneak away he said, "I guess we'd better talk."

"Um...not really. I mean, I don't have anything on my mind." She waited, scarcely breathing, then added, "Do you?"

He blinked. Was that confusion she saw on his face? Surely not. Hunter was the kind of man who never put a foot wrong, literally or figuratively.

"Oh, well...I guess we do need to talk about the forgery." Maggie the magnanimous.

"Maggie, what happened—I don't want you to think—"

But before she could discover what it was he didn't want her to think, Charlie emerged from the house. "Now we're even out of beer!"

Saved by the bell. It was clear from his expression that Ben was thinking the same thing she was. "I could go get some," Maggie volunteered. "Make out a grocery list and I'll be glad to go." Forty-five minutes there, half an hour to shop, forty-five minutes back...that should allow her plenty of time to put what had happened into perspective. Getting over it was another thing altogether.

Ben said, "I'll do it. I need a few things, anyway."

"Add it to the list," Maggie said without meeting his eyes.

Ben thought, dammit, she had no intention of hearing him out. Not that he knew what he was going to say, but she couldn't just ignore what had happened. She wasn't that kind of a woman, that much he did know.

She huffed up a little bit, turned to go and caught her shoe on the door sill. Lunging away from the porch rail, he managed to catch her. "Easy there, you don't want to tear up the woodwork."

Her face turned pink and he thought she was going to slug him. Instead, she laughed. "Don't say it. I need to lose these shoes. Well, I hate to disillusion you but I can be just as clumsy barefooted." She looked pointedly at his slick-soled, slant-heeled boots. Shaking her head, she said, "You'll get yours, just wait."

"Hey, these are my good luck boots."

And then they both laughed, not that it was particularly funny, but as a relief valve, laughter served the purpose. Ben held on to her arm, but gently—not like he was trying to take control. Women like Maggie, he told himself, needed delicate handling. Needed someone to smooth the way before they charged out to save the world.

Charlie was in the kitchen scribbling on a strip of paper. Glancing up, he said, "Skim milk, too, but wait'll after the next session. Silver's brought down some mattes. He's going to show us how to crop out the bad parts."

Still a little self-conscious, Ben said, "Hey, as long as we're here, we might as well learn how to crop out the bad parts, right?"

"I think he means the bad parts of our paintings," Maggie said dryly.

"I knew that." He took the list Charlie gave him and tucked it into his pocket.

Both Suzy and Ann were at the table when Maggie slid into place a few minutes later. Other than looking tired, Ann looked perfectly healthy. "I heard Perry did the loosening up thing this morning," she said softly.

"You should've been here," Suzy said. "I thought for a minute I was back at the Fit'n Trim Gym. Bend, sweep to the left, sweep to the right, twenty reps and then stand up and do it all over again."

"He's a good teacher," the quiet brunette said. "He's been drawing and painting since he was in grade school. He actually did a year at Pratt and met some of the big name artists."

Suzy said dryly, "I toured the capitol once, but that doesn't make me a politician."

At the front of the room, Silver had placed one of his own watercolors on a standing easel. He held up a small matte, then moved it over first one section, then another. "What we're looking for is something that can be salvaged even if we have to sacrifice those parts that aren't working."

Maggie wondered which parts of this week she would salvage, given the chance.

"Think of it as mining for precious gemstones." Silver shifted the small horizontal matte to frame a log tobacco barn, a dead tree and part of a cornfield, blocking out the farmhouse that had been the center of interest.

She would salvage today. Wise or not, she would

salvage every single moment she spent with Ben Hunter.

Suzy said, "I still don't know exactly what he means by not working."

"Do you care?" Maggie whispered back.

"You have a question, Miss Riley?"

Well, heck. She might as well get something out of this blasted class after all the money she'd wasted on it. Mary Rose would just have to take her word for what a creep the man was, because so far Maggie hadn't come up with a scrap of proof in spite of Suzy's efforts. "I said I'm not sure what you mean by not working."

"Come closer, dear, perhaps it's your eyes that aren't working."

Or her brain, Maggie admitted ruefully. The implication was clear, and not all that unfounded.

Over the next several minutes the class was treated to a demonstration of how elements as small as a speck of bright color or a broken cornstalk pointing the wrong way could lead the eye out of the picture plane. It never occurred to Maggie to ask what a picture plane was. She really didn't care.

While Perry droned on and on about muddy colors and paint quality—about the difference between planned bleeds and unplanned blotches—Maggie wondered where Ben was. He hadn't joined the class. She listened for the sound of a vehicle leaving the parking lot, but all she heard was the rumble of distant thunder.

By the time Silver relented, her head was reeling with useless knowledge, her feet were killing her and all she could think of was that Ben had made love to her and she was probably doomed to spinsterhood. No other man could ever come up to his standard. It had nothing whatsoever to do with technique, but with the man himself. Whatever it was—chemical, biological or something more mystical—she was stuck with it.

She was packing up her material with some vague idea of leaving for good when Perry Silver's mellifluous voice rang out again. "There's a truism among artists. When the general public likes your work, you're in trouble. Do you know what I say?" He looked expectantly at his disciples. "Faugh on that. Perry says, faugh, faugh, faugh!"

Faugh? Now there was a word for you, Maggie thought, amused. This entire week, she had to admit, had been a learning experience. A few of the lessons she could have done without.

"I paint for the masses," the instructor announced, "not for the elite. If the general public appreciates my work, I know I've succeeded."

Then he'd obviously succeeded, scam or no scam. She'd heard nothing but raves from most of his students, several of whom would probably part with enough money to buy whatever he was selling.

Finally the last class of the day ended. The last as far as Maggie was concerned, at any rate. Tonight's session she would skip, if she were still here. For all the progress she was making, either as a painter or a sleuth, she might as well pack up and go home.

Ben was waiting for her when she emerged from her room a few minutes later. Without a word spoken on either side, he steered her to the front door. And like the dumbest lamb in the flock, she went.

The western sky had blackened, creating a dramatic backdrop for the narrow streak of late sunlight that gilded the treetops. Instead of lingering to appreciate the view, he nodded toward the arbor on the edge of the clearing.

Maggie was suddenly reluctant. She'd heard of butterflies in the belly. Hers tended to go for the brain. If he wanted to act as if today had never happened, two could play that game. Affecting an offhand manner, she said, "Maybe we're doing the man an injustice, did you ever think of that?"

"Who, Silver? Yeah, I thought about it. According to Janie, the guy really does know his stuff. He's won a whole bunch of awards in the state and local arena. The only thing I have a problem with is selling reproductions and claiming they're a great investment."

Pausing to finger a pebble from her sandal, Maggie steadied herself by clinging to his arm. Straightening, she said, "Okay, so maybe he's the next best thing to whatsisname, that guy who paints the four-eyed, dissected ladies. Maybe he's even made a fortune selling his stuff—and I'm sorry about your grandmother, I really am—but that doesn't mean he's in love with Mary Rose and not her trust fund."

"So what are you saying? There's no such thing as love at first sight?"

Her heart shifted into overdrive. "Pure urban myth," she said breathlessly.

"Okay, then what about this one? When it comes to love, rich women don't stand a chance."

Halting, she turned to face him and then wished she hadn't. It was almost impossible to think clearly when she was this close. Her hormones had taken over earlier today. Now it was time for the gray cells to step forward. "All I'm saying is that if Perry made as much money on art as the Dilyses have on pickles, there's a slight chance he truly loves her for herself. I really, really hope that's the case, honestly, I do. But I don't think so."

Ben's eyes narrowed. "Has he come on to you?"

"Do I look rich? Of course he hasn't, but I asked Suzy to—to sort of flirt with him, drop a few hints about her family's business."

"The hell with that, has he made a move toward you?"

Maggie looked at him as if he'd lost his wits. "For Pete's sake, why would he go after me when he could have someone like Suzy—or even Ann?"

He shook his head slowly. "You still don't get it, do you?"

"Sure I get it. Whenever I want it." And then, hearing what she'd just said, Maggie slapped a hand over her mouth, inwardly cursing her tendency to resort to glibness when she was nervous. "I mean, I can get a date any time I want one, but that's not why I'm here. Oh, shoot!" She closed her eyes. "You get me so mixed up!"

A slow grin spread over his face. "Good. I'll take any advantage I can get."

"Oh, no you won't."

"We need to talk about that, too, but let's get this other stuff out of the way first. How old is this friend of yours?" They had stopped a dozen feet away from the arbor.

"I already told you, she's twenty-five. A *young*

twenty-five.'' She tapped her foot, daring him to challenge her. If he thought she was making too much of her own maturity, he didn't mention it. Just as well. She could still clobber him.

Mature. Right.

''Any reason she can't think for herself?'' His tone was suspiciously reasonable.

''Other than the fact that her father's always treated her like a hothouse rose, I can't think of any. I keep telling her she needs to move into a place of her own, but she's afraid of hurting her folks' feelings.''

Ben did something with his mouth that was both maddening and provocative. She knew what that mouth could do, dammit. She didn't need to be reminded. ''Tell me something,'' he said. ''Do you still live at home?''

''That's different.''

''I expect it is,'' was all he said. With an arm at her back, he steered her toward the vine-covered arbor. If she had a grain of sense she'd turn around right now and go back inside. Any talking they did needed to be done in plain view of anyone who cared to look. There was safety in numbers.

''I've known her forever.'' Maggie had this habit of filling any uncomfortable silence with words, whether or not they were relevant. ''When we were little we used to play together. My dad does all Mr. Dilys's insurance, did I tell you that?''

His arms moved to her shoulder as he led her over a patch of rocky terrain. She could smell his pine-scented soap. When she'd stripped off her clothes earlier, she had smelled something earthy and green.

Never would she be able to look at moss in the same way.

Rather than break away and run back to the house—her first impulse—she focused on not tripping and tried to ignore the feel of him, the scent of him, and how comfortable the weight of his arm felt on her shoulder. She wanted desperately for him to approve of her, which was a bad sign. An incredibly bad sign, because for the most part, Maggie didn't give a hoot what anyone thought of her. Her father called her heedless, and she had to admit that the trait occasionally landed her in trouble.

"What a pair you must have made," Ben mused. They were only a few yards away from the shadowy arbor, with its cozy two-person swing.

"We still do. She writes letters to my column under an assumed name when things are slow so it looks like I've got this huge readership, and I take her to places she's never heard of and introduce her to some really neat people."

Ben shook his head. "I'd like to meet a few of what you call 'neat people.' Sometimes a woman can fall in with the wrong crowd and find herself in more trouble than she bargained for. You ever think about that?"

"All the time. For instance—"

But before she could get to her "for instance," they arrived at the arbor and stopped dead. Ben said, "Charlie, what are you doing out here?"

Someone laughed, a soft, husky sound that identified her even before the peach colored hair came into view.

"'Scuse us," Ben said, and backed away. As they

turned toward the house again, Maggie told herself she wasn't disappointed, not really. If she had a single grain of sense—which at the moment, was debatable—she'd call it a lucky reprieve.

Ben chuckled and Maggie said, "Maybe we could make reservations. For the arbor, I mean."

Kick yourself, woman!

"Good idea. I've got an even better one. How about we head for town, pick up whatever groceries are on the list and have dinner while we're out?"

Spending time alone together was like waltzing through a minefield. Maggie knew it. She had a feeling Ben knew it, too, unless today had meant no more to him than scratching a temporary itch.

Ten

The rain began in earnest before they were even half-way to town. With the windshield wipers and head-lights on, Maggie leaned forward to switch on the defogger. Neither of them had brought any rain gear, but Ben said, "Miss Emma made me bring an um-brella. Told her I never used 'em, but she insisted."

"That's what grandmothers are for. Where is it?"

"Somewhere back there under a ton of junk." He nodded to the narrow space behind the driver's seat. "Rain'll be over by the time we get to town, any-way."

Before they'd set out he had glanced at a map, even though Maggie told him she knew the way. With rain coming down in curtains, maps were little help as they could barely see the road, much less the exit signs.

"Real frog strangler."

"Try for something more original. How about an ark floater? Ben, slow down," Maggie cautioned.

He slowed, but not too much. He didn't want to rear-end another vehicle, but neither did he want to slow up enough to risk being a road hazard. There was no sign of any taillights ahead, but that didn't mean they were the only ones on the highway. There were always a few nuts who thought that as long as they could see they didn't need lights.

Clutching her shoulder belt, Maggie leaned forward, peering through the wall of gray. "There ought to be an exit somewhere along here where we could—"

"Sit back. If I have to stop suddenly I don't want you—" He swore under his breath. "Sunovabitch!" Jerking the wheel sharply, he milked the brakes to a standstill within inches of a white van that had pulled off onto the shoulder at an angle, one corner projecting a few feet onto the highway.

Ben backed up a few feet, then steered cautiously onto the narrow shoulder, making sure he was completely off the highway. Maggie said, "I don't want to be here."

"Me, either." He waited a moment, then checked carefully for any sign of traffic before pulling out again. "Is there an overpass anywhere around here?"

She shook her head. "I don't think so. Anyway, it might not be wide enough if you were thinking about parking there until the rain slacked off."

"Yeah, you're probably right. Watch for an exit. We'd better find a place to wait it out."

*   *   *

The Laurel Lane Lodge looked as if it had survived the past half century unchanged. Of the five separate units, none appeared to be occupied, but there was a light on in the office.

"Sit tight." Ben ducked out and made a dash to the door.

The apron-clad woman behind the desk rose to meet him. "My mercy, would you look at this rain. Sauer's Branch is already up over the banks, I heard it on the radio. There's so much static you can't hardly hear anything. You need a place to stay?"

A few minutes later Ben slid into the truck again, soaked to the skin, but grinning. Brandishing a key, he said, "Any old port in a storm." His voice was barely audible over the sound of rain hammering down on the metal cab.

Maggie tried to pretend her pulse rate hadn't shot into the stratosphere. "If you wanted to show off your Texas roots, a broad-brimmed hat would've served a lot better than those boots."

"I'll match my boots against those things you're wearing any day. We drew number five, over there on the end." Inching along the short driveway, he pulled up in front of a small unit distinguished by a blue door and a single blue-shuttered window. "Stay here while I unlock."

Watching him dash toward the minuscule shelter, Maggie thought of all the motel jokes she'd ever heard. Under the circumstances, stopping was only sensible. It didn't necessarily mean they were going to dive into bed together. They could dry off and talk until the rain slacked off. Actually, it would be a good opportunity to get better acquainted—sharing childhood experiences, comparing notes on the progress of their individual missions. That should take all of two minutes. *Then* what?

As if she didn't know.

Deliberately she pushed away the thought that in a few days, once the workshop ended, they would each go their separate ways. Not that they would be all that far apart—not as long as he stayed with his grandmother. She hadn't asked about his future plans because first of all, it was none of her business. Now she was afraid to—afraid his plans didn't include her.

After only a short dash to the blue door they were both wet, thanks partly to the solid wall of water pouring off the roof. Maggie wouldn't have been surprised to see steam rising from Ben's shirt, the way it was plastered to his skin. His boots made a squeaky sound with every step. "Hope there's enough towels," he said, reaching the minuscule bathroom in three strides.

Self-conscious, Maggie studied the room that was dominated by a chenille-covered bed. Instead of the usual commercial carpet there were several scatter rugs on a varnished wood floor. "This reminds me of one of the illustrations in this book I used to have," she said, refusing to be intimidated by a bed. "I'm not sure if it was *Goldilocks* or *Little Red Riding Hood*."

"Easy to tell the difference." Ben dropped a towel over her hair and gave it a few gentle rubs. "Depends on whether there's a wolf or a bear in the bed."

So then of course they both stared at the bed, which suddenly seemed to grow until there was nothing else in the room. Ben cleared his throat. He seemed almost

as tense as she was. Moving abruptly, he crossed to
the window, discovered that it wouldn't open, and
opened the front door a crack. "Air's musty in here,"
he said gruffly. "Rain's not blowing from this direction.

He began unbuttoning his shirt and Maggie
thought, not like this...please. It's too soon. She
looked everywhere but at the man who absorbed all
the oxygen in the small room. "You know what? I
think this furniture is the real thing," she said
brightly. "I mean genuine wood." Swallowing hard,
she walked over and touched the leaf of a potted
plant. "This is real, too. Real dirt and everything."

*Marvelous, Maggie. Why not impress him with
your brilliant conversational skills?*

"Watch your step on these rugs, they're trippers,"
Ben cautioned. His shirt unbuttoned, he tugged it out
of his pants. Before she could inform him that she
didn't need a caretaker, he said, "Maggie, get out of
those damp clothes before you start sneezing."

She wilted. All right, so he was bossy. It was the
kindness in his voice that got to her. He wasn't just
interested in getting her naked so he could have his
way with her—not that his way wasn't hers, too.

"Oh, for Pete's sake," she muttered, turning away
just as he peeled off his wet shirt.

Unfortunately, she turned toward the oval dresser
mirror, and there he was again. Closing her eyes
didn't help. They could be stranded together in a
pitch-black cave and she would still be aware of him
with every cell in her body. It had to be chemical.
That pheromone thing, probably. She knew men who
were handsomer—even a few who were built as well,

but not a single one of them moved her at all. Somewhere inside her was an intricate lock, just waiting for the right key. And Ben Hunter was that key.

All right, she told herself—you're both adults. You've done it before, so what does it matter if you do it again? Where's the problem?

The problem was that she wanted more than sex.

"Maggie? You're frowning."

He appeared behind her in the mirror, his wide shoulders framing her narrower ones like a hawk hovering over a scared rabbit. "No'm not," she said, and forced a smile to prove it.

His hands closed over her shoulders. "Maggie, Maggie," he said with exaggerated patience. "Look, if you don't want to stay here we don't have to. We can wait in the truck for the rain to slack and head back. I know I promised you dinner, but it might have to wait."

"I'm fine. I mean this is only sensible. I mean, what if one of us had to go to the…" Chagrined, she closed her eyes. "Shut up, Maggie, just shut up."

Ben chuckled. "Take off your damp clothes. I can turn on the fan and they'll dry in no time."

They wouldn't, and they both knew it. Maggie might tell a white lie or two to spare someone's feelings, but she tried never to lie to herself. She had wanted this man almost from the first moment she'd seen him. Wanted him even before he'd kissed her. Out in the woods on a patch of moss beside a tiny waterfall, she had welcomed him into her arms, into her body. What had followed was a pleasure so profound she knew it would be with her 'til her dying day.

A realist, Maggie told herself that whatever happened now, it was an inevitable extension of what had happened earlier. It really didn't change anything.

"So," she said, her voice half an octave higher than usual. "Shall we...sit down? If we had a deck of cards..."

There wasn't a damned thing to do in here but go to bed. There wasn't even an old newspaper she could pretend to read. Nothing but the bed looming behind them.

Ben watched her in the mirror, trying to figure out what was going on under that shaggy mop of damp hair. He couldn't quite get a handle on Maggie Riley—possibly because she didn't play any of the games he'd come to expect from the women he took to bed.

She was nervous, which told him that despite what had happened earlier she didn't take this sort of thing for granted. As it couldn't be for lack of opportunity he could only conclude that few men had managed to break through her prickly defenses.

Still facing the mirror, he slipped his arms around her waist from behind. Under the clinging fabric of her dress, her small breasts were clearly visible, her nipples dark and alert. She closed her eyes as he began unfastening the row of pearl buttons. "Maggie?" he whispered, and she nodded.

He deliberately lingered over the task of undressing her, savoring each small step. Allowing the tension to build until it was all but irresistible. Her body might be slight, but there was no mistaking its maturity. Judging from the way she was pressing herself against his arousal, she was as eager as he was.

This woman won't be so easy to forget. Ignoring the soft, insistent whisper, he led her toward the bed. It was a double, not even a queen size. His inconvenient conscience urged him to issue the standard disclaimer to the effect that, despite what had happened earlier and what was about to happen now, there was nothing binding on either side.

But hell, she knew that. He didn't have to put it into words.

Turning her in his arms, he lowered his lips to hers. The fleeting thought crossed his mind as he deepened the kiss, savoring what was to come, that he could easily become addicted to this woman.

When she began tugging at his belt, he reached for the bottom of the silky undershirt thing she was wearing and eased it up under her arms. There was no way of getting it over her head without ending the kiss. Reluctantly, he lifted his head. Then, in an impromptu dance, she kicked off her sandals and wriggled the rest of the way out of her damp top.

Ben took a moment to appreciate the perfection of her, from her small, rounded thighs to her small rounded hips—to the waist he could practically span with his hands and the small, proud swell of her breasts.

Dropping his jeans around his knees, he attempted to step out of them and nearly tripped. He cursed under his breath, but managed to keep it brief and relatively clean.

"You might want to take off your boots first." Maggie's dry observation brought forth a snort of laughter that did nothing at all to reduce the tension.

"Yes, ma'am. Uh—how about closing the front

door.'' He'd forgotten they'd left it partly open to air out the room.

Naked but for a scrap of yellow silk that just missed being a thong, she lunged for the door, slammed it and fastened the chain. ''Oh, for gosh sakes, anyone passing by could've looked in!'' She switched off the overhead light but left on a forty-watt lamp on the dresser.

Ben shucked off his boots and socks, then peeled off his jeans and briefs in one swift motion. Glancing up, he said, ''Watch that rug.''

She wrinkled her nose at him. ''You know me too well.''

''Yeah, I do,'' he said, realizing it was no less than the truth.

With one knee on the edge of the mattress, she hesitated. ''Um—do you—that is—''

''I do,'' he said, and held up a foil packet.

''Good, because I don't, and we didn't earlier this afternoon.'' She said it in a half-joking way, trying to sound as if she did this sort of thing all the time.

Ben knew better. He really did know Maggie Riley, no matter if they had met only a few days ago. ''Come here,'' he said, his voice a rough caress.

There was none of the awkwardness that sometimes occurred between new lovers. Even the first time, there had been no real awkwardness, only eagerness—only a sense of inevitability.

Now, starting with another hungry kiss, they picked up where they had left off and quickly moved beyond. All senses alive, Ben felt the satiny heat of her skin—he breathed in the intoxicating scent of fruity shampoo and warm, aroused woman and heard the tiny whimpering sounds, the soft gasps she made as he explored her slender perfection. Her nipples were ripe cherries begging to be plucked. He plucked them, first with his fingertips, then with his lips and teeth.

Gasping, she ran her hands over his chest, raking his flat nipples until they stood up like small cartridges.

"Honey, maybe we'd better slow down," he said even as his hands made forays under the sheet that brought forth another shuddering gasp. *Slow down? Man, are you crazy?*

No guarantees on that front.

Her fingers twisted the flat curls that crossed his chest before spearing down to his groin. At this rate he'd better suit up fast, or it would be too late. Amazing, the degree of pressure that could build up when a man went too long without sex, he told himself, unwilling to admit that it was the woman herself and not the long, dry spell that had ended only hours earlier.

"I don't want to slow down. Make love to me, Ben."

With her small hands probing dangerously close to ground zero, he whispered roughly, "Neither do I." Using his teeth and his free hand, he ripped the corner off the foil packet he'd had the forethought to put within reach.

"Sweet—creamery—butter," he whispered roughly as he first gloved himself in protection and then in her warm, welcoming body. "Maggie, I don't want to rush you, but—"

"You're not." She was moving restlessly, each shuddering breath clearly audible. Her hands fluttered over whatever parts of him they could reach, igniting small brushfires along the way.

He pulled back, looming over her, his face tense with urgency. When she protested, he rolled over onto his back, carrying her with him so that she bracketed his hips with her thighs. He probably outweighed her by a good seventy-five pounds. He should have thought of that out by the waterfall, but he hadn't been thinking at all—at least not with his brain.

"Go, girl," he directed, his voice so strained as to be unrecognizable.

She needed no prompting. Lifting her hips, she centered herself and settled down again with such exquisite slowness he died several deaths before he could even remember to breathe. Steeling himself against snatching control and racing for the finish line, he let her move at her own pace, every muscle in his body quivering with tension.

Her pace started out slow and easy, but then, as if she'd lost the rhythm and couldn't get back in step, it became jerky and fast. She started to whimper. Clasping her shoulders, Ben melded his pace to hers until suddenly she ground herself hard against him, her eyes widening.

"Oh, oh, oh!" The soft sound of discovery cascaded over him like a benediction.

He held her tightly in place as a million volts of pure energy shot through him, echoing repeatedly throughout every cell of his body.

Eventually she collapsed, damp and panting. "Oh, my goodness," she whispered breathlessly.

"Yeah," he said as blood began to filter back to his brain. "My thoughts precisely."

* * *

The sky had mostly cleared by the time they ventured outside. Tufts of pink-edged clouds drifting overhead as traffic appeared to be running normally again, tires singing on wet pavement. The small parking area outside their cottage was littered with puddles and leaves from newly green trees.

"I'm hungry," Maggie said, a note of surprise in her voice. "Do we still have time to get something to eat?" There was none of the awkwardness she might have expected.

"You operating on a deadline?" Ben opened the passenger side door and helped her up. Her legs were short, the 4x4 was high, the running board little more than a narrow chrome bar. It occurred to him that he really didn't need four-wheel drive any longer.

The thought was followed by a shaft of unease. Just because a man had sex with a woman a few times, that was no cause to start changing his lifestyle. Maggie sure as hell wasn't making an issue of it. Some women wanted to talk afterward. All he'd ever wanted to do was sleep, preferably alone.

Not that he'd have minded talking to Maggie, but she'd clammed up tighter than a tick on a shorthaired dog and headed for the shower. Then, while she'd dressed, he had showered. There hadn't been a whole lot of opportunity for conversation.

"Barbecue all right with you?" he asked casually as they turned off highway 52 toward Pilot Mountain. There was a sign ahead that promised Lexington-style barbecue, which meant lean pork in a light, tomato-based sauce. It took some getting used to after the heavy-bodied beef 'que he was used to, but it wasn't bad. Not half-bad, in fact.

"Love it," she said brightly. A little too brightly, he suspected, but then he wasn't quite as relaxed as he was making out to be, either.

She sighed and continued to watch the scenery go by while he drove and tried not to think of either the immediate past or the future.

Neither of them did justice to the barbecue. Maggie nibbled on a sweet, greasy hushpuppy while Ben looked around for some hot sauce and used it liberally on his mild, eastern style sandwich. He said, "You put slaw on yours?"

She said, "You're supposed to."

"Not where I come from."

"So?"

And that settled that. East was east and west was west, and all the rest of it.

Outside a small independent grocery store a few minutes later, Maggie glanced over the list. Ben insisted on giving her a fifty-dollar bill and offered to help shop.

"Since I'm not used to help it would be more of a hindrance, but thanks."

He was waiting outside the truck when she emerged with a grocery cart. Together they crammed the bags onto the back seat. Neither of them spoke more than a few words on the drive back to Peddler's Knob as for once, Maggie found herself incapable of filling in an awkward silence with mindless chatter.

Only when they pulled into the parking lot did she speak. Unclipping her seat belt, she peered up at the house. "It looks like every light in the house is on. I wonder why."

"Because it's dark outside? Come on, I'll get Charlie to help bring in the supplies."

When they reached the steps, slick from the recent rain, he took her hand. Rather than make an issue of it, Maggie let him guide her up onto the porch. Was there a tactful way of letting him know she didn't expect anything from him? In case one of her readers ever asked her about the protocol for afternoon sex by a waterfall or evening sex in a rented room, she would have to refer them to Dr. Ruth or Dr. Laura. Miss Maggie hadn't a clue.

She slanted a sidelong glance at the man beside her and saw that he was frowning. She wanted to say, "Look, so we went to bed together a couple of times. We're consenting adults, a good time was had by all, and that's the end of that, period."

Only it wasn't. Not for her, at least. So she didn't say it.

Charlie met them at the door. "Where the hell have you two been? Are you both feeling all right?"

Maggie darted another look at Ben, wondering if it showed. Had she buttoned her dress wrong?

Ben said, "We got caught in a cloudburst, that's all. What's going on?"

"You didn't eat supper?"

Ben nodded and Maggie said, "We had barbecue. We could have brought some back if we'd thought of it. The supplies are—"

Charlie said, "Heck with that, long's you didn't eat here. They're dropping like flies. Janie and Georgia and I did the cooking tonight, but it wasn't that, I swear."

Eleven

Thank goodness she'd showered at the motel before they'd left, Maggie told herself, because the ladies' bathroom was not a particularly pleasant place. Three people so far had come down with symptoms of food poisoning. Two more were looking iffy.

Janie said, "I called a doctor. He said bring 'em in, but I don't know…"

"Pity they don't make house calls anymore," said a brisk, white-haired woman named Bea who was cooking rice. Seeing Maggie staring at the pot on the stove, she said, "It'll help some. Cola's for them that can keep it down. With all this rain, the saltines are limp as raw bacon."

Maggie said, "Oven. Crisp 'em in the oven." Good Lord, what was going on around here? She'd left an art workshop and come back to find a field hospital.

Janie stood in the middle of the kitchen and waved a cooking spoon. "Attention, everyone. I'll coordinate for the duration, all right? Charlie, you see that there's a bucket beside every bed. Round up the water containers from the studio. You, Maggie—and you, Ben—go up to the third floor and see where Perry's hiding out. He hasn't been downstairs since all this started."

"Probably on the phone with his lawyer right this minute," said Georgia.

Following Ben up to the second floor, Maggie couldn't believe that little more than an hour ago she'd been lying in his arms, trying not to think about wedding bells—about riding off into the sunset on a white horse with the cowboy of her choice.

Actually, she was a lot smarter than that, only sometimes her imagination got in the way of her common sense. Despite his boots and his accent, Ben wasn't John Wayne, she reminded herself. What he was, was an unemployed Texan who happened to be visiting a relative, who happened to live in North Carolina.

Moans, groans and more ominous sounds greeted them as they hurried along the second floor hall to the attic stairway. The door was always kept closed. For all she knew, it might even be locked.

It wasn't. "Maybe you'd better let me go up alone," Ben said.

"No way. You might need backup."

"Maggie—" He shook his head, opened the door and set off up the narrow, steep steps, with Maggie two steps behind him. The only light showing was a dim glow coming from the far end of a long, slope-

ceiling room. It was the light they'd seen from the
parking lot.

Two steps from the top, he paused. To steady herself, Maggie looped her fingers under his belt and
tried to peer around him through the clutter of boxes,
stacks of empty frames and what looked like a small
guillotine. As there was no blood, only a few scraps
of matte board under the wicked blade, Maggie managed to control her alarm.

Ann was seated at a desk at the far end. She
glanced up and her eyes widened. "What are you two
doing up here?"

Ben had to bend to avoid bumping his head.
"Watch it," he warned as Maggie followed close on
his heels.

"One good thing about being height challenged,"
she whispered. "I'm good with low clearances." And
then she said, "Why am I whispering? Ann, are you
all right? You do know what's going on downstairs,
don't you?"

Ann held a finger over her lips, casting her eyes
toward a door that had been hidden until now. "Shh,
Perry doesn't feel good. He's trying to get a nap before he heads back to town."

Avoiding the eaves, Ben dodged the cartons and
stacks. "If he's got the same symptoms as everybody
else, he'll be better off on the second floor—that is,
unless there's a john up here."

Ann's frown was replaced by a look of concern.
"Symptoms?"

"Food poisoning," Maggie supplied.

Ann sat down again. "You're kidding. I thought it

was just his wrist. He takes all this herbal stuff and sometimes it makes him feel, you know—yukky.''

"Did either of you eat here tonight?'' Ben asked.

Maggie was distracted by the label on several of the boxes. Good heavens, Hong Kong again? She was pretty sure Perry had said his three-hundred-pound watercolor paper was French, not Chinese.

"I haven't had time to eat since breakfast. Perry's been in his room since the late session. He stays over sometimes, but he's got an apartment in town.''

"Did either of you go down for supper?''

Ann shook her head slowly. "I made a sandwich and brought it up with me while I was...'' She glanced at the cluttered desk and looked away.

"Where is he, through here?'' Ben was halfway to the inconspicuous door when Ann blocked his way.

"Let me,'' she said. "I'm pretty sure he's okay, but like I said, he takes all this herbal stuff. I doubt if any of it's ever been FDA approved, but you know Perry—you can't tell him anything.''

Maggie moved slowly around the angular room, eyeing the stack of prints—reproductions or whatever they were called. Still with her hand on the doorknob, Ann said, "He's got that carpal tunnel thing now, but the truth is, he's always had some excuse to keep from doing whatever he doesn't want to do. He's my cousin on my mama's side, so I've tried to help— you know how it is with family—but honestly, there's times lately when I feel like telling him...''

Shaking her head, she quietly opened the door. "Perry? Are you awake?''

It was a subdued group that met in the kitchen later that night. The worst of the sickness was evidently over. "They'll live," said Charlie, "but they're feeling pretty drained."

Groans could be heard around the table, where an array of safe snacks had been set out. Charlie, who hadn't been affected, said, "Sorry. No pun intended. Stuff acts like salmonella. I figure it had to be either the raw cider or the sprouts. Not everybody put sprouts on their salad, and not everybody drank the cider, but I tossed the leftovers just in case."

"Godalmighty." After emptying pails for the past few hours Ben was too tired to watch his language. The brow-soothing and hand-holding had been left to Janie, Georgia and Maggie, while the woman called Bea had manned the kitchen, brewing tea, serving up warm ginger ale and oven-crisped saltines.

"How's Perry doing? Is Ann looking after him?" Bea asked.

"Evidently his stomach's fine," Maggie told her. "It's his carpal tunnel that's acting up."

"Just in time to keep him from being pressed into service in the bucket brigade," Ben commented.

Charlie slathered mustard on a corned beef sandwich. Evidently his appetite hadn't been affected. "Carpal tunnel? Must come from painting all those thousands of picket fences and dead twigs."

"That's what Ann says anyway, and she's known him all her life. They're cousins."

Nobody seemed to know what to say after that. Georgia twisted her wedding rings. Janie handed Charlie a paper napkin when his sandwich dripped mustard on his shirt, and Ben wheeled his chair around, stretched his long legs in front of him and sighed. "What now? We break camp, shut down and go home?"

"He can still talk. He doesn't have to use his wrist to teach," Georgia offered.

Maggie leaned forward, arms crossed on the long wooden table. She didn't want to go home. They were all exhausted, but if they packed up and left, where would Ben go? To his grandmother's house? Back to Texas? She felt like crying, and not only because it was late and she was bone tired.

"I left something in the truck," he said softly. They'd brought in the supplies earlier. "Maggie, how about a short walk to help you sleep?"

"I don't need a walk, thanks. I don't even need to be horizontal, all I need is to let my eyes close." Her lids were already drooping, but she got up and followed him to the door. Dead and in her grave she would probably follow him if he so much as crooked his little finger.

As Perry was fond of saying, Faugh!

Once outside, Ben told her he'd be leaving the next day. "First thing tomorrow, matter of fact." He eyed her uncertainly. When she didn't react, he said, "So I was just wondering…will you be all right?"

Stunned, she took only a moment to recover. "I think I'll stay on for the last couple of days. I'm really getting into this—this art stuff." It was a lie and they both knew it, but it was the best she could do on short notice.

"Maggie? You're sure you're okay?"

What had he expected her to do, throw herself in his arms and beg him never to leave her? She might look like a weakling on the outside, but inside she was tough as nails. "I'm sorry about your grand-mother, but at least maybe she'll enjoy her prints—reproductions—whatever."

Ben nodded. It wasn't Miss Emma's so-called prints he wanted to talk about. He'd already made up his mind to buy them from her, offering her twice what she'd paid. It would just about wipe out his bank account, but what the heck. He could tell her he knew of a man back in Texas who'd be glad to take them off his hands.

He would deal with Miss Emma tomorrow. Right now he had another problem that would never have become a problem if he hadn't suffered a major lapse in judgment. "Maggie, I have to go back to Dry Creek for a few days—maybe even a few weeks—but—"

"That's great! I mean, you must be getting home-sick. I know I would be if I had to—well, anyway, just drive safe, all right?"

He'd be flying, not driving. Not that he bothered to correct her. Before she turned away he saw a sus-picion of tears in her eyes.

Sweet Jesus, he didn't want to hurt this woman, but if he told her why he had to leave, he'd have to tell her the whole ugly story. He'd just as soon not leave her with that impression. Until he dealt with the past, though, he couldn't afford to think about the future.

"It's been a long day," she said with quiet dignity, and he watched her walk back to the shabby old man-sion. She stumbled only once on the steep, graveled path.

"Damned shoes," he swore softly. She wasn't

fooling anyone, and he had a feeling she knew it. Maggie wasn't a pretender. She was a straight-shooter. She expected the same of the people she let herself get close to, and God knows, they'd been close. So close it was threatening to undermine everything he'd always taken for granted. Such as being married to a cop was a high-risk position for any woman.

He waited until she was inside, then he called on his cell phone and booked his flight. Packing wouldn't take long. He had a few more goodbyes to say, but those would wait until morning. Whereas with Maggie...

Had she believed him when he said he'd be back?

Had he believed himself?

"Damn Ben Hunter, anyway." Maggie stumbled over the sandals she'd just kicked off. Why couldn't he have had the decency to ignore her? So what if she'd been attracted to him? What woman with a viable hormone wouldn't be? She should have known better than to sleep with him though, especially after dealing with the very same kind of heartbreak practically every week in her column.

Although admittedly, some of the letters were from Mary Rose.

And that was another thing, she thought as she rummaged through her suitcase for some of the snack foods she'd brought with her. Angrily, she bit into a Moon Pie, scattering crumbs down her nonexistent bosom. All things considered, this whole week had been a waste of time. She should have stayed home where at the very least she could have seen that her father ate decent meals and didn't smoke more than the one cigar a day his doctor allowed him.

After a largely sleepless night, Maggie had been tempted to throw her things into her car and take off, but sheer stubbornness prevailed. If she left first, Ben would know why, and that she couldn't have borne. If he'd even greeted her this morning with a smile instead of a wary nod, she might have felt better, but he hadn't. She watched as he spoke to Charlie, to Bea and a few others, and hugged Janie and Georgia.

Not so much as a smile in Maggie's direction.

She stirred a third spoonful of sugar into her breakfast coffee. Fine. They'd said their goodbyes last night, nothing more to be said. She would damn well show a little class if it killed her.

And then Perry showed up in the kitchen. Was it only her imagination, or did he look a bit apprehensive? Probably spent the past few hours poring over the fine print in his liability policy.

Ben cornered him and the two men stepped out into the hall. Maggie strained to hear what was said, but others were talking and she caught only a few words. Ben was speaking quietly, but Perry's voice suddenly cut through the desultory conversation.

"Don't threaten me, dammit! What do you know about anything? You wouldn't know a giclee from a serigraph, you're nothing but a—a security guard!"

Oh ho, she thought—this isn't about last night, after all. Way to go, Texas! She made up her mind on the spot to write a column exposing—

Exposing what? The truth was, she still didn't know enough about the subject to write about it.

Maybe she'd better stick to writing advice to the love-lorn. She definitely knew about being lovelorn, if "lorn" meant being depressed, discouraged and angry all at the same time. If it meant wanting to kick something or throw something, or just curl up and cry until she ran out of tears.

A thin-lipped Perry marched into the studio and slammed the door. Maggie remained in the kitchen, ignoring her cooling cup of coffee. Ben collected the two small bags he'd set by the front door and headed out to his truck.

Maggie watched from the house, her throat aching the way it did just before the hurt spilled over into tears. At least one of them had accomplished something. From now on Perry might not be so quick to offer his pretty pictures as investments. Personally, she couldn't tell the difference between a zircon and a diamond, but if she ever needed money in a hurry, a zircon wouldn't do her much good.

As for Mary Rose, she might just have to learn her lesson the hard way. Any rescuing Maggie did from now on would be strictly through her column.

Halfway to the parking lot she saw Ben drop his bags and turn back toward the house. Without even thinking, she headed outside, across the porch and down the steps.

They met halfway. For one long moment they simply looked at each other. Ben said, "I'll call you."

No you won't, Maggie thought. But she nodded, unable to think of a single thing to say that wouldn't betray her true feelings.

"Maggie, about yesterday…"

The worst actress in the world, she tipped back her

head and laughed. "You mean the food poisoning? What a mess! Thank goodness we ate in town."

Through the studio windows they could hear Perry speaking in triplicate again. Something about "Values, values, values!"

"Write down your phone number for me," he said. "Got a pencil?" She shook her head, so he patted his pockets down and came up with a stubby drawing pencil. "Here's my number. I always have my cell phone with me." He handed her the scrap of paper—a gas station receipt.

"I rarely carry mine," she said, just to be contrary. If she thought he might actually call her, she would sleep with the thing. Bathe with it. But she told him her number and he wrote that down on a card from his billfold.

In whisky-clear eyes, she should have been able to read all sorts of hidden messages. The books always talked about things like that—how a woman could read a man's true thoughts in his eyes.

Maggie couldn't read a blessed thing, maybe because her own eyes were burning with unshed tears. She blurted the first thing she could think of. "You were right—about the forgery, I mean. Ann was signing his name on all those pictures because of his wrist."

Ben nodded.

"That makes it even worse, I guess. I mean..."

"I know what you mean, Maggie." It was as if they were both speaking a foreign language that bore no relation to what was in their minds. At least, none to what Maggie was thinking.

Ben turned to go, then reversed once more. When

he swept her into his arms, her feet actually left the ground. The kiss, as sweet as it was, held more than a touch of desperation. It ended far too quickly.

"Later," he said gruffly, and turned away once again. This time he didn't come back. Maggie watched him all the way to the pickup, watched him open the door and swing himself inside.

Long-legged men, she thought wistfully. Long, lean, strong, graceful—all the beautiful things a man could be. There ought to be a law against them. At the very least, the federal meat inspectors should stamp a warning in purple ink on their sides.

When his dust died away—there wasn't much of it on account of yesterday's rain—she went back inside and actually considered joining the class. Before she did anything else, though, she was going to retrieve her cell phone, in case he thought of something else he wanted to say.

"You're pathetic, you know that?" she muttered.

Just as she reached the room, she heard the quiet buzz of the cell phone she'd left on the dresser. Startled, she stopped dead for an instant, then she nearly broke her neck lunging across the room.

"Hello?" Oh, God, please let him have changed his mind about leaving.

She hadn't even bothered to check the numbers when she heard a familiar voice. "Maggie, where in the world have you been, I've been trying to call you since forever! You'll never guess what's happened!" There was a pause while Maggie tried to swallow her disappointment. And then, "Mag, it's me, Mary Rose. Say something!"

Without waiting, her friend rushed on. "Guess

what, I've lost seven pounds—I know, I know, it's
mostly water weight so far, but my waistband's are
getting loose, and I'm getting a really terrific tan.
There's this new lotion—I'll tell you about it when I
get home. Look, do you think you could make me an
appointment with Zelle for a cut and maybe some
color for two weeks from now? Because, wait'll you
hear—I've met this really neat man…''

Two minutes later Maggie was still holding the tiny
instrument in her hand, staring dumbly at the wall.
''She met this really neat man,'' she repeated softly.
''Well, shoot!''

All the way back to Miss Emma's neat frame house
in Mocksville, Ben thought about his options and the
situation he'd got himself involved in. He'd called his
grandmother last night, letting her know he'd be stopping by before catching a late evening flight from
Greensboro International.

Maybe he should have explained to Maggie why
he had to leave, but then he'd have had to tell her
about the ugly mess he'd left behind. Dammit all to
hell and back, why couldn't someone else have uncovered the truth and turned over the evidence to
I.A.? The thing that worried him most was that
Mercy—the man who had saved his butt when he'd
been a street-smart kid headed down a dead-end
road—Mercy had gone along with it. Maybe he
hadn't been involved personally, but he'd known. He
had to have known. Hell, he'd admitted to just wanting to hang in there 'til he retired to secure his ben-
efits package.

Ben knew he could've told Maggie simply that he

had to go back and testify in a court case, but that he'd be back as soon as the trial was over in case she wanted to pick up where they'd left off, but—

That's where he pulled up short. Even if Maggie was willing, how far down that particular road did he want to go? As far as he was concerned, it was unexplored territory. And while he wasn't a coward, he never liked to go into any situation unprepared.

How the hell did a man prepare for falling in love?

Twelve

Purely because she hated to admit defeat, Maggie stayed to the bitter end. She helped Ann matte the new shipment of reproductions—she called them that deliberately. Soon Ann was calling them that, too. Several would go on display at the end-of-the-workshop exhibit along with two of his originals.

Evidently Ben had spread the word before he left, because she heard Georgia telling one of the librarians that she intended to buy a copy of *Stone Mill in Winter* to hang over the bookcase in her dining room—because she liked it, not because she considered it an investment. Janie entered the conversations, and the print versus original thing was openly discussed.

Ann winked at Maggie and whispered, "I'm glad they know. I couldn't say anything because Aunt Iola, Perry's mama, lent my brother a down payment on his house, and Brother hasn't paid her back yet."

There would be other workshops, other exhibits, and probably other people talked into buying reproductions as an investment. Ben had done all he could, but Maggie hadn't. She still had a column to write.

Ben had left his paints behind, including all his awful attempts at landscape painting. Maggie matted what she considered his best attempt for the exhibit and put the rest of his gear with her own. After tonight's festive ''opening'' she would load her car and get an early start tomorrow.

The celebration was dismal. Not even the wine helped. Charlie claimed he never drank screw-top wines as they gave him headaches. He and Janie were openly holding hands now. Maggie warmed to the thought that they'd been able to put the past behind them and look forward to a new future.

Don't waste time, she wanted to urge. Follow your heart!

But then, who was she to advise anyone? Just because she wrote an advice column...

Faugh, as Perry would say.

The next morning she hugged them all goodbye, even those she hadn't got to know very well. Even Perry. For all his faults, he was probably a competent painter and an excellent teacher. Not that he'd been able to teach her to paint, but at least she knew now that being an artist involved a lot more than splashing paint on a blank piece of paper and calling it art.

Home was just as she'd left it. The lawn needed mowing, the gutters still needed cleaning and there was a sinkful of dirty dishes, despite the fact that they had a dishwasher. Sooner or later she would get around to everything.

Her father wasn't home yet, but then he often worked on Sundays when he could have the office to himself. Maggie checked his room, collected the clothes that needed laundering, stripped his bed and remade it after opening several windows to air out the cigar smoke.

Her own room was just as she'd left it, too. She set up the laptop computer she hadn't bothered to open back at Peddler's Knob, already thinking about the column she would write as soon as she got something cooking for supper.

Her mind still free-ranging over possibilities, she sorted through the mail to see if there was anything for Miss Maggie. Only a single letter from a man wanting to know if a wife was obligated to do all the housework even if she had an outside job.

That one she would definitely answer. She might even invent a few more letters along the same lines to get her point across. As long as both partners were working outside the home, she thought, mentally phrasing her response while she scrubbed sweet potatoes, wrapped them in foil, and shoved them in the oven, then both partners should share equally in household chores.

She was catching up on the news on television later that night when her cell phone buzzed softly from the kitchen where she'd left it. She hurried to answer it before it could wake her father, who had fallen asleep reading the *Journal*.

The minute she heard that familiar gravelly drawl

she stopped breathing. "Maggie? Are you there? Hello?"

"Ben," she exclaimed when she could finally harness her brain to her tongue. "Did you make it home all right? Well, of course you didn't—it's too soon. How long does it take to get there, anyway?"

She forced herself to relax and take a deep breath.

Ignoring her questions, he said, "I wanted to tell you when I'll be back."

"Back as in…?" Her heart knocked out an extra beat.

"Back as in North Carolina. As in a few miles from where you live."

Some five minutes later she punched off and laid her phone aside, still dazed. He was coming back. Not only to see his grandmother, who apparently had discovered eBay and was turning into something of an art dealer, but to see her—Maggie.

Ben had said Miss Emma was making only enough profit to cover the cost of shipping and insurance, but Maggie could tell how proud he was. Not that he'd ever said much about his family, but she had a feeling his early life had been vastly different from her own. Even after her mother had left, she'd had her father, two aunts, an uncle and half a dozen cousins. All Ben had was the woman he called Miss Emma.

"And me," she whispered. "He's coming back, he's coming back," she sang, clasping her arms around herself.

Don't get your hopes up too high, a small voice warned.

In the lounge chair across the living room, her father snored softly. Maggie wondered how he would get along if she left home and moved to Texas. Could she do it?

Too many questions, too few answers. Not even Miss Maggie could predict the future.

It was almost three weeks later when a familiar dark green pickup pulled into the driveway. Maggie was on a ladder dodging oak branches while she cleaned out the gutters. They hadn't been cleaned since last fall. Already small oak trees were sprouting there.

There were a thousand green trucks on the highway, she told herself. A million. Nevertheless, she nearly broke her neck scrambling down the ladder.

"Wait!" Ben yelled, jogging the last few steps. "Don't move!"

Halfway down she froze, but only for a moment. That was all the time it took for him to reach up and grab her around the waist and swing her down into his arms.

"God, I missed you," he said fervently. "Your shoestring's untied."

Ben had taken time only to stop by his grandmother's house, leave his bags and get directions to Maggie's house. Miss Emma said she had a bridge date that night, but she'd leave a casserole in the oven in case he made it back.

Food was the last thing on his mind.

"Ah, Maggie, Maggie, you'll never believe how much I missed you," he growled. Wrapped around him like a honeysuckle vine, her legs around his waist, her arms around his neck, she was either laughing or sobbing, he couldn't tell which. Didn't much care as long as she let him hold her.

"Put me down and kiss me," she ordered.

"The two are not mutually exclusive," he told her, and then he proved it.

A long time later, Maggie told him he might as well stay and meet her father, who had remained downtown for a Chamber of Commerce meeting.

"You need to meet Miss Emma, too. You'll like her. You two are a whole lot alike in some ways."

"Are you going to be here long?" The hesitancy in her voice made him ache.

"Like I told you, I've finished my business in Dry Creek. I'm ready to make a move." He'd ended up having only to give one more written deposition. Several other witnesses had been found and were ready to testify. Chief Mercer had cut a deal, so the case was pretty much in the bag.

It was a lousy ending to some good years in his life—the best years, so far. But he had a strong feeling that was about to change.

"And?" Maggie asked the leading question, sounding half-hopeful, half-fearful. He hadn't come right out and said the words, but she had to know how he felt. Hell, he was here, wasn't he? He'd left his truck in long-term parking at the airport in Greensboro, knowing he would be back. That was a testament to something, wasn't it?

Nearly an hour later, lying on his back with one arm around Maggie, the other propped under his head, Ben studied the smears of green, gray and purple that had been framed and hung where it could be seen from the bed. Frowning, he said, ''That looks kind of familiar. Almost like...''

''Your last masterpiece? It is. The genuine thing, too, and not just a copy. Actually, it's kind of nice, once you stop thinking that it's supposed to look like something.''

If Ben had been in any doubt about what love felt like, that was no longer the case. Lust would carry a man only so far. Love was what carried him the rest of the way.

''The best of both worlds,'' he murmured, burying his face in her hair.

''Is that the title?''

''Yeah,'' he said with a satisfied smile. ''That's the title.''

* * * * *

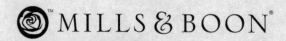

English edition prepared by First Edition Translations Ltd, Great Britain
Designed and produced by AA Publishing

Distributed in the United Kingdom by AA Publishing, Norfolk House,
Priestley Road, Basingstoke, Hampshire RG24 9NY

First published in 1992 as Wat & Hoe Frans,
©Uitgeverij Kosmos bv - Utrecht/Antwerpen
Van Dale Lexicografie bv - Utrecht/Antwerpen

This edition © The Automobile Association 1997

A CIP catalogue record for this book is available from the
British Library .

ISBN: 0 7495 1478 7

Published by AA Publishing (a trading name of Automobile Association
Developments Limited, whose registered office is Norfolk House,
Priestley Road, Basingstoke, Hampshire RG24 9NY.
Registered number 1878835).

Typeset by Anton Graphics Ltd, Andover, Hampshire.

Printed and bound by G. Canale C.SpA, Torino, Italy.

Cover photographs: Kapali Carsi, Istanbul, AA Photo Library
(A. Souter); Military Museum Band, Istanbul, AA Photo Library
(A. Souter); The Blue Mosque, Istanbul, Powerstock Photo Library

Introduction

● **Welcome to the AA's new Essential Phrase Books series, covering the most popular European languages and containing everything you'd expect from a comprehensive language series. They're concise, accessible and easy to understand, and you'll find them indispensable on your trip abroad.**

Each guide is divided into 15 themed sections and starts with a pronunciation table which explains the phonetic pronunciation to all the words and phrases you'll need to know for your trip, while at the back of the book is an extensive word list and grammar guide which will help you construct basic sentences in your chosen language.

Throughout the book you'll come across coloured boxes with a 🗨 beside them. These are designed to help you if you can't understand what your listener is saying to you. Hand the book over to them and encourage them to point to the appropriate answer to the question you are asking.

Other coloured boxes in the book - this time without the symbol - give alphabetical listings of themed words with their English translations beside them.

For extra clarity, we have put all English words and phrases in black, foreign language terms in red and their phonetic pronunciation in italic.

This phrase book covers all subjects you are likely to come across during the course of your visit, from reserving a room for the night to ordering food and drink at a restaurant and what to do if your car breaks down or you lose your traveller's cheques and money. With over 2,000 commonly used words and essential phrases at your fingertips you can rest assured that you will be able to get by in all situations, so let the Essential Phrase Book become your passport to a secure and enjoyable trip!

Pronunciation table

The pronunciation provided should be read as if it were English, bearing in mind the following main points:

Consonants

The Turkish **ğ** (soft g) is not pronounced, but it slightly lengthens the preceding vowel; it is represented as a colon(:).
Mostly, **h** is pronounced as in English, but in some words, there is a different, slightly guttural h sound. This is shown as **H**.
The Turkish **r** is slightly rolled, *and always audibly pronounced*. As a reminder that it should be pronounced every time, when it occurs in the middle or at the end of a word, it is written as **R**.
ç is like the English **ch**.
Ş is the same as **sh** in English.
j is given as **zh**.

Double consonants in Turkish (as in **dükkan**) take twice as long to say as single consonants. The effect is a little like saying them twice. In the transliterated phrases, words with double consonants have been hyphenated as a reminder (eg **res-sam**).

Vowels

a, **e**, **i**, and **o** are pronounced very much as they are in English. Please note that a capital I has a dot over the top like this: **İ**. A capital I without a dot is the upper case form of **ı** (see below).
u is almost exactly like the English sound **oo**.
ı is pronounced rather like the English sound **er** as in 'letter', or the sound **uh**. In the transcriptions it is given as **uh**.
ü is given as **ew**.
ö is transcribed here as **ur**, with a small **r**. *Do not confuse this with the slightly rolled consonant r (shown as **R** in the middle and at the end of words).*

Vowel blends **ai** and **ay** are pronounced like **i** as in 'side'. The symbol **í** is used to represent this sound.

As mentioned above, hyphens have been used to separate double consonants (which are pronounced separately). In other places, hyphens are also used to separate strings of letters which might otherwise be misread (eg **adaya** is read as **ada-ya**, not **aday-a**).

Stress

Turkish words are mostly very lightly stressed – usually on the last syllable. The commonest exception comes with verbs containing the negative *mi* suffix in them, where the stress is thrown back onto the syllable before the **mi**.

Place names have the stress on the first syllable (except for Antalya and Istanbul, where it is on the middle syllable). However, some foreign loan-words (Arabic and Persian) do not conform to Turkish rules at all, and here the stress is shown with bold lettering.

6

Useful lists

Useful lists

Useful lists

1.1 Today or tomorrow?

What day is it today?	Bugün günlerden ne? *boogewn gewnleRden neh?*
Today's Monday	Bugün günlerden pazartesi *boogewn gewnleRden pazaRtesi*
– Tuesday	Bugün günlerden salı *boogewn gewnleRden saluh*
– Wednesday	Bugün günlerden çarşamba *boogewn gewnleRden chaRshamba*
– Thursday	Bugün günlerden perşembe *boogewn gewnleRden peRshembeh*
– Friday	Bugün günlerden cuma *boogewn gewnleRden jooma*
– Saturday	Bugün günlerden cumartesi *boogewn gewnleRden joomaRtesi*
– Sunday	Bugün günlerden pazar *boogewn gewnleRden pazaR*
in January	ocakta *ojakta*
since February	şubattan beri *shoobat-tan beRi*
in spring	ilkbaharda *ilkba-haRda*
in summer	yazın/yazları *yazuhn/yazlaRuh*
in autumn	sonbaharda *sonba-haRda*
in winter	kışın/kışları *kuhshuhn/kuhshlaRuh*
1997	bin dokuz yüz doksan yedi *bin dokooz yewz doksan yedi*
the twentieth century	XX. (yirminci) yüzyıl *yiRminji yewzyuhl*
What's the date today?	Bugün ayın kaçı? *boogewn ayuhn kachuh?*
Today's the 24th	Bugün ayın 24'ü *boogewn ayuhn yiRmi durRdewnjew*
Monday 3 November 1998	Pazartesi, 3 Kasım 1998 *pazaRtesi, ewch kasuhm 1998*
in the morning	sabahleyin *sabaHleyin*
in the afternoon	öğleden sonra *urleden sonRa*
in the evening	akşamleyin *akshamleyin*
at night	geceleyin *gejeleyin*
this morning	bu sabah *boo sabaH*
this afternoon	bugün öğleden sonra *boogewn ur:leden sonRa*
this evening	bu akşam *boo aksham*

8

tonight	bu gece	
	boo gejeh	
last night	dün gece	
	dewn gejeh	
this week	bu hafta	
	boo hafta	
next month	gelecek ay	
	gelejek í	
last year	geçen sene	
	gechen seneh	
next...	gelecek...	
	gelejek...	
in...days/weeks/	...gün/hafta/ay/sene sonra	
months/years	*...gewn/hafta/i/seneh sonRa*	
...weeks ago	...hafta önce	
	...hafta urnjeh	
day off	tatil günü	
	tatil gewnewĕ	

 .2 Bank holidays

● **Public** holidays and **religious** observance:

Public holidays

1 January	Yılbaşı (New Year)
23 April	Ulusal Egemenlik ve Çocuk Bayramı (National Sovereignty and Children's Day)
19 May	Gençlik ve Spor Bayramı (Young People's and Sports Day)
30 August	Zafer Bayramı (Victory Day)
29 October	Cumhuriyet Bayramı (Republic Day)

Major Religious Festivals

The *Şeker Bayramı* (the Feast of Breaking Fast) is a three-day festival marking the end of Ramadan. Its date each year varies with the timing of Ramadan. Information on the precise date should be readily available before you travel.

The *Kurban Bayramı* (the Feast of Sacrifice) follows two months later, and is a four-day celebration which traditionally has been associated with the sacrifice of a ram.

Shops, banks and offices are closed on all these days.

If at any time you should wish to enter a mosque during your visit, be ready to remove your shoes at the entrance. Women should also cover their heads (a headscarf can often be borrowed from the mosque itself). Both shorts and short skirts are inappropriate.

You should also without fail remove your shoes before entering a private house.

.3 What time is it?

What time is it?	Saat kaç?	
	saht kach?	
It's nine o'clock	Saat dokuz	
	saht dokooz	
– five past ten	Saat onu beş geçiyor	
	saht onoo besh gechiyoR	
– a quarter past eleven	Saat on biri çeyrek geçiyor	
	saht on biRi cheyrek gechiyoR	

– twenty past twelve _____	Saat on ikiyi yirmi geçiyor *saht on ikiyi yiRmi gechiyoR*
– half past one _____	Saat bir buçuk *saht biR boochook*
– twenty–five to three _____	Saat üçe yirmi beş var *saht ewcheh yiRmi besh vaR*
– a quarter to four _____	Saat dörde çeyrek var *saht durRdeh cheyRek vaR*
– ten to five _____	Saat beşe on var *saht besheh on vaR*
– twelve noon _____	Öğlen saat on iki *ur:len saht on iki*
– midnight _____	Gece on iki *gejeh on iki*
half an hour _____	yarım saat *yaRuhm saht*
What time? _____	Saat kaçta? *saht kachta?*
What time can I come round? _____	Saat kaçta uğrayayım? *saht kachta u:Ra-ya-yuhm?*
At... _____	Saat...de *saht...deh*
After... _____	den...sonra *den...sonRa*
Before... _____	den...önce *den...urnjeh*
Between...and... _____	...le...arası *...ileh...aRasuh*
From...to... _____	...den...kadar *...den...kadaR*
In...minutes _____	...dakika sonra *...dakika sonRa*
– an hour _____	...saat sonra *...saht sonRa*
– a quarter of an hour _____	On beş dakika sonra *on besh dakika sonRa*
– three quarters of an hour _____	Kırk beş dakika sonra *kuhRk besh dakika sonRa*
early/late _____	çok erken/geç *chok eRken/gech*
on time _____	zamanında *zamanuhnda*
summertime _____	yaz mevsimi *yaz mevsimi*
wintertime _____	kış mevsimi *kuhsh mevsimi*

1.4 One, two, three...

0 _____	sıfır	*suhfuhR*
1 _____	bir	*biR*
2 _____	iki	*iki*
3 _____	üç	*ewch*
4 _____	dört	*durRt*
5 _____	beş	*besh*

6 _____	altı	*altuh*
7 _____	yedi	*yedi*
8 _____	sekiz	*sekiz*
9 _____	dokuz	*dokooz*
10 _____	on	*on*
11 _____	on bir	*on biR*
12 _____	on iki	*on iki*
13 _____	on üç	*on ewch*
14 _____	on dört	*on durRt*
15 _____	on beş	*on besh*
16 _____	on altı	*on altuh*
17 _____	on yedi	*on yedi*
18 _____	on sekiz	*on sekiz*
19 _____	on dokuz	*on dokooz*
20 _____	yirmi	*yiRmi*
21 _____	yirmi bir	*yiRmi biR*
22 _____	yirmi iki	*yiRmi iki*
30 _____	otuz	*otooz*
31 _____	otuz bir	*otooz biR*
32 _____	otuz iki	*otooz iki*
40 _____	kırk	*kuhRk*
50 _____	elli	*el-li*
60 _____	altmış	*altmuhsh*
70 _____	yetmiş	*yetmish*
80 _____	seksen	*seksen*
90 _____	doksan	*oksan*
100 _____	yüz	*yewz*
101 _____	yüz bir	*yewz biR*
110 _____	yüz on	*yewz on*
120 _____	yüz yirmi	*yewz yiRmi*
200 _____	iki yüz	*iki yewz*
300 _____	üç yüz	*ewch yewz*
400 _____	dört yüz	*durRt yewz*
500 _____	beş yüz	*besh yewz*
600 _____	altı yüz	*altuh yewz*
700 _____	yedi yüz	*yedi yewz*
800 _____	sekiz yüz	*sekiz yewz*
900 _____	dokuz yüz	*dokooz yewz*
1000 _____	bin	*bin*
1100 _____	bin yüz	*bin yewz*
2000 _____	iki bin	*iki bin*
10,000 _____	on bin	*on bin*
100,000 _____	yüz bin	*yewz bin*
1,000,000 _____	milyon	*mil-yon*

1st _____	birinci	*biRinji*
2nd _____	ikinci	*ikinji*
3rd _____	üçüncü	*ewchewnjew*
4th _____	dördüncü	*durRdewnjew*
5th _____	beşinci	*beshinji*
6th _____	altıncı	*altuhnjuh*
7th _____	yedinci	*yedinji*
8th _____	sekizinci	*sekizinji*
9th _____	dokuzuncu	*dokoozoonjoo*
10th _____	onuncu	*onoonjoo*
11th _____	on birinci	*on biRinji*

12th	on ikinci	*on ikinji*
13th	on üçüncü	*on ewchewnjew*
14th	on dördüncü	*on durRdewnjew*
15th	on beşinci	*on beshinji*
16th	on altıncı	*on altuhnjuh*
17th	on yedinci	*on yedinji*
18th	on sekizinci	*on sekizinji*
19th	on dokuzuncu	*on dokoozoonjoo*
20th	yirminci	*yiRminji*
21st	yirmi birinci	*yiRmi biRinji*
22nd	yirmi ikinci	*yiRmi ikinji*
30th	otuzuncu	*otoozoonjoo*
100th	yüzüncü	*yewzewnjew*
1000th	bininci	*bininji*

once	bir kere	*biR keReh*
twice	iki kere	*iki keReh*
double	iki katı	*iki katuh*
triple	üç katı	*ewch katuh*
half	yarısı	*yaRuhsuh*
a quarter	dörtte biri	*durRt-teh biRi*
a third	üçte biri	*ewchteh biRi*
a couple, a few, some	bir çift, birkaç, bazı	*biR chift, biRkach, bazuh*

2+4=6	iki artı dört eşittir altı	*iki aRtuh durRt eshit-tiR altuh*
4-2=2	dört eksi iki eşittir iki	*durRt eksi iki eshit-tiR iki*
2x4=8	iki çarpı dört eşittir sekiz	*iki chaRpuh durRt eshit-tiR sekiz*
4÷2=2	dört bölü iki eşittir iki	*durRt burlew iki eshit-tiR iki*
odd/even	tek/çift	*tek/chift*
total	toplam	*toplam*
6x9	altı çarpı dokuz	*altuh chaRpuh dokooz*

🕐 .5 The weather

Is the weather going to be good/bad?	Hava güzel mi/kötü mü olacak?	*hava gewzel mi/kurtew mew olajak?*
Is it going to get colder/hotter?	Hava soğuk mu/sıcak mı olacak?	*hava so:ook moo/suhjak muh olajak?*
What temperature is it going to be?	Hava kaç derece olacak?	*hava kach deRejeh olajak?*
Is it going to rain?	Yağmur mu yağacak?	*ya:mooR moo ya:ajak?*

Is there going to be a ___ storm?	Hava fırtınalı mı olacak?	
	hava fuhRtuhnaluh muh olajak?	
Is it going to snow? ___	Kar mı yağacak?	
	kahR muh ya:ajak?	
Is it going to freeze? ___	Don mu olacak?	
	don moo olajak?	
Is the thaw setting in? ___	Buzlar mı eriyecek?	
	boozlaR muh eRiyejek?	
Is it going to be foggy? ___	Hava sisli mi olacak?	
	hava sisli mi olajak?	
Is there going to be a ___ thunderstorm?	Fırtına mı çıkacak?	
	fuhRtuhna muh chuhkajak?	
The weather's changing ___	Hava değişiyor	
	hava de:ishiyoR	
It's cooling down ___	Hava soğuyor	
	hava so:ooyor	
What's the weather going to be like today/ tomorrow?	Bugün/yarın hava nasıl olacak?	
	Boogewn/yaruhn hava nasuhl olajak?	

aniden şiddetlenen rüzgar	güneşli	sağanak yağış
sudden squall	**sunny**	**heavy downpour**
az bulutlu	güzel	serin
almost cloudless	**beautiful**	**cool**
boğucu sıcaklık	hafif/şiddetli rüzgar	sıcak
stifling heat	**light/strong wind**	**hot**
bulut	ılımlı	sıcak hava dalgası
cloud	**moderate**	**heat wave**
bunaltıcı	kar	(sıfırın altında/üstünde)
oppressive	**snow**	...derece
çok bulutlu	kasırga	**...degrees below/above**
very cloudy	**cyclone,**	**zero**
dolu	**hurricane**	sis
hail	kırağı	**fog**
don	**hoar frost**	yağmur
ice	parçalı bulutlu	**rain**
fırtına	**with patchy cloud**	yağmurlu
storm	rüzgar	**rainy**
fırtınalı	**wind**	
stormy	rüzgarlı	
	windy	

.6 Here, there...

See also 5.1 Asking for directions

here/there ___	burada/orada
	booRada/oRada
somewhere/nowhere ___	herhangi bir yerde/hiç bir yerde
	heRhangi biR yeRdeh/hich biR yeRdeh
everywhere ___	her yerde
	heR yeRdeh
far away/nearby ___	uzak/yakın
	oozak/yakuhn

Useful lists

right/left	sağ/sol
	sa:/sol
to the right/left of	sağında/solunda
	sa:uhnda/soloonda
straight ahead	doğru
	do:Roo
via	...yoluyla
	...yolooyla
in	...içine/içinde
	...ichineh/ichindeh
on	...üzerine/üzerinde
	...ewzeRineh/ewzeRindeh
under	...altına/altında
	...altuhna/altuhnda
against	...karşı
	...kaRshuh
opposite	karşısında
	kaRshuhsuhnda
next to	...yanında
	...yanuhnda
near	...yakın
	...yakuhn
in front of	...önünde
	...urnewndeh
in the centre	ortada
	oRtada
forward	öne
	urneh
down	aşağı (aşağıya)
	asha:uh (asha:uh-ya)
up	yukarı (yukarıya)
	yookaRuh (yookaRuh-ya)
inside	içeri (içeriye)
	icheRi (icheRiyeh)
outside	dışarı (dışarıya)
	duhshaRuh (duhshaRuh-ya)
behind	arka (arkaya)
	aRka (aRka-ya)
at the front	ön tarafta
	urn taRafta
at the back	arka tarafta
	aRka taRafta
in the north	kuzeyde
	koozeydeh
to the south	güneye
	gewneyeh
from the west	batıdan
	batuhdan
from the east	doğudan
	do:oodan
...of	...de/da
	...-deh/-da

.7 What does that sign say?

See also 5.4 Traffic signs

açık/kapalı	fotoğraf çekmek	pasaj
open/closed	yasaktır	arcade
acil çıkış	**no photographs**	peron
emergency exit	giriş	platform
açılış saatleri	**entrance**	PTT
opening hours	girmek yasaktır	PTT (main post office
asansör	**no entry, no admittance**	and public
lift	gişe, vezne	telephones)
ateş yakmak yasaktır	**pay here**	resepsiyon
no open fires	istasyon	**reception**
bayanlar tuvaleti	**station**	satılık
ladies toilet	itiniz/çekiniz	**for sale**
bozuk	**push/pull**	seyahat acentası
out of order	kalkış	**travel agent**
çay bahçesi	**departure**	sigara içmek yasaktır
tea garden	kamping	**no smoking**
çıkış	**camping, camp-site**	tehlike
way out	karakol	**danger**
danışma, enformasyon	**police station**	tuvaletler
information	kasa	**toilets**
dikkat	**pay here**	vestiyer
take care, beware	...kat	**cloakroom**
dikkat köpek var	**...floor**	yangın merdiveni
beware of the dog	kiralık	**fire escape**
dolu	**for hire**	yangın tehlikesi
full	merdiven	**danger - fire**
durak	**stairs**	yerlere tükürmeyiniz
(bus) stop	merkez	**no spitting**
emanet	**centre**	yüksek voltaj
left luggage	otel	**high voltage**
erkekler tuvaleti	**hotel**	yürüyen merdiven
gentlemen's toilet	pansiyon	**escalator**
	bed and breakfast	

 .8 Telephone alphabet

a	*ah*	Adana	*adana*
b	*beh*	Bursa	*booRsa*
c	*jeh*	Cide	*jideh*
ç	*cheh*	Çanakkale	*chanak- kaleh*
d	*deh*	Denizli	*denizli*
e	*eh*	Edirne	*ediRneh*
f	*feh*	Fethiye	*fet-hiyeh*
g	*geh*	Giresun	*giResoon*
ğ	*yoomooshak geh (no Turkish words begin with ğ)*		
h	*heh*	Hatay	*hatí*
i	*i*	İzmir	*izmiR*
ı	*uh*	Isparta	*uhspaRta*

15

l	*leh*	Lüleburgaz	*lewlebooRgaz*
m	*meh*	Malatya	*malatya*
n	*neh*	Nevşehir	*nevshe-hiR*
o	*o*	Ordu	*oRdoo*
ö	*ur*	Ören	*urRen*
p	*peh*	Pamukkale	*pamook-kaleh*
r	*reh*	Rize	*rizeh*
s	*seh*	Sinop	*sinop*
ş	*sheh*	Şirvan	*shiRvan*
t	*teh*	Tokat	*tokat*
u	*oo*	Urfa	*ooRfa*
ü	*ew*	Üsküp	*ewskewp*
v	*veh*	Van	*van*
y	*yeh*	Yozgat	*yozgat*
z	*zeh*	Zonguldak	*zongooldak*

🕐 .9 Personal details

surname _____	soyadı *soy-aduh*
forename(s) _____	adı *aduh*
initials _____	ismin baş harfleri *ismin bash haRfleRi*
address (street/number) ___	adres (sokak/numara) *adRes (sokak/noomaRa)*
post code/town _____	posta kodu/oturduğu yer *posta kodoo/otooRdoo:oo yeR*
sex (male/female) _____	cinsiyeti (erkek, kadın) *jinsiyeti (eRkek/kaduhn)*
nationality _____	uyruğu *ooyRoo:oo*
date of birth _____	doğum tarihi *do:oom tahRi-hi*
place of birth _____	doğum yeri *do:oom yeRi*
occupation _____	mesleği *mesle:i*
married/single/divorced ___	evli/bekar/boşanmış *evli/bekahR/boshanmuhsh*
widowed _____	dul *dool*
(number of) children _____	çocukları (sayısı) *chojooklaRuh (sa-yuhsuh)*
passport/identity _____ card/driving licence number	pasaport/ehliyet numarası *pasapoRt/eHliyet noomaRasuh*
place and date of issue ___	verildiği tarih ve yer *veRildi:i taRiH veh yeR*

Courtesies

Courtesies

● Greetings are very popular, everyone is asked individually if they're all right. When introduced people shake hands, when they part they also shake hands.

If they know each other people kiss on both cheeks (usually man to man, woman to woman).

.1 Greetings

Hello, Mr John Smith	Merhaba John Bey *meR-haba John Bey*
Hello, Mrs Barbara Jones	Merhaba Barbara Hanim *meR-haba, Barbara Hanuhm*
Hello, Peter	Merhaba, Peter *meR-haba, Peter*
Hi, Helen	Selam, Helen *selam, Helen*
Good morning, madam	Günaydın hanımefendi *gewníduhn hanuhmefendi*
Good afternoon, sir	İyi günler beyefendi *iyi gewnleR bey-efendi*
Good evening	İyi akşamlar *iyi akshamlaR*
How are you?	Nasılsınız, iyi misiniz? *nasuhlsuhnuhz, iyi misiniz?*
Fine, thank you, and you?	Teşekkür ederim. Siz nasılsınız? *teshek-kewR edeRim. siz nasuhlsuhnuhz?*
Very well	Çok iyiyim, teşekkür ederim *chok iyiyim, teshek-kewR edeRim*
Not very well	İyi değilim *iyi de:ilim*
Not too bad	İdare eder *idaReh edeR*
I'd better be going	Ben gideyim artık *ben gideyim aRtuhk*
I have to be going	Gitmek zorundayım. Beni bekliyorlar *gitmek zoRoonda-yim. beni bekli-yoRlaR*
Someone's waiting for me Bye!	Görüşürüz! *gurRewshewRewz!*
Goodbye	Güle güle/Allaha ısmarladık *gewleh gewleh/al-laha uhsmaRladuhk*
See you soon	görüşmek üzere *gurRewshmek ewzeReh*
See you later	Sonra görüşmek üzere *sonRa gurRewshmek ewzeReh*
See you in a little while	En kısa zamanda görüşmek üzere *en kuhsa zamanda gurRewshmek ewzeReh*
Sleep well	İyi uykular *iyi ooykoolaR*
Good night	İyi geceler *iyi gejeleR*
All the best	Sağlıcakla kalın *sa:luhjakla kaluhn*
Have fun	İyi eğlenceler *iyi e:lenjeleR*

Good luck _____	İyi şanslar	
	iyi shanslaR	
Have a nice holiday _____	İyi tatiller	
	iyi tatil-leR	
Have a good trip _____	İyi yolculuklar	
	iyi yoljoolooklaR	
Thank you, you too_____	Teşekkürler, size de	
	teshek-kewRleR, sizeh deh	
Say hello to...for me_____	e... selamlarımı söyleyin	
	selamlaRuhmuh suhy-leh-yin	

.2 How to ask a question

Who?_____	Kim?	
	kim	
Who's that? _____	O kim?	
	o kim?	
What? _____	Ne?	
	neh?	
What's there to_____	Burada görülecek ne var?	
see here?	*booRada gurRewlejek neh vaR?*	
What kind of hotel_____	O nasıl bir otel?	
is that?	*o nasuhl biR otel?*	
Where? _____	Nerede?	
	neRedeh?	
Where's the toilet? _____	Tuvalet ne tarafta?	
	too-alet neh taRafta?	
Where are you going? _____	Nereye gidiyorsunuz?	
	neRe-yeh gidiyoRsoonooz?	
Where are you from? _____	Nerelisiniz?	
	neRelisiniz?	
How?_____	Nasıl?	
	nasuhl?	
How far is that? _____	Orası ne kadar uzak?	
	oRasuh neh kadaR oozak?	
How long does that take? _	Ne kadar sürer?	
	neh kadaR sewReR?	
How long is the trip? _____	Yolculuk ne kadar sürer?	
	yoljoolook neh kadaR sewReR?	
How much?_____	Ne kadar?	
	neh kadaR?	
How much is this?_____	Bunun fiyatı ne kadar?	
	boonoon fi-yatuh neh kadaR?	
What time is it? _____	Saat kaç?	
	saht kach?	
Which? _____	Hangi? Hangileri?	
	hangi? hangileRi?	
Which glass is mine? _____	Hangi bardak benim?	
	hangi baRdak benim?	
When? _____	Ne zaman?	
	neh zaman?	
When are you leaving? ____	Yola ne zaman çıkıyorsunuz?	
	yola neh zaman chuhkuh-yoRsoonooz?	
Why?_____	Niçin?	
	nichin?	
Could you...me?_____	Bana...?	
	bana...?	

Courtesies

19

Courtesies

Could you help me, _____ please?	Bana yardım edebilir misiniz? *bana yaRduhm edebiliR misiniz?*
Could you point that _____ out to me?	Onu bana gösterebilir misiniz? *onoo bana gursteRebiliR misisniz?*
Could you come _____ with me, please?	Benimle gelebilir misiniz? *benimleh beRabeR gelebiliR misiniz?*
Could you... _____	...-ir misiniz?/mısınız? *...-iR misiniz?/muhsuhnuz?*
Could you reserve some _____ tickets for me, please?	Benim için birkaç bilet ayırır mısınız, lütfen? *benim ichin biRkach bilet í-uhRuhR muhsuhnuhz?*
Do you know...? _____	...biliyor musunuz? *...biliyoR moosoonooz?*
Do you know another _____ hotel, please?	Başka bir otel biliyor musunuz? *bashka biR otel biliyoR moosoonooz?*
Do you have a...? _____	...var mı? *...vaR muh?*
Do you have a...for me? _____	Benim için...var mı? *benim ichin...vaR muh?*
Do you have a _____ vegetarian dish, please?	Etsiz bir yemeğiniz var mı? *etsiz bir yeme:iniz vaR muh?*
I'd like... _____	...istiyorum *...istiyoRoom*
I'd like a kilo of apples, _____ please	Bir kilo elma istiyorum *biR kilo elma istiyoRoom*
Can I...? _____	abilir/ebilir miyim? *-abiliR/-ebiliR miyim?*
Can I take this? _____	Bunu alabilir miyim? *boonoo alabiliR miyim?*
Can I smoke here? _____	Burada sigara içebilir miyim? *booRada sigaRa ichebiliR miyim?*
Could I ask you _____ something?	Bir şey sorabilir miyim? *BiR shey soRabiliR mi-yim?*

2 .3 How to reply

Yes, of course _____	Evet, tabii *evet tabee*
No, I'm sorry _____	Hayır, özür dilerim *ha-yuhR urzewR dileRim*
Yes, what can I do _____ for you?	Evet, size nasıl yardımcı olabilirim? *evet, sizeh nasuhl yaRduhmjuh olabiliRim?*
Just a moment, please _____	Bir saniye lütfen *biR sahniyeh lewtfen*
No, I don't have _____ time now	Hayır, şu anda hiç zamanım yok *ha-yiR shoo anda hich zamanuhm yok*
No, that's impossible _____	Hayır, imkansız *ha-yuhR imkahnsuhz*
I think so _____	Zannederim *zan-nedeRim*
I agree _____	Bence de *benjeh deh*
I hope so too _____	Umarım *oomaRuhm*
No, not at all _____	Hayır *ha-yuhR*
No, no-one _____	Hayır, hiç kimse *ha-yuhR hich kimseh*

No, nothing	Hayır, hiç bir şey
	ha-yuhR hich biR shey
That's (not) right	Doğru (doğru değil)
	do:Roo (do:Roo de:il)
I (don't) agree	Sizinle aynı fikirdeyim (fikirde değilim)
	sizinleh ıynuh fikiRdeyim (fikiRdeh de:ilim)
All right	İyi
	iyi
Okay	Tamam
	tamam
Perhaps	Belki
	belki
I don't know	Bilmiyorum
	bilmiyoRoom

2.4 Thank you

Thank you	Teşekkür ederim
	teshek-kewR edeRim
You're welcome	Bir şey değil
	biR shey de:il
Thank you very much	Çok teşekkür ederim
	chok teshek-kewR edeRim
Very kind of you	Çok naziksiniz
	chok naziksiniz
I enjoyed it very much	Benim için büyük bir zevkti
	benim ichin bew-yewk biR zevkti
Thank you for your trouble	Zahmet ettiniz, teşekkür ederim
	zaHmet et-tiniz, teshek-kewR edeRim
You shouldn't have	Bunu yapmamalıydınız
	boonoo yapmamaluhy-duhnuhz
That's all right	Hiç önemli değil
	hich urnemli de:il

2.5 Sorry

Sorry!	Pardon!
	paRdon!
Excuse me	Özür dilerim
	urzewR dileRim
I'm sorry, I didn't know...	Özür dilerim, ... bilmiyordum
	urzewR dileRim ... bilmiyoRdoom
I do apologise	Affedersiniz
	af-fedeRsiniz
I'm sorry	Çok üzgünüm
	chok ewzgewnewm
I didn't do it on purpose, it was an accident	Kasten yapmadım, yanlışlıkla oldu
	kasten yapmaduhm, yanluhshluhkla oldoo
That's all right	Önemli değil
	urnemli de:il
Never mind	Boş ver
	bosh veR
It could've happened to anyone	Herkesin başına gelebilir
	heRkesin bashuhna gelebiliR

.6 What do you think?

Which do you prefer?_____	Neyi tercih edersiniz? *neyi teRji-hedeRsiniz?*
What do you think?_____	Ne dersiniz? *neh deRsiniz?*
Don't you like dancing? ____	Dans etmeyi sevmiyor musun? *dans etmeyi sevmiyoR moosoon?*
I don't mind_____	Benim için fark etmez *benim ichin faRk etmez*
Well done! _____	Bravo! *bRavo!*
Not bad!_____	Fena değil! *fena de:il!*
Great! _____	Şahane! *sha-haneh!*
Wonderful! _____	Harika! *haRika!*
It's really nice here! _____	Burası ne eğlenceli! *booRasuh neh e:lenjili!*
How nice! _____	Ne hoş/güzel! *neh hosh/gewzel!*
How nice for you! _____	Sizin için ne iyi! *sizin ichin neh iyi!*
I'm (not) very happy_____ with...	...çok memnunum (memnun değilim) *...chok memnoonoom (memnoon de:ilim)*
I'm glad..._____	...memnun oldum *...memnoon oldoom*
I'm having a great time ____	Çok eğleniyorum *chok e:leniyoroom*
I'm looking forward to it ___	Sabırsızlıkla bekliyorum *sabuhRsuhzluhkla bekliyoRoom*
I hope it'll work out_____	Umarım olur *oomaRuhm oloor*
That's ridiculous!_____	Ne gülünç! *neh gewlewnch!*
That's terrible! _____	Ne iğrenç! *neh i:Rench!*
What a pity! _____	Ne yazık! *neh yazuhk!*
That's filthy! _____	Ne pis! *ne pis!*
What a load of rubbish! ___	Ne saçmalık! *neh sachmaluhk!*
I don't like..._____	...sevmiyorum *...sevmiyoRoom*
I'm bored to death _____	Canım çok sıkılıyor *januhm chok suhkuhluhyoR*
I've had enough_____	Bıktım *buhktuhm*
This is no good _____	Bu böyle olmaz *boo buhyleh olmaz*
I was expecting _____ something completely different	Tamamen başka bir şey bekliyordum *tamahmen bashka biR shey bekliyoRdoom*

Courtesies

22

Conversation

3 Conversation

3.1 I beg your pardon?

I don't speak any/ I speak a little...	...konuşmasını bilmiyorum/...biraz biliyorum *...konooshmasuhnuh bilmiyoRoom/...biRaz biliyoRoom*
I'm English	Ben İngilizim *ben ingilizim*
I'm Scottish	Ben İskoçyalıyım *ben iskochyaluh-yuhm*
I'm Irish	Ben İrlandalıyım *ben iRlandaluh-yuhm*
I'm Welsh	Ben Gallerliyim *ben gal-leRliyim*
Do you speak English/French/German?	İngilizce/Fransızca/Almanca konuşmasını biliyor musunuz? *ingilizje/fransuhzja/almanja konooshmasuhnuh biliyoR moosoonooz?*
Is there anyone who speaks...?	...konuşmasını bilen kimse var mı? *...konushmasuhnuh bilen kimseh var muh?*
I beg your pardon?	Ne dediniz? *neh dediniz?*
I (don't) understand	Sizi anlıyorum (anlamıyorum) *sizi anluhyoRoom (anlamuhyoRoom)*
Do you understand me?	Beni anlıyor musunuz? *beni anluhyoR moosoonooz?*
Could you repeat that, please?	Lütfen tekrar eder misiniz? *lewtfen tekRaR edeR misiniz?*
Could you speak more slowly, please?	Biraz daha yavaş konuşabilir misiniz? *biRaz da-ha yavash konooshabiliR misiniz?*
What does that (word) mean?	O/o sözcük ne demek? *o/o surzjewk neh demek?*
Is that similar to/the same as...?	...(hemen hemen) aynısı mı? *...(hemen hemen) ihnuhsuh muh?*
Could you write that down for me, please?	Onu benim için bir kağıda yazabilir misiniz? *onoo benim ichin biR ka:uhda yazabiliR misiniz?*
Could you spell that for me, please? *(See 1.8 Telephone alphabet)*	Onu benim için heceleyebilir misiniz? *onoo benim ichin hejeleyebiliR misiniz?*
Could you point that out in this phrase book, please?	Onu bana bu rehberde gösterebilir misiniz? *onoo bana boo reHbeRdeh gursteRebiliR misiniz?*
One moment, please, I have to look it up	Bir saniye, sözcüğü aramam gerek *biR sahniyeh, surzjew:ew aRamam geRek*
I can't find the word/the sentence	Sözcüğü/cümleyi bulamıyorum *surzjew:ew/jewmleyi boolamuhyoRoom*
How do you say that in...?	...ona ne diyorsunuz? *...ona neh diyoRsoonooz?*
How do you pronounce that?	Onu nasıl telaffuz ediyorsunuz? *onoo nasuhl telaf-fooz ediyoRsoonooz*

24

 **.2** Introductions

May I introduce myself? ___	Kendimi tanıtabilir miyim?
	kendimi tanuhtabiliR miyim?
My name's... _____	Benim adım...
	benim aduhm..
I'm... _____	Ben...
	ben...
What's your name? _____	Adınız ne?
	aduhnuhz neh?
May I introduce...? _____	Size...tanıtabilir miyim?
	size...tanuhtabiliR miyim?
This is my wife/ _____	Bu benim eşim/kızım/annem/kız arkadaşım.
daughter/mother/girlfriend	*boo benim eshim/kuhzuhm/an-nem/kuhz aRkadashuhm*
– my husband/son/ _____	Bu benim eşim/oğlum/babam/erkek arkadaşım.
father/boyfriend	*boo benim eshim/o:loom/babam/eRkek aRkadashuhm*
How do you do _____	Memnum oldum
	memnoom oldoom
Pleased to meet you_____	(Tanıştığımıza) memnun oldum
	(tanuhshtuh:uhmuhza) memnoon oldoom
Where are you from? _____	Nerelisiniz?
	neRelisiniz?
I'm from _____	Ben İngilizim/İskoçyalıyım/İrlandalıyım/
England/Scotland/Ireland/	Gallerliyim
Wales	*ben ingilizim/iskochyaluh-yuhm/iRlandaluh-yuhm/gal-leRliyim*
What city do you live in?___	Hangi şehirde oturuyorsunuz?
	hangi she-hiRdeh otooRooyoRsoonooz?
In..., It's near... _____	..., ...yakın
	..., ...yakuhn
Have you been here _____	Uzun zamandan beri mi buradasınız?
long?	*oozoon zamandan beRi mi booRadasuhnuhz?*
A few days _____	Birkaç günden beri buradayım
	biRkach gewnden beRi booRada-yuhm
How long are you _____	Burada ne kadar kalacaksınız?
staying here?	*booRada neh kadaR kalajaksuhnuhz?*
We're (probably) leaving___	(Büyük bir olasılıkla) yarın/iki hafta sonra yola
tomorrow/in two weeks	çıkacağız
	bewyewk biR olasuhluhkla yaRuhn/iki hafta sonRa yola chuhkaja:uhz
Where are you staying?____	Nerede kalıyorsunuz?
	neRedeh kaluhyoRsoonooz?
In a hotel/an apartment ___	Bir otelde/apartman dairesinde
	biR oteldeh/apaRtaman díResindeh
On a camp site_____	Bir kampingde
	biR kampingdeh
With friends/relatives _____	Bir arkadaşın/ailenin yanında
	biR aRkadashuhn/ílenin yanuhnda
Are you here on your_____	Burada yalnız mısınız?/ailenizle misiniz?
own/with your family?	*booRada yalnuhz muhsuhnuhz?/ilenizleh misiniz?*
I'm on my own_____	Yalnızım
	yalnuhzuhm
I'm with my_____	Eşimleyim
partner/wife/husband	*eshimleyim*

Conversation

25

– with my family	Ailemleyim	*ilemleyim*
– with relatives	Akrabalarlayım	*akRabalaRla-yuhm*
– with a boyfriend/girlfriend/ friends	Erkek arkadaşımlayım/kız arkadaşımlayım/arkadaşlarımlayım	*eRkek aRkadashuhmla-yuhm/kuhz aRkadashuhmla-yuhm/aRkadashlaRuhmla-yuhm*
Are you married?	Evli misiniz?	*evli misiniz?*
Do you have a steady boyfriend/girlfriend?	Erkek/kız arkadaşın var mı?	*eRkek/kuhz aRkadasuhn vaR muh?*
That's none of your business	Sizi ilgilendirmez	*sizi ilgilendiRmez*
I'm married	Evliyim	*evliyim*
– single	Bekarım	*be**kah**Ruhm*
– separated	Eşimden ayrı yaşıyorum	*eshimden íruh yashuhyoRoom*
– divorced	Boşandım	*boshanduhm*
– a widow/widower	Dulum	*dooloom*
I live alone/with someone	Yalnız/biriyle beraber yaşıyorum	*yalnuhz/biRiyleh beRabeR yashuhyoRoom*
Do you have any children/grandchildren?	Çocuklarınız/torunlarınız var mı?	*chojooklaRuhnuhz/toRoonlaRuhnuhz vaR muh?*
How old are you?	Kaç yaşındasınız?	*kach yashuhndasuhnuhz?*
How old is she/he?	O kaç yaşında?	*o kach yashuhnda?*
I'm...	...yaşındayım	*...yashuhnda-yuhm*
She's/he's...	O...yaşında	*o...yashuhnda*
What do you do for a living?	Ne iş yaparsınız?	*neh ish yapaRsuhnuhz?*
I work in an office	Bir büroda çalışıyorum	*biR bewRoda chaluhshuhyoRoom*
I'm a student/ I'm at school	Okuyorum	*okooyoRoom*
I'm unemployed	İşsizim	*ishsizim*
I'm retired	Emekliyim	*emekliyim*
I'm on a disability pension	İş görmezlik sigortasından para alıyorum	*ish gurRmezlik sigoRtasuhndan paRa aluhyoRoom*
I'm a housewife	Ev kadınıyım	*ev kaduhnuh-yuhm*
Do you like your job?	İşinizi seviyor musunuz?	*ishinizi seviyoR moosoonooz?*
Most of the time	Çoğu zaman	*cho:oo zaman*
I usually do, but I prefer holidays	Genellikle seviyorum, ama tatil daha eğlenceli	*genel-likleh seviyoRoom ama tatil da-ha e:lenjeli*

3.3 Starting/ending a conversation

Could I ask you _____ something?	Size bir şey sorabilir miyim? *sizeh biR shey soRabiliR miyim?*
Excuse me _____	Özür dilerim *urzewR dileRim*
Excuse me, could you _____ help me?	Özür dilerim, bana yardım edebilir misiniz? *urzewR dileRim, bana yaRduhm edebiliR misiniz?*
Yes, what's the problem? _____	Evet, sorun ne? *evet, soRun neh?*
What can I do for you? _____	Size ne şekilde yardımcı olabilirim? *sizeh neh shekildeh yaRduhmjuh olabiliRim?*
Sorry, I don't have time _____ now	Kusura bakmayın, şu anda hiç zamanım yok *koosooRa bakma-yuhn, shoo anda hich zamanuhm yok*
Do you have a light? _____	Ateşiniz var mı? *ateshiniz vaR muh?*
May I join you? _____	Yanınıza oturabilir miyim? *yanuhnuhza otooRabiliR miyim?*
Could you take a _____ picture of me/us? Press this button	Resmimi/resmimizi çeker misiniz? Bu düğmeye basın *resmimi/resmimizi chekeR misiniz? bu dew:meyeh basuhn*
Leave me alone _____	Beni rahat bırak *beni rahat buhRak*
Get lost _____	Çekil git *chekil git*
Go away or I'll scream _____	Gitmezseniz, bağırırım *gitmezseniz ba:uhRuhRuhm*

3.4 Congratulations and condolences

Happy birthday/many _____ happy returns	Doğum gününüz kutlu olsun *do:oom gewnewnewz kootloo olsoon*
Please accept my _____ condolences	Başınız sağ olsun *bashuhnuhz sa: olsoon*
I'm very sorry for you _____	Sizin için çok üzgünüm *sizin ichin chok ewzgewnewm*

3.5 A chat about the weather

See also 1.5 The weather

It's so hot/cold today! _____	Bugün hava ne kadar sıcak/soğuk! *boogewn hava neh kadaR suhjak/so:ook*
Nice weather, isn't it? _____	Hava güzel, değil mi? *hava gewzel, de:il mi?*
What a wind/storm! _____	Bu ne rüzgar/fırtına! *boo neh rewzgaR/fuhRtuhna!*
All that rain/snow! _____	Bu ne yağmur/kar! *boo neh ya:mooR/kahR!*
All that fog! _____	Bu ne sis! *boo neh sis!*
Has the weather been _____ like this for long here?	Hava uzun zamandan beri mi böyle? *hava oozoon zamandan beRi mi buhyleh?*

Conversation

3

Is it always this hot/cold here?	Burası her zaman mı bu kadar sıcak/soğuk?
	booRasuh heR zaman muh boo kadaR suhjak/so:ook?
Is it always this dry/wet here?	Burası her zaman mı bu kadar kurak/yağışlı?
	booRasuh heR zaman muh boo kadaR kooRak/ya:uhshluh?

.6 Hobbies

Do you have any hobbies?	Boş zamanlarınızı nasıl değerlendirirsiniz?
	bosh zamanlaRuhnuhz nasuhl de:eRlendiRiRsiniz?
I like painting/ reading/photography/ DIY	Resim yapmayı/kitap okumayı/fotoğraf çekmeyi/ufak tefek tamir işleri ile uğraşmayı severim
	urRgew urRmeyi/kitap okooma-yuh/foto:Raf chekmeyi/ufak tefek tahmir ishleRi ileh oo:Rashma-yuh seveRim
I like music	Müzik dinlemeyi severim
	mewzik dinlemeyi seveRim
I like playing the guitar/piano	Gitar/piyano çalmayı severim
	gitaR/piyano chalma-yuh seveRim
I like going to the movies	Sinemaya gitmeyi severim
	sinema-ya gitmeyi seveRim
I like travelling/ sport/fishing/walking	Seyahat etmeyi/spor yapmayı/balık tutmayı/yürümeyi severim
	seyahat etmeyi/spoR yapma-yuh/baluhk tootma-yuh/yewRewmeyi seveRim

.7 Being the host(ess)

See also 4 Eating out

Can I offer you a drink?	Size içecek bir şey ikram edebilir miyim?
	sizeh ichejek biR shey ikRahm edebiliR miyim?
What would you like to drink?	Ne içersiniz?
	neh icheRsiniz?
Something non-alcoholic, please	Alkolsüz bir şey, lütfen
	alkolsewz biR shey, lewtfen
Would you like a cigarette/cigar/to roll your own?	Sigara/puro/sarma sigara içer misiniz?
	sigaRa/pooRo/saRma sigaRa icheR misiniz?
I don't smoke	Sigara kullanmam
	sigaRa kul-lanmam

.8 Invitations

Are you doing anything tonight?	Bu akşam meşgul müsünüz?
	boo aksham meshgool mewsewnewz?
Do you have any plans for today/this afternoon/tonight?	Bugün/bugün öğleden sonra/bu akşam için planlarınız var mı?
	boogewn/boogewn ur:leden sonRa/boo aksham ichin planlaRuhnuhz vaR muh?
Would you like to go out with me?	Benimle çıkmak ister misiniz?
	benimleh chuhkmak isteR misiniz?
Would you like to go dancing with me?	Benimle dansa gelmek ister misiniz?
	benimleh dansa gelmek isteR misiniz?

Would you like to have ____ lunch/dinner with me?	Benimle öğle yemeğe/akşam yemeğe çıkmak ister misiniz?
	benimleh ur:leh yeme:eh/aksham yeme:eh chuhkmak isteR misiniz?
Would you like to come____ to the beach with me?	Benimle plaja gelmek ister misiniz?
	benimleh plazha gelmek isteR misiniz?
Would you like to come____ into town with us?	Bizimle şehire inmek ister misiniz?
	bizimleh sheh-hireh inmek isteR misiniz?
Would you like to come____ and see some friends with us?	Bizimle arkadaşlara gelmek ister misiniz?
	bizimleh aRkadashlaRa gelmek isteR misiniz?
Shall we dance?_____	Dans edelim mi?
	dans edelim mi?
– sit at the bar? _____	Bara geliyor musun?
	baRa geliyoR moosoon?
– get something to drink? __	Bir şeyler içmeye gidelim mi?
	biR sheyleR ichmeyeh gidelim mi?
– go for a walk/drive?_____	Biraz yürüyelim mi/arabayla gezelim mi?
	biRaz yewRewyelim mi/aRabıla gezelim mi?
Yes, all right _____	Tamam, olur
	tamam, olooR
Good idea _____	İyi fikir
	iyi fikiR
No (thank you) _____	Hayır (teşekkür ederim)
	ha-yuhR teshek-kewR edeRim
Maybe later_____	Belki daha sonra
	belki da-ha sonRa
I don't feel like it _____	Canım istemiyor
	januhm istemiyoR
I don't have time _____	Zamanım yok
	zamanuhm yok
I already have a date _____	Başka bir randevum var
	bashka biR randevoom vaR
I'm not very good at_____ dancing/volleyball/ swimming	Ben dansta/voleybolda/yüzmede pek iyi değilim
	dansta/voleybolda/yewzmedeh pek iyi de:ilim

3.9 Paying a compliment

You look wonderful! _____	Sizi çok iyi gördüm!
	sizi chok iyi gurRdewm!
I like your car! _____	Ne güzel araba!
	neh gewzel aRaba!
I like your ski outfit! _____	Ne güzel kayak kıyafeti!
	neh gewzel ka-yak kuh-yafeti!
You're a nice boy/girl _____	Çok iyi bir çocuksun/kızsın
	chok iyi biR chojooksoon/kuhzsuhn
What a sweet child! _____	Ne şirin çocuk!
	neh shiRin chojook!
You're a wonderful _____ dancer!	Çok güzel dans ediyorsunuz!
	chok gewzel dans ediyoRsoonooz!
You're a wonderful _____ cook!	Çok güzel yemek pişiriyorsunuz!
	chok gewzel yemek pishiRiyoRsoonooz!
You're a terrific soccer _____ player!	Çok iyi futbol oynuyorsunuz!
	chok iyi footbol oynooyoRsoonooz!

Conversation

3

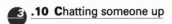

3.10 Chatting someone up

I like being with you	Seninle beraber olmaktan hoşlanıyorum *seninleh beRabeR olmaktan hoshlanuhyoRoom*
I've missed you so much	Seni öyle özledim ki *seni uhyleh urzledim ki*
I dreamt about you	Rüyamda seni gördüm *rew-amda seni gurRdewm*
I think about you all day	Bütün gün seni düşünüyorum *bewtewn gewn seni dewshewnew-yoRoom*
You have such a sweet smile	Çok tatlı gülüyorsun *chok tatluh gewlew-yoRsoon*
You have such beautiful eyes	O kadar güzel gözlerin var ki *o kadaR gewzel gurzleRin vaR ki*
I'm in love with you	Sana aşığım *sana ashuh:uhm*
I'm in love with you too	Ben de sana *ben deh sana*
I love you	Seni seviyorum *seni seviyoRoom*
I love you too	Ben de seni *ben deh seni*
I don't feel as strongly about you	Bu duyguları sana karşı duymuyorum *boo dooygoolaRuh sana kaRshuh dooymoo-yoroom*
I already have a boyfriend/girlfriend	Benim erkek arkadaşım/kız arkadaşım var *benim eRkek aRkadashuhm/kuhz aRkadashum vaR*
I'm not ready for that	Henüz o noktaya gelmedim *henewz o nokta-ya gelmedim*
This is going too fast for me	Her şey çok çabuk oluyor *heR shey chok chabook olooyoR*
Take your hands off me	Benden uzak dur *benden oozak door*
Okay, no problem	Tamam, sorun değil *tamam soRoon de:il*
Will you stay with me tonight?	Bu gece bende kalır mısın? *bu gejeh bendeh kaluhR muhsuhn?*
I'd like to go to bed with you	Seninle sevişmek istiyorum *seninleh sevishmek istiyoRoom*
Only if we use a condom	Sadece prezervatif ile *sadejeh pReseRvatif ileh*
We have to be careful about AIDS	Aids hastalığı yüzünden dikkatli olmamız gerekiyor *ehds hastaluh:uh yewzewnden dik-katluh olmamuhz geRekiyoR*
That's what they all say	Herkes aynı şeyi söylüyor *heRkes ihnh shey surlew-yor*
We shouldn't take any risks	İşi şansa bırakmayalım *ishi shansa buhRakma-yaluhm*
Do you have a condom?	Prezervatifin var mı? *pReseRvatifin vaR muh?*
No? In that case we won't do it	Yok mu? O halde sevişemeyiz *yok moo? o haldeh sevishemeyiz*

3.11 Arrangements

When will I see you again?	Sizi tekrar ne zaman göreceğim? *sizi tekRaR neh zaman gurReje:im?*
Are you free over the weekend?	Bu hafta sonu zamanınız var mı? *boo hafta sonoo zamanuhnuhz vaR muh?*
What shall we arrange?	Nasıl yapalım? *nasuhl yapaluhm?*
Where shall we meet?	Nerede buluşalım? *neRedeh boolooshaluhm?*
Will you pick me/us up?	Beni/bizi alacak mısınız? *beni/bizi alajak muhsuhnuhz?*
Shall I pick you up?	Sizi alayım mı? *sizi ala-yuhm muh?*
I have to be home by...	Saat....evde olmam gerekiyor *saht....evdeh olmam geRekiyoR*
I don't want to see you anymore	Sizi bir daha görmek istemiyorum *sizi biR da-ha gurRmek istemiyoRoom*

3.12 Saying goodbye

Can I take you home?	Sizi evinize götürebilir miyim? *sizi evinizeh gurtewRebiliR miyim?*
Can I write/call you?	Size mektup yazabilir miyim/telefon açabilir miyim? *sizeh mektoop yazabiliR miyim/telefon achabiliR miyim?*
Will you write/call me?	Bana mektup yazar mısınız/telefon açar mısınız? *bana mektoop yazaR muhsuhnuhz/telefon achaR muhsuhnuhz?*
Can I have your address/phone number?	Adresinizi/telefon numaranızı alabilir miyim? *adResinizi/telefon noomaRasuhnuhzuh alabiliR miyim?*
Thanks for everything	Her şey için çok teşekkür ederim *heR shey ichin chok teshek-kewR edeRim*
It was very nice	Her şey çok güzeldi *heR shey chok gewzeldi*
Say hello to...	...selamlarımı söyle *...selamlaRuhmuh suhyleh*
All the best	Size her şeyin en iyisini dilerim *sizeh heR sheyin en iyisini dileRim*
Good luck	İyi şanslar *iyi shanslaR*
When will you be back?	Tekrar ne zaman geleceksiniz? *tekRaR neh zaman gelejeksiniz?*
I'll be waiting for you	Sizi bekleyeceğim *sizi bekleyeje:im*
I'd like to see you again	Sizi tekrar görmeyi çok isterim *sizi tekRaR gurRmeyi chok isteRim*
I hope we meet again soon	Umarım en kısa zamanda tekrar görüşürüz *oomaRuhm en kuhsa zamanda tekRaR gurRewshewRewz*
This is our address. If you're ever in the UK...	Bu bizim adresimiz. İngiltere'ye uğrarsanız... *boo bizim adResimiz. ingilteRe'yeh oo:RaRsanuhz...*
...You'd be more than welcome	Her zaman bekleriz *heR zaman bekleRiz*

31

Conversation

4 Eating out

Eating out

● **Mealtimes in Turkey** are as follows:

1. *Kahvaltı* (breakfast) - any time between 7.30 and 10 am. Typically there will be bowls of olives *(zeytin)* and pieces of cheese *(beyaz peynir)* for you to nibble. There will be bread *(ekmek)* with two or three types of jam *(reçel)* or honey *(bal)*. There may be spreading yoghurt *(süzme yoğurt)* – use it instead of butter, and combine it with jam. Turkish tea *(çay)* is served black, but you can ask for it to be strong *(demli)* or weak *(açık)*. If you prefer, it can be drunk with lemon *(limon)* on request.

2. *Öğle yemeği* (lunch) – between 12.30 and 2.30 – often a hot meal, but lighter than supper. It is often followed by Turkish coffee, which is very strong. This can be without sugar *(şekersiz or sade)*, very sweet *(şekerli)* or medium *(orta)*. If you prefer just a little sugar, ask for *az şekerli*.

3. *Akşam yemeği* is the main meal of the day and it can be as early as 7 pm or as late as 10pm. It usually includes a very sweet pudding *(tatlı)* but if you prefer, there is often fruit *(meyva)*. Try the melon – it can be delicious.

4.1 **O**n arrival

I'd like to book a table ____ for seven o'clock, please	Saat yedi için bir masa ayırtabilir miyim? *saht yedi ichin biR masa i-uhRtabiliR miyim?*
I'd like a table for two, ____ please	İki kişilik bir masa lütfen *iki kishilik biR masa lewtfen*
We've/we haven't booked __	Yer ayırtmıştık (ayırtmamıştık) *yeR i-uhRtmushtuhk (i-uhRtmamuhshtuhk)*
Is the restaurant open ____ yet?	Restoran açık mı? *restoRan achuhk muh?*
What time does the _____ restaurant open/close?	Restoran saat kaçta açılıyor/kapanıyor? *restoRan saht kachta achuhluhyoR/kapanuhyoR?*
Can we wait for a table? ___	Boş bir masa için bekleyebilir miyiz? *bosh biR masa ichin bekleyebiliR miyiz?*
Do we have to wait long? __	Çok beklememiz gerekiyor mu? *chok beklememiz geRekiyoR moo?*
Is this seat taken? _____	Burası boş mu? *booRasuh bosh moo?*
Could we sit here/there? ___	Buraya/oraya oturabilir miyiz? *booRa-ya/oRa-ya otooRabiliR miyiz?*
Can we sit by the_____ window?	Cam kenarına oturabilir miyiz? *jam kenahRuhna otooRabiliR miyiz?*
Can we eat outside? _____	Dışarıda da yiyebilir miyiz? *duhshaRuhda da yiyebiliR miyiz?*
Do you have another _____ chair for us?	Bir sandalyeniz daha var mı? *biR sandal-yeniz da-ha vaR muh?*

Yer ayırtmış mıydınız? _____	Do you have a reservation?
Adınız lütfen? _____	What name, please?
Bu taraftan lütfen _____	This way, please
Bu masa reserve edildi _____	This table is reserved
On beş dakika sonra bir masa _____ boşalacak	We'll have a table free in fifteen minutes
Masa boşalana kadar barda _____ beklemek ister miydiniz?	Would you like to wait (at the bar)?

33

Do you have a highchair? ___	Çocuk için bir sandalyeniz var mı?
	chojook ichin biR sandal-yeniz vaR muh?
Is there a socket for ___ this bottle-warmer?	Bu biberon ısıtıcısı için bir priziniz var mı?
	boo bibeRon uhsuhtuhjuhsuh ichin biR pRiziniz vaR muh?
Could you warm up ___ this bottle/jar for me?	Bu biberonu/kavanozu ısıtabilir misiniz?
	boo bibeRonoo/kavanozoo uhsuhtabiliR misiniz?
Not too hot, please ___	Çok sıcak olmasın lütfen
	chok suhjak olmasuhn lewtfen
Is there somewhere I ___ can change the baby's nappy?	Bebeğin altını değiştirebileceğim bir yer var mı?
	bebe:in altuhnuh de:ishtiRebileje:im biR yeR vaR muh?
Where are the toilets? ___	Tuvalet ne tarafta?
	too:alet neh taRafta?

4 .2 Ordering

Waiter! ___	Garson!
	gaRson!
Madam! ___	Hanımefendi!
	hanuhmefendi!
Sir! ___	Beyefendi!
	beyefendi!
We'd like something to ___ eat/a drink	Bir şeyler yemek/içmek istiyoruz
	biR sheyleR yemek/ichmek istiyoRooz
Could I have a quick ___ meal?	Çabucak bir şeyler yiyebilir miyim?
	chaboojak biR sheyleR yiyebiliR miyim?
We don't have much ___ time	Fazla zamanımız yok
	fazla zamanuhmuhz yok
We'd like to have a ___ drink first	Önce bir şeyler içmek istiyoruz
	uhnje biR sheyleR ichmek istiyoRooz
Could we see the ___ menu/wine list, please?	Yemek listesini/şarap listesini rica edebilir miyim?
	yemek listesini/shaRap listesini rija edebiliR miyim?
Do you have a menu ___ in English?	İngilizce yemek listeniz var mı?
	ingilizje yemek listeniz vaR muh?
Do you have a dish ___ of the day?	Günlük menünüz/turistik menünüz var mı?
	gewnlewk menewnewz/tooRistik menewnewz vaR muh?
We haven't made a ___ choice yet	Henüz seçimimizi yapmadık
	henewz sechimimizi yapmaduhk
What do you ___ recommend?	Ne tavsiye edersiniz?
	neh tavsiyeh edeRsiniz?
What are the specialities ___ of the region/the house?	Bu yörenin/restoranın spesyalitesi nedir?
	boo yuhRenin/restoRanuhn spesyalitesi nediR?
I like strawberries/olives ___	Çileği/zeytini severim
	chile:i/zeytini seveRim
I don't like meat/fish... ___	Balığı/eti/...sevmem
	baluh:uh/eti/...sevmem
What's this? ___	Bu ne?
	boo neh?
Does it have...in it? ___	İçinde...var mı?
	ichinde...vaR muh?
What does it taste like? ___	Tadı neye benziyor?
	taduh neyeh benziyoR?

Is this a hot or a _____ cold dish?	Bu yemek sıcak mı yoksa soğuk mu? *boo yemek suhjak muh yoksa so:ook moo?*
Is this sweet? _____	Bu yemek tatlı mı? *boo yemek tatluh muh?*
Is this spicy? _____	Bu yemek acı/baharatlı mı? *boo yemek ajuh/bahaRatluh muh?*
Do you have anything _____ else, please?	Başka bir yemeğiniz var mı? *bashka biR yeme:iniz vaR muh?*
I'm on a salt-free diet _____	Tuzsuz yemek perhizindeyim *toozsooz yemek peRhizindeyim*
I can't eat pork _____	Domuz eti yemem yasak *domooz eti yemem yasak*
– sugar _____	Şeker kullanmam yasak *shekeR kul-lanmam yasak*
– fatty foods _____	Yağlı yemek yemem yasak *ya:luh yemek yemem yasak*
– (hot) spices _____	Baharatlı yemek yemem yasak *bahaRatluh yemek yemem yasak*
I'll/we'll have what those _____ people are having	Onlarınkinin aynısını istiyorum *onlaRuhnkinin ínuhsuhnuh istiyoRoom*
I'd like... _____	...istiyorum *...istiyoRoom*
We're not having a _____ starter	Meze istemiyoruz *mezeh istemiyoRooz*
The child will share what _____ we're having	Çocuk bizim yemeğimizden yiyecek *chojook bizim yeme:imizden yiyejek*
Could I have some _____ more bread, please?	Biraz daha ekmek getirir misiniz lütfen? *biRaz da-ha ekmek getiRiR misiniz lewtfen?*
– a bottle of water/wine _____	Bir şişe su/şarap getirir misiniz lütfen? *biR shisheh su/shaRap getiRiR misiniz lewtfen?*
– another helping of... _____	Bir porsiyon...getirir misiniz lütfen? *biR poRSiyon...getiRiR misiniz lewtfen?*
– some salt and pepper _____	Tuz ve karabiber getirir misiniz lütfen? *tooz ve kaRabibeR getiRiR misiniz lewtfen?*
– a napkin _____	Bir peçete getirir misiniz lütfen? *biR pecheteh getiRiR misiniz lewtfen?*
– a spoon _____	Bir kaşık getirir misiniz lütfen? *biR kashuhk getiRiR misiniz lewtfen?*
– an ashtray _____	Bir kül tablası getirir misiniz lütfen? *biR kewl tablasuh getiRiR misiniz lewtfen?*

Aperatif alır mıydınız? _____	Would you like a drink first?
Seçiminizi yaptınız mı? _____	Have you decided?
Ne içersiniz? _____	What would you like to drink?
Afiyet olsun _____	Enjoy your meal
Bifteğiniz nasıl olsun? _____	Would you like your steak rare, medium or well done?
Tatlı/kahve alır mıydınız? _____	Would you like a dessert/coffee?

– some matches _____	Bir kutu kibrit getirir misiniz lütfen?
	biR kootoo kibrit getiRiR misiniz lewtfen?
– some toothpicks _____	Birkaç tane kürdan getirir misiniz lütfen?
	biRkach taneh kewRdan getiRiR misiniz lewtfen?
– a glass of water _____	Bir bardak su getirir misiniz lütfen?
	biR baRdak soo getiRiR misiniz lewtfen?
– a straw (for the child) ___	(Çocuk için) bir kamış getirir misiniz lütfen?
	(chojook ichin) biR kamuhsh getiRiR misiniz lewtfen?
Enjoy your meal! _____	Afiyet olsun!
	afiyet olsoon!
You too! _____	Size de!
	sizeh deh!
Cheers! _____	Şerefe!
	sheRefeh!
The next round's on me ___	Bir dahaki sefer sıra bende
	biR da-haki sefeR suhRa bendeh
Could we have a doggy ___ bag, please?	Kalanları paket yapar mısınız?
	kalanlaRuh paket yapaR muhsuhnuhz?

4 .3 The bill

See also 8.2 Settling the bill

How much is this dish? ___	Bu yemeğin fiyatı ne kadar?
	boo yeme:in fiyatuh neh kadaR?
Could I have the bill, _____ please?	Hesap lütfen
	hesap lewtfen
All together _____	Hepsi bir arada
	hepsi biR aRada
Everyone pays separately __	Herkes kendi hesabını ödeyecek
	heRkes kendi hesabuhnuh urdeyejek
Could we have the menu ___ again, please?	Yemek listesine bir göz atabilir miyiz?
	yemek listesine biR gurz atabiliR miyiz?
The...is not on the bill _____	...hesapta yok
	...hesapta yok

4 .4 Complaints

It's taking a very _____ long time	Çok uzun sürüyor
	chok oozoon sewRew-yor
We've been here an _____ hour already	Bir saatten beri buradayız
	biR saht-ten beRi booRada-yuhz
This must be a mistake ___	Bir yanlışlık olmalı
	bir yanluhshluhk olmaluh
This is not what I _____ ordered	Ben bunu ısmarlamamıştım
	ben boonoo uhsmaRlamamuhshtuhm
I ordered... _____	...istemiştim
	...istemishtim
There's a dish missing _____	Yemeklerden biri eksik
	yemekleRden biRi eksik
This is broken/not clean ___	Bu kırık/kirli
	boo kuhRuhk/kiRli
The food's cold _____	Yemek soğuk
	yemek so:ook

– not fresh _____	Yemek taze değil
	yemek tazeh de:il
– too salty/sweet/spicy _____	Yemek çok tuzlu/tatlı/baharatlı
	yemek chok toozloo/tatluh/bahaRatluh
The meat's not done _____	Et iyi pişmemiş
	et iyi pishmemish
– overdone _____	Et çok haşlanmış
	et chok hashlanmuhsh
– tough _____	Et çok sert
	et chok seRt
– off _____	Et bozuk
	et bozook
Could I have something ___ else instead of this?	Bunun yerine bana başka bir şey verebilir misiniz?
	boonoon yeRineh bana bashka biR shey veRebiliR misiniz?
The bill/this amount is _____ not right	Hesapta bir yanlışlık var
We didn't have this_____	*hesapta bir yanluhshluhk vaR*
	Biz bunu yemedik
	biz boonoo yemedik
There's no paper in the ___ toilet	Tuvalette tuvalet kağıdı kalmamış
Do you have a _____ complaints book?	*too-alet-te too-alet ka:uhduh kalmamuhsh*
	Şikayet defteriniz var mı?
Will you call the_____ manager, please?	*shika-yet defteRiniz vaR muh?*
	Şefinizi çağırır mısınız lütfen?
	shefinizi cha:uhRuhR muhsuhnuhz lewtfen?

4.5 Paying a compliment

That was a wonderful _____ meal	Yemeklerinizi çok beğendik
	yemekleRinizi chok be:endik
The food was excellent ____	Yemekleriniz çok lezizdi
	yemekleRiniz chok lezizdi
The...in particular was _____ delicious	Özellikle...çok lezzetliydi
	urzel-likleh...chok lez-zetliydi

4.6 The menu

alkollü içkiler	kahvaltı	şarap listesi
alcoholic drinks	**breakfast**	**wine list**
alkolsüz içkiler	KDV dahil	sebze yemekleri
non-alcoholic drinks	**including VAT**	**vegetable dishes**
aperatif	kokteyller	servis dahil
aperitif	**cocktails**	**service included**
balık çeşitleri	menü	servis hariç
choice of fish dishes	**menu**	**service not included**
çorba çeşitleri	meyva	sıcak yemekler
choice of soups	**fruit**	**hot dishes**
etli yemekler	mezeler	soğuk yemekler
meat dishes	**starters**	**cold dishes**
etsiz yemekler	pasta çeşitleri	tatlılar
vegetarian dishes	**choice of cakes**	**sweets (puddings)**
ızgara	salatalar	
grills	**salads**	

4.7 Alphabetical list of drinks and dishes

alabalık	biftek	çikolatalı dondurma
trout	**steak**	**chocolate ice cream**
armut	bira	çilek
pear	**beer**	**strawberries**
aşure	bisküvi	cızbız köfte
sweet dish made from	**biscuits**	**grilled meatballs**
fruit and many kinds	böbrek	çoban salatası
of nut	**kidneys**	**cucumber, tomato and**
ayran	bonfile	**onion salad**
yoghurt drink	**best cut (beef)**	çorba
ayşe kadın fasulyesi	börek	**soup**
green beans	**pastry**	dana eti
ayva	brüksel lahanası	**veal**
quince	**Brussels sprouts**	dil
badem ezmesi	bulgur	**tongue**
ground almonds	**bulgar wheat**	dil balığı
bakla	but	**sole**
broad beans	**leg (of meat)**	domates
baklava	buz	**tomatoes**
sticky pastry	**ice**	domates çorbası
balık	cacık	**tomato soup**
fish	**cucumber and yoghurt**	domates dolması
beyaz peynir	çay	**stuffed tomatoes**
white cheese (like feta)	**tea**	domates salatası
beyaz şarap	çerkez tavuğu	**tomato salad**
white wine	**chicken with walnuts**	domates salçası
bezelye	ceviz	**sauce made from**
peas	**walnut**	**tomatoes**
biber	ciğer	domuz eti
peppers	**liver**	**pork**
biber dolması	çikolata	dondurma
stuffed peppers	**chocolate**	**ice cream**

döner	**spit-roast**
düğün çorbası	**meat and yoghurt soup**
ekmek	**bread**
elma	**apple**
enginar	**globe artichoke**
erik	**plum**
et	**meat**
et suyu	**meat stock**
etli bezelye	**peas cooked with meat**
fasulye	**beans**
fındık	**hazelnuts**
fırında	**oven-roast**
gazoz	**fizzy lemonade**
güveç	**meat and vegetable casserole**
hamsi	**anchovy**
hardal	**mustard**
havuç	**carrot**
helva	**halva**
hindi	**turkey**
hurma	**dates**
iç pilav	**rice stuffing**
imam bayıldı	**stuffed aubergine**
incir	**fig**
irmik helvası	**semolina helva**
işkembe çorbası	**tripe soup**
ıspanak	**spinach**
ıstakoz	**lobster**
istiridye	**oysters**
ızgara	**grill/grilled**
izmir köftesi	**meatballs in tomato sauce**
jöle	**jelly**
kabak	**courgettes/marrow**
kabak dolması	**stuffed courgettes**
kadınbudu köfte	**meat and rice rissoles**
kahve	**coffee**
kalkan balığı	**turbot**
karabiber	**black pepper**
karides	**shrimps**
karışık	**mixed**
karnabahar	**cauliflower**
karnıyarık	**aubergine stuffed with minced meat**
karpuz	**water melon**
kaşar peyniri	**cheese (cheddar-type, sometimes dry, usually mature)**
kavun	**melon**
kayısı	**apricot**
kebap	**kebab**
keçi	**goat**
kekik	**thyme**
keklik	**partridge**
kereviz	**celery**
kestane	**chestnut**
ketçap	**ketchup**
kiraz	**cherry**
kırlangıç	**swallow (bird)**
kırmızı biber	**red pepper**
kırmızı lahana	**red cabbage**
kırmızı şarap	**red wine**
kırmızı turp	**radishes**
kıyma	**mince**
kızartılmış ekmek	**toast**
köfte	**meat-balls**
kokoreç	**sheep's chitterlings cooked on a spit**
komposto	**stewed fruit**
koyun eti	**mutton**
kuru fasulye	**dried beans**
kuşkonmaz	**asparagus**
kuzu budu	**leg of lamb**
kuzu eti	**lamb**
lahana	**cabbage**
lahana dolması	**stuffed cabbage**
lahmacun	**Turkish pizza made with minced meat, spices and onions**
levrek	**bass**
limon	**lemon**
limonata	**lemonade**
lokum	**Turkish delight**
maden sodası	**soda water**
maden suyu	**mineral water**
makarna	**macaroni**

mandalina
tangerine, mandarin
mantar
mushroom
maydanoz
parsley
mayonez
mayonnaise
menemen
omlette with tomatoes,
  onion and paprika
mercimek çorbası
lentil soup
meyva suyu
fruit juice
mezgit
whiting
midye
mussels
midye dolması
stuffed mussels
midye pilakisi
mussel stew (cold)
midye tava
fried mussels
mısır
sweetcorn
mücver
courgette croquettes
mürekkep balığı
squid
muz
banana
nar
pomegranate
omlet
omlette
ördek
duck
pancar
beetroot
pastırma
pressed (spiced)
  meat
patates
potatoes
patates kızartması
chips
patates püresi
mashed potatoes
patates salatası
potato salad
patlıcan
aubergine
patlıcan kızartması
fried aubergine

patlıcan musakkası
moussaka
patlıcan salatası
aubergine salad
peynir
cheese
pide
(flat) bread
pilav
rice
piliç
small chicken
pırasa
leek
pirzola
cutlet
portakal
orange
portakal suyu
orange juice
rafadan yumurta
lightly-
  boiled egg
rakı
aniseed spirit served
  mixed with a little
  water
ringa balığı
herring
roka
rocket (salad
  vegetable)
salata
salad
salatalık
cucumber
salmon
salmon
şam fıstığı
pistachio
şarap
wine
sardalya
sardines
sarımsak
garlic
sazan
carp
sebze
vegetable
sebze çorbası
vegetable soup
şeftali
peach
şeker
sugar

şekerpare
small cakes cooked in
  sweet syrup
sığır eti
beef
sirke
vinegar
şiş kebap
sish kebab
sivri biber
long green pepper
siyah zeytin
black olives
sos
sauce
su
water
süt
milk
tarçın
cinnamon
tarhana çorbası
soup made from grain,
  yoghurt and tomatoes
tas kebabı
braised lamb
tavada
fried
tavşan
rabbit
tavuk
chicken
tavuk çorbası
chicken soup
tavuk göğsü
milk pudding
  cooked with
  chicken breast
taze
fresh
terbiyeli
with a sauce
tereyağı
butter
tereyağlı
made with butter
turna balığı
pike
turp
radishes
turşu
pickled
tuz
salt
tuzlu
with added salt, salty

tuzsuz	viski	yeşil zeytin
without salt	**whisky**	**green olives**
un	vişne	yoğurt
flour	**morello**	**yoghurt**
un kurabiyesi	cherries	yoğurt çorbası
cake made with	yağlı et	**yoghurt soup**
almond and nuts	**meat (not lean)**	yumurta
uskumru	yağsız et	**eggs**
mackerel	**lean meat**	zeytin
üzüm	yaprak dolması	**olives**
grapes	**stuffed vine**	zeytin yağı
vanilya	**leaves**	**olive oil**
vanilla	yayla çorbası	zeytin yağlı
vanilyalı dondurma	**parsley and yoghurt**	**made with olive oil**
vanilla ice-cream	**soup**	
vermut	yengeç	
vemouth	**crab**	

Eating out

On the road

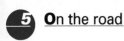

5 On the road

5.1 Asking for directions

Excuse me, could I ask you something?	Özür dilerim, size bir şey sorabilir miyim? *urzewR dileRim, sizeh biR shey soRabiliR miyim?*
I've lost my way_____	Yolumu kaybettim *yoloomoo kibet-tim*
Is there a(n)... _____ around here?	Bu civarda bir...var mı? *boo jivaRda biR...vaR muh?*
Is this the way to...? _____	...giden yol bu mu? *...giden yol boo moo?*
Could you tell me _____ how to get to the... (name of place) by car/on foot?	Bana...arabayla/yaya nasıl gidebileceğimi söyleyebilir misiniz? *bana...aRabíla/ya-ya nasuhl gidebileje:imi suhyleyebiliR misiniz?*
What's the quickest_____ way to...?	...en çabuk nasıl gidebilirim? *...en chabook nasuhl gidebiliRim?*
How many kilometres ____ is it to...?	...kaç kilometre kaldı? *...kach kilometReh kalduh?*
Could you point it _____ out on the map?	Haritada gösterebilir misiniz? *haRitada gursteRebiliR misiniz?*

Bilmiyorum, buralı değilim _____	I don't know, I don't know my way around here
Yanlış yoldasınız _____	You're going the wrong way
... geri dönmelisiniz _____	You have to go back to...
Oradan levhaları takip ediniz _____	From there on just follow the signs
Oraya varınca tekrar sorun _____	When you get there, ask again

doğru **straight ahead**	sokak **the street**	bağlantı yolu the flyover
sola **left**	trafik ışıkları **the traffic lights**	köprü **the bridge**
sağa **right**	tünel **the tunnel**	hemzemin geçit **the level crossing/the**
dönmek **turn**	'yol ver' işareti **the `give way' sign**	**boom gates**
takip etmek **follow**	bina **the building**	... giden yolu gösteren levha **the sign pointing to...**
karşıya geçmek **cross**	köşede at the corner	
kavşak **the intersection**	ırmak/nehir the river	

5.2 Customs

● **Before you set out,** you will need a valid passport. On arrival, you will have to acquire a visa, which is normally issued automatically. Queue for the visa before passport control. Drivers need an international driving licence, green card, UK plates, insurance which is valid in Turkey and also their car registration documents.
You may take 5 litres of spirits into the country, and up to 200 cigarettes.

Pasaportunuz lütfen _____	Your passport, please
Yeşil kartınız lütfen _____	Your green card, please
Araba ruhsatınız lütfen _____	Your vehicle documents, please
Vizeniz lütfen _____	Your visa, please
Nereye gidiyorsunuz? _____	Where are you heading?
Ne kadar kalmayı düşünüyorsunuz? _____	How long are you planning to stay?
Beyan edecek bir şeyiniz var mı?_____	Do you have anything to declare?
Bunu açar mısınız? _____	Open this, please

My children are entered ___ Çocuklar pasaportuma kayıtlı
  on this passport   *chojooklaR pasapoRtooma kayuhtluh*
I'm travelling through _____ Ülkenizden geçiyordum
                            ewlkenizden gechiyoRdoom
I'm going on holiday to... __ ...tatile gidiyorum
                            ...tatileh gidiyoRoom
I'm on a business trip _____ İş seyahatindeyim
                            ish sey-ahatindeyim
I don't know how long_____ Ne kadar kalacağımı daha bilmiyorum
  I'll be staying yet   *neh kadaR kalaja:uhmuh da-ha bilmiyoRoom*
I'll be staying here for _____ Bir hafta sonu kalacağım
  a weekend   *biR hafta sonoo kalaja:uhm*
– for a few days _____ Birkaç gün kalacağım
                            biRkach gewn kalaja:uhm
– for a week_____ Bir hafta kalacağım
                            biR hafta kalaja:uhm
– for two weeks _____ İki hafta kalacağım
                            iki hafta kalaja:uhm
I've got nothing to_____ Beyan edecek bir şeyim yok
  declare   *beyahn edejek biR sheyim yok*
I've got...with me_____ Yanımda...var
                            yanuhmda...vaR
– ...cartons of cigarettes ___ Yanımda bir karton sigara var
                            yanuhmda biR kaRton sigaRa vaR
– ...bottles of... _____ Yanımda bir şişe...var
                            yanuhmda biR shisheh...vaR
– some souvenirs _____ Yanımda birkaç hediyelik eşya var
                            yanuhmda biRkach hediyelik eshya vaR

44

These are personal _____ effects	Bunlar benim şahsi eşyalarım
	boonlaR benim shasi eshyalaRuhm
These are not new _____	Bu eşyalar yeni değil
	boo eshyalaR yeni de:il
Here's the receipt _____	Makbuzu burada
	makboozoo booRada
This is for private use ____	Bu kişisel kullanım için
	boo kishisel kool-lanuhm ichin
How much import duty ____ do I have to pay?	Ne kadar gümrük vergisi ödemem gerek?
	neh kadaR gewmRewk veRgisi urdemem geRek?
Can I go now? _____	Gidebilir miyim?
	gidebiliR miyim?

5.3 Luggage

Porter! _____	Hamal!
	hamal!
Could you take this _____ luggage to...?	Bu bagajı...götürür müsünüz lütfen?
	boo bagazhuh...gurtewRewR mewsewnewz lewtfen?
How much do I _____ owe you?	Borcum ne kadar?
	boRjoom neh kadaR?
Where can I find a _____ luggage trolley?	Nerede bir bagaj vagonu bulabilirim?
	neRedeh biR bagazh vagonoo boolabiliRim?
Could you store this _____ luggage for me?	Bu bagajı emanete verebilir miyim?
	boo bagazhuh emahneteh veRebiliR miyim?
Where are the luggage ____ lockers?	Bagaj saklama dolapları nerede?
	bagazh saklama dolaplaRuh neRedeh?
I can't get the locker _____ open	Bagaj saklama dolabını açamıyorum
	bagazh saklama dolabuhnuh achamuhyoRoom
How much is it per item ____ per day?	Parça başına günlüğü ne kadar?
	paRcha bashuhna gewnlew:ew neh kadaR?
This is not my bag/ _____ suitcase	Bu benim çantam/bavulum değil
	boo benim chantam/bavooloom de:il
There's one item/bag/ _____ suitcase missing still	Bir parça/çanta/bavul eksik
	biR paRcha/chanta/bavool eksik
My suitcase is damaged ____	Bavulum hasara uğramış
	bavooloom hasaRa oo:Ramuhsh

5.4 Traffic signs

Beklemek yasaktır	H (hastane)	Tamirat
no waiting	**H (hospital)**	**roadworks**
Bozuk yol	Havaalanı	Tek yön
poor road surface	**airport**	**one way**
D (durak)	Jandarma	Tünel
D (bus stop)	**gendarmarie**	**tunnel**
Dikkat	Park etmek yasaktır	Viraj
caution	**no parking**	**bend**
Dur	Polis	Yangın tehlikesi
stop	**police**	**danger of fire**
Gümrük	Şehir merkezi	Yavaş
customs	**city centre**	**slow**

See the diagram on page 49.

● **Speed limits** are 50km/h in built-up areas and 90km/h on the open road (for cars with trailers, limits are 40 and 70 respectively).
All accidents must be reported to the police whether or not personal injury occurs. In the event of an accident, you may find the other driver has *tek taraflı* insurance which covers only his or her own claims, or *çift taraflı* which should cover yours, too.
In country areas, Turkish drivers are always on the look-out for the occasional unexpected obstruction on the road (farm machinery or herds of animals) and in the towns, when the traffic lights show green, they may well prudently check that no car is about to cross their path against the red. Turkish driving standards are often high, but always be ready for exceptions.
On open roads, *take particular care on bends, as adverse cambers are not unknown.*

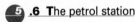
.6 The petrol station

● **Petrol is not particularly expensive** in Turkey, and out-of town filling stations often have excellent facilities for refreshment. Attendant service is normal.

How many kilometres to ___ the next petrol station, please?	Bir sonraki benzin istasyonuna kaç kilometre var?
	biR sonRaki benzin istas-yonoona kach kilometReh vaR?
I would like...litres of..., ___ please	...litre...istiyorum
	...litReh...istiyoRoom
– super ___	...litre kurşunlu benzin istiyorum
	...litReh kooRshoonloo benzin istiyoRoom
– leaded ___	...litre kurşunsuz benzin istiyorum
	...litReh kooRshoonsooz benzin istiyoRoom
– unleaded ___	...litre süper benzin istiyorum
	...litReh sewpeR benzin istiyoRoom
– diesel ___	...litre dizel istiyorum
	...litReh dizel istiyoRoom
I would like...liras' ___ worth of petrol, please	...liralık benzin istiyorum
	...liRaluhk benzin istiyoRoom
Fill her up, please ___	Doldurun lütfen
	doldooRoon lewtfen
Could you check...? ___	...kontrol eder misiniz?
	...kontRol edeR misiniz?
– the oil level ___	Yağ seviyesini kontrol eder misiniz?
	ya: seviyesini kontRol edeR misiniz?
– the tyre pressure ___	Lastiklerdeki hava basıncını kontrol eder misiniz?
	lastikleRdeki hava basuhnjuhnuh kontRol edeR misiniz?
Could you change the ___ oil, please?	Yağı değiştirebilir misiniz?
	ya:uh de:ishtiRebiliR misiniz?
Could you clean the ___ windows/the windscreen, please?	Camları/ön camı silebilir misiniz?
	jamlaRuh/on camuh silebiliR misiniz?
Could you give the car___ a wash, please?	Arabamı yıkayabilir misiniz?
	aRabamuh yuhka-yabiliR misiniz?

I'm having car trouble. _____ Could you give me a hand?	Arabam arızalandı. Yardım edebilir misiniz? *aRabam aRuhzalanduh. yaRduhm edebiliR misiniz?*
I've run out of petrol _____	Benzinim bitti *benzinim bit-ti*
I've locked the keys _____ in the car	Anahtarları arabanın içinde unuttum *anaHtaRlaRuh aRabanuhn ichinde oonoot-toom*
The car/motorbike/ _____ moped won't start	Arabam/motosikletim/mopetim çalışmıyor *aRabam/motosikletim/mopetim chalushmuhyoR*
Could you contact the _____ recovery service for me, please?	Benim için Türkiye Turing ve Otomobil Kurumunu arayabilir misiniz? *benim ichin tewRkiyeh tooRing ve otomobil kooRoomoonu ara-yabiliR misiniz?*
Could you call a garage_____ for me, please?	Bir araba tamircisini arayabilir misiniz? *biR aRaba tahmiRcisini aRa-yabiliR misiniz?*
Could you give me _____ a lift to...?	Sizinle...kadar gelebilir miyim? *sizinleh...kadaR gelebiliR miyim?*
– a garage/into town?_____	Sizinle bir araba tamircisine/şehire kadar gelebilir miyim? *sizinleh biR aRaba tahmiRjisineh/she-hiReh kadaR gelebiliR miyim?*
– a phone booth?_____	Sizinle bir telefon kulübesine kadar gelebilir miyim? *sizinleh biR telefon koolewbesineh kadaR gelebiliR miyim?*
– an emergency phone? _____	Sizinle en yakın telefona kadar gelebilir miyim? *sizinleh en yakuhn telefona kadaR gelebiliR miyim?*
Can we take my _____ bicycle/moped?	Bisikletimi/mobiletimi de alabilir miyiz? *bisikletimi/mobiletimi deh alabiliR miyiz?*
Could you tow me to _____ a garage?	Arabamı bir araba tamircisine kadar çekebilir misiniz? *aRabamuh biR aRaba tahmiRjisineh kadaR chekebiliR misiniz?*
There's probably _____ something wrong with...(See 49)	Büyük bir olasılıkla...arızalı *bewyewk biR olasuhluhkla...aRuhzaluh*
Can you fix it? _____	Tamir edebilir misiniz? *tahmiR edebiliR misiniz?*
Could you fix my tyre? _____	Lastiğimi tamir edebilir misiniz? *lasti:imi tahmiR edebiliR misiniz?*
Could you change this _____ wheel?	Bu tekerleği değiştirebilir misiniz? *boo tekeRle:i de:ishtiRebiliR misiniz?*
Can you fix it so it'll _____ get me to...?	...varana kadar idare edecek bir şekilde tamir edebilir misiniz? *...vaRana kadaR idaReh edejek biR shekildeh tahmiR edebiliR misiniz?*
Which garage can _____ help me?	Bana hangi tamircide yardımcı olabilirler? *bana hangi tahmiRjideh yaRduhmjuh olabiliRleR?*
When will my car/bicycle _____ be ready?	Arabam/bisikletim ne zaman hazır olur? *aRabam/bisikletim neh zaman hazuhR olooR?*
Can I wait for it here?_____	Burada bekleyebilir miyim? *booRada bekleyebiliR miyim?*

On the road

47

The parts of a car
(the diagram shows the numbered parts)

1	battery	akümülatör	akewmewlaturR
2	rear light	arka lamba	aRka lamba
3	rear-view mirror	ayna	ína
	reversing light	geri vites lambası	geRi vites lambasuh
4	aerial	anten	anten
	car radio	radyo	radyo
5	petrol tank	yakıt deposu	yakuht deposoo
	inside mirror	iç ayna	ich ína
6	sparking plugs	buji	boozhi
	fuel filter/pump	yakıt filtresi/pompası	yakuht filtResi/pompasuh
7	wing mirror	dış ayna	duhsh ína
8	bumper	tampon	tampon
	carburettor	karbüratör	kaRbewRaturR
	crankcase	karter	kaRteR
	cylinder	silindir	silindiR
	ignition	kontak	kontac
	warning light	kontrol lambası	kontRol lambasuh
	dynamo	dinamo	dinamo
	accelerator	gaz pedalı	gaz pedaluh
	handbrake	el freni	el fReni
	valve	subap	soobap
9	silencer	ses kesici	ses kesiji
10	boot	bagaj	bagazh
11	headlight	far	faR
	crank shaft	krank	kRank
12	air filter	hava filtresi	hava filtResi
	fog lamp	sis lambası	sis lambasuh
13	engine block	motorblok	motoRblok
	camshaft	kamlı mil	kamluh mil
	oil filter/pump	yağ filtresi/pompası	ya: filtResi/pompasuh
	dipstick	yağ seviye kontrol çubuğu	ya: seviyeh kontRol chooboo:oo
	pedal	pedal	pedal
14	door	kapı	kapuh
15	radiator	radyatör	rad-yaturR
16	brake disc	fren diski	fRen diski
	spare wheel	yedek tekerlek	yedek tekeRlek
17	indicator	yön gösterici	yurn gursteRiji
18	windscreen wiper	cam sileceği	jam sileje:i
19	shock absorbers	amortisör	amoRtisurR
	sunroof	tente	tenteh
	spoiler	arka kapak	aRka kapak
	starter motor	marş motoru	maRsh motoRoo
20	steering column	direksiyon kutusu	diReksiyon kootoosoo
21	exhaust pipe	egzoz borusu	egzoz boRoosoo
22	seat belt	emniyet kemeri	emniyet kemeRi
	fan	vantilatör	vantilaturR
23	distributor cables	distribütör kablosu	distRibewturR kablosoo

On the road 5

48

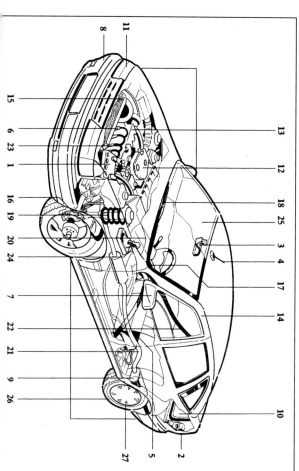

24	gear lever	vites kolu	vites koloo
25	windscreen	ön cam	urn jam
	water pump	su pompası	soo pompasuh
26	wheel	tekerlek	tekeRlek
27	hubcap	tekerlek poyrası	tekeRlek poyRasuh
	piston	piston	piston

How much will it cost?	`Ne kadar tutacak? *neh kadaR tootajak?*
Could you itemise the bill?	Hesabı makbuza ayrıntılı olarak geçirebilir misiniz? *hesabuh makbooza íRuhntuhluh olaRak gechiRebiliR misiniz?*
Can I have a receipt for the insurance?	Sigorta için bir makbuz verir misiniz? *sigoRta ichin biR makbooz veRiR misiniz?*

5.8 The bicycle/moped

See the diagram on page 53.

● **Turks use bicycles** only for short-distance journeys, and cycling by tourists is only gradually becoming more common.
Motorcycles are subject to the same speed limits as cars with trailers (40 km/h in town and 70 on the open road).

5.9 Renting a vehicle

I'd like to rent a...	...kiralamak istiyorum *...kiRalamak istiyoRoom*
Do I need a (special) licence for that?	Onun için (özel) bir ehliyetim olması gerekiyor mu? *onoon ichin (urzel) biR eHliyetim olmasuh geRekiyoR moo?*
I'd like to rent the...for...	... ...kiralamak istiyorum *... ...kiRalamak istiyoRoom*
– one day	...bir günlüğüne kiralamak istiyorum *...biR gewnlew:ewneh kiRalamak istiyoRoom*
– two days	...iki günlüğüne kiralamak istiyorum *...iki gewnlew:ewneh kiRalamak istiyoRoom*
How much is that per day/week?	Günlüğü/haftalığı ne kadar? *gewnlew:ew/haftaluh:uh neh kadaR?*
How much is the deposit?	Ne kadar kaparo ödemem gerek? *neh kadaR kapaRo urdemem geRek?*
Could I have a receipt for the deposit?	Sizden kaparoyu ödediğime dair bir makbuz alabilir miyim? *sizden kapaRoyu urdedi:ime díR biR makbooz alabiliR miyim?*
How much is the surcharge per kilometre?	Kilometre başına ek olarak ne kadar ödemem gerek? *kilometReh bashuhnuh ek olaRak neh kadaR urdemem geRek?*
Does that include petrol?	Benzin dahil mi? *benzin da-hil mi?*
Does that include insurance?	Sigorta dahil mi? *sigoRta da-hil mi?*

Arabanız/bisikletiniz için gerekli _____ yedek parçalar elimde yok	I don't have parts for your car/bicycle
Yedek parçaları başka bir yerden _____ almam gerek	I have to get the parts from somewhere else
Yedek parçaları ısmarlamam gerek_____	I have to order the parts
Yarım gün sürer _____	That'll take half a day
Bir gün sürer _____	That'll take a day
Birkaç gün sürer _____	That'll take a few days
Bir hafta sürer _____	That'll take a week
Arabanız hurda olmuş _____	Your car is a write-off
Yapılacak hiç bir şey yok _____	It can't be repaired
Arabanız/motosikletiniz/mobiletiniz/ _____ bisikletiniz saat...hazır olur	The car/motor bike/moped/bicycle will be ready at...o'clock

What time can I pick _____ the...up tomorrow?	...yarın saat kaçta gelip alabilirim?
	...yaRuhn saht kachta gelip alabiliRim?
When does the...have _____ to be back?	...ne zaman geri getirmem gerek?
	...neh zaman geRi getiRmem geRek?
Where's the petrol tank? ___	Yakıt deposu nerede?
	yakuht deposoo neRedeh?
What sort of fuel does _____ it take?	Depoyu hangi tür yakıt ile doldurmam gerek?
	depoyoo hangi tewR yakuht ileh doldooRmam geRek?

.10 Hitchhiking

● **Short-distance hitch-hiking** is very common in Turkey, but you will be expected to offer to pay the driver (*Borcum ne kadar?*). As a visitor, your offer will almost certainly be declined, but it is rude not to make the gesture.

For long distances, check out the bus prices. They can be surprisingly inexpensive, just as much a social opener, and much more dependable than hitching.

Where are you heading? ___	Nereye gidiyorsunuz?
	neReyeh gidiyoRsoonooz?
Can I come along? _____	Sizinle gelebilir miyim?
	sizinleh gelebiliR miyim?
Can my boyfriend/ _____ girlfriend come too?	Erkek/kız arkadaşım da gelebilir mi?
	eRkek/kuhz aRkadashuhm da gelebiliR mi?
I'm trying to get to... _____	...gitmem gerek
	...gitmem geRek
Is that on the way to...? ___	...yolu üzerinde mi?
	...yoloo ewzeRindeh mi?
Could you drop me off...? ___	Beni...indirebilir misiniz?
	beni...indiRebiliR misiniz?
– here? _____	Beni burada indirebilir misiniz?
	beni booRada indiRebiliR misiniz?
– at the...exit? _____	Beni...giden yolda indirebilir misiniz?
	beni...giden yolda indiRebiliR misiniz?
– in the centre? _____	Beni şehir merkezinde indirebilir misiniz?
	beni she-hiR meRkezindeh indiRebiliR misiniz?

The parts of a bicycle
(the diagram shows the numbered parts)

1 rear lamp	arka lamba	*aRka lamba*
2 rear wheel	arka tekerlek	*aRka tekeRlek*
3 (luggage) carrier	port bagaj	*poRt bagazh*
4 fork crown	direksiyon mili	*diReksiyon mili*
5 bell	zil	*zil*
inner tube	iç lastik	*ich lastik*
tyre	dış lastik	*duhsh lastik*
6 crank	pedal kolu	*pedal koloo*
7 gear change	zincir dişlisi	*zinjiR dishlisi*
wire	kablo	*kablo*
dynamo	dinamo	*dinamo*
bicycle trailer	iki tekerlek yük arabası	*iki tekeRlek yewk aRabasuh*
frame	karkas	*kaRkas*
8 dress guard	çamurluk	*chamooRlook*
	(bayan elbisesi için)	*(ba-yan elbisesi ichin)*
9 chain	zincir	*zinjiR*
chain guard	zincir muhafazası	*zinjiR moohafazasuh*
lock and chain	zincir kiliti	*zinjiR kiliti*
milometer	kilometre sayacı	*kilometReh sa-yajuh*
child's seat	çocuk oturacağı	*hojook otooRaja:uh*
10 headlamp	far	*faR*
bulb	ampul	*ampool*
11 pedal	pedal	*pedal*
12 pump	bisiklet pompası	*bisiklet pompasuh*
13 reflector	reflektör	*reflekturR*
14 break pad	fren kampanası	*fRen kampanasuh*
15 brake cable	fren teli	*fRen teli*
16 ring lock	dairesel kilit	*diResel kilit*
17 carrier straps	bagaj lastiği	*bagazh lastik*
speedometer	hız göstergesi	*huhz gursteRgesi*
18 spoke	jant teli	*zhant teli*
19 mudguard	çamurluk	*chamooRlook*
20 handlebar	direksiyon	*diReksiyon*
21 chain wheel	çark	*chaRk*
toe clip	tutma aleti	*tootma aleti*
22 crank axle	pedal kolu mili	*pedal koloo mili*
drum brake	makaralı fren	*makaRaluh fRen*
rim	jant	*zhant*
23 valve	subap	*subap*
24 valve sleeve	subap hortumu	*subap hoRtoomoo*
25 gear cable	vites teli	*vites teli*
26 front fork	ön tekerlek çatalı	*urn tekeRlek chataluh*
27 front wheel	ön tekerlek	*urn tekeRlek*
28 seat	sele	*seleh*

On the road

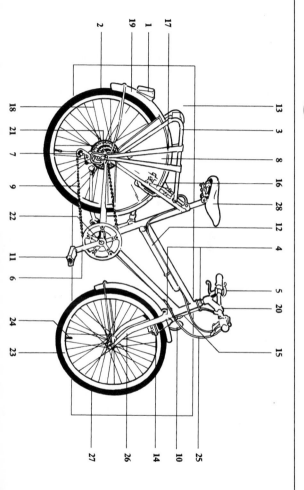

– at the next roundabout? Beni bir sonraki dönel kavşakta indirebilir misiniz?
beni biR sonRaki durnel kavshakta indiRebiliR misiniz?

Could you stop here, please? Burada durur musunuz lütfen?
booRada dooRooR moosoonooz lewtfen?

I'd like to get out here Burada inmek istiyorum
booRada inmek istiyoRoom

How much do I owe you? Borcum ne kadar?
borjoom neh kadaR?

Thanks for the lift Otostop için teşekkür ederim
otostop ichin teshek-kewR edeRim

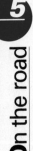

On the road

Public transport

6 Public transport

6.1 In general

● **Train travel** is not the automatic option for long-distance travel.
The rail network is relatively restricted, and journey times can be very
long.

Bus travel, on the other hand, is surprisingly cheap and very efficient,
so ask first about bus timetables and fares, and check out competing
companies. The bus-station (*otogar*) may be on the edge of town, but a
minibus service often provides a city-centre link. Seats are numbered,
and bookable in advance; you would do well to avoid the sunny side of
the bus.

Your fellow-passengers will be friendly, and ensure that you get off at
the stop you want. Each bus has an attendant (*yardımcı*) and the
upmarket companies provide a hostess (*hostes*). The *yardımcı* or
hostes will provide cologne for passengers to splash on their hands
and hair, and, when asked, will give anyone water to drink.
Refreshment breaks come every hour and a half.

Announcements

...giden (10:40) treninin...5 dakika rötarı var	The [10:40] train to...has been delayed by 15 minutes
...giden/...gelen (10:40) tren 5. perona girmek üzeredir	The train now arriving at platform 5 is the [10:40] train to.../from...
...giden (10:40) tren 5. peronda hala bekliyor	The [10:40] train to...is about to leave from platform 5
...giden tren...perondan hareket etmektedir	The train to...will leave from platform...
...istasyonuna girmek üzereyiz	We're now approaching...

Where does this train go to?	Bu tren nereye gidiyor? *boo tRen neReyeh gidiyoR?*
Does this boat go to...?	Bu vapur...gidiyor mu? *boo vapooR...gidiyoR moo?*
Can I take this bus to...?	...gitmek için bu otobüse mi binmem gerekiyor? *...gitmek ichin boo otobewseh mi binmem geRekiyoR?*
Does this train stop at...?	Bu tren...duruyor mu? *boo tRen...dooRooyoR moo?*
Is this seat taken/free/ reserved?	Burası dolu mu/boş mu/ayırtılmış mı? *booRasuh doloo moo/bosh moo/a-yuhRtuhlmuhsh muh?*
I've booked...	Ben...yer ayırtmıştım *ben...yeR a-yuhRtmuhshtuhm*
Could you tell me where I have to get off for... ?	Nerede inmem gerektiğini söyler misiniz? *neRedeh inmem geRekti:ini suhyleR misiniz?*

56

Could you let me _____ know when we get to...?	...geldiğimizde beni uyarır mısınız?	*...geldi:imizdeh beni ooy-aRuhR muhsuhnuhz?*
Could you stop at the _____ next stop, please?	Bir sonraki durakta durur musunuz lütfen?	*biR sonRaki dooRakta dooRooR moosoonooz lewtfen?*
Where are we now? _____	Neredeyiz?	*neRedeyiz?*
Do I have to get off here? __	Burada mı inmem gerekiyor?	*booRada muh inmem geRekiyoR?*
Have we already _____ passed...?	...geçtik mi?	*...gechtik mi?*
How long have I been _____ asleep?	Ne kadar uyumuşum?	*neh kadaR ooy-oomooshoom?*
How long does... _____ stop here?	...burada ne kadar kalacak?	*...booRada neh kadaR kalajak?*
Can I come back on the ____ same ticket?	Bu bilet dönüşte de geçerli mi?	*boo bilet durnewshteh deh gecheRli mi?*
Can I change on this _____ ticket?	Bu biletle aktarma yapabilir miyim?	*boo biletleh aktaRma yapabiliR miyim?*
How long is this ticket _____ valid for?	Bu bilet ne zamana kadar geçerli?	*boo bilet neh zamana kadaR gecheRli?*

.2 Questions to passengers

Ticket types

Birinci sınıf mı yoksa ikinci sınıf mı? _____	First or second class?
Tek gidiş mi yoksa gidiş dönüş mü? _____	Single or return?
Sigara içilir mi içilmez mi?_____	Smoking or non-smoking?
Cam kenarına mı koridor tarafına mı?	Window or aisle?
Ön tarafa mı yoksa arka tarafa mı?	Front or back?
Koltuk mu kuşet mi? _____	Seat or couchette?
Üstte mi, ortada mı yoksa altta mı? _____	Top, middle or bottom?
Turistik sınıf mı yoksa birinci sınıf mı?	Tourist class or business class?
Kamara mı yoksa koltuk mu?_____	Cabin or seat?
Tek kişilik mi yoksa iki kişilik mi?_____	Single or double?
Kaç kişisiniz?_____	How many are travelling?

.3 Tickets

Where can I...? _____	Nerede...?	*neRedeh...?*
– buy a ticket?_____	Nerede bir bilet satın alabilirim?	*neRedeh biR bilet satuhn alabiliRim?*
– make a reservation? _____	Nerede bir yer ayırtabilirim?	*neRedeh biR yeR a-yuhRtabiliRim?*
– book a flight?_____	Nerede bir uçak bileti ayırtabilirim?	*neRedeh biR oochak bileti a-yuhRtabiliRim?*
Could I have a...to...,_____ please?	... ...istiyorum	*... ...istiyoRoom*

Destination

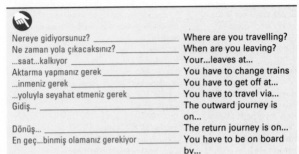

Nereye gidiyorsunuz? _____	Where are you travelling?
Ne zaman yola çıkacaksınız? _____	When are you leaving?
...saat...kalkıyor _____	Your...leaves at...
Aktarma yapmanız gerek _____	You have to change trains
...inmeniz gerek _____	You have to get off at...
...yoluyla seyahat etmeniz gerek _____	You have to travel via...
Gidiş... _____	The outward journey is on...
Dönüş... _____	The return journey is on...
En geç...binmiş olamanız gerekiyor _____	You have to be on board by...

Inside the vehicle

Biletiniz lütfen _____	Your ticket, please
Yer ayırdığınızı gösteren belge lütfen _____	Your reservation, please
Pasaportunuz lütfen _____	Your passport, please
Yanlış yere oturmuşsunuz _____	You're in the wrong seat
Yanlış ... binmişsiniz _____	You're on/in the wrong...
Bu yer ayırtılmıştır _____	This seat is reserved
Bir miktar ek olarak ödemeniz gerekiyor _____	You'll have to pay a supplement
... ...dakika rötarlı _____	The...has been delayed by...minutes

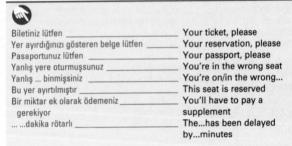

– a single _____	...tek gidiş istiyorum *...tek gidish istiyoRoom*
– a return _____	...gidiş dönüş istiyorum *...gidish durnewsh istiyoRoom*
first class _____	birinci sınıf *biRinji suhnuhf*
second class _____	ikinci sınıf *ikinji suhnuhf*
tourist class _____	turistik sınıf *tooRistik suhnuhf*
business class _____	Birinci sınıf *biRinji suhnuhf*
I'd like to book a _____ seat/couchette/cabin	Bir koltuk/kuşet/kamara ayırtmak istiyorum *biR koltook/kooshet/kamaRa a-yuhRtmak istiyoRoom*
I'd like to book a berth in __ the sleeping car	Kuşetli bir yer ayırtmak istiyorum *kooshetli biR yeR a-yuhRtmak istiyoRoom*
top/middle/bottom _____	üst/orta/alt *ewst/oRta/alt*
smoking/no smoking _____	sigara içilir/içilmez *sigaRa ichiliR/ichilmez*
by the window _____	cam kenarına *jam kenaRuhna*
single/double _____	tek kişilik/iki kişilik *tek kishilik/iki kishilik*

Public transport 6

58

at the front/back _____	ön tarafta/arka tarafta
	urn taRafta/aRka taRafta
There are...of us _____	... kişiyiz
	... kishiyiz
a car _____	Bir araba ileyiz
	biR aRaba ileyiz
a caravan _____	Bir karavan ileyiz
	biR kaRavan ileyiz
...bicycles _____	...bisiklet ileyiz
	...bisiklet ileyiz
Do you also have...? _____	...var mı?
	...vaR muh?
– season tickets? _____	Abone biletiniz de var mı?
	aboneh biletiniz deh vaR muh?
– weekly tickets? _____	Haftalık abone biletiniz de var mı?
	haftaluhk aboneh biletiniz deh vaR muh?
– monthly season _____	Aylık abone biletiniz de var mı?
tickets?	*iluhk aboneh biletiniz deh vaR muh?*

6.4 Information

Public transport

Where's? _____	...nerede?
	...neRedeh?
Where's the information ___	Danışma bürosu nerede?
desk?	*danuhshma bewRosoo neRedeh?*
Where can I find a _____	Tren/otobüs tarifesi nerede?
timetable?	*tRen/otobews taRifesi neRedeh?*
Where's the...desk? _____	...gişesi nerede?
	...gishesi neRedeh
Do you have a city map ___	şehrin otobüs/metro ağını gösteren bir haritanız
with the bus/the	var mı?
underground routes on it?	*sheHRin otobews/metRo a:uhnuh gursteRen*
	biR haRitanuhz vaR muh?
Do you have a _____	Tren/otobüs tarifeniz var mı?
train/bus timetable?	*tRen/otobews taRifeniz vaR muh?*
I'd like to confirm/ _____	...olan rezervasyonumu/yolculuğumu konfirme
cancel/change my	etmek/iptal etmek/değiştirmek istiyorum
booking for/trip to...	*...olan rezeRvasyonoomoo/yoljooloo:oomoo*
	konfriRmeh etmek/iptahl etmek/de:ishtiRmek
	istiyoRoom
Will I get my money _____	Paramı geri alabilir miyim?
back?	*paRamuh geRi alabiliR miyim?*
I want to go to... _____	...gitmek istiyorum. (En çabuk) nasıl gidebilirim?
How do I get there?	*...gitmek istiyoRoom. (en chabook) nasuhl*
(What's the quickest way	*gidebiliRim?*
there?)	
How much is a _____	...tek gidiş/gidiş dönüş ne kadar?
single/return to...?	*...tek gidish/gidish durnewsh neh kadaR?*
Do I have to pay a _____	Ek olarak bir şey ödemem gerekiyor mu?
supplement?	*ek olaRak biR shey urdemem geRekiyoR moo?*
Can I interrupt my _____	Bu biletle yolculuğuma ara verebilir miyim?
journey with this ticket?	*boo biletleh yoljooloo:ooma aRa veRebiliR*
How much luggage _____	*miyim?*
am I allowed?	Yanıma ne kadar bagaj alabilirim?
Can I send my luggage ___	*yanuhma neh kadaR bagazh alabiliRim?*
in advance?	Bagajlarımı önceden gönderebilir miyim?
	bagazhlaRuhmuh urnjeden gurndeRebiliR miyim?

59

Does this...travel direct? ___	Bu...dosdoğru mu gidiyor?
	boo...dosdo:Roo moo gidiyoR?
Do I have to change? _____ Where?	Aktarma yapmam gerekiyor mu? Nerede?
	aktaRma yapmam geRekiyoR moo? neRedeh?
Will there be any _____ stopovers?	Uçak aktarmalı uçuş mu yapıyor?
	oochak aktaRmaluh oochoosh moo yapuhyoR?
Does the boat call in at ___ any ports on the way?	Bu vapur yolculuk sırasında başka limanlara da uğruyor mu?
	boo vapooR yoljoolook suhRasuhnda bashka limanlaRa da oo:RooyoR moo?
Does the train/ _____ bus stop at...?	Bu tren/otobüs...duruyor mu?
	boo tRen/otobews...dooRooyoR moo?
Where should I get off? ___	Nerede inmem gerekiyor?
	neRedeh inmem geRekiyoR?
Is there a connection _____ to...?	...giden araca hemen aktarma yapmam mümkün mü?
	...giden aRaja hemen aktaRma yapmam mewmkewn mew?
How long do I have to ____ wait?	Ne kadar beklemem gerekiyor?
	neh kadaR beklemem geRekiyoR?
When does...leave? _____	...ne zaman kalkıyor?
	...neh zaman kalkuhyoR?
What time does the _____ first/next/last...leave?	İlk/bir sonraki/en son...saat kaçta kalkıyor?
	ilk/biR sonRaki/en son...saht kachta kalkuhyoR?
How long does...take? ____	Yolculuk kaç saat sürüyor?
	yoljoolook kach saht sewRew-yoR?
What time does...arrive ____ in...?	...saat kaçta...varıyor?
	...saht kachta...vaRuh-yoR?
Where does the...to... _____ leave from?	...giden...nereden kalkıyor?
	...giden...neReden kalkuh-yoR?
Is this...to...? _____	...giden...bu mu?
	...giden...boo muh?

6.5 Aeroplanes

● **At arrival at a Turkish airport** (*havaalanı*), you will find the following signs:

geliş	iç hatlar	dış hatlar
arrivals	domestic flights	international
gidiş		
departures		

🔵 .6 Trains

● **If you prefer** train to bus, be sure to choose the express trains (*mavi tren, ekspres,* or *mototren*). Avoid the 'passenger' (*yolcu*) or mail (*posta*) trains, as these can be astonishingly slow.

When reading timetables, remember that the station name, not the city name, will generally be used. If in doubt, ask.

🔵 .7 Taxis

● **The regular taxis** are not the only option. Ask about the *dolmuş* service. These follow a pre-set route, but can be flagged down (or will allow you to get off) at any point on the way. They are either minibuses or big old cars, and have a distinctive yellow stripe.

If you do take a regular taxi, just be sure the driver starts his meter as you get in. If he forgets, remind him *('Taksimetreyi açar mısınız').* It may save a lot of argument later. The Turks themselves do not normally expect to tip taxi drivers, and you are quite within your rights to refuse. However, since foreign travellers do so often offer tips, you could volunteer one if you wished. Don't feel coerced, though.

boş	dolu	taksi durağı
for hire	booked	taxi rank

Taxi! _____	Taksi!
	taksi!
Could you get me a taxi, ___ please?	Benim için bir taksi çağırabilir misiniz?
	benim ichin biR taksi cha:uhRabiliR misiniz?
Where can I find a taxi____ around here?	Bu civarda nerede bir taksi bulabilirim?
	boo jivaRda neRedeh biR taksi boolabiliRim?
Could you take me to..., ___ please?	Beni...götürün lütfen
	beni...gurtewRewn lewtfen
– this address _____	Beni bu adrese götürün lütfen
	beni boo adReseh gurtewRewn lewtfen
– the...hotel _____	Beni...oteline götürün lütfen
	beni...otelineh gurtewRewn lewtfen
– the town/city centre_____	Beni şehir merkezine götürün lütfen
	beni shehiR meRkezineh gurtewRewn lewtfen
– the station _____	Beni istasyona götürün lütfen
	beni istas-yona gurtewRewn lewtfen
– the airport _____	Beni havaalanına götürün lütfen
	beni hava-alanuhna gurtewRewn lewtfen
How much is the _____ trip to...?	...gitmek ne kadar tutar?
	...gitmek neh kadaR tootaR?
How far is it to...? _____	...kaç kilometre?
	...kach kilometReh?
Could you turn on the ____ meter, please?	Taksimetreyi açar mısınız lütfen?
	taksimetReyi achaR muhsuhnuhz lewtfen?
I'm in a hurry _____	Acelem var
	ajelem vaR
Could you speed up/ _____ slow down a little?	Daha hızlı/yavaş gidebilir misiniz?
	da-ha huhzluh/yavash gidebiliR misiniz?

Public transport

61

Could you take a _____ different route?	Başka bir yoldan gidebilir misiniz? *bashka biR yoldan gidebiliR misiniz?*
I'd like to get out here,_____ please.	Beni burada indirin, lütfen *beni booRada indiRin lewtfen*
You have to go...here _____	Buradan...gidin/dönün *booRadan...gidin/durnewn*
You have to go straight _____ on here	Buradan doğru gidin *booRadan do:Roo gidin*
You have to turn left_____ here	Buradan sola dönün *booRadan sola durnewn*
You have to turn right _____ here.	Buradan sağa dönün *booRadan sa:a durnewn*
This is it _____	Burası *booRasuh*
Could you wait a minute____ for me, please?	Bir saniye bekler misiniz? *biR **sah**niyeh bekleR misiniz?*

6

Public transport

Overnight accommodation

Overnight accommodation

7.1 General

● **There is a five star rating system** for hotels, with luxury hotels exactly the same as in any other country. Two or three star hotels can provide all the facilities expected by most European travellers, and offer a more than adequate standard of comfort.

Prices can be very reasonable indeed.

If you have enough money to spare, ask for information about hotels in former Ottoman mansions. They can be outstanding for their exotic atmosphere, and can be a memorable part of your stay. By Turkish standards they are not cheap, however. For those who need to be careful with money, a bed-and-breakfast *pansiyon* will offer a perfectly adequate place to stay. Even cheaper (but not very attractive) accommodation can be found in a hostel (*yurt*) or student hostel (*öğrenci yurdu*).

There are also camp-sites (with varying facilities) but mostly these are located in the major tourist areas.

Ne kadar kalacaksınız?	How long will you be staying?
Bu formu doldurur musunuz lütfen?	Fill out this form, please
Pasaportunuzu görebilir miyim?	Could I see your passport?
Kaparo ödemeniz gerek	I'll need a deposit
Peşin olarak ödemeniz gerek	You'll have to pay in advance

My name's...I've made a reservation over the phone/by mail	Adım...(telefonla/yazılı olarak) yer ayırtmıştım *aduhm...(telefonla/yazuhluh olaRak) yeR a-yuhRtmuhshtuhm*
How much is it per night/week/ month?	Bir geceliği/haftalığı/aylığı ne kadar? *biR gejeli:i/haftaluh:uh/iluh:uh neh kadaR?*
We'll be staying at least...nights/weeks	En az...gece/hafta kalacağız *en az...gejeh/hafta kalaja:uhz*
We don't know yet	Tam olarak bilmiyoruz *tam olaRak bilmiyoRooz*
Do you allow pets (cats/dogs)?	Ev hayvanlarını (kedi/köpek) kabul ediyor musunuz? *ev hívanlaRuhnuh (kedi/kurpek) kabool ediyoR moosoonooz?*
What time does the gate/door open/close?	Demir parmaklık/kapı saat kaçta açılıyor/kapanıyor? *demiR paRmakluhk/kapuh saht kachta achuhluhyoR/kapanuhyoR?*
Could you get me a taxi, please?	Benim için bir taksi çağırır mısınız? *benim ichin biR taksi cha:uhRuhR muhsuhnuhz?*
Is there any mail for me?	Bana posta var mı? *bana posta vaR muh?*

64

See the diagram on page 67.

Yerinizi kendiniz seçebilirsiniz _____	You can pick your own site
Yeriniz gösterilecek _____	You'll be allocated a site
Yer numaranız bu _____	This is your site number
Bunu arabanıza yapıştırır mısınız? _____	Stick this on your car, please
Lütfen, bu kartı kaybetmeyiniz _____	Please don't lose this card

Where's the manager? ____	Yönetici nerede? *yurnetiji neRedeh?*
Are we allowed to _____ camp here?	Burada kamp kurabilir miyiz? *booRada kamp kooRabiliR miyiz?*
There are...of us and _____ ...tents	...kişi ve...çadırlayız *...kishi veh...chaduhRla-yuhz*
Can we pick our _____ own pitch?	Çadır kurabileceğimiz yeri kendimiz seçebilir miyiz? *chaduhR kooRabileje:imiz yeRi kendimiz sechebiliR miyiz?*
Do you have a quiet _____ spot for us?	Bizim için sakin bir yeriniz var mı? *bizim ichin **sak**in biR yeRiniz vaR muh?*
Do you have any other ____ pitches available?	Başka boş yeriniz yok mu? *bashka bosh yeRiniz vaR muh?*
It's too windy/sunny/ _____ shady here.	Burası çok rüzgarlı/güneşli/gölgeli *booRasuh chok rewzgaRluh/gewneshli/gurlgeli*
It's too crowded here _____	Burası çok kalabalık *booRasuh chok kalabaluhk*
The ground's too _____ hard/uneven	Yer çok sert/pürüzlü *yeR chok seRt/pewRewzlew*
Do you have a level _____ spot for the camper/caravan/folding caravan?	Minibüs/karavan/açılır kapanır karavan için düz bir yeriniz var mı? *minibews/kaRavan/achuhluhR kapanuhR kaRavan ichin dewz biR yeRiniz vaR muh?*
Could we have adjoining ____ pitches?	Yan yana iki yer alabilir miyiz? *yan yana iki yeR alabiliR miyiz?*
Can we park the car _____ next to the tent?	Arabayı çadırın yanına park edebilir miyiz? *aRaba-yuh chaduhRuhn yanuhna paRk edebiliR miyiz?*
How much is it per _____ person/tent/caravan/car?	Kişi/çadır/karavan/araba başına ne kadar tutar? *kishi/chaduhR/kaRavan/aRaba bashuhnuh neh kadaR tootaR?*
Are there any cabins for ____ hire?	Kiralık kulübeniz var mı? *kiRaluhk koolewbeniz vaR muh?*

Camping equipment

(the diagram shows the numbered parts)

	luggage space	bagaj yeri	*bagazh yeRi*
	can opener	konserve açacağı	*konseRveh achaja:uh*
	butane gas bottle	tüp gaz	*tewp gaz*
1	pannier	bisiklet çantası	bisiklet chantasuh
2	gas cooker	tüp ocağı	tewp oja:uh
3	groundsheet	zemin örtüsü	zemin urRtewsew
	mallet	çekiç	chekich
	hammock	hamak	hamak
4	jerry can	bidon	bidon
	campfire	kamp ateşi	kamp ateshi
5	folding chair	portatif sandalye	poRtatif sandalyeh
6	insulated picnic box	termos kutusu	teRmos kootoosoo
	ice pack	paket buz	paket booz
	compass	pusula	poosoola
	(incandescent) gas mantle	lamba gömleği	lamba gurmle:i
	corkscrew	tirbuşon	tiRbooshon
7	airbed	şişirme yatak	shishiRmeh yatak
8	airbed plug	şişirme yatak hava tıpası	shishiRmeh yatak hava tuhpasuh
	pump	pompa	pompa
9	awning	güneşlik	gewneshlik
10	karimat	döşek	durshek
11	pan	tencere	tenjeReh
12	pan handle	kap kacak tutacağı	kap kajak tootaja:uh
	primus stove	parafin ocağı	parafin oja:uh
	zip	fermuar	feRmoo-aR
13	backpack	sırt çantası	suhRt chantasuh
14	guy rope	germe ipi	geRmeh ipi
	sleeping bag	uyku tulumu	ooykoo tooloomoo
15	storm lantern	gemici feneri	gemiji feneRi
	camp bed	portatif kamp yatağı	poRtatif kamp yata:uh
	table	masa	masa
16	tent	çadır	chaduhR
17	tent peg	çadır kazığı	chaduhR kazuh:uh
18	tent pole	çadır direği	chaduhR diRe:i
	vacuum flask	termos	teRmos
19	water bottle	portatif su bidonu	poRtatif soo bidonoo
	clothes peg	mandal	mandal
	clothes line	çamaşır ipi	chamashuhR ipi
	windbreak	rüzgarlık	rewzgaRluhk
20	torch	el feneri	el feneRi
	pocket knife	çakı	chakuh

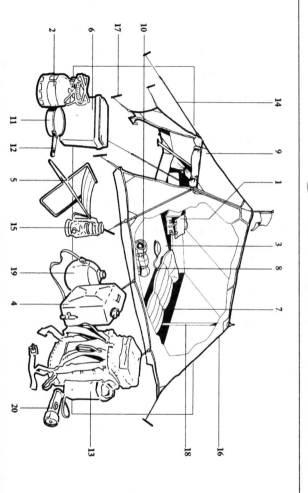

Are there any...?	...var mı?
	...vaR muh?
– hot showers?	Duşlar sıcak sulu mu?
	dooshlaR suhjak sooloo moo?
– washing machines?	Çamaşır makinesi var mı?
	chamashuhR makinesi vaR muh?
Is there a...on the site?	Bu arazide bir...var mı?
	boo aRahzideh biR...vaR muh?
Is there a children's play area on the site?	Bu arazide bir çocuk bahçesi var mı?
	boo aRahzideh biR chocook baHjesi vaR muh?
Are there covered cooking facilities on the site?	Bu arazide bir mutfak var mı?
	boo aRahzideh biR mootfak vaR muh?
Can I rent a safe here?	Burada bir kasa kiralayabilir miyim?
	booRada biR kasa kiRalayabiliR miyim?
Are we allowed to barbecue here?	Burada mangal yakabilir miyiz?
	booRada mangal yakabiliR miyiz?
Are there any power points?	Elektrik bağlantısı var mı?
	elektRik ba:lantuhsuh vaR muh?
Is there drinking water?	İçme suyu var mı?
	ichmeh soo-yoo vaR muh?
When's the rubbish collected?	Çöp ne zaman alınıyor?
	churp neh zaman aluhnuhyoR?
Do you sell gas bottles (butane gas/propane gas)?	Tüp gaz (bütan/propan) satıyor musunuz?
	tewp gaz (bewtan/pRopan) satuhyoR moosoonooz?

7.3 Hotel/B&B/apartment/holiday house

Do you have a single/double room available?	Tek/iki kişilik boş odanız var mı?
	tek/iki kishilik bosh odanuhz vaR muh?
per person/per room	kişi başına/oda başına
	kishi bashuhna/oda bashuhna
Does that include breakfast/lunch/dinner?	Kahvaltı/öğle yemeği/akşam yemeği dahil mi?
	kaHvaltuh/ur:leh yeme:i/aksham yeme:i dah-hil mi?
Could we have two adjoining rooms?	Yanyana iki odanız var mı?
	yanyana iki odanuhz vaR muh?
with/without toilet/bath/shower	tuvaletli/tuvaletsiz/banyolu/banyosuz/duşlu/duşsuz
	too-aletli/too-aletsiz/banyoloo/banyosooz/dooshloo/dooshsooz
(not) facing the street	sokağa bakan (bakmayan)
	soka:a bakan (bakma-yan)
with/without a view of the sea	deniz manzaralı/deniz manzarası olmayan
	deniz manzaRaluh/deniz manzaRasuh olma-yan
Is there...in the hotel?	Otelde...var mı?
	oteldeh...vaR muh?
Is there a lift in the hotel?	Otelde asansör var mı?
	oteldeh asansurR vaR muh?
Do you have room service?	Otelde oda servisi var mı?
	oteldeh oda seRvisi vaR muh?
Could I see the room?	Odayı görebilir miyim?
	odayuh gurRebilir miyim?

7

Overnight accommodation

68

I'll take this room_____	Bu odayı tutuyorum
	boo odayuh tootooyoRoom
We don't like this one ____	Bunu beğenmedik
	boonoo be:enmedik
Do you have a larger/____	Daha büyük/ucuz bir odanız var mı?
less expensive room?	*da-ha bew-yewk biR odanuhz vaR muh?*
Could you put in a cot? ___	Odaya bir çocuk karyolası yerleştirebilir misiniz?
	odaya biR chojook kaR-yolasuh yeRleshtiRebiliR misiniz?
What time's breakfast? ____	Kahvaltı saat kaçta?
	kaHvaltuh saht kachta?
Where's the dining _____	Yemek salonu ne tarafta?
room?	*yemek salonoo neh taRafta?*
Can I have breakfast_____	Kahvaltıyı odamda edebilir miyim?
in my room?	*kaHvaltuh odamda edebiliR miyim?*
Where's the emergency____	Acil çıkış/yangın merdiveni ne tarafta?
exit/fire escape?	**ah-jil** chuhkuhsh/yan-guhn meRdiveni neh taRafta?
Where can I park my _____	Arabamı nereye emniyetle park edebilirim?
car (safely)?	*aRabamuh neReyeh emniyetleh paRk edebiliRim?*

Tuvalet ve duş aynı katta/odanızda _____ mevcut	You can find the toilet and shower on the same floor/en suite
Bu taraftan lütfen_____	This way, please
Odanız...katta, oda numaranız... _____	Your room is on the...floor,

The key to room..., _____	...numaralı odanın anahtarı lütfen
please	*...noomaRuhluh odanuhn anaHtaRuh lewtfen*
Could you put this in _____	Bunu emanete verebilir miyim?
the safe, please?	*boonoo emahneteh veRebiliR miyim?*
Could you wake me _____	Beni yarın saat...uyandırır mısınız?
at...tomorrow?	*beni yaRuhn saht...ooy-anduhRuhR muhsuh-nuhz?*
Could you find a _____	Bana bir çocuk bakıcısı bulabilir misiniz?
babysitter for me?	*bana biR chojook bakuhjuhsuh boolabiliR misiniz?*
Could I have an extra_____	Fazladan bir battaniyeniz var mı?
blanket?	*fazladan biR bat-taniyeniz vaR muh?*
What days do the _____	Haftanın hangi günleri temizlik yapılıyor?
cleaners come in?	*haftanuhn hangi gewnleRi temizlik yapuhluhyoR?*
When are the sheets/ _____	Çarşaflar/havlular/mutfak bezleri ne zaman değiştiriliyor?
towels/tea towels changed?	*chaRshaflaR/havloolaR/mutfak bezleRi neh zaman de:ishtiRiliyoR?*

.4 Complaints

We can't sleep for _____ the noise	Gürültüden uyuyamıyoruz *gewRewltewden ooy-ooy-amuhyoRooz*
Could you turn the _____ radio down, please?	Radyonun sesini biraz kısar mısınız? *radyonun sesini biRaz kuhsaR muhsuhnuhz?*
We're out of toilet paper ___	Tuvalet kağıdı bitmiş *too-alet ka:uhduh bitmish*
There aren't any.../there's _ not enough...	Hiç/yeterince...yok *hich/yeteRinjeh...yok*
The bed linen's dirty_____	Çarşaflar kirli *chaRshaflaR kiRli*
The room hasn't been _____ cleaned.	Oda temizlenmemiş *oda temizlenmemish*
The kitchen is not clean____	Mutfak temiz değil *mootfak temiz de:il*
The kitchen utensils are____ dirty	Mutfak eşyaları pis *mootfak eshyalaRuh pis*
The heater's not_____ working	Kalorifer çalışmıyor *kaloRifeR chaluhshmuhyoR*
There's no (hot) _____ water/electricity	(Sıcak) su akmıyor/elektrikler kesik *(suhjak) soo akmuh-yoR/elektRikleR kesik*
...is broken_____	...bozuk *...bozook*
Could you have that _____ seen to?	Onu yaptırabilir misiniz? *onoo yaptuhRabiliR misiniz?*
Could I have another _____ room/site?	Başka bir oda/çadır için başka bir yer istiyorum *bashka biR oda/chaduhR ichin bashka biR yeR istiyoRoom*
The bed creaks terribly ____	Yatak çok gıcırdıyor *yatak chok guhjuhRduhyoR*
The bed sags _____	Yatak çok çöküyor *yatak chok churkew-yoR*
There are bugs/insects____ in our room	Döşeğin altına koyabileceğim bir tahtanız var mı? *Durshe:in altuhna koyabileje:im bir taHtanuhz vaR muh?*
This place is full_____ of mosquitos	Burası sivrisinek dolu *booRasuh sivRisinek dolooo*
– cockroaches_____	Burası hamam böceği dolu *booRasuh hamam burje:i dolooo*
– Brits _____	Burası İngilizlerle dolu *booRasuh ingilizleRleh doloo*

.5 Departure

See also 8.2 Settling the bill

I'm leaving tomorrow. _____ Could I settle my bill, please?	Yarın yola çıkıyorum. Hesabı ödeyebilir miyim? *yaRuhn yola chuhkuhyoRoom. hesabuh urdeyebiliR miyim?*
What time should we_____ vacate?	...saat kaçta boşaltmamız gerek? *...saht kachta boshaltmamuhz geRek?*
Could I have my deposit/ __ passport back, please?	Kaparoyu/pasaportumu geri verir misiniz? *kapaRo-yoo/pasapoRtoomoo geRi veRiR misiniz?*

Overnight accommodation

We're in a terrible hurry ___ Çok acelemiz var
chok ajelemiz vaR

Could you forward _____
my mail to this address? Bana gelen mektupları bu adrese yollayabilir
misiniz?
bana gelen mektooplaRuh boo adReseh yol-la-yabiliR misiniz?

Could we leave our_____
luggage here until we
leave? Yola çıkana kadar bavullarımızı buraya
bırakabilir miyiz?
yola chuhkana kadaR bavool-laRuhmuhzuh booRaya buhRakabiliR miyiz?

Thanks for your _____
hospitality Misafirperverliğinize çok teşekkür ederim
misahfiRpeRveRli:inizeh chok teshek-kewR edeRim

Money matters

8

Money matters

● **Before you travel** (or at the airport when you arrive), change just a 'survival' amount of UK currency into TL, as you will probably get a better rate at the high-street exchange offices. (These are, incidentally, quicker and have fewer formalities than banks.) You should be given a receipt. Keep all receipts carefully, as you could be asked to show them at border crossings to justify purchases made in Turkey.
Banks – if you need them – are open from 8.30 or 9 through to 12 or 12.30, then from 1.30 to 5 or 5.30. They are closed on Saturdays.

.1 Banks and currency exchange offices

Where can I find a _____ bank/an exchange office around here?	Bu civarda nerede bir banka/kambiyo bürosu var? *boo jivaRda neRedeh biR banka/kambiyo bewRosoo vaR?*
Where can I cash this _____ traveller's cheque/giro cheque?	Bu seyahat/posta çekini nerede bozdurabilirim? *boo seya-hat/posta chekini neRedeh bozdooRabiliRim?*
Can I cash this...here? ____	Bu...burada bozdurabilir miyim? *boo...booRada bozdooRabiliR miyim?*
Can I withdraw money _____ on my credit card here?	Burada kredi kartıyla para çekebilir miyim? *booRada kRedi kaRtuhyla paRa chekebiliR miyim?*
What's the minimum/ _____ maximum amount?	En az/en fazla ne kadar çekebilirim? *en az/en fazla neh kadaR chekebiliRim?*
Can I take out less _____ than that?	Bundan daha az para çekebilir miyim? *boondan da-ha az paRa chekebiliR miyim?*
I've had some money _____ transferred here. Has it arrived yet?	Adıma para transfer edilmişti. Geldi mi acaba? *aduhma paRa tRansfeR edilmishti. geldi mi ajaba?*
These are the details of ____ my bank in the UK	Bunlar benim İngiltere'deki bankamın verileri *boonlaR benim ingilteRedeki bankamuhn veRileRi*
This is my bank/giro _____ number	Bu benim banka hesabımın/posta çeki hesabımın numarası *boo benim banka hesabuhmuhn/posta cheki hesabuhmuhn noomaRasuh*
I'd like to change _____ some money	Para bozdurmak istiyorum *paRa bozdooRmak istiyoRoom*
– pounds into... _____	...sterlin... *...steRlin...*
– dollars into... _____	...dola ... *...dolaR...*
What's the exchange _____ rate?	Günlük döviz kuru ne kadar? *gewnlewk durviz kooRoo neh kadaR?*
Could you give me _____ some small change with it?	Bir kısmını bozuk para olarak verebilir misiniz? *biR kuhsmuhnuh bozook paRa olaRak veRebiliR misiniz?*
This is not right _____	Bir yanlışlık olmalı *biR yanluhshluhk olmaluh*

Burayı imzalayın	Sign here, please
Bunu doldurun	Fill this out, please
Pasaportunuzu görebilir miyim?	Could I see your passport, please?
Nüfus cüzdanınızı görebilir miyim?	Could I see some identification, please?
Posta çeki kartınızı görebilir miyim?	Could I see your girobank card, please?
Banka kartınızı görebilir miyim?	Could I see your bank card, please?

.2 Settling the bill

Could you put it on my bill?	Hesabıma geçirebilir misiniz? _hesabuhma gechiRebiliR misiniz?_
Does this amount include service?	(Bu hesaba) servis dahil mi? _(boo hesaba) seRvis **dah**-hil mi?_
Can I pay by...?	ile ödeyebilir miyim...? _ileh urdeyebiliR miyim...?_
Can I pay by credit card?	Kredi kartı ile ödeyebilir miyim? _kRedi kaRtuh ileh urdeyebiliR miyim?_
Can I pay by traveller's cheque?	Seyahat çeki ile ödeyebilir miyim? _seya-hat cheki ileh urdeyebiliR miyim?_
Can I pay with foreign currency?	Döviz ile ödeyebilir miyim? _durviz ileh urdeyebiliR miyim?_
You've given me too much/you haven't given me enough change	Paranın üstünü fazla/eksik verdiniz _paRanuhn ewstewnew fazla/eksik veRdiniz_
Could you check this again, please?	Bunu bir daha hesaplar mısınız? _boonoo biR da-ha hesaplaR muhsuhnuhz?_
Could I have a receipt, please?	Bana bir makbuz/fiş verebilir misiniz? _bana biR makbooz/fish veRebiliR misiniz?_
I don't have enough money on me	Yanımda yeterince para yok _yanuhmda yeteRinjeh paRa yok_
This is for you	Buyurun, bu sizin _booyooRoon, boo sizin_
Keep the change	Paranın üstü kalsın _paRanuhn ewstew kalsuhn_

Kredi kartı/seyahat çeki/döviz kabul etmiyoruz	We don't accept credit cards/traveller's cheques/foreign currency

Post and telephone

Post and telephone

9 .1 Post

For giros, see 8 Money matters

● **Post offices** The central post offices in cities (PTTs) are open from 8 am till 8 pm, or even later, Monday to Saturday, and from 9 till 7 on Sundays. Smaller post offices are open for normal business hours. Postal services are comparable with those on offer throughout Europe. Delivery times are a little slower than in some countries, but are by no means the slowest in Europe.

havale	pul	telgraf
money order	stamps	telegrams
paketler		
parcels		

Where's...?	...nerede?
	...neRedeh?
Where's the post office?	Bu civarda nerede bir postane var?
	boo jivaRda neRedeh biR postaneh vaR?
Where's the main post office?	Merkez postane nerede?
	meRkez postaneh neRedeh?
Where's the postbox?	Bu civarda nerede bir posta kutusu var?
	boo jivaRda neRedeh biR posta kootoosoo vaR?
Which counter should I go to...?	Hangi gişede...?
	hangi gishedeh...?
– to send a fax	Hangi gişede faks çektirebilirim?
	hangi gishedeh faks chektiRebiliRim?
– to change money	Hangi gişede para bozdurabilirim?
	hangi gishedeh paRa bozdooRabiliRim?
– to change giro cheques	Hangi gişede posta çeki bozdurabilirim?
	hangi gishedeh posta cheki bozdooRabiliRim?
– for a Telegraph Money Order?	Hangi gişede havale çektirebilirim?
	hangi gishedeh havaleh chektiRebiliRim?
Poste restante	Postrestant
	postRestant
Is there any mail for me. My name's...	Bana posta var mı? Adım...
	bana posta vaR muh? aduhm...

Stamps

What's the postage for a...to...?	...gidecek...için kaç liralık posta pulu yapıştırmam gerek?
	...gidejek...ichin kach liRaluhk posta pooloo yapuhshtuhRRam geRek?
Are there enough stamps on it?	Yeterince pul yapıştırmış mıyım?
	yeteRinjeh pool yapuhshtuhRmuhsh muhyuhm?
I'd like... ...Lira stamps	...liralık...tane posta pulu istiyorum
	...liRaluhk...taneh posta pooloo istiyoRoom
I'd like to send this...	Bunu...yollamak istiyorum
	boono...yol-lamak istiyoRoom

76

– express _____	Bunu acele posta servisi ile yollamak istiyorum
	boonoo ahjeleh posta seRvisi ileh yol-lamak istiyoRoom
– by air mail _____	Bunu uçak ile yollamak istiyorum
	boonoo oochak ileh yol-lamak istiyoRoom
– by registered mail _____	Bunu iadeli taahhütlü yollamak istiyorum
	*boonoo i-**ahdeli tah**-hewtlew yol-lamak istiyoRoom*

Telegram / fax

I'd like to send a _____ telegram to...	...telgraf çekmek istiyorum
	...telegRaf chekmek istiyoRoom
How much is that _____ per word?	Kelimesi kaç lira?
	kelimesi kach liRa?
This is the text I want_____ to send	Bu yollamak istediğim metin
	boo yol-lamak istedi:im metin
Shall I fill out the form_____ myself?	Formu kendim doldurayım mı?
	foRmoo kendim doldooRa-yuhm muh?
Can I make photocopies/___ send a fax here?	Burada fotokopi/faks çekebilir miyim?
	booRada fotokopi/faks chekebiliR miyim?
How much is it_____ per page?	Sayfası kaç lira?
	sifasuh kach liRa?

9 .2 Telephone

See also 1.8 Telephone alphabet

● **The PTTs have public phones** as well as postal facilities.
These may be better for international calls than the phone-booths in
the street. Public telephones do not take coins but tokens (jetons)
available from the PTT. Particularly for long-distance or international
calls, it is far easier to buy a phonecard (also from
the PTT).
As in most countries, dial 00 44 for the UK, or 00 1 for the USA, then
miss out the initial zero from the area code.

Is there a phone box _____ around here?	Bu civarda bir telefon kulübesi var mı?
	boo jivaRda biR telefon koolewbesi vaR muh?
Could I use your _____ phone, please?	Telefonunuzu kullanabilir miyim?
	telefonoonoozoo kul-lanabiliR miyim?
Do you have a _____ (city/region)...phone directory?	Sizde (şehrinin/yöresinin)...telefon rehberi var mı?
	sizdeh (seHrinin/yurResinin)...telefon reHbeRi vaR muh?
Where can I get a _____ phone card?	Nereden telefon kartı satın alabilirim?
	neReden telefon kaRtuh satuhn alabiliRim?
Could you give me...? _____	...verir misiniz?
	...veRiR misiniz?
– the number for _____ international directory enquiries	Bana yurt dışı istihbarat numarasını verir misiniz?
	bana yooRt duhshuh istiHbaRat noomaRasuhnuh veRiR misiniz?
– the number of room... ___	...numaralı odanın telefon numarasını verir misiniz?
	...noomaRaluh odanuhn telefon noomaRasuhnuh veRiR misiniz?

– the international _____ access code	Bana yurt dışı arama kodunu verir misiniz?
	bana yooRt duhshshuh aRama kodoonoo veRiR misiniz?
– the country code for... _____	...ülke kod numarasını verir misiniz?
	...ewlkeh kod noomaRasuhnuh veRiR misiniz?
– the trunk code for... _____	...şehir kod numarasını verir misiniz?
	...shehiR kod noomaRasuhnuh veRiR misiniz?
– the number of... _____	...telefon numarasını verir misiniz?
	...telefon noomaRasuhnuh veRiR misiniz?
Could you check if this _____ number's correct?	Bu numaranın doğru mu yanlış mı olduğunu soruşturabilir misiniz?
	boo noomaRanuhn do:Roo moo yanluhsh muh oldoo:oonoo soRooshtooRabiliR misiniz?
Can I dial international _____ direct?	Yurt dışına otomatik olarak telefon açabilir miyim?
	yooRt duhshuhna otomatik olaRak telefon achabiliR miyim?
Do I have to go through _____ the switchboard?	Santral aracılığı ile mi aramam gerek?
	santral aRajuhluh:uh ileh mi aRamam geRek?
Do I have to dial '0' first? _____	Önce sıfırı mı çevirmem gerekiyor?
	urnje suhfuhRuh muh cheviRmem geRekiyoR?
Do I have to book _____ my calls?	Numarayı bağlatmam mı gerekiyor?
	noomaRa-yuh ba:latmam muh geRekiyoR?
Could you dial this _____ number for me, please?	Benim için bu numarayı arar mısınız?
	benim ichin boo noomaRa-yuh aRaR muhsuhnuhz?
Could you put me _____ through to.../extension..., please?	Beni...numara/... numaralı hat ile bağlayabilir misiniz?
	beni...noomaRa/...noomaRaluh hat ileh ba:la-yabiliR misiniz?
I'd like to place a _____ reverse-charge call to...	...numarayı ödemeli olarak aramak istiyorum
	...noomaRa-yuh urdemeli olaRak aRamak istiyoRoom
What's the charge per _____ minute?	Dakikası kaç lira?
	dakikasuh kach liRa?
Have there been any _____ calls for me?	Beni arayan oldu mu?
	beni aRa-yan oldoo moo?

The conversation

Hello, this is... _____	İyi günler, ...ile görüşüyorsunuz
	iyi gewnleR, ...ileh gurRewshew-yoRsoonooz
Who is this, please? _____	Kiminle görüşüyorum?
	kiminleh gurRewshew-yoRoom?
Is this...? _____	... ile mi görüşüyorum?
	... ileh mi gurRewshew-yoRoom?
I'm sorry, I've dialled _____ the wrong number	Özür dilerim, yanlış numarayı çevirmişim
	urzewR dileRim, yanluhsh noomaRa-yuh cheviRmishim
I can't hear you _____	Sizi duyamıyorum
	sizi dooy-amuhyoRoom
I'd like to speak to... _____	...ile görüşmek istiyorum
	...ileh gurRewshmek istiyoRoom
Is there anybody _____ who speaks English?	İngilizce konuşmasını bilen biri var mı?
	ingilizjeh konooshmahsuhnuh bilen biRi vaR muh?
Extension..., please _____	...numaralı hattı bağlar mısınız?
	...noomaRaluh hat-tuh ba:laR muhsuhnuhz?

Could you ask him/her _____ Beni aramasını söyler misiniz?
to call me back? *beni aRamasuhnuh suhyleR misiniz?*
My name's... _____ Adım...Telefon numaram...
My number's... *aduhm...telefon noomaRa ...*
Could you tell him/her _____ Aradığımı kendisine iletir misiniz?
I called? *aRaduh:uhmuh kendisineh iletiR misiniz?*
I'll call back tomorrow _____ Kendisini yarın tekrar ararım
kendisini yaRuhn tekRaR aRaRuhm

Size telefon var _____ There's a phone call for you

Önce sıfırı çevirmeniz gerekiyor _____ You have to dial '0' first

Bir saniye lütfen _____ One moment, please

Cevap vermiyor _____ There's no answer

Telefon meşgul _____ The line's engaged

Lütfen bekleyiniz _____ Do you want to hold?

Sizi bağlıyorum _____ Putting you through

Elinizdeki numara yanlış _____ You've got a wrong number

Kendileri şu anda burada yok _____ He's/she's not here right now

Kendileri...kadar burada olacak _____ He'll/she'll be back...

Bu...telesekreteri _____ This is the answering machine of...

Post and telephone

9

79

Shopping

<u>**10**</u>

10 **S**hopping

● **Opening times:** Shops are open from 9 am to 7 pm or even later. Some shops (bakers and food-shops) are open on Sunday mornings.

alış veriş merkezi	dükkan	mobilyacı
shopping centre	shop	furniture shop
ayakkabı mağazası	eczane	müzikçi
shoe shop	chemist	music shop
ayakkabı tamircisi	elektrikli cihazlar	nalbur
cobbler	electrical appliances	hardware shop
baharatçı	fırın	oyuncakçı
herbalist	bakery	toy shop
bakkal	fotoğraf stüdyosu	parfümeri
grocer's shop	photographer's	cosmetics and perfume
baklavacı	studio	shop/department
baklava shop	gazete bayii	pasaj
balıkçı	newsagent's	arcade
fishmonger	giyim mağazası	pastane
berber	clothes shop	cake shop
barber	gözlükçü	pazar
bijuteri	optician's	market
jeweller	güzellik merkezi	postane
bisiklet tamircisi	beauty centre	post office
cycle repair shop	hediyelik eşya	saat tamircisi
büfe	gift shop	watch and clock repair
free-standing kiosk	kapalı çarşı	shop
selling newspapers,	covered market (in	şarküteri
cigarettes, milk and	Istanbul Grand Bazaar)	delicatessen
cold drinks	kasap	satış mağazası
butik	butchers	direct factory sales
boutique	kırtasiye	outlet
çay bahçesi	stationery shop	spor mağazası
tea garden	kitabevi	sports shop
çiçekçi	book shop	süpermarket
florist	kuaför	supermarket
çömlekçi	hairdresser's	tekel
shop selling	kürk mağazası	off-licence, wine shop
(earthenware) pots	furriers	terzi
deri giyim mağazası	kuru temizleme	tailor (either gents or
leather-wear shop	dry cleaners	ladies)
dondurmacı	manav	
ice-cream seller	greengrocers	

10 .1 **S**hopping conversations

Where can I get...? _____	Hangi dükkandan...satın alabilirim?
	*hangi dewk-**kahn-dan** satuhn alabiliRim?*
When does this shop _____	Bu dükkan saat kaçta açılıyor?
open?	*boo dewk-**kahn** saht kachta achuhluhyoR?*
Could you tell me _____	Bana...reyonunu gösterebilir misiniz?
where the...department is?	*bana...reyonoonoo gursterebiliR misiniz?*
Could you help me, _____	Bana yardım edebilir misiniz?...arıyorum
please? I'm looking for...	*bana yaRduhm edebiliR misiniz?...aRuhyoRoom*

81

Do you sell English/ _____ American newspapers?	İngiliz ve Amerikan gazetesi satıyor musunuz? *ingilizj ve ameRikan gazetesi satuhyoR moosoonooz?*

Size yardımcı olan var mı? _____	**Are you being served?**

No, I'd like... _____	Hayır...istiyordum *ha-yuhR...istiyoRdoom*
I'm just looking, _____ if that's all right	Mahsuru yoksa sadece bakıyorum *maHsooRoo yoksa sadejeh bakuhyoRoom*

Başka bir şey ister miydiniz? _____	**Anything else?**

Yes, I'd also like... _____	Evet, bana...verin *evet...bana veRin*
No, thank you. That's all ____	Hayır, teşekkür ederim. Bu kadar *ha-yuhr, teshek-kewR edeRim. boo kadaR*
Could you show me...? ___	Bana...gösterebilir misiniz? *bana...gursteRebiliR misiniz?*
I'd prefer... _____	...tercih ediyorum *...teRji-h-ediyoRum*
This is not what I'm _____ looking for	Aradığım bu değil *aRaduh:uhm boo de:il*
Thank you. I'll keep _____ looking	Teşekkür ederim. Birkaç yere daha bakacağım *teshek-kewR edeRim. biRkach yeReh da-ha bakaja:uhm*
Do you have _____ something...?	Daha...bir şeyiniz yok mu? *da-ha...biR sheyiniz yok moo?*
– less expensive? _____	Daha ucuz bir şeyiniz yok mu? *da-ha oojooz biR sheyiniz yok moo?*
– something smaller? _____	Daha küçük bir şeyiniz yok mu? *da-ha kewchewk biR sheyiniz yok moo?*
– something larger? _____	Daha büyük bir şeyiniz yok mu? *da-ha bew-yewk biR sheyiniz yok moo?*
I'll take this one _____	Bunu alıyorum *boonoo aluhyoRoom*
Does it come with _____ instructions?	İçinde kullanma talimatı var mı? *ichindeh kul-lanma talimatuh vaR muh?*
It's too expensive _____	Çok pahalı *chok pa-haluh*
I'll give you... _____	...liraya verirseniz, alırım *...liRa-ya veRiRseniz, aluhRuhm*
Could you keep this for ____ me? I'll come back for it later	Bunu benim için bir kenara ayırır mısınız? Biraz sonra gelir alırım *boonoo benim ichin biR kenaRa a-yuhRuhR muhsuhnuhz? biRaz sonRa geliR aluhRuhm*

10 Shopping

Have you got a bag _____ for me, please?	Naylon torbanız var mı?
	nilon toRbanuhz vaR muh?
Could you giftwrap _____ it, please?	Hediyelik kağıda sarar mısınız?
	hediyelik ka:uhda saRaR muhsuhnuhz?

Kusura bakmayın, elimizde yok _____	I'm sorry, we don't have that
Kusura bakmayın, sonuncusu da satıldı _____	I'm sorry, we're sold out
Kusura bakmayın,...gelecek _____	I'm sorry, that won't be in until...
Kasaya ödeyiniz _____	You can pay at the cash desk
Kredi kartı kabul etmiyoruz _____	We don't accept credit cards
Seyahat çeki kabul etmiyoruz _____	We don't accept traveller's cheques
Döviz kabul etmiyoruz _____	We don't accept foreign currency

10 .2 Food

I'd like a hundred _____ grams of..., please	Yüz gram...istiyorum
	yewz gRam...istiyoRoom
– five hundred grams/ _____ half a kilo of...	Yarım kilo...istiyorum
	yaRuhm kilo istiyoRoom
– a kilo of... _____	Bir kilo...istiyorum
	biR kilo...istiyoRoom
Could you...it for me, _____ please?	Bunu benim için...?
	boonoo benim ichin...?
Could you slice it/ _____ dice it for me, please?	Bunu benim için dilimler/keser misiniz?
	boonoo benim ichin dilimleR/keseR misiniz?
Could you grate it _____ for me, please?	Bunu benim için rendeler misiniz?
	boonoo benim ichin rendeleR misiniz?
Can I order it? _____	Ismarlıyabilir miyim?
	uhsmaRluhyabiliR miyim?
I'll pick it up tomorrow/ _____ at...	Yarın/saat...gelir alırım
	yaRuhn/saht...geliR aluhRuhm
Can you eat/drink this? _____	Bu yiyecek/içecek mi?
	boo yiyejek/ichejek mi?
What's in it? _____	İçinde ne var?
	ichindeh neh vaR?

10 .3 Clothing and shoes

I saw something in the _____ window. Shall I point it out?	Vitrinde bir şey gördüm. Göstereyim mi?
	vitRindeh biR shey gurRdewm. gursteReyim mi?
I'd like something to _____ go with this	Buna uyan bir şey istiyorum
	boona ooyan biR shey istiyoRoom
Do you have shoes _____ to match this?	Bu renk ayakkabınız var mı?
	boo renk a-yak-kabuhnuhz vaR muh?
I'm a size...in the UK _____	İngiltere'de...bedenim
	ingilteRedeh...bedenim

Can I try this on?	Bunu deneyebilir miyim? *boonoo deneyebiliR miyim?*
Where's the fitting room?	Kabin nerede? *kabin neRedeh?*
It doesn't fit	Olmadı *olmaduh*
This is the right size	Bu beden iyi *boo beden iyi*
It doesn't suit me	Yakışmadı *yakuhshmaduh*
Do you have this/ these in...?	Bunun...rengi var mı? *boonoon...rengi vaR muh?*
The heel's too high/low	Topuğu çok yüksek/alçak *topoo:oo chok yewksek/alchak*
Is this/are these genuine leather?	Bu/bunlar hakiki deri mi? *boo/boonlaR hakiki deRi mi?*
I'm looking for a... for a...-year-old baby/child	...yaşındaki bebek/çocuk için...arıyorum *...yashuhndahki bebek/chojook ichin...aRuhyoRoom*
I'd like a... ...	...bir...istiyorum *biR...istiyoRoom*
– silk	İpekten bir...istiyorum *ipekten biR...istiyoRoom*
– cotton	Pamuklu bir...istiyorum *pamookloo bi ...istiyoRoom*
– woollen	Yün bir...istiyorum *yewn biR...istiyoRoom*
– linen	Keten bir...istiyorum *keten biR...istiyoRoom*
What temperature can I wash it at?	Bunu kaç derecede yıkayabilirim? *boonoo kach deRejedeh yuhka-yabiliRim?*
Will it shrink in the wash?	Yıkandığında çeker mi? *yuhkanduh:uhnda chekeR mi?*

| ütülemeyin
Do not iron | Islak asın
Drip dry | Elde yıkayın
Hand wash |
| Sıkmayın
Do not spin dry | Kuru temizleme
Dry clean | Makinede yıkanır
Machine wash |

At the cobbler's

Could you mend these shoes?	Bu ayakkabıları tamir edebilir misiniz? *boo a-yak-kabuhlaRuh tahmiR edebiliR misiniz?*
Could you put new soles/heels on these?	Köseleyi/topukları yenileyebilir misiniz? *kursheleyi/topooklaRuh yenileyebiliR misiniz?*
When will they be ready?	Ne zaman hazır olurlar? *neh zaman hazuhR olooRlaR?*
I'd like..., please	...istiyorum *...istiyoRoom*
– a tin of shoe polish	Bir kutu ayakkabı boyası istiyorum *biR kootoo ayuhk-kabuhsuh boyasuh istiyoRoom*
– a pair of shoelaces	Bir çift ayakkabı bağı istiyorum *biR chift ayak-kabuh ba:uh istiyoRoom*

10 Shopping

84

10 .4 Photographs and video

'd like a film for this camera, please	Bu makine için bir film istiyorum *boo makineh ichin biR film istiyoRoom*
- a cartridge _____	Bu makine için bir kaset film istiyorum *boo makineh ichin biR kaset film istiyoRoom*
- a one twenty-six cartridge	Bu makine için yüz yirmi altılık bir kaset film istiyorum *boo makineh ichin yewz yiRmi altuhluhk biR kaset film istiyoRoom*
- a slide film _____	Bu makine için bir slayt istiyorum *boo makineh ichin biR slit istiyoRoom*
- a film cartridge _____	Bu makine için film kaseti istiyorum *boo makineh ichin film kaseti istiyoRoom*
- a videotape _____	Video kaseti istiyorum *video kaseti istiyoRoom*
colour/black and white____	renkli/siyah beyaz *renkli/siyaH beyaz*
super eight _____	süper sekiz *sewpeR sekiz*
12/24/36 exposures _____	on iki/yirmi dört/otuz altı pozluk *on iki/yiRmi durRt/otooz altuh pozlook*
ASA/DIN number_____	ASA/DIN sayısı *asa/din sa-yuhsuh*
daylight film _____	doğal ışık için film *do:al uhshuhk ichin film*
film for artificial light _____	yapay ışık için film *yapi uhshuhk ichin film*

Problems

Could you load the film for me, please?	Filmi makineye takar mısınız? *filmi makineyeh takaR muhsuhnuhz?*
Could you take the film out for me, please?	Filmi makineden çıkarır mısınız? *filmi makineden chuhkaRuhR muhsuhnuhz?*
Should I replace the batteries?	Pilleri değiştirmem gerekir mi? *pil-leRi de:ishtiRmem geRekiR mi?*
Could you have a look at my camera, please? It's not working	Makineme bir bakar mısınız? Çalışmıyor *makinemeh biR bakaR muhsuhnuhz? chaluhshmuhyoR*
The...is broken _____	...bozuk *...bozook*
The film's jammed _____	Film takılmış *film takuhlmuhsh*
The film's broken_____	Film yırtılmış *film yuhRtuhlmuhsh*
The flash isn't working ___	Flaş çalışmıyor *flash chaluhshmuhyoR*

10

Processing and prints

I'd like to have this film ____ developed/printed, please	Bu filmi banyo ettirmek/bastırmak istiyorum *boo filmi banyo et-tiRmek/bastuhRmak istiyoRoom*
I'd like...prints from_____ each negative	Her negatiften...baskı istiyorum *heR negatiften...baskuh istiyoRoom*
glossy/mat_____	parlak/mat *paRlak/mat*
6x9_____	altı çarpı dokuz *altuh chaRpuh dokooz*
I'd like to re-order _____ these photos	Bu fotoğrafları çoğaltırmak istiyorum *boo foto:Raflaruh cho:alt-tuhRmak istiyoRoom*
I'd like to have this _____ photo enlarged	Bu fotoğrafı büyüttürmek istiyorum *boo foto:Rafuh bew-yewt-tewRmek istiyoRoom*
How much is_____ processing?	Banyo ettirmek ne kadar tutar? *banyo et-tiRmek neh kadaR tootaR?*
– printing _____	Fotoğrafları bastırmak ne kadar tutar? *foto:RaflaRuh bastuhRmak neh kadaR tootaR?*
– it to re-order _____	Fotoğrafları çoğaltırmak ne kadar tutar? *foto:RaflaRuh cho:alt-tuhRmak neh kadaR tootaR?*
– the enlargement_____	Fotoğrafları büyüttürmek ne kadar tutar? *foto:RaflaRuh bew-yewt-tewRmek neh kadaR tootaR?*
When will they_____ be ready?	Ne zaman hazır olurlar? *neh zaman hazuhR olooRlaR?*

10.5 At the hairdresser's

Do I have to make an ____ appointment?	Randevu almam gerekiyor mu? *randevoo almam geRekiyoR moo?*
Can I come in straight ____ away?	Bana şimdi yardımcı olabilir misiniz? *bana shimdi yaRduhmjuh olabiliR misiniz?*
How long will I have_____ to wait?	Ne kadar beklemem gerekiyor? *neh kadaR beklemem geRekiyoR?*
I'd like a shampoo/ _____ haircut	Saçımı yıkatmak/kestirmek istiyorum *sachumuh yuhkatmak/kestiRmek istiyoRoom*
I'd like a shampoo for ____ oily/dry hair, please	Yağlı/kuru saç için şampuan istiyorum *ya:luh/kooRoo sach ichin shampooan istiyoRoom*
– an anti-dandruff _____ shampoo	Kepekli saç için şampuan istiyorum *kepekli sach ichin shampooan istiyoRoom*
– a shampoo for_____ permed/coloured hair	Permalı saç/boyalı saç için şampuan istiyorum *peRmaluh sach/boy-aluh sach ichin shampooan istiyoRoom*
– a colour rinse shampoo __	Boyalı şampuan istiyorum *boy-aluh shampooan istiyoRoom*
– a shampoo with _____ conditioner	Kremli şampuan istiyorum *kRemli shampooan istiyoRoom*
– highlights _____	Saçlarıma röfle yaptırmak istiyorum *sachlaRuhma rurfleh yaptuhRmak istiyoRoom*
Do you have a colour_____ chart, please?	Renk kataloğunuz var mı? *renk katalo:oonooz vaR muh?*

want to keep it the same colour	Saçımın aynı renk kalmasını istiyorum *sachuhmuhn ínuh renk kalmasuhnuh istiyoRoom*
'd like it darker/lighter	Saçımın daha koyu/açık olmasını istiyorum *sachuhmuhn da-ha koyoo/achuhk olmasuhnuh istiyoRoom*
'd like/I don't want hairspray	Saç spreyi istiyorum (istemiyorum) *sach spreyi istiyoRoom (istemiyoRoom)*
- gel	Saçıma jöle sürmenizi istiyorum (istemiyorum) *sachuhma zhurleh sewRmenizi istiyoRoom (istemiyoRoom)*
- lotion	Saçıma losyon sürmenizi istiyorum (istemiyorum) *sachuhma losyon sewRmenizi istiyoRoom (istemiyoRoom)*
'd like a short fringe	Kakülümün kısa olmasını istiyorum *kahkewlewmewn kuhsa olmasuhnuh istiyoRoom*
Not too short at the back	Saçımın arkasından çok almayın *sachuhmuhn aRkasuhndan chok alma-yuhn*
Not too long here	Burasını çok uzun bırakmayın *booRasuhnuh chok oozoon buhRakma-yuhn*
'd like/I don't want (many) curls	(çok) dalgalı olsun (olmasın) *(chok) dalgaluh olsoon (olmasuhn)*
t needs a little/ a lot taken off	Saçımın çok az/saçımın kısa kesilmesi gerek *sachuhmuhn chok az/sachuhmuhn kuhsa kesilmesi geRek*
want a completely different style	Değişik bir model istiyorum *de:ishik biR model istiyoRoom*
'd like it the same...	Saçımın...gibi olmasını istiyorum *sachuhmuhn...gibi olmasuhnuh istiyoRoom*
- as that lady's	Saçımın o bayanınki gibi olmasını istiyorum *sachuhmuhn o ba-yanuhnki gibi olmasuhnuh istiyoRoom*
- as in this photo	Saçımın bu resimdeki gibi olmasını istiyorum *sachuhmuhn boo resimdeki gibi olmasuhnuh istiyoRoom*
Could you put the drier up/down a bit?	Saç kurutma makinesini açar/kısar mısınız? *sach kooRootma makinesini achaR/kuhsaR muhsuhnuhz?*
'd like a facial	Yüzüme temizleyici maske yaptırmak istiyorum *yewzewme temizleyiji maskeh yaptuhRmak istiyoRoom*
- a manicure	Manikür yaptırmak istiyorum *manikewR yaptuhRmak istiyoRoom*
- a massage	Masaj yaptırmak istiyorum *masazh yaptuhRmak istiyoRoom*
Could you trim my fringe?	Kakülümün ucundan alır mısınız? *kakewlewmewn oojoondan aluhR muhsuhnuhz?*
- my beard?	Sakalımın ucundan alır mısınız? *sakaluhmuhn oojoondan aluhR muhsuhnuhz?*
- my moustache?	Bıyığımın ucundan alır mısınız? *buhyuhmuhn oojoondan aluhR muhsuhnuhz?*

I'd like a shave, please	Sakal tıraşı lütfen
	sakal tuhRashuh lewtfen
I'd like a wet shave, please	Tıraş olmak istiyorum
	tuhRash olmak istiyoRoom

Saçınızın nasıl kesilmesini isterdiniz?	How do you want it cut?
Hangi modeli isterdiniz?	What style did you have in mind?
Saçınızın hangi renge boyanmasını isterdiniz?	What colour did you want it?
Bu sıcaklık iyi mi?	Is the temperature all right for you?
Okuyacak bir şey ister misiniz?	Would you like something to read?
Bir şey içer misiniz?	Would you like a drink?
Nasıl, beğendiniz mi?	Is this what you had in mind?

At the Tourist Information Centre

11 .1 **P**laces of interest

Where's the Tourist Information, please?	Danışma bürosu nerede? *danuhshma bewRosoo neRedeh?*
Do you have a city map?	Sizde şehrin haritası var mı? *sizdeh sheHrin haRitasuh vaR muh?*
Could you give me some information about...?	Bana...hakkında bilgi verebilir misiniz? *bana...hak-kuhnda bilgi veRebiliR misiniz?*
How much is that?	Borcum ne kadar? *boRjum neh kadaR?*
What are the main places of interest?	Görülmeye değer ne var? *gurRewlmeyeh de:eR neh vaR?*
Could you point them out on the map?	Haritada gösterebilir misiniz? *haRitada gursteRebiliR misiniz?*
What do you recommend?	Ne tavsiye edersiniz? *neh tavsiyeh edeRsiniz?*
We'll be here for a few hours	Burada birkaç saat kalacağız *booRada biRkach saht kalaja:uhz*
– a day	Burada bir gün kalacağız *booRada biR gewn kalaja:uhz*
– a week	Burada bir hafta kalacağız *booRada biR hafta kalaja:uhz*
We're interested in...	...ilgimizi çekiyor *...ilgimizi chekiyoR*
Is there a scenic walk around the city?	Şehirde gezinti yapmak için güzel yerler var mı? *sheHiRdeh gezinti yapmak ichin gewzel yeRleR vaR muh?*
How long does it take?	Ne kadar sürer? *neh kadaR sewReR?*
Where does it start/end?	Başlangıç/bitiş noktası nerede? *bashlan-guhch/bitish noktasuh neRedeh?*
Are there any boat cruises here?	Burada gezi vapurları var mı? *booRada gezi vapooRlaRuh vaR muh?*
Where can we board?	Nereden binebiliriz? *neReden binebiliRiz?*
Are there any bus tours?	Otobüsle gezi turu var mı? *otobewsleh gezi tooRoo vaR muh?*
Where do we get on?	Nereden binebiliriz? *neReden binebiliRiz?*
Is there a guide who speaks English?	İngilizce konuşmasını bilen bir rehber var mı? *ingilizjeh konooshmasuhnuh bilen biR reHbeR vaR muh?*
What trips can we take around the area?	Çevrede ne gibi gezintiler yapmak mümkün? *chevRedeh neh gibi gezintileR yapmak mewmkewn?*
Are there any excursions?	Turistik geziler var mı? *tooRistik gezileR vaR muh?*
Where do they go to?	Nereye gezi var? *neReyeh gezi vaR?*
We'd like to go to...	... gitmek istiyoruz *... gitmek istiyoRooz*

90

How long is the trip? _____	Gezi ne kadar sürer?
	gezi neh kadaR sewReR?
How long do we _____ stay in...?	...ne kadar kalacağız?
	...neh kadaR kalaja:uhz?
Are there any guided _____ tours?	Rehber eşliğinde gezileriniz var mı?
	reHbeR eshli:indeh gezileRiniz vaR muh?
How much free time _____ will we have there?	Gezmek için ne kadar zamanımız var?
	gezmek ichin neh kadaR zamanuhmuhz vaR?
We want to go hiking _____	Hiking yapmak istiyoruz
	híking yapmak istiyoRooz
Can we hire a guide? _____	Bir rehber kiralayabilir miyiz?
	biR reHbeR kiRala-yabiliR miyiz?
Can I book mountain _____ huts?	Dağ kulübesi ayırtabilir miyim?
	da: koolewbesi a-yuhRtabiliR miyim?
What time does... _____ open/close?	...saat kaçta açılıyor/kapanıyor?
	...saht kachta achuhluhyoR/kapanuhyoR
What days is...open/ _____ closed?	...haftanın hangi günleri açık/kapalı?
	...haftanuhn hangi gewnleRi achuhk/kapaluh?
What's the admission _____ price?	Giriş ücreti ne kadar?
	giRish ewchReti neh kadaR?
Is there a group _____ discount?	Gurup indirimi yapıyor musunuz?
	gooRoop indiRimi yapuhyoR moosoonooz?
Is there a child _____ discount?	Çocuklara indirim var mı?
	chojooklaRa indiRim vaR muh?
Is there a discount _____ for pensioners?	Emeklilere indiriminiz var mı?
	emeklileReh indiRiminiz vaR muh?
Can I take (flash) _____ photos/can I film here?	Burada (flaşla) fotoğraf/film çekebilir miyim?
	booRada (flashla) foto:Raf/film chekebiliR miyim?
Do you have any _____ postcards of...?	üzerinde...olan kartpostal satıyor musunuz?
	ewzeRindeh...olan kaRtpostal satuhyoR moosoonooz?
Do you have an _____ English...?	İngilizce bir...var mı?
	ingilizjeh biR...vaR muh?
- an English catalogue? _____	İngilizce bir kataloğunuz var mı?
	ingilizjeh biR katalo:oonooz vaR muh?
- an English programme? _____	İngilizce bir programınız var mı?
	ingilizjeh biR pRogRamuhnuhz vaR muh?
- an English brochure? _____	İngilizce bir broşürünüz var mı?
	ingilizjeh biR bRoshewRewnewz vaR muh?

● **In Turkish theatres,** you will be shown to your seat by an attendant who will also (usually) give you a free leaflet about the play. You should offer a tip (maybe 5 or 10 percent of the ticket price)

Most films are dubbed into Turkish (Türkçe seslendirilmiş) but those which are subtitled will be advertised as alt yazılı or orijinali.

At the Tourist Information Centre

Do you have this _____ week's/month's entertainment guide?	Sizde bu haftanın/ayın etkinlik dergisi var mı? *sizdeh boo haftanuhn/i-uhn etkinlik deRgisi vaR muh?*
What's on tonight? _____	Bu akşam yapılacak ne var? *boo aksham yapuhlajak neh vaR?*
We want to go to... _____	...gitmek istiyoruz *...gitmek istiyoRooz*
Which films are _____ showing?	Hangi filmler gösteriliyor? *hangi filmleR gursteRiliyoR?*
What sort of film is that?___	Nasıl bir film? *nasuhl biR film?*
Suitable for the whole _____ family	her yaş için *heR yash ichin*
not suitable for_____ children under 16 years	16 yaşından küçükler giremez *16 yashuhndan kewchewkleR giRemez*
original version _____	orijinali *orizhinali*
subtitled _____	alt yazılı *alt yazuhluh*
dubbed_____	Türkçe seslendirilmiş *tewRkcheh seslendiRilmish*
Is it a continuous_____ showing?	Gösteri aralıksız mı? *gursteRi aRaluhksuhz muh?*
What's on at...? _____	...ne var? *...neh vaR?*
– the theatre? _____	Tiyatroda ne var? *tiyatRoda neh vaR?*
– the concert hall? _____	Konser merkezinde ne var? *konseR meRkezindeh neh vaR?*
– the opera? _____	Operada ne var? *opeRada neh vaR?*
Where can I find a good ___ disco around here?	Bu civarda nerede iyi bir diskotek var? *boo jivaRda neRedeh iyi biR diskotek vaR?*
Is it members only? _____	Üye olmak şart mı? *ewyeh olmak shaRt muh?*
Where can I find a good ___ nightclub around here?	Bu civarda nerede iyi bir gece kulübü var? *boo jivaRda neRedeh iyi biR gejeh koolewbew vaR?*
Is it evening wear only? ___	Gece kıyafeti şart mı? *gejeh kuhyafeti shaRt muh?*
Should I/we dress up? _____	Gece kıyafeti isteniyor mu? *gejeh kuhyafeti isteniyoR moo?*
What time does the _____ show start?	Gösteri saat kaçta başlıyor? *gursteRi saht kachta bashluhyoR?*
When's the next soccer ___ match?	Bir sonraki futbol maçı ne zaman? *biR sonRaki footbol machuh neh zaman?*
Who's playing?_____	Maç hangi takımlar arasında? *mach hangi takuhmlaR aRasuhnda?*

11

Hangi gösteri için yer ayırtmak istiyorsunuz? _____	Which performance do you want to book for?
Ne tarafta oturmak isterdiniz? _____	Where would you like to sit?
Bilet kalmadı _____	Everything's sold out
Sadece ayakta yer var _____	It's standing room only
Sadece balkonda yer var _____	We've only got balcony seats left
Sadece galeride yer var _____	We've only got seats left in the gallery
Sadece salonda yer var _____	We've only got stalls seats left
Sadece ön tarafta yer var _____	We've only got seats left at the front
Sadece arka tarafta yer var _____	We've only got seats left at the back
Kaç bilet istiyorsunuz? _____	How many seats would you like?
Biletleri saat...önce almanız gerekiyor _____	You'll have to pick up the tickets before...o'clock
Biletinizi görebilir miyim? _____	Tickets, please
Yeriniz burası _____	This is your seat
Yanlış yerde oturuyorsunuz _____	You're in the wrong seats

🤝 .3 Booking tickets

Could you book some _____ tickets for us?	Bizim için yer ayırabilir misiniz? *bizim ichin yeR a-yuhRabiliR misiniz?*
We'd like to book... _____ seats/a table...	...yer/bir masa istiyoruz *...yeR/biR masa istiyoRooz*
- in the stalls _____	Salonda...yer/bir masa istiyoruz *salonda...yeR/biR masa istiyoRooz*
- on the balcony _____	Balkonda...yer/bir masa istiyoruz *balkonda...yeR/biR masa istiyoRooz*
- box seats _____	Locada...yer istiyoruz *lojada...yeR istiyoRooz*
- a table at the front _____	Ön tarafta...bir masa istiyoruz *urn taRafta...biR masa istiyoRooz*
- in the middle _____	Ortada...bir masa istiyoruz *oRtada...biR masa istiyoRooz*
- at the back _____	Arka tarafta...bir masa istiyoruz *aRka taRafta...biR masa istiyoRooz*
Could I book...seats for the...o'clock performance?	Saat...gösteri için...bilet ayırtabilir miyim? *saht...gursteRi ichin...bilet a-yuhRtabiliR miyim?*
Are there any seats left for tonight?	Bu akşamki gösteri için biletiniz var mı? *boo akshamki gursteRi ichin biletiniz vaR muh?*
How much is a ticket? _____	Bir biletin fiyatı ne kadar? *biR biletin fiyatuh neh kadaR?*
When can I pick the _____ tickets up?	Biletleri saat kaçta gelip alabilirim? *biletleRi saht kachta gelip alabiliRim?*
I've got a reservation _____	Yer ayırtmıştım *yeR a-yuhRtmuhshtuhm*
My name's... _____	Adım... *aduhm...*

12 **S**ports

12 **S**ports

12 **.1 S**porting questions

Where can we..._____ around here?	Burada nerede...? *booRada neRedeh...?*
Is there a..._____ around here?	Bu civarda bir...var mı? *boo jivaRda biR...vaR muh?*
Can I hire a...here? _____	Burada bir...kiralayabilir miyim? *booRada biR...kiRala-yabiliR miyim?*
Can I take...lessons? _____	...dersi alabilir miyim? *...deRsi alabiliR miyim?*
How much is that per_____ hour/per day/a turn?	Saati/günlüğü/bir kereliği ne kadar? *sahti/gewnlew:ew/biR keReli:i neh kadaR?*
Do I need a permit _____ for that?	Ruhsat gerekli mi? *ruHsat geRekli mi?*
Where can I get _____ the permit?	Bu ruhsatı nereden alabilirim? *boo ruHsatı neReden alabiliRim?*

12 **.2 B**y the waterfront

Is it a long way to _____ the sea still?	Denize daha çok uzak mı? *denizeh da-ha chok oozak muh?*
Is there a...around here? ___	Bu civarda bir...var mı? *boo jivaRda biR...vaR muh?*
– an outdoor/indoor/_____ public swimming pool	Bu civarda bir yüzme havuzu var mı? *boo jivaRda biR yewzmeh havoozoo vaR muh?*
– a sandy beach_____	Bu civarda bir kumsal var mı? *boo jivaRda biR koomsal vaR muh?*
– a nudist beach_____	Bu civarda bir çıplaklar plajı var mı? *boo jivaRda biR chuhplaklaR plazhuh vaR muh?*
– mooring _____	Bu civarda bir yat limanı var mı? *boo jivaRda biR yat limanuh vaR muh?*
Are there any rocks_____ here?	Burası kayalık mı? *booRasuh ka-yaluhk da vaR muh?*
When's high/low tide? _____	Deniz ne zaman kabarıyor/alçalıyor? *deniz neh zaman kabaRuhyoR/alchaluhyoR?*
What's the water _____ temperature?	Su kaç derece? *soo kach deRejeh?*
Is it (very) deep here? _____	Burası (çok) derin mi? *booRasuh (chok) deRin mi?*
Can you stand here?_____	Burada ayakta durulabilir mi? *booRada a-yakta dooRoolabiliR mi?*
Is it safe to swim here? ____	Burada yüzmek (çocuklar için) tehlikeli değil mi? *booRada yewzmek (chojooklaR ichin) teHlikeli de:il mi?*
Are there any currents? ____	Akıntı var mı? *akuhntuh vaR muh?*
Are there any rapids/_____ waterfalls in this river?	Bu nehrin hızlı akıntı yeri/şelalesi var mı? *boo neHRin huhzluh akuhntuhluh yeRi/shelalesi vaR muh?*
What does that flag/_____ buoy mean?	O bayrak/şamandıra ne anlamına geliyor? *o bírak/shamanduhRa neh anlamuhna geliyoR?*
Is there a life guard_____ on duty here?	Burada bir cankurtaran var mı? *booRada biR jankooRtaRan vaR muh?*

Are dogs allowed here?____	Köpeklerin girmesi yasak mı?
	kurpekleRin giRmesi yasak muh?
Is camping on the _____	Plajda kamp kurmak yasak mı?
beach allowed?	*plazhda kamp kooRmak yasak muh?*
Are we allowed to_____	Burada ateş yakmak yasak mı?
build a fire here?	*booRada atesh yakmak yasak muh?*

Balık tutmak yasaktır	Sadece ruhsat ile	Tehlike
No fishing	Only with a permit	Danger
Balık tutulur	Sörf yapmak yasaktır	Yüzmek yasaktır
Fishing water	No surfing	No swimming

12.3 In the snow

Can I take ski lessons_____	Burada kayak dersi alabilir miyim?
here?	*booRada ka-yak deRsi alabiliR miyim?*
for beginners/advanced____	Yeni başlayanlar/(biraz) ilerlemiş olanlar
	yeni bashla-yanlaR/(biRaz) ileRlemish olanlaR
How large are the _____	Guruplar kaç kişilik?
groups?	*gooRooplaR kach kishilik?*
What language are _____	Dersler hangi dilde veriliyor?
the classes in?	*deRsleR hangi dildeh veRiliyoR?*
I'd like a lift pass,_____	Bir kayak (telesiyej/teleferik) pasosu istiyorum
please	*biR ka-yak (telesiyezh/telefeRik) pasosoo*
	istiyoRoom
Must I give you a_____	Vesikalık fotoğraf gerekir.
passport photo?	*vesikaluhk foto:Raf geRekiR*
Where can I have a _____	Nerede vesikalık fotoğraf çektirebilirim?
passport photo taken?	*neRedeh vesikaluhk foto:raf chektiRebiliRim?*
Where are the_____	Yeni başlayanlar için kayak pisti nerede?
beginners' slopes?	*yeni bashla-yanlaR ichin ka-yak pisti neRedeh?*
Are the...in operation? ____	...açık mı?
	...achuhk muh?
– the ski lifts _____	Teleferik açık mı?
	telefeRik achuhk muh?
– the chair lifts _____	Telesiyej açık mı?
	telesiyezh achuhk muh?

Sports

12

96

Sickness

13.1 Call (fetch) the doctor

Could you call/fetch a_____ doctor quickly, please?	Hemen bir doktor çağırır mısınız lütfen?
	hemen biR dokoR cha:uhRuhR muhsuhnuhz lewtfen?
When does the doctor _____ have surgery?	Doktorun görüşme saatleri ne zaman?
	doktoRoon gurRewshmeh sahtleRi neh zaman?
When can the doctor _____ come?	Doktor ne zaman gelebilir?
	doktoR neh zaman geliR?
I'd like to make an_____ appointment to see the doctor	Benim için doktordan bir randevu alabilir misiniz?
	benim ichin doktoRdan biR randevoo alabiliR misiniz?
I've got an appointment ___ to see the doctor at...	Saat...doktorla randevum var
	saht...doktoRla randevoom vaR
Which doctor/chemist _____ has night/weekend duty?	Hangi doktorun/eczanenin gece/hafta sonu nöbeti var?
	hangi doktoRoon/ejzanenin gejeh/hafta sonoo nurbeti vaR?

13.2 Patient's ailments

I don't feel well _____	Kendimi iyi hissetmiyorum
	kendimi iyi his-setmiyoRoom
I'm dizzy_____	Başım dönüyor
	bashuhm durnew-yoR
– ill_____	Hastayım
	hasta-yuhm
– sick _____	Midem bulanıyor
	midem boolanuhyoR
I've got a cold_____	Nezleyim
	nezleyim
It hurts here _____	Buram ağrıyor
	booRam a:RuhyoR
I've been throwing up _____	İstifrağ ettim
	istifra: et-tim
I've got... _____	...şikayetçiyim
	...shika-yet-chiyim
I'm running a _____ temperature...degrees	Ateşim...derece
	ateshim...deRejeh
I've been stung by_____ a wasp	Beni eşek arısı soktu
	beni eshek aRuhsuh soktoo
I've been stung by an_____ insect	Beni böcek ısırdı
	beni burjek uhsuhRduh
I've been bitten by _____ a dog	Beni köpek ısırdı
	beni kurpek uhsuhRduh
I've been stung by_____ a jellyfish	Bana deniz anası değdi
	bana deniz anasuh de:di
I've been bitten by _____ a snake	Beni yılan ısırdı
	beni yuhlan uhsuhRduh
I've been bitten by _____ an animal	Beni bir hayvan ısırdı
	beni biR hívan uhsuhRduh
I've cut myself _____	kendimi kestim
	kendimi kestim

I've burned myself _____	kendimi yaktım *kendimi yaktuhm*
I've grazed myself _____	kendimi yüzdüm *kendimi yewzdewm*
I've had a fall _____	Düştüm *dewshtewm*
I've sprained my ankle _____	Ayak bileğimi burktum *a-yak bile:imi booRktoom*
I've come for the pill	Doğum kontrol hapı istiyorum, lütfen *do:oom kontRol hapuh istiyoRoom, lewtfen*

🚑 .3 The consultation

📣	
Şikayetiniz nedir? _____	What seems to be the problem?
Bu şikayetleriniz başlayalı ne kadar _____ oluyor?	How long have you had these symptoms?
Bu şikayetleriniz geçmişte de var mıydı? _____	Have you had this trouble before?
Ateşiniz kaç derece? _____	How high is your temperature?
Lütfen, soyununuz _____	Get undressed, please
Belden yukarsını çıkarın _____	Strip to the waist, please
Şurada soyunabilirsiniz _____	You can undress there
Sağ/sol kolunuzu sıvar mısınız? _____	Roll up your left/right sleeve, please
Buraya uzanın _____	Lie down here, please
Acıyor mu? _____	Does this hurt?
Derin nefes alıp verin _____	Breathe deeply
Ağzınızı açın _____	Open your mouth

Patient's medical history

I'm a diabetic _____	Şeker hastasıyım *shekeR hastasuhyuhm*
I have a heart condition ___	Kalp hastasıyım *kalp hastasuhyuhm*
I have asthma _____	Astım hastasıyım *astuhm hastasuhyuhm*
I'm allergic to... _____	...karşı alerjim var *...kaRshuh aleRzhim vaR*
I'm...months pregnant _____	...aylık hamileyim *...íluhk hahmileyim*
I'm on a diet _____	Perhizdeyim *peRhizdeyim*
I'm on medication/the pill ___	İlaç/doğum kontrol hapı kullanıyorum *ilach/do:oom kontRol hapuh kul-lanuhyoRoom*
I've had a heart attack _____ once before	Daha önce de kalp krizi geçirdim *da-ha urnjeh deh kalp kRizi gechiRdim*
I've had a(n)...operation ___	...ameliyat oldum *...ameliyat oldoom*
I've been ill recently _____	Bir müddet önce hastaydım *biR mewd-det urnjeh hastíduhm*

Herhangi bir şeye karşı alerjiniz var mı? _____	Do you have any allergies?
İlaç kullanıyor musunuz? _____	Are you on any medication?
Perhizde misiniz? _____	Are you on a diet?
Hamile misiniz? _____	Are you pregnant?
Tetanoz aşısı oldunuz mu? _____	Have you had a tetanus injection?

The diagnosis

Pek bir şeyiniz yok _____	It's nothing serious
...kırmışsınız _____	Your...is broken
...berelenmişsiniz _____	You've got a/some bruised...
...kopmuş _____	You've got (a) torn...
İltihaplanma var _____	You've got an inflammation
Apandisitiniz var _____	You've got appendicitis
Bronşitiniz var _____	You've got bronchitis
Cinsel bir hastalığa yakalanmışsınız _____	You've got a venereal disease
Gripe yakalanmışsınız _____	You've got the flu
Kalp krizi geçirmişsiniz _____	You've had a heart attack
Mikrop kapmışsınız _____	You've got an infection (viral, bacterial)
Zatürree olmuşsunuz _____	You've got pneumonia
Ülseriniz var _____	You've got an ulcer
Kasınızı zorlayıp incitmişsiniz _____	You've pulled a muscle
Vajinal enfeksiyonunuz var _____	You've got a vaginal infection
Yediğiniz gıdadan zehirlenmişsiniz _____	You've got food poisoning
Sizi güneş çarpmış _____	You've got sunstroke
... karşı alerjiniz var _____	You're allergic to...
Hamilesiniz _____	You're pregnant
Kanınızı/idrarınızı/dışkınızı araştırtmak istiyorum _____	I'd like to have your blood/urine/stools tested
Dikiş atılması gerek _____	It needs stitching
Sizi bir uzman doktora/hastaneye gönderiyorum _____	I'm referring you to a specialist/sending you to hospital
Röntgen fotoğraflarının çekilmesi gerek _____	You'll need to have some x-rays taken
Bir süre daha bekleme odasında oturmanız gerek _____	Could you wait in the waiting room, please?
Ameliyat olmanız gerek _____	You'll need an operation

Sickness

13

I've got an ulcer _____	Ülserim var	
	ewlseRim vaR	
I've got my period _____	Adet kanamam başladı	
	adet kanamam bashladuh	
Is it contagious? _____	Bulaşıcı mı?	
	boolashuhjuh muh	
How long do I have to ____ stay...?	... ne kadar kalmam gerek?	
	... neh kadaR kalmam geRek?	
– in bed _____	Yatakta ne kadar kalmam gerek?	
	yatakta neh kadaR kalmam geRek?	
– in hospital _____	Hastanede ne kadar kalmam gerek?	
	hastanedeh neh kadaR kalmam geRek?	
Do I have to go on a special diet?	Perhiz yapmak zorunda mıyım?	
	peRhiz yapmak zoRoonda muhyuhm?	
Am I allowed to travel? ____	Seyahat edebilir miyim?	
	seyahat edebiliR miyim?	
Can I make a new appointment?	Yeni bir randevu alabilir miyim?	
	yeni biR randevoo alabiliR miyim?	
When do I have to _____ come back?	Tekrar ne zaman gelmem gerek?	
	tekRaR neh zaman gelmem geRek?	
I'll come back tomorrow	Yarın tekrar gelirim	
	yaRuhn tekRaR geliRim	

Yarın/...gün sonra yeniden _____ gelmelisiniz	Come back tomorrow/in...days' time.

🖐 .4 Medication and prescriptions

How do I take this medicine?	Bu ilaçları nasıl almam gerekiyor?
	boo ilachlaR nasuhl almam geRekiyoR?
How many capsules/ drops/injections/spoonfuls/ tablets each time?	Her seferinde kaç kapsül/damla/iğne/kaşık/tablet?
	heR sefeRindeh kach kapsewl/damla/i:neh/kashuhk/tablet?
How many times a day? ____	Günde kaç defa?
	gewndeh kach defa?
I've forgotten my medication. At home I take...	İlaçlarımı unutmuşum. İngiltere'de...kullanıyorum
	ilachlaRuhm oonootmooshoom. ingilteRedeh...kool-lanuhyoRoom
Could you make out a prescription for me?	Bana bir reçete verebilir misiniz?
	bana biR recheteh veRebiliR misiniz?

Sickness

13

Size antibiyotik/şurup/sakinleştirici/ağrı _____ kesici yazıyorum	I'm prescribing antibiotics/a mixture/a tranquillizer/pain killers
Dinlenmelisiniz _____	Have lots of rest
Dışarı çıkmamalısınız _____	Stay indoors
Yatakta kalmalısınız _____	Stay in bed

bu ilaçarı aldıktan sonra araba kullanmayınız	injections	tablets
	kapsül	tedaviyi tamamlayın
	capsules	finish the course
do not drive after taking this medicine	merhem	tümünü yutun
	ointment	swallow whole
	...saatte bir	yemeklerden önce
damla	every...hours	before meals
drops	sadece dıştan kullanılır	(yemek/çay) kaşığı
...gün boyunca	not for internal use	spoonfuls (table-spoons/teaspoons)
throughout the day	sürün	
	rub on	yutun
günde...kere	suyla karıştırın	swallow
...times a day	dissolve in water	
iğne	tablet	

📻 .5 At the dentist's

Do you know a good _____ dentist?	Bana iyi bir diş doktoru tavsiye edebilir misiniz? *bana iyi biR dish doktoRoo tavsiyeh edebiliR misiniz?*
Could you make a _____ dentist's appointment for me? It's urgent	Benim için diş doktorundan randevu alabilir misiniz? Acelem var *benim ichin dish doktooRoondan randevoo alabiliR misiniz? ajelem vaR*
Can I come in today, _____ please?	Bugün gelebilir miyim lütfen? *boogewn gelebiliR miyim lewtfen?*
I have (terrible) _____ toothache	Dişim (felaket) ağrıyor *dishim (felahket) a:RiyoR*
Could you prescribe/ _____ give me a painkiller?	Ağrı kesici yazabilir mısınız/verebilir misiniz? *a:Ruh kesiji yazabiliR misiniz?/veRebiliR misiniz?*
A piece of my tooth _____ has broken off	Dişimin bir parçası kırıldı *dishimin biR paRchasuh kuhRuhlduh*
My filling's come out _____	Dolgum düştü *dolgoom dewshtew*
I've got a broken crown _____	Dişimin köprüsü kırıldı *dishimin kurpRewsew kuhRuhlduh*
I'd like/I don't want a _____ local anaesthetic	Lokal anestezi istiyorum/istemiyorum *lokal anestezi istiyoRoom/istemiyoRoom*
Can you do a makeshift _____ repair job?	Bana bir müddet idare edecek şekilde yardım edebilir misiniz? *bana biR mewd-det idaRe edejek shekildeh yaRduhm edebiliR misiniz?*
I don't want this tooth _____ pulled	Bu dişin çekilmesini istemiyorum *boo dishin chekilmesini istemiyoRoom*
My dentures are broken. _____ Can you fix them?	Takma dişim kırıldı. Tamir edebilir misiniz? *takma dishim kuhRuhlduh. **tah**mir edebiliR misiniz?*

Hangi dişiniz ağrüyor? _____	Which tooth hurts?
Abseniz var _____	You've got an abscess.
Kanal tedavisi yapmam gerekiyor _____	I'll have to do a root canal
Lokal anestezi yapacağüm _____	I'm giving you a local anaesthetic
Bu dişi doldurmam/çekmem/törp_____ lemem gerekiyor	I'll have to fill/pull/file this tooth down
Dişinizi delmem gerekiyor _____	I'll have to drill
Ağzünüzü açün _____	Open wide, please
Ağzünüzü kapayün_____	Close your mouth, please
Ağzünüzü çalkalayün_____	Rinse, please
Hala ağrüyor mu? _____	Does it hurt still?

14

In trouble

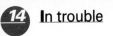

14 In trouble

14 .1 Asking for help

Help!	İmdat!
	imdat!
Fire!	Yangın!
	yanguhn!
Police!	Polis!
	polis!
Quick!	Çabuk!
	chabook!
Danger!	Tehlike!
	teHlikeh!
Watch out!	Dikkat!
	dik-kat!
Stop!	Dur!
	dooR
Be careful!	Dikkat et!
	dik-kat et!
Don't!	Yapma!
	yapma!
Let go!	Bırak!
	buhRak!
Stop that thief!	Hırsız var, yakalayın!
	huhRsuhz vaR, yakala-yuhn!
Could you help me, please?	Bana yardım eder misiniz?
	bana yaRduhm edeR misiniz?
Where's the police station/emergency exit/fire escape?	Karakol/acil çıkış/yangın merdiveni nerede?
	kaRakol/ah-jil chuhkuhsh/yanguhn meRdiveni neredeh?
Where's the nearest fire extinguisher?	Yangın söndürücüsü nerede?
	yanguhn surndewRewjewsew neRedeh?
Call the fire brigade!	İtfaiyeyi çağırın!
	itfah-iyeyi cha:uhRuhn!
Call the police!	Polisi arayın
	polisi aRa-yuhn
Call an ambulance!	Bir ambülans çağırın
	biR ambewlans cha:uhRuhn
Where's the nearest phone?	Telefon nerede?
	telefon neRedeh?
Could I use your phone?	Telefonunuzu kullanabilir miyim?
	telefonoonoozoo kool-lanabiliR miyim?
What's the emergency number?	Acil servis numarası ne?
	ah-jil seRvis noomaRasuh neh?
What's the number for the police?	Karakolun telefon numarası ne?
	kaRakoloon telefon noomaRasuh neh?

In trouble

14

14.2 Loss

I've lost my purse/_____ wallet	Cüzdanımı/evrak çantamı kaybettim *jewzdanuhm/evRak chantamuh kíbet-tim*
I lost my...yesterday _____	Dün...unuttum *dewn...oonoot-toom*
I left my...here _____	...buraya bırakmıştım *...booRa-ya buhRakmuhshtuhm*
Did you find my...? _____	Benim...buldunuz mu? *benim...booldoonooz moo?*
It was right here_____	Buradaydı *booRadíduh*
It's quite valuable _____	Çok değerli *chok de:eRli*
Where's the lost_____ property office?	Kayıp eşya bürosu nerede? *kí-uhp eshya bewRosoo neRedeh?*

14.3 Accidents

There's been an accident __	Bir kaza oldu *biR kaza oldoo*
Someone's fallen into _____ the water	Biri suya düştü *biRi sooya dewshtew*
There's a fire_____	Yangın var *yanguhn vaR*
Is anyone hurt? _____	Yaralanan var mı? *yaRalanan vaR muh?*
Some people have _____ been/no one's been injured	Yaralı var (yok) *yaRaluh vaR (yok)*
There's someone in _____ the car/train still	Arabada/trende biri daha var *aRabada/trendeh biRi da-ha vaR*
It's not too bad. Don't_____ worry	Pek bir şey yok. Merak etmeyin *pek biR shey yok. meRak etmeyin*
Leave everything the _____ way it is, please	Hiç bir şeyin yerini değiştirmeyiniz *hich biR sheyin yeRini de:ishtiRmeyiniz*
I want to talk to the_____ police first	Önce polisle görüşmek istiyorum *urnjeh polisleh gurRewshmek istiyoRoom*
I want to take a _____ photo first	Önce bir fotoğraf çekmek istiyorum *urnjeh biR foto:Raf chekmek istiyoRoom*
Here's my name_____ and address	Buyurun, adım ve adresim *booy-ooRoon aduhm ve adResim*
Could I have your _____ name and address?	Adınızı ve adresinizi alabilir miyim? *aduhnuhzuh ve adResinizi alabiliR miyim?*
Could I see some_____ dentification/your insurance papers?	Nüfus cüzdanınızı/sigorta poliçenizi görebilir miyim? *newfoos cewzdanuhnuhz/sigoRta polichenizi gurRebiliR miyim?*
Will you act as a _____ witness?	Görgü tanıklığı eder misiniz? *gurRgew tanuhkluh:uh edeR misiniz?*
I need the details for _____ the insurance	Verileri sigorta için bilmem gerek *veRileRi sigoRta ichin bilmem geRek*
Are you insured?_____	Sigortalı mısınız? *sigoRtaluh muhsuhnuhz?*

In trouble

14

Third party or _____ comprehensive?	Tek taraflı mı yoksa çift taraflı mı? *tek taRafluh muh yoksa chift taRafluh muh?*
Could you sign here, _____ please?	Burayı imzalar mısınız? *booRaya imzalaR muhsuhnuhz?*

🔟 .4 Theft

I've been robbed _____	Soyuldum *soyooldoom*
My...has been stolen _____	...çalındı *...chaluhnduh*
My car's been _____ broken into	Arabama zorla girildi *aRabama zoRla giRildi*

🔟 .5 Missing person

I've lost my child/ _____ grandmother	Çocuğumu/büyük annemi kaybettim *chojoo:uhmuh/bew-yewk an-nemi kibet-tim*
Could you help me _____ find him/her?	Aramama yardım eder misiniz? *aRamama yaRduhm edebiliR misiniz?*
Have you seen a _____ small child?	Küçük bir çocuk gördünüz mü? *kewchewk biR chojook gurRdewnewz mew?*
He's/she's...years old _____	...yaşında *...yashuhnda*
He's/she's got _____ short/long/blond/red/ brown/black/grey/curly/ straight/frizzy hair	Kısa/uzun/sarı/kızıl/kahverengi/siyah/beyaz/dalgalı /düz/kıvırcık saçlı *kuhsa/oozoon/saruh/kuhzuhl/kaHveRengi/siyah/be yaz/dalgaluh/dewz/kuhvuhRjuhk sachluh*
with a ponytail _____	saçı at kuyruklu *sachuh at kooyRookloo*
with plaits _____	saçı örgülü *sachuh urRgewlew*
in a bun _____	saçı topuz *sachuh topooz*
He's/she's got _____ blue/brown/green eyes	Gözleri mavi/kahverengi/yeşil *gurzleRi mavi/kaHveRengi/yeshil*
He's wearing swimming ___ trunks/mountaineering boots	Üzerinde mayosu/ayağında dağcılık ayakkabıları vardı *ewzeRindeh mayosoo/a-ya:uhnda da:juhluhk a-yak-kabuhlaRuh vaRduh*
with/without glasses/ _____ a bag	gözlüklü/gözlüksüz/çantalı/çantasız *gurzlewklew/gurzlewksewz/chantaluh/chantasuhz*
tall/short_____	kısa/uzun boylu *kuhsa/oozoon boyloo*
This is a photo of _____ him/her	Bu onun resmi *boo onoon resmi*
He/she must be lost _____	Eminim kayboldu *eminim kiboldoo*

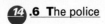

14.6 The police

An arrest

I don't speak Turkish_____	Türkçe konuşmasını bilmiyorum
	tewRkcheh konooshmasuhnuh bilmiyoRoom
I didn't see the sign _____	Levhayı görmedim
	levha-yuh gurRmedim
I don't understand_____ what it says	Ne demek istendiğini anlamıyorum
	neh demek istedi:ini anlamuhyoRoom
I was only doing..._____ kilometres an hour	Saatte...kilometre ile gidiyordum
	saht-teh...kilometReh ileh gidiyoRdoom
I'll have my car checked ___	Arabama baktıracağım
	aRabama baktuhRaja:uhm
I was blinded by _____ oncoming lights	Karşıdan gelen araç yüzünden bir şey göremez oldum
	kaRshuhdan gelen aRach yewzewnden biR shey gurRemez oldoom

Ruhsatınız lütfen _____	Your registration papers, please
Arabanızı çok süratli kullanıyordunuz _____	You were speeding
Yanlış park etmişsiniz _____	You're not allowed to park here
Park ücretini ödememişsiniz _____	You haven't put money in the meter
Işıklarınız yanmıyo _____	Your lights aren't working
...liralık bir ceza ödemek zorundasınız_____	That's a...lira fine
Şimdi ödemek ister misiniz?_____	Do you want to pay on the spot?
Şimdi ödemek zorundasınız_____	You'll have to pay on the spot

At the police station

I want to report a_____ collision/missing person/rape	Bir çarpışma/kayıp/tecavüz nedeniyle zabıt tutturmak istiyorum
	biR chaRpuhshma/ki-uhp/tejahvewz nedeniyleh zabuht toot-tooRmak istiyoRoom
Could you make out _____ a report, please?	Tutanağa geçirir misiniz?
	tootana:a gechiRiR misiniz?
Could I have a copy _____ for the insurance?	Bir nüshasını sigorta için alabilir miyim?
	biR news-hasuhnuh sigoRta ichin alabiliR miyim?
I've lost everything _____	Her şeyimi kaybettim
	heR sheyimi kibet-tim
I've run out of money ____	Param bitti, ne yapacağımı bilmiyorum
	paRam bit-ti, neh yapaja:uhmuh bilmiyoRoom
Can you lend me some ____ money	Bir miktar borç para verebilir misiniz?
	biR miktaR boRch paRa veRebiliR misiniz?
I'd like an interpreter _____	Tercüman istiyorum
	teRjewman istiyoRoom
I'm innocent _____	Ben suçsuzum
	ben soochsoozoom

In trouble

14

108

I don't know anything _____ about it	Benim hiç bir şeyden haberim yok *benim hich biR sheyden habeRim yok*
I want to speak to _____ someone from the British consulate	İngiltere konsolosluğundan biri ile görüşmek istiyorum *ingiltere konsolosloo:oondan biRi ileh gurRewshmek istiyoRoom*
I need to see someone ____ from the British embassy	İngiltere büyük elçiliğinden biri ile görüşmek istiyorum *ingiltere bew-yewk elchili:inden biRi ileh gurRewshmek istiyoRoom*
I want a lawyer who _____ speaks English	İngilizce konuşmasını bilen bir avukat istiyorum *ingilizjeh konooshmasuhnuh bilen biR avookat istiyoRoom*

Nerede oldu? _____	Where did it happen?
Ne kaybettiniz? _____	What's missing?
Ne çalındı?_____	What's been taken?
Nüfus cüzdanınızı görebilir miyim? _____	Could I see some identification?
Saat kaçta oldu? _____	What time did it happen?
Başka kimlerin ilişkisi var? _____	Who was involved?
Görgü tanıkları var mı?_____	Are there any witnesses?
Bunu doldurur musunuz? _____	Fill this out, please
Burayı imzalayın lütfen _____	Sign here, please
Tercüman ister misiniz? _____	Do you want an interpreter?

In trouble

14

15

Word list

Word list English - Turkish

● **This word list** is meant to supplement the previous chapters. In a number of cases, words not contained in this list can be found elsewhere in this book, namely alongside the diagrams of the car, the bicycle and the tent. Many food terms can be found in the Turkish-English list in 4.7.

A

about	yaklaşık olarak	yaklashuhk olaRak
above	...üstünde	...ewstewndeh
abroad	yurt dışı	yooRt duhshuh
accident	kaza	kaza
adder	engerek yılanı	engeRek yuhlanuh
addition	toplama	toplama
address	adres	adRes
admission	giriş	giRish
admission price	giriş fiyatı	giRish fiyatuh
advice	öneri, tavsiye	urneRi, tavsiyeh
after	sonra	sonRa
afternoon (in the)	öğleden sonra	ur:leden sonRa
aftershave	tıraş losyonu	tuhRash los-yonoo
again	yeniden	yeniden
against	karşı	kaRshuh
age	yaş	yash
Aids	Aids hastalığı	eehds hastaluh:uh
air conditioning	havalandırma	havalanduhRma
air mattress	şişirme yatak	shishiRmeh yatak
air sickness bag	istifrağ torbası	istifra: toRbasuh
aircraft	uçak	oochak
airmail, by	uçak ile	uchak ileh
airport	havaalanı	havaalanuh
alarm	alarm	alaRm
alarm clock	çalarsaat	chalaRsaht
alcohol	alkol	alkol
all the time	daima	dima
allergic	alerjik	aleRzhik
alone	yalnız	yalnuhz
always	her zaman	heR zaman
ambulance	ambülans	ambewlans
amount	miktar	miktaR
amusement park	lunapark	loona-paRk
anaesthetize	uyuşturmak	ooyooshtooRmak
anchovy	hamsi	hamsi
and	ve	veh
angry	kızgın	kuhzguhn
animal	hayvan	hívan
ankle	ayak bileği	a-yak bile:i
answer	cevap, yanıt	jevap, yanuht
ant	karınca	kaRuhnja
antibiotics	antibiyotik	antibiyotik
antifreeze	antifriz	antifRiz
antique	antika	antika
antiques	antika	antika
anus	anüs	anews
apartment	apartman dairesi	apaRtman díResi
aperitif	aperatif	apeRatif

Word list

15

apologize	özür dilemek	*urzewR dilemek*
apple	elma	*elma*
apple juice	elma suyu	*elma soo-yoo*
apple pudding	elma tatlısı	*elma tatluhsuh*
apple sauce	elma sosu	*elma sosoo*
appointment	randevu	*randevoo*
apricot	kayısı	*kí-uhsuh*
April	nisan	*nisan*
architecture	mimarlık	*mimaRluhk*
area	civar	*jivaR*
area code	şehirlerarası	*sheh-hiRleR-aRasuh*
	kod numarası	*kod noomaRasuh*
arm	kol	*kol*
arrange	sözleşmek	*surzleshmek*
arrive	varmak	*vaRmak*
arrow	ok	*ok*
art	sanat	*sanat*
artery	atardamar	*ataRdamaR*
artichokes	enginar	*enginaR*
article	malzeme	*malzemeh*
artificial respiration	suni tenefüs	*sooni tenefews*
ashtray	kül tablası	*kewl tablasuh*
ask	sormak	*soRmak*
ask	rica etmek	*rija etmek*
asparagus	kuşkonmaz	*kooshkonmaz*
aspirin	aspirin	*aspiRin*
assault	sarkıntılık	*saRkuhntuhluhk*
at night	geceleyin	*gejeleyin*
at the back	arkada	*aRkada*
at the front	önde	*urndeh*
aubergine	patlıcan	*patluhjan*
August	ağustos	*a:oostos*
automatic	otomatik	*otomatik*
autumn	sonbahar	*sonba-haR*
avalanche	çığ	*chuh*
awake	uyanık	*ooyanuhk*
awning	güneşlik	*gewneshlik*

B

baby	bebek	*bebek*
baby food	bebek maması	*bebek mamasuh*
babysitter	çocuk bakıcısı	*chojook bakuhjuhsuh*
back	sırt	*suhRt*
backpack	sırt çantası	*suhRt chantasuh*
bad	kötü	*kurtew*
bag	çanta	*chanta*
baker	fırın	*fuhRuhn*
balcony (theatre)	loca	*loja*
balcony (to building)	balkon	*balkon*
ball	top	*top*
ballet	bale	*baleh*
ballpoint pen	tükenmez kalem	*tewkenmez kalem*
banana	muz	*mooz*
bandage	sargı	*saRguh*
bank (river)	sahil	*sa-hil*
bank	banka	*banka*
bank card	banka kartı	*banka kaRtuh*

bar (café)	bar	baR
bar (drinks cabinet)	minibar	minibaR
barbecue	mangal	mangal
bath	banyo	banyo
bath attendant	cankurtaran	jankooRtaRan
bath foam	banyo köpüğü	banyo kurpew:ew
bath towel	banyo havlusu	banyo havloosoo
bathing cap	bone	boneh
bathing cubicle	banyo kabini	banyo kabini
bathing suit	mayo	ma-yo
bathroom	banyo	banyo
battery	pil	pil
battery (car)	akümülatör	akewmewlaturR
beach	plaj	plazh
beans	(kuru) fasulye	(kooRoo) fasoolyeh
beautiful	güzel	gewzel
beauty parlour	güzellik merkezi	gewzel-lik meRkezi
bed	yatak	yatak
bee	arı	aRuh
beef	sığır eti	suh:uhR eti
beer	bira	biRa
beetroot	pancar	panjaR
begin	başlamak	bashlamak
beginner	yeni başlayan	yeni bashla-yan
behind	...arkasında	...aRkasuhnda
belt	kemer	kemeR
berth	kuşet	kooshet
better	daha iyi	da-ha iyi
bicarbonate of soda	karbonat	kaRbonat
bicycle	bisiklet	bisiklet
bicycle pump	bisiklet pompası	bisiklet pompasuh
bicycle repairman	bisiklet tamircisi	bisiklet **tah**miRjisi
bikini	bikini	bikini
bill	hesap	hesap
billiards, to play	bilardo oynamak	bilaRdo oynamak
birthday	doğum günü	do:oom gewnew
biscuit	bisküvi	biskwi
bite	ısırmak	uhsuhRmak
bitter	acı	ajuh
black	siyah	si-yaH
bland	tatsız	tatsuhz
blanket	battaniye	bat-taniyeh
bleach	ağartmak	a:aRtmak
blister	su toplaması	soo toplamasuh
blond	sarışın	saRuhshuhn
blood	kan	kan
blood pressure	tansiyon	tansiyon
blouse	bluz	blooz
blow dry	saç kurutma	sach kooRootma
blue	mavi	mavi
blunt	kör	kurR
boat	gemi, vapur	gemi, vapooR
body	vücut	vewjoot
body milk	vücut losyonu	vewjoot losyonoo
boiled	haşlanmış	hashlanmuhsh
boiled ham	jambon	zhambon
bonbon	şekerleme	shekeRlemeh

W o r d   l i s t

15

113

bone	kemik	*kemik*
bonnet	motor kapağı	*motoR kapa:uh*
book (verb)	yer ayırtmak	*yeR a-yuhRtmak*
book	kitap	*kitap*
book	yer ayırtmak	*yeR a-yuhRtmak*
booked	rezerveli	*rezeRveli*
booking office	bilet gişesi	*bilet gishesi*
bookshop	kitabevi	*kitabevi*
border	sınır	*suhnuhR*
bored, to be	sıkılmak	*suhkuhlmak*
boring	can sıkıcı	*jan suhkuhjuh*
born	doğumlu	*do:oomloo*
borrow	borç almak	*boRch almak*
botanical gardens	botanik bahçesi	*botanik baHchesi*
both	her ikisi	*heR ikisi*
bottlewarmer	biberon ısıtıcı	*bibeRon uhsuhtuhjuh*
bottle (baby's)	biberon	*bibeRon*
box	kutu	*kootoo*
box	loca	*loja*
boy	oğlan	*o:lan*
bra	sutyen	*soot-yen*
bracelet	bilezik	*bilezik*
brake	fren	*fRen*
brake fluid	fren sıvısı	*fRen suhvuhsuh*
brake oil	fren yağı	*fRen ya:uh*
brass	pirinç	*piRinch*
bread	ekmek	*ekmek*
break	kırmak	*kuhRmak*
breakfast	kahvaltı	*kaHvaltuh*
breast	göğüs	*gur:ews*
bridge	köprü	*kurpRew*
briefs	külot	*kewlot*
bring	getirmek	*getiRmek*
brochure	broşür	*bRoshewR*
broken	bozuk	*bozook*
brother	erkek kardeş	*eRkek kaRdesh*
brown	kahverengi	*kaHveh-Rengi*
bruise	berelemek	*beRelemek*
brush	fırça	*fuhRcha*
Brussels sprouts	Brüksel lahanası	*bRewksel la-hanasuh*
bucket	kova	*kova*
bug	mikrop	*mikRop*
bugs	böcek	*burjek*
building	bina	*bina*
buoy	şamandıra	*shamanduhRa*
burglary	hırsızlık	*huhRsuhzluhk*
burn	yanmak	*yanmak*
burnt	yanık	*yanuhk*
bus	otobüs	*otobews*
bus station	otogar	*otogaR*
bus stop	otobüs durağı	*otobews dooRa:uh*
business class	birinci sınıf	*biRinji suhnuhf*
business trip	iş seyahati	*ish seya-hati*
busy	kalabalık	*kalabuhluk*
butane camping gas	bütan kamp gazı	*bewtan kamp gazuh*
butcher	kasap	*kasap*
butter	tereyağı	*teRe-ya:uh*

114

buttered roll	tereyağılı ufak ekmek	*teRe-ya:uhluh oofak ekmek*
button	düğme	*dew:meh*
buy	satın almak	*satuhn almak*

C

cabbage	lahana	*la-hana*
cabin	kamara	*kamaRa*
cake	pasta	*pasta*
cake shop	pastane	*pastaneh*
call	telefon etmek	*telefon etmek*
called, to be	adlı	*adluh*
camera	fotoğraf makinesi	*foto:Raf makinesi*
camp	kamp kurmak	*kamp kooRmak*
camp shop	kamp malzemeleri satan mağaza	*kamp malzemeleRi satan ma:aza*
camp site	kamping, kamp sahası	*kamping, kamp sa-hasuh*
camper	kamper	*kampeR*
campfire	kamp ateşi	*kamp ateshi*
camping guide	kamp kılavuzu	*kamp kuhla-oozoo*
camping permit	kamp kurma ruhsatı	*kamp kooRma rooHsatuh*
canal boat	gezi vapuru	*gezi vapooRoo*
cancel	iptal etmek	*iptahl etmek*
candle	mum	*moom*
canoe (verb)	kano yapmak	*kano yapmak*
canoe	kano	*kano*
car	araba, otomobil	*aRaba, otomobil*
carriage	vagon	*vagon*
car deck	otomobil guvertesi	*otomobil gewveRtesi*
car documents	araba ruhsat belgeleri	*aRaba rooHsat belgeleRi*
car seat	araba koltuğu	*aRaba koltoo:oo*
car trouble	motor arızası	*motoR aRuhzasuh*
carafe	sürahi	*sewRah-hi*
caravan	karavan	*kaRavan*
cardigan	hırka	*huhRka*
careful	dikkatli	*dik-katli*
carrot	havuç	*havooch*
carton	karton	*kaRton*
cascade	şelale	*shelaleh*
cash desk	kasa	*kasa*
casino	kumarhane	*koomaRhaneh*
cassette	kaset	*kaset*
castle	kale	*kaleh*
cat	kedi	*kedi*
catalogue	katalog	*katalog*
cauliflower	karnıbahar	*kaRnuhba-haR*
cave	mağara	*ma:aRa*
CD	kompakt disk	*kompakt disk*
celebrate	kutlamak	*kootlamak*
cellotape	selobant	*selobant*
cemetery	mezarlık	*mezahRluhk*
centimetre	santimetre	*santimetReh*
central heating	kalorifer	*kaloRifeR*
centre	orta	*oRta*

Word list

15

centre	merkez	meRkez
chair	sandalye	sandal-yeh
chambermaid	oda hizmetçisi	oda hizmetchisi
champagne	şampanya	shampan-ya
change (coins)	bozuk para	bozook paRa
change (verb)	değiştirmek	de:ishtiRmek
change (trains, buses)	aktarmak	aktaRmak
change (money)	para bozdurmak	paRa bozdooRmak
change the baby's nappy	bebe:in altını	bebe:in altuhnuh
	değiştirmek	de:ishtiRmek
change the oil	yağ değiştirmek	ya: de:ishtiRmek
charter flight	çarter uçuş	chaRteR oochoosh
chat up	flört etmek	flurRt etmek
check	kontrol etmek	kontRol etmek
check in	yolcu kabul	yoljoo kabool
cheers	şerefe	sheRefeh
cheese (tasty, mild)	peynir (lezzetli, hafif)	peyniR (lez-zetli, hafif)
chef	şef	shef
chemist	eczane	ejzaneh
cheque	çek	chek
cherries	kiraz	kiRaz
chess, to play	satranç oynamak	satRanch oynamak
chewing gum	sakız, çiklet	sakuhz, chiklet
chicken	tavuk	tavook
child	çocuk	chojook
child's seat	çocuk oturacağı	chojook otooRaja:uh
chilled	soğutulmuş	so:ootoolmoosh
chin	çene	cheneh
chips	patates kızartması	patates kuhzaRtmasuh
chocolate	çikolata	chikolata
choose	seçmek	sechmek
chop	pirzola	piRzola
cigar	puro	pooRo
cigar shop	tütüncü	tewtewnjew
cigarette	sigara	sigaRa
cigarette paper	sigara kağıdı	sigaRa ka:uhduh
cine camera	film makinesi	film makinesi
circle	daire, çember	diReh, chembeR
circus	sirk	siRk
city	şehir	she-hiR
city map	şehir haritası	she-hiR haRitasuh
classical concert	klasik konser	klasik konseR
clean (verb)	temizlemek	temizlemek
clean	temiz	temiz
clear	net	net
clearance	indirimli satışlar	indiRimli satuhshlaR
clock	duvar saati	doovaR sahti
closed	kapalı	kapaluh
closed off	kapalı (yol)	kapaluh (yol)
clothes	konfeksiyon	konfeksiyon
clothes hanger	askı	askuh
clothes peg	mandal	mandal
clothing	giyim	giyim
coat	palto	palto
cockroach	hamam böceği	hamam burje:i
cocoa	kakao	kaka-o
cod	morina balığı	moRina baluh:uh

coffee	kahve	kaHveh
coffee filter	kahve filtresi	kaHveh filtResi
cognac	konyak	kon-yak
cold	soğuk	so:ook
cold (medical)	soğuk algınlığı	so:ook alguhnluh:uh
cold cuts	salam çeşitleri	salam cheshitleRi
collarbone	köprücük kemiği	kurpRewjewk kemi:i
colleague	meslektaş	meslektash
collision	çarpışma	chaRpuhshma
cologne	kolonya	kolon-ya
colour	renk	renk
colour pencils	boya kalemi	boya kalemi
colour TV	renkli televizyon	renkli televizyon
colouring book	boyama kitabı	boyama kitabuh
comb	tarak	taRak
come	gelmek	gelmek
come back	geri gelmek	geRi gelmek
compartment	kompartman	kompaRtman
complain (verb)	şikayetçi olmak	shika-yet-chi olmak
complaint	şikayet	shika-yet
complaints book	şikayet defteri	shika-yet defteRi
completely	tamamen	tamahmen
compliment	iltifat	iltifat
compulsory	mecburi, zorunlu	mejbooRi, zoRoonloo
concert	konser	konseR
concert hall	konser salonu	konseR salonoo
concussion	beyin sarsıntısı	beyin saRsuhntuhsuh
condom	prezervatif	pReseRvatif
congratulate	tebrik etmek	tebRik etmek
connection	bağlantı	ba:lantuh
constipation	kabızlık	kabuhzluhk
consulate	konsolosluk	konsoloslook
consultation	konsültasyon	konsewltas-yon
contact lens	kontak lens	kontak lens
contact lens solution	lens bakım solüsyonu	lens bakuhm solews-yonoo
contagious	bulaşıcı	boolashuhjuh
contraceptive	doğum kontrol metodu	do:oom kontRol metodoo
contraceptive pill	doğum kontrol hapı	do:oom kontRol hapuh
cook (verb)	pişirmek	pishiRmek
cook	aşçı	ash-chuh
copper	bakır	bakuhR
copy	kopya nüsha	kop-ya news-ha
corkscrew	tirbuşon	tiRbooshon
corner	köşe	kursheh
cornflour	mısır unu	muhsuhR oonoo
correct	doğru	do:Roo
correspond	yazışmak	yazuhshmak
corridor	koridor	koRidoR
costume	kostüm	kostewm
cot	çocuk karyolası	chojook kaR-yolasuh
cotton	pamuklu	pamookloo
cotton wool	idrofil pamuk	idRofil pamook
cough	öksürük	urksewRewk
cough mixture	öksürük şurubu	urksewRewk shooRooboo

Word list

15

117

counter	tezgah	tezgahH
country	ülke	ewlkeh
country (countryside)	taşra	tashRa
country code	ülke telefon kodu	ewlkeh telefon kodoo
courgette	kabak	kabak
course	tedavi	tedavi
cousin	kuzen	koozen
crab	yengeç	yengech
cream	kaymak	kímak
credit card	kredi kartı	kRedi kaRtuh
crisps	patates çipsi	patates chipsi
croissant	kruason (Fransız	kRooason (fRansuhz
	kahvaltı böreği)	kaHvaltuh burRe:i)
crosscountry run	kır koşusu	kuhR koshoosoo
cross the road	karşıya geçmek	kaRshuhya gechmek
crossing	yaya geçidi	yaya gechidi
crossing	geçiş	gechish
cry	ağlamak	a:lamak
cubic metre	metre küp	metReh kewp
cucumber	salatalık	salataluhk
cuddly toy	oyuncak hayvan	oyoonjak hayvan
cuff links	manşet düğmeleri	manshet dew:meleRi
culottes	pantalon etek	pantalon etek
cup	fincan	finjan
curly	kıvırcık	kuhvuhRjuhk
current	akıntı	akuhntuh
cushion	yastık	yastuhk
custard	krema	kRema
customary	normal	noRmal
customs	gümrük	gewmRewk
customs check	gümrük kontrolü	gewmRewk kontRolew
cut	kesmek	kesmek
cut	kesmek	kesmek
cutlery	çatal bıçak takımı	chatal buhchak
		takuhmuh
cycling	bisiklet sporu	bisiklet spoRoo

D

dairy	süt mamülleri	sewt mamewl-leRi
	dükkanı	dewk-kahnuh
damaged	hasara uğramış	hasaRa oo:Ramuhsh
dance	dans etmek	dans etmek
dandruff	kepek	kepek
danger	tehlike	teHlikeh
dangerous	tehlikeli	teHlikeli
dark	karanlık	kaRanluhk
date	randevu	randevoo
daughter	kız	kuhz
day	gün	gewn
day after tomorrow	yarın değil öbür gün	yaRuhn de:il
		urbewR gewn
day before yesterday	evvelki gün	ev-velki gewn
dead	ölü	urlew
decaffeinated	kafeinsiz	kafeynsiz
December	aralık	aRaluhk
deck chair	şezlong	shezlong
declare (customs)	beyan etmek	**beyahn** etmek

deep	derin	deRin
deep sea diving	deniz dalgıçlığı	deniz dalguhchluh:uh
deepfreeze	dondurucu	dondooRoojoo
degrees	derece	deRejeh
delay	rötar	rurtaR
delicious	nefis	nefis
dentist	dişçi	dishchi
dentures	takma diş	takma dish
deodorant	deodorant	deodorant
department	reyon	reyon
department store	büyük mağaza	bewyewk ma:aza
departure	gidiş	gidish
departure time	gidiş saati	gidish sahti
depilatory cream	tüy dökücü krem	tewy durkewjew kRem
deposit (verb)	emanete vermek	e**mah**neteh veRmek
deposit	kaparo	kapaRo
dervish dancers	semazenler	semazenleR
dessert	tatlı	tatluh
destination	gidilen yer	gidilen yeR
develop	banyo etmek	banyo etmek
diabetic	şeker hastası	shekeR hastasuh
dial	çevirmek	cheviRmek
diamond	elmas	elmas
diarrhoea	ishal	is-hal
dictionary	sözlük	surzlewk
diesel	dizel	dizel
diesel oil	mazot	mazot
diet	perhiz	peRhiz
difficulty	zorluk	zoRlook
dining room	yemek salonu	yemek salonoo
dining/buffet car	yemekli vagon	yemekli vagon
dinner	akşam yemeği	aksham yeme:i
dinner jacket	smokin	smokin
dinner, to have	akşam yemeği yemek	aksham yeme:i yemek
direction	yön	yurn
directly	dosdoğru	dosdo:Roo
dirty	kirli	kiRli
disabled	sakat	sakat
disco	diskotek	diskotek
discount	indirim	indiRim
dish	yemek	yemek
dish of the day	günün yemeği	gewnewn yeme:i
disinfectant	dezenfekte edici	dezenfekteh ediji
distance	mesafe	mesafeh
distilled water	arı su	aruh soo
disturb	rahatsız etmek	ra-hatsuhz etmek
disturbance	rahatsızlık	ra-hatsuhzluhk
dive	dalmak	dalmak
diving	dalgıçlık sporu	dalguhchluhk spoRoo
diving board	tramplen	tRamplen
diving gear	dalgıçlık takımı	dalguhchluhk takuhmuh
divorced	boşanmış	boshanmuhsh
dizziness	baş dönmesi	bash durnmesi
do	yapmak	yapmak
doctor	doktor	doktoR
dog	köpek	kurpek
doll	oyuncak bebek	oynoojak bebek

Word list

15

119

domestic	yurt içi	yooRt ichi
done (well cooked)	pişmiş	pishmish
door	kapı	kapuh
double	iki kişilik	iki kishilik
down	aşağı	asha:uh
draught	cereyan	jeReyan
draughts, to play	dama oynamak	dama oynamak
dream	rüya görmek	rewya gurRmek
dress	elbise	elbiseh
dressing gown	sabahlık	sabaHluhk
drink	içecek	ichejek
drinking chocolate	kakaolu süt	kaka-oloo sewt
drinking water	içme suyu	ichmeh soo-yoo
drive	araba kullanmak	aRaba kool-lanmak
driver	şoför	shofurR
driving licence	ehliyet	eHliyet
drought	kuraklık	kooRakluhk
dry (verb)	kurutmak	kooRootmak
dry	kuru	kooRoo
dry clean	kuru temizleme	kooRoo temizlemeh
dry cleaner's	kuru temizleyici	kooRoo temizleyiji
dry shampoo	kuru saçlar için	kooRoo sachlaR ichin
	şampuan	shampoo-an
dummy	yalancı meme	yalanjuh memeh
during	boyunca	boyoonja
during	esnasında	esnasuhnda
during the day	gündüz	gewndewz

E

ear	kulak	koolak
ear, nose and throat	kulak burun boğaz	koolak booRoon bo:az
(ENT) specialist	(KBB) uzmanı	oozmanuh
earache	kulak ağrısı	koolak a:Ruhsuh
eardrops	kulak damlası	koolak damlasuh
early	erken	eRken
earrings	küpe	kewpeh
earth	toprak	topRak
earthenware	çömlek	churmlek
east	doğu	do:oo
easy	kolay	kolí
eat	yemek	yemek
eczema	egzama	egzama
eel	yılan balığı	yuhlan baluh:uhn
egg	yumurta	yoomooRta
elastic band	lastik bant	lastik bant
electric	elektrikli	elektRikli
electricity	elektrik	elektRik
embassy	büyük elçilik	bewyewk elchilik
emergency brake	acil fren	**ah-jil** fRen
emergency exit	acil çıkış	**ah-jil** chuhkuhsh
emergency number	acil servis numarası	**ah-jil** seRvis
		noomaRasuh
emergency triangle	reflektör	reflekturR
emery board	tırnak törpüsü	turRnak turRpewsew
empty	boş	bosh
engaged	dolu	doloo
engaged	meşgul	meshgool

Word list

15

English language	İngilizce	*ingilizjeh*
enjoy	zevk almak	*zevk almak*
entertainment guide	etkinlik dergisi	*etkinlik deRgisi*
envelope	zarf	*zaRf*
evening	akşam	*aksham*
evening wear	gece kıyafeti	*gejeh kuhyafeti*
event	olay	*olí*
everything	her şey	*her shey*
everywhere	her yerde	*heR yeRdeh*
examine	muayene etmek	*moo-a-yeneh etmek*
excavation	arkeolojik kazı	*aRkeolozhik kazuh*
excellent	çok iyi	*chok iyi*
exchange	değiştirmek	*de:ishtiRmek*
exchange office	kambiyo bürosu	*kambio bewRosoo*
exchange rate	döviz kuru	*durviz kooRoo*
excursion	turistik gezi	*tooRistik gezi*
exhibition	sergi	*seRgi*
exit	çıkış	*chuhkuhsh*
expenses	masraf	*masRaf*
expensive	pahalı	*pa-haluh*
explain	açıklamak	*achuhklamak*
express train	mavi tren, ekspres	*mavi tRen, ekspRes*
external	dış	*duhsh*
eye	göz	*gurz*
eye drops	göz damlası	*gurz damlasuh*
eye shadow	göz boyası	*gurz boyasuh*
eye specialist	göz doktoru	*gurz doktoRoo*
eyeliner	göz kalemi	*gurz kalemi*

F

face	yüz	*yewz*
factory	fabrika	*fabRika*
fall	düşmek	*dewshmek*
family	aile	*íleh*
famous	ünlü, meşhur	*ewnlew, mesh-hooR*
far away	uzak	*oozak*
farewell	veda	*veda*
farm	çiftlik	*chiftlik*
farmer	çiftçi	*chiftchi*
farmer's wife	çiftçi kadın	*chiftchi kaduhn*
fashion	moda	*moda*
fast	çabuk	*chabook*
father	baba	*baba*
fault	hata	*hata*
fax, to send a	faks çekmek	*faks chekmek*
February	şubat	*shoobat*
feel	hissetmek	*his-setmek*
feel like	canı istemek	*januh istemek*
fence	çit	*chit*
ferry	vapur, feribot	*vapuR, feRibot*
fever	ateş	*atesh*
fill	dolgu yapmak	*dolgoo yapmak*
fill out	doldurmak	*doldooRmak*
filling (dental)	dolgu	*dolgoo*
film	film	*film*
filter	filtre	*filtReh*
find	bulmak	*boolmak*

fine	para cezası	paRa jezasuh
finger	parmak	paRmak
fire	ateş, yangın	atesh, yanguhn
fire brigade	itfaiye	it**fa**-iyeh
fire escape	yangın merdiveni	yanguhn meRdiveni
fire extinguisher	yangın söndürücüsü	yanguhn surndewRewjewsew
first	birinci	biRinji
first aid	ilk yardım	ilk yaRduhm
first class	birinci sınıf	biRinji suhnuhf
first name	ad	ad
fish (verb)	balık tutmak	baluhk tootmak
fish	balık	baluhk
fishing rod	olta	olta
fit	uymak	ooymak
fitness centre	spor merkezi	spoR meRkezi
fitness training	egzersiz	egzeRsiz
fitting room	kabin	kabin
fix	tamir etmek	tahmiR etmek
flag	bayrak	biRak
flash bulb	flaş lambası	flash lambasuh
flash cube	flaş lambası	flash lambasuh
flash gun	flaş	flash
flat	apartman dairesi	apaRtman díResi
flea market	bit pazarı	bit pazaRuh
flight	uçuş	oochoosh
flight number	uçuş numarası	oochoosh noomaRasuh
flood	sel	sel
floor	kat	kat
flour	un	oon
flu	grip	gRip
flyover	bağlantı yolu	ba:lantuh yoloo
fly (insect)	sinek	sinek
fly (verb)	uçmak	oochmak
fog	sis	sis
foggy, to be	sis basmak	sis basmak
folkloristic	folklorik	folkloRik
follow	takip etmek	takip etmek
food	gıda	guhda
food poisoning	gıda zehirlenmesi	guhda zeh-hiRlenmesi
foot	ayak	a-yak
for	için	ichin
for hire	kiralık	kiRaluhk
forbidden	yasak	yasak
forehead	alın	aluhn
foreign	yabancı	yabanjuh
forget	unutmak	oonootmak
fork	çatal	chatal
form	form	foRm
fort	hisar	hisaR
forward	yollamak	yol-lamak
fountain	çeşme	cheshmeh
frame	çerçeve	cheRcheveh
free (seat)	boş	bosh
free	bedava, ücretsiz	bedahva, ewjRetsiz
free time	boş zaman	bosh zaman
freeze	donmak	donmak

French bread	francala	fRanjala
French language	Fransızca	fRansuhzja
fresh	taze	tazeh
Friday	cuma	jooma
fried	kızartılmış	kuhzaRtuhlmuhsh
fried egg	yağda yumurta	ya:da yoomooRta
friend	arkadaş	aRkadash
friendly	candan, cana yakın	jandan, jana yakuhn
frightened	korkmuş	koRkmoosh
fringe	kakül	kakewl
front (at the)	ön tarafta	urn taRafta
fruit	meyva	meyva
fruit juice	meyva suyu	meyva soo-yoo
frying pan	tava	tava
full	dolu	doloo
fun	eğlence	e:lenjeh
funfair	lunapark	loona-paRk

G

gallery	galeri	galeRi
game	oyun	oyoon
garage	garaj	gaRazh
garbage bag	çöp torbası	churp toRbasuh
garden	bahçe	baHcheh
gastroenteritis	mide iltihabı	mideh iltihahbuh
gauze	gazlı bez	gazluh bez
gear	vites	vites
gel	jöle	zhurleh
German language	Almanca	almanja
get off	inmek	inmek
gift	hediye	hediyeh
gilt	yaldızlı	yalduhzluh
ginger	zencefil	zenjefil
girl	kız	kuhz
girlfriend	kız arkadaş	kuhz aRkadash
giro cheque	posta çeki	posta cheki
giro pass	posta çeki kartı	posta cheki kaRtuh
glacier	buzul	boozool
glass (tumbler)	bardak	baRdak
glasses (sun -)	gözlük	gurzlewk
	(güneş gözlüğü)	gewnesh gurzlew:ew)
glide	planörle uçmak	planurRleh oochmak
glove	eldiven	eldiven
glue	tutkal	tootkal
gnat	sivrisinek	sivRisinek
go	gitmek	gitmek
go back	geri dönmek	geRi durnmek
go out	çıkmak	chuhkmak
goat's cheese	keçi peyniri	kechi peyniRi
gold	altın	altuhn
golf course	golf sahası	golf sa-hasuh
gone	kayıp	ka-yuhp
good afternoon	iyi günler	iyi gewnleR
good evening	iyi akşamlar	yi akshamlaR
good morning	günaydın	gewníduhn
good night	iyi geceler	iyi gejeleR
goodbye	hoşça kal	hosh-cha kal

gram	gram	gRam
grandchild	torun	toRoon
grandfather	dede	dedeh
grandmother	büyük anne	bewyewk an-neh
grape juice	üzüm suyu	ewzewm soo-yoo
grapefruit	greyfrut	gReyfRoot
grapes	üzüm	ewzewm
grave	mezar	mezaR
greasy	yağlı	ya:luh
green	yeşil	yeshil
green card	yeşil kart	yeshil kaRt
greet	selam vermek	selahm veRmek
grill	ızgara yapmak	uhzgaRa yapmak
grilled	kızartılmış	kuhzaRtuhlmuhsh
grocer	bakkal	bak-kal
ground	yer	yeR
group	gurup	gooRoop
guest house	pansiyon	pansiyon
guide (book)	kılavuz, rehber	kuhla-ooz, reHbeR
guide (person)	rehber	reHbeR
guided tour	rehberli tur	reHbeRli tooR
gynaecologist	kadın doktoru	kaduhn doktoRoo

H

hair	saç	sach
hairbrush	saç fırçası	sach fuhRchasuh
hairdresser	kuaför; berber	koo-afurR, beRbeR
hairpins	saç tokası	sach tokasuh
hairspray	saç spreyi	sach spReyi
half	yarım	yaRuhm
half	yarı	yaRuh
half full	yarı dolu	yaruh doloo
hammer	çekiç	chekich
hand	el	el
hand brake	el freni	el fReni
handbag	el çantası	el chantasuh
handkerchief	mendil	mendil
handmade	el işi	el ishi
happy	memnun	memnoon
harbour	liman	liman
hard	sert	seRt
hat	şapka	shapka
hay fever	saman nezlesi	saman nezlesi
hazelnut	fındık	fuhnduhk
head	baş	bash
headache	baş ağrısı	bash a:Ruhsuh
health	sağlık	sa:luhk
health food shop	doğal gıda satan dükkan	do:al guhda satan dewk-kahn
hear	duymak	dooymak
hearing aid	işitme cihazı	ishitmeh ji-hazuh
heart	kalp	kalp
heart patient	kalp hastası	kalp hastasuh
heat	sıcaklık	suhjakluhk
heater	kalorifer	kaloRifeR
heavy	ağır	a:uhR
heel	ayak topuğu	a-yak topoo:oo

heel	topuk	*topook*
hello	merhaba	*meRhaba*
helmet	kask	*kask*
help (verb)	yardım etmek	*yarduhm etmek*
help	yardım	*yaRduhm*
helping	porsiyon	*poRsiyon*
herbal tea	baharlı çay	*ba-haRluh chí*
herbs	baharat	*ba-haRat*
here	burada	*booRada*
here you are	buyurun	*booyooRoon*
herring	ringa balığı	*ringa baluh:uh*
high	yüksek	*yewksek*
high tide	kabarma	*kabaRma*
highchair	çocuk sandalyesi	*chojook sandaliyesi*
hiking	hiking	*híking*
hiking trip	gezi	*gezi*
hip	kalça	*kalcha*
hire	kiralamak	*kiRalamak*
hitchhike	otostop yapmak	*otostop yapmak*
hobby	hobi	*hobi*
holdup	soyulma	*soyoolma*
holiday (national)	bayram tatili	*bíRam tatili*
holiday	tatil	*tatil*
holiday house	yazlık	*yazluhk*
holiday park	tatil köyü	*tatil kuryew*
home, at	evde	*evdeh*
homesickness	özlem	*urzlem*
honest	dürüst	*dewRewst*
honey	bal	*bal*
horizontal	yatay	*yatí*
horrible	iğrenç	*i:Rench*
horse	at	*at*
hospital	hastane	*hastaneh*
hospitality	misafirperverlik	*misahfiR-peRveRlik*
hot	sıcak	*suhjak*
hotwater bottle	sıcak su torbası	*suhjak soo toRbasuh*
hot	acı	*ajuh*
hotel	otel	*otel*
hour	saat	*saht*
house	ev	*ev*
household items	ev eşyaları	*ev eshyalaRuh*
houses of parliament	parlamento binası	*paRlamento binahsuh*
housewife	ev kadını	*ev kaduhnuh*
how far?	ne kadar?	*neh kadaR?*
how long?	ne kadar uzak?	*neh kadaR oozak?*
how much?	ne kadar?	*neh kadaR?*
how?	nasıl?	*nasuhl?*
hundred grams	yüz gram	*yewz gRam*
hungry, to be	acıkmak	*ajuhkmak*
hurricane	kasırga	*kasuhRga*
hurry	acele	*ajeleh*
husband	eş	*esh*
hut	kulübe	*koolewbeh*
hyperventilation	hiper ventilasyon	*hipeR ventilas-yon*

I

ice cream	dondurma	dondooRma
ice cubes	buz parçası	booz paRchasuh
ice skate	buz pateni	booz pateni
idea	fikir	fikiR
identification	kimlik kartı, nüfus cüzdanı	kimlik kaRtuh, newfoos cewzdanuh
identify	kimliğini tespit etmek	kimli:ini tespit etmek
ignition key	kontak anahtarı	kontak anaHtaRuh
ill	hasta	hasta
illness	hastalık	hastaluhk
imagine	sanmak	sanmak
immediately	hemen	hemen
import duty	gümrük vergisi	gewmRewk veRgisi
impossible	imkansız	imkahnsuhz
in	...içine; içinde	...ichineh, ichindeh
in the evening	akşamleyin	akshamleyin
included	dahil	**da**-hil
indicate	göstermek	gursteRmek
indicator	yön gösterici	yurn gursteRiji
inexpensive	ucuz	oojooz
infection (viral, bacterial)	enfeksiyon	enfeksiyon
inflammation	iltihap	iltihap
information	bilgi	bilgi
information office	danışma bürosu	danuhshma bewRosoo
injection	aşı, iğne	ashuh, i:neh
injured	yaralı	yaRaluh
inner ear	iç kulak	ich koolak
inner tube	iç lastik	ich lastik
innocent	suçsuz	soochsooz
insect	böcek	burjek
insect bite	böcek ısırması	burjek uhsuhRmasuh
insect repellant	sinek koruyucu krem	sinek koRooyoojoo kRem
inside	...içinde	...ichindeh
insole	ayakkabının iç tabanı	a-yak-kabuhnuhn ich tabanuh
instructions	kullanılış şekli	kool-lanuhluhsh shekli
insurance	sigorta	sigoRta
intermission	ara	aRa
international	uluslararası	oolooslaRaRasuh
interpreter	tercüman	teRjooman
intersection	kavşak	kavshak
introduce oneself	kendini tanıtmak	kendini tanuhtmak
invite	davet etmek	davet etmek
iodine	tentürdiyot	tentewRdiyot
iron (metal)	demir	demiR
iron (verb)	ütülemek	ewtewlemek
iron	ütü	ewtew
ironing board	ütü masası	ewtew masasuh
island	ada	ada
Italian language	İtalyanca	ital-yanja
itch	kaşıntı	kashuhntuh

J

jack	kriko	kRiko
jacket	ceket	jeket
jam	reçel	rechel
January	ocak	ojak
jaw	çene	cheneh
jellyfish	deniz anası	deniz anasuh
jeweller	kuyumcu	kooyoomjoo
jewellery	mücevherat	mewjev-heRat
jog	koşu yapmak	koshoo yapmak
joke	şaka	shaka
July	temmuz	tem-mooz
jump leads	marş kablosu	maRsh kablosoo
jumper	kazak	kazak
June	haziran	haziRan

K

key	anahtar	anaHtaR
kilo	kilo	kilo
kilometre	kilometre	kilometReh
king	kral	kRal
kiss (verb)	öpmek	urpmek
kiss	öpücük	urpewjewk
kitchen	mutfak	mootfak
knee	diz	diz
knee socks	diz altı çorap	diz altuh choRap
knife	bıçak	buhchak
knit	örgü örmek	urRgew urRmek
know	bilmek	bilmek

L

lace	dantel	dantel
lace	ayakkabı bağı	a-yak-kabuh ba:uh
ladies'	bayanlar tuvaleti	ba-yanlaR too-aleti
lake	göl	gurl
lamp	lamba	lamba
land	inmek	inmek
lane	şerit	sheRit
language	dil	dil
large	büyük	bewyewk
last	geçen	gechen
last	son	son
last night	dün gece	dewn gejeh
late	geç	gech
later	sonra	sonRa
latest, at the	en son	en son
laugh	gülmek	gewlmek
launderette	çamaşırhane	chamashuhR-haneh
law	hukuk	hookook
laxative	müshil ilacı	mews-hil ilajuh
leak	sızıntı	suhzuhntuh
leather	deri	deRi
leather goods	deri mamülleri	deRi mamewl-leRi
leave	yola çıkmak	yola chuhkmak
leek	pırasa	puhRasa
left	sol	sol
left luggage	emanet	emahnet

Word list

15

left, to the	sola	sola
leg	bacak	bajak
lemon	limon	limon
lend	borç vermek	boRch veRmek
lens	mercek	meRjek
lentils	mercimek	meRjimek
less	daha az	da-ha az
lesson	ders	deRs
letter	mektup	mektoop
lettuce	marul	maRool
level crossing	hemzemin geçit	hemzemin gechit
library	kütüphane	kewtewp-haneh
lie	uzanmak	oozanmak
lies, to tell	yalan söylemek	yalan suhylemek
lift (hitchhike)	otostop	otostop
lift (in building)	asansör	asansurR
lift (ski)	telesiyej	telesiyezh
light (not dark)	aydınlık	íduhnluhk
light (not heavy)	hafif	hafif
light	lamba	lamba
lighter (cigarette)	çakmak	chakmak
lighthouse	fener	feneR
lightning	şimşek	shimshek
like (verb)	hoşlanmak, sevmek	hoshlanmak, sevmek
line	çizgi	chizgi
linen	keten	keten
lipstick	ruj	roozh
liqueur	likör	likuhR
liquid gas	likit gaz	likit gaz
listen	dinlemek	dinlemek
literature	edebiyat	edebiyat
litre	litre	litReh
little	az	az
little (a)	biraz	biRaz
live	oturmak	otooRmak
live together	beraber yaşamak	beRabeR yashamak
lobster	istakoz	istakoz
local	lokal	lokal
lock	kilit	kilit
long	uzun	oozoon
look	bakmak	bakmak
look for	aramak	aRamak
look up (in dictionary)	aramak	aRamak
lorry	kamyon	kam-yon
lose	kaybetmek	kíbetmek
loss	kayıp	kí-uhp
lost	kayıp	kí-uhp
lost item	kayıp eşya	kí-uhp eshya
lost property office	kayıp eşya bürosu	kí-uhp eshya bewRosoo
lost, to be	kaybolmak	kaybolmak
lotion	losyon	losyon
loud	gürültülü, yüksek sesli	gewRewltewlew, yewksek sesli
love (verb)	sevmek	sevmek
love	sevgi (aşk)	sevgi (ashk)
love, be in - with	-e aşık olmak	-eh ashuhk olmak

low	alçak	*alchak*
low tide	alçak gel-git	*alchak gel-git*
luck	şans	*shans*
luggage	bagaj	*bagazh*
luggage locker	bagaj dolabı	*bagazh dolabuh*
lunch	öğle yemeği	*ur:leh yeme:i*
lunchroom	yemek salonu	*yemek salonoo*
lungs	akciğer	*akji:eR*

M

macaroni	makarna	*makaRna*
madam	bayan	*ba-yan*
magazine	dergi	*deRgi*
mail	posta	*posta*
main post office	merkez postane	*meRkez postaneh*
main road	ana yol	*ana yol*
make an appointment	randevu almak	*randevoo almak*
make love	sevişmek	*sevishmek*
makeshift	geçici	*gechiji*
man	erkek	*eRkek*
manager	müdür	*mewdewR*
mandarin	mandalina	*mandalina*
manicure	manikür	*manikewR*
map	harita	*haRita*
marble	mermer	*meRmeR*
March	mart	*maRt*
margarine	margarin	*maRgaRin*
marina	yat limanı	*yat limanuh*
market	pazar	*pazaR*
marriage	evlilik	*evlilik*
married	evli	*evli*
married, get	evlenmek	*evlenmek*
massage	masaj	*masazh*
mat	mat	*mat*
match	maç	*mach*
matches	kibrit	*kibRit*
May	mayıs	*ma-yuhs*
maybe	belki	*belki*
mayonnaise	mayonez	*ma-yonez*
mayor	belediye başkanı	*belediyeh bashkanuh*
meal	yemek	*yemek*
mean	...anlamına gelmek	*...anlamuhna gelmek*
meat	et	*et*
medication	ilaç	*ilach*
medicine	ilaç	*ilach*
meet	tanışmak	*tanuhshmak*
melon	karpuz; kavun	*kaRpooz, kavoon*
membership	üyelik	*ew-yelik*
menstruate	adet görmek	*adet gurRmek*
menstruation	adet kanaması	*adet kanamasuh*
menu	menü	*menew*
menu of the day	günün menüsü	*gewnewn menewsew*
message	mesaj, not	*mesazh, not*
metal	metal	*metal*
meter	taksimetre	*taksimetReh*
metre	metre	*metReh*
migraine	migren	*migRen*

mild (tobacco)	hafif	hafif
milk	süt	sewt
millimetre	milimetre	milimetReh
milometer	kilometre sayacı	kilometReh sa-yajuh
minaret	minare	minaReh
mince	kıyma	kuhyma
mineral water	maden suyu	maden soo-yoo
minute	dakika	dakika
mirror	ayna	ína
miss	özlemek	urzlemek
missing person	kayıp kişi	ka-yuhp kishi
missing, to be	kayıp olmak	ka-yuhp olmak
mistake	yanlışlık	yanluhshluhk
mistaken, to be	yanılmak	yanuhlmak
misunderstanding	yanlış anlama	yanluhsh anlama
mixture	şurup	shooRoop
mocha	yemen kahvesi	yemen kaHvesi
modern art	günümüz sanatı	gewnewmewz sanatuh
molar	azı (dişi)	azuh (dishi)
moment	saniye, an	**sah**niyeh, an
monastery	dergah	deRgah
Monday	pazartesi	pazaRtesi
money	para	paRa
month	ay	í
moped	mobilet	mobilet
morning, in the	sabahleyin	sabaHleyin
mosque	cami	jami
mosque prayers	namaz	namaz
motel	motel	motel
mother	anne	an-neh
motor cross	motokros	moto-kRos
motorbike	motosiklet	motosiklet
motorboat	deniz motoru	deniz motoRoo
motorway	otoyol	oto-yol
mountain	dağ	da:
mountain hut	dağ kulübesi	da: koolewbesi
mountaineering	dağcılık sporu	da:juhluhk spoRoo
mountaineering shoes	dağcılık ayakkabıları	da:juhluhk a-yak-kabuhlaRuh
mouse	fare	faReh
mouth	ağız	a:uhz
much/many	çok	chok
multistorey car park	çok katlı otopark	chok katluh otopaRk
muscle	kas	kas
muscle spasms	kas kasılması	kas kasuhlmasuh
museum	müze	mewzeh
mushrooms	mantar	mantaR
music	müzik	mewzik
musical	müzikal	mewzikal
mussels	midye	mid-yeh
mustard	hardal	haRdal

N

nail (finger)	tırnak	turRnak
nail	çivi	chivi
nail polish	oje	ozheh
nail polish remover	aseton	aseton

nail scissors	tırnak makası	turRak makasuh
naked	çıplak	chuhplak
nappy	çocuk bezi	chojook bezi
National Health	sosyal sigorta kurumu	sosyal sigoRta kooRoomoo
nationality	uyruk	uyRook
natural	doğal	do:al
nature	doğa	do:a
naturism	doğacılık	do:ajuhluhk
nausea	mide bulantısı	mideh boolantuhsuh
near	...yakın	...yakuhn
nearby	yakın	yakuhn
necessary	gerekli	geRekli
neck	boyun	boyoon
necklace	kolye	kol-yeh
nectarine	tüysüz şeftali	tewysewz sheftali
needle	iğne	i:neh
negative	negatif	negatif
neighbours	komşular	komshoolaR
nephew	yeğen (erkek)	ye:en (eRkek)
never	asla	asla
new	yeni	yeni
news	haberler	habeRleR
news stand	gazete bayisi	gazeteh bí-isi
newspaper	gazete	gazeteh
next	gelecek	gelejek
next to	...yanında	...yanuhnda
nice (friendly)	cana yakın	jana yakuhn
nice (to the eye)	hoş	hosh
nice (tasty)	lezzetli	lez-zetli
niece	yeğen (kız)	ye:en (kuhz)
night	gece	gejeh
night duty	gece nöbeti	gejeh nurbeti
nightclub	gece kulübü	gejeh koolewbew
nightlife	gece hayatı	gejeh ha-yatuh
no one	hiç kimse	hich kimseh
no	hayır	ha-yuhR
no overtaking	geçme yasağı	gechmeh yasa:uh
noise	gürültü	gewRewltew
nonstop	duraklamadan	dooRaklamadan
normal	normal	noRmal
north	kuzey	koozey
nose	burun	booRoon
nose drops	burun damlası	booRoon damlasuh
nosebleed	burun kanaması	booRoon kanamasuh
notepaper	dosya kağıdı	dosya ka:uhduh
nothing	hiç bir şey	hich biR shey
November	kasım	kasuhm
nowhere	hiç bir yerde	hich biR yeRdeh
nudist beach	çıplaklar plajı	chuhplaklaR plazhuh
number	numara	noomaRa
number plate	plaka	plaka
nurse	hemşire	hemshiReh
nutmeg	küçük hindistan cevizi	kewchewk hindistan jevizi
nuts	fındık fıstık	fuhnduhk fuhstuhk

Word list

15

131

O

October	ekim	ekim
off licence	tekel	tekel
off	bozuk	bozook
offer	ikram etmek	ikRam etmek
office	büro	bewRo
oil	yağ	ya:
oil level	yağ seviyesi	ya: seviyesi
ointment	merhem	meRhem
ointment for burns	yanık merhemi	yanuhk meRhemi
okay	tamam	tamam
old	yaşlı	yashluh
olive oil	zeytin yağı	zeytin ya:uh
olives	zeytin	zeytin
omelette	omlet	omlet
on	...üzerine; üzerinde	...ewzeRindeh, ewzeRindeh
on board	gemide	gemideh
on the way	yolda	yolda
oncoming car	karşı yönden gelen araba	kaRshuh yurnden gelen aRaba
one-way traffic	tek yönlü yol	tek yurnlew yol
onion	soğan	so:an
open	açık	achuhk
open	açmak	achmak
opera	opera	opeRa
operate	ameliyat etmek	ameliyat etmek
operator (telephone)	operatör	opeRaturR
operetta	operet	opeRet
opposite	karşısında	kaRshuhsuhnda
optician	gözlükçü	gurzlewkchew
orange	portakal rengi	poRtakal rengi
orange	portakal	poRtakal
orange juice	portakal suyu	poRtakal soo-yoo
order (in -, tidy)	yolunda (derli toplu)	yoloonda (deRli toploo)
order	sipariş	sipaRish
order (verb)	ısmarlamak	uhsmaRlamak
other	başka	bashka
other side	karşı taraf	kaRshuh taRaf
outside	...dışında	...duhshuhnda
overtake	geçmek	gechmek
oysters	istiridye	istiRid-yeh

P

packed lunch	hazır öğle yemeği paketi	hazuhR ur:leh yeme:i paketi
page	sayfa	sīfa
pain	ağrı	a:Ruh
painkillers	ağrı kesici	a:Ruh kesiji
paint	boya	boya
painting (art)	ressamlık	res-samluhk
painting (object)	resim	resim
palace	saray	saRí
pan	tencere	tenjeReh
pancake	krep süzet	kRep sewzet
pane	cam	jam
pants	pantalon	pantalon

panty liner	ped	ped
paper	kağıt	ka:uht
paprika	kırmızı biber	kuhrRmuhzuh bibeR
paraffin oil	gaz yağı	gaz ya:uh
parasol	güneşten koruyan	gewneshten koRooyan
	şemsiye	shemsiyeh
parcel	paket	paket
pardon	pardon	paRdon
parents	anne ve baba	an-neh veh baba
park	park	paRk
park	park etmek	paRk etmek
parking space	park yeri	paRk yeRi
parsley	maydanoz	mídanoz
part	yedek parça	yedek paRcha
partner	eş	esh
party	parti	paRti
passable	geçilir	gechiliR
passenger	yolcu	yoljoo
passport	pasaport	pasapoRt
passport photo	vesikalık fotoğraf	vesikaluhk foto:Raf
patient	hasta	hasta
pavement	kaldırım	kalduhRuhm
pay	ödemek	urdemek
pay the bill	hesabı ödemek	hesabuh urdemek
peach	şeftali	sheftali
peanuts	fıstık	fuhstuhk
pear	armut	aRmoot
peas	bezelye	bezel-yeh
pedal	pedal	pedal
pedestrian crossing	yaya geçidi	ya-ya gechidi
pedicure	pedikür	pedikewR
pen	kalem	kalem
pencil	kurşun kalem	kooRshoon kalem
penis	penis	penis
pepper	biber	bibeR
performance	gösteri	gursteRi
perfume	parfüm	paRfewm
perm (verb)	perma yapmak	peRma yapmak
perm	perma	peRma
permit	ruhsat	rooHsat
person	kişi	kishi
personal	kişisel	kishisel
petrol	benzin	benzin
petrol station	benzin istasyonu	benzin istas-yonoo
pets	ev hayvanları	ev hívanlaRuh
pharmacy	eczane	ejzaneh
phone (verb)	telefon etmek	elefon etmek
phone	telefon	telefon
phone box	telefon kulübesi	telefon koolewbesi
phone directory	telefon rehberi	telefon reHbeRi
phone number	telefon numaras	telefon noomaRasuh
photo	fotoğraf, resim	foto:Raf, resim
photocopier	fotokopi makinesi	fotokopi makinesi
photocopy (verb)	fotokopi çekmek	fotokopi chekmek
photocopy	fotokopi	fotokopi
pick up	almak	almak
picnic	piknik	piknik

piece of clothing	giyecek	giyejek
pier	iskele	iskeleh
pigeon	güvercin	gewveRjin
pill (contraceptive)	doğum kontrol hapı	do:oom kontRol hapuh
pillow	yastık	yastuhk
pillowcase	yastık yüzü	yastuhk yewzew
pin	iğne	i:neh
pineapple	ananas	ananas
pipe	pipo	pipo
pipe tobacco	pipo tütünü	pipo tewtewnew
pity	yazık	yazuhk
place of entertainment	eğlence yeri	e:lenjeh yeRi
place of interest	görülmeye değer	gurRewlmeyeh de:eR
plan	plan	plan
plant	bitki	bitki
plasters	yara bandı	yaRa banduh
plastic	plastik	plastik
plastic bag	naylon torba	nílon toRba
plate	tabela	tabela
platform	peron	peRon
play (theatre)	piyes	pi-yes
play	oynamak	oynamak
play basketball	basketbol oynamak	basketbol oynamak
play golf	golf oynamak	golf oynamak
play tennis	tenis oynamak	tenis oynamak
playground	çocuk bahçesi	chojook baHchesi
playing cards	iskambil kağıtları	iskambil ka:uhtlaruh
pleasant	hoş	hosh
please	lütfen	lewtfen
pleasure	zevk	zevk
plum	erik	eRik
pocket knife	çakı	chakuh
point	göstermek	gursteRmek
poison	zehir	ze-hiR
police	polis	polis
police station	karakol	kaRakol
policeman	polis memuru	polis memooRoo
pond	gölet	gurlet
pony	midilli	midil-li
pop concert	pop konseri	pop konseRi
population	nüçus	newfoos
port	porto şarabı	poRto shaRabuh
porter	hamal	hamal
porter	kapıcı	kapuhjuh
post code	posta kodu	post kodoo
post office	postane	postaneh
postage	posta ücreti	posta ewjReti
postbox	posta kutusu	posta kootoosoo
postcard	kartpostal	kaRtpostal
postman	postacı	postajuh
potato	patates	patates
poultry	kümes hayvanları	kewmes hívanlaRuh
powdered milk	süt tozu	sewt tozoo
power point	priz	pRiz
pram	çocuk arabası	chojook aRabasuh
prawns	karides	kaRides
precious	değerli	de:eRli

prefer	tercih etmek	*teRji-h-etmek*
preference	tercih	*teRjih*
pregnant	hamile	*hahmileh*
present (available)	mevcut	*mevjoot*
present	hediye	*hediyeh*
press	basmak	*basmak*
pressure	basınç	*basuhnch*
price	fiyat	*fiyat*
price list	fiyat listesi	*fiyat listesi*
print (verb)	basmak	*basmak*
probably	büyük bir olasılıkla	*bewyewk biR olasuhluhkla*
problem	sorun	*soRoon*
profession	meslek	*meslek*
programme	program	*pRogRam*
pronounce	telaffuz etmek	*telaf-fooz etmek*
propane camping gas	propan kamp gazı	*pRopan kamp gazuh*
prune	kuru erik	*kooRoo eRik*
pudding	tatlı	*tatluh*
pull	çekmek	*chekmek*
pulled muscle	kas kopması	*kas kopmasuh*
pure	saf	*saf*
purple	mor	*moR*
purse	para cüzdanı	*paRa jewzdanuh*
push	itmek	*itmek*
puzzle	bulmaca	*boolmaja*
pyjamas	pijama	*pizhama*

Q

quarter	dörtte biri	*durRt-teh biRi*
quarter of an hour	on beş dakika	*on besh dakika*
queen	kraliçe	*kRaliceh*
question	soru	*soRoo*
quick	çabuk	*chabook*
quiet	sakin	***sa**kin*

R

radio	radyo	*radyo*
railways	demiryolu işletmesi	*demiR-yoloo ishletmesi*
rain (verb)	yağmur yağmak	*ya:mooR ya:mak*
rain	yağmur	*ya:mooR*
raincoat	yağmurluk	*ya:mooRlook*
raisins	kuru üzüm	*kooRoo ewzewm*
rape	tecavüz	*tejavewz*
rapids	hızlı akıntı yeri	*huhzluh akuhntuh yeRi*
raspberries	ahududu	*ahoodoodoo*
raw	çiğ	*chi:*
raw vegetables	çiğ sebze	*chi: sebzeh*
razor blades	jilet	*zhilet*
read	kitap okumak	*kitap okoomak*
ready	hazır	*hazuhR*
really	aslında	*asluhnda*
receipt	makbuz	*makbooz*
recipe	yemek tarifi	*yemek taRifi*
reclining chair	şezlong	*shezlong*
recommend	tavsiye etmek	*tavsiyeh etmek*
recovery service	TTOK	*teh teh o keh*

rectangle	dikdörtgen	*dikdurRtgen*
red	kırmızı	*kuhRmuhzuh*
red wine	kırmızı şarap	*kuhRmuhzuh shaRap*
reduction	indirim	*indiRim*
refrigerator	buzdolabı	*boozdolabuh*
regards	selamlar	*selamlaR*
region	bölge	*burlgeh*
registered (letter)	iadeli taahhütlü	*iahdeli tah-hewtlew*
registration	kayıt	*ka-yuht*
relatives	aile, akraba	*íleh, akRaba*
reliable	güvenilir	*gewveniliR*
religion	din	*din*
rent out	kiraya vermek	*kiRa-ya veRmek*
repair (verb)	tamir etmek	**tah**miR *etmek*
repairs	tamir	**tah**miR
repeat	tekrar etmek	*tekRaR etmek*
report	rapor	*rapoR*
resent	içerlemek	*icheRlemek*
responsible	sorumlu	*soRoomloo*
rest	dinlenmek	*dinlenmek*
restaurant	restoran	*restoRan*
result	sonuç	*sonooch*
retired	emekli	*emekli*
return (ticket)	gidiş dönüş	*gidish durnewsh*
reverse (vehicle)	geri yürütmek	*geRi yewRewtmek*
rheumatism	romatizma	*romatizma*
rice	pilav	*puhlow*
ridiculous	gülünç	*gewlewnch*
riding (horseback)	ata binmek	*ata binmek*
riding school	binicilik okulu	*binijilik okooloo*
right	sağ	*sa:*
right of way	öncelik	*urnjelik*
right, on the	sağa	*sa:a*
ripe	olgun	*olgoon*
risk	risk	*risk*
river	nehir, ırmak	*ne-hiR, uhRmak*
road	yol	*yol*
roadway	şose	*shoseh*
roasted	kavrulmuş	*kavRoolmoosh*
rock	kaya	*ka-ya*
roll	ufak ekmek	*oofak ekmek*
rolling tobacco	tütün (sarma sigara için)	*tewtewn (saRma sigaRa ichin)*
roof rack	araba üst bagajı	*aRaba ewst bagazhuh*
room	oda	*oda*
room number	oda numarası	*oda noomaRasuh*
room service	oda servisi	*oda seRvisi*
rope	halat	*halat*
rosé	pembe şarap	*pembeh shaRap*
roundabout	dönel kavşak	*durnel kavshak*
route	yol	*yol*
rowing boat	sandal	*sandal*
rubber	lastik	*lastik*
rubbish	saçmalık	*sachmaluhk*
rucksack	küçük sırt çantası	*kewchewk suhRt chantasuh*
rude	kaba	*kaba*

| ruins | harabe | haRabeh |
| run into | karşılaşmak | kaRshuhlashmak |

S

sad	üzgün	ewzgewn
safari	safari	safaRi
safe	emin	emin
safe	kasa	kasa
safety pin	çengelli iğne	chengel-li i:neh
sail	yelken açmak	yelken achmak
sailing boat	yelkenli	yelkenli
salad	salata	salata
salad oil	zeytinyağı	zeytin-ya:uh
salami	salam	salam
sale	indirimli satışlar	indiRimli satuhshlaR
salt	tuz	tooz
same	aynısı	ínuhsuh
sandy beach	kumsal	koomsal
sanitary pad	ped	ped
sardines	sardalya	saRdalya
satisfied	memnun	memnoon
Saturday	cumartesi	joomaRtesi
sauce	sos	sos
sauna	sauna	saoona
sausage	sosis	sosis
savoury	tatlı olmayan	tatluh olma-yan
say	söylemek	suhylemek
say one's farewells	vedalaşmak	vedalashmak
scarf	eşarp, fular	eshaRp, foolaR
scenic walk	manzaralı gezinti	manzaRuhluh gezinti
school	okul	okool
scissors	makas	makas
scooter	skuter	skooteR
scorpion	akrep	akRep
screw	vida	vida
screwdriver	tornavida	toRnavida
sculpture	heykeltıraşlık	heykeltuhRashluhk
sea	deniz	deniz
seasick (to be)	deniz tutmak	deniz tootmak
seat	yer	yeR
secondhand	elden düşme	elden dewshmeh
second	saniye	sahniyeh
second	ikinci	ikinji
sedative	sakinleştirici hap	sakinleshtiRiji hap
see	görmek	gurRmek
self timer	otomatik deklanşör	otomatik deklanchurR
send	yollamak	yol-lamak
sentence	cümle	jewmleh
September	eylül	eylewl
serious	ciddi	jid-di
service	servis	seRvis
serviette	peçete	pecheteh
set (ladies' hair)	öndüle yapmak	urndewleh yapmak
sewing thread	iplik	iplik
shade	gölge	gurlgeh
shallow	sığ	suh:
shammy	güderi	gewdeRi

shampoo	şampuan	*shampooan*
shark	köpek balığı	*kurpek baluh:uh*
shave (verb)	tıraş olmak	*tuhRash olmak*
shaver	tıraş makinesi	*tuhRash makinesi*
shaving brush	tıraş fırçası	*tuhRash fuhRchasuh*
shaving cream	tıraş kremi	*tuhRas kRemi*
shaving soap	tıraş sabunu	*tuhRash saboonoo*
sheet	çarşaf	*chaRshaf*
sherry	şeri	*sheRi*
shirt	gömlek	*gurmlek*
shoe	ayakkabı	*a-yak-kabuh*
shoe polish	ayakkabı boyası	*a-yak-kabuh boyasuh*
shoe shop	ayakkabı mağazası	*a-yak-kabuh ma:azasuh*
shoemaker	kunduracı	*koondooRajuh*
shop	dükkan	*dewk-kahn*
shop (verb)	alış veriş yapmak	*aluhsh veRish yapmak*
shop assistant	tezgahtar	*tezgahHtaR*
shop window	vitrin	*vitRin*
shopping centre	alış veriş merkezi	*aluhsh veRish meRkezi*
short	kısa	*kuhsa*
short circuit	kısa devre	*kuhsa devReh*
shorts	şort	*shoRt*
shoulder	omuz	*omooz*
show	gösteri	*gursteRi*
shower	duş	*doosh*
shutter	obtüratör	*obtewRaturR*
sieve	süzgeç	*sewzgech*
sign	imzalamak	*imzalamak*
signature	imza	*imza*
silence	sessizlik	*ses-sizlik*
silver	gümüş	*gewmews*
silverplated	gümüş kaplama	*gewmewsh kaplama*
simple	basit	*basit*
single (unmarried)	bekar	*bekahR*
single (one way)	tek gidiş	*tek gidish*
single (one person)	tek kişilik	*tek kishilik*
sir	bey	*bey*
sister	kızkardeş	*kuhzkaRdesh*
sit	oturmak	*otooRmak*
size	numara	*noomaRa*
ski	kayak yapmak	*kíyak mak*
ski boots	kayak ayakkabıları	*kíyak ayak-kabuhlRuh*
ski goggles	kayak gözlüğü	*kíyak gurzlew:ew*
ski instructor	kayak hocası	*kíyak hojasuh*
ski lessons/class	kayak dersi	*kíyak deRsi*
ski lift	telesiyej, teleferik	*telesiyezh, telefeRik*
ski pants	kayak pantalonu	*kíyak pantalonoo*
ski pass	kayak pasosu	*kíyak pasosoo*
ski slope	kayak pisti	*kíyak pisti*
ski stick	kayak değneği	*kíyak de:ne:i*
ski suit	kayak kıyafeti	*kíyak kuhyafeti*
ski wax	kayak çilası	*kíyak chilasuh*
skimmed milk	yağı alınmış süt	*ya:uh aluhnmuhsh sewt*
skin	cilt	*jilt*
skirt	etek	*etek*
skis	kayak	*kíak*

sleep	uyumak	*ooyoomak*
sleeping car	kuşetli vagon	*kooshetli vagon*
sleeping pills	uyku hapı	*ooykoo hapuh*
slide	slayt	*slít*
slip	jüpon	*jewpon*
slip road	tali yol	*tahli yol*
slow	yavaş	*yavash*
slow train	yolcu/posta treni	*yoljoo/posta tReni*
small	küçük	*kewchewk*
small change	bozuk para	*bozook paRa*
smell	kokmak	*kokmak*
smoke	duman	*dooman*
smoke	sigara içmek	*sigaRa ichmek*
smoked	füme	*fewmeh*
smoking compartment	sigara içilebilen vagon	*sigaRa ichilebilen vagon*
snake	yılan	*yuhlan*
snorkel	snorkel	*snoRkel*
snow (verb)	kar yağmak	*kaR ya:mak*
snow	kar	*kaR*
snow chains	araba zinciri	*aRaba zinjiRi*
soap	sabun	*saboon*
soap box	sabun kutusu	*saboon kootoosoo*
soap powder	çamaşır tozu	*chamashuhR tozoo*
soccer	futbol	*footbol*
soccer match	futbol maçı	*footbol machuh*
socket	priz	*pRiz*
socks	çorap	*choRap*
soft drink	meşrubat	*meshRoobat*
sole	taban	*taban*
sole (fish)	dil balığı	*dil baluh:uh*
solicitor	avukat	*avookat*
someone	biri	*biRi*
sometimes	bazen	*bazen*
somewhere	bir yerde	*biR yeRdeh*
son	oğul	*o:ool*
soon	biraz sonra	*biRaz sonRa*
sorbet	şerbet	*sheRbet*
sore	yara	*yaRa*
sore throat	boğaz ağrısı	*bo:az a:Ruhsuh*
sorry	özür dilerim	*urzewR diliRim*
sort	çeşit	*cheshit*
soup	çorba	*choRba*
sour	ekşi	*ekshi*
source	kaynak	*kínak*
south	güney	*gewney*
souvenir	hediyelik eşya	*hediyelik eshya*
spaghetti	spagetti	*spaget-ti*
spanner (open ended)	İngiliz anahtarı	*ingiliz anaHtaRuh*
spanner	cıvata anahtarı	*juhvata anaHtaRuh*
spare	yedek	*yedek*
spare parts	yedek parça	*yedek paRcha*
spare tyre	yedek lastik	*yedek lastik*
spare wheel	yedek tekerlek	*yedek tekeRlek*
speak	konuşmak	*konooshmak*
special	özel	*urzel*
specialist	uzman	*oozman*
speciality	spesiyalite	*spesiyaliteh*

speed limit	azami hız	azami huhz
spell	hecelemek	hejelemek
spicy	baharatlı	ba-haRatluh
splinter	kıymık	kuhymuhk
spoon	kaşık	kashuhk
spoonful	kaşık dolusu	kashuhk doloosoo
sport	spor	spoR
sports centre	spor merkezi	spoR meRkezi
spot	yer	yeR
sprain	burkmak	booRkmak
spring	ilkbahar	ilkba-haR
square	meydan	meydan
square (geometric)	kare	kaReh
square metres	metre kare	metReh kaReh
squash, to play	skuoş oynamak	skoo-osh oynamak
stadium	stadyum	stad-yoom
stain	leke	lekeh
stain remover	leke giderici	lekeh gideRiji
stairs	merdiven	meRdiven
stalls	salon	salon
stamp	posta pulu	posta pooloo
start	çalıştırmak	chaluhshtuhRmak
station	istasyon	istasyon
statue	heykel	heykel
stay (verb)	kalmak	kalmak
stay	zaman	zaman
steal	çalmak	chalmak
steel	çelik	chelik
stench	pis koku	pis kokoo
sting (insect only)	ısırmak	uhsuhRmak
stitch (med.)	dikiş	dikish
stitch (verb)	dikmek	dikmek
stock	et suyu	et soo-yoo
stockings	çorap	choRap
stomach	mide	mideh
stomach ache	mide ağrısı	mideh a:Ruhsuh
stomach cramps	karın spazmı	kaRuhn spazmi
stools	dışkı	dushkuh
stop (verb)	durmak	dooRmak
stop	durak	dooRak
stopover	aktarma	aktaRma
storm	fırtına	fuhRtuhna
straight	doğru	do:Roo
straight ahead	doğru	do:Roo
straw	kamış	kamuhsh
strawberries	çilek	chilek
street	sokak	sokak
street side	sokağa bakan	soka:a bakan
strike	grev	gRev
strong (tea)	demli	demli
study	okumak	okoomak
stuffing	içi	ichi
subscriber's number	abone telefon numarası	aboneh telefon noomaRasuh
subtitled	alt yazılı	alt yazuhluh
succeed	başarmak	bashaRmak
sugar	şeker	shekeR

sugar lumps	kesmeşeker	kesmeshekeR
suit	takım elbise	takuhm elbiseh
suitcase	bavul, valiz	bavool, valiz
summer	yaz	yaz
summertime	yaz mevsimi	yaz mevsimi
sun	güneş	gewnesh
sun hat	güneş şapkası	gewnesh shapkasuh
sunbathe	güneşlenmek	gewneshlenmek
Sunday	pazar	pazaR
sunglasses	güneş gözlüğü	gewnesh gurzlew:ew
sunrise	gün doğması	gewn do:masuh
sunset	gün batımı	gewn batımı
sunstroke	güneş çarpması	gewnesh chaRpmasuh
suntan lotion	güneş kremi	gewnesh kRemi
suntan oil	güneş yağı	gewnesh ya:uh
supermarket	süpermarket	sewpeRmaRket
surcharge	ek	ek
surf	sörf yapmak	surRf yapmak
surf board	sörf kayağı	surf ka-ya:uh
surgery	muayene odası	moo-a-yeneh odasuh
surname	soyadı	soyaduh
surprise	sürpriz	sewRpriz
swallow	yutmak	yootmak
swamp	bataklık	batakluhk
sweat	ter	teR
sweet (charming)	şekerli	shekeRli
sweet (pudding)	şirin	shiRin
sweet	tatlı	tatluh
sweet corn	mısır	muhsuhR
sweeteners	tatlılaştırıcı	tatlulashtuhRuhjuh
sweets	şekerleme	shekeRlemeh
swim	yüzmek	yewzmek
swimming pool	yüzme havuzu	yewzmeh havoozoo
swimming trunks	mayo	ma-yo
swindle	dolandırıcılık	dolanduhRuhjuhluhk
switch	şalter	shalteR
synagogue	sinagog	sinagog

T

table	masa	masa
table tennis (to play)	masa tenisi oynamak	masa tenisi oynamak
tablet	ilaç tableti	ilach tableti
take	almak	almak
take pictures	fotoğraf çekmek	foto:Raf chekmek
taken	dolu	doloo
talcum powder	talk pudrası	talk poodRasuh
talk	konuşmak	konooshmak
tall	uzun boylu	oozoon boyloo
tampons	tamponlar	tamponlaR
tanned	bronzlaşmış	bRonzlashmuhsh
tap	musluk	mooslook
tap water	musluk suyu	mooslook soo-yoo
taste	güzel zevk	gewzel zevk
tax free shop	gümrüksüz mağaza	gewmRewksewz ma:aza
taxi	taksi	taksi
taxi stand	taksi durağı	taksi dooRa:uh

tea	çay	chí
teapot	çaydanlık	chídanluhk
teaspoon	çay kaşığı	chí kashuh:uh
teat (baby's bottle)	plastik meme	plastik memeh
telegram	telgraf	telegRaf
telephoto lens	teleobjektif	tele-obzhektif
television	televizyon	televizyon
telex	teleks	teleks
temperature	sıcaklık	suhjakluhk
temporary filling	geçici dolgu	gechiji dolgoo
tender	yumuşak	yoomooshak
tennis ball	tenis topu	tenis topoo
tennis court	tenis kortu	tenis koRtoo
tennis racket	tenis raketi	tenis raketi
tenpin bowling	bovling	bohling
tent	çadır	chaduhR
tent peg	çadır kazığı	chaduhR kazuh:uh
terrace	teras	teRas
terribly	müthiş	mewt-hish
thank	teşekkür etmek	teshek-kewR etmek
thank you	teşekkür ederim	teshek-kewR edeRim
thanks	teşekkürler	teshek-kewRleR
thaw	erimek	eRimek
theatre	tiyatro	tiyatRo
theft	hırsızlık	huhRsuhzluhk
there	orada	oRada
thermal bath	kaplıca	kapluhja
thermometer	termometre	teRmometReh
thick	kalın	kaluhn
thief	hırsız	huhRsuhz
thigh	üst bacak	ewst bajak
thin	ince	injeh
things	eşya	eshya
think	düşünmek	dewshewnmek
third	üçte biri	ewchteh biRi
thirsty, to be	susamış olmak	soosamuhsh olmak
this afternoon	bugün öğleden sonra	boogewn urleden sonRa
this evening	bu akşam	boo aksham
this morning	bu sabah	boo sabaH
thread	iplik	iplik
throat	boğaz	bo:az
throat lozenges	pastil	pastil
throw up	kusmak	koosmak
thunderstorm	fırtına	fuhRtuhna
Thursday	perşembe	peRshembeh
ticket (admission)	bilet	bilet
ticket (travel)	bilet	bilet
tickets	biletler	biletleR
tidy (verb)	toplamak	toplamak
tie	kravat	kRavat
tights	külotlu çorap	kewlotloo choRap
time	zaman	zaman
times	kere, defa	keReh, defa
timetable	tarife	taRifeh
tin	konserve	konseRveh
tip	bahşiş	baH-shish
tissues	kağıt mendil	ka:uht mendil

toast	kızarmış ekmek	*kuhzaRmuhsh ekmek*
tobacco	tütün	*tewtewn*
toboggan	kızak	*kuhzak*
today	bugün	*boogewn*
toe	ayak parmağı	*a-yak paRma:uh*
together	beraber	*beRabeR*
toilet	tuvalet	*too-alet*
toilet paper	tuvalet kağıdı	*too-alet ka:uhduh*
toilet seat	tuvalet oturağı	*too-alet otooRa:uh*
toiletries	kozmetik malzemeleri	*kozmetik malzemeleRi*
tomato	domates	*domates*
tomato purée	domates salçası	*domates salchasuh*
tomato sauce	domates sosu	*domates sosoo*
tomorrow	yarın	*yaRuhn*
tongue	dil	*dil*
tonic water	tonik	*tonik*
tonight	bu gece	*boo gejeh*
too much	fazla	*fazla*
tools	araç gereç	*aRach geRech*
tooth	diş	*dish*
toothache	diş ağrısı	*dish a:Ruhsuh*
toothbrush	diş fırçası	*dish fuhRchasuh*
toothpaste	diş macunu	*dish majoonoo*
toothpick	kürdan	*kewRdan*
top up	doldurmak	*doldooRmak*
total	toplam	*toplam*
tough	sert	*seRt*
tour	tur	*tur*
tour guide	tur rehberi	*tooR reHbeRi*
tourist card	turist kartı	*tooRist kaRtuh*
tourist class	turistik sınıf	*tooRistik suhnuhf*
Tourist Information office	danışma bürosu	*danuhshma bewRosoo*
tourist menu	turistik menü	*tooRistik menew*
tow	çekmek	*chekmek*
tow cable	çekme halatı	*chekmeh halatuh*
towel	havlu	*havloo*
tower	kule	*kooleh*
town	kasaba	*kasaba*
town hall	belediye sarayı	*belediyeh saRi-uh*
toys	oyuncak	*oyoonjak*
traffic	trafik	*tRafik*
traffic light	trafik ışıkları	*tRafik uhshuhklaRuh*
trailer tent	açılır kapanır karavan	*achuhluhR kapanuhR kaRavan*
train	tren	*tRen*
train ticket	tren bileti	*tRen bileti*
train timetable	tren tarifesi	*tRen taRifesi*
training shoes	spor ayakkabısı	*spoR a-yak-kabuhsuh*
translate	tercüme etmek	*teRjewmeh etmek*
travel	seyahat etmek	*seya-hat etmek*
travel agent	seyahat acentası	*seya-hat ajentasuh*
travel guide	seyahat rehberi	*seya-hat reHbeRi*
traveller	yolcu	*yoljoo*
traveller's cheque	seyahat çeki	*seya-hat cheki*
treacle/syrup	şeker pekmezi/şurup	*shekeR pekmezi/shooRoop*
treatment	tedavi	*tedahvi*

Word list

15

143

triangle	üçgen	ewchgen
trim	ucundan almak	oojoondan almak
trip	gezi	gezi
trouble	şikayet	shika-yet
trout	alabalık	alabaluhk
trunk call	şehirlerarası telefon	she-hiRleRaRasuh
	konuşması	telefon konooshmasuh
trustworthy	güvenilir	gewveniliR
try on	denemek	denemek
tube	tüp	tewp
Tuesday	salı	saluh
tumble drier	çamaşır kurutma	chamashuhR
	makinesi	kooRootma
		makinesi
tuna	ton balığı	ton baluh:uh
tunnel	tünel	tewnel
Turkish	Türkçe	tewRkcheh
turn	sıra	suhRa
TV	televizyon	televizyon
TV guide	televizyon rehberi	televizyon reHbeRi
tweezers	cımbız	juhmbuhz
tyre	dış lastik	duhsh lastik
tyre lever	salapurya	salapooR-ya
tyre pressure	hava basıncı	hava basuhnjuh

U

ugly	çirkin	chiRkin
umbrella	şemsiye	shemsiyeh
under	...altında	...altuhnda
underground	metro	metRo
underground	metro ağı	metRo a:uh
railway system		
underground station	metro istasyonu	metRo istasyonoo
underpants	külot	kewlot
understand	anlamak	anlamak
underwear	iç çamaşırı	ich chamashuhRuh
undress	soyunmak	soyoonmak
unemployed	işsiz	ishsiz
uneven	pürüzlü	pewRewzlew
university	üniversite	ewniveRsiteh
unleaded	kurşunsuz benzin	kooRshoonsooz benzin
up	yukarı	yookaRuh
urgent	acil	ah-jil
urgently	acilen	ahjilen
urine	idrar	idRaR
usually	çoğunlukla	cho:oonlookla

V

vacate	boşaltmak	boshaltmak
vaccinate	aşılamak	ashuhlamak
vagina	vajina	vazhina
vaginal infection	vajinal enfeksiyon	vazhinal enfeksiyon
valid	geçerli	gecheRli
valley	vadi	vadi
valuable	değerli	de:eRli
van	kamyonet	kam-yonet
vanilla	vanilya	vanilya

vase	vazo	*vazo*
vaseline	vazelin	*vazelin*
veal	dana eti	*dana eti*
vegetable soup	sebze çorbası	*sebzeh choRbasuh*
vegetables	sebze	*sebzeh*
vegetarian	vejetaryen	*vezhetaR-yen*
vein	damar	*damaR*
(vending) machine	otomatik satış makinesi	*otomatik satuhsh makinesi*
venereal disease	cinsel hastalık	*jinsel hastaluhk*
via	...yoluyla	*...yolooyla*
video recorder	video	*video*
video tape	video kaseti	*video kaseti*
view	manzara	*manzaRa*
village	köy	*kuhy*
visa	vize	*vizeh*
visit	ziyaret etmek	*ziyaRet etmek*
vitamin tablets	vitamin hapları	*vitamin haplaRuh*
vitamins	vitamin	*vitamin*
volcano	yanardağ	*yanaRda:*
volleyball	voleybol	*voleybol*
vomit	istifrağ etmek	*istifRa: etmek*

W

wait	beklemek	*beklemek*
waiter	garson	*gaRson*
waiting room	bekleme odası	*beklemeh odasuh*
waitress	bayan garson	*ba-yan gaRson*
wake up	uyandırmak	*ooyanduhRmak*
walk	yürüşmek	*yewRewshmek*
walk	yürümek	*yewRewmek*
wallet	cüzdan	*jewzdan*
wardrobe	elbise dolabı	*elbiseh dolabuh*
warm	ılık	*uhluhk*
warn	uyarmak	*ooyaRmak*
warning	uyarı	*ooyaRuh*
wash	yıkamak	*yuhkamak*
washing powder	çamaşır tozu	*chamashuhR tozoo*
washing	çamaşır	*chamashuhR*
washing line	çamaşır ipi	*chamuhshuhR ipi*
washing machine	çamaşır makinesi	*chamashuhR makinesi*
wasp	eşek arısı	*eshek aRuhsuh*
watch	kol saati	*kol sahti*
water	su	*soo*
water ski	su kayağı yapmak	*soo ka-ya:uh yapmak*
waterproof	su geçirmez	*soo gechiRmez*
wavepool	suni dalgalı havuz	*sooni dalgaluh havooz*
way	yol	*yol*
we	biz	*biz*
weak (tea)	açık	*achuhk*
weather	hava	*hava*
weather forecast	hava raporu	*hava rapoRoo*
wedding	düğün	*dew:ewn*
Wednesday	çarşamba	*chaRshamba*
week	hafta	*hafta*
weekend	hafta sonu	*hafta sonoo*
weekend duty	hafta sonu nöbeti	*hafta sonoo nurbeti*

Word list

15

weekly ticket	haftalık abone bileti	*haftaluhk aboneh bileti*
welcome	hoş geldiniz	*hosh geldiniz*
well	iyi	*iyi*
west	batı	*batuh*
wet	ıslak	*ihslak*
wet (weather)	yağmurlu	*ya:mooRloo*
wetsuit	sörf kıyafeti	*surRf kuhyafeti*
what?	ne?	*neh?*
wheel	tekerlek	*tekeRlek*
wheelchair	tekerlekli sandalye	*tekeRlekli sandal-yeh*
when?	ne zaman?	*neh zaman?*
where?	nerede?	*neRedeh?*
which?	hangi?	*hangi?*
whipped cream	krem şanti	*kRem shanti*
white	beyaz	*beyaz*
white-haired	ak saçlı	*ak sachluh*
who?	kim?	*kim?*
wholemeal	kepekli	*kepekli*
wholemeal bread	kepekli ekmek	*kepekli ekmek*
why?	niçin?	*nichin?*
wide angle lens	geniş açılı mercek	*genish achuhluh meRjek*
widow	dul	*dool*
widower	dul	*dool*
wife	eş	*esh*
wind	rüzgar	*rewzgaR*
windbreak	rüzgarlık	*rewzgaRluhk*
windmill	değirmen	*de:iRmen*
window	pencere	*penjeReh*
window (pay desk)	gişe, vezne	*gisheh, vezneh*
windscreen wiper	cam sileceği	*jam sileje:i*
wine	şarap	*shaRap*
wine glass	şarap bardağı	*shaRap baRda:uh*
wine list	şarap listesi	*shaRap listesi*
winter	kış	*kuhsh*
witness	görgü tanığı	*gurRgew tanuh:uh*
woman	kadın	*kaduhn*
wonderful	şahane	*sha-haneh*
wood	tahta	*taHta*
wool	yün	*yewn*
word	sözcük, kelime	*surzjewk, kelimeh*
work	iş	*ish*
working day	iş günü	*ish gewnew*
worn	aşınmış	*ashuhnmuhsh*
worried	endişeli	*endisheli*
wound	yara	*yaRa*
wrap	paketlemek	*paketlemek*
wrist	bilek	*bilek*
write	yazmak	*yazmak*
write down	not etmek	*not etmek*
writing pad	bloknot	*bloknot*
writing paper	dosya kağıdı	*dosya ka:uhduh*
written	yazılı	*yazuhluh*
wrong	yanlış	*yanluhsh*

Y

yacht	yat	*yat*
year	sene, yıl	*seneh, yuhl*
yellow	sarı	**saRuh**
yes	evet	*evet*
yes, please	lütfen	*lewtfen*
yesterday	dün	*dewn*
yoghurt	yoğurt	*yo:ooRt*
you	siz	*siz*
you too	size de	*sizeh deh*
youth hostel	gençlik yurdu	*genchlik yooRdoo*

Z

zip	fermuar	*feRmooaR*
zoo	hayvanat bahçesi	*hívanat baHchesi*

Basic grammar

1 The importance of suffixes, and their varying forms

A very distinctive feature of Turkish is the way it builds up increasingly complex meanings from simple words. This is done with suffixes – either in the middle of words or on the end. English, in contrast, adds other, quite separate words for the same effect, eg:

Eng.	Turk.
I am going	**gidiyorum**
I am not going	**gitmiyorum**
I will be able to go	**gidebileceğim**

However, these suffixes change their form to echo the vowels in the particular words in which they occur. Plurals, for instance, can end in **-ler** or **-lar**.

Another example is the 'detached' question suffix with four variants. In the 'you' form, polite or plural, these are: **misiniz, mısınız, müsünüz** and **musunuz**. Choosing the right one rapidly becomes instinctive, but it is first necessary to understand what determines the variant.

2 Vowel harmony

Vowels are classed as front or back. Front vowels are **e, i, ö** and **ü**; back vowels are **a, ı, o** and **u**. A native Turkish word is made up solely of either front or back vowels (e.g. **güneşli**, sunny) – it never mixes front and back – and all suffixes must obey a similar harmony. The only exceptions are foreign loan words.

There are two typical variations of suffix harmony: in the first, all front vowels are echoed by **e**, and all back vowels by **a** (giving plurals **-ler** and **-lar**). In the second type, the last syllable in the root word is echoed, and this is how:
e and **i** are echoed by **i**
ö and **ü** by **ü**
a and **ı** by **ı**
o and **u** by **u**

These shape the question suffixes:

güzel mi?	is it beautiful?	**sütlü mü?**	is it milky?
kırmızı mı?	is it red?	**bozuk mu?**	is it broken?

They also shape the personal suffixes. After a consonant, and where the last vowel was **e** or **i** these are:
-im (my), **-in** (your), **-i** (his, hers, its),
-imiz (our) **-iniz** (polite 'your' singular, or 'your' plural) and **-leri** (their)

With **iş** (job) this gives:
işim (my job) **işin** (your job) **işi** (her job)
işimiz (our job) **işiniz** (your job) **işleri** (their job)

But the echo changes as the vowel changes: **buzum** - my ice (**buz** = ice), **gülün** - your rose (**gül** = rose) and **atı** - his horse (**at** = horse).

Note that **-leri** is slightly different – it has only two forms. It is **-leri** for all front-vowel words, and **ları** for all back vowels.

3 The missing verbs: 'to be' and 'to have'

This is perhaps the moment to point out that there is no verb 'to have' in Turkish, nor is there a 'to be' either – or not in the present tense, at least. Instead another, slightly different set of suffixes is added to nouns or adjectives – again with the same four-fold echo. These are (after an **i** or **e**):

-(y)im – I am; **-sin** – you are; **-dir** (very often omitted) he, she it is; **-(y)iz** – we are; **-siniz** – you are (plural or polite form); **-(dir)ler** – they are.

Examples are:
iyiyim (I am well)
iyisin (you are well)
iyi misin? (are you well?)
iyi (he, she is well), etc.
But the harmonising echoes also give:

Türksün	you are Turkish
kadınsın	you are a woman
adam mısın?	are you a man? and so on.

Two very useful words supplement these suffixes:

var (there is, there are) and **yok** (there is no, there are no).

Para var means there is money, and **para yok** means 'there is no money'.

But if the personal suffixes (see previous section) are combined with **para,** there is a complete change of meaning. The effect is the same as our verb 'to have'.

Param var means 'I have (some) money', and **param yok** is 'I have no money'. The same harmonising echoes recur: **arkadaşın** var (you have a friend), sorunu var (he, she has a problem) and then again **Çözümüz var** (we have a solution). (Root words are **arkadaş, sorun** and **çözüm.**)

4 Direct objects, 'to', 'from' and 'at'

The direct object of the sentence ('the man' in the sentence 'I saw the man') is modified in form if its English equivalent has the article 'the', 'my' (etc) or is a person's name, and not if it goes with 'a' or 'some'. The suffix which modifies the direct object has eight different variants - **(y)i, -(y)ı, -(y)ö,** or **-(y)u.**

Examples: **annemi gördüm** - I saw my mother (**anne** = mother); **Fatmayı gördüm** - I saw Fatma; but **bir kedi gördüm** - I saw a cat (**kedi** = cat). Note that the verb is at the end of the sentence, which is its normal position.

'To', 'from' and 'at' are expressed in Turkish with suffixes obeying the same two-fold -e/-a harmony mentioned above. Using **ev** (home/house) and **okul** (school):

eve = to home/the house
evden = from home/the house
evde = at home/the house

okula = to (the) school
okuldan = from (the) school
okulda = at (the) school

5 'You' - polite and familiar forms

Turkish is very like French, German and Italian in having polite and familiar forms of 'you' and 'your'. With people who know each other well, or are in informal situations, the familiar form is natural. If in any doubt, however, be polite.

6 More about verbs and tenses...

Here is another verb form using endings somewhat similar to those already illustrated for the present tense of 'to be'. It is shown with a front-vowel verb (**görmek** - to see) and a back-vowel verb (**yapmak** - to do).

The present continuous tense: 'I see/am seeing' - 'I do/am doing'

görüyorum	görüyoruz
yapıyorum	yapıyoruz
görüyorsun	görüyorsunuz
yapıyorsun	yapıyorsunuz
görüyor	görüyorlar
yapıyor	yapıyorlar

... and ever increasing complexities

Different suffixes provide all the different forms which verbs need to take; in every case the meaning is contained in a single word (except in the case of the detached question suffixes mentioned above).

Here are some examples:

-ecek/-acak	the future tense
-di, -dı, -dü, -du	the past tense
-meli/-malı	should or ought
-iyordu	past continuous
-ebil/-abi	I can, be able

eg(using **gelmek** to come) **gelecek** (he will come) **geldi** (he came) **gelmeli** (he ought to come) **geliyordu** (he was coming) **gelebilir** (he can or may come).

There are several combinations of tenses like **-iyordu**. One very useful such combination is the future-in-the-past **-ecekti** (the **d** of **-di** becomes a **t** in order to harmonise with the unvoiced **k**). It means 'I was going to'.

Others, much less commonly used, can give very subtle shades of meaning, such as 'I may not be able to', and 'I gather that I may not be able to'; there is even a tense with the meaning 'I am (quite) able not to' or 'it is possible that I am not' again using just a single word (eg **gelmiyebilirim**). But the beauty is that these complexities are built out of basic components and a remarkably simple logic.